THE WAR OF THE JEWELS

THE HISTORY OF MIDDLE-EARTH

J. R. R. TOLKIEN

THE WAR OF
THE JEWELS

The Later Silmarillion
Part Two
The Legends of Beleriand

Edited by Christopher Tolkien

Boston   New York
HOUGHTON MIFFLIN COMPANY
1994

CIP data is available.
ISBN 0-395-71041-3

Printed in the United States of America

AGM 10 9 8 7 6 5 4 3 2 1

CONTENTS

FOREWORD

The War of the Jewels is a companion to and continuation of *Morgoth's Ring*, Volume 10 in *The History of Middle-earth*. As I explained in that book, the two together contain virtually all of my father's narrative writing on the subject of the Elder Days in the years after *The Lord of the Rings*, but the division into two is made 'transversely': between the first part of 'The Silmarillion' ('the Legends of Aman') and the second ('the Legends of Beleriand'). I use the term 'Silmarillion', of course, in a very wide sense: this though potentially confusing is imposed by the extremely complex relationship of the different 'works' – especially but not only that of the *Quenta Silmarillion* and the *Annals*; and my father himself employed the name in this way. The division of the whole corpus into two parts is indeed a natural one: the Great Sea divides them. The title of this second part, *The War of the Jewels*, is an expression that my father often used of the last six centuries of the First Age: the history of Beleriand after the return of Morgoth to Middle-earth and the coming of the Noldor, until its end.

In the foreword to *Morgoth's Ring* I emphasised the distinction between the first period of writing that followed in the early 1950s the actual completion of *The Lord of the Rings*, and the later work that followed its publication; in this book also, therefore, two distinct 'phases' are documented.

The number of new works that my father embarked upon in that first 'phase', highly creative but all too brief, is astonishing. There were the new *Lay of Leithian*, of which all that he wrote before he abandoned it was published in *The Lays of Beleriand*; the *Annals of Aman* and new versions of the *Ainulindalë*; the *Grey Annals*, abandoned at the end of the tale of Túrin; the new *Tale of Tuor and the Fall of Gondolin* (published in *Unfinished Tales*), abandoned before Tuor actually entered the city; and all the new tale of Túrin and Niënor from Túrin's return to Dor-lómin to their deaths in Brethil (see p. 144 in this book). There were also an abandoned prose saga of Beren and Lúthien (see V.295); the story of Maeglin; and an extensive revision of the *Quenta Silmarillion*, the central work of the last period before *The Lord of the Rings*, interrupted near the beginning of the tale of Túrin in 1937 and never concluded.

I expressed the view in the foreword to *Morgoth's Ring* that 'despair of publication, at least in the form that he regarded as essential' (i.e. the conjunction of *The Silmarillion* and *The Lord of the Rings* in a single work) was the fundamental cause of the collapse of this new endeavour; and that this break destroyed all prospect that what may be called 'the older Silmarillion' would ever be completed. In *Morgoth's Ring* I have documented the massive upheaval, in the years that followed, in his conception of the old myths: an upheaval that never issued in new and secure form. But we come now to the last epoch of the Elder Days, when the scene shifts to Middle-earth and the mythical element recedes: the High-elves return across the Great Sea to make war upon Morgoth, Dwarves and Men come over the mountains into Beleriand, and bound up with this history of the movement of peoples, of the policies of kingdoms, of momentous battles and ruinous defeats, are the heroic tales of Beren One-hand and Túrin Turambar. Yet in *The War of the Jewels* the record is completed of all my father's further work on that history in the years following the publication of *The Lord of the Rings*; and even with all the labour that went into the elaboration of parts of 'the Saga of Túrin' it is obvious that this bears no comparison with his aims or indeed his achievements in the early 1950s.

In Part Two of this book it will be seen that in this later phase of his work the *Quenta Silmarillion* underwent scarcely any further significant rewriting or addition, other than the introduction of the new chapter *Of the Coming of Men into the West* with the radically altered earlier history of the Edain in Beleriand; and that (the most remarkable fact in the whole history of *The Silmarillion*) the last chapters (the tale of Húrin and the dragon-gold of Nargothrond, the Necklace of the Dwarves, the ruin of Doriath, the fall of Gondolin, the Kinslayings) remained in the form of the *Quenta Noldorinwa* of 1930 and were never touched again. Only some meagre hints are found in later writings.

For this there can be no simple explanation, but it seems to me that an important element was the centrality that my father accorded to the story of Húrin and Morwen and their children, Túrin Turambar and Niënor Níniel. This became for him, I believe, the dominant and absorbing story of the end of the

Elder Days, in which complexity of motive and character, trapped in the mysterious workings of Morgoth's curse, sets it altogether apart. He never finally achieved important passages of Túrin's life; but he extended the 'great saga' (as he justly called it) into 'the Wanderings of Húrin', following the old story that Húrin was released by Morgoth from his imprisonment in Angband after the deaths of his children, and went first to the ruined halls of Nargothrond. The dominance of the underlying theme led to a new story, a new dimension to the ruin that Húrin's release would bring: his catastrophic entry into the land of the People of Haleth, the Forest of Brethil. There were no antecedents whatsoever to this tale; but antecedents to the manner of its telling are found in parts of the prose 'saga' of the Children of Húrin (*Narn i Chîn Húrin*, given in *Unfinished Tales*), of which 'Húrin in Brethil' is a further extension. That 'saga' went back to the foundations in *The Book of Lost Tales*, but its great elaboration belongs largely to the period after the publication of *The Lord of the Rings*; and in its later development there entered an immediacy in the telling and a fullness in the recording of event and dialogue that must be described as a new narrative impulse: in relation to the mode of the 'Quenta', it is as if the focus of the glass by which the remote ages were viewed had been sharply changed.

But with Húrin's grim and even it may seem sardonic departure from the ruin of Brethil and dying Manthor this impulse ceased – as it appears. Húrin never came back to Nargothrond and Doriath; and we are denied an account, in this mode of story-telling, of what should be the culminating moment of the saga after the deaths of his children and his wife – his confrontation of Thingol and Melian in the Thousand Caves.

It might be, then, that my father had no inclination to return to the *Quenta Silmarillion*, and its characteristic mode, until he had told on an ample scale, and with the same immediacy as that of his sojourn in Brethil, the full tale of Húrin's tragic and destructive 'wanderings' – and their aftermath also: for it is to be remembered that his bringing of the treasure of Nargothrond to Doriath would lead to the slaying of Thingol by the Dwarves, the sack of Menegroth, and all the train of events that issued in the attack of the Fëanorians on Dior Thingol's heir in Doriath and, at the last, the destruction of the Havens of Sirion. If my father had done this, then out of it might have come, I suppose, new chapters of the *Quenta Silmarillion*, and a return to that quality in the older writing that I attempted to describe in my foreword to *The Book of Lost Tales*: 'The compendious or epitomising form and manner of *The Silmarillion*, with its suggestion of ages of poetry and "lore" behind it, strongly evokes a sense of "untold tales", even in the telling of them ... There is no narrative urgency, the pressure and fear of the immediate and unknown event. We do not actually see the Silmarils as we see the Ring.'

But this is entirely speculative, because none of it came about: neither the 'great saga' nor the *Quenta Silmarillion* were concluded. Freely as my father often wrote of his work, he never so much as hinted at his larger intentions for the structure of the whole. I think that it must be said that we are left, finally, in the dark.

'The Silmarillion', again in the widest sense, is very evidently a literary entity of a singular nature. I would say that it can only be defined in terms of its history; and that history is with this book largely completed ('largely', because I have not entered further into the complexities of the tale of Túrin in those parts that my father left in confusion and uncertainty, as explained in *Unfinished Tales*, p. 6). It is indeed the only 'completion' possible, because it was always 'in progress'; the published work is not in any way a completion, but a construction devised out of the existing materials. Those materials are now made available, save only in a few details and in the matter of 'Túrin' just mentioned; and with them a criticism of the 'constructed' *Silmarillion* becomes possible. I shall not enter into that question; although it will be apparent in this book that there are aspects of the work that I view with regret.

In *The War of the Jewels* I have included, as Part Four, a long essay of a very different nature: *Quendi and Eldar*. While there was no possibility of making *The History of Middle-earth* a history of the languages as well, I have not wished to eschew them altogether even when not essential to the narrative (as Adunaic is in *The Notion Club Papers*); I have wished to give at least some indication at different stages of the presence of this vital and evolving element, especially in regard to the meaning of names – thus the appendices to *The Book of Lost Tales* and the *Etymologies* in *The Lost Road*. *Quendi and Eldar* illustrates perhaps more than any other writing of my father's the significance of names, and of linguistic change affecting names, in his histories. It gives also an account of many things found nowhere else, such as the gesture-language of the Dwarves, and all that will ever be known, I believe, of Valarin, the language of the Valar.

I take this opportunity to give the correct text of a passage in *Morgoth's Ring*. Through an error that entered at a late stage and was not observed a line was dropped and a line repeated in note 16 on page 327; the text should read:

> There have been suggestions earlier in the *Athrabeth* that Andreth was looking much further back in time to the awakening of Men (thus she speaks of 'legends of days when death came less swiftly and our span was still far longer', p. 313); in her words here, 'a rumour that has come down through years uncounted', a profound alteration in the conception seems plain.

I have received a communication from Mr Patrick Wynne concerning Volume IX, *Sauron Defeated*, which I would like to record here. He has pointed out that several of the names in Michael Ramer's account of his experiences to the Notion Club are 'not just Hungarian in style but actual Hungarian words' (Ramer was born and spent his early childhood in Hungary, and he refers to the influence of Magyar on his 'linguistic taste', *Sauron Defeated* pp. 159, 201). Thus the world of the story that he wrote and read to the Club was first named *Gyönyörü* (*ibid.* p. 214, note 28), which means 'lovely'. His name for the planet Saturn was first given as *Gyürüchill* (p. 221, note 60), derived from Hungarian *gyürü* 'ring' and *csillag* 'star' (where *cs* is pronounced as English *ch* in *church*); *Gyürüchill* was then changed to *Shomorú*, probably from Hungarian *szomorú* 'sad' (though that is pronounced '*somorú*'), and if so, an allusion to the astrological belief in the cold and gloomy temperament of those born under the influence of that planet. Subsequently these names were replaced by others (*Emberü*, and *Eneköl* for Saturn) that cannot be so explained.

In this connection, Mr Carl F. Hostetter has observed that the Elvish star-name *Lumbar* ascribed to Saturn (whether or not my father always so intended it, see *Morgoth's Ring* pp. 434–5) can be explained in the same way as Ramer's *Shomorú*, in view of the Quenya word *lumbë*, 'gloom, shadow', recorded in the Elvish Etymologies (*The Lost Road and Other Writings*, p. 170).

Mr Hostetter has also pointed out that the name *Byrde* given to Finwë's first wife Míriel in the *Annals of Aman* (*Morgoth's Ring*, pp. 92, 185) is not, as I said (p. 103), an Old English word meaning 'broideress', for that is not found in Old English. The name actually depends on an argument advanced (on very good evidence) by my father that the word *byrde* 'broideress' must in fact have existed in the old language, and that it survived in the Middle English *burde* 'lady, damsel', its original specific sense faded and forgotten. His discussion is found in his article *Some Contributions to Middle-English Lexicography* (*The Review of English Studies* I.2, April 1925).

I am very grateful to Dr Judith Priestman for her generous help in providing me with copies of texts and maps in the Bodleian Library. The accuracy of the intricate text of this book has been much improved by the labour of Mr Charles Noad, unstintedly given and greatly appreciated. He has read the first proof with extreme care and with critical understanding, and has made many improvements; among these is an interpretation of the way in which the narrow path, followed by Túrin and afterwards by Brandir the Lame, went down through the woods above the Taeglin to Cabed-en-Aras: an interpretation that justifies expressions of my father's that I had taken to be merely erroneous (pp. 157, 159).

There remain a number of writings of my father's, other than those that are expressly philological, that I think should be included in this *History of Middle-earth*, and I hope to be able to publish a further volume in two years' time.

PART ONE

THE
GREY ANNALS

THE GREY ANNALS

The history of the *Annals of Beleriand* began about 1930, when my father wrote the earliest version ('**AB 1**') together with that of the *Annals of Valinor* ('**AV 1**'). These were printed in Vol.IV, *The Shaping of Middle-earth*; I remarked there that 'the *Annals* began, perhaps, in parallel with the *Quenta* as a convenient way of driving abreast, and keeping track of, the different elements in the ever more complex narrative web.' Second versions of both sets of *Annals* were composed later in the 1930s, as part of a group of texts comprising also the *Lhammas* or Account of Tongues, a new version of the *Ainulindalë*, and the central work of that time: a new version of 'The Silmarillion' proper, the unfinished *Quenta Silmarillion* ('**QS**'). These second versions, together with the other texts of that period, were printed in Vol.V, *The Lost Road and Other Writings*, under the titles *The Later Annals of Valinor* ('**AV 2**') and *The Later Annals of Beleriand* ('**AB 2**').

When my father turned again, in 1950–1, to the Matter of the Elder Days after the completion of *The Lord of the Rings*, he began new work on the *Annals* by taking up the AV 2 and AB 2 manuscripts from some 15 years earlier and using them as vehicles for revision and new writing. In the case of AV 2, correction of the old text was limited to the opening annals, and the beginnings of a new version written on the blank verso pages of this manuscript likewise petered out very quickly, so that there was no need to take much account of this preliminary work (X.47). In AB 2, on the other hand, the preparatory stages were much more extensive and substantial.

In the first place, revision of the original AB 2 text continues much further – although in practice this can be largely passed over, since the content of the revision appears in subsequent texts. (In some cases, as noted in V.124, it is not easy to separate 'early' (pre-*Lord of the Rings*) revisions and additions from 'late' (those of the early 1950s).) In the second place, the beginning of a new and much fuller version of the *Annals of Beleriand* on the blank verso pages of AB 2 extends for a considerable distance (13 manuscript pages) – and the first part of this is written in such a careful script, before it begins to degenerate, that it may be thought that my father did not at first intend it as a draft. This is entitled 'The Annals of Beleriand', and could on that account be referred to as 'AB 3', but I shall in fact call it '**GA 1**' (see below).

The final text is a good clear manuscript bearing the title 'The Annals of Beleriand or the Grey Annals'. I have chosen to call this work the *Grey Annals*, abbreviated '**GA**', in order to mark its distinctive nature in relation to the earlier forms of the Annals of Beleriand and its close association with the *Annals of Aman* ('**AAm**'), which also bears a title different from that of its predecessors. The abandoned first version just mentioned is then more suitably called 'GA 1' than 'AB 3', since for most of its length it was followed very closely in the final text, and is to be regarded as a slightly earlier variant: it will be necessary to refer to it, and to cite passages from it, but there is no need to give it in full. Where it is necessary to distinguish the final text from the aborted version I shall call the former '**GA 2**'.

There is some evidence that the *Grey Annals* followed the *Annals of Aman* (in its primary form), but the two works were, I feel certain, closely associated in time of composition. For the structure of the history of Beleriand the *Grey Annals* constitutes the primary text, and although much of the latter part of the work was used in the published *Silmarillion* with little change I give it in full. This is really essential on practical grounds, but is also in keeping with my intention in this 'History', in which I have traced the development of the Matter of the Elder Days from its beginning to its end within the compass of my father's actual writings: from this point of view the published work is not its end, and I do not treat his later writing primarily in relation to what was used, or how it was used, in '*The Silmarillion*'. – It is a most unhappy fact that he abandoned the *Grey Annals* at the death of Túrin – although, as will be seen subsequently (pp. 251 ff.), he added elements of a continuation at some later time.

I have not, as I did in the case of the *Annals of Aman*, divided the *Grey Annals* into sections, and the commentary, referenced to the numbered paragraphs, follows the end of the text (p. 103). Subsequent changes to the manuscript, which in places were heavy, are indicated as such.

At the top of the first page of the old AB 2 text, no doubt before he began work on the enormously enlarged new version, my father scribbled these notes: 'Make these the Sindarin Annals of Doriath and leave out most of the . . .' (there are here two words that probably read 'Nold[orin] stuff'); and 'Put in notes about Denethor, Thingol, etc. from AV'.

Two other elements in the complex of papers constituting the *Grey Annals* remain to be mentioned. There are a number of disconnected rough pages bearing the words 'Old material of Grey Annals' (see p. 29); and there is an amanuensis typescript in top copy and carbon that clearly belongs with that of the *Annals of Aman*, which I tentatively dated to 1958 (X.47).

THE ANNALS OF BELERIAND
OR
THE GREY ANNALS

§1   These are the Annals of Beleriand as they were made by the Sindar, the Grey Elves of Doriath and the Havens, and enlarged from the records and memories of the remnant of the Noldor of Nargothrond and Gondolin at the Mouths of Sirion, whence they were brought back into the West.

§2   Beleriand is the name of the country that lay upon either side of the great river Sirion ere the Elder Days were ended. This name it bears in the oldest records that survive, and it is here retained in that form, though now it is called Belerian. The name signifies in the language of that land: the country of Balar. For this name the Sindar gave to Ossë, who came often to those coasts, and there befriended them. At first, therefore, this name was given to the land of the shores, on either side of Sirion's mouths, that face the Isle of Balar, but it spread until it included all the ancient coast of the North-west of Middle-earth south of the Firth of Drengist and all the inner land south of Hithlum up to the feet of Eryd Luin (the Blue Mountains). But south of the mouths of Sirion it had no sure boundaries; for there were pathless forests in those days between the unpeopled shores and the lower waters of Gelion.

VY 1050

§3   Hither, it is said, at this time came Melian the Maia from Valinor, when Varda made the great stars. In this same time the Quendi awoke by Kuiviénen, as is told in the Chronicle of Aman.

1080

§4   About this time the spies of Melkor discovered the Quendi and afflicted them.

1085

§5   In this year Oromë found the Quendi, and befriended them.

1090

§6   At this time the Valar came hither from Aman for their assault upon Melkor, whose stronghold was in the North beyond Eryd Engrin (the Iron Mountains). In these regions, therefore, were fought the first battles of the Powers of the West and the North, and all this land was much broken, and it took then that shape which it had until the coming of Fionwë. For the Great Sea broke in upon the coasts and made a deep gulf to the southward, and many lesser bays were made between the Great Gulf and Helkaraxë far in the North, where Middle-earth and Aman came nigh together. Of these bays the Bay of Balar was the chief; and into it the mighty river Sirion flowed down from the new-raised highlands northwards: Dorthonion and the mountains about Hithlum. At first these lands upon either side of Sirion were ruinous and desolate because of the War of the Powers, but soon growth began there, while most of Middle-earth slept in the Sleep of Yavanna, because the Valar of the Blessed Realm had set foot there; and there were young woods under the bright stars. These Melian the Maia fostered; and she dwelt most in the glades of Nan Elmoth beside the River Celon. There also dwelt her nightingales.

1102–5

§7   Ingwë, Finwë, and Elwë were brought to Valinor by Oromë as ambassadors of the Quendi; and they looked upon the Light of the Trees and yearned for it. Returning they counselled the Eldar to go to the Land of Aman, at the summons of the Valar.

1115

§8   Even as the Valar had come first to Beleriand as they went eastward, so later Oromë leading the hosts of the Eldar westwards towards Aman brought them to the shores of Beleriand. For there the Great Sea was less wide and yet free from the perils of the ice that lay further north. In this year of the Valar, therefore, the foremost companies of the Vanyar and Noldor passed through the vale of Sirion and came to the sea-coast between Drengist and the Bay of Balar. But because of their fear of the Sea, which they had before neither seen nor imagined, the Eldar drew back into the woods and highlands. And Oromë departed and went to Valinor and left them there for a time.

1128

§9   In this year the Teleri, who had lingered on the road,

came also at last over Eryd Luin into northern Beleriand. There they halted and dwelt a while between the River Gelion and Eryd Luin. At that time many of the Noldor dwelt westward of the Teleri, in those regions where afterwards stood the forests of Neldoreth and Region. Finwë was their lord, and with him Elwë lord of the Teleri had great friendship; and Elwë was wont often to visit Finwë in the dwellings of the Noldor.

1130

§10   In this year King Elwë Singollo of the Teleri was lost in the wilderness. As he journeyed home from a meeting with Finwë, he passed by Nan Elmoth, and he heard the nightingales of Melian the Maia, and followed them deep into the glades. There he saw Melian standing beneath the stars, and a white mist was about her, but the Light of Aman was in her face. Thus began the love of Elwë Greymantle and Melian of Valinor. Hand in hand they stood silent in the woods, while the wheeling stars measured many years, and the young trees of Nan Elmoth grew tall and dark. Long his people sought for Elwë in vain.

1132

§11   Now Ulmo, at the command of the Valar, came to the shores of Beleriand and summoned the Eldar to meet him; and he spoke to them, and made music upon his conches, and changed the fear of all who heard him into a great desire for the Sea. Then Ulmo and Ossë took an island, which stood far out in the Sea, and they moved it, and brought it, as it were a mighty ship, into the Bay of Balar; and the Vanyar and Noldor embarked thereon, and were drawn over Sea, until they came at last to the Land of Aman. But a part of that island which was deep-grounded in the shoals off the mouths of Sirion was broken away and remained; and this was the Isle of Balar to which afterward Ossë often came.

§12   For the Teleri had not embarked, but remained behind. Many indeed were dwelling at that time afar off in eastern Beleriand and heard the summons of Ulmo too late; and many others searched still for Elwë their king, and were not willing to depart without him. But when the Teleri learned that their kinsfolk, the Vanyar and the Noldor, were gone, the most part hastened to the shore and dwelt thereafter nigh the mouths of Sirion, in longing for their friends that had left them. And they took Olwë, Elwë's brother, for their lord. Then Ossë and Uinen came to them, and dwelt in the Isle of Balar, and became the friends of the Teleri and taught them all manner of sea-lore and sea-music.

1149–50

§13   In this year Ulmo returned to Beleriand. To this he was most moved by the prayers of the Noldor and of Finwë their king, who grieved at their sundering from the Teleri, and besought Ulmo to bring Elwë and his people to Aman, if they would come. And all those who followed Olwë were now willing to depart; but Ossë was sad at heart. For he went seldom to the shores of Aman, and loved the Teleri, and he was ill-pleased that their fair voices should be heard no longer by the strands of Middle-earth, which were his domain.

§14   Ossë therefore persuaded many to remain in Beleriand, and when King Olwë and his host were embarked upon the isle and passed over the Sea they abode still by the shore; and Ossë returned to them, and continued in friendship with them. And he taught to them the craft of shipbuilding and of sailing; and they became a folk of mariners, the first in Middle-earth, and had fair havens at Eglarest and Brithombar; but some dwelt still upon the Isle of Balar. Cirdan the Shipwright was the lord of this people, and all that shoreland between Drengist and Balar that he ruled was called the Falas. But among the Teleri were none yet so hardy of heart, and of their ships none so swift and strong that they might dare the deeps of the Great Sea or behold even from afar the Blessed Realm and the Light of the Trees of Valinor. Wherefore those that remained behind were called Moriquendi, Elves of the Dark.

1150

§15   The friends and kinsfolk of Elwë also remained; but they would fain have departed to Valinor and the Light of the Trees (which Elwë indeed had seen), if Ulmo and Olwë had been willing to tarry yet longer while they sought still for Elwë. But when Ulmo had tarried a full Year (and a Year of the Valar is in length well nigh as are ten of the years that now are) he departed, and the friends of Elwë were left behind. Therefore they called themselves the Eglath, the Forsaken People; and though they dwelt in the woods and hills rather than by the Sea, which filled them with sorrow, their inmost hearts yearned ever Westward.

1152

§16 At this time, it is told, Elwë Singollo awoke from his long trance. And he came forth from Nan Elmoth with Melian, and they dwelt thereafter in the woods in the midst of the land; and though Elwë had greatly desired to see again the light of the Trees, in the face of Melian the fair he beheld the Light of Aman as in an unclouded mirror, and in that light he was content. Then his folk gathered about him in joy; and they were amazed, for fair and noble as he had been, now he appeared as it were a lord of the Maiar, tallest of all the Children of Ilúvatar, his hair as grey silver, and his eyes like unto stars. King of the Eglath he became, and Melian was his Queen, wiser than any daughter of Middle-earth.

1200

§17 It is not known to any among Elves or Men when Lúthien, only child of Elwë and Melian, came into the World, fairest of all the Children of Ilúvatar that were or shall be. But it is held that it was at the end of the first age of the Chaining of Melkor, when all the Earth had great peace and the glory of Valinor was at its noon, and though Middle-earth for the most [part] lay in the Sleep of Yavanna, in Beleriand under the power of Melian there was life and joy and the bright stars shone like silver fires. In the Forest of Neldoreth it is said that she was born and cradled under the stars of heaven, and the white flowers of *niphredil* came forth to greet her, as stars from the earth.

1200–50

§18 In this time the power of Elwë and Melian reached over all Beleriand. Elu Thingol he was called in the tongue of his people, King Greymantle, and all the Elves of Beleriand from the mariners of Cirdan to the wandering huntsmen of the Blue Mountains took him for lord. And they are called, therefore, the Sindar, the Grey Elves of starlit Berleriand. And albeit they were Moriquendi, under the lordship of Thingol and the teaching of Melian they became the fairest and the most wise and skilful of all the Elves of Middle-earth.

1250

§19 In this year the Norn-folk came first over the mountains into Beleriand. This people the Noldor after named the Naugrim, whom some Men call Dwarves. Their most ancient dwellings were far to the East, but they had delved for themselves great halls and mansions, after the manner of their kind, on the east-side of Eryd Luin, north and south of Mount Dolmed, in those places which the Eldar named Belegost and Nogrod (but they Gabilgathol and Tumunzahar). Thence they now came forth and made themselves known to the Elves; and the Elves were amazed, for they had deemed themselves to be the only living things in Middle-earth that spoke with words or wrought with hands; and that all others were beasts and birds only.

§20   Nonetheless they could understand no word of the tongue of the Naugrim, which to their ears was cumbrous and unlovely; and few ever of the Eldar have achieved the mastery of it. But the Dwarves were swift to learn (after a fashion), and indeed were more willing to learn the Elven-tongue than to teach to aliens their own; and soon there was much parley between the peoples. Ever cool was their friendship, though much profit they had one of the other. But at that time those griefs that lay between them had not yet come to pass, and they were welcomed by King Thingol.

§21   How the Dwarves came into the world the Eldar know not for certain, though the loremasters have elsewhere recorded the tales of the Naugrim themselves (such as they would reveal) concerning their beginning. They say that Aulë the Maker, whom they call Mahal, brought them into being; and however that may be, certain it is that they were great smiths and masons, though of old there was little beauty in their works. Iron and copper they loved to work more than silver or gold, and stone more than wood.

1300

Of the building of Menegroth

§22   Now Melian had after the manner of the Maiar, the people of Valinor, much foresight. And when two of the ages of the Chaining of Melkor had passed, she counselled Thingol that the Peace of Arda would not last for ever; and he therefore bethought him how he should make for himself a kingly dwelling, and a place that should be strong, if evil were to awake again in Middle-earth. He called therefore upon the Enfeng, the Longbeards of Belegost, whom he had befriended, and sought their aid and counsel. And they gave it willingly, for they were unwearied in those days, and eager for new works.

And though the Dwarves ever demanded a price for all that they did, whether with delight or with toil, at this time they held themselves paid. For Melian taught them much wisdom, which they were eager to get; whereas Thingol rewarded them with many fair pearls. These Cirdan gave to him, for they were got in great number in the shallow waters about the Isle of Balar; but the Naugrim had not before seen their like, and they held them dear. And one there was great as a dove's egg, and its sheen was as the starlight upon the foam of the sea; Nimphelos it was named, and the chieftain of the Enfeng prized it above a mountain of wealth.

§23 Therefore the Naugrim laboured long and gladly for Thingol, and devised for him mansions after the fashion of their folk, delved deep in the earth. Where the River Esgalduin flowed down, dividing Neldoreth from Region, there was in the midst of the forest a rocky hill, and the river ran at its feet. There they made the gates of the halls of Thingol, and they built a bridge of stone over the river, by which alone the gates could be entered. But beyond the gates wide passages ran down to high halls and chambers far below that were hewn in the living stone, so many and so great that that dwelling was named Menegroth, the Thousand Caves.

§24 But the Elves also had part in that labour, and Elves and Dwarves together, each with their own skills, there wrought out the visions of Melian, images of the wonder and beauty of Valinor beyond the Sea. The pillars of Menegroth were hewn in the likeness of the beeches of Oromë, stock, bough, and leaf, and they were lit with lanterns of gold. The nightingales sang there as in the gardens of Lorien; and there were fountains of silver, and basins of marble, and floors of many-coloured stones. Carven figures of beasts and of birds there ran upon the walls, or climbed upon the pillars, or peered among the branches entwined with many flowers. And as the years passed Melian and her maidens filled the halls with webs of many hues, wherein could be read the deeds of the Valar, and many things that had befallen in Arda since its beginning, and shadows of things that were yet to be. That was the fairest dwelling of any king that hath ever been east of the Sea.

1300–50

§25 After the building of Menegroth was achieved, there was peace in the realm of Thingol. The Naugrim would come ever and anon over the mountains and visit Menegroth and go in traffick about the land, though they went seldom to the Falas, for they hated the sound of the Sea and feared to look on it; but otherwise there came to Beleriand no rumour or tidings of the world without. But it came to pass that the Dwarves were troubled, and they spoke to King Thingol, saying that the Valar had not rooted out utterly the evils of the North, and now the remnant, having long multiplied in the dark, were coming forth once more and roaming far and wide. 'There are fell beasts,' said they, 'in the land east of the mountains, and the dark-elves that dwell there, your ancient kindred, are flying from the plains to the hills.'

1330

§26   And ere long (in the year 1330 according to the annals that were made in Doriath) the evil creatures came even to Beleriand, over passes in the mountains, or up from the south through the dark forests. Wolves there were, or creatures that walked in wolf-shapes, and other fell beings of shadow.

§27   Among these were the Orkor indeed, who after wrought ruin in Beleriand; but they were yet few and wary and did but smell out the ways of the land, awaiting the return of their Lord. Whence they came, or what they were, the Elves knew not then, deeming them to be Avari, maybe, that had become evil and savage in the wild. In which they guessed all too near, it is said.

§28   Therefore Thingol bethought [him] of arms, which before his folk had not needed, and these at first the Naugrim smithied for him. For they were greatly skilled in such work, though none among them surpassed the craftsmen of Nogrod, of whom Telchar the Smith was the greatest in renown. A warlike race of old were all the Naugrim, and they would fight fiercely with whomsoever aggrieved them: folk of Melkor, or Eldar, or Avari, or wild beasts, or not seldom with their own kin, Dwarves of other mansions and lordships. Their smith-craft indeed the Sindar soon learned of them; yet in the tempering of steel alone of all crafts the Dwarves were never outmatched even by the Noldor, and in the making of mail of linked rings (which the Enfeng first contrived) their work had no rival.

§29   At this time therefore the Sindar were well armed, and they drove off all creatures of evil, and had peace again; but Thingol's armouries were stored with axes (the chief weapons of the Naugrim, and of the Sindar), and with spears and swords, and tall helms, and long coats of bright mail: for the hauberks of the Enfeng were so fashioned that they rusted not and shone ever as were they new-burnished. This proved well for Thingol in the time that was to come.

1350

The coming of Denethor

§30 Now as is elsewhere recounted, one Dân of the host of Olwë forsook the march of the Eldar at that time when the Teleri were halted by the shores of the Great River upon the borders of the westlands of Middle-earth. And he led away a numerous people and went south down the river, and of the wanderings of that people, the Nandor, little is now known. Some, it is said, dwelt age-long in the woods of the Vale of the Great River, some came at last to the mouths of Anduin, and there dwelt by the Sea, and others passing by the White Mountains came north again and entered the wilderness of Eriador between Eryd Luin and the far Mountains of Mist. Now these were a woodland folk and had no weapons of metal, and the coming of the fell beasts of the North affrayed them sorely, as the Naugrim reported. Therefore Denethor, the son of Dân, hearing rumour of the might of Thingol and his majesty, and of the peace of his realm, gathered such host of his scattered folk as he could and led them over the mountains into Beleriand. There they were welcomed by Thingol, as kin long lost that return, and they dwelt in Ossiriand in the south of his kingdom. For it was a great country, and yet little peopled; and it was so named, the Land of Seven Rivers, because it lay between the mighty stream of Gelion and the mountains, from which there flowed into Gelion the swift rivers: Ascar, Thalos, Legolin, Brilthor, Duilwen, and Adurant. In that region the forests in after days were tall and green, and the people of Denethor there dwelt warily and seldom seen, because of their raiment of the colour of leaves; and they were called therefore the Green-elves.

§31 Of the long years of peace that followed after the coming of Denethor there is little tale; for though in this time Dairon the minstrel, it is said, who was the chief loremaster of the kingdom of Thingol, devised his Runes,* [*added later in margin:* Cirth] they were little used by the Sindar for the keeping of records, until the days of the War, and much that was held in memory has perished in the ruin of Doriath. Yet verily of bliss and glad life there is little to be said, ere it endeth; as works fair and wonderful, while still they endure for eyes to see, are their own record, and only when they are in peril or broken for ever do they pass into song. In Beleriand in those days the Elves walked, and the rivers flowed, and the stars shone, and the night-flowers gave forth their scents; and the beauty of Melian was as the noon, and the beauty of Lúthien was as the dawn in spring. In Beleriand King Thingol upon his throne was as the sons of the Valar, whose power is at rest, whose joy is as an air that they breathe in all their days, whose thought flows in a tide untroubled from the heights to the deeps. In Beleriand still at whiles rode Oromë the great, passing like a wind over the mountains, and the sound of his horn came down the leagues of the starlight, and the Elves feared him for the splendour of his countenance and the great noise of the onrush of Nahar; but when the Valaróma echoed in the hills, they knew well that all evil things were fled far away.

1495

§32   It came to pass at last that the end of Bliss was at hand, and the noontide of Valinor was drawing to its twilight. For as is known to all, being written elsewhere in lore and sung in many songs, Melkor slew the Trees of the Valar with the aid of Ungoliantë, and escaped and came back to the north of Middle-earth. And hereafter he shall be known by that name that Fëanor gave him, the Dark Foe, Morgoth the Accursed.

§33   Far to the North befell the strife of Morgoth and Ungoliantë; but the great cry of Morgoth echoed through Beleriand, and all its folk shrank for fear; for though few knew what it foreboded, they heard then the herald of death.

§34   Soon after, indeed, Ungoliantë fled from the North and came into the realm of King Thingol, and a terror of darkness

---

* These, it is said, he contrived first ere the building of Menegroth, and after bettered them. The Naugrim, indeed, that came to Thingol learned the Runes of Dairon, and were well-pleased with the device, esteeming Dairon's skill higher than did the Sindar, his own folk; and by the Naugrim they [*later* > the Cirth] were taken east over the mountains and passed into the knowledge of many peoples.

was about her. But by the power of Melian she was stayed, and entered not into Neldoreth, but abode long while under the shadow of the precipices in which Dorthonion fell southward. Therefore they became known as Eryd Orgoroth, the Mountains of Terror, and none dared go thither, or pass nigh to them; for even after Ungoliantë herself departed and went whither she would back into the forgotten South of the world, her foul offspring dwelt there in form as spiders and wove there their hideous webs. There light and life were strangled, and there all waters were poisoned.

§35   Morgoth, however, came not himself to Beleriand, but went to the Iron Mountains, and there with the aid of his servants that came forth to meet him he delved anew his vast vaults and dungeons. These the Noldor after named Angband: the Iron Prison; and above their gates Morgoth reared the vast and threefold peaks of Thangorodrim, and a great reek of dark smoke was ever wreathed about them.

1497

§36   In this year Morgoth made his first assault upon Beleriand, which lay south of Angband. Indeed it is said that the gates of Morgoth were but one hundred and fifty leagues distant from the bridge of Menegroth; far and yet all too near.

§37   Now the Orcs that had multiplied in the bowels of the earth grew strong and fell, and their dark lord filled them with a lust of ruin and death; and they issued from Angband's gates under the clouds that Morgoth sent forth, and passed silently into the highlands of the north. Thence on a sudden a great army came to Beleriand and assailed King Thingol. Now in his wide realm many Elves wandered free in the wild or dwelt at peace in small kindreds of quiet folk far sundered. Only about Menegroth in the midst of the land, and along the Falas in the country of the mariners were there numerous peoples; but the Orcs came down upon either side of Menegroth, and from camps in the east between Celon and Gelion, and west in the plains between Sirion and Narog, they plundered far and wide; and Thingol was cut off from Cirdan at Eglarest.

§38   Therefore he called upon Denethor, and the Elves came in force from Region over Aros and from Ossiriand, and fought the first battle in the Wars of Beleriand. And the eastern host of the Orcs was taken between the armies of the Eldar, north of the Andram and midway between Aros and Gelion, and there they were utterly defeated, and those that fled north from the great slaughter were waylaid by the axes of the Naugrim that issued from Mount Dolmed: few indeed returned to Angband.

§39   But the victory of the Elves was dearbought. For the Elves of Ossiriand were light-armed, and no match for the Orcs, who were shod with iron and iron-shielded and bore great spears with broad blades. And Denethor was cut off and surrounded upon the hill of Amon Ereb; and there he fell and all his nearest kin about him, ere the host of Thingol could come to his aid. Bitterly though his fall was avenged, when Thingol came upon the rear of the Orcs and slew them aheaps, the Green-elves lamented him ever after and took no king again. After the battle some returned to Ossiriand, and their tidings filled the remnant of their folk with great fear, so that thereafter they came never forth in open war, but kept themselves by wariness and secrecy. And many went north and entered the guarded realm of Thingol and were merged with his folk.

§40   And when Thingol came again to Menegroth he learned that the Orc-host in the west was victorious and had driven Cirdan to the rim of the Sea. Therefore he withdrew all his folk that his summons could reach within the fastness of Neldoreth and Region, and Melian put forth her power and fenced all that dominion round about with an unseen wall of shadow and bewilderment: the Girdle of Melian, that none thereafter could pass against her will or the will of King Thingol (unless one should come with a power greater than that of Melian the Maia). Therefore this inner land which was long named Eglador was after called Doriath, the guarded kingdom, Land of the Girdle. Within it there was yet a watchful peace; but without there was peril and great fear, and the servants of Morgoth roamed at will, save in the walled havens of the Falas.

Of the Coming of the Noldor

§41   But new tidings were at hand, which none in Middle-earth had foreseen, neither Morgoth in his pits nor Melian in Menegroth; for no news came out of Aman, whether by messenger, or by spirit, or by vision in dream, after the death of the Trees and the hiding of Valinor. In this same year of the Valar (but some seven years after in the later reckoning of time) Fëanor came over Sea in the white ships of the Teleri, and landed in the Firth of Drengist, and there burned the ships at Losgar.

§42   Now the flames of that burning were seen not only by
Fingolfin, whom Fëanor had deserted, but also by the Orcs and
the watchers of Morgoth. No tale hath told what Morgoth
thought in his heart at the tidings that Fëanor his bitterest foe
had brought a host out of the West. Maybe he feared him little,
for he had not yet had proof of the swords of the Noldor, and
soon it was seen that he purposed to drive them back into the
Sea.

§43   Drengist is a long firth which pierces the Echoing Hills
of Eryd Lómin that are the west-fence of the great country of
Hithlum. Thus the host of Fëanor passed from the shores into
the inner regions of Hithlum, and marching about the northern
end of the Mountains of Mithrim they encamped in that part
which was named Mithrim and lay about the great lake amid
the mountains that bore the same name.

§44   But the host of Melkor, orcs and werewolves, came
through the passes of Eryd-wethrin and assailed Fëanor on a
sudden, ere his camp was fullwrought or put in defence. There
now on the grey fields of Mithrim was fought the second battle
of the Wars of Beleriand, and the first meeting of the might of
Morgoth with the valour of the Noldor. *Dagor-nuin-Giliath* it is
named, the Battle under the Stars, for the Moon had not yet
risen. In that battle, albeit outnumbered and taken at unawares,
the Noldor were swiftly victorious. Strong and fair were they
yet, for the light of Aman was not yet dimmed in their eyes;
swift they were, and deadly in wrath, and long and terrible were
their swords. The Orcs fled before them, and they were driven
forth from Mithrim with great slaughter, and hunted over that
great plain that lay north of Dorthonion, and was then called
Ardgalen. There the armies that had passed south into the vales
of Sirion and had beleagured Cirdan came up to their succour,
and were caught in their ruin. For Celegorn Fëanor's son,
having news of them, waylaid them with a part of the Elven-
host, and coming down upon them out of the hills nigh Eithel
Sirion drove them into the Fen of Serech. Evil indeed were the
tidings that came at last unto Angband, and Morgoth was
dismayed. Ten days that battle endured, and from it returned
of all the hosts that he had prepared for the conquest of the
kingdoms of the Eldar no more than a handful of leaves.

§45   Yet cause he had for great joy, though it was hidden
from him for a while. For the heart of Fëanor, in his wrath
against the Enemy, blazed like a fire, and he would not halt, but

pressed on behind the remnant of the Orcs, thinking, it is said, so to come at Morgoth himself. And he laughed aloud as he wielded his sword, and rejoiced that he had dared the wrath of the Valar and the evils of the road that he might see that hour of his vengeance. He knew naught of Angband or the great strength of defence that Morgoth had so swiftly prepared; but had he known, it would not have deterred him, for fey he was, consumed by the flame of his own wrath. Thus it was that he drew far ahead of the van of his host, and seeing this the servants of Morgoth turned to bay, and there issued from Angband Balrogs to aid them. There upon the confines of Dor Daedeloth, the land of Morgoth, Fëanor was surrounded, with few friends about him. Soon he stood alone; but long he fought on, and laughed undismayed, though he was wrapped in fire and wounded with many wounds. But at the last Gothmog,* Lord of the Balrogs, smote him to the ground, and there he would have perished, but Maidros and three other of his sons in that moment came up with force to his aid, and the Balrogs fled back to Angband.

§46   Then his sons raised up their father and bore him back towards Mithrim. But as they drew near to Eithel Sirion and were upon the upward path to the pass over the mountains, Fëanor bade them halt. For his wounds were mortal, and he knew that his hour was come. And looking out from the slopes of Eryd-wethrin with his last sight he beheld afar the peaks of Thangorodrim, mightiest of the towers of Middle-earth, and knew with the foreknowledge of death that no power of the Noldor would ever overthrow them; but he cursed the name of Morgoth, and laid it upon his sons to hold to their oath, and to avenge their father. Then he died; but he had neither burial nor tomb, for so fiery was his spirit that, as it passed, his body fell to ash and was borne away like a smoke, and his likeness has never again appeared in Arda, neither has his spirit left the realm of Mandos. Thus ended the mightiest of the Noldor, of whose deeds came both their greatest renown and their most grievous woe.

§47   Tidings of these great deeds came to Menegroth and to Eglarest, and the Grey-elves were filled with wonder and with hope, for they looked to have great help in their defence against

---

* [*Marginal note:*] whom Ecthelion afterward slew in Gondolin.

Morgoth from their mighty kindred that thus returned un-looked-for from the West in their very hour of need, believing indeed at first that they came as emissaries of the Valar to deliver their brethren from evil. Now the Grey-elves were of Telerian race, and Thingol was the brother of Olwë at Alqua-londë, but naught yet was known of the kinslaying, nor of the manner of the exile of the Noldor, and of the oath of Fëanor. Yet though they had not heard of the Curse of Mandos, it was soon at work in Beleriand. For it entered into the heart of King Thingol to regret the days of peace when he was the high lord of all the land and its peoples. Wide were the countries of Beleriand and many empty and wild, and yet he welcomed not with full heart the coming of so many princes in might out of the West, eager for new realms.

§48 Thus there was from the first a coolness between him and the sons of Fëanor, whereas the closest friendship was needed, if Morgoth were to be withstood; for the [House >] sons of Fëanor were ever unwilling to accept the overlordship of Thingol, and would ask for no leave where they might dwell or might pass. When, therefore, ere long (by treachery and ill will, as later is told) the full tale of the deeds in Valinor became known in Beleriand, there was rather enmity than alliance between Doriath and the House of Fëanor; and this bitterness Morgoth eagerly inflamed by all means that he could find. But that evil lay as yet in the days to come, and the first meeting of the Sindar and the Noldor was eager and glad, though parley was at first not easy between them, for in their long severance the tongue of the Kalaquendi in Valinor and the Moriquendi in Beleriand had drawn far apart.

Excursus on the languages of Beleriand

I interrupt the text here since the complex variant material that follows in the two manuscripts cannot well be accommodated in the commentary.

In place of GA 2 §48 just given, GA 1 (making no reference to the active hostility that developed between Thingol and the Fëanorians) has only the following (after the words 'eager for new realms'):

Moreover in their long severance the tongues of the Sindar and the Noldor had drawn apart, and at first parley was not easy between them.

This is followed by a long 'excursus' (marked on the manuscript as an intrusion into the main text) on the development and relations of

Noldorin and Sindarin in Beleriand, the end of which is also the end of GA 1. This discussion reappears, rewritten, in GA 2, and then this revised form was itself substantially altered. It seems desirable to give all the versions of this passage, of central importance in the linguistic history of Middle-earth. The numbered notes to this section are found on p. 28.

The original version in GA 1 reads as follows.

It was indeed at the landing of Fëanor three hundred and sixty-five long years of the Valar[1] since the Noldor had passed over the Sea and left the Teleri behind them. Now that time was in length well nigh as three thousand and five hundred years of the Sun. In such an age the tongues of mortal Men that were far sundered would indeed change out of knowledge, unless it were as written records of song and wisdom. But in Valinor in the days of the Trees change was little to be perceived, save that which came of will and design, while in Middle-earth under the Sleep of Yavanna it was slow also, though before the Rising of the Moon all things had been stirred from slumber in Beleriand, as has before been told.[2] Therefore, whereas the tongue of the Noldor had altered little from the ancient tongue of the Eldar upon the march – and its altering had for the most part come in the making of new words (for things old and new) and in the softening and harmonizing of the sounds and patterns of the Quendian tongue to forms that seemed to the Noldor more beautiful – the language of the Sindar had changed much, even in unheeded growth as a tree may imperceptibly change its shape: as much maybe as an unwritten mortal tongue might change in five hundred years or more.[3] It was already ere the Rising of the Sun a speech greatly different to the ear from the Noldorin, and after that Rising all change was swift, for a while in the second Spring of Arda very swift indeed. To the ear, we say, because though Dairon the minstrel and loremaster of Menegroth had devised his Runes already by V.Y. 1300 (and after greatly bettered them), it was not the custom of the Sindar to write down their songs or records, and the Runes of Dairon (save in Menegroth) were used chiefly for names and brief inscriptions cut upon wood, stone, or metal. (The Naugrim[4] learned the Runes of Dairon from Menegroth, being well-pleased with the device and esteeming Dairon higher than [did] his own folk; and by the Naugrim they were brought east over the Mountains.)[5]

Soon, however, it came to pass that the Noldor in daily use

took on the Sindarin tongue, and this tongue enriched by words and devices from Noldorin became the tongue of all the Eldar in Beleriand (save in the country of the Green[-elves]) and the language of all the Eldar, either in Middle-earth, or that (as shall be told) went back from exile into the West and dwelt and dwell now upon Eressëa. In Valinor the ancient Elven-speech is maintained, and the Noldor never forsook it; but it became for them no longer a cradle-tongue, a mother-tongue, but a learned language of lore, and of high song and noble and solemn use. Few of the Sindar learned it, save in so far as they became, outside Doriath, merged in one people with Noldor and followed their princes; as indeed ere long happened indeed except for few scattered companies of Sindar in mountainous woods, and except also for the lordship of Cirdan, and the guarded kingdom of Thingol.

Now this change of tongue among the Noldor took place for many divers reasons. First, that though the Sindar were not numerous they far outnumbered the hosts of Fëanor and Fingolfin, such as in the end survived their dreadful journeys and reached Beleriand. Secondly and no less: that the Noldor having forsaken Aman themselves began to be subject to change undesigned while they were yet upon the march, and at the Rising of the Sun this change became swift – and the change in their daily tongue was such that, whether by reason of the like clime and soil and the like fortunes, whether by intercourse and mingling of blood, it changed in the same ways as did the Sindarin, and the two tongues grew towards one another. Thus it came that words taken from Noldorin into Telerin entered not in the true forms of High Speech but as it were altered and fitted to the character of the tongue of Beleriand. Thirdly: because after the death of Fëanor the overlordship of the Exiles (as shall be recounted) passed to Fingolfin, and he being of other mood than Fëanor acknowledged the high-kingship of Thingol and Menegroth, being indeed greatly in awe of that king, mightiest of the Eldar save Fëanor only, and of Melian no less. But though Elu-Thingol, great in memory, could recall the tongue of the Eldar as it had been ere riding from Finwë's camp he heard the birds of Nan Elmoth, in Doriath the Sindarin tongue alone was spoken, and all must learn it who would have dealings with the king.

It is said that it was after the Third Battle Dagor Aglareb[6] that the Noldor first began far and wide to take the Sindarin as they settled and established realms in Beleriand; though maybe the Noldorin survived (especially in Gondolin) until Dagor Arnediad[7] or until the Fall of Gondolin – survived, that is, in the spoken form that it had in Beleriand as different both from the Quenya (or Ancient Noldorin) and from the Sindarin: for the Quenya never perished and is known and used still by all such as crossed the Sea ere the Trees were slain.

This is the first general linguistic statement since the *Lhammas*, written long before, and there have been major shifts from the earlier theory. The third version of the *Lhammas*, '*Lammasethen*', the latest and shortest of the three, gives a clear statement of what is more diffusely expressed in the longer versions, and I cite a part of it (from V.193–4):

> Now ancient Noldorin, as first used, and written in the days of Fëanor in Tûn, remained spoken by the Noldor that did not leave Valinor at its darkening, and it abides still there, not greatly changed, and not greatly different from Lindarin. It is called *Kornoldorin*, or *Finrodian* because Finrod and many of his folk returned to Valinor and did not go to Beleriand. But most of the Noldor went to Beleriand, and in the 400 years of their wars with Morgoth their tongue changed greatly. For three reasons: because it was not in Valinor; because there was war and confusion, and much death among the Noldor, so that their tongue was subject to vicissitudes similar to those of mortal Men; and because in all the world, but especially in Middle-earth, change and growth was very great in the first years of the Sun. Also in Beleriand the tongue and dialects of the Telerian Ilkorins was current, and their king Thingol was very mighty; and Noldorin in Beleriand took much from Beleriandic especially of Doriath. Most of the names and places in that land were given in Doriathrin form. Noldorin returned, after the overthrow of Morgoth, into the West, and lives still in Toleressëa, where it changes now little; and this tongue is derived mainly from the tongue of Gondolin, whence came Eärendel; but it has much of Beleriandic, for Elwing his wife was daughter of Dior, Thingol's heir; and it has somewhat of Ossiriand, for Dior was son of Beren who lived long in Ossiriand.

There was also the book-tongue, 'Elf-Latin', Quenya, concerning which the *Lammasethen* gives a different account from that in the other versions (see V.195). The 'Elf-Latin', it is said (V.172), was brought to Middle-earth by the Noldor, it came to be used by all the Ilkorindi, 'and all Elves know it, even such as linger still in the Hither Lands'.

Thus in the *Lhammas* account we are concerned essentially with three tongues in Beleriand after the Return of the Noldor:

Quenya, the high language and book-tongue, brought from Valinor by the Noldor;

Noldorin, the language of the Noldor in Kôr, greatly changed in Beleriand and much influenced by the Ilkorin speech especially that of Doriath. (It is said in the *Lhammas*, V.174, that the Noldorin tongue of Kôr, *Korolambë* or *Kornoldorin*, was itself much changed from ancient times through the peculiar inventiveness of the Noldor.)

Beleriandic, the Ilkorin tongue of Beleriand, which had become in long ages very different from the tongues of Valinor.

The Noldorin speech of Gondolin was the language that survived in Tol Eressëa after the end of the Elder Days, though influenced by other speech, especially the Ilkorin of Doriath during the sojourn at Sirion's Mouths (see V.177–8).

In GA 1 we have still the conception that the language of the Noldor in Valinor was changed by Noldorin inventiveness, though it is emphasized that it had altered little 'from the ancient tongue of the Eldar upon the march'; and the profound difference between the Noldorin of the new-come Exiles out of Valinor and the ancient Telerian tongue of Beleriand (now called Sindarin) likewise remains – indeed it is the remark that at first communication between Noldor and Sindar was not easy that leads to this excursus. But in GA 1 it is said that, while the Sindarin tongue was 'enriched by words and devices from Noldorin', *Sindarin nevertheless became the language of all the Eldar of Middle-earth and was the language of Tol Eressëa after the Return*; while Noldorin of Valinor became a 'learned' tongue – equivalent in status to the 'Elf-Latin' or Quenya of the *Lhammas*, but learned by few among the Sindar; and indeed the 'Ancient Noldorin' is equated with Quenya (p. 22, at the end of the text). Among the reasons given for this development is that spoken Noldorin in Beleriand and Sindarin 'grew towards' each other, and it is made clear in the last paragraph of the text that there was at the end of the Elder Days a profound difference between the spoken Noldorin of Beleriand, where it survived, and 'Ancient Noldorin' or Quenya.

The statement that Fingolfin as 'overlord' of the Exiles 'acknowledged the high-kingship of Thingol and Menegroth', being 'greatly in awe of that king', is notable (cf. QS §121: 'and mighty though the Kings of the Noldor were in those days ... the name of Thingol was held in awe among them'). This is indeed one of the reasons given for the adoption of Sindarin by the Noldor in Beleriand – for in Thingol's domain only Sindarin might be used; but it is clear that as yet the idea of an actual ban on the use of the Noldorin speech among the Sindar had not arisen.

At the end of this linguistic passage in GA 1 my father wrote in rapid pencil:

Alter this. Let Sindar and Noldor speak much the same tongue owing (a) to changelessness in Valinor (b) to slow change in Middle-earth (c) to long memories of the Elves. But there were of course differences – new words in Noldorin and Sindarin. In both cases more by invention than involuntary. But after Rising of Sun change was sudden and swift – and the Noldor brought a special curse of changefulness with them (designed to cut them off from converse with Valinor?). The two tongues there changed and grew alike. Generally in Beleriand a Noldorized (slightly) Sindarin was spoken. In Doriath less Noldorin if any. [?Ossiriand] to be like Beleriandic.

The difference here from the primary text lies in a denial of any very significant difference between the language of Beleriand and the language of the incoming Noldor, with the subsequent history (as it appears, from the brief and hasty words) being rather one of the coalescence of the languages than of the abandonment of Noldorin.

The excursus on languages in GA 2, written in a much smaller script than that of the main body of the text, reads as follows.

It was indeed at the landing of Fëanor three hundred and sixty-five long years of the Valar since the Noldor had passed over the Sea and left the Sindar behind. Now that time was in length well nigh as three thousand and five hundred years of the Sun. In such an age the tongues of Men that were far sundered would indeed change out of knowledge, save such as were written down in records of song and wisdom. But in Valinor in the days of the Trees change was little to be perceived, save that which came of will and design, while in Middle-earth under the Sleep of Yavanna the change of growth was slow also. Nonetheless in Beleriand the Sleep before the coming of the Sun had been stirred (as elsewhere is told) and the language of the Sindar had in the long years changed much, even in unheeded growth, as a tree may imperceptibly change its shape: as much, maybe, as an unwritten tongue of the later days woud change in five hundred years or more. Whereas the Noldorin tongue, albeit still far nearer in most ways to the ancient common speech of the Eldar, had been altered by will (to forms that seemed to those in Aman more sweet upon the tongue or in the ear) and by the invention of many new words unknown to the Sindar. But speech between the two kindreds became easy and free in this wise. First that after the Rising of the Sun the change of all things in Arda was sudden and swift, and in the days of the Wars both the tongue of the Noldor and that of the Sindar changed greatly: moreover, whether by reason of the like clime, and soil, and the like fortunes, whether by intercourse and the mingling of the peoples, the two tongues changed in similar ways and drew together again. Secondly because in time it came to pass that most of the Noldor indeed forsook their own tongue in daily use and took the tongue of Beleriand instead, though they enriched it with many words of their own. Only in Gondolin, which was early peopled (by Noldor alone)[8] and cut off from intercourse with others, did the Noldorin tongue endure unto the end of the city; whereas in Doriath only was the Sindarin tongue maintained untouched by the Noldorin and less changed than the language of those without. Now this change in the speech of the Noldor came about in this wise. First: though the Sindar were not numerous they much outnumbered the hosts of Fëanor and Fingolfin, such as survived their dreadful journey. Secondly: because of the mingling of the peoples, whereby in all the countries save only in Doriath though the princes of the Noldor were the kings their followers were largely Sindarin by race. Thirdly: because after the death of Fëanor the overlordship of the Exiles passed to Fingolfin (save among the followers of Fëanor's sons), and he acknowledged the high-kingship of Thingol, being indeed in awe of that king, mightiest of the Eldar save Fëanor, and of Melian no less. But Thingol, because of the grievance of the Teleri against the Noldor, would not speak the Noldorin tongue and forbade his subjects to do so. Moreover it came to pass that the Noldor, having of their own will forsaken Aman in rebellion, became subject to change undesigned in a measure beyond even that of the Sindar, and their own tongue in daily use swiftly became unlike the high tongue of Valinor. But the Noldor, being loremasters, retained that high tongue in lore, and ceased not to use it for noble purposes and to teach it to their children. Therefore the form of their speech in daily use came to be held as debased, and the Noldor would use either the High Tongue as a learned language, or else in daily business and in all matters that concerned all the Eldar of Beleriand in general they would use rather the tongue of that land. It is said that it was after the Third Battle, Dagor Aglareb, that the Noldor first began far and wide to take the Sindarin tongue, as they settled and established their realms in Beleriand.

This restructuring and partial rewriting of the text does not change very substantially the ideas expressed in the earlier form of it: my father did not take up his pencilled note of projected alterations given on p. 24. The passage concerning Dairon and the Runes is omitted, but that had been introduced earlier in GA 2 (§31). It is now emphasized that the Sindarin of Doriath was to some degree archaic, and 'untouched' by Noldorin: this is not stated in GA 1, though it is said there that 'in Doriath the Sindarin tongue alone was spoken'. The acknowledgement by Fingolfin of Thingol's 'high-kingship' is retained (with the reservation 'save among the followers of Fëanor's sons'), but there now appears the ban on the Noldorin tongue imposed by Thingol on his subjects when he learned of the Kinslaying at Alqualondë as one of the reasons for the abandonment of their own tongue by the Noldor. Noldorin is now said to have changed even more rapidly in Middle-earth after the Rising of the Sun than Sindarin, and this is associated with their rebellion in Aman (cf. the words in the pencilled comments at the end of the GA 1 text, p. 24: 'the Noldor brought a special curse of changefulness with them'); while the opinion coming to be held among the Noldor themselves that their spoken tongue was debased provides a further explanation of its abandonment.

My father then (probably after no long interval) rejected the whole of this second text after the words 'and by the invention of many new words unknown to the Sindar' (p. 24) and replaced it as follows:

But it came to pass ere long that the Exiles took up the tongue of Beleriand, as the language of daily use, and their ancient tongue was retained only as a high speech and a language of lore, especially in the houses of the Noldorin lords and among the wise. Now this change of speech was made for many reasons. First, the Noldor were fewer in number than the Sindar, and, save in Doriath [*struck our later:* and Gondolin],[9] the peoples soon became much mingled. Secondly, the Noldor learned the Sindarin tongue far more readily than the Sindar could learn the ancient speech; moreover, after the kinslaying became known, Thingol would hold no parley with any that spake in the tongue of the slayers at Alqualondë, and he forbade his folk to do so. Thus it was that the common speech of Beleriand after the Third Battle, Dagor Aglareb, was the speech of the Grey-elves, albeit somewhat enriched by words and devices drawn from Noldorin (save in Doriath where the language remained purer and less changed by time). [*Struck out later:* Only in Gondolin did the tongue of the Noldor remain in daily use until the end of that city; for it was early peopled by Turgon with Noldor only, from the North-west of the land, and was long hidden and cut off from all converse with others.[10] *The following replacement passage was written in the margin:*]

but the Noldor preserved ever the High-speech of the West as a language of lore, and in that language they would still give names to mighty men or to places of renown. / But all the days of the Wars of Beleriand, [wellnigh >] more than six hundred years, were times of great change, not only because of the labours and troubles of those years, but because in the first years of the Sun and the second Spring of Arda the growth and change of all living things was sudden and swift. Far other at the end of the Wars were [both the Sindarin and Noldorin tongues later >] the tongues of Beleriand[11] than they were at the landing of Fëanor, and only the High Speech being learned anew from letters remained unaltered. But these histories were made after the Last Battle and the end of the Elder Days, and therefore they were made in the tongue of the remnant of the Elves as it then was, ere it passed again into the West, and the names of those that they record and of the places that are remembered have for the most part that form which they had in the spoken speech at the last.

> Here ends that part which was drawn mainly from the Grey Annals, and there follows matter drawn in brief from the *Quenta Noldorinwa*, and mingled with the traditions of Doriath.[12]

In this revised version, nothing is said about Sindarin and Noldorin 'drawing together' again, and there is no suggestion that the later tongue of the Noldor came to be regarded as 'debased'; spoken Noldorin endured (as the passage was originally written) in the wholly Noldorin city of Gondolin until its fall. The whole conception becomes in fact far simpler: the Noldor retained their own tongue as a High Speech, but Sindarin became their language of daily use (and this was because of the numerical inferiority of the Noldor and the mingling of the peoples outside Doriath, the difficulty that the Sindar found in acquiring the High Speech, and the ban imposed by Thingol). Sindarin received 'loanwords' from Noldorin, but not in Doriath, where the language remained somewhat archaic. By later changes to the text (see notes 8–11) the idea that Noldorin remained in daily use in Gondolin was abandoned.

It is interesting to read, at the end of this last version, that 'these histories' were made '*after* the Last Battle and the end of the Elder Days, and therefore they were made in the tongue of the remnant of the Elves as it then was, *ere* it passed again into the West.'

NOTES

1 365 years of the Valar: 1132–1497 (see GA §11).

2 On the awakening of Beleriand from the Sleep of Yavanna see §§6, 17, and the commentary on §§6, 10.

3 A rough draft of this passage is extant, and this has here:

> Therefore whereas the tongue of the Noldor had changed for the most part only in the making of new words (for things new and old), and in the wilful altering of the ancient tongue of the Quendi to forms and patterns that seemed to the Eldar more beautiful – in which Vanyar, Noldor, and Teleri differed and drew apart – the tongue of the Sindar had changed as living things change by growth – yet only so as in the later world might pass in 400 years.

4 Earlier in GA 1 the form is *Nauglath*: see the commentary on §19.

5 On this passage concerning the Runes of Dairon see §31 and commentary.

6 *Dagor Aglareb*, the Glorious Battle, was formerly the Second Battle (see commentary on §§36 ff.).

7 *Dagor Arnediad*: the Battle of Unnumbered Tears (*Nírnaith Arnediad*).

8 This represents my father's original view that there were no Grey-elves among the people of Gondolin; see note 9.

9 The removal of the words 'and Gondolin' shows the entry of the later conception (see note 8) that many Sindar dwelling in Nivrost at the coming of the Noldor took Turgon to be their lord, and that there were in fact more Elves of Sindarin origin than of Noldorin in the people of Gondolin; see §§107, 113 and commentary.

10 This passage was removed at the same time and for the same reason as the words 'and Gondolin' earlier in this revised text (note 9).

11 The change of 'both the Sindarin and Noldorin tongues' to 'the tongues of Beleriand' was made later than the changes referred to in notes 9 and 10, but presumably for the same reason, since the reference was to the spoken Noldorin of Gondolin. The plural 'tongues' in the revised wording is rather puzzling; perhaps my father was thinking of the speech of the Green-elves of Ossiriand, or possibly he meant the varieties (dialects) of Sindarin.

12 The term *Quenta Noldorinwa* appears in the title of Q (IV.77). I cannot say what conception my father had formed of the historical tradition when he wrote these concluding words.

As I have said, the manuscript GA 1 does not continue after the end of the discussion of the languages, but for the next section of GA 2 there is a text on loose pages which may be regarded as a continuation of GA 1. It constitutes part of the material labelled 'Old material of Grey Annals' referred to on p. 4. This text runs from the (second) beginning of the annal 1497 ('Now Morgoth being dismayed ...') to the end of annal YS 20 (and for the annals 6 and 7 there is a very rough preliminary draft as well). To this text the GA 2 manuscript is very close indeed, and is scarcely more than a fine copy of it with changes of wording here and there; a few interesting points of difference are noticed in the commentary.

I return now to the text of GA 2, which need not now be distinguished by a number.

1497

§49 Now Morgoth being dismayed by the rout of his armies and the unlooked-for valour of the Noldor, and desiring time for new designs, sent emissaries to Maidros, and feigned that he was willing to treat with him. And Maidros feigned that he for his part was also willing, and either purposed evil to the other. Therefore against covenant each came with great force to the parley, but Morgoth with the more, and Maidros was defeated and taken captive.

§50 Then Morgoth held Maidros as a hostage, and swore only to release him, if the Noldor would march away, either to Valinor, or else far from Beleriand into the South of the world; and if they would not do this, then he would put Maidros to torment. But the other sons of Fëanor knew that Morgoth would betray them, and would not release Maidros, whatsoever they might do; and they were constrained also by their oath, and might not for any cause forsake the war against their Enemy.

1498

§51 Therefore Morgoth took Maidros, and setting a band of hellwrought steel about his right wrist hung him thereby above a precipice upon the west-tower of Thangorodrim, where none could reach him. But his brethren drew back and fortified a great camp in Hithlum.

1500

§52 In this time Fingolfin and those that followed him crossed the grinding ice of Helkaraxë, and so came at last with great woe and loss into the North of Endar; and their hearts were filled with bitterness. And even as they set foot upon Middle-earth, the ages of the Stars were ended, and the time of the Sun and Moon was begun, as is told in the Chronicle of Aman.

YS 1

§53 Here the Moon and the Sun, wrought by the Valar after the death of the Trees, rose new in the heaven. First the Moon came forth, and even as it rose above the darkness in the West Fingolfin let blow his silver trumpets, and began his march into Middle-earth; and the shadows of his host went long and black before them.

§54 The Elves of Middle-earth looked up with hope and delight at this new thing; but the servants of Morgoth were amazed; and Morgoth sent spirits of darkness to assail Tilion, the guardian of the moon, and there was strife in heaven. But soon after there came the first Dawn of the Sun, and it was like a great fire upon the towers of the Pelóri, and the clouds of Middle-earth were kindled, and all the mists of the world smoked and glowed like gold. Then Fingolfin unfurled his blue and silver banners, and flowers awoke from the Sleep of Yavanna and sprang up beneath the feet of his host.

§55 Then indeed Morgoth was dismayed, and he descended into the uttermost depths of Angband, and withdrew his servants, sending forth great reek and dark cloud to hide his land from the light of the Daystar. Therefore Fingolfin marched from the North unopposed through the fastness of the realm of Morgoth, and he passed over Dor-Daedeloth, and his foes hid beneath the earth; but the Elves smote upon the gates of Angband, and the challenge of their trumpets shook the towers of Thangorodrim. And Maidros heard them amid his torment and cried aloud, but his voice was lost in the echoes of the stone.

§56 From this time are reckoned the Years of the Sun. Swifter and briefer are they than the long Years of the Trees in Valinor. Lo! in that time the growth and the changing and ageing of all things was hastened exceedingly; and all living things spread and multiplied in the Second Spring of Arda, and the Eldar increased, and Beleriand grew green and fair.

§57 At the first Sunrise, it is said, Men, the younger children of Ilúvatar, awoke in Hildórien in the midmost regions of the

world. The Atani they were named; but the Eldar called them
also the Hildi, the Followers. Into the tale of Beleriand they
came ere the end.

2

§58 Now Fingolfin, being of other temper than Fëanor, and
wary of the wiles of Morgoth, after sounding his challenge
withdrew from Dor-Daedeloth and turned towards Mithrim,
for he had heard tidings that there he should find the sons of
Fëanor, and he desired also to have the shield of the mountains,
while his folk rested and grew strong; for he had seen the
strength of Angband and deemed not that it would fall to the
sound of trumpets only. Therefore coming at length to Hithlum
he made his first camp and dwelling by the north-shore of Lake
Mithrim.

§59 But no love was there in the hearts of Fingolfin and his
folk for the people of Fëanor; and though Fingolfin learned that
Fëanor was dead, he held his sons the accomplices of their
father, and there was peril of war between the two hosts.
Grievous as were their losses upon the road, the people of
Fingolfin and Inglor son of Finrod were still more numerous
than the followers of Fëanor; wherefore they withdrew before
Fingolfin and removed their dwelling to the south-shore, and
the Lake lay between the peoples.

§60 Many indeed of Fëanor's folk repented them sorely of
the deed at Losgar, and were astounded at the valour which had
brought the friends that they abandoned over the Ice of the
North, and they would have welcomed them humbly had they
dared for shame. Thus because of the curse that lay on them the
Noldor achieved nothing, while Morgoth was dismayed and his
servants still cowed by the sudden light. And Morgoth let make
vast smokes and vapours in the pits of Angband, and they came
forth from the reeking tops of the Iron Mountains, and the east
wind bore them over Hithlum and darkened the new sun, and
they fell, coiling about field and hollow, and lying upon the
waters of Mithrim, drear and poisonous.

5

§61 Here Fingon the Valiant resolved to heal the feud that
divided the Noldor, ere their Enemy should be ready for war;
for the earth trembled in the north-lands with the thunder of the
forges of Morgoth. Moreover the thought of his ancient

friendship with Maiðros stung his heart with grief (though he knew not yet that Maidros had not forgotten him at the burning of the ships). Therefore he dared a deed which is justly renowned among the feats of the princes of the Noldor: alone, and without the counsel of any, he set forth in search of Maidros; and aided by the very darkness that Morgoth had made he came unseen into the fastness of his foes. In the *Quenta* it is told how at the last he found Maidros, by singing a song of Valinor alone in the dark mountains, and was aided by Thorondor the Eagle, who bore him aloft unto Maidros; but the bond of steel he could in no wise release and must sever the hand that it held. Thus he rescued his friend of old from torment, and their love was renewed; and the hatred between the houses of Fingolfin and Fëanor was assuaged. Thereafter Maidros wielded his sword in his left hand.

6

§62   Now the Noldor, being again united, set a watch upon the borders of Dor-Daedeloth, and held their main force in the north of the land, but they sent forth messengers far and wide to explore the countries of Beleriand and to treat with the folk that dwelt there.

§63   Beyond the Girdle of Melian those of Finrod's house were suffered to pass, for they could claim close kinship with King Thingol himself (their mother Ëarwen being his brother's daughter). Now Angrod was the first of the Exiles to come to Menegroth, as messenger of Inglor, and he spoke long with the King, telling him of the deeds of the Noldor in the north, and their numbers, and the ordering of their force; but being true and wisehearted and deeming all griefs now forgiven, he spoke naught of the deeds of Fëanor save his valiant death.

§64   And King Thingol hearkened, and he said to Angrod ere he went: 'Thus thou shalt speak for me to those that sent thee. In Hithlum indeed the Noldor have leave to do as they will, and in Dor Thonion they may dwell, and in the countries east of Doriath even to the feet of the mountains of Eryd Luin there is room and to spare. But elsewhere there are many of my folk, and I would not have them restrained of their freedoms, still less ousted from their homes. Beware therefore how ye princes of the West bear yourselves, for I am the Lord of Beleriand and all who seek to dwell there shall hear my word.

Into Doriath none shall come to abide there, but only such as I call as guests, or who seek me in great need.'

7

§65   Now the Noldor held council in Mithrim to ponder all such matters, and to resolve how they should deal in friendship with the Grey-elves, and yet best gather force and dispose it for the war upon Morgoth. For that cause they had come to Middle-earth; yet to many the northlands seemed chill and the south countries fairer, and they desired greatly new homes where their folk might increase in peace far from the camps of war in the highlands.

§66   To this council came Angrod out of Doriath bearing the words of King Thingol, and their welcome seemed cold to the Noldor. The sons of Fëanor indeed were wroth thereat; and Maidros laughed, saying: 'He is a king that can hold his own, or else his title is vain. Thingol does but grant us lands where his power does not run. Indeed Doriath only would be his realm this day, but for the coming of the Noldor. Therefore in Doriath let him reign, and be glad that he hath the sons of Finwë for neighbours, not the Orcs of Morgoth that we found. Elsewhere it shall go as seems good to us.'

§67   But Cranthir, who loved not the sons of Finrod, and was the harshest of the brethren and the most quick to anger, cried aloud: 'Yea more! Let not the sons of Finrod run hither and thither with their tales to this Dark-elf in his caves! Who made them our spokesmen to deal with him? And though they be come indeed to Beleriand, let them not so swiftly forget that their father was a lord of the Noldor, though their mother was of other kin.'

§68   Then Angrod was exceedingly wroth and went forth from the council. Maidros indeed rebuked Cranthir; but the greater part of the Noldor, of both followings, hearing his words were troubled in heart, fearing the fell spirit of the sons of Fëanor that, it seemed, would ever be like to burst forth in rash word or violence.

§69   Therefore when the council came to the choosing of one to be the overlord of the Exiles and the head of all their princes, the choice of all save few fell on Fingolfin. And even as the choice was made known, all those that heard it recalled the words of Mandos that the House of Fëanor should be called the Dispossessed for ever. None the less ill for that did the sons of

Fëanor take this choice, save Maidros only, though it touched him the nearest. But he restrained his brethen, saying to Fingolfin: 'If there lay no grievance between us, lord, still the choice would come rightly to thee, the eldest here of the house of Finwë, and not the least wise.'

§70   But the sons of Fëanor departed then from the council, and soon after they left Mithrim and went eastward to the countries wide and wild between Himring and Lake Helevorn under Mount Rerir. That region was named thereafter the March of Maidros; for there was little defence there of hill or river against assault from the North; and there Maidros and his brethren kept watch, gathering all such folk as would come to them, and they had little dealings with their kinsfolk westward, save at need.

§71   It is said, indeed, that Maidros himself devised this plan, to lessen the chances of strife, and because he was very willing that the chief peril of assault (as it seemed) should fall upon himself; and he remained for his part in friendship with the houses of Fingolfin and Finrod, and would come among them at whiles for common counsel. Yet he also was bound by the Oath, though it slept now for a time.

20

§72   In this year Fingolfin, King of the Noldor, called a great council and made a high feast, that was long after remembered as Mereth Aderthad, the Feast of Reuniting. And it was held nigh the fair pools of Ivrin (whence the swift Narog arose), for there the lands were green and fair at the feet of the mountains that shielded them from the North. Thither came many of the chieftains and people of Fingolfin and Inglor; and of the sons of Fëanor Maidros and Maglor with warriors of the March; and there they were joined by Cirdan and many folk of the Havens, and great concourse of the Grey-elves from woods and fields far and near, and even from Ossiriand there came some of the Nandor on behalf of their folk. But Thingol came not himself from Doriath, and sent but two messengers, Dairon and Mablung, bringing his greetings. At Mereth Aderthad many counsels were taken in good will, and oaths were sworn of league and friendship, and there was much mirth and good hope; and indeed there followed after a fair time of peace, of growth and blossoming, and all the land was glad, though still the Shadow brooded in the North.

§73 (At this feast it is recorded that the tongue of the Grey-elves was most spoken even by the Noldor, for whereas the Noldor readily learned the speech of the land, the Sindar were slow to master the tongue of Aman.)

50

§74 Here after long peace, as Inglor and Turgon journeyed together, and lay by night near the Twilight Meres, Ulmo laid a deep sleep upon them and troubled them in dreams. And thereafter each sought separately for places of strength and refuge in the land, lest Morgoth should burst from Angband as their dreams foreboded. [*Added later:* But Turgon found not what he sought, and returned to Nivrost.]

52

§75 In this year Inglor and his sister Galaðriel were long the guests of Thingol their kinsman. And Inglor was filled with wonder at the beauty and strength of Menegroth, and he desired greatly to make for himself a strong place in like manner. Therefore he opened his heart to Thingol, telling him of his dreams; and Thingol spoke to him of the caves under the High Faroth on the west-bank of Narog, and when he departed gave him guides to lead him to that place of which few yet knew. Thus Inglor came to the Caverns of Narog and began there to establish deep halls and armouries, after the manner of Menegroth; and that stronghold was called Nargothrond. Wherefore the Noldor named him Felagund, Lord of Caves, and that name he bore until his end. But Galaðriel did not depart [*added later:* from Doriath], and remained long with Melian, for there was much love between them.

53

§76 [Turgon journeying alone, by the favour of Ulmo *later* >] In this year Ulmo appeared to Turgon upon the shores of Nivrost, and at his bidding went forth alone, and by the favour of Ulmo he / discovered that hidden vale amid the encircling mountains where afterwards Gondolin was built. Of this he spoke to none yet, but began secretly to devise the plan of a city after the manner of Tirion upon Túna, for which his heart now yearned in exile.

60
The Third Battle

§77   Here Morgoth, believing the report of his spies that the lords of the Eldar were wandering abroad with little thought of war, made trial of the strength and watchfulness of his enemies. Once more, with little warning, his might was stirred, and suddenly there were earthquakes in the North, and fires came from fissures in the earth, and the Iron Mountains vomited flame; and an army of Orcs thrust down the Vale of Sirion and attempted to pierce to the heart of Beleriand. But Fingolfin and Maidros were not sleeping, and gathering swiftly great force of both Noldor and Sindar they destroyed all the scattered bands of the Orcs that had stolen into the land; but the main host they repelled, and drove out onto the fields of Ardgalen, and there surrounded it and destroyed it, to the least and last, within sight of Angband. This was the Third Battle of the Wars, and was called *Dagor Aglareb*, the Glorious Battle.

§78   A victory it was, and yet a warning; and the chieftains took heed of it, and thereafter drew closer their leaguer, and strengthened and ordered their watch, setting the Siege of Angband, which lasted wellnigh four hundred years. And Fingolfin boasted that (save by treason among themselves) Morgoth could never again burst from the leaguer of the Eldar. Yet neither could the Noldor take Angband nor regain the Silmarils. And war never wholly ceased in all that time of the Siege; for Morgoth was secretly forging new weapons, and ever and anon he would make trial of his enemies. Moreover, he was not encircled upon the uttermost north; and though the ice and snow restrained his enemies from keeping watch in the frozen wilderness, it hindered not his spies and messengers from secret going and coming.

> The following passage as the text was originally written began thus: 'At this time also Morgoth began a new evil. He bade his servants to take alive any of the Eldar ...' This was replaced by the long rider (written on a separate page) that follows here (§§79–81), returning to the original text at 'He now bade the Orkor to take alive any of the Eldar', the second sentence of §81.

§79   Nor himself, an he would go. Indeed we learn now in Eressëa from the Valar, through our kin that dwell still in Aman, that after Dagor-nuin-Giliath Melkor was so long in assailing the Eldar with strength for he himself had departed from

Angband, for the last time. Even as before at the awakening of the Quendi, his spies were watchful, and tidings soon came to him of the arising of Men. This seemed to him so great a matter that secretly under shadow he went forth into Middle-earth, leaving the command of the War to Sauron his lieutenant. Of his dealings with Men the Eldar knew naught at that time, and know little now, for neither the Valar nor Men have spoken to them clearly of these things.

§80   But that some darkness lay upon the hearts of Men (as the shadow of the kinslaying and the doom of Mandos lay upon the Noldor) the Eldar perceived clearly even in the fair folk of the Elf-friends that they first knew. To corrupt or destroy whatsoever arose new and fair was ever the chief desire of Morgoth; but as regards the Eldar, doubtless he had this purpose also in his errand: by fear and lies to make Men their foes, and bring them up out of the East against Beleriand. But this design was slow to ripen, and was never wholly achieved, for Men (it is said) were at first very few in number, whereas Morgoth grew afraid of the tidings of the growing power and union of the Eldar and came back to Angband, leaving behind at that time but few servants, and those of less might and cunning.

§81   Certain it is that at this time (which was the time of his return, if the aforesaid account be true, as we must believe) Morgoth began a new evil, desiring above all to sow fear and disunion among the Eldar in Beleriand. He now bade the Orkor to take alive any of the Eldar that they could and bring them bound to Angband. For it was his intent to use their lore and skill under duress for his own ends; moreover he took pleasure in tormenting them, and would besides by pain wring from them at times tidings of the deeds and counsels of his enemies. Some indeed he so daunted by the terror of his eyes that they needed no chains more, but walked ever in fear of him, doing his will wherever they might be. These he would unbind and let return to work treason among their own kin. In this way also was the curse of Mandos fulfilled, for after a while the Elves grew afraid of those who claimed to have escaped from thraldom, and often those hapless whom the Orcs ensnared, even if they broke from the toils would but wander homeless and friendless thereafter, becoming outlaws in the woods.

§82   And though it was long ere all these evils began to appear, it is said that even after the victory of the Third Battle some of the Eldar (either caught by robber bands in the woods, or over rash in pursuit of the foe) were thus seized and taken to Morgoth. And thus he learned much of all that had befallen since the rebellion of Fëanor, and rejoiced seeing therein the seed of many dissensions among his foes. But thus also it became known to the Eldar that the Silmarils yet lived, and were set in the Iron Crown that Morgoth wore upon his dark throne. For the Noldor were a mighty race yet, and few of them could he so daunt that they would do his will, but escaping they became oft his deadliest foes.

§83　In the *Quenta Noldorinwa* it is recounted in what manner after Dagor Aglareb the lords of the Noldor and Sindar ordered the land, during the Siege of Angband. Here it suffices to say that [*added:* westernmost at first Turgon abode in Nivrost south of Drengist between Eryd Lómin and the Sea; but] Fingolfin and Fingon held Hithlum and had their abode and chief fortress at Eithel Sirion; and they had horsemen also that rode upon the fields of Ardgalen, for from few their horses had increased swiftly, and the grass of Ardgalen was yet rich and green. Of those horses many of the sires came from Valinor, and were given to Fingolfin by Maidros in atonement of his losses, for they had been carried by ship to Losgar.

§84　The sons of Finrod held the land from Hithlum unto the eastern end of Dorthonion. Inglor and Orodreth held the pass of Sirion, but Angrod and Egnor held the north slopes of Dorthonion as far as Aglon where began the March of Maidros aforesaid.

§85　Behind this leaguer from the Sea to Eryd Luin the wide countries of Beleriand, west and east of Sirion, were held in this wise. Though Fingolfin of Hithlum was overlord of all the Noldor, Inglor, well-beloved of all Elves, became indeed the greatest prince in the land. For King Felagund he was in Nargothrond, whereas his brothers Angrod and Egnor were lords of Dorthonion and his vassals; and he had also a fort and place of battle in the north, in the wide pass between Eredwethrin and Dorthonion through which Sirion flowed south. There stood an isle amid the river, and upon it Inglor built a mighty watchtower: Minnas-tirith: and there, when Nargothrond was made, he set Orodreth as warden. But upon either side of Narog all the folk of either race that dwelt in the lands took him for their lord, as far south as the Mouths of Sirion, and from

Nenning in the West to the borders of Doriath eastward. But in Eglarest, and west of Nenning to the Sea, Cirdan the Shipwright was lord, yet ever he was close in friendship with Nargothrond.

§86   Doriath in the midst of the land was the realm of King Thingol; and east the wide countries south of the March of Maidros, even to the borders of Ossiriand were held to be the domain of the sons of Fëanor. But few dwelt there save hunters and Grey-elves wandering, and there Damrod and Díriel abode and came seldom northward while the Siege lasted. Thither other of the Elven-lords would ride at whiles, even from afar, to hunt in the green-woods; but none ever passed east over Eryd Luin or looked upon Eriador, save the Green-elves only, who had kindred that dwelt yet in the further lands. Thus little news and late came to Beleriand of what passed in the regions of the East.

60–445

§87   For the most part the time of the Siege of Angband was a time of gladness, and the earth had peace under the new light, while the swords of the Noldor restrained the malice of Morgoth, and his thought being bent on their ruin he gave the less heed to aught else in Middle-earth. In this time therefore Men waxed and multiplied, [and they had converse with the Dark-elves of the Eastlands >] and among them were some that had converse with the Elves of Middle-earth, / and learned much of them. [From them it is said that they took the first beginnings of the many tongues of Men. Thus they heard rumour of the Blessed Realms [*sic*] of the West and of the Powers that dwelt there, and many of the Fathers of Men, the *Atanatári*, in their wanderings moved ever westward. *This passage was rewritten to read:*] From them it is said that they took the first beginnings of the western tongues of Men; and from them also they heard rumour of the Blessed Realms of the West and of the Powers of Light that dwelt there. Therefore many of the Fathers of Men, the *Atanatári*, in their wanderings moved ever westward, fleeing from the darkness that had ensnared them. For these Elf-friends were Men that had repented and rebelled against the Dark Power, and were cruelly hunted and oppressed by those that worshipped it, and its servants.

64

§88 Now the unquiet that Ulmo set in his heart returned to Turgon in Nivrost, and he gathered therefore his folk together, even to a third part of the Noldor of Fingolfin's people (nor were any of the Sindar among them), and with their wives and their goods they departed secretly along the south of Ered-wethrin, and few knew whither they were gone. But Turgon came to Gondolin, and there his folk pressed on with the building of the city that he had devised in his heart; and they set a guard upon it that none might come upon it from without. [*This annal was later changed to read:*]

§89 Now the unquiet that Ulmo set in his heart returned to Turgon in Nivrost, and he gathered therefore many of his most skilled folk together and led them secretly to Gondolin, and there they began the building of the strong city that Turgon had devised in his heart; and they set a guard upon it that none might come upon their work from without.

65

§90 Here with the aid of the Noldor (whose skill far surpassed that of the Sindar) Brithombar and Eglarest were walled about with great walls, and fair towns were raised within, and harbours with quays and piers of stone. And the Tower of Ingildon was set up upon the cape west of Eglarest to watch the Sea; though needlessly, as it proved. For at no time ever did Morgoth essay to build ships or to make war by sea. Water all his servants shunned, and to the Sea none would willing go nigh, save in dire need.

66

§91 Now Galaðriel Finrod's daughter, as hath been told, dwelt with Melian, and was dear to her. And at times they would speak together of Valinor and the bliss of old; but beyond the dark hour of the death of the Trees Galaðriel would not go, but fell ever silent.

§92 And on a time Melian said: 'There is some woe that lies upon thee and thy kin. That I can see in thee, but all else is hidden from me; for by no vision or thought can I perceive aught that passed or passes in the West: a shadow lies over all the Land of Aman, and reaches far out over the Sea. [Wilt thou not >] Why wilt thou not tell me more?'

'For that woe is past,' answered Galaðriel; 'and I would take what joy is here left untroubled by memory. And maybe there is woe enough yet to come, though still hope may seem bright.'

§93 Then Melian looked in her eyes, and said: 'I believe not that the Noldor came forth as messengers of the Valar, as was said at first: not though they came in the very hour of our need. For lo! they speak never of the Valar, nor have their high lords brought any message to Thingol, whether from Manwë, or Ulmo, or even from Olwë the king's brother and his own folk that went over the Sea. For what cause, Galaðriel, were the high people of the Noldor driven forth as exiles from Aman? Or what evil lies on the sons of Fëanor that they are so haughty and fell? Do I not strike near the truth?'

§94 'Near, lady,' answered Galadriel, 'save that we were not driven forth, but came of our own will, and against that of the Valar. And through great peril and in despite of the Valar for this purpose we came: to take vengeance upon Morgoth, [or >] and regain what he stole.' Then Galaðriel spoke to Melian of the Silmarils, and of the slaying of King Finwë. But still she said no word of the Oath, nor of the Kinslaying, nor of the burning of the ships.

§95 But Melian, who looked still in her eyes as she spoke, said: 'Now much thou tellest me, and yet more I perceive. A darkness thou wouldst cast still over the long road from Tirion, but I see evil there, which Thingol should learn for his guidance.'

'Maybe,' said Galaðriel, 'but not of me.'

§96 And Melian spoke then no more of these matters with Galaðriel; but she told to King Thingol all that she had heard of the Silmarils. 'This is a great matter,' said she, 'a greater indeed than the Noldor themselves understand. For lo! the Light of Aman and the fate of Arda lie now locked in these things, the work of Fëanor, who is gone. They shall not be recovered, I foretell, by any power of the Eldar; and the world shall be broken in battles that are to come, ere they are wrested from Morgoth. See now! Fëanor they have slain (and many another I guess); but first of all the deaths they have brought and yet shall bring was Finwë thy friend. Morgoth slew him, ere he fled from Aman.'

§97 Then Thingol was silent a while with grief and foreboding; but at length he said: 'Now at last I understand the coming of the Noldor out of the West, at which I wondered much before. Not to our aid came they (save by chance); for those that remain upon Middle-earth the Valar will leave to their own devices, until the uttermost need. For vengeance and redress of their loss the Noldor came. Yet all the more sure shall they be as allies against Morgoth, with whom it is not now to be thought that they shall ever make treaty.'

§98   But Melian said: 'Truly for these causes they came; but for others also. Beware of the sons of Fëanor! The shadow of the wrath of the Gods lies upon them; and they have done evil, I perceive, both in Aman and to their own kin. A grief but lulled to sleep lies between the princes of the Noldor.'

§99   And Thingol said: 'What is that to me? Of Fëanor I have heard but report, which maketh him great indeed. Of his sons I hear little to my pleasure; yet they are likely to prove the deadliest foes of our foe.'

'Their words and their counsels shall have two edges,' said Melian; and afterward they spake no more of this matter.

67

§100   It was not long ere whispered tales began to pass among the Sindar concerning the deeds of the Noldor ere they came to Beleriand. Whence they came is now clear (though it was not so then), and as may well be thought, the evil truth was enhanced and poisoned with lies. Morgoth chose the Sindar for this first assault of his malice, because they knew him not, and were yet unwary and trustful of words. Therefore Cirdan, hearing these dark tales, was troubled. Wise he was, and perceived swiftly that, true or false, these tales were put about at this time with malice; but the malice he deemed was that of the princes of the Noldor because of the jealousy of their houses. Therefore he sent messengers to Thingol to tell all that he had heard.

§101   And it chanced that at that time the sons of Finrod were again the guests of Thingol, for they wished to see their sister Galaðriel. Then Thingol, being greatly moved, spake in ire to Inglor, saying: 'Ill hast thou done to me, kinsman, to conceal so great matters from me. For behold! I have learned of all the evil deeds of the Noldor.'

§102   But Inglor answered: 'What ill have I done thee, lord? Or what evil deed have the Noldor done in all thy realm to grieve thee? Neither against thy kingship nor against any of thy folk have they thought evil or done evil.'

§103 'I marvel at thee, son of Eärwen,' said Thingol, 'that thou wouldst come to the board of thy kinsman thus red-handed from the slaying of thy mother's kin, and yet say nought in defence, nor yet seek any pardon!'

§104 And Inglor was sorely troubled, but he was silent, for he could not defend himself, save by bringing charges against the other princes of the Noldor; and this he was loath to do before Thingol. But in Angrod's heart the memory of the words of Cranthir welled up again with bitterness, and he cried: 'Lord, I know not what lies thou hast heard, nor whence. But we come not redhanded. Guiltless we came forth, save maybe of folly, to listen to the words of fell Fëanor, and become as folk besotted with wine, and as briefly. No evil did we do on our road, but suffered ourselves great wrong. And forgave it. For which we are named tale-bearers to thee and treasonable to the Noldor. Untruly as thou knowest, for we have of our loyalty been silent before thee, and thus earned thy anger. But now these charges are not longer to be borne, and the truth thou shalt know.' Then he spake bitterly against the sons of Fëanor, telling of the blood at Alqualondë, and the doom of Mandos, and the burning of the ships at Losgar. 'Wherefore should we that endured the Grinding Ice bear the names of kinslayers and traitors?' he cried.

§105 'Yet the shadow of Mandos lies on you also,' said Melian. But Thingol was long silent ere he spoke. 'Go now!' he said. 'For my heart is hot within me. Later ye may return, if you will. For I will not shut my doors for ever against you my kin, that were ensnared in an evil that ye did not aid. With Fingolfin and his folk also I will keep friendship, for they have bitterly atoned for such ill as they did. And in our hatred of the Power that wrought all this woe our griefs shall be lost.

§106 'But hear this! Never again in my ears shall be heard the tongue of those who slew my folk in Alqualondë! Nor in all my realm shall that tongue be openly spoken, while my power endureth. All the Sindar shall hear my command that they shall neither speak with the tongue of the Noldor nor answer to it. And all such as use it shall be held slayers of kin and betrayers of kin unrepentant.'

§107 Then the sons of Finrod departed from Menegroth with heavy hearts, perceiving how the words of Mandos would ever be made true, and that none of the Noldor that followed after Fëanor could escape from the shadow that lay upon his house. And it came to pass even as Thingol had spoken; for the Sindar heard his word and thereafter throughout Beleriand they refused the tongue of the Noldor, and shunned those that spoke it aloud; but the Exiles took the Sindarin tongue in all their daily uses, [save only in Gondolin where Noldor dwelt unmingled, but that was yet hidden. >] and the High Speech of the West was spoken only by the lords of the Noldor among themselves, yet it lived ever as a language of lore wherever any of that folk dwelt.

102

§108   About this time it is recorded that Nargothrond was full-wrought, and Finrod's sons were gathered there to a feast and Galadriel came from Doriath and dwelt there a while. Now King Inglor Felagund had no wife, and Galadriel asked him why this was; but foresight came upon Felagund as she spoke, and he said: 'An oath I too shall swear, and must be free to fulfill it and go into darkness. Nor shall anything of all my realm endure that a son should inherit.'

§109   But it is said that not until that hour had such cold thoughts ruled him; for indeed she whom he had loved was Amárië of the Vanyar, and she was not permitted to go with him into exile.

116

§110   In this year according to the records of that city Gondolin was full-wrought, in fifty years after the coming of Turgon from Nivrost. But no tidings of this came over the mountains, nor were any of Turgon's kin bidden to a feast. [*This annal was later struck out and replaced by the following rider,* §§111–13:]

§111   In this year Gondolin was full-wrought, after fifty [*added:* and 2] years of secret toil. Now therefore Turgon prepared to depart from Nivrost, and leave his fair halls in Vinyamar beneath Mount Taras; and then [for the last time Ulmo himself came to him >] Ulmo came to him a second time / and said: 'Now thou shalt go at last to Gondolin, Turgon; and I will set my power in the Vale of Sirion, so that none shall mark thy going, nor shall any find there the hidden entrance to thy land against thy will. Longest of all the realms of the Eldalië shall Gondolin stand against Melkor. But love it not too well, and remember that the true hope of the Noldor lieth in the West and cometh from the Sea.'

§112   And Ulmo warned Turgon that he also lay under the Doom of Mandos, which Ulmo had no power to remove. 'Thus it may come to pass,' he said, 'that the curse of the Noldor shall find thee too ere the end, and treason shall awake within thy walls. Then shall they be in peril of fire. But if this peril draweth nigh, then even from Nivrost one shall come to warn thee, and from him beyond ruin and fire hope shall be born for Elves and Men. Leave, therefore, in this house arms and a sword, that in years to come he may find them, and thus shalt thou know him and be not deceived.' And Ulmo showed to Turgon of what kind and stature should be the mail and helm and sword that he left behind.

§113   Then Ulmo returned to the Sea; and Turgon sent forth all his folk (even to a third part of the Noldor of Fingolfin's House, and a yet greater host of the Sindar), and they passed away, company by company, secretly, under the shadows of Eryd Wethion, and came unseen with their wives and goods to Gondolin, and none knew whither they were gone. And last of all Turgon arose and went with his lords and household silently through the hills and passed the gates in the mountains, and they were shut. But Nivrost was empty of folk and so remained until the ruin of Beleriand.

150

§114   The people of Cranthir Fëanor's son dwelt beyond the upper waters of Gelion, about Lake Helevorn under the shadow of the Blue Mountains. At this time it is said that they first climbed into the mountains and looked eastward, and wide and wild it seemed to them was Middle-earth. Thus it was that Cranthir's folk first came upon the Naugrim, who after the onslaught of Morgoth and the coming of the Noldor had ceased their traffick into Beleriand. Now, though either people loved skill and was eager to learn, there was little love between the Noldor and the Dwarves. For the Dwarves were secret and quick to resentment, whereas Cranthir was haughty and scarce concealed his scorn for the unloveliness of the Naugrim, and his folk followed their lord. Nonetheless, since both peoples feared and hated Morgoth they made alliance, and had of it great profit. For the Naugrim learned many secrets of craft in those days, so that the smiths and masons of Nogrod and Belegost became renowned among their kin; but the Noldor got great wealth of iron, and their armouries became filled with store of weapons and harness of war. Moreover thereafter, until the power of Maidros was overthrown, all the traffick of the dwarf-mines passed first through the hands of Cranthir, and thus he won great riches.

155

§115 Here after long quiet Morgoth endeavoured to take Fingolfin at unawares (for he knew of the vigilance of Maidros); and he sent forth an army into the white north, and it turned then west and again south and came by the coasts to the firth of Drengist, and so would enter into the heart of the realm of Hithlum. But it was espied in time and taken in a trap among the hills at the head of the firth, and the most of the Orcs were driven into the sea. This was not reckoned among the great battles, and was but the most dangerous of the many trials and thrusts that Angband would make ever and anon against the leaguer. Thereafter there was peace for many years, and no open assault; for Morgoth perceived now that the Orcs unaided were no match for the Noldor, save in such numbers as he could not yet muster. Therefore he sought in his heart for new counsel, and he bethought him of dragons.

260

§116 Here Glaurung, the first of the *Urulóki*, the fire-drakes of the North, came forth from Angband's gate by night. He was yet young and scarce half-grown (for long and slow is the life of those worms), but the Elves fled before him to Erydwethrin and to Dorthonion in dismay; and he defiled the fields of Ardgalen. Then Fingon, prince of Hithlum, rode against him with archers upon horseback, and hemmed him round with a ring of swift riders. And Glaurung in turn was dismayed, for he could not endure their darts, being not yet come to his full armoury; and he fled back to hell, and came not forth again for many years. But Morgoth was ill pleased that Glaurung had disclosed himself over soon; and after his defeat there was the long peace of wellnigh two hundred years. In that time there was naught but affrays on the north-marches, and all Beleriand prospered and grew rich, and the Noldor built many towers and fair dwellings and made many things of beauty, and many poesies and histories and books of lore. And in many parts of the land the Noldor and Sindar became welded into one folk and spoke the same tongue; though ever this difference remained between them, that the Noldor of purer race had the greater power of mind and body, being both the mightier warriors and sages, and they built with stone, and loved rather the hill-slopes and open lands. Whereas the Sindar had the fairer voices and were more skilled in music (save only Maglor son of Fëanor), and loved the woods and riversides, and some still would wander far and wide without settled abode, and they sang as they went.

[Isfin and Ëol]

At this point in the manuscript my father inserted an annal entry for the year 316 concerning Isfin and Ëol, replacing the annal that stood in the manuscript under 471, which was struck out. He wrote the new annal on the back of a page from an engagement calendar for November 1951; and on the same page he added two further annals on the same subject, for the years 320 and 400. It is clearest and most convenient to give all four annals (i.e. the original one for 471 and the three later ones) together here.

§117 [*Rejected annal for the year 471*] In this year Isfin the White, sister of Turgon, wearying of the city, and desiring to look again upon Fingon her brother, went from Gondolin against the will and counsel of Turgon; and she strayed into Brethil and was lost in the dark forest. There Ëol, the Dark-elf, who abode in the forest, found her and took her to wife. In the depths of the wood he lived and shunned the sun, desiring only the starlight of old; for so he had dwelt since the first finding of Beleriand, and took no part in all the deeds of his kin.

316

§118 Here Isfin the White, sister of Turgon, wearying of the city, went from Gondolin against the [will >] wish of Turgon. And she went not to Fingon, as he bade, but sought the ways to the East, to the land of Celegorm and his brethren, her friends of old in Valinor. But she strayed from her escort in the shadows of Nan Dungorthin, and went on alone; and she came at last to Nan Elmoth. There she came into the enchantments of Ëol the Dark-elf, who abode in the wood and shunned the sun, desiring only the starlight of old. And Ëol took her to wife, and she abode with him, and no tidings of her came to any of her kin; for Ëol suffered her not to stray far, nor to fare abroad save in the dark or the twilight.

320

§119   Here Isfin the White bore a son in Nan Elmoth to Ëol the Dark-elf; and she would name him (?) Fingol [added: dur], but Ëol named him Glindûr [later > Maeglin]; for that was the name of the metal of Ëol, which he himself devised, and it was dark, supple, and yet strong; and even so was his son.

400

§120   Here Isfin and her son Glindûr [later > Maeglin] fled from Ëol the Dark-elf in Nan Elmoth, and came to Gondolin, and they were received with joy by Turgon, who had deemed his sister dead or lost beyond finding. But Ëol, following them with stealth, found the Hidden Way, and was brought by the Guard to Turgon. Turgon received him well, but he was wroth and filled with hatred of the Noldor, and spoke evilly, and demanded to depart with his son. And when that was denied to him he sought to slay Glindûr [not emended] with a poisoned dart, but Isfin sprang before her son, and was wounded, and died in that day. Therefore Ëol was doomed to death, and cast from the high walls of Gondolin; and he cursed his son as he died, foreboding that he should die a like death. But Glindûr [later > Maeglin] abode in Gondolin and became great among its lords.

370

§121   Here Bëor, eldest of the Fathers of Men of the West, was born east of the mountains.

388

§122   Here Haleth the Hunter was born in Eriador.

390

§123   Here also in Eriador was born Hador the Golden-haired, whose house was after the most renowned of all the kindreds of the Elf-friends.

400

§124   Here King Inglor Felagund went a-hunting in the eastern woods, as is told in the *Quenta*, and he passed into Ossiriand, and there came upon Bëor and his men, that were new-come over the mountains. Bëor became a vassal of

Felagund, and went back with him into the west-country, and
dwelt with him until his death. There was great love between
them. In eastern Beleriand was born Bregolas son of Bëor.

402

§125   Here there was fighting on the north-marches, more
bitter than there had been since the routing of Glaurung; for the
Orcs attempted to pierce the pass of Aglon. There Maidros and
Maglor were aided by the sons of Finrod, and Bëor was with
them, the first of Men to draw sword in behalf of the Eldar.
In this year Barahir son of Bëor was born, who after dwelt in
Dorthonion.

413

§126   Hundor son of Haleth was born.

417

§127   Galion the Tall, son of Hador, was born [beneath the
shadows of Eryd Lindon >] in Eriador.

419

§128   Gundor son of Hador was born beneath the shadows
of Eryd Lindon.

420

§129   In this year Haleth the Hunter came into Beleriand
out of Eriador. Soon after came also Hador the Goldenhaired
with great companies of Men. Haleth remained in Sirion's vale,
and his folk wandered much in hunting, owning allegiance to
no prince; but their dwellings were deep in the forest of Brethil
between Taiglin and Sirion, where none before had dwelt
because of the greatness and darkness of the trees. Hador hearing that there was room and need of folk in Hithlum, and being
come of a northland people, became a vassal of Fingolfin; and
he strengthened greatly the armies of the king, and he was given
wide lands in Hithlum in the country of Dor-Lómin. There was
ever great love between the Eldar and the house of Hador, and
the folk of Hador were the first of Men to forsake their own
tongue and speak the elven-tongue of Beleriand.

§130   It is said that in these matters none save Inglor took
counsel with King Thingol. And he was ill pleased, for that
reason and because he was troubled with dreams concerning the

coming of Men, ere ever the first tidings of them were heard. Therefore he commanded that Men should take no lands to dwell in save in the north, in Hithlum and Dorthonion, and that the princes whom they served should be answerable for all that they did. And he said: 'Into Doriath shall no Man come while my realm lasts, not even those of the house of Bëor who serve Inglor the beloved.'

§131   Melian said naught to him at that time, but she said after to Galadriel: 'Now the world runs on swiftly to great tidings. And lo! one of Men, even of Bëor's house, shall indeed come, and the Girdle of Melian shall not restrain him, for doom greater than my power shall send him; and the songs that shall spring from that coming shall endure when all Middle-earth is changed.'

422

§132   Here at the prayer of Inglor Thingol granted to Haleth's people to live in Brethil; for they were in good friendship with the woodland Elves.

§133   In this time, the strength of Men being added to the Noldor, their hope rose high, and Morgoth was more straitly enclosed; for the folk of Hador, being hardy to endure cold and long wandering, feared not at times to go far into the North and keep watch on any movements of the Enemy. Now Fingolfin began to ponder an assault upon Angband; for he knew that they lived in danger while Morgoth was free to labour in his deep mines, devising what evils none could foretell ere he should reveal them. But because the land was grown so fair most of the Eldar were content with matters as they were and slow to begin an assault in which many must surely perish, were it in victory or defeat. Therefore his designs were delayed and came in the end to naught.

§134   The Men of the Three Houses now grew and multiplied; and they learned wisdom and craft and fair speech of the Eldar, and became more like to them than any other race have been, yet they were gladly subject to the Elf-lords and loyal; and there was as yet no grief between the two kindreds.

§135   The men of Bëor were dark or brown of hair, but fair of face, with grey eyes; of shapely form, having courage and endurance, yet they were no greater in stature than the Eldar of that day. For the Noldor indeed were tall as are in the latter days men of great might and majesty. But the people of Hador were of yet greater strength and stature, mighty among the Children of Eru, ready in mind, bold and steadfast. Yellowhaired they were for the most part and blue-eyed* and their women were tall and fair. Like unto them were the woodmen of Haleth, yet somewhat broader and less high.

423

§136   Hador's folk entered Dorlómin. [*This annal was a late pencilled addition.*]

[425 >] 424

§137   Baragund son of Bregolas son of Bëor was born in Dorthonion.

428

§138   Belegund his brother was born.

432

§139   Beren son of Barahir son of Bëor was born in Dorthonion, who was after named *Erchamion* the One-handed and *Camlost* the Emptyhanded. His mother was Emeldir the Manhearted.

436

§140   Hundor son of Haleth wedded Glorwendil daughter of Hador.

441

§141   Húrin the Steadfast son of Galion son of Hador was born in Hithlum. In the same year was born Handir son of Hundor.

[445 >] 443

§142   Morwen Eleðwen, the Elf-sheen, was born, daughter of Baragund. She was the fairest of all mortal maidens of the Elder Days.

444

§143   Huor brother of Húrin was born.

* Not so was Túrin, but his mother was of Bëor's house.

450

§144 Rían daughter of Belegund, mother of Tuor the Blessed, was born. In this year Bëor the Old, father of Men, died of [old age >] age. The Eldar saw then for the first time [the death of weariness, without wound or sickness; *by late pencilled change* >] the swift waning of the life of Men and the coming of death without wound or grief; and they wondered at the fate of Men, grieving greatly at the short span that was allotted to them. Bregolas then ruled the people of Bëor.

455

§145 *The Fell Year.* Here came an end of peace and mirth. In the winter, at the year's beginning, Morgoth unloosed at last his long-gathered strength, and he sought now to break with one great blow the leaguer of Angband, and to overthrow the Noldor and destroy Beleriand utterly. The Battle began suddenly on the night of mid-winter, and fell first and most heavily upon the sons of Finrod. This is named the *Dagor Bragollach*, the Battle of Sudden Flame. Rivers of fire ran down from Thangorodrim, and Glaurung, Father of Dragons, came forth in his full might. The green plains of Ardgalen were burned up and became a drear desert without growing thing; and thereafter they were called *Anfauglith*, the Gasping Dust.

§146 In the assault upon the defences of Dorthonion Angrod and Egnor, sons of Finrod, fell, and with them Bregolas was slain and a great part of the warriors of Bëor's folk. But Barahir his brother was in the fighting further westward nigh the passes of Sirion. There King Inglor Felagund, hastening from the south, was defeated and was surrounded with small company in the Fen of Serech. But Barahir came thither with the doughtiest of his men, and broke the leaguer of the Orcs and saved the Elven-king. Then Inglor gave to Barahir his ring, an heirloom of his house, in token of the oath that he swore unto Barahir to render whatsoever service was asked in hour of need to him or to any of his kin. Then Inglor went south to Nargothrond, but Barahir returned to Dorthonion to save what he could of the people of Bëor.

§147 Fingolfin and Fingon had marched indeed from Hithlum to the aid of the sons of Finrod, but they were driven back to the mountains with grievous loss. Hador, now aged [*later* > old *and* '65' *added*], fell defending his lord at Eithel

Sirion, and with him fell Gundor his [*added later:* younger] son, pierced with many arrows. Then Galion the Tall took the lordship of the House of Hador.

§148   Against the March of Maidros there came also a great army and the sons of Fëanor were overwhelmed. Maidros and Maglor held out valiantly upon the Hill of Himring, and Morgoth could not yet take the great fortress that they had there built; but the Orcs broke through upon either side, through Aglon and between Gelion and Celon, and they ravaged far into East Beleriand driving the Eldar before them, and Cranthir and Damrod and Díriel fled into the south. Celegorn and Curufin held strong forces behind Aglon, and many horsed archers, but they were overthrown, and Celegorn and Curufin hardly escaped, and passed westward along the north borders of Doriath with such mounted following as they could save, and came thus at length to the vale of Sirion.

§149   Turgon was not in that battle, nor Haleth, nor any but few of Haleth's men. [*The following passage, to the end of §150, was struck out later:* It is said that in the autumn before the Sudden Flame, Húrin son of Galion was dwelling as fosterson (as the custom was among the northern men) with Haleth, and Handir and Húrin, being of like age, went much together; and hunting in Sirion's vale they found [by chance or fate *later* >] by fate or the will of Ulmo / the hidden entrance into the valley of Tumladin where stood Gondolin the guarded city. There they were taken by the watch and brought before Turgon, and looked upon the city of which none that dwelt outside yet knew aught, save Thorondor King of Eagles. But Turgon welcomed them, for [messages and dreams sent by Ulmo, Lord of Waters, up the streams of Sirion had warned him that a time of grief approached in which he would have need of the help of Men. >] Ulmo, Lord of Waters, had warned him to look kindly upon the folk of the House of Hador, from whom great help should come to him at need.

§150   It is said that Turgon had great liking for the boy Húrin, and wished to keep him in Gondolin; but Thorondor brought dread tidings of the great battle, and Handir and Húrin wished to depart to share the troubles of their folk. Therefore Turgon let them go, but they swore to him oaths of secrecy and never revealed Gondolin; yet at this time Húrin learned something of the counsels of Turgon, though he kept them hidden in his heart.]

§151   When [*later* > But when] Turgon learned of the breaking of the leaguer of Angband, he sent secret messengers to the mouths of Sirion and to the Isle of Balar and there they [*the following passage was struck out and replaced at the time of writing:* built many swift ships. Thence many set sail upon Turgon's errand, seeking for Valinor, to ask for pardon and for aid of the Valar, but none came ever to the West and few returned.

§152   Now it seemed to Fingolfin, King of the Noldor, that he beheld the utter ruin of his people, and the defeat beyond redress of all their houses, and he was filled with wrath and despair. Then he rode forth alone to the gates of Angband] endeavoured to build ships that might sail into the uttermost West on Turgon's errand, seeking for Valinor, there to ask for pardon and the aid of the Valar. But the Noldor had not the art of shipbuilding, and all the craft that they built foundered or were driven back by the winds. But Turgon ever maintained a secret refuge upon the Isle of Balar, and the building of ships was never wholly abandoned.

§153   [*Original date here* 456 *struck out at the time of writing*] Morgoth learning now of the defeat of the sons of Finrod, and the scattering of the people of Fëanor, hemmed Fingolfin in Hithlum and sent a great force to attack the westward pass into the vales of Sirion; and Sauron his lieutenant (who in Beleriand was named *Gorsodh*) led that assault, and his hosts broke through and besieged the fortress of Inglor, Minnas-tirith upon Tolsirion. And this they took after bitter fighting, and Orodreth the brother of Inglor who held it was driven out. There he would have been slain, but Celegorn and Curufin came up with their riders, and such other force as they could gather, and they fought fiercely, and stemmed the tide for a while; and thus Orodreth escaped and came to Nargothrond. Thither also at last before the might of Sauron fled Celegorn and Curufin with small following; and they were harboured in Nargothrond gratefully, and the griefs that lay between the houses of Finrod and Fëanor were for that time forgotten.

§154   But Sauron took Minnas-tirith and made it into a watch-tower for Morgoth, and filled it with evil; for he was a sorcerer and a master of phantoms and terror. And the fair isle of Tolsirion became accursed and was called *Tol-in-Gaurhoth*, Isle of Werewolves; for Sauron fed many of these evil things.

456

§155 Now Fingolfin, King of the Noldor, beheld (as him seemed) the utter ruin of his people, and the defeat beyond redress of all their houses, and he was filled with wrath and despair. Therefore he did on his silver arms, and took his white helm, and his sword Ringil, and his blue shield set with a star of crystal, and mounting upon Rochallor his great steed he rode forth alone and none might restrain him. And he passed over the Anfauglith like a wind amid the dust, and all that beheld his onset fled in amaze, deeming that Oromë himself was come, for a great madness of ire was upon him, so that his eyes shone like the eyes of the Valar. Thus he came alone to Angband's gate and smote upon it once again, and sounding a challenge upon his silver horn he called Morgoth himself to come forth to combat, crying: 'Come forth, thou coward king, to fight with thine own hand! Den-dweller, wielder of thralls, liar and lurker, foe of Gods and Elves, come! For I would see thy craven face.'

§156 Then Morgoth came. For he could not refuse such a challenge before the face of his captains. But Fingolfin withstood him, though he towered above the Elven-king like a storm above a lonely tree, and his vast black shield unblazoned overshadowed the star of Fingolfin like a thundercloud. Morgoth fought with a great hammer, Grond, that he wielded as a mace, and Fingolfin fought with Ringil. Swift was Fingolfin, and avoiding the strokes of Grond, so that Morgoth smote only the ground (and at each blow a great pit was made), he wounded Morgoth seven times with his sword; and the cries of Morgoth echoed in the north-lands. But wearied at last Fingolfin fell, beaten to the earth by the hammer of Angband, and Morgoth set his foot upon his neck and crushed him.

§157 In his last throe Fingolfin pinned the foot of his Enemy to the earth with Ringil, and the black blood gushed forth and filled the pits of Grond. Morgoth went ever halt thereafter. Now lifting the body of the fallen king he would break it and cast it to his wolves, but Thorondor coming suddenly assailed him and marred his face, and snatching away the corse of Fingolfin bore it aloft to the mountains far away and laid it in a high place north of the valley of Gondolin; there the eagles piled a great cairn of stones. There was lamentation in Gondolin when Thorondor brought the tidings, for [the people of the hidden city were all *later* >] many of the people of the hidden city were / Noldor of Fingolfin's house. Now Rochallor had stayed beside the king until the end, but the wolves of Angband assailed him, and he escaped from them because of his great swiftness, and ran at last to Hithlum, and broke his heart and died. Then in great sorrow Fingon took the lordship of the house of Fingolfin and the kingdom of the Noldor. [*Late pencilled addition:* But his young son (?Findor) [*sic*] Gilgalad he sent to the Havens.]

§158   Now Morgoth's power overshadowed the north-lands, but [*struck out:* still] Barahir would not retreat and defended still the remant of his land and folk in Dorthonion. But Morgoth hunted down all that there remained of Elves or Men, and he sent Sauron against them; and all the forest of the northward slopes of that land was turned into a region of dread and dark enchantment, so that it was after called *Taur-nu-Fuin*, the Forest under Nightshade.

§159   At last so desperate was the case of Barahir that Emeldir the Manhearted his wife (whose mind was rather to fight beside her son and husband than to flee) gathered together all the women and children that were still left, and gave arms to those that would bear them, and led them into the mountains that lay behind, and so by perilous paths, until they came with loss and misery at last to Brethil. And some were there received into Haleth's folk, and some passed on to Dorlómin and the people of Galion Hador's son. (Among these were Morwen Eledhwen daughter of Baragund, and Rían daughter of Belegund.) But none ever again saw the menfolk that they had left. For these were slain one by one, or fled, until at last only Barahir and Beren his son, and Baragund and Belegund sons of Bregolas, were left, and with them [eight >] nine desperate men whose names were long remembered in song: Dagnir and Ragnor, Raðhruin and Dairuin and Gildor, Urthel and Arthad and Hathaldir, and Gorlim Unhappy. Outlaws without hope they became, for their dwellings were destroyed, and their wives and children slain or taken or fled with Emeldir. No help came to them and they were hunted as wild beasts.

458

§160   Here Haleth and his men fought with the Orcs that came down Sirion. In this battle they had help out of Doriath (for they dwelt upon its west-march), and Beleg the Bowman chief of the march-wards of Thingol brought great strength of the Eglath armed with axes into Brethil; and issuing from the deeps of the forest they took an Orc-legion at unawares and destroyed it. Thus for a while the black tide out of the North was stemmed in that region and the Orcs did not dare to cross the Taiglin for many years after.

At this point my father inserted into the manuscript an extensive rider, replacing the rejected passage in annal 455 (§§149–50). This rider was written on the backs of two sheets from the engagement calendar for 1951 (see p. 47), covering weeks in August–September and December of that year.

§161   It is said that at this time Húrin and Huor, the sons of Galion, were dwelling with Haleth [*added later:* their kinsman] as fostersons (as the custom then was among northern Men); and they went both to battle with the Orcs, even Huor, for he would not be restrained, though he was but thirteen years in age. And being with a company that was cut off from the rest, they were pursued to the ford of Brithiach; and there they would have been taken or slain, but for the power of Ulmo, which was still strong in Sirion. Therefore a mist arose from the river and hid them from their enemies, and they escaped into Dimbar, and wandered in the hills beneath the sheer walls of the Crisaegrim. There Thorondor espied them, and sent two Eagles that took them and bore them up and brought them beyond the mountains to the secret vale of Tumladen and the hidden city of Gondolin, which no man else had yet seen.

§162   Then they were led before King Turgon, and he welcomed them, for Ulmo had counselled him to deal kindly with the House of Hador, whence great help should come to him at need. And Húrin and Huor dwelt as his guests for well nigh a year; and it is said that at this time Húrin learned something of the counsels and purposes of Turgon. For Turgon had great liking for Húrin, and for Huor his brother, and spoke much with them; and he wished to keep them in Gondolin, out of love and not for his law only. Now it was the law of the king that no stranger who found the way in, or looked on the guarded realm, should ever depart again until such time as the king should [come forth from hiding >] open the leaguer and the hidden people should come forth.

§163   But Húrin and Huor desired to return to their own kin, and share in the wars and griefs that now beset them. And

Húrin said to Turgon: 'Lord, we are but mortal men, and unlike the Eldar. They may endure long years, awaiting battle with their enemies in some far distant day. But for us time is short, and our hope and strength soon withereth. Moreover we found not the road hither, and indeed we know not surely where this city standeth; for we were brought in fear and wonder by the high ways of the air, and in mercy our eyes were veiled.'

§164   Then Turgon yielded to their prayer, and said: 'By the way that ye came ye have leave to depart, if Thorondor is willing. I grieve at this parting, yet in a little while, as the Eldar account it, we may meet again.'

§165   But it is said that [Glindûr *later* >] Maeglin, the king's sister-son, grieved not at all at their going, [save only *later* >] though he begrudged it/ that in this the king showed them favour, for he loved not the kindred of Men; and he said: 'Your grace is greater than ye know, and the law is become less stern than aforetime, or else no choice would be given you but to abide here to your life's end.'

§166   'The king's grace is great indeed,' answered Húrin; 'but if we have not thy trust then oaths we will take.' And the brethren swore never to reveal the counsels of Turgon and to keep secret all that they had seen in his realm. Then they took their leave, and the Eagles coming bore them away and set them down in Dor Lómin; and their kinsfolk rejoiced to see them, for messages from Brethil had reported that they were slain or taken by the Orcs. But though they told that they had dwelt a while in honour in the halls of King Turgon, to none, kin or stranger, would they ever speak of the manner of his land, or its ordering, or where upon earth it might be found. Nonetheless the strange fortune of the sons of Galion, and their friendship with Turgon, became known far and wide, and reached the ears of the servants of Morgoth.

The rider ends here, and I return to the original text of the *Annals*.

460

§167   The forest of Dorthonion rose southward into mountainous moors. There lay a lake, Tarn-aeluin, in the east of those highlands, and wild heaths were about it, and all that land was pathless and untamed; for even in the days of the Long Peace none had dwelt there. But the waters of Tarn-aeluin were held in reverence; for they were clear and blue by day and by night were

a mirror for the stars. Melian herself, it was said, had hallowed that water in days of old. Thither Barahir and his outlaws withdrew, and there made their lair, and Morgoth could not discover it. But the rumour of the deeds of Barahir and his twelve men went far and wide, and enheartened those that were under the thraldom of Morgoth; and he therefore commanded Sauron to find and destroy the rebels speedily. Elsewhere in the *Quenta* and the *Lay of Leithian* is much told of this, and how Sauron ensnared Gorlim by a phantom of his wife Eilinel, and tormented him and cozened him, so that he betrayed the hidings of Barahir. Thus at last the outlaws were surrounded and all slain, save Beren son of Barahir. For Barahir his father had sent him on a perilous errand to spy upon the ways of the Enemy, and he was far afield when the lair was taken, and returned only to find the bodies of the slain.

§168   Then Beren pursued the Orcs that had slain his father, and coming upon their camp, at Rivil's Well above Serech, he entered it and slew the captain even as he boasted that he was the slayer of Barahir; and he snatched from him the hand of Barahir that had been cut off as a token for Sauron. Thus he regained the Ring of Felagund that his father had worn.

§169   Thereafter escaping from the Orcs Beren dwelt still in those lands as a solitary outlaw for four years, and did such deeds of single-handed daring that Morgoth put a price on his head no less than upon the head of Fingon King of the Noldor.

462

§170   Here Morgoth renewed his assaults, seeking to advance further into Beleriand and secure his hold southwards. For great though his victory had been in the Bragollach, and he had done grievous damage then and in the year after to his enemies, yet his own loss had been no less. And now the Elda' had recovered from their first dismay and were slowly regainin what they had lost. Dorthonion he now held and had estal lished Sauron in the pass of Sirion; but in the east he had bee foiled. Himring stood firm. The army that had driven into Ea Beleriand had been broken by Thingol on the borders Doriath, and part had fled away south never to return to hi part retreating north had been stricken by a sortie of Maidi while those that ventured near the mountains were hunted the Dwarves. And still upon his flank Hithlum stood firm.

§171   He resolved, therefore, now to send force aga

Hithlum; for in the eastward war he hoped ere long to have new help unforeseen by the Eldar. The assault upon Hithlum was bitter, but it was repelled from the passes of Erydwethrin. There, however, in the siege of the fortress of Eithel Sirion Galion was slain, for he held it on behalf of King Fingon. Húrin his son was but then new come to manhood, but he was mighty in heart and strength, and he defeated the Orcs and drove them with loss from the walls into the sands of Anfauglith. Thereafter he ruled the House of Hador. [*Added subsequently:*] Of less stature was he than his father (or his son after him), but tireless and enduring in body; lithe and swift he was, after the manner of his mother's kin, the daughter of Haleth.

§172   But King Fingon with most of the Noldor was hard put to it to hold back the army of Angband that came down from the north. Battle was joined upon the very plains of Hithlum, and Fingon was outnumbered; but timely help came from Cirdan. His ships in great strength sailed into Drengist and there landed a force that came up in the hour of need upon the west flank of the enemy. Then the Eldar had the victory and the Orcs broke and fled, pursued by the horsed archers even to the Iron Mountains.

463

§173   In this year new tidings came to Beleriand: the Swarthy Men came out of Eriador, and passing north about the Eryd Luin entered into Lothlann. Their coming was not wholly unlooked-for, since the Dwarves had warned Maidros that hosts of Men out of the further East were journeying towards Beleriand. They were short and broad, long and strong in the arm, and grew much hair on face and breast; their locks were dark as were their eyes, and their skins were sallow or swart. But they were not all of one kind, in looks or in temper, or in tongue. Some were not uncomely and were fair to deal with; some were grim and ill-favoured and of little trust. Their houses were many, and there was little love among them. They had small liking for the Elves, and for the most part loved rather the Naugrim of the mountains; but they were abashed by the lords of the Noldor, whose like they had not before encountered.

§174   But Maidros, knowing the weakness of the Noldor and the Elf-friends, whereas the pits of Angband seemed to hold store inexhaustible and ever renewed, made alliance with these new-come Men, and gave them dwellings both in Lothlann

north of the March, and in the lands south of it. Now the two chieftains

> From this point there are two parallel versions of the text (the remainder of the annal concerning the Swarthy Men and the story of Beren and Lúthien); on the manuscript a secretary wrote 'Version I' (the first and much shorter version) and 'Version II' (much longer), and similarly on the typescript of the *Grey Annals*, where both forms are given. There can be no doubt at all that Version II was written second (even though it has the earlier form *Borthandos* while Version I has the later *Borthand*), for Version I is integral with the whole text of the *Annals*, whereas Version II ends before the bottom of a page. I give first the whole text of Version I, continuing from the point in the annal for 463 on the Swarthy Men where the text was broken off above.

that had the greatest followings and authority were named Bór and Ulfang. The sons of Bór were Borlas and Boromir and Borthand, and they followed Maidros and were faithful. The sons of Ulfang the swart were Ulfast and Ulwarth and Uldor the Accursed; and they followed Cranthir and swore allegiance to him and were faithless.*

464

§175   In the beginning of this year Beren was pressed so hard that at last he was forced to flee from Dorthonion. In time of winter and snow, therefore, he forsook the land and grave of his father and climbed into the Eryd Orgorath, and thence found a way down into Nan Dungorthin, and so came by paths that no Man nor Elf else dared to tread to the Girdle of Melian. And he passed through, even as Melian had foretold, for a great doom lay on him. In this year, in the spring, Húrin Galion's son of the House of Hador wedded Morwen Elfsheen daughter of Baragund of the House of Bëor [*this sentence was later marked for transposition to the beginning of the annal*]. [*Later insertion:*] In this year Túrin son of Húrin was born in Dorlómin.

§176   In this year at the mid-summer Beren son of Barahir met Lúthien Thingol's daughter in the forest of Neldoreth, and

---

* It was after thought that the people of Ulfang were already secretly in the service of Morgoth ere they came to Beleriand. Not so the people of Bór, who were worthy folk and tillers of the earth. Of them, it is said, came the most ancient of the Men that dwelt in the north of Eriador in the Second Age and [? *read* in] after-days.

because of her great beauty and his love a spell of dumbness was laid on him, and he wandered long in the woods of Doriath.

465

§177 In this year at the first spring Beren was released from his spell, and spoke to Lúthien, calling her *Tinúviel*, the Nightingale. Thus began the love of Beren the most renowned and Lúthien the most fair of which the *Lay of Leithian* was made.

§178 Beren was brought before King Thingol, who scorned him, and desiring to send him to death, said to him in mockery that he must bring a Silmaril from the crown of Morgoth as the bride-price of Lúthien. But Beren took the quest upon himself and departed, and came to Nargothrond and sought the aid of King Felagund. Then Felagund perceived that his oath had returned to bring him to death, but he was willing to lend to Beren all the aid of his kingdom, vain though it must prove.

§179 [Celegorm >] Celegorn and Curufin however hindered the quest, for their Oath was roused from slumber, and they swore that even should the quest be achieved they would slay any that kept the Silmaril or gave it to any hands but their own. And because of their fell words great fear fell on the folk of Nargothrond, and they withheld their aid from the king.

§180 King Inglor Felagund and Beren set forth, with ten companions only, and went northward; but they were waylaid by Sauron and cast into a pit in Tol-in-Gaurhoth. There they were devoured one by one by wolves; but Felagund fought the wolf that was sent to devour Beren, and slew it, and was slain. Thus perished from Middle-earth the fairest of the children of Finwë, and returned never again; but dwells now in Valinor with Amárië.

§181 Lúthien desired to follow Beren, but was held captive by her father, until she escaped and passed into the wild. There she was found by Celegorn and Curufin, and taken to Nargothrond. And evil entered into the hearts of the brethren, and they designed to seize the kingship of Nargothrond, and wed Lúthien to Celegorn and compel Thingol to alliance, and so make the sons of Fëanor the greatest House of the Noldor again.

§182 But Lúthien escaped them and came to Sauron's isle and with the aid of Húan the Hound of Valinor overthrew the werewolves and Sauron himself, and rescued Beren. And when these tidings were heard in Nargothrond Orodreth took the crown of Felagund and drove forth Celegorn and Curufin. And they riding east in haste found Beren and Lúthien near the borders of Doriath, and would seize Lúthien. But they were foiled, and rode away; yet Beren was sorely wounded.

§183 When Beren was healed he led Lúthien to her own land and there left her sleeping and went forth alone on his quest, but Lúthien following overtook him upon the borders of the Anfauglith.

[*Added:*] In the winter of this year, Túrin son of Húrin was born with omens of sorrow. [*Written against this later:* Place in 464]

466

§184 In disguise Beren and Lúthien came to Angband, and Lúthien cast Carcharoth the Wolf-warden of the gate into a slumber; and they descended to Morgoth's throne. There Lúthien laid her spell even upon Morgoth, so that he fell asleep against his will, and the Iron Crown rolled from his head.

§185 Lúthien and Beren bearing a Silmaril were waylaid at the gate by Carcharoth, and Carcharoth bit off the hand of Beren that held the jewel, and being filled with madness fled away. Then Thorondor and his eagles lifted up Beren and Lúthien, and bore them away and set them within the borders of Doriath. Long Lúthien fought with death, until Beren was again healed. And in the spring of the year she led him back to Menegroth. And when Thingol heard all that had befallen them, his mood was softened, for he was filled with wonder at the love of Lúthien and Beren, and perceived that their doom might not be withstood by any power of the world. For thus was it appointed that the two kindreds, the elder and the younger children of Eru, should be joined. Then Beren took the hand of Lúthien before the throne of her father.

§186 But soon after Carcharoth by the power of the Silmaril burst into Doriath, and the Wolf-hunt of Carcharoth was made. In that hunt were King Thingol, and Beren of the One Hand, and Beleg and Mablung and Húan the Hound of Valinor. And Carcharoth hurt Beren to the death, but Húan slew him and then died. From the belly of the Wolf Mablung cut the Jewel and Beren took it and gave it to Thingol, and said 'Now the Quest is achieved', and afterwards spoke no more. But ere he died Lúthien bade him farewell before the gates of

Menegroth, and said to him: 'Await me beyond the Western Sea.'

Thus ended the Quest of the Silmaril.

As has been seen (p. 61), 'Version II' takes up at a point in annal 463 concerning the Swarthy Men, following the words 'Now the two chieftains'; my father copied out the end of that annal simply because it stood at the head of the page on which the story of Beren and Lúthien began, as originally written. He inevitably introduced some differences, however, and I give the second text in full.

(Conclusion of annal 463 in Version II)

[Now the two chieftains] that had the greatest followings and authority were named Bór and Ulfang. The sons of Bór were Borlas and Boromir and Borthandos, and they were goodly men, and they followed Maidros and Maglor and were faithful. The sons of Ulfang the Swart were Ulfast and Ulwarth and Uldor the Accursed; and they followed Cranthir and swore allegiance to him, and were faithless. (It was after thought that the people of Ulfang were already secretly in the service of Morgoth ere they came to Beleriand.)*

464

§187   In the beginning of this year Beren was pressed so hard that at last, [in the winter >] soon after the mid-winter, he was forced to choose between flight and capture. He forsook then Dorthonion and passed into the Eryd Orgorath and found a way down into Nan Dungorthin, and so came by paths that neither Man nor Elf else ever dared to tread to the Girdle of Doriath. And he passed through, even as Melian had foretold to Galadriel; for a great doom lay on him.

In this year in the spring Húrin of the House of Hador wedded Morwen Elfsheen of the people of Bëor [*this sentence was later marked for transposition to the beginning of the annal, as in §175*].

§188   In this year at the midsummer Beren son of Barahir met Lúthien Thingol's daughter in the forest of Neldoreth, and becoming enamoured of her wandered long in the woods of Doriath, for a spell of dumbness was upon him. [*Later insertion, as in §175:*] Túrin son of Húrin was born in Dor Lómin.

---

* Of the people of Bór, it is said, came the most ancient of the Men that dwelt in the north of Eriador afterwards in the Second Age.

465

§189   In this year at the first spring Beren was released from his spell and spoke to Lúthien, calling her *Tinúviel*, the Nightingale (for he knew not her name yet, nor who she was). Thus began the love of Beren the blessed and Lúthien the most fair, of which the *Lay of Leithian* was made. Their meetings were espied by Dairon the minstrel (who also loved Lúthien) and were bewrayed to King Thingol. Then Thingol was wroth indeed, but Lúthien brought Beren to Menegroth, and Beren showed to him the ring of Inglor his kinsman. But Thingol spoke in anger scorning mortal Men, saying that the service of Beren's father to another prince gave the son no claim to walk in Doriath, still less to lift his eyes to Lúthien. Then Beren being stung by his scorn swore that by no power of spell, wall or weapon should he be withheld from his love; and Thingol would have cast him into prison or put him to death, if he had not sworn to Lúthien that no harm should come to Beren. But, as doom would, a thought came into his heart, and he answered in mockery: 'If thou fearest neither spell, wall nor weapons, as thou saist, then go fetch me a Silmaril from the crown of Morgoth. Then we will give jewel for jewel, but thou shalt win the fairer: Lúthien of the First-born and of the Gods.' And those who heard knew that he would save his oath, and yet send Beren to his death.

§190   But Beren looked in the eyes of Melian, who spake not, and he took upon himself the Quest of the Silmaril, and went forth from Menegroth alone.

§191   Now Beren went west to Nargothrond, and sought out King Felagund. And when Felagund heard of the quest he knew that the oath he had sworn was come upon him for his death (as long before he had said to Galadriel). But he kept his oath, and would have mustered all his host for the service of Beren, vain though all his strength must be in such a venture.

§192   But Celegorn and Curufin were in Nargothrond (as was before told), and the quest roused from sleep the Oath of Fëanor. And the brethren spoke against Felagund, and with their words set such a fear in the hearts of the people of Nargothrond that they would not obey their king, neither for many years after would they go to any open war.

§193   Then [Finrod >] Inglor cast off his crown and made ready to go forth alone with Beren, but ten of his most faithful knights stood beside him, and Edrahil, their chief, lifted the crown and bade the king give it in keeping to Orodreth his brother. But Celegorn said: 'Know this: thy going is vain; for could ye achieve this quest it would avail nothing. Neither thee nor this Man should we suffer to keep or to give a Silmaril of Fëanor. Against thee would come all the brethren to slay thee rather. And should Thingol gain it, then we would burn Doriath or die in the attempt. For we have sworn our Oath.'

§194   'I also have sworn an oath,' said Felagund, 'and I seek no release from it. Save thine own, until thou knowest more. But this I will say to you, [son of Fëanor >] Celegorn the fell, by the sight that is given me in this hour, that neither thou nor any son of Fëanor shall regain the Silmarils ever unto world's end. And this that we now seek shall come indeed, but never to your hands. Nay, your oath shall devour you, and deliver to other keeping the bride-price of Lúthien.'

§195   Thus King Felagund and Beren and their companions went forth, and waylaying a company of Orcs beyond the Taiglin they passed towards [Tolsirion >] Tol-in-Gaurhoth, disguised as soldiers of Morgoth. There they were questioned and laid bare by Sauron, and cast into a pit.

§196   Now Lúthien resolved in heart to follow Beren, but seeking the counsel of Dairon (who was of old her friend) she was again bewrayed to Thingol, and he in dismay set her in a prison high in the trees. But she escaped by arts of enchantment upon a rope of her own hair and passed into the wild. There she was found by Celegorn and Curufin, as they were a-hunting, and taken to Nargothrond, and there closely kept. For Celegorn being enamoured of her beauty resolved to wed her, and compel King Thingol's assent.

§197   But Lúthien with the aid of Húan, the hound of Valinor, who followed Celegorn but was won to the love of Lúthien, escaped from Nargothrond and came to Tol-in-Gaurhoth.

§198   There in the pits of Sauron one by one the twelve companions were slain and devoured by werewolves, until at last only Beren and Felagund remained. But none had betrayed them, and Sauron could not learn the errand upon which they went. He left the Elven-king to the last, for he knew who he was, and deemed that he was the mover in whatever venture was devised. But when the wolf came to Beren, Felagund with his last strength broke his bonds, and wrestled naked-handed with the wolf and slew it, and was slain.

§199   Thus perished Inglor Felagund son of Finrod, fairest and most beloved of the children of Finwë, and returned never again to Middle-earth. But it is said that released soon from Mandos, he went to Valinor and there dwells with Amárië.

§200   Beren sank down now into a darkness of sorrow and despair. In that hour Lúthien and Húan came to the bridge that led to Sauron's isle, and Lúthien sang a song of Doriath. Then Beren awoke from his darkness; and the towers of Sauron trembled, and he sent forth Draugluin the greatest of his werewolves. But Húan slew Draugluin, and when Sauron himself came forth in wolf-hame he overthrew him. Thus Sauron was constrained to yield up Tol-sirion, ere bereft of his bodily form he passed away as a black shadow into Taur-nu-Fuin.

§201   Thus Lúthien rescued Beren, and set free many hapless prisoners of Sauron. These prisoners Húan led back to Nargothrond, for his loyalty constrained him to return to Celegorn, his master. But when the tidings came to Nargothrond of the death of Felagund, and the great deeds of the Elf-maid, then Celegorn and Curufin were hated, and Orodreth took the crown of Nargothrond, and drove them forth; and they fled eastward to Himring.

§202   Lúthien and Beren wandered in the wild together in brief joy; and Beren led Lúthien back towards Doriath. Thus by ill chance Celegorn and Curufin came upon them as they rode to the north-borders with Húan. There Celegorn would ride Beren down, and Curufin seized Lúthien; but Beren overthrew Curufin, and took his horse and his knife, and was saved from death at the hands of Celegorn by Húan; who in that hour forsook his master and served Lúthien. Then Celegorn and Curufin rode away upon one horse, and Curufin shooting back smote Beren with an arrow and he fell.

466

§203   Lúthien and Húan guarded Beren in the woods, and Lúthien brought him back at last from the edge of death. But when he was healed, and they had passed into Doriath, Beren remembering his oath and proud words to Thingol, was unwilling to return to Menegroth, neither would he lead Lúthien upon his hopeless quest. Therefore in great grief he left her as she slept in a glade, and committing her to the care of Húan, rode away north upon his horse that he took from

Curufin. And since Tol-in-Gaurhoth was now destroyed he came at last to the north-slopes of Taur-nu-Fuin and looked across the Anfauglith to Thangorodrim and despaired.

§204 There he sent away his horse, and bade farewell to life and to the love of Lúthien, and prepared to go forth alone to death. But Lúthien was borne swiftly after him by Húan, and she came upon him in that hour, and would not be parted from him. Then with the aid of Húan and her arts, Lúthien disguised Beren as a wolf in the hame of Draugluin, and herself as the vampire Thuringwethil, and they passed over Anfauglith and came to Angband, but Húan abode in the woods.

§205 At Angband's gate Lúthien cast down the warden of the gate, Carcharoth mightiest of all wolves, into a deep slumber, and Beren and Lúthien came into the dreadful realm of Morgoth, and descended even into his uttermost hall and came before his throne. There Beren slunk in wolf-form beneath the very chair of Morgoth, but the disguise of Lúthien did not deceive Morgoth and she was revealed to him. Yet she eluded his foul grasp, and even as he watched her dancing, held as in a spell by her beauty, she set a deep slumber upon all the hall, and at last Morgoth himself was overcome and fell from his seat into a blind sleep, but the Iron Crown rolled from his head.

§206 Then Lúthien roused Beren and stripping off the wolf-hame he took the dwarf-knife of Curufin and cut from Morgoth's crown a Silmaril. But desiring suddenly to go beyond doom and rescue all the jewels he was betrayed by the knife which snapped, and a splinter smote Morgoth and disturbed his sleep.

§207 Then Beren and Lúthien fled, but at the gates they found Carcharoth once more awake, and he leaped upon Lúthien; and before she could use any art Beren sprang before and would daunt the wolf with the hand that held the Silmaril. But Carcharoth seized the hand and bit it off, and straightway the Silmaril burned him, and madness seized him and he fled away; but his howls roused all the sleepers in Angband. Then Lúthien knelt by Beren, as he lay in a swoon as it were of death, and all their quest seemed in ruin. But even as she drew forth the venom from Beren's wound with her lips, Thorondor came with Lhandroval and Gwaihir, his mightiest vassals, and they lifted up Lúthien and Beren and bore them south, high over Gondolin, and set them down on the borders of Doriath.

§208 There Húan found them and again they tended Beren

and won him from death, and as spring grew fair they passed into Doriath and came to Menegroth. Glad was their welcome in Doriath, for a spell of shadow and silence had lain upon all the land since Lúthien fled; and Dairon seeking her in sorrow had wandered far away and was lost.

§209 Thus once more Lúthien led Beren to the throne of her father, and he marvelled at him, but was not appeased; and he said to Beren: 'Didst thou not say that thou wouldst not return to me save with a jewel from the crown of Morgoth?' And Beren answered: 'Even now a Silmaril is in my hand.' And Thingol said: 'Show it to me!' But Beren said: 'That I cannot do; for my hand is not here.' And he held up his right arm; and from that hour he named himself *Camlost*.

§210 Then Thingol's mood was softened, for it seemed to him that this Man was unlike all others, and among the great in Arda, whereas the love of Lúthien was of a strength greater than all the kingdoms of West or East. And Beren took Lúthien's hand and laid it upon his breast before the throne of her father, and thus they were betrothed.

But now Carcharoth by the power of the Silmaril burst into Doriath.

Here Version II breaks off abruptly, and not at the foot of a page. The page on which Version I ends, with the words 'Thus ended the Quest of the Silmaril' (p. 64), continues with the annal for 467.

467

§211 In this year at the first breaking of Spring Lúthien Tinúviel laid her body as a white flower on the grass and her spirit fled from Middle-earth, and she went unto Mandos, as it saith in the *Lay*. But a winter as it were the hoar age of mortal Men came upon Thingol.

468

§212 In this time Maidros began those counsels for the raising of the fortunes of the Eldar that are called the Union of Maidros. For new hope ran through the land, because of the deeds of Beren and Lúthien, and it seemed to many that Morgoth was not unconquerable, and that fear only gave him his power. Yet still the Oath of Fëanor lived and hindered all good, and not least the evil that Celegorn and Curufin had done because of it. Thus Thingol would lend no aid to any son of

Fëanor; and small help came from Nargothrond: there the Noldor trusted rather to defend their hidden stronghold by secrecy and stealth. But Maidros had the help of the Naugrim, both in armed force and in great store of weapons; and he gathered together again all his brethren and all the folk that would follow them; and the men of Bór and of Ulfang were marshalled and trained for war, and given fair arms, and they summoned yet more of their kinsfolk out of the East. And in Hithlum Fingon, ever the friend of Maidros, prepared for war, taking counsel with Himring. To Gondolin also the tidings came to the hidden king, Turgon, and in secret also he prepared for great battle. And Haleth gathered his folk in Brethil, and they whetted their axes; but he died of age ere the war came, and Hundor his son ruled his people.

469

§213   In the spring of this year Maidros made the first trial of his strength though his plans were not yet full-wrought. In which he erred, not concealing his stroke until it could be made suddenly with all strength, as Morgoth had done. For the Orcs indeed were driven out of Beleriand once more, and even Dorthonion was freed for a while, so that the frontiers of the Noldor were again as they were before the Bragollach, save that the Anfauglith was now a desert possessed by neither side. But Morgoth being warned of the uprising of the Eldar and the Elf-friends took counsel against them, and he sent forth many spies and workers of treason among them, as he was the better able now to do, for the faithless men of his secret allegiance were yet deep in the secrets of Fëanor's sons.

§214   In this year, it hath been [thought >] said, Beren and Lúthien returned to the world, for a while. For Lúthien had won this doom from Manwë that Beren might return to live again, and she with him; but only so that she too thereafter should be mortal as he, and should soon die indeed and lose the world and depart from the numbers of the Eldalië for ever. This doom she chose. And they appeared again unlooked for in Doriath, and those that saw them were both glad and fearful. But Lúthien went to Menegroth and healed the winter of Thingol with the touch of her hand; yet Melian looked in her eyes and read the doom that was written there, and turned away: for she knew that a parting beyond the end of the World had come between them, and no grief of loss hath been heavier than the grief of the heart of Melian Maia in that hour (unless only it were the grief of Elrond and Arwen). But Lúthien and Beren passed then out of the knowledge of Elves and Men, and dwelt a while alone by the green waters of Ossiriand in that land which the Eldar named therefore *Gwerth-i-guinar*, the land of the Dead that Live. Thereafter Beren son of Barahir spoke not again with any mortal Man.

470

§215   In this year was the birth of Dior Aranel the Beautiful in Gwerth-i-Guinar, who was after known as Dior Thingol's heir, father of the Halfelven.

The annal that follows now in GA, for 471, concerning Isfin and Ëol, was struck out; the revised version of the story appears on a rider inserted at an earlier point, under the year 316 (see §§117–18, where the rejected annal for 471 has been given). A new annal for 471 was added later in pencil:

471

§216   In this year Huor wedded Rían daughter of Belegund.

472

§217   *This is the Year of Lamentation.* At last Maidros resolved to assault Angband from east and from west. With the main host that he gathered, of Elves and Men and Dwarves, he purposed to march with banners displayed in open force from the east over Anfauglith. But when he had drawn forth, as he hoped, the armies of Morgoth in answer, then at a signal Fingon should issue from the passes of Hithlum with all his strength. Thus they thought to take the might of Morgoth as between anvil and hammer, and so break it to pieces.

§218   [Huor son of Galion wedded Rían daughter of Belegund upon the eve of battle, and marched with Húrin his brother in the army of Fingon. *Changed in pencil to read:*] Huor son of Galion wedded Rían daughter of Belegund in the first days of spring. But when he had been but two months wed, the summons came for the mustering of the hosts, and Húrin marched away with his brother in the army of Fingon.

§219   Here at midsummer was fought the Fifth Battle *Nírnaeth Arnediad*, Unnumbered Tears, upon the sands of the Anfauglith before the passes of Sirion. [*Struck out later:* The place of the chief slaughter was long marked by a great hill in which the slain were heaped, both Elves and Men: *Hauð-na-Dengin*, upon which alone in all Anfauglith the grass grew green.]

§220   In this battle Elves and Men were utterly defeated and the ruin of the Noldor was achieved. For Maidros was hindered at his setting out by the guile of Uldor the Accursed: first he gave false warning of an attack from Angband; then he must tarry for not all his men were willing to march. And the army in the West awaited the signal, and it came not, and they grew impatient, and there were whispers of treason among them.

§221   Now the army of the West contained the host of Hithlum, both Elves and Men, and to it was added both folk of the Falas, and a great company from Nargothrond [*and many of the woodmen out of Brethil. This was struck out and the following substituted:*] And many of the woodmen came also with Hundor of Brethil; and with him marched Mablung of Doriath with a small force of Grey-elves, some with axes, some with bows; for Mablung was unwilling to have no part in these great deeds, and Thingol gave leave to him to go, so long as he served not the sons of Fëanor. Therefore Mablung joined him to the host of Fingolfin [*read:* Fingon] and Húrin. / And lo! to the joy and wonder of all there was a sounding of great trumpets, and there marched up to war a host unlooked for. This was the army of Turgon that issued from Gondolin, ten thousand strong, with bright mail and long swords; and they were stationed southwards guarding the passes of Sirion.

§222   Then Morgoth, who knew much of what was done, chose his hour, and trusting in his servants to hold back Maidros and prevent the union of his foes, he sent forth a force seeming great (and yet but part of all that he had made ready) and marched them on Hithlum. Then hot of heart Fingon wished to assail them upon the plain, thinking he had the greater strength; but Húrin spoke against this, bidding him await the signal of Maidros, and let rather the Orcs break themselves against his strength arrayed in the hills.

§223   But the Captain of Morgoth in the West had been commanded to draw forth Fingon into open battle swiftly, by whatsoever means he could. Therefore when his van had come even to the inflowing of Rivil into Sirion and still none came forth to withstand him, he halted, and sent forth riders with tokens of parley; and they rode up close to the lines of their enemies upon the west-shore of Sirion at the feet of the mountains.

§224   Now they led with them Gelmir son of Guilin, a lord of Nargothrond, whom they had taken in the Bragollach and had blinded; and they showed him forth, crying: 'We have many more such at home, but ye must make haste, if ye would find them. For we shall slay them when we return, even so.' And they hewed off Gelmir's hands and feet, and his head last, within sight of the Elves.

§225   But by ill chance across the water stood Gwindor Guilin's son, and he indeed against the will of Orodreth had marched to the war with all the strength that he could muster because of his grief for his brother. Therefore his wrath [*struck out:* could no longer be restrained, but] was kindled to a flame, and the men of Nargothrond sprang over the stream and slew the riders, and drove then on against the main host. And seeing this all the host of the West was set on fire, and Fingon sounded his trumpets and leaped forth from the hills in sudden on-slaught; and many also of the army of Gondolin joined in the battle ere Turgon could restrain them.

§226   And behold! the light of the drawing of the swords of the Noldor was like a fire in a field of reeds; and so fell was their onset that almost the designs of Morgoth went astray. Ere the army that he had sent westward could be strengthened, it was swept away; [and assailed from west and south it was hewn down as it stood, and the greatest slaughter of the Orcs was then made that yet had been achieved. >] and the banners of Fingolfin [? *read* Fingon] passed over Anfauglith and were raised before the walls of Angband. / Gwindor son of Guilin and the folk of Nargothrond were in the forefront of that battle, and they burst through the outer gates and slew the Orcs [even in the very tunnels of Morgoth >] within the very fortress of Morgoth, and he trembled upon his deep throne, hearing them beat upon his doors.

§227   But at the last Gwindor was taken and his men slain; for none had followed them, and no help came. By other secret doors in the mountains of Thangorodrim Morgoth had let forth his main host that was held in waiting, and Fingon was beaten back with great loss from the walls.

§228   Then in the plain of Anfauglith, on the [third >] fourth day of the war, began the *Nírnaeth Arnediad*, for no song can contain all its grief. The host of Fingon retreated over the sands of the desert, and there fell Hundor son of Haleth [*struck out:* in the rearguard] and most of the men of Brethil. But as night fell, and they were still far from [Ered-wethion >] Eryd-wethrin, the Orcs surrounded the army of Fingon, and they fought until day, pressed ever closer. Even so, all was not yet lost. In the morning were heard the horns of Turgon who brought up now his main host to the rescue [*struck out:* unlooked-for by the Orcs]; and the Noldor of Gondolin were strong and clad in mail, and they broke [the leaguer, and once again the might of Angband was defeated. >] through the ranks of the Orcs, and Turgon hewed his way to the side of Fingon, his brother. And it is said that the meeting of Turgon with Húrin who stood by his king was glad in the midst of the battle./

§229   And in that very day, at the third hour of morning, lo! at last the trumpets of Maidros were heard coming up from the east; and the banners of the sons of Fëanor assailed the enemy in the rear. It has been said that even then the Eldar might have won the day, had all their hosts proved faithful; for the Orcs wavered, and their onslaught was stayed, and already some were turning to flight.

§230   But even as the vanguard of Maidros came upon the Orcs, Morgoth loosed his last strength, and Angband was emptied. There came wolves, and wolfriders, and there came Balrogs a thousand, and there came worms and drakes, and Glaurung, Father of Dragons. And the strength and terror of the Great Worm were now grown great indeed, and Elves and Men withered before him; and he came between the hosts of Maidros and Fingon and swept them apart.

§231   Yet neither by wolf, balrog, nor dragon would Morgoth have achieved his end, but for the treachery of Men. In this hour the plots of Ulfang were revealed; for many of the Easterlings turned and fled, their hearts being filled with lies and fear; but the sons of Ulfang went over suddenly to the side of Morgoth and drove in upon the rear of the sons of Fëanor. And in the confusion that they wrought they came near to the standard of Maidros. They reaped not the reward that Morgoth promised them, for Maglor slew Uldor the Accursed, the leader in treason, and Bór and his sons slew Ulfast and Ulwarth ere they themselves were slain. But new strength of evil men came up that Uldor had summoned and kept hidden in the eastern hills, and the host of Maidros being assailed now on three sides, by the Orcs, and the beasts, and by the Swarthy Men, was dispersed and fled this way and that. Yet fate saved the sons of Fëanor, and though all were wounded, none were slain, for they drew together and gathering a remnant of Noldor and of the Naugrim about them they hewed a way out of the battle and escaped towards Mount Dolmed.

§232   Last of all the eastern force to stand firm were the Enfeng of [Nogrod >] Belegost, and thus won renown. Now the Naugrim withstood fire more hardily than either Elves or Men, and it was the custom moreover of the Enfeng to wear great masks [*struck out:* or vizors] in battle hideous to look upon, which stood them in good stead against the drakes. And but for them Glaurung and his brood would have withered all that was left of the Noldor. But the Naugrim made a circle about him when he assailed them, and even his mighty armour was not full proof against the blows of their great axes; and when in his rage he turned and struck down Azaghâl of Belegost and crawled over him, with his last stroke Azaghâl drove a knife into his belly and so wounded him that he fled the field and the beasts of Angband in dismay followed after him. Had Azaghâl but borne a sword great woe would have been spared to the Noldor that after befell [*added:*] but his knife went not deep enough. / But then the Enfeng raised up the body of Azaghâl and bore it away; and with slow steps they walked behind, singing a dirge in their deep voices, as it were a funeral pomp in their own country, and gave no heed more to their foes; and indeed none dared to stay them.

§233   But now in the western battle Fingon was surrounded by a tide of foes thrice greater than all that was left to him [*struck out:* and the Balrogs came against him]. There at last fell the King of the Noldor, and flame sprang from his helm when it was cloven. He was overborne by the Balrogs and beaten to the earth and his banners blue and silver were trodden into dust.

§234   The day was lost, but still Húrin and Huor with the men of Hador stood firm, and the Orcs could not yet win the passes of Sirion. Thus was the treachery of Uldor redressed; and the last stand of Húrin and Huor is the deed of war most renowned among the Eldar that the Fathers of Men wrought in their behalf. For Húrin spoke to Turgon saying: 'Go now, lord, while time is! For last art thou of the House of Fingolfin, and in thee lives the last hope of the Noldor. While Gondolin stands, strong and guarded, Morgoth shall still know fear in his heart.'

'Yet not long now can Gondolin be hidden, and being discovered it must fall,' said Turgon.

§235 'Yet [a while it must stand,' said Húrin; 'for out of Gondolin >] if it stands but a little while,' said [Húrin >] Huor, 'then out of [Gondolin *later* >] thy house / shall come the hope of Elves and Men. This I say to thee, lord, with the eyes of death; though here we part for ever, and I shall never look on thy white walls, from thee and me shall a new star arise. Farewell!'

§236 [*Struck out:* Then Turgon withdrew and all the Noldor of Gondolin went back down Sirion and vanished into the hills. But all the remnant of the host of the west gathered about the brethren and held the pass behind them.]

§237 [*Added subsequently:*] And [Glindûr *later* >] Maeglin, Turgon's sister-son, who stood by heard these words and marked them well, [*struck out later:* and looked closely at Huor,] but said naught.

§238 Then Turgon accepted the valiant words of the brethren, and summoning all that remained of the folk of Gondolin, and such of Fingon's host as could be gathered, he [withdrew >] fought his way southward,/ and escaped down Sirion, and vanished into the mountains and was hidden from the eyes of Morgoth. For Húrin and Huor held the pass behind him, so that no foe could follow him, and drew the remnant of the mighty men of Hithlum about them.

§239 Slowly they withdrew, until they came behind the Fen of Serech, and had the young stream of Sirion before them, and then they stood and gave way no more, for they were in the narrow gorge of the pass. Then all the host of Morgoth swarmed against them, and they bridged the stream with the dead, and encircled the remnant of Hithlum as a gathering tide about a rock.

§240 Huor fell pierced with a venomed arrow in the eye, and all the valiant men of Hador were slain about him in a heap, and the Orcs hewed their heads and piled them as a mound of gold; for the sun was shining on the [fourth >] sixth and last / day of the battle and their yellow locks shone amid the blood. Last of all Húrin stood alone. Then he cast aside his shield and wielded his axe two-handed; and it is sung that in that last stand he himself slew an hundred of the Orcs. But they took him alive at last, by the command of Morgoth, who thought thus to do him more evil than by death. Therefore his servants grappled him with their hands, which clung still to him though he hewed off their arms; and ever their numbers were renewed until at the last he fell buried beneath them. Then binding him they dragged him to Angband with mockery. Thus ended the *Nírnaeth Arnediad*, and the sun sank red over Hithlum, and there came a great storm on the winds of the West.

§241   Great indeed now was the triumph of Morgoth; and his design was accomplished in a manner after his own heart; for Men took the lives of Men, and betrayed the Eldar, and fear and hatred were aroused among those that should have been united against him. From that day indeed began the estrangement of Elves from Men, save only from those of the Three Houses of Bëor, Hador, and Haleth, and their children.

§242   The March of Maidros was no more. The fell sons of Fëanor were broken and wandered far away in the woods as leaves before the wind. The Gorge of Aglon was filled with Orcs, and the Hill of Himring was garrisoned by soldiers of Angband; the pass of Sirion was pierced and Tol-sirion retaken and its dread towers rebuilt. All the gates of Beleriand were in the power of Morgoth. The realm of Fingon was no more [*struck out:* for few ever of the host of Hithlum, Elves or Men, came ever back over the mountains to their land]. To Hithlum came back never one of Fingon's host, nor any of the Men of Hador, nor any tidings of the battle and the fate of their lords.

§243   Doriath indeed remained, and Nargothrond was hidden, and Cirdan held the Havens; but Morgoth gave small heed to them as yet, either for he knew little of them, or because their hour was not yet come in the deep purposes of his malice. But one thought troubled him deeply, and marred his triumph; Turgon had escaped the net, whom he most desired to take. For Turgon came of the great house of Fingolfin, and was now by right King of all the Noldor, [*struck out:* and from of old he hated him, scarce less than Fëanor, and feared him more. For never in Valinor would Turgon greet him, being a friend of Ulmo and of Tulkas; and moreover, ere yet darkness overwhelmed him and the blindness of malice, he looked upon Turgon and knew that from him should come, in some time that doom held, the end of all hope.] and Morgoth feared and hated most the house of Fingolfin, because they had scorned him in Valinor, and had the friendship of Ulmo, and because of the wounds that Fingolfin gave him in battle. Moreover of old his eye had lighted on Turgon, and a dark shadow fell on his heart, foreboding that, in some time that lay yet hidden in doom, from Turgon ruin should come to him.

§244   Therefore Húrin was brought before Morgoth, and defied him; and he was chained and set in torment. But Morgoth who would ever work first with lies and treachery, if they might avail, came to him where he lay in pain, and offered him freedom, and power and wealth as one of his great captains, if he would take service in his armies and lead a host against Turgon, or even if he would but reveal where that king had his stronghold. For he had learned that Húrin knew the secret counsels of Turgon. But again Húrin the Steadfast mocked him.

§245   Then Morgoth restrained his wrath and spoke of Húrin's wife and son now helpless in Hithlum [*written above later:* Dorlómin], and at his mercy to do what he would with them.

§246   'They know not the secrets of Turgon,' said Húrin. 'But an they did, thou shouldst not come at Turgon so; for they are of the houses of Hador and Bëor, and we sell not our troth for any price of profit or pain.'

§247   Then Morgoth cursed Húrin and Morwen and their offspring and set a doom upon them of sorrow and darkness; and taking Húrin from prison he set him in a chair of stone upon a high place of Thangorodrim. There he could see afar the land of Hithlum westward and the lands of Beleriand southward. There Morgoth standing beside him cursed him again, and set his power upon him so that he could not stray from that place, nor die, unless Morgoth released him.

§248   'Sit now there!' said Morgoth. 'Look upon the lands where the uttermost woe shall come upon those whom thou hast delivered unto me. Yea, verily! Doubt not the power of Melkor, Master of the fates of Arda! And with my eyes shalt thou see it, [*struck out:* and nought shall be hidden from thee, and all that befalls those thou holdest dear shall swiftly be told to thee] and with my ears shalt thou hear all tidings, and nought shall be hidden from thee!'

§249   And even so it came to pass; but it is not said that Húrin asked ever of Morgoth either mercy or death, for himself or for any of his kin.

§250   Now the Orcs in token of the great triumph of

.

Angband gathered with great labour all the bodies of their enemies that were slain, and all their harness and weapons, and they piled them, Elves and Men, in a great hill in the midst of the Anfauglith. [Hauð-na-D(engin) > Hauð-i-Nengin *later* >] Hauð-ina-Nengin was the name of that mound, and it was like unto a hill. But thither alone in all the desert the grass came, and grew again long and green, and thereafter no Orc dared tread upon the earth beneath which the swords of the Noldor crumbled into rust.

§251 Rían wife of Huor hearing no tidings of her lord went forth into the wild, and there gave birth to Tuor her son; and he was taken to foster by [the Dark-elves *later* >] Annael of the Grey-elves of Mithrim. But Rían went to [Hauð-i-Nengin *later* > Hauð-na-nDengin >] Hauð-in-nDengin and laid her there and died. And in Brethil Glorwendil, Hador's daughter, died of grief. But Morwen wife of Húrin abode in Hithlum, for she was with child.

§252 Morgoth now broke his pledges to the Easterlings that had served him, and denied to them the rich lands of Beleriand which they coveted, and he sent away these evil folk into Hithlum, and there commanded them to dwell. And little though they now loved their new king, yet they despised the remnant of the folk of Hador (the aged and the women and the children for the most part), and they oppressed them, and took their lands and goods, and wedded their women by force, and enslaved their children. And those of the Grey-elves that had dwelt there fled into the mountains, or were taken to the mines of the North and laboured there as thralls.

§253 Therefore Morwen unwilling that Túrin her son, being then seven years old, should become a slave, sent him forth with two aged servants, and bade them find if they could a way to Doriath, and there beg fostering for the son of Húrin, and kinsman of Beren (for her father was his cousin).

473

§254 In the [*added:*] first/beginning of this year was born to Morwen Elfsheen a maid-child, daughter of Húrin; and she was named Nienor, which is Mourning. And at about this time Túrin came through great perils to Doriath and was there received by Thingol, who took him to his own fostering, as he were king's son, in memory of Húrin. For Thingol's mood was now changed towards the houses of the Elf-friends.

§255   In this year Morgoth having rested his strength, and given heed to his own hurts and great losses, renewed the assault upon Beleriand, which now lay open to him; and the orcs and wolves passed far into the lands, even as far as the borders of Ossiriand upon one side, and Nan Tathren upon the other, and none were safe in field or wild.

§256   Many now fled to the Havens and took refuge behind Cirdan's walls, and the mariner folk passed up and down the coast and harried the enemy with swift landings. Therefore the first assault of Morgoth was against Cirdan; and ere the winter was come he sent great strength over Hithlum and Nivrost, and they came down the Rivers Brithon and Nenning, and ravaged all the Falas, and besieged the walls of Brithombar and Eglarest. Smiths and miners and masters of fire they brought with them, and set up great engines, and though they were stoutly resisted they broke the walls at last. Then the Havens were laid in ruin, and the Tower of Ingildon cast down, and all Cirdan's folk slain or enthralled, save those that went aboard and escaped by sea [*added:*] and some few that fled north to Mithrim.

§257   Then Cirdan took his remnant by ship, and they sailed to the Isle of Balar, [*struck out:* and mingled with Turgon's outpost there,] and made a refuge for all that could come thither. For they kept also a foothold at the mouths of Sirion, and there many light swift ships lay hid in the creeks and waters where the reeds were dense as a forest. [And seven ships at Turgon's asking Cirdan sent out into the West, but they never returned. >] And when Turgon heard of this he sent again his messengers to Sirion's Mouths, and besought the aid of Cirdan the Shipwright. And at his bidding Cirdan let build seven swift ships, and they sailed out into the West, and were never heard of again – save one and the last. Now the captain of this ship was Voronwë, and he toiled in the sea for many years, until returning at last in despair his ship foundered in a great storm within sight of land, and he alone survived, for Ulmo saved him from the wrath of Ossë, and the waves bore him up and cast him ashore in Nivrost./

481

§258   Túrin waxed fair and strong and wise in Doriath, but was marked with sorrow. In this his sixteenth year he went forth to battle on the marches of Doriath, and became the companion in arms of Beleg the Bowman. [*Later pencilled addition:*] Túrin donned the Dragon-helm of Galion.

484

§259 Here Túrin was a guest at Menegroth in honour for his deeds of valour. But he came from the wild, and was unkempt and his gear and garments were wayworn. And Orgof taunted him, and the people of Hithlum, and in his wrath he smote Orgof with a cup and slew him at the king's board. Then fearing the anger of Thingol he fled, and became an outlaw in the woods, and gathered a desperate band, of Elves and of Men [*struck out:* beyond the Girdle of Melian].

487

§260 Here Túrin's band captured Beleg and bound him; but Túrin returning released him, and they renewed their friendship. And Túrin learned of the king's pardon, but would not go back to Menegroth, and remained upon the marches. And since no foe yet could pass the Girdle of Melian, and he desired only to take vengeance on the Orcs, he made a lair in the woods between Sirion and Mindeb in the country of Dimbar.

The following passage was rewritten several times and it is not possible to be perfectly certain of the detail of development at each stage. As first written it seems to have read:

§261 Here Tuor son of Huor, being now fifteen years of age, came to Hithlum seeking his kin, but they were no more, for Morwen and Nïenor had been carried away to Mithrim and none remembered them.

This seems to have been cancelled as soon as written, and a second form probably reads thus:

§262 Here Tuor son of Huor, being now fifteen years of age, came to Hithlum seeking his kin, but he found them not. For though the Elves that fostered him knew indeed their names, they knew not where they dwelt of old, or dwelt now in the change of the land. But Morwen and Nïenor alone remained, and they dwelt still in Dor Lómin; therefore Tuor searched in Hithlum in vain, and the Easterlings seized him and enslaved him. But he escaped and became an outlaw in the wild lands about Lake Mithrim.

In the final form of the passage the date 488 was added:

488

§263   Here Tuor son of Huor, being now sixteen years of age, seeking to escape from Dorlómin, was made captive and enslaved by Lorgan chief of the Easterlings; and he endured thraldom for [seven years *immediately* >] three years, ere he escaped and became an outlaw in the hills of Mithrim.

[*Struck out:* 488]

§264   Here Haldir Orodreth's son of Nargothrond was trapped and hung on a tree by Orcs. Thereafter the Elves of Nargothrond were yet more wary and secret, and would not suffer even Elves to stray in their lands.

489

§265   In this year Gwindor Guilin's son escaped from Angband. Blodren Ban's son was an Easterling, and being taken by Morgoth, and tormented because he was one of the faithful that withstood Uldor, entered the service of Morgoth and was released, and sent in search of Túrin. And he entered the hidden company in Dimbar, and served Túrin manfully for two years. But seeing now his chance he betrayed the refuge of Beleg and Túrin to the Orcs, as his errand was. Thus it was surrounded and taken, and Túrin was captured alive and carried towards Angband; but Beleg was left for dead among the slain. Blodren was slain by a chance arrow in the dark. [*Pencilled against this annal:* What happened to the Dragon-helm?]

§266   Beleg was found by Thingol's messengers, and taken to Menegroth and healed by Melian. At once he set forth in search of Túrin [*pencilled in margin:* bearing the Dragon-helm that Túrin had left in Menegroth]. He came upon Gwindor bewildered in Taur-na-Fuin (where Sauron now dwelt) and together they pursued the captors of Túrin. From an orc-camp on the edge of the desert they rescued him as he slept in drugged sleep, and carried him to a hidden dell. But Beleg as he laboured to unloose Túrin's fetters pricked his foot, and he was roused, and dreaming that he was surrounded by Orcs that would torment him, seized Beleg's sword and slew him ere he knew him. Gwindor buried Beleg, and led Túrin away, for a dumb madness of grief was on him.

490

§267 Through great perils Gwindor led Túrin towards Nargothrond, and they came to the pools of Ivrin, and there Túrin wept and was healed of his madness. Gwindor and Túrin came at last to Nargothrond, and were admitted; for Finduilas daughter of Orodreth, to whom Gwindor had been betrothed, alone of his people knew him again after the torments of Angband.

490-5

§268 During this time Túrin dwelt in Nargothrond, and became great in counsel and renown. The Noldor took Beleg's sword which Túrin had kept, and re-forged it, and it was made into a black sword with edges as of fire. Now Túrin [added:] had begged Gwindor to conceal his right name, for the horror he had of his slaying of Beleg and dread lest it were learned in Doriath; and he / had given out his name as *Iarwaeth* [*struck out:* the blood-stained], but now it was changed to *Mormegil* the Blacksword, because of the rumour of his deeds with that weapon in vengeance for Beleg; but the sword itself he named *Gurthang* Iron of Death. Then the heart of Finduilas was turned from Gwindor (who because of his pains in Angband was half crippled) and her love was given to Túrin; and Túrin loved her, but spoke not, being loyal to Gwindor. [*Added:*] Then Finduilas being torn in heart became sorrowful; and she grew wan and silent. / But Gwindor seeing what had befallen was bitter at heart, and cursed Morgoth, who could thus pursue his enemies with woe, whithersoever they might run. 'And now at last,' he said, 'I believe the tale of Angband that Morgoth hath cursed Húrin and all his kin.'

§269 And he spoke on a time to Finduilas, saying: 'Daughter of the House of Finrod, let no grief lie between us, for, though Morgoth hath laid my life in ruin, thee still I love. But go thou whither love leads thee! Yet beware! Not meet is it that the Elder Children should stoop to the Younger. Neither will fate suffer it, save once or twice only for some high cause of doom. But this Man is not Beren. A doom indeed lies on him, as seeing eyes may well read in him, but a dark doom. Enter not into it! And if thou wilt, then thy love shall betray thee to bitterness and death. For behold! this is not *Iarwaeth* nor *Mormegil*, but Túrin son of Húrin.'

§270   And Gwindor told how Húrin's torment and curse was known to all in Angband; and said: 'Doubt not the power of Morgoth Bauglir! Is it not written in me?' But Finduilas was silent.

§271   And later in like manner Gwindor spoke to Túrin; but Túrin answered: 'In love I hold thee for rescue and safe-keeping. And even were it not so, still I would do thee no hurt willingly, who hast suffered such great wrongs. Finduilas indeed I love, but fear not! Shall the accursed wed, and give as morrowgift his curse to one that he loves? Nay, not even to one of his own people. But now thou hast done ill to me, friend, to bewray my right name, and call my doom upon me, from which I had thought to lie hidden.'

§272   But when it became known to Orodreth [and the folk of Nargothrond that Iarwaeth was indeed the son of Húrin, then greater became his honour among them, and they would do >] that Iarwaeth was indeed the son of Húrin, he gave him great honour, and did / all that he counselled. And he being troubled by this new grief (for ever the love of Finduilas that he would not take grew greater) found solace only in war. And in that time the folk of Nargothrond forsook their secrecy, their war of ambush and hunting, and went openly to battle; and they [*struck out:* allied themselves with Handir of Brethil, and] built a bridge over the Narog from the great doors of Felagund for the swifter passage of their arms. And they drove the Orcs and beasts of Angband out of all the land between Narog and Sirion eastward, and westward to the Nenning and the borders of the desolate Falas. Thus Nargothrond was revealed to the wrath and malice of Morgoth, but still at Túrin's prayer his true name was not spoken, and rumour spoke only of Mormegil of Nargothrond.

The following entry, for the year 492, was struck out later. Its replacement, an inserted annal for the year 400, has been given earlier (§120).

§273   [*Rejected annal for the year 492*] Here Meglin son of Ëol was sent by his mother Isfin to Gondolin, and Turgon rejoiced to hear tidings of his sister whom he had deemed lost, and he received Meglin with honour as his sister-son. But it is said that Meglin, having been nurtured in the shadows of Brethil, was never wholly at ease in the light of Gondolin.

494

§274   In this time, when because of the deeds of Mormegil of Nargothrond the power of Morgoth was stemmed west of Sirion, Morwen and Niënor fled at last from Dor Lómin and came to Doriath, seeking tidings of Túrin. But they found him gone, and in Doriath no tidings had been heard of his name, since the Orcs took him, five years before. [*Added:*] Morwen and Niënor remained as guests of Thingol, and were treated with honour, but they were filled with sorrow, and yearned ever for tidings of Túrin. /

495

§275   Here [*added:*] Handir of Brethil was slain in the spring in fighting with Orcs that invaded his land. The Orcs gathered in the passes of Sirion. Late in the year having thus mustered great strength / Morgoth assailed Nargothrond. Glaurung the Urulókë passed [into Hithlum and there did great evil, and he came thence out of Dorlómin over the Erydwethrin >] over Anfauglith, and came thence into the north vales of Sirion and there did great evil, and he came thence under the shadows of the Erydwethrin / with a great army of Orcs in his train, and he defiled the Eithil Ivrin. Then he passed into the realm of Nargothrond, burning the Talath Dirnen, the Guarded Plain, between Narog and Sirion. Then Orodreth and Túrin [*struck out:* and Handir of Brethil; *added later:*] and Gwindor / went up against him, but they were defeated upon the field of Tum-halad; and Orodreth was slain [*struck out:* and Handir. *Added later:*] and Gwindor. [*Pencilled in margin:* Túrin in the battle wore the Dragon-helm.] Túrin bore Gwindor out of the rout, and escaping to a wood there laid him on the grass.

§276   And Gwindor said, 'Let bearing pay for bearing! But hapless was mine, and vain is thine. For now my body is marred, and I must leave Middle-earth; and though I love thee, son of Húrin, yet I rue the day I took thee from the Orcs. But for thy prowess, still I should have love and life, and Nargothrond should stand. Now if you love me, leave me! Haste thee to Nargothrond and save Finduilas. And this last I say to thee: she alone stands between thee and thy doom. If thou fail her, it shall not fail to find thee. Farewell!'

§277   Therefore Túrin sped now back to Nargothrond, mustering such of the rout as he met on the way. [*Added:*] And the leaves fell from the trees in a great wind as they went, for the autumn was passing to a dire winter. And one, Ornil, said: 'Even so fall the people of Nargothrond, but for them there shall come no Spring.' And Túrin hastened, / but Glaurung and his army were there before him (because of his succouring of Gwindor), and they came suddenly, ere those that were left on guard were aware of the defeat. In that day the bridge that Túrin let build over Narog proved an evil; for it was great and mightily made and could not swiftly be destroyed, and thus the enemy came readily over the deep river, and Glaurung came in full fire against the Doors of Felagund, and overthrew them, and passed within.

§278   And even as Túrin came up the ghastly sack of Nargothrond was wellnigh achieved. The Orcs had slain or driven off all that remained in arms, and they were even then ransacking all the great halls and chambers, plundering and destroying; but those of the women and maidens that were not burned or slain they had herded on the terrace before the doors, as slaves to be taken to Angband. Upon this ruin and woe Túrin came, and none could withstand him; or would not, though he struck down all before him, and passed over the bridge, and hewed his way towards the captives.

§279   And now he stood alone, for the few that had followed him had fled into hiding. But behold! in that moment Glaurung the fell issued from the gaping Doors of Felagund, and lay behind, between Túrin and the bridge. Then suddenly he spoke by the evil spirit that was in him, saying: 'Hail, son of Húrin. Well met!'

§280   Then Túrin sprang about, and strode against him, and fire was in his eyes, and the edges of Gurthang shone as with flame. But Glaurung withheld his blast, and opened wide his serpent-eyes and gazed upon Túrin. And without fear Túrin looked in those eyes as he raised up his sword, and lo! straightway he fell under the dreadful spell of the dragon, and was as one turned to stone. Thus long they stood unmoving, silent before the great Doors of Felagund. Then Glaurung spoke again, taunting Túrin. [*Pencilled against this paragraph:* For while he wore the Dragon-helm of Galion he was proof against the glance of Glaurung. Then the Worm perceiving this (*sic*)]

§281   'Evil have been all thy ways, son of Húrin,' said he. 'Thankless fosterling, outlaw, slayer of thy friend, thief of love, usurper of Nargothrond, captain foolhardy, and deserter of thy kin. [*Struck out:* How long wilt thou live to bring ruin upon all that love thee?] As thralls thy mother and sister live in Dorlómin, in misery and want. Thou art arrayed as a prince, but they go in rags. For thee they yearn, but thou reckest not of that. Glad may thy father be to learn that he hath such a son, as learn he shall.' And Túrin being under the spell of Glaurung, harkened to his words, and saw himself as in a mirror misshapen by malice, and loathed that which he saw. And while he was yet held by the eyes of Glaurung in torment of mind, and could not stir, at a sign from the dragon the Orcs drove away the herded captives, and they passed nigh to Túrin and went over the bridge. And behold! among them was Finduilas, and she held out her arms to Túrin, and called him by name. But not until her cries and the wailing of the captives was lost upon the northward road did Glaurung release Túrin, and he might not even stop his ears against that voice that haunted him after.

§282　Then suddenly Glaurung withdrew his glance, and waited; and Túrin stirred slowly as one waking from a hideous dream. Then coming to himself with a loud cry he sprang upon the dragon. But Glaurung laughed, saying: 'If thou wilt be slain, I will slay thee gladly. But small help will that be to Morwen and Niënor. No heed didst thou give to the cries of the Elf-woman. Wilt thou deny also the bond of thy blood?'

§283　But Túrin drawing back his sword stabbed at his eyes; and Glaurung coiling back swiftly towered above him, and said: 'Nay! At least thou art valiant. Beyond all whom I have met. And they lie who say that we of our part do not honour the valour of foes. Behold! I offer thee freedom. Go to thy kin, if thou canst. Get thee gone! And if Elf or Man be left to make tale of these days, then surely in scorn they will name thee, if thou spurnest this gift.'

§284　Then Túrin, being yet bemused by the eyes of the dragon, as were he treating with a foe that could know pity, believed the words of Glaurung, and turning away sped over the bridge. But as he went Glaurung spake behind him, saying in a fell voice: 'Haste thee now, son of Húrin, to Dorlómin! Or maybe the Orcs shall come before thee, once again. And if thou tarry for Finduilas, then never shalt thou see Morwen or Niënor again; and they will curse thee.' [*Pencilled in margin:* Glaurung taunts him with the Dragon-helm.]

§285　But Túrin passed away on the northward road, and Glaurung laughed once more, for he had accomplished the errand of his Master. Then he turned to his own pleasure, and sent forth his blast, and burned all about him. But all the Orcs that were busy in the sack he routed forth, and drove them away, and denied them their plunder even to the least thing of worth. The bridge then he broke down and cast into the foam of Narog, and being thus secure, he gathered all the hoard and riches of Felagund and heaped them, and lay then upon them in the innermost hall, and rested a while.

§286   Now Túrin hastened along the ways to the North, through the lands now desolate, between Narog and Taiglin, [*added:*] and the Fell Winter came down to meet him; for that year snow fell ere autumn was passed, and spring came late and cold. / Ever it seemed to him as he went that he heard the cries of Finduilas, calling his name by wood and by hill, and great was his anguish; but his heart being hot with the lies of Glaurung, and seeing ever in his mind the Orcs burning the house of Húrin or putting Morwen and Niënor to torment, he held on his way, turning never aside.

> There follows here a section of the text where the original writing was heavily emended, after which the greater part of the section was struck out and replaced. I give first the form as originally written. For the antecedents of the *Grey Annals* (other than the entries concerning Tuor) from this point to the end of the tale of Túrin (§349) see the commentary on §§287 ff.

§287   At last worn and hungry by long days of journey, as the sad autumn drew on he came to the pools of Ivrin, where before he had been healed. But they were broken and defiled, and he could not drink there again. An ill token it seemed to him.

§288   Thus he came through the passes into Dorlómin, and even as winter fell with snow from the North, he found again the land of his childhood. Bare was it and bleak. And Morwen was gone. Empty stood her house, broken and cold. It was more than a year since she departed to Doriath. Brodda the Easterling (who had wedded Morwen's kinswoman Airin) had plundered her house, and taken all that was left of her goods. Then Túrin's eyes were opened, and the spell of Glaurung was broken, and he knew the lies wherewith he had been cheated. And in his anguish and his wrath for the evils that his mother had suffered he slew Brodda in his own hall, and fled then out into the winter, a hunted man.

§289   Tidings came soon to Thingol in Doriath of the fall of Nargothrond; and [it was revealed now that Mormegil was indeed Túrin son of Húrin >] fear walked on the borders of the Hidden Kingdom.

§290   In this same year Tuor son of Huor was led by the sendings of Ulmo to a secret way that led from Mithrim, by a channel of water running under earth, and so came to the deep cleft at the head of Drengist, and passed out of the knowledge of the spies of Morgoth. Then journeying alone warily down the coasts he came through the Falas and the ruined Havens and so reached at the year's end the Mouths of Sirion. [*Added and then struck out:* In the spring of this year also Handir of Brethil was slain in fighting with the Orcs that ventured into Brethil.]

496

§291   Too late now Túrin sought for Finduilas, roaming the woods under the shadow of Eryd Wethion, wild and wary as a beast; and he waylaid all the roads that went north to the pass of Sirion. Too late. For all trails had grown old, or had perished in the winter. But thus it was that Túrin passing southwards down Taiglin came upon some of the folk of Haleth that dwelt still in the forest of Brethil. They were dwindled now by war to a small people, and dwelt for the most part secretly within a stockade upon the Amon Obel deep in the forest. Ephel Brandir was that place named; for Brandir son of Handir was now their lord since [Handir had not returned from the stricken field of Tum-halad. >] since Handir his father had been slain. And Brandir was no man of war, being lame by a misadventure in childhood; and he was gentle moreover in mood, loving wood rather than metal, and the knowledge of all things that grow in the earth rather than other lore.

At this point the rejected section of the narrative, beginning at §287, ends. The text that replaced it belongs to the time of the writing of the manuscript.

§292   At last worn by haste and the long road (for [eighty >] forty leagues had he journeyed without rest) he came with the first ice of winter to the pools of Ivrin, where before he had been healed. But they were now but a frozen mire, and he could not drink there again.

§293   Thus he came hardly by the passes of Dorlómin,

through bitter snows from the North, and found again the land of his childhood. Bare was it and bleak. And Morwen was gone. Empty stood her house, broken and cold, and no living thing now dwelt nigh.

§294   It so befell that Túrin came then to the hall of Brodda the Incomer, and learned of an old servant of Húrin that Brodda had taken to wife by force Airin Húrin's kinswoman, and had oppressed Morwen; and therefore in the year before she had fled with Niënor, none but Airin knew whither.

§295   Then Túrin strode to Brodda's table, and with threats learned from Airin that Morwen went to Doriath to seek her son. For said Airin: 'The lands were freed then from evil by the Blacksword of the South, who now hath fallen, they say.'

§296   Then Túrin's eyes were opened, and the last shreds of Glaurung's spell left him, and for anguish, and wrath at the lies that had deluded him, and hatred of the oppressors of Morwen, a black rage seized him, and he slew Brodda in his hall, and other Easterlings that were his guests, and then he fled out into the winter, a hunted man.

§297   But he was aided by some that remained of Hador's people and knew the ways of the wild, and with them he escaped through the falling snow and came to an outlaws' refuge in the southern mountains of Dorlómin. Thence Túrin passed again from the land of his childhood, and returned to Sirion's vale. His heart was bitter, for to Dorlómin he had brought only greater woe upon the remnant of his people, and they were glad of his going; and this comfort alone he had: that by the prowess of the Blacksword the ways to Doriath had been laid open to Morwen. And he said in his heart: 'Then those deeds wrought not evil to all! And where else might I have better bestowed my dear kin, even if I had come sooner? For if the Girdle of Melian is broken, then last hope is ended. Nay, it is better as it hath turned out. For behold! a shadow I cast wheresoever I come. Let Melian keep them! But I will leave them in peace unshadowed for a while.'

496

§298   Here Tuor son of Huor met Bronwë of the Noldor at the mouths of Sirion; and they began a journey northward along the great river. But as they dwelt in Nan Tathrin, and delayed because of the peace and beauty of that country in the spring, Ulmo himself came up Sirion and appeared to Tuor, and the yearning for the Great Sea was ever after in his heart. But now at Ulmo's command he went up Sirion, and by the power that Ulmo set upon them Tuor and Bronwë found the guarded entrance to Gondolin. There Tuor was brought before King Turgon, and spake the words that Ulmo had set in his mouth, bidding him depart and abandon the fair and mighty city that he had built, and go down to the Sea. But Turgon would not listen to this counsel; and [Meglin *later* >] Glindûr his sister-son spoke against Tuor. But Tuor was held in honour in Gondolin, for his kindred's sake.

This annal was much emended and added to (and the date changed to 495), and then (since the text was now in a very confused state) struck out as far as 'bidding him depart' and replaced by the following version on a detached slip:

495

§299 Now Tuor Huor's son had lived as an outlaw in the caves of Androth above Mithrim for four years, and he had done great hurt to the Easterlings, and Lorgan set a price upon his head. But Ulmo, who had chosen him as the instrument of his designs, caused him to go by secret ways out of the land of Dorlómin, so that his going was hidden from all the servants of Morgoth; and he came to Nivrost. But there, becoming enamoured of the Sea, he tarried long; and in the autumn of the year Ulmo himself appeared to Tuor, and bade him to depart, and go to the hidden city of Turgon. And he sent to him Voronwë, last of the mariners of Turgon, to guide him; and Voronwë led Tuor eastward along the eaves of Eryd Wethion to Ivrin. (And there they saw Túrin pass, but spoke not with him.) And at the last by the power that Ulmo set upon them they came to the guarded gate of Gondolin. There Tuor was brought before the king, and spoke the counsel of Ulmo, bidding Turgon [*the following is the text already given in* §298] depart and abandon the fair and mighty city that he had built, and go down to the Sea. But Turgon would not listen to this counsel; and [Meglin *later* >] Glindûr his sister-son spoke against Tuor. But Tuor was held in honour in Gondolin, for his kindred's sake.

[496]

§300 Now Túrin coming down from Eryd Wethion sought for Finduilas in vain, roaming the woods under the shadow of the mountains, wild and wary as a beast; and he waylaid all the roads that went north to the passes of Sirion. Too late. For all the trails had grown old, or were washed away by the winter. But thus it was that, passing southwards down Taiglin, Túrin came upon some of the Men of Brethil, and delivered them from Orcs that had entrapped them. For the Orcs fled from Gurthang.

§301   He named himself Wildman of the Woods, and they besought him to come and dwell with them; but he said that he had an errand yet unachieved: to seek Finduilas Orodreth's daughter. Then Dorlas, leader of the woodmen, told the grievous tidings of her death. For the woodmen at the Crossings of Taiglin had waylaid the orc-host that led the captives of Nargothrond, hoping to rescue them; but the Orcs had at once cruelly slain their prisoners, and Finduilas they pinned to a tree with a spear. So she died, saying at the last: 'Tell the Mormegil that Finduilas is here.' Therefore they had laid her in a mound near that place, and named it *Hauð-en-Ellas*.

§302   Túrin bade them lead him thither, and there he fell down into a darkness of grief, and was near to death. Then Dorlas by his black sword, the fame whereof had come even into the deeps of Brethil, and by his quest of the king's daughter, knew that this Wildman was indeed the Mormegil of Nargoth-rond [*added:*] (whom rumour said was the son of Húrin of Dorlómin). The woodmen therefore lifted him up, and bore him away to their homes. These were set in a stockade upon a high place in the forest, Ephel Brandir upon Amon Obel; for the folk of Haleth were now dwindled by war to a small people, and Brandir son of Handir who ruled them was a man of gentle mood, and lame also from childhood, and he trusted rather in secrecy than in deeds of war to save them from the power of the North.

§303   Therefore he feared the tidings that Dorlas brought, and when he beheld the face of Túrin as he lay on the bier a cloud of foreboding lay on his heart. Nonetheless being moved by his woe, he took him into his own house and tended him; for he had skill in healing. And with the beginning of spring Túrin cast off his darkness, and grew hale again; and he arose, and he thought that he would remain in Brethil, hidden, and put his shadow behind him, forsaking the past. He took therefore a new name, *Turambar*, and besought the woodmen to forget that he was a stranger among them or ever bore any other name. Nonetheless he would not wholly leave deeds of war, for he could not endure that the Orcs should come to the Crossings of Taiglin or draw nigh Hauð-en-Ellas, and he made that a place of dread for them so that they shunned it. But he laid his black sword by, and used rather the bow.

§304   Now new tidings came to Doriath concerning Nargothrond, for some that had escaped from the defeat and the sack, and had survived the fell winter in the wild, came at last to Thingol, seeking refuge. But their tales were at variance, some saying that Nargothrond was empty, others that Glaurung abode there; some saying that all the lords and captains were slain, others that, nay, the Mormegil had returned to Nargothrond and there was made a prisoner under the spell of the dragon. But all declared that it was known to many in Nargothrond ere the end that the Mormegil was none other than Túrin Húrin's son. [*Pencilled addition:* And when she heard of the Dragon-helm Morwen knew this was true.]

§305   Then Morwen was distraught, and refusing the counsel of Melian, she rode forth alone into the wild to seek her son, or some true tidings of him. Thingol, therefore, sent Mablung after her, with many hardy march-wards, and some riders, to guard her, and to learn what news they might; but Nïenor joined this company secretly in disguise, for she hoped that when Morwen saw that her daughter would go with her into peril, if she went on, then she would be willing to return to Doriath and leave the seeking of tidings to Mablung. But Morwen, being fey, would not be persuaded, and Mablung perforce led the ladies with him; and they passed out over the wide plain and came to Amon Ethir, a league before the bridge of Nargothrond. There Mablung set a guard of riders about Morwen and her daughter, and forbade them go further. But he, seeing from the hill no sign of any enemy, went down with his scouts to the Narog, as stealthily as they could go.

§306   But Glaurung was aware of all that they did, and he came forth in heat of wrath, and lay into the river; and a vast vapour and foul reek went up, in which Mablung and his company were blinded and lost. Then Glaurung passed east over Narog.

§307   Seeing the onset of Glaurung the guards upon Amon Ethir sought to lead the ladies away, and fly with them with all speed back eastwards; but the wind bore the blank mists upon them, and their horses were maddened by the dragon-stench, and were ungovernable, and ran this way and that, so that some were dashed against trees and slain, and others were borne far away. Thus the ladies were lost, and of Morwen indeed no sure tidings came ever to Doriath after. But Niënor, being thrown by her steed yet unhurt, groped her way back to Amon Ethir, there to await Mablung, and came thus above the reek into the sunlight. [Thus she came alone face to face with Glaurung himself, who had climbed up from the other side. >] And looking west she looked straight into the eyes of Glaurung, whose head lay upon the hill-top.

§308   Her will strove with him for a while, but he put forth his power, and having learned who she was (as indeed he guessed full well) he constrained her to gaze into his eyes, and laid a spell of utter darkness and forgetfulness, so that she could remember nothing that had ever befallen her, nor her own name, nor the name of any other thing; and for many days indeed she could neither hear, nor see, nor stir by her own will. Then Glaurung left her standing alone upon Amon Ethir, and he went back to Nargothrond.

§309   Now Mablung, who greatly daring had explored the halls of Felagund when Glaurung left them, fled from them at the approach of the dragon, and returned to Amon Ethir. The sun sank and night fell as he climbed the hill, and to his dismay he found none there, save Niënor standing alone under the stars as an image of stone. No word she spoke or heard, but would follow, if he took up her hand. Therefore in great grief he led her away, though it seemed to him vain; for they were both like to perish, succourless, in the wild.

§310   But they were found by three of Mablung's companions, and slowly they journeyed northward and eastward to the fences of Doriath where, nigh to the inflowing of Esgalduin, there was the secret gate by which those of its folk that returned from without were wont to enter. Slowly the strength of Niënor returned as they drew nearer to Doriath and further from Glaurung, but as yet she could not speak or hear, and walked blindly as she was led.

§311   But even as they drew near the fences at last she closed her wild staring eyes, and would sleep; and they laid her down and she slept; and they rested also, for they were utterly outworn. Being thus less heedful than was wise, they were there assailed by an Orc-band, such as now roamed often as nigh the fences of Doriath as they dared. But Niënor in that hour recovered hearing and sight, and being awakened by the cries of the Orcs, sprang up in terror as a wild thing, and fled ere they could come to her.

§312 Then the Orcs gave chase, and the Elves after; but though they overtook the Orcs indeed and slew them ere they could harm her, Nienor escaped them. For she fled as in a madness of fear, swifter than a deer, and tore off all her raiment as she ran, until she was naked [*bracketed later:*] but for a short kirtle. And she passed out of their sight, running northward, and though they sought her long they found her not, nor any trace of her. And at last Mablung in despair returned to Menegroth and told all his tidings. [*Added:* Greatly grieved were Thingol and Melian; but Mablung went forth and for three years sought in vain for tidings of Morwen and Nienor.]

§313 But Nienor ran on into the woods, until she was spent, and then fell and slept, and awoke; and behold it was a bright morning, and she rejoiced in light as it were a new thing, and all things else that she saw seemed new and strange, for she had no names for them. Nothing did she remember save a darkness that lay behind her, and a shadow of fear; therefore warily she went as a hunted beast, and became famished, for she had no food and knew not how to seek it. But coming at last to the Crossings of Taiglin she went over, seeking the shelter of the great trees of Brethil, for she was afraid, and it seemed to her that the darkness was overtaking her again from which she had fled.

§314 But it was a great storm of thunder that came up from the South, and in terror she cast herself down by the mound, Hauð-en-Ellas [*pencilled in margin:* Elleth], stopping her ears from the thunder, but the rain smote her and drenched her, and she lay like a wild beast that is dying.

§315 There Turambar found her, as he came to the Crossings of Taiglin, having heard a rumour of Orcs that roamed near. And seeing in a flare of lightning the body of a slain maiden (as it seemed) lying upon the mound of Finduilas, he was stricken [suddenly with fear >] to the heart. But the woodmen lifted her up, and Turambar cast his cloak about her, and they took her to a lodge nearby, and bathed her and warmed her and gave her food. And as soon as she looked upon Turambar she was comforted; for it seemed to her that she had found something at last that she long sought in her darkness; and she laid her hand in his and would not be parted from him.

§316   But when he asked her concerning her name and her kin and her misadventure, then she became troubled as a child that perceives that something is demanded but cannot understand what it be. And she burst into tears. Therefore Turambar said: 'Be not troubled! Doubtless thy tale is too sad yet to tell. It shall wait. But a name thou must have, and I will call thee *Níniel* (tear-maiden).' And at that name she shook her head, but said *Níniel*. That was the first word she spoke after her darkness, and it remained her name among the woodmen ever after.

§317   The next day they bore her towards Ephel Brandir, but at the falls of Celebros a great shuddering came upon her (wherefore afterwards that place was called Nen Girith), and ere she came to the home of the woodmen she was sick of a fever. She lay long in her sickness, but was healed by the skill of Brandir and the care of the leech-women of Brethil; and the women taught her language as to an infant. Ere autumn came she was hale again, and could speak, but remembered nothing before she was found by Turambar. Brandir loved her dearly, but all her heart was given to Turambar. All that year since the coming of Níniel there was peace in Brethil, and the Orcs did not trouble the woodmen.

497

§318   Turambar still remained at peace and went not to war. His heart turned to Níniel, and he asked her in marriage; but for that time she delayed in spite of her love. For Brandir foreboded he knew not what, and sought to restrain her, rather for her sake than his own or rivalry with Turambar; and he revealed to her that Turambar was Túrin son of Húrin, and though she knew not the name a shadow fell on her heart. This Turambar learned and was ill pleased with Brandir.

498

§319   In the spring of this year Turambar asked Níniel again, and vowed that he would now wed her, or go back to war in the wild. And Níniel took him with joy, and they were wedded at the mid-summer, and the Woodmen of Brethil made a great feast. But ere the end of the year Glaurung sent Orcs of his dominion against Brethil; and Turambar sat at home deedless, for he had promised Níniel that he would go to battle only if their home was assailed. But the woodmen were worsted, and Dorlas upbraided him that he would not aid the folk that he had taken for his own. Then Turambar arose and brought forth again his black sword, and he gathered a great force of the Men of Brethil, and they defeated the Orcs utterly. But Glaurung heard tidings that the Black Sword was in Brethil, and he pondered what he had heard, devising new evil.

499

§320   Níniel conceived in the spring of this year, and became wan and sad. At the same time there came to Ephel Brandir the first rumours that Glaurung had issued from Nargothrond. And Turambar sent out scouts far afield, for he now ordered things as he would, and few gave heed to Brandir.

§321   And as it drew near to summer Glaurung came to the borders of Brethil, and lay near the west-shore of Taiglin, and then there was great fear among the wood-folk, for it was now plain that the Great Worm would assail them and ravage their land, and not pass by, returning to Angband, as they had hoped. They sought therefore the counsel of Turambar. And he counselled them that it was vain to go against the Worm with all their force. Only by cunning and good fortune could they defeat him. He offered therefore himself to seek Glaurung on the borders of the land, and bade the rest of the people to remain at Ephel Brandir, but to prepare for flight. For if Glaurung had the victory, he would come first to the woodmen's homes to destroy them, and they could not hope to withstand him; but if they then scattered far and wide, then many might escape, for Glaurung would not take up his dwelling in Brethil and would return soon to Nargothrond.

§322   Then Turambar asked for companions willing to aid him in his peril, and Dorlas stood forth, but no others. Then Dorlas upbraided the people, and spoke scorn of Brandir who could not play the part of the heir of Haleth; and Brandir was shamed before his people, and was bitter at heart. But Torbarth [*pencilled above:* Gwerin] kinsman of Brandir asked his leave to go in his stead. Then Turambar said farewell to Níniel and she was filled with fear and foreboding, and their parting was sorrowful; but Turambar set out with his two companions and went to Nen Girith.

§323   Then Níniel being unable to endure her fear, and unwilling to wait in the Ephel tidings of Turambar's fortune, set forth after him, and a great company went with her. At this Brandir was filled more than ever before with dread, [*struck out:* but she heeded not his counsels] and he sought to dissuade her and the folk that would go with her from this rashness, but they heeded him not. Therefore he renounced his lordship, and all love for the people that had scorned him, and having naught left but his love for Níniel, he girt himself with a sword, and went after her; but being lame he fell far behind.

§324   Now Turambar came to Nen Girith at sundown and there learned that Glaurung lay on the brink of the high shores of the Taiglin, and was like to move when night fell. Then he called those tidings good; for the Worm lay at [Cabad-en-Aras >] Cabed-en-Aras, where the river ran in a deep and narrow gorge that a hunted deer might o'erleap, and Turambar deemed that he would seek no further, but would attempt to pass over the gorge. Therefore he purposed to creep down at dusk, and descend into the ravine under night, and cross over the wild water, and then climb up the further cliff (which was less sheer) and so come at the Worm beneath his guard.

§325   This counsel he then took, but the heart of Dorlas failed when they came to the races of Taiglin in the dark, and he dared not attempt the perilous crossing, but drew back and lurked in the woods burdened with shame. Turambar and Torbarth, nonetheless, crossed over in safety, for the loud roaring of the water drowned all other sounds, and Glaurung slept. But ere the middle-night the Worm roused, and with a great noise and blast cast his forward part across the chasm and began to draw his bulk after. Turambar and Torbarth were well-night overcome by the heat and the stench, as they sought in haste for a way up to come at Glaurung; and Torbarth was slain by a great stone that, dislodged from on high by the passage of the dragon, smote him upon the head and cast him into the River. So ended the last of the right kin of Haleth, and not the least valiant.

§326   Then Turambar summoned all his will and courage and climbed the cliff alone, and he thrust Gurthang into the soft belly of the Worm, even up to the hilts. But when Glaurung felt his death-pang he screamed, and in his dreadful throe he heaved up his bulk and hurled himself across the chasm, and there lay lashing and coiling in his agony. And he set all in a blaze about him, and beat all to ruin, until at last his fires died, and he lay still.

§327   Now Gurthang had been wrested from Turambar's

hand in the throe of Glaurung, and clave to the belly of the Worm. Turambar, therefore, crossed the water once more, desiring to recover his sword, and look on his foe. And he found him stretched at his length, and rolled upon one side; and the hilts of Gurthang stood in his belly. Then Turambar seized the hilts and set his foot upon the belly, and cried in mockery of the Worm and his words at Nargothrond: 'Hail, Worm of Morgoth! Well met again! Die now and the darkness have thee! Thus is Túrin son of Húrin avenged.'

§328   Then he wrenched out the sword, but a spout of black blood followed it, and fell on his hand, and the venom burned it. And thereupon Glaurung opened his eyes and looked upon Turambar with such malice, that it smote him as a blow; and by that stroke and the anguish of the venom he fell into a dark swoon, and lay as one dead, and his sword was beneath him.

§329   The yells of Glaurung rang in the woods and came to the folk that waited at Nen Girith; and when those that looked forth heard the scream of the Worm and saw from afar the ruin and burning that he made, they deemed that he had triumphed and was destroying those that assailed him. And Níniel sat and shuddered beside the falling water, and at the voice of Glaurung her darkness crept upon her again, so that she could not stir from that place of her own will.

§330   Even so Brandir found her, for he came to Nen Girith at last, limping wearily. And when he heard that the Worm had crossed the river and had beaten down his foes his heart yearned towards Níniel in pity. Yet he thought also: 'Turambar is dead, but Níniel lives. Now maybe she will come with me and I will lead her away and so we shall escape the Worm together.'

§331   After a while therefore he stood by Níniel and said: 'Come! It is time to go. If thou wilt, I will lead thee.' And he took her hand, and she arose silently, and followed him; and in the darkness none saw them go.

§332   But as they went down the path toward the Crossings the moon arose, and cast a grey light on the land, and Níniel said: 'Is this the way?' And Brandir answered that he knew no way, save to flee as they might from the Worm, and escape into the wild. But Níniel said: 'The Black Sword was my beloved and my husband. To seek him only do I go. What else couldst thou think?' And she sped on before him. Then she came towards the Crossings of Taiglin and beheld Hauð-en-Ellas in the white moonlight, and great dread came on her. Then with a cry she turned away, casting off her cloak, and fled southward along the river, and her white raiment shone in the moon.

§333   Thus Brandir saw her from the hill-side and turned to cross her path, but was still behind her, when she came to the ruin of Glaurung nigh the brink of [Cabad-en-Aras >] Cabed-en-Aras. There she saw the Worm lying, but heeded him not, for a man lay beside him; and she ran to Turambar and called his name in vain. Then, finding his hand that was burned, she laved it with tears and bound it about with a strip of her raiment, and kissed him and cried on him again to awake. Thereat Glaurung stirred for the last time ere he died, and he spoke with his last breath saying: 'Hail, Nienor daughter of Húrin. This is thy brother! Have joy of your meeting, and know him: Túrin son of Húrin, treacherous to foes, faithless to friends, and [a] curse unto his kin. And to thee worst of all, as now thou shalt feel!'

§334   Then Glaurung died, and the veil of his malice was taken from her, and she remembered all her life; and she sat as one stunned with horror and anguish. Then Brandir who had heard all, standing stricken upon the edge of the ruin, hastened towards her; but she leapt up and ran like a hunted deer, and came to [Cabad-en-Aras >] Cabed-en-Aras, and there cast herself over the brink, and was lost in the wild water.

§335   Then Brandir came and looked down into Cabad-en-Aras, and turned away in horror, and though he no longer desired life, he could not seek death in that roaring water. And thereafter no man looked ever again upon Cabad-en-Aras, nor would any beast or bird come there, nor any tree grow; and it was named Cabad Naeramarth, the Leap of Dreadful Doom.

§336   But Brandir now made his way back to Nen Girith, to bring tidings to the people; and he met Dorlas in the woods, and slew him (the first blood that ever he had spilled and the last). And he came to Nen Girith, and men cried to him: 'Hast thou seen her? Lo! Níniel is gone.'

§337   And he answered saying: 'Yea, Níniel is gone for ever. The Worm is dead, and Turambar is dead: and those tidings are good.' And folk murmured at these words, saying that he was crazed. But Brandir said: 'Hear me to the end! Níniel the beloved is also dead. She cast herself into the Taiglin desiring life no more. For she learned that she was none other than Nienor daughter of Húrin, ere her forgetfulness came upon her, and that Turambar was her brother, Túrin son of Húrin.'

§338 But even as he had ceased and the people wept, Túrin himself came before them. For when the Worm died, his swoon left him, and he fell into a deep sleep of weariness. But the cold of the night troubled him, and the hilts of Gurthang drove into his side, and he awoke. Then he saw that one had tended his hand, and he wondered much that he was left nonetheless to lie upon the cold ground; and he called and hearing no answer, he went in search of aid, for he was weary and sick.

§339 But when the people saw him they drew back in fear thinking that it was his unquiet spirit; and he said: 'Nay, be glad; for the Worm is dead, and I live. But wherefore have ye scorned my counsel, and come into peril? And where is Níniel? For her I would see. And surely ye did not bring her from her home?'

§340 Then Brandir told him that it was so and Níniel was dead. But the wife of Dorlas cried out: 'Nay, lord, he is crazed. For he came here saying that thou wert dead, and called it good tidings. But thou livest.'

§341 Then Turambar was wroth, and believed that all that Brandir said or did was done in malice towards himself and Níniel, begrudging their love; and he spoke evilly to Brandir, naming him Club-foot. Then Brandir reported all that he heard, and named Níniel Niënor daughter of Húrin, and cried out upon Turambar with the last words of Glaurung, that he was a curse unto his kin and to all that harboured him.

§342 Then Turambar fell into a fury, and charged Brandir with leading Níniel to her death, and publishing with delight the lies of Glaurung (if he devised them not himself indeed), and he cursed Brandir and slew him, and fled from the people into the woods. But after a while his madness left him, and he came to Hauð-en-Ellas and there sat and pondered all his deeds. And he cried upon Finduilas to bring him counsel; for he knew not whether he would do now more ill to go to Doriath to seek his kin, or to forsake them for ever and seek death in battle.

§343 And even as he sat there Mablung with a company of Grey-elves came over the Crossings of Taiglin, and he knew Túrin and hailed him, and was glad to find him living. For he had learned of the coming forth of Glaurung and that his path led to Brethil, and at the same time he had heard report that the Black Sword of Nargothrond now abode there. Therefore he came to give warning to Túrin and help if need be. But Túrin said: 'Too late thou comest. The Worm is dead.'

§344   Then they marvelled, and gave him great praise, but he cared nothing for it, and said: 'This only I ask: give me news of my kin, for in Dorlómin I learned that they had gone to the Hidden Kingdom.'

§345   Then Mablung was dismayed, but needs must tell to Túrin how Morwen was lost, and Niënor cast into a spell of dumb forgetfulness, and how she escaped them upon the borders of Doriath and fled northward. Then at last Túrin knew that doom had overtaken him, and that he had slain Brandir unjustly, so that the words of Glaurung were fulfilled in him. And he laughed as one fey, crying: 'This is a bitter jest indeed!' But he bade Mablung go, and return to Doriath, with curses upon it. 'And a curse too on thy errand!' he said. 'This only was wanting. Now comes the night!'

§346   Then he fled from them like the wind, and they were amazed, wondering what madness had seized him; and they followed after him. But Túrin far out-ran them, and came to Cabad-en-Aras, and heard the roaring of the water, and saw that all the leaves fell sere from the trees, as though winter had come. Then he cursed the place and named it Cabad Naeramarth, and he drew forth his sword, that now alone remained to him of all his possessions, and he said: 'Hail Gurthang! No lord or loyalty dost thou know, save the hand that wieldeth thee. From no blood wilt thou shrink. Wilt thou therefore take Túrin Turambar, wilt thou slay me swiftly?'

§347   And from the blade rang a cold voice in answer: 'Yea, I will drink thy blood gladly, that so I may forget the blood of Beleg my master, and the blood of Brandir slain unjustly. I will slay thee swiftly.'

§348   Then Túrin set the hilts upon the ground, and cast himself upon the point of Gurthang, and the black blade took his life. But Mablung and the Elves came and looked on the shape of the Worm lying dead, and upon the body of Túrin, and they were grieved; and when men of Brethil came thither, and they learned the reasons of Túrin's madness and death, they were aghast; and Mablung said bitterly: 'Lo! I also have been meshed in the doom of the Children of Húrin, and thus with my tidings have slain one that I loved.'

§349   Then they lifted up Túrin and found that Gurthang had broken asunder. But Elves and Men gathered then great store of wood and made a mighty burning, and the Worm was consumed to ashes. But Túrin they laid in a high mound where he had fallen, and the shards of Gurthang were laid beside him. And when all was done, the Elves sang a lament for the Children of Húrin, and a great grey stone was set upon the mound, and thereon was carven in the Runes of Doriath:

Here the manuscript comes to an end, at the foot of a page, and the typescript also. Later, and probably a good while later, since the writing is in ball-point pen, my father added in the margin of the manuscript:

TURIN TURAMBAR DAGNIR

GLAURUNGA

and beneath they wrote also:

NIENOR NINIEL ·

But she was not there, nor was it ever known whither the cold waters of Taiglin had taken her. [Thus endeth the *Narn i Chîn Húrin*: which is the longest of all the lays of Beleriand, and was made by Men.]

It always seemed to me strange that my father should have abandoned the *Grey Annals* where he did, without at least writing the inscription that was carved on the stone; yet the facts that the amanuensis typescript ended at this point also, and that he added in the inscription in rough script on the manuscript at some later time, seemed proof positive that this was the case. Ultimately I discovered the explanation, which for reasons that will be seen I postpone to the beginning of Part Three (p. 251).

COMMENTARY

In this commentary the following abbreviations are used:

AV   *Annals of Valinor* (see p. 3)

AAm   *Annals of Aman* (text with numbered paragraphs in Vol.X)

AB   *Annals of Beleriand* (see p. 3). I use the revised dating of the annals in AB 2 (see V.124).

GA   *Grey Annals* (GA 1 abandoned opening, **GA 2** the final text when distinguished from GA 1: see pp. 3–4)

Q   *The Quenta* (text in Vol.IV)

QS   *Quenta Silmarillion* (text with numbered paragraphs in Vol.V)

NE   The last part of the *Narn i Chîn Húrin*, given in *Unfinished Tales* (pp. 104–46), and referenced to the pages in that book; see pp. 144–5.

§1   This opening paragraph is absent from the abandoned version GA 1. Cf. the direction scribbled on the old AB 2 manuscript (p. 4)

to 'make these the Sindarin Annals of Doriath'. For the beginning of
the Annals in GA 1 see under §2 below.
§2   This is a much more definite statement of the development of the
geographical concept of 'Beleriand' than that found in GA 1, where
the Annals begin thus:

The name Beleriand is drawn from the tongue of the Sindar, the
Grey-elves that long dwelt in that country; and it signifies the land
of Balar. For this name the Sindar gave to Ossë, who came much
to those coasts, and there befriended them. In ancient days, ere
the War of Utumno, it was but the northern shoreland of the long
west-coast of Middle-earth, lying south of Eryd Engrin (the Iron
Mountains) and between the Great Sea and Eryd Luin (the Blue
Mountains).

This is in any case not easy to understand, since Beleriand 'in the
ancient days' is defined as 'but' the northern shoreland of the west-
coast of Middle-earth, yet extending south of the Iron Mountains
and from the Great Sea to the Blue Mountains, an area in fact much
greater than that described in GA 2 as its later extension of meaning. The latter agrees with the statement on the subject in QS §108,
where 'Beleriand was bounded upon the North by Nivrost and
Hithlum and Dorthonion'.

A possible explanation of the opening passage of GA 1 may be
found, however, by reference to the *Ambarkanta* map IV (IV.249),
where it will be seen that 'Beleriand' could well be described as 'but
the northern shoreland of the long west-coast of Middle-earth, lying
south of the Iron Mountains and between the Great Sea and the
Blue Mountains'. The meaning of the opening of GA 1 may be,
therefore, not that this geographical description was the original
reference of the name 'Beleriand', but that before the War of
Utumno (when Melkor was chained) Beleriand was 'but the
northern shoreland of the long west-coast of Middle-earth', whereas
in the ruin of that war there was formed the Great Gulf to the
southward (referred to in GA §6, both texts; see *Ambarkanta*
map V, IV.251), after which Beleriand could not be so described.

In the List of Names of the 1930s (V.404) 'Beleriand' was said as
in GA 2 to have been originally the 'land about southern Sirion'; but
is there said to have been 'named by the Elves of the Havens from
Cape *Balar*, and Bay of *Balar* into which Sirion flowed'. In the
Etymologies (V.350, stem BAL) *Beleriand* was likewise derived from
(the isle of) *Balar*, and *Balar* in turn 'probably from *bálāre*, and so
called because here Ossë visited the waiting Teleri.' At that time
Ossë was a *Bala* (*Vala*).

On the later form *Belerian* see my father's note on Sindarin
Rochand > *Rochan* (*Rohan*) in *Unfinished Tales* p. 318 (note 49 to
Cirion and Eorl).
§3   Cf. the entry added to the annal for Valian Year 1050 in AAm

§40 (X.72, 77), concerning Melian's departure from Valinor. In the preceding annal 1000–1050 in AAm it is told that Varda 'made stars newer and brighter'.

§§3–5   The second sentence of the annal 1050 and the annals 1080 and 1085 were added to the manuscript subsequently. It is curious that there was no mention of the Awakening of the Elves in GA 1 nor in GA 2 as written; but among the rough draft pages referred to on p. 4 there is in fact a substantial passage beginning: 'In this same time the Quendi awoke by the waters of Kuiviénen: of which more is said in the Chronicles of Aman.' The text that follows in this draft is very close – much of it indeed virtually identical – to the long passage interpolated into AAm (§§43–5) on the fear of Oromë among the Quendi, the ensnaring of them by the servants of Melkor, and the breeding of the Orcs from those captured. There are no differences of substance between this text and the passage in AAm; and it is obvious that the latter followed, and was based on, the former, originally intended for inclusion in the *Grey Annals*.

In AAm the same dates are given for the Awakening of the Elves (1050) and for their discovery by Oromë (1085); no date is given in AAm for their discovery by Melkor, but it is said (AAm §43) that this was 'some years ere the coming of Oromë'.

§6   In GA 1 the sentence 'it took then that shape which it had until the coming of Fionwë' reads '… which it had until the Change of the World', using that expression not to refer to the World Made Round at the Drowning of Númenor but to the destruction of Beleriand in the final overthrow of Morgoth, at the end of the Elder Days.

The Great Gulf (shown and thus named on the *Ambarkanta* map V, IV.251) was referred to in QS §108: 'Beyond the river Gelion the land narrowed suddenly, for the Great Sea ran into a mighty gulf reaching almost to the feet of Eredlindon …' See under §2 above.

Unique to the *Grey Annals* is the statement that because the Valar had set foot in the lands about Sirion, when they came from Aman for the assault on Utumno, growth soon began there again 'while most of Middle-earth slept in the Sleep of Yavanna', and that Melian fostered the 'young woods under the bright stars'. See further under §10 below.

§7   This annal was a later addition to the manuscript; the date was first written 1102, then changed to 1102–5. AAm (§§54–6) has entries concerning the three ambassadors, their going in 1102 and their return to Kuiviénen in 1104.

§8   In AAm the dates were so often changed and became so confused that in rendering the text I gave only the final ones (see X.47–8); but in this part of AAm all the dates were in fact originally 100 Valian Years later – thus 1115, the year in which the Eldar reached the Anduin (X.82) was an emendation of 1215. Already in GA 1 the dates are in the 1100s as first written, showing that it followed AAm, if at no long interval. But it is curious that in GA (both texts) the coming of the Vanyar and Noldor to the Great Sea is placed in 1115; in AAm the march began in 1105, the Anduin was reached in 1115, and the Sea in 1125.

§10 This annal has close relations not only with that in AAm for the same year (§65) but also with the passage in the 'Silmarillion' tradition (X.172, §32).

With 'the young trees of Nan Elmoth' cf. the change made on one of the typescripts of AAm (X.91) of 'the trees of Nan Elmoth' to 'the sapling trees of Nan Elmoth', though this was made years later. The 'young trees' are no doubt to be connected with the phrase in GA §9 'where *afterwards stood* the forests of Neldoreth and Region'; and it seems clear that the trees were all young because, as is said in GA §6, 'the lands upon either side of Sirion were ruinous and desolate because of the War of the Powers, but soon growth began there, while most of Middle-earth slept in the Sleep of Yavanna, because the Valar of the Blessed Realm had set foot there; and there were young woods under the bright stars.'

The conception that there were trees in a world illumined only by starlight was a datum of the mythology (though years after the writing of the *Grey Annals* my father rejected it: 'Neither could there be woods and flowers &c. on earth, if there had been no light since the overthrow of the Lamps!', X.375); on the other hand, there appears in AAm (§30) the story, not present in the 'Silmarillion' tradition, that Yavanna 'set a sleep upon many fair things that had arisen in the Spring [i.e. before the fall of the Lamps], both tree and herb and beast and bird, so that they should not age but should wait for a time of awakening that yet should be.' In the other tradition (X.158, §18) 'While the Lamps had shone, growth began there which now was checked, because all was again dark. But already the oldest living things had arisen: in the sea the great weeds, and on the earth the shadow of great trees ... In those lands and forests Oromë would often hunt ...'

How these conceptions relate to each other is far from clear on the basis of these texts; but now, in the *Grey Annals* (§6), the peculiar nature of Beleriand is asserted, in that there alone growth began again under the stars on account of the passage of the Valar from Aman, and (§17) 'though Middle-earth for the most part lay in the Sleep of Yavanna, in Beleriand under the power of Melian there was life and joy and the bright stars shone like silver fires.'

§§11–12 This annal 1132 is very close to that in AAm (§66), largely identical in structure and near in phraseology; the only important feature in which it differs is the reference to the legend that a part of the island that became Tol Eressëa was broken off and became the

Isle of Balar. This story appears in a footnote to the next of QS §35 (V.221, X.174).

§§13–15   The annals 1149–50 and 1150 are again close to those in AAm (§§70–1), and were I think based on them (it may be noted that in GA 1, of which GA 2 is here for the most part scarcely more than a fair copy, my father first wrote in §15 'The friends and kinsfolk of Elwë also were unwilling to depart', as in AAm, but changed the last words in the act of writing to 'also remained').

§14   The whole extent of the coastal region from the Firth of Drengist south to Cape Balar is here named the Falas (cf. QS §109: 'the country of the Falas (or Coast), south of Nivrost'), and thus Cirdan is made the ruler of the shorelands of Nivrost (later Nevrast).

The last part of the annal 1149–50, concerning the fact that the Elves of the Havens did not cross the Great Sea (though there was no ban on their attempting to do so), is not in GA 1. It is indeed an answer to a question that has not emerged in any previous writing – though it becomes implicit from the first emergence of the sailing-elves of the Havens (Elves persuaded by Ossë to remain on the shores of Middle-earth are first mentioned in Q, IV.87).

§16   The annal 1152 is closely related to that in AAm (§74). The question arises why, if these Annals were the work of the Sindar (see §1), should they have such obvious affinity to those of Aman? Perhaps it should be supposed that both sets of Annals, as received, derive from the editorial work of Pengoloð in Tol Eressëa.

§17   There is nothing corresponding to the interesting annal 1200 in AAm. On the reference to the Sleep of Yavanna and the life and joy in Beleriand see under §10 above. Melian's power and presence in Beleriand is now given a greater significance. – Here *niphredil* appears from *The Lord of the Rings*.

§18   The idea of the 'higher culture' of the Dark-elves of Beleriand (the Sindar) goes back to the very early 'Sketch of the Mythology' (IV.21): 'Only in the realm of Doriath, whose queen was of divine race, did the Ilkorins equal the Koreldar'; this phrase with a slight modification survived through Q (IV.100) into QS (§85).

§19   Cf. the passage inserted into annal 1250 in AAm (§84), a Beleriandic interpolation by Pengoloð, against which my father later noted: 'Transfer to A[nnals of] B[eleriand]' (X.102, note 7). That passage (very greatly expanded here in GA) begins:

> In this time also, it is said among the Sindar, the Nauglath [*written above:* Naugrim] whom we also name the Nornwaith (the Dwarves) came over the mountains into Beleriand and became known to the Elves.

The present annal in GA 1 begins: 'In this year, it is recorded among the Sindar, the Nauglath came first over the mountains into

Beleriand. This people the Noldor after named the Norn-folk ...' In GA 2 the words 'it is recorded among the Sindar' are absent, and *Naugrim* replaces *Nauglath*.

In QS §124 the Dwarvish names of the cities in Eryd Luin were Gabilgathol (Belegost, the Great Fortress) and Khazaddûm (Nogrod, the Dwarfmine); Tumunzahar now first appears (also in QS revised, p. 206, §7).

§20 For statements in the *Lhammas* and in QS on the languages of the Dwarves see V.178–9, 273. – The concluding sentences of this paragraph ('Ever cool was their friendship ...') are very close to what is said in AAm (§84).

§21 This cautious and sceptical view of the story of the origin of the Dwarves – ascribing it entirely to the Dwarves themselves – seems to contrast with earlier texts, where it is said to be derived from 'the wise in Valinor' (V.129, 273). – The name *Mahal* of Aulë has not appeared before.

§22 *Enfeng, the Longbeards of Belegost.* In the old *Tale of the Nauglafring* the *Indrafangs* or Longbeards were the Dwarves of Belegost, while Dwarves of Nogrod were the *Nauglath* (see II.247). In Q the Indrafangs had become those of Nogrod (IV.104), and this reappears in QS (§124): 'those who dwelt in Nogrod they [the Gnomes] called Enfeng, the Longbeards, because their beards swept the floor before their feet.' In the passage in AAm (§84) the Long-beards, as here, are again the Dwarves of Belegost. – The conclusion of this paragraph is wholly different in GA 1:

> For Melian taught them much wisdom (which also they were eager to get), and she gave to them also the great jewel which alone she had brought out of Valinor, work of Fëanor, [*struck out but then ticked as if to stand*: for he gave many such to the folk of Lórien.] A white gem it was that gathered the starlight and sent it forth in blue fires; and the Enfeng prized it above a mountain of wealth.

This was an idea that did not fit the chronology, for Melian left Valinor in 1050, the year of the Awakening of the Elves, as stated both in AAm (see X.77) and GA (Fëanor was born more than a hundred Valian years later, AAm §78); and in GA 2 the story of the great pearl Nimphelos was substituted.

§§23–4 Thingol's early association with the Dwarves is mentioned in QS §122 (from their cities in the Blue Mountains the Dwarves 'journeyed often into Beleriand, and were admitted at times even into Doriath'), but the aid of the Longbeards of Belegost in the building of Menegroth did not appear until the interpolation in AAm (§84). That brief mention is here greatly expanded into a description of the Thousand Caves; cf. the *Lay of Leithian* (III.188–9, lines 980–1008), and for the earliest conception – before the rise of Thingol to his later wealth and majesty – see II.63, 128–9, 245–6.

§§25–9   In GA 1 the whole passage given here in the annals 1300–50 and 1330 is placed under 1320: the actual event in 1320 was the speaking of the Dwarves to Thingol concerning their fears ('In this year, however, the Dwarves were troubled . . .', where GA 2 has 'But it came to pass that the Dwarves were troubled . . .'), and it was 'not long thereafter' that 'evil creatures came even to Beleriand'. In a note to the year 1320 on the typescript of AAm (X.106, §85) my father added: 'The Orcs first appear in Beleriand'; in GA 2 (§26) the event is dated ten Valian Years later, in 1330.

§25   The Dwarves' hatred and fear of the Sea has not been mentioned before.

§26   GA 1 has 'over passes in the mountains, or up from the south where their heights fell away': probably referring to the region of the Great Gulf (*Ambarkanta* map V, IV.251).

§27   This paragraph was an addition to GA 1, though not long after the primary text was made. This is the later conception, introduced into AAm (see X.123, §127), according to which the Orcs existed before ever Oromë came upon the Elves, being indeed bred by Morgoth from captured Elves; the older tradition, that Morgoth brought the Orcs into being when he returned to Middle-earth from Valinor, survived unchanged in the final form of the *Quenta Silmarillion* (see X.194, §62). See further under §29 below.

§28   Telchar of Nogrod is not named here in GA 1. He goes back a long way in the history, appearing first in the second version of the *Lay of the Children of Húrin* (III.115), and in Q (IV.118) – where he is of Belegost, not Nogrod.

§29   Axes were 'the chief weapons of the Naugrim, and of the Sindar': cf. the name 'Axe-elves' of the Sindar, X.171. – Of the appearance of Orcs and other evil beings in Eriador and even in Beleriand long before (some 165 Valian Years) the return of Melkor to Middle-earth, and of the arming of the Sindar by the Dwarves, there has been no previous suggestion (see under §27 above).

§30   The coming of Denethor to Beleriand is more briefly recorded in an annal interpolated into AAm (§86) under the same date, 1350 – an interpolation by Pengoloð which (like that referred to under §19 above) was marked later for transfer to the *Annals of Beleriand*. With the mention of the halting of the Teleri on the shores of the Great River cf. the fuller account in AAm, annal 1115 (§§60–1). In GA 1 the name *Nandor* is interpreted, 'the Turners-back': this expression is found also in a note to one of the texts of the *Lhammas*, V.188.

It has not (of course) been said before that the coming of Denethor over the Blue Mountains was brought about by the emergence of 'the fell beasts of the North'. The later history and divisions of the Nandor are now much more fully described: those who 'dwelt age-long' in the woods of the Vale of Anduin (the Elves of Lothlórien and Mirkwood, see *Unfinished Tales* p. 256), and those who went down Anduin, of whom some dwelt by the Sea, while others passed by the White Mountains (the first mention of Ered Nimrais in the writings concerned with the Elder Days) and entered Eriador. These last were the people of Denethor (of whom it is said in AAm that 'after long wanderings they came up into Beleriand from the South', see §86 and commentary, X.93, 104).

The words 'in after days' in 'In that region the forests in after days were tall and green' are perhaps significant: the association of green with the Elves of Ossiriand emerged after the rising of the Sun. See further under §44 below.

§31   The passage corresponding to this in GA 1 is very much briefer:

Of the long years of peace that followed after the coming of Denethor there is no tale, save only that Oromë would come at whiles to the land, or pass over the mountains, and the sound of his horn came over the leagues of the starlight ...

(concluding as in GA 2). But the passage in GA 2 concerning Dairon and his runes is largely derived from a later passage in GA 1 (absent in GA 2), for which see p. 20.

The word *Cirth* first appears here, though as a later addition to the manuscript (perhaps at the time when my father was preparing Appendix E to *The Lord of the Rings*). It is said in the footnote to the paragraph that Dairon contrived his runes 'ere the building of Menegroth' (begun in 1300, according to GA); so also in GA 1 'Dairon ... had devised his Runes already by V.Y.1300'. An annal added to the typescript of AAm (X.106, §85) has '1300   Daeron, loremaster of Thingol, contrives the Runes.' For an earlier view of the origin of the Runes of Dairon (an invention of 'the Danian Elves of Ossiriand', elaborated in Doriath) see *The Treason of Isengard* pp. 453–5; there the name 'Alphabet of Dairon' is ascribed simply to the fact of 'the preservation in this script of some fragments of the songs of Dairon, the ill-fated minstrel of King Thingol of Doriath, in the works on the ancient Beleriandic languages by Pengolod the Wise of Gondolin'. See also my father's later statement concerning the Alphabet of Daeron at the beginning of Appendix E (II) to *The Lord of the Rings*.

§33   On the great cry of Morgoth see X.109, 296. Where GA 2 has 'few knew what it foreboded' GA 1 has 'few (save Melian and Thingol) knew what it foreboded'.

§34   So also in AAm (§126) and in the late *Quenta Silmarillion* text 'Of the Thieves' Quarrel' (X.297) Ungoliantë after her rout by the Balrogs went down into Beleriand and dwelt in Nan Dungorthin (Nan Dungortheb); but it is not said in those texts that the power of

Melian prevented her entry into the Forest of Neldoreth. In both it is said that that valley was so named because of the horror that she bred there, but the statement here that the Mountains of Terror came to be so called after that time is not found elsewhere. That Ungoliantë departed into the South of the world is said also in AAm, but in 'Of the Thieves' Quarrel' (X.297) 'whither she went after no tale tells'.

§35   The stage of development in the tradition of Morgoth's fortress is that of QS and AAm, in which Angband was built on the ruins of Utumno (see X.156, §12). – In GA 1 the name *Thangorodrim* is translated 'the Tyrannous Towers'; cf. the later translation 'the Mountains of Oppression' (X.298).

§§36 ff.   This is the first full account of 'the First Battle of Beleriand' (a term previously applied to the Battle-under-Stars, which now becomes the Second Battle). In the pre-*Lord of the Rings* texts the first assault of the Orcs on Beleriand had been briefly described; thus in the second version (AV 2) of the *Annals of Valinor* it was said (V.114):

> Thingol with his ally Denithor of Ossiriand for a long while held back the Orcs from the South. But at length Denithor son of Dan was slain, and Thingol made his deep mansions in Menegroth, the Thousand Caves, and Melian wove magic of the Valar about the land of Doriath; and most of the Elves of Beleriand withdrew within its protection, save some that lingered about the western havens, Brithombar and Eglorest beside the Great Sea, and the Green-elves of Ossiriand who dwelt still behind the rivers of the East . . .

In QS §115 the account ran thus:

> Of old the lord of Ossiriand was Denethor, friend of Thingol; but he was slain in battle when he marched to the aid of Thingol against Melko, in the days when the Orcs were first made and broke the starlit peace of Beleriand. Thereafter Doriath was fenced with enchantment, and many of the folk of Denethor removed to Doriath and mingled with the Elves of Thingol; but those that remained in Ossiriand had no king, and lived in the protection of their rivers.

§36   Between Menegroth and Thangorodrim on the second Silmarillion map (as drawn: not in my reproduction, V.409) the length is 14 cm, and the scale is stated to be 50 miles to 3·2 cm. (the length of the sides of the squares); the distance was therefore 218·75 miles, or just under 73 leagues (for my father's later interpretation of the scale in inches, not centimetres, see p. 332, but the difference has no significance here). The distance given here of 150 leagues (450 miles) from Menegroth to Angband's gate, more than doubling that shown on the second map, seems to imply a great extension of the northern plain. The geography of the far North is discussed in

V.270–2; but since it is impossible to say how my father came to conceive it I discreetly omitted all indication of the Iron Mountains and Thangorodrim from the map drawn for the published *Silmarillion*.

§38   GA 1 has here:

Therefore he called on Denethor [*struck out:* and on the Enfengs] and the First Battle was fought in the Wars of Beleriand. And the Orcs in the east were routed and slain aheaps, and as they fled before the Elves they were waylaid by the axes of the Enfengs that issued from Mount Dolmed: few returned to the North.

In GA 2 'Region over Aros' refers to that part of the Forest of Region between the rivers Aros and Celon (see p. 183, square F 10). The implication of the sentence seems clearly to be that these Elves owed allegiance to Denethor; and this does not seem to be consistent with what is said in §39, that after the First Battle many of the Green-elves of Ossiriand 'went north and entered the guarded realm of Thingol and were merged with his folk'. Against this sentence in the typescript of GA my father wrote in the margin 'Orgol' and 'of the Guest-elves in Arthórien', marking these with carets to indicate that something should be said of them. In *Unfinished Tales*, p. 77, occurs the following passage:

Saeros . . . was of the Nandor, being one of those who took refuge in Doriath after the fall of their lord Denethor upon Amon Ereb, in the first battle of Beleriand. These Elves dwelt for the most part in Arthórien, between Aros and Celon in the east of Doriath, wandering at times over Celon into the wild lands beyond; and they were no friends to the Edain since their passage through Ossiriand and settlement in Estolad.

This was largely derived from an isolated note, very rapidly written and not at all points intelligible, among the *Narn* papers, but somewhat reduced. It is remarked in this note that 'the Nandor had turned away, never seen the Sea or even Ossë, and had become virtually Avari. They had also picked up various Avari before they came back west to Ossiriand.' Of those Nandor who took refuge in Doriath after the fall of Denethor it is said: 'In the event they did not mingle happily with the Teleri of Doriath, and so dwelt mostly in the small land Eglamar, Arthórien under their own chief. Some of them were "darkhearted", though this did not necessarily appear, except under strain or provocation.' 'The chief of the "Guest-elves", as they were called, was given a permanent place in Thingol's council'; and Saeros (in this note called in fact *Orgoph* or *Orgol*) was 'the son of the chief of the Guest-elves, and had been for a long time resident in Menegroth'.

I think it very probable that my father wrote 'Orgol' and 'of the Guest-elves in Arthórien' on the typescript of GA as the same time as he wrote this note.

Arthórien was entered on the second map (p. 183, square F 10). The application of the name *Eglamar* to Arthórien in this note is puzzling (see p. 189, §57).

The intervention of the Dwarves has not been referred to previously.

§40   The words 'unless one should come with a power greater than that of Melian the Maia' replaced at the time of writing 'unless haply some power greater than theirs should assail them'. – *Eglador*: my father pencilled this name under *Doriath* on the second map (see p. 186, §14).

§41   At the end of this paragraph the *Annals of Aman* cease to record the events in the *Grey Annals*, and comparison is with QS (V.248 ff.), together with the conclusion of AV 2 (V.117 ff.) and with AB 2 (V.125 ff.). In this commentary I do not generally refer to later developments in the *Quenta Silmarillion* tradition.

§44   For *Eryd-wethrin, the valour of the Noldor,* and *Dagor-nuin-Giliath* GA 1 has *Erydwethion, the valour of the Gnomes,* and *Dagor-nui-Ngiliath* (as in QS §88, marginal note).

This is the first occurrence of *Ardgalen* in the texts as here presented, replacing *Bladorion* as the original name of the great northern plain before its devastation. It is notable that *Ardgalen* 'the green region' is expressly stated to have been the name at this time before the rising of the Sun; cf. the change made long before to the passage in Q describing the Battle-under-Stars (when the battle was fought on the plain itself, not in Mithrim): 'yet young and green (it stretched to the feet of the tall mountains)' > 'yet dark beneath the stars' (IV.101, 103).

The Orc-hosts that passed southwards down the Vale of Sirion are not of course mentioned in previous accounts of the Battle-under-Stars. The attack on the Noldor in Mithrim is now taken up into a larger assault out of Angband, and the victory of the Noldor brought into relation with the newly-developed conception of the beleaguered Sindar.

In the account of the destruction of the western Orc-host by Celegorn is the first appearance of the Fen of Serech: this was first named in an addition to the second map the Fen of Rivil, subsequently changed to the Fen of Serech (p. 181, §3). Rivil was the stream that rising at Rivil's Well on Dorthonion made the fen at its inflowing into Sirion.

§45   In AV 2 (V.117) and QS (§88) the Balrogs were in the rearguard of Morgoth's host, and it was they who turned to bay. – Of the rescue of Fëanor GA 1 (following QS) has only: 'But his sons coming up with force rescued their father, and bore him back to Mithrim' (see under §46).

§46   The story of Fëanor's dying sight of Thangorodrim and his cursing of the name of Morgoth first appeared in Q (IV.101), where the Battle-under-Stars was fought on the plain of Bladorion (Ardgalen). In AV 1 and AV 2 (IV.268, V.117) the battle was fought in Mithrim, and Fëanor was mortally wounded when he advanced too far upon the plain, but he was brought back to Mithrim and died there; his sight of Thangorodrim and curse upon Morgoth do not appear. In QS (§88) my father combined the accounts: Fëanor died in Mithrim, but it is also told that he 'saw afar the peaks of Thangorodrim' as he died, and 'cursed the name of Morgoth thrice'; GA 1 follows this story (see under §45 above). It must have been the consideration that from Mithrim Thangorodrim was not visible on account of the heights of Eryd-wethrin that led to the story in GA 2 that Fëanor caused his sons to halt as they began the climb above Eithel Sirion, and that he died in that place.

§47   The initial misapprehension among the Grey-elves concerning the return of the Noldor is a wholly new element in the narrative, as is also the cold view taken by Thingol, seeing in it a threat to his own dominion. In the old versions his coolness does not appear until his refusal to attend the Feast of Reuniting (Mereth Aderthad) in the year 20 of the Sun, and arises rather from his insight into what the future might bring: 'Thingol came not himself, and he would not open his kingdom, nor remove its girdle of enchantment; for wise with the wisdom of Melian he trusted not that the restraint of Morgoth would last for ever' (QS §99, and very similarly in AB 2, V.126).

§49   The date 1497 is repeated from §36. – The Balrogs that constituted the force that Morgoth sent to the parley in QS (§89 and commentary) have disappeared.

§52   As in AAm §§157–8, 163 the form *Endar* ('Middle-earth') is clear, but here as there the typist put *Endor* (see X.126, §157).

§53   The paragraph opens in the manuscript with a large pointing hand.

§§54–5   In this passage, while there are echoes of the earlier texts, the writing is largely new, and there are new elements, notably the cry of Maidros on Thangorodrim.

§54   The story of Morgoth's assault on Tilion is told in AAm §179, where however it took place after both Sun and Moon were launched into the heavens. It is told in AAm that 'Tilion was the victor: as he ever yet hath been, though still the pursuing darkness overtakes him at whiles', evidently a reference to the eclipses of the Moon.

§57   On the placing of Hildórien see AV 2 (V.120, note 13) and QS §82 and commentary; also pp. 173–4. On the name *Atani* see X.7, 39.

§§58–60   While this annal for the second year of the Sun is obviously closely related to and in large part derived from QS §§92–3, it contains new elements, as the more explicit portrayal of Fingolfin's anger against the Fëanorians, and also the repentance of many of the latter for the burning of the ships at Losgar.

§61   The reference to the *Quenta* is to the much fuller account of the rescue of Maidros in QS §§94–7. In AAm (§160) it is told that Maidros was 'on a time a friend of Fingon ere Morgoth's lies came between', and (§162) that he alone stood aside at the burning of the ships. – The spelling *Maiðros*: at earlier occurrences in GA the name is spelt *Maidros*, and *Maidros* appears again in the following line; while in the draft text referred to on p. 29 the form is mostly *Maiðros* (cf. the later form *Maedhros*, X.177, adopted in the published *Silmarillion*, beside *Maedros* X.293, 295).

§§63–4   The content of this passage is largely new; there has been no previous mention of the coming of Angrod to Thingol and his silence about many matters in respect of the Return of the Noldor. The actual nature of Thingol's claim to overlordship, whereby he 'gave leave' to the princes of the Noldor to dwell in certain regions, is now specified (the acceptance by Fingolfin of Thingol's claim is referred to in the earlier forms of the linguistic excursus in GA, pp. 21, 25; cf. also the anticipatory words in §48, 'the sons of Fëanor were ever unwilling to accept the overlordship of Thingol, and would ask for no leave where they might dwell or might pass'). – The Telerin connection of the Third House of the Noldor through the marriage of Finrod (> Finarfin) to Eärwen Olwë's daughter appears in AAm §§85, 156, and see X.177.

§§65–71   The content of the annal for the year 7 is largely new, save that in QS (§98) there is told of the waiving of the high-kingship of the Noldor by Maidros, and the secret disavowal of this among some at least of his brothers ('to this his brethen did not all in their hearts agree'). In GA there is no mention of what is told in QS, that 'Maidros begged forgiveness for the desertion in Eruman, and gave back the goods of Fingolfin that had been borne away in the ships' (but see §83 and commentary); on the other hand we learn here of the scornful rejection of Thingol's claim by the Fëanorians (with no mention of Fingolfin's acceptance of it, see under §§63–4 above), of Cranthir's harsh disposition and his insulting speech at the council, of the *choosing* of Fingolfin as overlord of the Noldor, of the opinion that Maidros was behind the swift departure of the Fëanorians into the eastern lands (in order to lessen the chances of strife and to bear the brunt of the likeliest assault), and of his remaining in friendship with the other houses of the Noldor, despite the isolation of the Fëanorians.

§67   Curiously, the draft text has here and in §68 *Caranthir* (the later form), while the final text reverts to *Cranthir*. In the very rough initial draft for the annals 6 and 7 (see p. 29) the son of Fëanor who was 'the harshest and the most quick to anger' was Curufin, changed to Caranthir. On Caranthir's scornful reference to Thingol as 'this Dark-elf' see my note in the Index to the published *Silmaril-lion*, entry *Dark Elves*. – In the draft text Caranthir says 'let them not so quickly forget that they were Noldor!'

§72   In AB 2 (V.126) and QS (§99) Mereth Aderthad was held in Nan Tathren, the Land of Willows. GA is more specific concerning those who were present than are the earlier texts: Maidros and Maglor; Cirdan; and Dairon and Mablung as the only two representatives from Doriath (on Thingol's aloofness see §47 and commentary).

§73   That the Noldor learned Sindarin far more readily than the Sindar learned Noldorin has been stated already in the final form of the linguistic excursus, p. 26. It is stated in all three versions of the excursus that it was after Dagor Aglareb (in the year 60) that Sindarin became the common speech of Beleriand.

§74   In AB 2 (V.126) Turgon discovered the hidden vale of Gondolin in the same year (50) as Inglor Felagund discovered Nargothrond – the year of their dreams.

§75   This is the first mention (as the texts are presented) of Galadriel in Middle-earth in the Elder Days. The spelling *Galaðriel* is note-worthy, implying the association of her name with *galadh* 'tree' (*galað*): see X.182 and *Unfinished Tales* p. 267.

In AB 2 (V.126) and QS (§101) there is no suggestion that Inglor Felagund was aided by Thingol to his discovery of the caves where he established Nargothrond. In QS 'the High Faroth' are named, at a later point in the narrative, *Taur-na-Faroth* (see QS §112 and commentary). The great highlands west of Narog were originally called the Hills of the Hunters or the Hunters' Wold; see III.88, IV.225, and the *Etymologies* in V.387, stem SPAR.

The passage beginning 'Thus Inglor came to the Caverns of Narog' as far as 'that name he bore until his end' was an addition to the manuscript, but seems certainly to have been made at the time of the original writing. In view of the close relationship of this annal to the later development of the story in the QS tradition, where a very similar passage is found, I think that my father merely left it out inadvertently and at once noticed the omission (see pp. 177–8, §101).

§76   It is said in QS (§116) only that Gondolin was 'like unto Tûn of Valinor'. This idea perhaps goes far back: see II.208.

§77   *Dagor Aglareb*, the Glorious Battle, was originally the Second Battle in the Wars of Beleriand (see p. 21 and note 6).

§78   The Siege of Angband 'lasted wellnigh four hundred years': from 60 to 455 (see V.257–8).

§§79–81   This inserted passage, which returns to the original text near the beginning of §81, concerns Morgoth's departure from Angband and his attempt to corrupt the first Men in the East, and is of great interest. While in QS (§63) it was said of Morgoth that 'it was never his wont to leave the deep places of his fortress', in AAm

(§128, X.110) 'never but once only, while his realm lasted, did he depart for a while secretly from his domain in the North'; but it is not said or hinted for what purpose he went. (It is worth noting that a rough draft for the present rider in GA is found on the same page as a draft for the expansion of the passage in AAm, on which see X.121 note 10.)

The insertion is carefully written in the same style as the main text, and seems likely to belong to much the same time. It is notable that the reverse of the page used for it carries drafting for the final form of the insertion in AAm (§§43–5) concerning the ensnaring of the Quendi by the servants of Melkor in the lands about Kuiviénen (cf. the words in §79, 'Even as before at the awakening of the Quendi, his spies were watchful'). See further under §87 below.

§79 'Nor himself, an he would go': i.e., nor did the ice and snow hinder Morgoth himself, if he wished to go. – 'Indeed we learn now in Eressëa': cf. the end of the final version of the 'linguistic excursus' (p. 27): 'these histories were made after the Last Battle and the end of the Elder Days', and also the opening paragraph of the *Grey Annals* (p. 5).

§83 The reference to the *Quenta Noldorinwa* (see p. 27 and note 12) is to Chapter 9 'Of Beleriand and its Realms' in QS (V.258).

In QS §116 it is mentioned that 'many of the sires' of the horses of Fingolfin and Fingon came from Valinor. The horses are here said to have been '*given to* Fingolfin by Maidros *in atonement of* his losses, for they had been carried by ship to Losgar'. In an earlier passage in GA (see the commentary on §§65–71) the reference in QS §98 to the *return* of Fingolfin's goods that had been carried away in the ships is absent.

§85 *Eredwethrin*: earlier in GA the form is *Erydwethrin* (also *Eryd Lómin*, *Eryd Luin*); cf. under §113 below. – This is the first occurrence of the river-name *Nenning* for earlier *Eglor* (at whose mouth was the haven of Eglorest), named in AB 2 (V.128, 139) and on the second map (V.408). On the map my father later struck out *Eglor* and wrote in two names, *Eglahir* and *Nenning*, leaving both to stand (p. 187, §22).

In QS (§109) it is said that the Dark-elves of Brithombar and Eglorest 'took Felagund, lord of Nargothrond, to be their king'; see the commentary on this passage, V.267. My father seems to have been uncertain of the status of Cirdan: in a late change to the text of AB 2 (the passage given in V.146, note 13) he wrote that 'in the Havens the folk of the Falas were ruled by Cirdan of the Grey-elves; but he was ever close in friendship with Felagund and his folk' (agreeing with what is said here in GA), but he at once substituted: 'And in the west Cirdan the Shipwright who ruled the mariners of the Falas took Inglor also for overlord, and they were ever close in friendship.'

§87   The words '[Morgoth's] thought being bent on their ruin he gave the less heed to aught else in Middle-earth' seem hardly to agree with the inserted passage concerning Morgoth's departure from Angband (§§79–80). It may be suggested, however, that that passage is precisely concerned with the period *before* the attack on Beleriand in the year 60 (*Dagor Aglareb*) – which was postponed so long because of Morgoth's operations in the East, whence he returned in alarm at 'the growing power and union of the Eldar' (§80).

By alteration to the original passage in this annal concerning the beginning of the languages of Men a Dark-elvish origin is ascribed only to the 'western tongues'. I think that this represents a clarification rather than the entry of a new conception. It was said already in *Lhammas B* (V.179, §10):

The languages of Men were from their beginning diverse and various; yet they were for the most part derived remotely from the language of the Valar. For the Dark-elves, various folk of the Lembi, befriended wandering Men in sundry times and places in the most ancient days, and taught them such things as they knew. But other Men learned also wholly or in part of the Orcs and of the Dwarves; while in the West ere they came into Beleriand the fair houses of the eldest Men learned of the Danas, or Green-elves.

The very interesting addition at the end of the annal belongs with the insertion about Morgoth's departure into the East. There it is said (§80): 'But that some darkness lay upon the hearts of Men … the Eldar perceived clearly even in the fair folk of the Elf-friends that they first knew'; but the present passage is the first definite statement that Men in their beginning fell to the worship of Morgoth, and that the Elf-friends, repentant, fled west to escape persecution. In the long account of his works written for Milton Waldman in 1951, and so very probably belonging to the same period, my father had said: 'The first fall of Man … nowhere appears – Men do not come on the stage until all that is long past, and there is only a rumour that for a while they fell under the domination of the Enemy and that some repented' (*Letters* no.131, pp. 147–8; see X.354–5).

§89   The new story in the revised form of the annal for 64, that Turgon at this time led only a part of his people – those skilled in such work – to Tumladen in order that they should begin the building of Gondolin, is extended further in a greatly expanded version of the annal for 116: see §§111–13.

§90   *The Tower of Ingildon*: this replaces the old name Tower of Tindobel (Tindabel), which survived in QS (§120) and AB 2 (V.129); see p. 197, §120. It is not said in GA as it was in QS that Inglor was the builder of the tower; this is perhaps to be connected with what is said in §85, that Cirdan was lord of the lands 'west of Nenning to the Sea'.

§§91–107   The entire content of the annals for 66 and 67 is new. Highly 'un-annalistic' in manner, with its long and superbly sustained discourse, this narrative is developed from the earlier passage in GA (§48) – or perhaps rather, reveals what my father had in mind when he wrote it:

> When, therefore, ere long (by treachery and ill will, as later is told) the full tale of the deeds in Valinor became known in Beleriand, there was rather enmity than alliance between Doriath and the House of Fëanor; and this bitterness Morgoth eagerly inflamed by all means that he could find.

A complete text of these annals is extant in a preliminary draft, but the form in GA followed this draft closely and the development was almost entirely stylistic. A few of the differences are worth noting:

§93   After 'not though they came in the very hour of our need' my father added to the draft text: 'The new lights of heaven are the sending of the Valar, not the Noldor, mighty though they be', and this was not taken up in GA.

§95   Draft text: '... over the long road from the Kalakiryan'. – After ' "Maybe," said Galaðriel, "but not of me" ' the draft continues:

> and being perplexed and recalling suddenly with anger the words of Caranthir she said ere she could set a guard on her tongue: 'For already the children of Finrod are charged with talebearing and treason to their kindred. Yet we at least were guiltless, and suffered evil ourselves.' And Melian spoke no more of these things with Galaðriel.

This passage was bracketed, and later in the draft the bitterness of the memory of Cranthir's words of sixty years before appears in Angrod's mouth, as in GA (§104). The draft has *Caranthir* in the first passage, *Cranthir* in the second; see under §67 above.

§105   In the draft Thingol says: 'for my heart is hot as the fire of Losgar'.

§107   After 'the words of Mandos would ever be made true' the draft has: 'and the curse that Fëanor drew upon him would darken all that was done after.'

On the spelling *Galaðriel* see under §75 above. In §94 appears *Galadriel*; the draft text begins with *Galaðriel* but then changes to *Galadriel*. This distinction is however probably artificial, since it is merely a question of the insertion or omission of the cross-line on the *d*, written in both cases in a single movement (a reversed 6).

§107   The revision at the end of the annal for 67 depends on the later story that the population of Gondolin was by no means exclusively Noldorin, and is similar to those made to the final version of the 'linguistic excursus' (see p. 26 and notes 9 and 10), a consequence of the rejection of the old conception that in Gondolin, and in Gondolin only, which was peopled by Noldor and cut off from intercourse with all others, the Noldorin tongue survived in daily use; see §113 and commentary.

§§108–9   The content of this annal, extended from the opening sentence recording the completion of Nargothrond (AB 2, V.129), is also entirely new. For the earlier story that Felagund did have a wife, and that their son was Gilgalad, see pp. 242–3.

§110   According to the chronology of the *Grey Annals* Turgon left Nivrost in the year 64 (§88), and thus the figure here of fifty years is an error for fifty-two. The error was repeated, but corrected, at the beginning of the revised annal for 116. Possibly my father had reverted in a momentary forgetfulness to the original dating, when the years were 52 and 102 (V.127, 129). See the commentary on §111.

§111   The change in the opening sentence of the new annal for 116 depends on the revised annal for 64 (§89), whereby Turgon did not definitively leave Vinyamar in that year but began the building of Gondolin. The erroneous fifty years, corrected to fifty-two, since the start of the work was presumably merely picked up from the rejected annal (see under §110).

§§111–12   Entirely new is the appearance of Ulmo to Turgon at Vinyamar on the eve of his departure, his warning, his prophecy, and his instruction to Turgon to leave arms in his house for one to find in later days (cf. II.208, where I suggested that the germ of this was already present in the original tale of *The Fall of Gondolin* – 'Thy coming was set in our books of wisdom'). But Ulmo's foretelling that Gondolin should stand longest against Morgoth goes back through Q (IV.136–7) to the *Sketch of the Mythology* (IV.34).

§113   The later story that there were many Sindar among Turgon's people has led to various changes already met in the text of GA: see the commentary on §107. – The reversion to the old form *wethion* in *Eryd Wethion* is curious (see commentary on §44).

At the foot of the page carrying the revised annal for 116 is the following rapidly pencilled note:

Set this rather in the *Silmarillion* and substitute a short notice:

'In this year as is said in the *Quenta* Gondolin was fully wrought, and Turgon arose and went thither with all his people, and Nivrost was emptied of folk and so remained. But the march of Turgon was hidden by the power of Ulmo, and none even of his kin in Hithlum knew whither he had gone.

Against this my father wrote 'Neglect this'; but since a new chapter was inserted into the *Quenta Silmarillion* which was largely based on the present rider (see pp. 198–9) this was presumably an instruction that was itself neglected.

§114   The date of this annal was first written 154, which was the revised date of the meeting of Cranthir's people with the Dwarves in the Blue Mountains in AB 2 (V.129, and cf. QS §125). The passage describing the relations of Cranthir's folk with the Dwarves is new. It was stated in AB 2 (V.129–30) that the old Dwarf-road into Beleriand had become disused since the return of the Noldor, and in a late rewriting of that passage (precursor of the present annal) it is said:

> But after the coming of the Noldor the Dwarves came seldom any more by their old roads into Beleriand (until the power of Maidros fell in the Fourth Battle [i.e. the Dagor Bragollach in 455]), and all their traffic passed through the hands of Cranthir, and thus he won great riches.

The meaning is therefore that after the meeting of Cranthir's people with the Dwarves their renewed commerce with the Elves passed for three hundred years over the mountains much further north, into the northern parts of Thargelion about Lake Helevorn.

§115   The route of the Orc-army that departed from Angband 'into the white north' remains unchanged from AB 2 (V.130); cf. the account in QS §103, and my discussion of the geography in V.270–1.

§116   *Glaurung* here appears for earlier *Glómund*, together with *Urulóki* 'fire-serpents': cf. the original tale of *Turambar and the Foalókë* in *The Book of Lost Tales* (and 'this *lókë* (for so do the Eldar name the worms of Melko)', II.85).

In QS §104 it was not said that Morgoth was 'ill pleased' that the dragon 'had disclosed himself over soon', but on the contrary that Glómund issued from Angband 'by the command of Morgoth; for he was unwilling, being yet young and but half-grown.'

The content of the latter part of the annal has no antecedent in the old versions. I take the words 'the Noldor of purer race' to mean those Noldor who had no or little intermingling of Dark-elven character, with perhaps the implication that they were more faithful to their ancient nature as it had evolved in Aman.

§§117–20   The story, or rather the existence of a story, about Isfin and Eöl goes back to the beginning, and I shall briefly rehearse here what can be learnt of it before this time.

In the original tale of *The Fall of Gondolin* (II.165, 168) Isfin appears as Turgon's sister, and there is a reference to the 'tale of Isfin and Eöl', which 'may not here be told'. Meglin was their son.

In the fragmentary poem *The Lay of the Fall of Gondolin* Fingolfin's wife and daughter (Isfin) were seeking for him when Isfin was captured by Eöl 'in Doriath's forest'; and Isfin sent Meglin her son to Gondolin (III.146).

In the *Sketch of the Mythology* (IV.34–5) Isfin was lost in Taur-na-Fuin after the Battle of Unnumbered Tears and entrapped by Eöl; Isfin sent Meglin to Gondolin (which at that stage was not founded until after the Battle of Unnumbered Tears).

In Q (IV.136), similarly, Isfin was lost in Taur-na-Fuin after the Battle of Unnumbered Tears, and captured by Eöl; in addition, it is said that 'he was of gloomy mood, and had deserted the hosts ere the battle'. It is subsequently said (IV.140) that Isfin and Meglin came together to Gondolin at a time when Eöl was lost in Taur-na-Fuin.

In AB 1 (IV.301), in the year 171 (the year before the Battle of Unnumbered Tears), it is told that Isfin strayed out of Gondolin and was taken to wife by Eöl. [An error in the printed text of AB 1 here may be mentioned: 'Isfin daughter of Turgon' for 'Isfin sister of Turgon'.] In 192 'Meglin comes to Gondolin and is received by Turgon as his sister's child', without mention of Isfin. This was repeated in AB 2 (V.136, 139), with changed dates (271, 292, later > 471, 492), but now it is expressly stated that Meglin was sent to Gondolin by Isfin, and that he went alone (thus reverting to the story in the *Sketch of the Mythology*).

QS has no mention of the story.

§117   In GA as originally written the loss of Isfin is still placed in the year (471) before the Battle of Unnumbered Tears, but the motive is introduced that she left Gondolin in weariness of the city and wishing to see her brother Fingon; and she was lost in Brethil and entrapped by Eöl, who had lived there 'since the first finding of Beleriand' – which must mean that he withdrew into secrecy and solitude when the Elves of the Great March first entered Beleriand. The implication of the last words, 'took no part in all the deeds of his kin', is not explained.

§118   In the replacement annal 316 something more is suggested of Eöl's nature, and the element enters that disregarding Turgon's bidding Isfin went eastwards from Gondolin, seeking 'the land of Celegorm and his brethren, her friends of old in Valinor'. A description of Isfin on a page from an engagement calendar dated October 1951 (and so belonging to the same time as the new annals in GA discussed here) was attached to the account of the princes of the Noldor in QS (see X.177, 182), and in this account it is said that in Valinor Isfin 'loved much to ride on horse and to hunt in the forests, and there was often in the company of her kinsmen, the sons of Fëanor'. It is further told in the new annal for 316 that she became separated from her escort in Nan Dungorthin and came to Nan Elmoth, where Eöl's dwelling is now placed. She now leaves Gondolin long before the Battle of Unnumbered Tears.

§119   The name *Fingol* is not in fact written with a capital, but is preceded by an altered letter that I cannot interpret (it might possibly be intended as an O). As the annal was written *Glindûr* (replacing the primitive and long-enduring name *Meglin*) was primarily the name of the metal devised by Eöl, and with the later change of *Glindûr* to *Maeglin* this remained true of the name *Maeglin*.

§120 The story now reverts to that told in Q (IV.140): Isfin and Glindûr (Maeglin) came together to Gondolin; and the essential features of the final drama now appear. The original text (see pp. 316 ff.) of the fully told story of Isfin and Eöl and their son (Chapter 16 in the published *Silmarillion*, *Of Maeglin*) belongs to this period, and indeed it was already in existence when these new annals were written: they are a very condensed résumé. (For the rejected annal of which this is a replacement see §273 and commentary.)

§121 The date of Bëor's birth remains unchanged from that in AB 2 (as revised: 170 > 370, V.130), as do the dates of the following annals.

§122–3 The statements in the annals for 388 and 390 that Haleth and Hador were born in Eriador were not made in AB 2.

§124 The reference to the *Quenta* is to QS §§126 ff. – Against the first sentence of this annal my father afterwards pencilled an X, with a scribbled note: 'This is too late. It should be the date of the invitation of the [?Sires] of Men to come west'. This was struck through, apart from the first four words: these are the first indication of major changes in the chronology that would enter at a later time.

§125 This annal is substantially extended from that in AB 2, where no more was said than 'there was war on the East Marches, and Bëor was there with Felagund'.

§127 *Galion* replaces *Gumlin* of QS §127 (and AB 2 as early revised, V.146 note 20: originally in this text the names of the sons of Hador were in the reverse positions, Gundor being the elder). Later, the name *Galion* was replaced by *Galdor*. The change to 'in Eriador' was probably made for this reason: Hador entered Beleriand in 420; thus Galion was born while his father was somewhere in Eriador, in 417, but by the time of Gundor's birth in 419 Hador was already in the eastern foothills of the Blue Mountains (§128).

§129 The first paragraph of the annal for 420 is close to that in AB 2 (V.130–1), with some additions: that Brethil had never before been inhabited on account of the density of the forest, that Hador was the more ready to settle in Hithlum 'being come of a northland people', and that his lands in Hithlum were 'in the country of Dor-Lómin'. In the margin against this last my father later scribbled: '[427 >] 423 Hador's folk come to Dor-lómin', but struck this out; see §136 and commentary. The old view that the people of Hador abandoned their own language in Hithlum is retained (see V.149, annal 220).

§§130–2 The content of the latter part of the annal for 420 and the opening of that for 422 is wholly new: Thingol's dreams concerning Men before they appeared, his ban on their settlement save in the North and on the entry of any Man (even of Bëor's house) into Doriath, Melian's prophecy to Galadriel, and Thingol's permission to the people of Haleth to dwell in Brethil, despite his hostility to Men in general and his edict against their taking land so far south.

§133   This passage follows closely the annal in AB 2 (V.131), but with the interesting addition that the people of Hador would go far into the cold North to keep watch.

§135   With the notable sentence (not in AB 2) 'For the Noldor indeed were tall as are in the latter days men of great might and majesty' cf. the collected references to the relative stature of Men and Elves in the oldest writings, II.326. In the early texts it was said more than once that the first Men were smaller than their descendants, while the Elves were taller, and thus the two races were almost of a size; but the present passage is not clear in this respect.

As the last sentence but one of the paragraph was originally written it read: 'Yellowhaired they were and blue-eyed (not so was Túrin but his mother was of Bëor's house) and their women were tall and fair.' The words 'for the most part' were added; they had appeared in a closely similar passage in QS chapter 10 (V.276, §130).

§136   That Hador's folk were given lands in Dor-lómin was mentioned in the annal for 420, to which my father added afterwards, but then struck out, '[427 >] 423   Hador's folk come to Dor-lómin' (commentary on §129). The implication is presumably that for a few years they dwelt in some other part of Beleriand.

§139   Beren's mother Emeldir 'Manhearted' is not named in the earlier texts.

§142   In AB 2 the birth of Morwen was in 445. When the date was changed in GA to 443 the entry was moved.

§144   Tuor has not previously been given the title of 'the Blessed'.

§§145–7   In AB 2 (V.131–2) the Battle of Sudden Fire, recorded in the annal for 455, 'began suddenly on a night of mid-winter'; but the passage beginning 'Fingolfin and Fingon marched to the aid of Felagund' has a new date, 456. I suggested (V.150) that this was because the Battle of Sudden Fire began at midwinter of the year 455, i.e. at the end of the year. In GA, on the other hand, it is expressly stated (§145) that the assault out of Angband came 'at the year's beginning', 'on the night of mid-winter'; thus the new year began at the mark of mid-winter, and the battle was dated the first day of the year 455. See commentary on §147.

§145   There are here the first appearances of the names *Dagor Bragollach* (for *Dagor Vreged-úr* in QS, earlier *Dagor Húr-Breged* in AB 2) and *Anfauglith* (for *Dor-na-Fauglith*).

§147   In QS (V.282, §140) Hador, who was born in 390, is said to have been 'sixty and six years of age' at his death, not as here 65 (see commentary on §§145–7).

§§149–50   This passage, later struck from the manuscript apart from the opening sentence of §149, remained very close to that in AB 2 (V.132) with some influence in its structure from the story as told in QS (V.288), except in one important particular: Húrin's companion was not, as in AB 2 and QS, Haleth the Hunter himself, but Haleth's grandson Handir, born in the same year as Húrin. – The story of Húrin in Gondolin reappears in GA in a long rider to the annal 458 (§§161–6).

§§151–2   As this passage concerning Turgon's messengers was first written it followed closely that in AB 2 (V.132–3, and cf. the version in QS, V.288); as revised it introduces the ideas of the inability of the Noldor to build seaworthy ships, and of Turgon's nonetheless keeping a secret outpost and place of shipbuilding on the Isle of Balar thereafter.

§153   In the earlier accounts (AB 2 in V.132–3 with notes 25 and 29, and QS §141 and commentary) the story of how Celegorn and Curufin came to Nargothrond after their defeat in the east was shifting and obscure, but there was at any rate no suggestion that they played any part in the defence of Minnas-tirith on Tolsirion. My father made a note at this time on the AB 2 manuscript, suggesting a possible turn in the story: Celegorn and Curufin were driven west and helped manfully in the siege of Minnas-tirith, saving Orodreth's life: and so when Minnas-tirith was taken Orodreth could not help but harbour them in Nargothrond. He struck this out; but the story was now reintroduced and developed in the *Grey Annals*.

The date of the capture of Minnas-tirith was changed in the *Grey Annals*. In AB 2 the date was 457 (following the fall of Fingolfin in 456); so also in QS §143 'For nearly two years the Gnomes still defended the west pass ... and Minnastirith withstood the Orcs', and it was 'after the fall of Fingolfin' that Sauron came against Tolsirion. In GA the present passage, describing the assault on the Pass of Sirion, was first dated 456, but the date was struck out, so that these events fall within the Fell Year, 455; and the fall of Fingolfin follows (still dated 456).

§154   The later form *Tol-in-Gaurhoth* (for earlier *Tol-na-Gaurhoth*) now appears.

§§155–7   The story of Fingolfin's death in AB 2 (V.133) had been compressed into a few lines. Introducing a much extended account into the new *Annals*, my father drew largely upon the story as it had been told in QS (§§144–7 and commentary), with some regard also to Canto XII of the *Lay of Leithian* (on which the QS version was largely based). In content the differences are mostly small, but there enters here the great ride of Fingolfin across Anfauglith on his horse Rochallor, and the horse's flight from Angband and death in Hithlum. In AB 2 (as in AB 1 and Q) it was Thorondor who built

Fingolfin's cairn, whereas in QS it was Turgon (see the commentary on QS §147); now in the *Grey Annals* the building of the cairn is ascribed to 'the eagles'.

§157   The change of 'the people of the hidden city were all Noldor' to 'many of the people ... were Noldor' depends on the development whereby there were many Elves of Sindarin origin in Gondolin: see commentary on §107 and references given there.

In the late addition at the end of this paragraph (present in the GA typescript) appears the parentage of Gilgalad as adopted in the published *Silmarillion*; see further pp. 242–3.

§158   The form *Taur-nu-Fuin* (for earlier *Taur-na-Fuin*) now appears.

§159   In AB 2 (V.133), and in a closely similar passage in QS (§139), it was said that the wives of Baragund and Belegund were from Hithlum, and that when the Battle of Sudden Fire began their daughters Morwen and Rían were sojourning there among their kinsfolk – hence they were the only survivors. This story is now superseded and rejected: Emeldir Beren's mother led the surviving women and children of Bëor's people away over the mountains in the aftermath of the battle, and it was thus that Morwen and Rían came to Dor-lómin (by way of Brethil). It is not made clear whether their mothers were still women of Hithlum.

In AB 2 the full list of Barahir's band was not given, with a suggestion that only certain names were remembered, but it appears in QS (§139). The only name that differs in GA is *Arthad* for *Arthod*. *Radhruin* of QS is here written *Raðhruin* (*Radruin* by emendation of *Radros* in AB 2, V.147 note 31), but this may not be significant.

§160   This paragraph derives from the annal for 458 in AB 2 (V.133). In the story as told in QS (§152) Beleg came to the aid of Haleth 'with many archers'; cf. GA §29, 'Thingol's armouries were stored with axes (the chief weapons of the Naugrim, and of the Sindar)', and the name 'Axe-elves' of the Sindar (transferred from the Nandor), X.171. On the name *Eglath* ('The Forsaken') see X.85, 164, 170.

§161   Huor now at last appears as Húrin's companion in Gondolin, replacing Handir grandson of Haleth in the earlier, rejected passage in GA (§149).

Haleth was the kinsman of Húrin and Huor (as noticed in a late addition to the manuscript) through the marriage in 436 (§140) of Haleth's son Hundor to Glorwendil, daughter of Hador and sister of their father Galion. But the genealogy was further developed in the annal for 462 (see §171 and commentary) by the marriage of Galion to Haleth's daughter, so that Haleth was the grandfather of Húrin and Huor; and it seems very probable that this was the reason for the addition of the words 'their kinsman' here.

The story now becomes decisively different from the old version in AB 2 and QS, and still present in GA as originally written (§149); for Húrin and his companion (now his brother Huor) were not hunting in the Vale of Sirion before the Battle of Sudden Flame, but the fact of the fostering of Húrin (and now of his brother also) among the people of Haleth is brought into association with the defeat of the Orcs in 458 by the men of Brethil, aided by Elves out of Doriath, three years after the battle. There enters now also the story that Húrin and Huor were taken to Gondolin by the Eagles. – On the ford of Brithiach see p. 228, §28.

§§162–6 The story now reaches virtually its final form, with the major innovation of Maeglin's hostility to the young men but also of their being permitted to leave Gondolin despite the king's ban, here first stated in its full rigour, on departure from the city of any stranger who came there; and this permission was granted because of their ignorance of how it might be found. (The riders on the story of Isfin and Ëol, §§118–20, were written at the same time as the present one.)

§165 On the change of *Glindûr* to *Maeglin* see §119 and commentary.

§166 On the carbon copy of the typescript of GA my father wrote against the words 'But though they told that they had dwelt a while in honour in the halls of King Turgon': 'They did not reveal Turgon's name.' See p. 169.

§170 'The army that had driven into East Beleriand' must refer to the invasions of the year 455: cf. AB 2, annal 456; QS §142; and again in GA §148, in all of which the phrase 'far into East Beleriand' occurs. In AB 2, in the renewed assaults of the year 462 (V.134), 'the invasion of the Orcs encompassed Doriath, both west down Sirion, and east through the passes beyond Himling.' Of this there is no mention here in GA (nor in QS, §156); but there has also been no mention before the present passage of Thingol's victory after the Dagor Bragollach or indeed of the subsequent total destruction (as it appears) of the eastern invading force.

§171 The statement that 'in the eastward war [Morgoth] hoped ere long to have new help unforeseen by the Eldar' is a premonitory reference to the coming of the Swarthy Men; cf. QS §150, where, immediately before their entry into Beleriand, it is said that Morgoth 'sent his messengers east over the mountains', and that 'some were already secretly under the dominion of Morgoth, and came at his call'. In GA (§174, footnote) it is said that 'it was after thought that the people of Ulfang were already secretly in the service of Morgoth ere they came to Beleriand.' See further §§79–81 and commentary.

Of the assault on Hithlum no more was said in AB 2 (V.134) than that 'Morgoth went against Hithlum, but was driven back as yet'; in

QS (§156) it was Fingon, not Húrin, who 'drove [the Orcs] in the end with heavy slaughter from the land, and pursued them far across the sands of Fauglith.'

At the end of the paragraph, by later addition, is the first reference to the short stature of Húrin, and also to the 'double marriage' of Hador's son Galion and daughter Glorwendil to Haleth's daughter (unnamed) and son Hundor. It seems likely that this extension of the genealogy arose here, and was the basis of the addition of 'their kinsman' to the annal for 458 discussed in the commentary on §161.

§172   In QS (§156) there seems only to have been an assault on Hithlum from the east, from Fauglith, for it is said that 'the Orcs won many of the passes, and some came even into Mithrim'. In the present annal it seems that Galion and his son Húrin defeated the attack from the east, while Fingon attempted to defend Hithlum from the north (the intervention of Cirdan is of course entirely new). On the puzzling question of the geographical configuration of the north of Hithlum see V.270–1 (and cf. what is said in GA of the route of the attack out of Angband in the year 155, §115 and commentary). The present passage does not clarify the matter, though the statement that the horsed archers of the Eldar pursued the Orcs 'even to the Iron Mountains' possibly suggests that Hithlum was to some degree open to the north. This would indeed be very surprising, since it would make Hithlum by far the most vulnerable of the territories of the Eldar, and Morgoth would have had little need to attempt to break through the vast natural defence of the Shadowy Mountains. But this is the merest speculation, and I know of no other evidence bearing on the matter.

§§173–4   New elements in this account of the Easterlings (cf. AB 2, V.134, and QS §151) are the explicit statement that they did not enter Beleriand over the Blue Mountains but passed to the north of them; the warning of the Dwarves to Maidros concerning their westward movement; the diversity of their tongues and their mutual hostility; their dwellings in Lothlann and south of the March of Maidros (in QS it is said only that they 'abode long in East Beleriand', §152). The form *Lothlann* appears for earlier *Lothland*; *Lothlann (Lhothlann)* is found in the *Etymologies* (stems LAD, LUS, V.367, 370).

§174   On the first sentence of the footnote to this paragraph see the commentary on §171. With the following remarks in the footnote concerning the descendants of the people of Bór in Eriador in the Second Age cf. QS chapter 16, §15 (V.310–11): 'From that day [Nírnaith Arnediad] the hearts of the Elves were estranged from Men, save only from those of the Three Houses, the peoples of Hador, and Bëor, and Haleth; for the sons of Bór, Boromir, Borlas, and Borthandos, who alone among the Easterlings proved true at need, all perished in that battle, and they left no heirs.' This suggests that the people of Bór ceased to be of any account after 472; but it is perhaps to be presumed in any case that these Men of Eriador were a branch of that people who never entered Beleriand.

§§175–210   I have described in V.295 how, after *The Lord of the Rings* was finished, my father began (on the blank verso pages of the manuscript of AB 2) a prose 'saga' of Beren and Lúthien, conceived on a large scale and closely following the revised *Lay of Leithian*; but this went no further than Dairon's betrayal to Thingol of Beren's presence in Doriath. Unless this work belongs to a time after the abandonment of the *Grey Annals*, which seems to me very improbable, the two versions of the tale that appear here in the *Annals* are the last of the many that my father wrote (for a full account of the complex history of the QS versions and drafts see V.292 ff.).

It will be seen that Version I is a précis of the narrative with no new elements, or elements inconsistent with the 'received tradition', apart from the reference to Amárië (see commentary on §180). Version II, if at the outset conceived on a fairly ample scale, again soon becomes another précis, though much fuller than Version I, and a great deal that is told in the completed QS text ('QS II', see V.292–3) is either not present or is treated much more cursorily: thus for example, nothing is said in GA of Húan's understanding of speech or speaking three times before his death, nor of his doom (*The Silmarillion* pp. 172–3), and much else that there is no need to detail here. But the structure of the two narratives remains very close.

It is curious to observe that the relation of the two versions in GA is the reverse of that between the two versions that my father made for the *Quenta Silmarillion*. The fuller form of the latter ('QS I') was very clearly an integral element in the QS manuscript as it proceeded, but he abandoned it and replaced it by the shorter form QS II because (as I have said, V.292) 'he saw that it was going to be too long, overbalancing the whole work. He had taken more than 4000 words to reach the departure of Beren and Felagund from Nargothrond'. In the case of the *Grey Annals*, on the other hand, it was the shorter form (Version I) that was integral to the text as written, while the fuller form (Version II) was intended to supplant it (though it was not finished).

For passages in the published *Silmarillion* derived from the *Grey Annals* see V.298–301.

§175   *Eryd Orgorath*: on the typescript of AAm *Ered Orgoroth* was changed to *Ered Gorgorath* (X.127, §126).

'And he passed through, even as Melian had foretold': see the words of Melian to Galadriel, §131.

In AB 2 (V.135) Húrin wedded Morwen in 464, as in GA, but Túrin was born in the winter of 465 'with sad omens'. This insertion in GA makes Túrin's birth in the year of his parents' marriage. See further the commentary on §183.

§178   The word 'bride-price' of the Silmaril demanded by Thingol had been used by Aragorn when he told the story on Weathertop.

§179   *Celegorm* was the original form, appearing in the *Lost Tales* (II.241). The name became *Celegorn* in the course of the writing of QS (V.226, 289), and this remained the form in AAm and GA; later it reverted to *Celegorm* (X.177, 179). The change of *m* to *n* here was made at the time of or very soon after the writing of this passage, and *Celegorm* was probably no more than a slip.

§180   With '[Felagund] dwells now in Valinor with Amárië' cf. QS I (V.300): 'But Inglor walks with Finrod his father among his kinsfolk in the light of the Blessed Realm, and it is not written that he has ever returned to Middle-earth.' In Version II (§199) it is said that 'released soon from Mandos, he went to Valinor and there dwells with Amárië.' It has been told in the annal for 102 (§109) that 'she whom [Felagund] had loved was Amárië of the Vanyar, and she was not permitted to go with him into exile.'

§183   Túrin's birth ('with sad omens') was likewise given in the year 465 in AB 2. The present entry was only inserted later, I think, because my father had inadvertently omitted it while concentrating on the story of Beren and Lúthien. Following the direction here 'Place in 464' a pencilled addition was made to the annal for that year in both versions (see §175 and commentary, §188).

§185   It appears from the penultimate sentence of this paragraph that the joining of the Two Kindreds is ascribed to the purpose of Eru. This is not in QS (I) (see *The Silmarillion* p. 184), nor in Version II of the story in the *Grey Annals* (§210).

§187   With the revised reading 'soon after the mid-winter' cf. the commentary on §§145–7.

§189   '[Thingol] answered in mockery': his tone is indeed less sombre and more briefly contemptuous than in QS (I) (*The Silmarillion* p. 167). In the *Lay of Leithian* (III.192, lines 1132–3) Thingol's warriors 'laughed loud and long' at his demand that Beren should fetch him a Silmaril; see my remarks on this, III.196.

§190   The detail of the glance passing between Melian and Beren at this juncture is not found in the other versions.

§191   The words 'as long before he had said to Galadriel' refer to Felagund's prophetic words in Nargothrond recorded in the annal for 102 (§108).

§193   The naming of Inglor 'Finrod' was perhaps no more than a slip without significance; but in view of the occurrence of 'Finrod Inglor the Fair' in a text associated with drafting for Aragorn's story on Weathertop (VI.187–8) it seems possible that my father had considered the shifting of the names (whereby Inglor became Finrod and Finrod his father became Finarfin) long before their appearance in print in the Second Edition of *The Lord of the Rings*.

§§193–4 In the long version QS (I), which ends at this point, when Felagund gave the crown of Nargothrond to his brother Orodreth 'Celegorm and Curufin said nothing, but they smiled and went from the halls' (*The Silmarillion* p. 170). The words of Celegorn and Felagund that follow here are a new element in the story.

The foresight of Felagund is undoubtedly intended to be a true foresight (like all such foresight, though it may be ambiguous). If full weight is given to the precise words used by Felagund, then it may be said that the conclusion of QS (V.331), where it is told that Maidros and Maglor did each regain a Silmaril for a brief time, is not contradicted.

§198 In QS (*The Silmarillion* p. 174) it is not said that Sauron 'left the Elven-king to the last, for he knew who he was', but only that he 'purposed to keep Felagund to the last, for he perceived that he was a Gnome of great might and wisdom.' See the *Lay of Leithian*, lines 2216–17 and 2581–2609 (III.231, 249).

§201 It is not told in other versions that Húan led the prisoners of Tolsirion back to Nargothrond; in QS it is said only that 'thither now returned many Elves that had been prisoners in the isle of Sauron' (*The Silmarillion* p. 176).

§203 The new year is placed at a slightly later point in the narrative in Version I, §184. In AB 2 all the latter part of the story of Beren and Lúthien, from their entry into Angband, was placed under the annal for the year 465 (V.135).

§204 The absence of any mention of the story that Húan and Lúthien turned aside to Tol-in-Gaurhoth on their way north, and clad in the wolfcoat of Draugluin and the batskin of Thuringwethil came upon Beren at the edge of Anfauglith (*The Silmarillion* pp. 178–9), is clearly due simply to compression. It was not said in QS (*ibid.* p. 179) that 'Húan abode in the woods' when Beren and Lúthien left him on their journey to Angband.

§207 It is not made clear in QS (*The Silmarillion* pp. 181–2) that it was the howls of Carcharoth that aroused the sleepers in Angband. – On the names Gwaihir and Lhandroval, which appear here in QS but not in the published *Silmarillion* (p. 182), see V.301 and IX.45.

§211 This annal is very close to a passage in QS (*The Silmarillion* p. 186).

§§212 ff. The text of QS is no longer the fine manuscript that was interrupted when it was sent to the publishers in November 1937, but the intermediate texts that my father wrote while it was away. These have been described in V.293–4: a rough but legible manuscript 'QS(C)' that completed the story of Beren and Lúthien, and extending through the whole of QS Chapter 16 *Of the Fourth Battle: Nírnaith Arnediad* was abandoned near the beginning of Chapter 17 (the story of Túrin); and a second manuscript 'QS(D)' which took up in the middle of Chapter 16 and extended somewhat further into Chapter 17, at which point the *Quenta Silmarillion* in that phase came to an end as a continuous narrative. From the beginning of Chapter 16 I began a new series of paragraph-numbers from §1 (V.306).

§212   In this annal (468) my father followed that in AB 2 (465–70, V.135) closely, and thus an important element in the 'Silmarillion' tradition is absent: the arrogant demand of the Fëanorians upon Thingol for the surrender of the Silmaril, followed by the violent menaces of Celegorn and Curufin against him, as the prime cause of his refusal to aid Maidros (see QS §6, and the passage in Q from which that derives, IV.116–17). In AB 2 Thingol's refusal is ascribed to 'the deeds of Celegorm and Curufin', and this is followed in GA. Again, the story in QS §7, absent in AB 2, that only a half of Haleth's people came forth from Brethil on account of 'the treacherous shaft of Curufin that wounded Beren', is not found in GA.

Notably, it is said in GA that Maidros had the help of the Dwarves 'in armed force' as well as in weapons of war; this was not said in AB 2 and was expressly denied in QS, where the Dwarves were represented as cynically engaged in the profitable enterprise of 'making mail and sword and spear for many armies' (see QS §3 and commentary).

§213   The annal in AB 2 from which this paragraph derives is dated 468. The present annal is much more explicit about the unwisdom of Maidros in revealing his power untimely than were the earlier accounts. – In QS (§3) it is said that at this time 'the Orcs were driven out of the northward regions of Beleriand', to which it is now added in GA that 'even Dorthonion was freed for a while'.

§214   The span of the second lives of Beren and Lúthien was said in the QS drafts to have been long, but the final text has 'whether the second span of his life was brief or long is not known to Elves or Men' (see V.305–6 on the development of the passage concerning the return of Beren and Lúthien and its form in the published *Silmarillion*). It seems possible that '[Lúthien] should *soon* die indeed' in the present text does not imply a short mortal span, but a mortal span in contrast to that of the Eldar.

The final text of QS says that Beren and Lúthien 'took up again their mortal form in Doriath', but the account here of their return to Thingol and Melian in Menegroth is entirely new (as also, of course, is the reference to Elrond and Arwen).

The land of the Dead that Live is named in QS(B) *Gwerth-i-Cuina* and in the final text of QS *Gyrth-i-Guinar* (V.305).

§215   In AB 2 the latter part of the legend of Beren and Lúthien, from their entry into Angband to their return from the dead, was placed under the year 465, whereas in GA it appears under 466, and the death of Lúthien in 467 (§211). The birth of Dior (whose name *Aranel* now appears) is here moved forward three years from the date in AB 2, 467.

§216 The wedding of Huor and Rían was given in AB 2 in the annal for 472, and was said to have taken place 'upon the eve of battle'. See §218 and commentary.

§§217 ff. In the very long account of the Nírnaeth Arnediad that follows my father made use both of the 'Silmarillion' and of the 'Annals' tradition, i.e. QS Chapter 16 and the account in AB 2. The QS chapter was itself largely derived from an interweaving of Q and AB 2 (see V.313). – A later version of the story of the battle, closely based on that in GA but with radical alterations, is given in Note 2 at the end of this commentary (pp. 165 ff.).

§218 This passage was not removed when the record of Huor's marriage to Rían was entered under 471 (§216); the typescript of GA, however, has only the later 471 entry.

§219 The Nírnaeth Arnediad, formerly the fourth battle in the wars of Beleriand, now becomes the fifth battle: see commentary on §§36 ff. The time of the year was not stated in the earlier accounts.

The placing of the passage on the subject of the Hill of Slain follows AB 2 (V.136); rejected here, it was replaced by another at the end of the story of the Nírnaeth Arnediad in GA (§250): cf. QS §19. On the name *Hauð-na-Dengin* see V.314, §19; also GA §§250–1.

§220 The actual nature of Uldor's machinations was not stated in the earlier accounts.

§221 'a great company from Nargothrond': earlier in GA (§212) it is said that 'small help came from Nargothrond' (cf. QS §5: 'only a small company'). – The addition concerning Mablung's presence, not in AB 2, comes from QS (§6), deriving from Q (IV.117); but in those texts Beleg ('who obeyed no man', 'who could not be restrained') came also to the battle. Thingol's qualified permission to Mablung is new in GA; in the *Quenta* tradition such permission was given by Orodreth to the company from Nargothrond. – The succession of Hundor on the death of his father, Haleth the Hunter, is recorded in the annal for 468 (§212). (Much later, when the genealogy of the People of Haleth was transformed, *Hundor* was replaced by '*Haldir* and *Hundar*'; on this see p. 236.)

On the unsatisfactory account of Turgon's emergence from Gondolin in QS, amalgamating the inconsistent stories in Q and AB 2, see V.313–15. In the *Grey Annals* the confusion is resolved. Turgon came up from Gondolin *before* battle was joined (in the AB story he and his host only came down from Taur-na-Fuin as Fingon's host withdrew southwards towards the Pass of Sirion, V.136–7), but only shortly before, and was stationed in the south guarding the Pass of Sirion.

§222   The story of the opening of the battle as told here differs from that in QS §10 (following Q), where Fingon and Turgon becoming impatient at the delay of Maidros sent their heralds into the plain of Fauglith to sound their trumpets in challenge to Morgoth.

§§224–5   There now appears the final link in this element of the narrative: the captured herald (see commentary on §222) slaughtered in provocation on the plain of Fauglith (QS §11) disappears and is replaced by Gelmir of Nargothrond, Gwindor's brother, who had been taken prisoner in the Battle of Sudden Flame. It was Gwindor's grief for his brother that had brought him from Nargothrond against the will of Orodreth the king, and his rage at the sight of Gelmir's murder was the cause of the fatal charge of the host of Hithlum. I have described the evolution of the story in IV.180.

§226   In §221 'the host of Fingolfin' is obviously a slip of the pen, for 'the host of Fingon', and so probably 'the banners of Fingolfin' here also: QS (§12) has 'the banners of Fingon'.

§228   'in the rearguard', struck out in GA, is found both in AB 2 and in QS (§13). – It is not said either in AB 2 or in QS that the host of Hithlum was surrounded, only that the enemy came between them and Erydwethion, so that Fingon was forced to retreat towards the Pass of Sirion.

It seems clear that Turgon emerged from the Pass only a brief time before the coming of the decoy force out of Angband; therefore he had not yet actually encountered Húrin.

§230   The Balrogs were still at this time conceived to exist in large numbers; cf. AAm §50 (X.75): '[Melkor] sent forth on a sudden a host of Balrogs' – at which point my father noted on the typescript of AAm: 'There should not be supposed more than say 3 or at most 7 ever existed' (X.80).

§231   In AB 2 and in QS (§15) it was Cranthir, not Maglor, who slew Uldor the Accursed. It is not said in those texts that 'new strength of evil men came up that Uldor had summoned and kept hidden in the eastern hills', nor, of course, that the Fëanorians, fleeing towards Mount Dolmed, took with them a remnant of the Naugrim, for it was only with the *Grey Annals* that the Dwarves took part in the battle (commentary on §212).

§232   Earlier in GA (§22) the *Enfeng* are the Dwarves of Belegost, but there was a period (Q, QS) when they were those of Nogrod (see commentary on §22); this no doubt explains *Nogrod* here, which was struck out and replaced by *Belegost* as soon as written. – The entire paragraph, and all its detail, is original in GA.

§233   In QS (§17) the banners of Fingon were white. In the account in GA of the fall of Fingolfin (§155) his shield was blue set with a star of crystal, and his arms silver; this is found also in the QS version (§144).

§§234–5   The speeches between Turgon, Húrin, and Huor are

entirely new. In §235 one might expect Huor to have said: 'I shall never look on thy white walls *again*' (as he does in the published *Silmarillion*, p. 194), since he had been to Gondolin, fourteen years before; but see p. 169.

§§235–6   Virtually all the changes in these paragraphs were made at the time of the writing of the manuscript.

§237   The name *Glindûr* has appeared in other passages introduced into the primary text: §§119–20, 165.

§240   Original details in GA are the striking of Huor's eye by the venomed arrow, and the piling of the dead men of Hador's house 'as a mound of gold'.

§241   This paragraph is derived from passages in QS (§§15–16) that occur at an earlier point in the narrative; but there is no mention in GA of the sons of Bór (see commentary on §174).

§242   The statement here that 'Tol-sirion [was] retaken and its dread towers rebuilt', not previously made, is clearly in plain contradiction of what was said in QS (V.300): 'They buried the body of Felagund upon the hill-top of his own isle, and it was clean again, and ever after remained inviolate; for Sauron came never back thither.' In the published *Silmarillion* this passage in QS was changed.

§243   'Cirdan held the Havens' is of course an addition to the passage in QS (§20) which is here being closely followed. – The references to Morgoth's peculiar fear of Turgon, and to Ulmo's friendship towards the house of Fingolfin, who scorned Morgoth in Valinor, have no antecedents in earlier texts. It can be seen from the rejected lines (rough and with many changes in the manuscript) that my father was to some extent working out the thought as he wrote. The words 'from Turgon ruin should come to him' are a reference to Eärendil and his embassage to Valinor.

§§244–9   The encounter of Húrin with Morgoth as told in GA is based on and for the most part follows closely the story in QS (§§21–3), but with some expansions: Morgoth's words concerning Húrin's wife and son now helpless in Hithlum, Húrin's sight of Hithlum and Beleriand far off from his stone seat on Thangorodrim. See further p. 169.

§251   It is at this point in the narrative that the draft manuscripts QS(C) and QS(D), having concluded the 'Nírnaith' chapter with the setting of Húrin on Thangorodrim, give a new heading, in QS(C) 'Of Túrin the Hapless' and in QS(D) 'Of Túrin Turamarth or Túrin the Hapless'. This, which was to be the next chapter (17) in QS, begins with the birth of Tuor and the death of Rían on the Hill of Slain (to which the *Grey Annals* likewise now turn); but QS(C) goes only so far as Túrin's departure from Menegroth to go out to fight on the marches of Doriath wearing the Dragon-helm, and QS(D) continues beyond this point only to Túrin's self-imposed outlawry after the slaying of Orgof (GA §259).

The fostering of Tuor by Dark-elves was recorded both in AB 2 (V.137) and in QS (§24); rejected in GA, there appears instead the first mention of Annael and the Grey-elves of Mithrim (see commentary on §252). Glorwendil's death of grief for her husband Hundor son of Haleth is referred to in the course of the narrative of the Nírnaith Arnediad in QS (§13).

§252   In both AB 2 (V.138) and in QS (§19) it was recorded that 'the Elves of Hithlum' were enslaved in the mines of Morgoth at this time, such of them as did not escape into the wild, and one would naturally assume that this referred to Noldorin Elves of Fingolfin's people – although the very reference to Tuor's fostering by 'Dark-elves' shows that there were other Elves in Hithlum, and 'Grey-elves' may be simply a later term for the Dark-elves of Beleriand owning allegiance to Thingol. In his message to the new-come Noldor by the mouth of Angrod (GA §64) Thingol did not indeed suggest that there were any of his people (Grey-elves) in Hithlum: among the regions where the Noldor might dwell he named Hithlum, adding that 'elsewhere there are many of my folk, and I would not have them restrained of their freedoms, still less ousted from their homes.'

§253   At the end of this paragraph my father pencilled: '(September–Dec.)'; this clearly refers to the months of Túrin's journey from Hithlum to Doriath in the latter part of 472 (the Battle of Unnumbered Tears was fought at midsummer of that year, §219). According to the earlier dating (§183) he was born in the winter of 465; this was changed (§§175, 188) to 464, but without indication of the time of the year. If he were born in the winter of 464, he would still have been seven years old in the autumn of 472.

§256   The whole content of this paragraph is new to the history. In the sentence 'Smiths and miners and masters of fire' the published *Silmarillion* (p. 196), which derives from this passage, has 'makers of fire': this was a misreading of the manuscript.

§257   It was said earlier in GA (§§151–2) that after the Dagor Bragollach Turgon sent Elves of Gondolin to the mouths of Sirion and to the Isle of Balar to attempt shipbuilding (it is perhaps a question, why did he not approach Cirdan at that time?), and that he 'ever maintained a secret refuge upon the Isle of Balar'. But the phrase in the present passage 'and mingled with Turgon's outpost there' was struck out, and the subsequent 'when Turgon heard of this he sent again his messengers to Sirion's Mouths' suggests of itself that the idea of a permanent outpost from Gondolin on Balar had been abandoned.

Here, in an alteration to the text, Voronwë's story is extended back, and he appears in a new rôle as captain of the last of the seven ships sent out into the Western Ocean by Cirdan (it is not said that he was an Elf of Gondolin). In earlier texts he has of course played no such part. In Q (IV.141) Tuor at the mouths of Sirion met Bronweg (> Bronwë) who had been of old of the people of Turgon and had escaped from Angband. With §§256–7 cf. the story of Tuor in *Unfinished Tales*, pp. 34–5 and note 13.

§258   If Túrin were born in the winter of 464 (see commentary on §253) he would have been in his seventeenth year in 481; it seems therefore that the older date (465) for his birth is retained. The *Annals*, very cursory, do not mention the occasion of Túrin's going to war (the ceasing of all tidings out of Hithlum).

The scribbled note 'Túrin donned the Dragon-helm of Galion' is not in the typescript of GA. The Dragon-helm goes back to the old *Lay of the Children of Húrin*, and was described in Q (IV.118), in the context of Húrin's not having worn it at the Battle of Unnumbered Tears; in the *Lay* (not in Q) Túrin's taking it to war at this time is mentioned (III.16, line 377: 'then Húrin's son took the helm of his sire').

§259   It is here that QS came to an end as a continuous narrative (see V.321, 323).

§260   The first two sentences of this annal are derived from Q (IV.123) and AB 2 (V.138); but those texts do not give the place of Túrin's lair, here said to be in Dimbar.

§261   The first part of this follows AB 2 (on Tuor's 'coming to Hithlum' see V.151), but the statement that Morwen and Niënor 'had been carried away to Mithrim' seems altogether aberrant.

§263   The final form of the annal concerning Tuor, with the date changed to 488 and his age changed to sixteen, and the appearance of Lorgan chief of the Easterlings, is probably derived from the story in *Of Tuor and his Coming to Gondolin* (*Unfinished Tales* pp. 18–19): in the manuscript of that work the date 488 was inserted against the paragraph beginning 'Therefore Annael led his small people ...' (p. 18), and Tuor's age was changed from fifteen to sixteen in the same sentence. On the other hand that text has 'after three years of thraldom' (p. 19) as it was written, whereas in GA 'three' is a change from 'seven'.

§264   This is the original annal for 488. When the preceding passage on Tuor was given the date 488 the entry concerning Haldir of Nargothrond became a continuation of that year. The event was referred to in the *Lay of the Children of Húrin* (III.75, lines 2137–8), where Orodreth's son was named *Halmir*; *Halmir* in AB 2 was changed to *Haldir* (V.138 and note 38), which is the form in the *Etymologies* (explained as meaning 'hidden hero', stem SKAL[1], V.386).

§265   In Q Blodrin was a Gnome, with the later addition that he was a Fëanorian (IV.123 and note 5); the story told here that he was one of the faithful Easterlings who became a traitor after his capture by Morgoth is a new development. In Q his evil nature was ascribed to his having 'lived long with the Dwarves', and this was derived from the *Lay* (III.32). – On the pencilled query concerning the Dragon-helm see §266.

§266   In Q Thingol's messengers arrived on the scene because they had been sent to summon Túrin and Beleg to a feast (IV.123). – The attempt to develop the subsequent history of the Dragon-helm and weave it into the existing story was inherently very difficult. Here, the questions arise at once: (1) Why was the Dragon-helm in Menegroth? This may be answered by supposing that when Túrin came to Menegroth for the feast at which he slew Orgof (§259) he brought the Helm with him from Dimbar, and after the slaying he fled from the Thousand Caves without it; on this assumption, the Helm remained in Doriath during the following years (484–9). But (2) if this is granted, why should Beleg now carry it off into the wilds on what must have seemed an almost certainly vain search for Túrin, who had been captured by Orcs and haled off to Angband? In my father's later work on the Túrin legend he concluded finally that Túrin left the Dragon-helm in Dimbar when he went to Menegroth for the fatal feast, and that (in the later much more complex story) Beleg brought it from there when he came to Amon Rûdh in the winter snow: hence in the (extremely artificial) passage in the published *Silmarillion*, p. 204, 'he brought out of Dimbar the Dragon-helm of Dor-lómin'.

§267   In the *Lay*, likewise, it was Finduilas who asserted against the disbelief and suspicion in Nargothrond that it was indeed Flinding (Gwindor) who had returned (III.69–71).

§268   In this passage a new element enters the story: Túrin's assumption of a riddling name, *Iarwaeth* (cf. the later *Agarwaen* 'Bloodstained', *The Silmarillion* p. 210), and his asking Gwindor to conceal his true name 'for the horror he had of his slaying of Beleg and dread lest it were learned in Doriath'; and here also appears the final form of the name of the re-forged sword, *Gurthang* 'Iron of Death' for earlier *Gurtholfin* > *Gurtholf* (V.139 and note 39) 'Wand of Death' (*Gurthang* is a change on the manuscript from a rejected name that cannot be read: the second syllable is *tholf* but the first is not *Gur*, and the meaning given is probably 'Wand of Death'). The form *Mormegil* appears in the earliest *Annals* (AB 1), emended to *Mormael* (IV.304 and note 52); Q had *Mormaglir* and AB 2 *Mormael*.

§§269–72   The greater part of this narrative appears for the first time in the *Grey Annals*: Gwindor's revelation to Finduilas of Túrin's identity, his warning to her, and his assertion that all in Angband knew of the curse upon Húrin; Túrin's assurance to Gwindor concerning Finduilas and his displeasure with him for what he had done; the honour done to Túrin by Orodreth when he learned who he was and the king's acceptance of his counsels; Túrin's unhappy love for Finduilas leading him to seek escape from his trouble in warfare.

§271 *morrowgift*: the gift of the husband to the wife on the morning ('morrow') after the wedding.

§272 The alliance of the Elves of Nargothrond with Handir of Brethil goes back to the earliest *Annals* (IV.305); I do not know why this element in the story was removed. See further the commentary on §300. – The bridge over Narog is not said here to have been built on Túrin's counsel, but this appears subsequently (§277).

§273 This rejected annal for 492 adheres to the old story that Meglin was sent by Isfin to Gondolin (although the later story that Isfin and Meglin came together to Gondolin appeared long before in Q: see §120 and commentary), and there is no trace of the story of Ëol's pursuit, the death of Isfin from Ëol's dart aimed at Maeglin, and Ëol's execution and dying curse on his son.

§275 The somewhat later insertion at the beginning of the annal replaces the subsequent statement in this paragraph that Handir was slain in the battle of Tum-halad, which derives from AB 2 (V.139).

The removal of Glaurung's passage through Hithlum on his way to Nargothrond (recorded in AB 2) is a great improvement to the probabilities of the narrative. – *Eithil Ivrin*: formerly *Ivrineithel* (V.139), 'Ivrin's Well', source of the Narog. This is the first reference to the defiling of Ivrin by Glaurung.

The site of the battle is not made clear. In Q it was 'upon the Guarded Plain, north of Nargothrond' (IV.126), and in AB 2 (V.139) 'between Narog and Taiglin'. In later work on the *Narn* my father wrote in one of a series of narrative-outlines:

They contact the Orc-host which is greater than they knew (in spite of Túrin's boasted scouts). Also none but Túrin could withstand the approach of Glaurung. They were driven back and pressed by the Orcs into the Field of Tumhalad between Ginglith and Narog and there penned. There all the pride and host of Nargothrond withered away. Orodreth was slain in the forefront of battle, and Gwindor wounded to death. Then Túrin came to him and all fled him, and he lifted Gwindor and bore him out of battle and [*several words illegible*] he swam the Narog and bore Gwindor to [?a wood] of trees. But Glaurung went down east of Narog and hastened [?on ?in] to Nargothrond with a great number of Orcs.

This is, I believe, the only statement that the site of the battle was between Ginglith and Narog; but my father pencilled in the name *Tumhalad* between those rivers, towards their confluence, on the map (p. 182, square E 5). In GA Túrin's escape with Gwindor 'to a wood' is mentioned, but not his swimming of the Narog. This is a curious detail: presumably he swam the Narog to escape from the battle, and then went down the east bank of the river to the Bridge of Nargothrond.

But it is hard to know what to make of this late conception of the site of Tumhalad. It would seem that my father now conceived Glaurung and the Orc-host to have come south from Ivrin on the west side of Narog; but the text states that they 'went down east of Narog' to Nargothrond, and therefore they also must have crossed the river – by swimming, as Túrin had done? In the published *Silmarillion* (pp. 212–13) I was probably mistaken to follow this very hastily written and puzzling text, and on the map accompanying the book to mark the site of Tumhalad in accordance with it. But in any case I feel sure that the original site, in the plain east of Narog, was still present in GA.

With regard to the pencilled note 'Túrin in the battle wore the Dragon-helm', the Helm was last mentioned in these marginal notes on the subject when Beleg carried it with him from Menegroth on the journey in search of Túrin which led to his death (see §266 and commentary). My father must have supposed therefore that Gwindor and Túrin carried it with them to Nargothrond. This raises the obvious difficulty that the Helm would at once have revealed the identity of Túrin; but in *Unfinished Tales* (pp. 154–5) I have referred to an isolated piece of writing among the *Narn* material which 'tells that in Nargothrond Túrin would not wear the Helm again "lest it reveal him", but that he wore it when he went to the Battle of Tumhalad.' The passage in question reads:

> Beleg searching the orc-camp [in Taur-nu-Fuin] finds the dragon-helm – or was it set on Túrin's head in mockery by the Orcs that tormented him? Thus it was borne away to Nargothrond; but Túrin would not wear it again, lest it reveal him, until the Battle of Dalath Dirnen.

(*Dalath Dirnen*, the Guarded Plain, was the earlier form; the name was so spelt when entered on the map, but changed subsequently as in the texts to *Talath Dirnen* (p. 186, §17).)

§276   Against the first line of this paragraph my father wrote a date: 'Oct.13'; against the first line of §278 he wrote 'Oct.25'; and against the first line of §288 he wrote 'Nov.1'. These very uncharacteristic additions must refer to the actual days of his writing, in (as I presume) 1951.

In AB 2 all that is said here is that 'Gwindor died, and refused the succour of Túrin.' The same was said in Q (IV.126), and also that he died reproaching Túrin: as I noted (IV.184), 'the impression is given that the reproaches of Flinding (Gwindor) as he died were on account of Finduilas. There is indeed no suggestion here that Túrin's policy of open war was opposed in Nargothrond'. Here in GA appears the motive that Gwindor held his death and the ruin of Nargothrond against Túrin – or more accurately, reappears, since it is clearly present in the old *Tale of Turambar* (II.83–4). Gwindor's words in GA concerning Túrin and Finduilas are altogether different from those given to him in Q, and there now appears the idea of the supreme importance to Túrin of his choice concerning Finduilas: but this is again a reappearance, from the *Tale*, where his choice is explicitly condemned (II.87).

§277   It is a new element in the narrative that it was Túrin's rescue of Gwindor that allowed Glaurung and his host to reach Nargothrond before he did.

This is a convenient place to describe a text whose relation to the *Grey Annals* is very curious. The text itself has been given in *Unfinished Tales*, pp. 159–62: the story of the coming of the Noldorin Elves Gelmir and Arminas to Nargothrond to warn Orodreth of its peril, and their harsh reception by Túrin. There is both a manuscript (based on a very rough draft outline written on a slip) and a typescript, with carbon copy, made by my father on the typewriter that he seems to have used first about the end of 1958 (see X.300). The manuscript has no title or heading, but begins (as also does the rough draft and the typescript) with the date '495'. The top copy of the typescript has a heading added in manuscript: 'Insertion for the longer form of the *Narn*', while the carbon copy has the heading, also added in manuscript, 'Insertion to *Grey Annals*', but this was changed to the reading of the top copy.

The curious thing is that while the manuscript has no 'annalistic' quality apart from the date 495, the typescript begins with the annalistic word 'Here' (a usage derived from the *Anglo-Saxon Chronicle*):

> Here Morgoth assailed Nargothrond. Túrin now commanded all the forces of Nargothrond, and ruled all matters of war. In the spring there came two Elves, and they named themselves Gelmir and Arminas ...

Moreover, while the manuscript extends no further than the text printed in *Unfinished Tales*, ending with the words 'For so much at least of the words of Ulmo were read aright', the typescript does not end there but continues:

> Here Handir of Brethil was slain in the spring, soon after the departure of the messengers. For the Orcs invaded his land, seeking to secure the crossings of Taiglin for their further advance; and Handir gave them battle, but the Men of Brethil were worsted and were driven back into their woods. The Orcs did not pursue them, for they had achieved their purpose for that time; and they continued to muster their strength in the passes of Sirion.
>
> Late in the year, having [*struck out:* gathered his strength and] completed his design, Morgoth at last loosed his assault upon Nargothrond. Glaurung the Urulókë passed over the Anfauglith,

[§277]

and came thence into the north vales of Sirion, and there did great evil; and he came at length under the shadow of Eryd Wethian [*sic*], leading the great army of the Orcs in his train . . .

The text then continues, almost exactly as in the *Grey Annals* §§275–6, concluding with Gwindor's words at the end of §276: 'If thou fail her, it shall not fail to find thee. Farewell!' The only significant difference from the text in the *Annals* is the statement that at the battle of Tum-halad 'Túrin put on the Dragon-helm of Hador'; this however had been said in a marginal note to GA §275.

This is very puzzling. So far as the content of the original manuscript of 'Gelmir and Arminas' is concerned, there seems nothing against the supposition that my father wrote it as an insertion to the *Grey Annals*, and indeed in appearance and style of script it could derive from the time when he was working on them, before the publication of *The Lord of the Rings*. The puzzle lies in my father's motive for making, years later, a typescript of the text and *adding to it* material taken directly from the *Grey Annals*, specifically reinforcing the place of 'Gelmir and Arminas' in the annalistic context – together with his uncertainty, shown in the headings to the carbon copy, as to what its place actually was to be. Subsequently, indeed, he bracketed on the typescript the date and opening words '495   Here Morgoth assailed Nargothrond', and struck out the words 'Here' and 'in the spring' at the beginning of the passage cited above, thus removing the obviously annalistic features; but the conclusion seems inescapable that when he made the typescript he could still conceive of the *Annals* as an ingredient in the recorded tradition of the Elder Days. (A curious relation is seen between a continuation of the *Annals* made after the main manuscript had been interrupted and the opening of the late work *The Wanderings of Hurin*: see pp. 251–4, 258–60.)

It should be mentioned that certain names in the text of 'Gelmir and Arminas' as printed in *Unfinished Tales* were editorial alterations made for the sake of consistency: in both manuscript and typescript Gelmir refers to Orodreth as 'Finrod's son', changed to 'Finarfin's son'; *Iarwaeth* was changed to *Agarwaen* (the later name found in the *Narn* papers); and *Eledhwen* was retained from the manuscript (*Eleðwen*) for the typescript *Eðelwen* (the form used in *The Wanderings of Húrin*).

§§278–85   This passage describing the fateful encounter of Túrin and Glaurung very greatly develops the bare narrative in Q (IV.126–7), but for the most part it is not at odds in essentials with the old version, and in places echoes it. On the other hand there is an important difference in the central motive. In Q (IV.126) the dragon offered him his freedom either 'to rescue his "stolen love" Finduilas, or to do his duty and go to the rescue of his mother and sister ... But he must swear to abandon one or the other. Then Túrin in anguish and in doubt forsook Finduilas against his heart ...' In the story in the *Grey Annals*, on the other hand, Túrin had no choice: his will was under Glaurung's when Finduilas was taken away, and he was physically incapable of movement. The Dragon does indeed say at the end: 'And if thou tarry for Finduilas, then never shalt thou see Morwen or Niënor again; and they will curse thee'; but this is a warning, not the offering of a choice. In all this Glaurung appears as a torturer, with complete power over his victim so long as he chooses to exert it, morally superior and superior in knowledge, his pitiless corruption able to assume an air almost of benevolence, of knowing what is best: 'Then Túrin ... as were he treating with a foe that could know pity, believed the words of Glaurung'.

§280   The further pencilled note here on the subject of the Dragon-helm, observing that while Túrin wore it he was proof against Glaurung's eyes, can be somewhat amplified. I have given at the end of the commentary on §275 a note on the recovery of the Dragon-helm when Túrin was rescued from the Orcs in Taur-nu-Fuin, whence it came to Nargothrond. That note continues with an account of the meeting of Túrin with Glaurung before the Doors of Felagund (see *Unfinished Tales* p. 155). Here it is said that Glaurung desired to rid Túrin of the aid and protection of the Dragon-helm, and taunted him, saying that he had not the courage to look him in the face.

> And indeed so great was the terror of the Dragon that Túrin dared not look straight upon his eye, but had kept the visor of his helmet down, shielding his face, and in his parley had looked no higher than Glaurung's feet. But being thus taunted, in pride and rashness he thrust up the visor and looked Glaurung in the eye.

At the head of the page my father noted that something should be said about the visor, 'how it protected the eyes from all darts (and from dragon-eyes)'.

This text, or rather the idea that it contains, is obviously behind the note in GA, and the last words of that note 'Then the Worm perceiving this' would no doubt have introduced some phrase to the effect that Glaurung taunted Túrin with cowardice in order to get him to remove it (cf. the note in the margin at §284 – which is scarcely in the right place). A further statement on the subject of the visor of the Helm is found in the *Narn* (*Unfinished Tales* p. 75, an expansion of the passage in QS Chapter 17, V.319): 'It had a visor (after the manner of those that the Dwarves used in their forges for the shielding of their eyes), and the face of one that wore it struck fear into the hearts of all beholders, but was itself guarded from dart and fire.' It is said here that the Helm was originally made for Azaghâl Lord of Belegost, and the history of how it came to Húrin is told.

In the published *Silmarillion* (p. 210) I adopted a passage from another text in the vast assemblage of the *Narn* papers, telling how Túrin found in the armouries of Nargothrond 'a dwarf-mask all gilded', and wore it into battle. It seems probable that this story arose at a stage when my father was treating the Dragon-helm as lost and out of the story (from the end of Dor-Cúarthol, the Land of Bow and Helm, when Túrin was taken by the Orcs), and I extended Túrin's wearing of it to the battle of Tumhalad (p. 212).

§§287 ff.   From the Battle of Tumhalad to the end of the tale of Túrin the text of the *Grey Annals* was virtually the sole source of the latter part of Chapter 21 'Of Túrin Turambar' in the published *Silmarillion* (pp. 213–26). There now enters an element in the history, however, of which I was unaware, or more accurately misinterpreted, when I prepared the text of the *Narn* for publication in *Unfinished Tales*, and which must be made clear. At that time I was under the impression that the last part of the *Narn* (from the beginning of the section entitled *The Return of Túrin to Dor-lómin* to the end, *Unfinished Tales* pp. 104–46) was a relatively late text, belonging with all the other *Narn* material that (in terms of the narrative) precedes it; and I assumed that the story in the *Grey Annals* (to which the last part of the *Narn* is obviously closely related, despite its much greater length) preceded it by some years – that it was in fact an *elaboration* of the story in the *Annals*.

This view is wholly erroneous, and was due to my failure to study sufficiently closely the material (preserved in a different place) that preceded the final text of the story in the *Narn*. In fact, it soon becomes plain (as will be seen in the commentary that follows) that the long narrative in the *Grey Annals* was *based directly on* the final text of that in the *Narn*, and was a *reduction* of that text, congruent with it at virtually all points. The manuscript of this latter is very similar in appearance and style of script to that of the *Annals of Aman* and the *Grey Annals*, and undoubtedly belongs to the same period (presumptively 1951). Thus the massive development and enhancement of the final tragedy in Brethil is yet another major work of the prolific time that followed the completion of *The Lord of the Rings* (see *Morgoth's Ring*, pp. vii and 3).

The manuscript was headed (later) 'The Children of Húrin: last part', and at the top of the first page my father wrote 'Part of the "Children of Húrin" told in full scale'. I shall devote a good deal of the following commentary to showing how, in more important instances, my father developed the narrative in the *Narn*. It is to be remembered that the last version he had written was the very compressed story in the *Quenta* (Q) of 1930 (IV.127–30), behind which lay 'the earliest Silmarillion' or 'Sketch of the Mythology' (IV.30–1), and behind that the old *Tale of Turambar and the Foalókë* (II.88–112).

I shall not make a detailed comparison of the new narrative with the older forms, nor of the last part of the *Narn* with the *Grey Annals*. Since it is obviously out of the question to reprint the last part of the *Narn* in this book, I must refer to the text in *Unfinished Tales*, which is very close to the final form of the text in the manuscript, but introduces some unimportant changes in wording; the use of 'you' for 'thou' and 'thee' of the original; and some later forms of names. In order to avoid ambiguity I shall identify the last part of the *Narn* by the letters 'NE' (i.e. 'End of the *Narn*'); thus 'NE p. 132' is to be understood as meaning the text of the *Narn* in *Unfinished Tales* on p. 132. Where necessary I distinguish the actual manuscript, or manuscripts, from the printed text. There is also a later amanuensis typescript of NE.

§290 The addition concerning the death of Handir of Brethil, rejected here, reappears at the beginning of the annal for 495 (§275).

§291 The names *Amon Obel* and *Ephel Brandir* now first appear; they were marked in on the second map (see the redrawing on p. 182, square E 7). On the emendation concerning Handir of Brethil see §275 and commentary.

§292 The opening of NE (p. 104) is almost the same as that of the rewritten section in GA, rather than its original form (§287). This is to be explained, I think, on the supposition that my father was working (here at any rate) on the two versions at the same time. – In both texts 'eighty leagues' was changed to 'forty leagues'; the distance on the second map from Nargothrond to Ivrin measured in a straight line is 8 cm. or 41·6 leagues (see V.412).

§293 Against *Dorlómin* my father wrote in the margin the Quenya form *Lóminórë*, but he did not strike out *Dorlómin*.

§294 It is made clear in the later text from which the section *The Departure of Túrin* in the *Narn* is derived that Brodda forcibly wedded Húrin's kinswoman Aerin (later form for Airin) before Túrin left Dor-lómin (see *Unfinished Tales* p. 69); in GA Túrin only learns of it now, on his return, and this was certainly the case also in NE. Airin now becomes Húrin's kinswoman, not Morwen's, as she was in Q and QS, and still in the rejected form (§288) of the present passage.

It is seen from NE (p. 106) that the story of Túrin's childhood friendship with the lame Sador Labadal was already in being, although it had not yet been written (the parts of the *Narn* narrative preceding NE being unquestionably later); in GA there is no suggestion of this story, but I think it certain that this is due merely to the extreme condensation of the narrative here: the long conversation in NE between Túrin and Sador, and Sador's 'recognition', before ever Túrin entered Brodda's hall, is reduced to a few lines in the *Annals*. In that conversation and subsequently the text of

NE uses 'thou' and 'thee' throughout, but afterwards my father sometimes changed them to 'you' and sometimes not. It seems possible that where the changes were made it was because the speakers were using the 'polite plural' (as Sador to Túrin when he found out who he was); but in the published text I adopted 'you' throughout. – Where in NE (p. 105) Sador speaks of 'Húrin Galdor's son' the manuscript has 'Húrin Galion's son', *Galion* being still at that time the name of Húrin's father.

§§295–7   The whole episode in NE (pp. 106–9) following Túrin's entry into Brodda's hall, a massive development of the bare words of Q (IV.127 and note 9), is again greatly reduced in these paragraphs, and much is omitted: thus there is no mention of the general fighting, of Airin's firing of the hall, or of Asgon, the man of Dor-lómin (who will reappear).

§298   This annal concerning Tuor, dated 496, follows on from the entry about his departure from Mithrim at the end of the annal for 495 in the rejected section of the manuscript (§290). It is based on that in AB 2 (V.140), and adheres still to the old story that Tuor met Bronwë (Voronwë) at the mouths of Sirion; thus it was written before the addition was made to §257 whereby Voronwë became the sole survivor of the seven ships sent into the West and was cast ashore in Nivrost (see the commentary on that paragraph).

§299   Tuor was born in 472 (§251), was enslaved by Lorgan in 488 when he was sixteen years old and endured thraldom for three years, thus until 491 (§263), and in 495 had lived as an outlaw in the hills of Mithrim for four years.

This annal replaces both the preceding entries concerning Tuor (§§290, 298). Here the very old story of Tuor's going down to the mouths of Sirion is at last abandoned, and Ulmo appears to Tuor in Nivrost; Voronwë, cast ashore in Nivrost, now leads Tuor eastwards to Gondolin along the southern faces of the Shadowy Mountains. Here also appears the story that they saw Túrin at Ivrin on his journey northward from Nargothrond, and it may well be that this accounts for the change of date from 496 to 495; but the coming of Tuor to Turgon's ancient dwelling of Vinyamar and finding the arms left there long before at Ulmo's counsel is not referred to.

For the bidding of Ulmo to Turgon in Q, where it appears in two versions, see IV.142, 146–7, and my remarks IV.193–4. In GA there is no suggestion of Ulmo's counsel that Turgon should prepare for a great war against Morgoth and that Tuor should be his agent in the bringing of new nations of Men out of the East to his banners.

Elsewhere in GA the change is always *Glindûr* > *Maeglin*; *Meglin* > *Glindûr* here depends on the time of writing, for while my father was working on the *Annals* the series went *Meglin* > *Glindûr* > *Maeglin*.

§300   The manuscript has no date here, but it is clear that there should be (it is obviously 496 later in the annal, where 'with the beginning of spring Túrin cast off his darkness', §303); in the rejected version of the text the date 496 is given at this point (§291), and in the manuscript of NE also. The omission is due to the (second) rejected entry concerning Tuor (§298) having been dated 496.

The spelling *Taiglin* is found in NE also; *Teiglin* in both the published texts is an editorial alteration to a later form (see pp. 228, 309–10).

The story of Túrin's rescue of the men of Brethil from an attack by Orcs, derived from the lively account of the incident in NE (p. 110), is a new element in the narrative. It is to be noted, however, that as NE was first written there was no mention of it; the original text tells simply that when Túrin fell in with some of the folk of Haleth in Brethil

... the men that saw Túrin welcomed him, and even thus as a wild wanderer they knew him for the Mormegil, the great captain of Nargothrond, and the friend of Handir; and they marvelled that he had escaped, since they had heard that none had come out alive from the fortress of Felagund. Therefore they bade him come and rest among them for a while.

Following this is a brief preliminary passage in which Túrin's rescue of the men of Brethil from the Orc-attack is introduced, and finally the full account of the incident as it stands in NE. It is thus clearly seen that this story arose in the course of the writing of NE, as also did the motive that the woodmen *deduced* that the stranger was the Mormegil after Túrin had fallen into his swoon of grief. Both these elements are present in the GA version. This is one of many unquestionable evidences that the last part of the *Narn* preceded the *Grey Annals*.

It is also said in the rejected passage of NE that when Túrin told the woodmen of his quest for Finduilas

... they looked on him with grief and pity. 'Seek no more!' said one. 'For behold! the few of our men that escaped from Tum-halad brought us warning of an Orc-host that came from Nargothrond towards the crossings of Taiglin, marching slowly because of the number of their captives. ...'

In the final text the statement that the woodmen fought at Tumhalad disappears (and Dorlas says of their ambush of the Orc-host from Nargothrond 'we thought to deal our small stroke in the war', NE p. 111). This is to be related to the information in GA which was struck out, that the Elves of Nargothrond 'allied themselves with Handir' (§272 and commentary), and that Handir was slain at Tumhalad (§275 and commentary).

§§301–3   The narrative (condensed from that of NE, pp. 109–12)

greatly expands that of Q (IV.127): new elements are 'Wildman of the Woods', Dorlas, and the Hauð-en-Ellas where Finduilas was laid near the Crossings of Taiglin, which have not been named before; Dorlas' realisation that the stranger must be the Mormegil, rumoured to be Túrin son of Húrin (in Q there is no indication that the woodmen knew who he was until the end); Brandir's foreboding when he saw Túrin on the bier, and his healing of Túrin; Túrin's setting aside of the black sword. The old story in Q (IV.129) that Túrin became lord of the woodmen is now abandoned: Brandir, as will be seen later in the narrative (§323, NE p. 132), remained the titular ruler (and in NE, p. 129, at the council held before Túrin's setting out for the encounter with Glaurung, he 'sat indeed in the high-seat of the lord of the assembly, but unheeded').

§301   *Hauð-en-Ellas*: the later form *-Elleth* was pencilled in on both the NE and GA manuscripts, and *Haudh-en-Elleth* is found in a plot-sequence among the later *Narn* papers (p. 256); this was adopted in both NE and *The Silmarillion*. The translation 'Mound of the Elf-maid', not in GA, was introduced into *The Silmarillion* from NE (p. 112), and comparison of the texts will show a number of other instances, not recorded here, of this conflation.

§302   Against the name *Ephel Brandir* in NE (p. 110) my father wrote faintly on the amanuensis typescript that was made from the manuscript: *Obel Halad* and '.... of the chieftain'; the illegible word might be 'Tower', but looks more like 'Town'. 'Town of the Chieftain' is quite possibly the correct interpretation, if *town* is used in the ancient sense of 'enclosed dwelling-place' (see II.292, and my remarks on the name *Tavrobel* in V.412). On *Obel Halad* see pp. 258, 263.

§303   In GA Brandir's foreboding concerning Turambar came upon him after he had heard 'the tidings that Dorlas brought', and therefore knew who it was that lay on the bier; whereas in NE (p. 111) his foreboding is more prophetic and less 'rational' (see *Unfinished Tales* p. 111 and note 21). In NE Turambar 'laid his black sword by' in response to Brandir's warning (p. 112), but this is lost in GA.

§305   The new narrative is here further developed from Q (IV.128), where 'Thingol yielded so far to the tears and entreaties of Morwen that he sent forth a company of Elves toward Nargothrond to explore the truth. With them rode Morwen ...'; now she rides forth alone and the Elves are sent after her. Niënor's motive in joining the Elvish riders in disguise is now more complex; and Mablung, entirely absent from the story in Q (and AB 2), enters the narrative.

There is a very great reduction in GA of the elaborate story told in NE (pp. 112–16), but the narrative structure is the same (the flight of Morwen followed by the company led by Mablung). In NE

Thingol already had the idea of sending out a party to Nargothrond, independently of Morwen's wish to go.

In Q it seems certain that Niënor's presence was never revealed to
the company, including Morwen (see my remarks, IV.185). The
discovery of her at the passage of the Twilit Meres is not mentioned
in GA, but that she was at some point revealed is implied by the
words 'But Morwen ... would not be persuaded' (i.e. by the presence
of Niënor); and Niënor was set with Morwen on the Hill of Spies.
The condensation in the *Annals* of the story in NE here produces
some obscurity, and in the passage in *The Silmarillion* (p. 217)
corresponding to this paragraph I made use of both versions (and
also Q), although at the time I misunderstood the relations between
them.

The reference in NE (p. 114) to the hidden ferries at the Twilit
Meres, not mentioned before, is lost in GA. In NE the sentence 'for
by that way messengers would pass to and fro between Thingol and
his kin in Nargothrond' continues in the manuscript 'ere the victory
of Morgoth' (i.e. at Tumhalad), and these last words were changed
to 'ere the death of Felagund'. This was omitted in the published
text, in view of the later reference (*Unfinished Tales* p. 153) to
the close relations of Orodreth with Menegroth: 'In all things
[Orodreth] followed Thingol, with whom he exchanged messengers by secret ways'.

There appears here (in both versions) the Elvish name *Amon
Ethir* of the Hill of Spies (the Spyhill, NE), and also (in NE only) its
origin, which has never been given before: 'a mound as great as a
hill that long ago Felagund had caused to be raised with great
labour in the plain before his Doors'. In both versions it is a league
from Nargothrond; in Q (IV.128) it was 'to the east of the Guarded
Plain', but Morwen could see from its top the issuing of Glaurung.
On the first map (following p. 220 in Vol.IV) it seems to be a long
way east, or north-east, of Nargothrond (though 'Hill of Spies' is
named on the map it is not perfectly clear where it is, IV.225); on the
second map it is not named, but if it is the eminence marked on
square F 6 (p. 182) it was likewise a long way from Nargothrond
(about 15 leagues).

§306 'But Glaurung was aware of all that they did': where NE
(p. 117) says of Glaurung that his eyes 'outreached the far sight of
the Elves' a rejected form of the passage has the notable statement:
'Indeed further reached the sight of his fell eyes than even the eyes of
the Elves (which thrice surpass those of Men).' Also, where it is said
in NE that Glaurung 'went swiftly, for he was a mighty Worm, and
yet lithe', there followed in the manuscript, but placed in brackets
later, 'and he could go as speedily as a man could run, and tire not in
a hundred leagues.'

§307 'Thus the ladies were lost, and of Morwen indeed no sure tidings came ever to Doriath after': so also in NE at a later point (p. 121): 'Neither then nor after did any certain news of her fate come to Doriath or to Dor-lómin', but against this my father wrote an X in the margin of the typescript. In NE the passage (p. 118) describing how one of the Elf-riders saw her as she disappeared into the mists crying *Niënor* replaced the following:

> After a while Morwen passed suddenly out of the mists, and near at hand there were two of the elf-riders; and whether she would or no her horse bore her with them swiftly away towards Doriath. And the riders comforted her, saying: 'You must go in our keeping. But others will guard your daughter. It is vain to tarry. Fear not! For she was mounted, and there is no horse but will make best speed away from the dragon-stench. We shall meet her in Doriath.'

This is another example of the precedence of NE as first written over GA; for this rejected text was apparently following the old story of Q (IV.128), that Morwen returned to Doriath. – In Q Niënor, whose presence was never revealed (see commentary on §305), did not go to the Hill of Spies with Morwen, but met with the Dragon on the banks of the Narog.

In the passage in NE (p. 118) describing the eyes of Glaurung when Niënor came face to face with him on the hill-top, the words 'they were terrible, being filled with the fell spirit of Morgoth, his master' contain an editorial alteration: the manuscript reads 'the fell spirit of Morgoth, who made him' (cf. IV.128). My father underlined the last three words in pencil, and faintly and barely legibly at the foot of the page he noted: 'Glaurung must be a demon [??contained in worm form].' On the emergence at this time of the view that Melkor could make nothing that had life of its own see X.74, 78.

§§309–12 There is a further great development in this passage (condensed from NE, pp. 119–21), following the enspelling of Niënor. There enters now Mablung's exploration of the deserted halls of Nargothrond; his discovery of Niënor on Amon Ethir in the early night; the meeting with the three other Elves of Mablung's company; the secret entrance into Doriath near the inflowing of Esgalduin; the attack by Orcs as they slept, and the slaying of the Orcs by Mablung and his companions; the flight of Niënor naked; and Mablung's return to Doriath and subsequent three-year-long search for Morwen and Niënor. In Q there is none of this; and it was Turambar with a party of the woodmen who slew the Orcs that pursued Niënor (IV.128–9).

§310 Where GA has 'the secret gate' into Doriath near the inflowing of Esgalduin into Sirion, NE (p. 120) has 'the guarded bridge'. A bridge is indeed more to be expected than a gate, for the West-march of Doriath, *Nivrim*, was within the Girdle of Melian (V.261–2).

§312 Similarly in the manuscript of NE, after 'until she went naked' (p. 121), the words 'but for the short elven-kirtle above the knee that she had worn in her disguise' were bracketed for exclusion.

§317 *The falls of Celebros.* In NE the passage beginning 'In the morning they bore Níniel towards Ephel Brandir' (pp. 122–3) replaced an earlier text, as follows:

In the morning they bore Níniel towards Ephel Brandir. Now there was a fair place on the way, a green sward amid white birches. There a stream leaping down from Amon Obel to find its way to the Taiglin went over a lip of worn stone, and fell into a rocky bowl far below, and all the air was filled with a soft spray, in which the sun would gleam with many colours. Therefore the woodmen called those falls *Celebros*, and loved to rest there a while.

The name *Celebros* first appeared in Q, 'the Falls of Silver-bowl' > 'the Falls of Celebros, Foam-silver', and the falls were in the Taiglin (see IV.129 and note 14). In GA the falls are still called *Celebros*, as in the passage just cited from NE from which it derives, but as in that passage my father would obviously have now placed them in the tributary stream falling down from Amon Obel towards the Taiglin.

In the NE manuscript, however, the passage was rewritten, and it is the rewritten text that stands in *Unfinished Tales* pp. 122–3: 'In the morning they bore Níniel towards Ephel Brandir, and the road went steeply upward towards Amon Obel until it came to a place where it must cross the tumbling stream of Celebros', &c. Thus *Celebros* becomes the name of the tributary stream, and in the continuation of this rewritten passage the falls themselves become *Dimrost*, the Rainy Stair. This change was not entered on the text of GA, but was incorporated in *The Silmarillion* (p. 220).

On the curious matter of the use in both versions of the name *Nen Girith* 'Shuddering Water' as if it were due to the fact of Níniel's fit of shuddering when she first came there, rather than to the prophetic nature of that shuddering whose meaning was not seen until she and Turambar were dead, see IV.186–7, where I discussed it fully.

§318 In Q (IV.129) it was said here that Brandir yielded the rule of the woodmen to Turambar (see commentary on §§301–3), and that 'he was ever true to Turambar; yet bitter was his soul when he might not win the love of Níniel.' This is not said in GA (or NE); but on the other hand there was nothing in Q about Níniel's delaying of the marriage, nor of Brandir's seeking to restrain her on account of his forebodings, nor yet of Brandir's revealing to her who Turambar was – indeed in Q, as I have mentioned (commentary on §§301–3), there is no indication that the woodmen knew his identity.

In NE, following the story in Q, the first draft of the passage begins: 'Turambar asked her in marriage, and she went to him gladly, and at the midsummer they were wed, and the woodmen made a great feast for them' (see NE pp. 124–5). In a second stage Brandir counselled Níniel to wait, but did not tell her that Turambar was Túrin son of Húrin: that entered with a further revision to the manuscript. GA has this final form. In NE (p. 125), however, Turambar's displeasure with Brandir was at his counsel of delay: in GA it was (apparently) at Brandir's revelation to Níniel of his identity. – The motive of Níniel's delaying of the marriage goes back to the *Tale* (II.102): 'she delayed him, saying nor yea nor no, yet herself she knew not why'.

§§322–5 Following the words in NE (p. 129) 'the tale of the scouts that had seen [Glaurung] had gone about and grown in the telling' the text as originally written continued:

Then Brandir who stood [before his house in the open place of Ephel Brandir >] nigh spoke before them and said: 'I would fain come with thee, Captain Black Sword, but thou wouldst scorn me. Rightly. But

This was changed immediately to the text printed, with Dorlas' crying scorn on Brandir, who sat 'unheeded', 'in the high-seat of the lord of the assembly'.

Up to this point, drafting for the manuscript of NE consists of little more than scribbled slips. From here on, however, there are in effect two manuscripts: one (which I shall refer to as 'the draft manuscript') being the continuation of the original, which became so chaotic with rewriting that my father subsequently copied it out fair. The draft manuscript in this part of the narrative has much interest as showing my father's development of the story from the form it had reached in Q (IV.129–30).

The words given in NE to Brandir's kinsman Hunthor (Torbarth in GA) were given first to Brandir, speaking in self-defence:

'Thou speakest unjustly, Dorlas. How can it be said that my counsels were vain, when they were never taken? And I say to thee that Glaurung comes now to us, as to Nargothrond before, because our deeds have bewrayed us to him, as I feared. But the son of Handir asketh none to take his place at need. I am here and will gladly go. The less loss of a cripple unwedded than of many others. Will not some stand by me, who have also less care to leave behind?'

Then five men came and stood by him. And Turambar said: 'That is enough. These five I will take. But, lord, I do not scorn thee, and any who do so are fools. But see! We must go in great haste ...'

[§§322-5]

This follows, in structure, the story in Q, where 'six of his boldest men begged to come with him'. In the draft manuscript 'Turambar with Dorlas and their five companions took horse and rode away in haste to Celebros'; and when later Turambar crossed the Taiglin (NE p. 133), 'in the deep dark he counted his following. They were four. "Albarth fell," said Dorlas, "and Taiglin took him beyond aid. The other two, I deem, were daunted, and skulk now yonder."' Albarth, who here first appears, seems to have been first written *Albard*.

The draft manuscript continues:

Then after a rest they that remained climbed, foot by foot, up the steep slope before them, till they came nigh the brink. There so foul grew the reek that their heads reeled, and they clung to the trees as best they could. The night was now passing, but there was a flicker above them as of smouldering fires, and a noise of some great beast sleeping; but if he stirred the earth quivered.

Dawn came slowly; and its glimmer came to Turambar as he strove with dark dreams of dread in which all his will had been given only to clinging and holding, while a great tide of blackness had sucked and gnawed at his limbs. And he woke and looked about in the wan light, and saw that only Dorlas remained by him.

'Seven wounds I hoped to give him,' he thought. 'Well, if it be two only, then they must go deep.'

But when day came indeed all passed as Turambar had hoped. For suddenly Glaurung bestirred himself, and drew himself slowly to the chasm's edge; and he did not turn aside, but prepared to spring over with his clawed forelegs and then draw his bulk after. Great was the horror of his coming, for he began the passage not right above Turambar, but many paces to the northward, and from under they could see his hideous head and gaping jaws as he peered over the brink. Then he let fly a blast, and the trees before him withered, and rocks fell into the river, and with that he cast himself forward and grappled the further bank and began to heave himself over the narrow chasm.

Now there was need of great haste, for though Turambar and Dorlas had escaped from the blast since they lay not right in Glaurung's path, they could not now come at him, and soon all the device of Turambar was in point to fail utterly. Heedless now of all else he clambered down, and Dorlas followed him. Then swiftly he came beneath the Worm; but there so deadly was the heat and the stench that he tottered and was almost blinded. And Dorlas because of the reek, or being daunted at last, clung to a tree by the water, and would not move   fell and lay as in a swoon [*sic; the sentence changed to:*] But Dorlas was overcome, and his

[§§322-5]

will daunted at last, and he stumbled and fell and was engulfed in the water.

Then Turambar said aloud: 'Now thou art alone at the end, Master of Doom. Fail now or conquer!' And he summoned to him all his will, and all his hatred of the Worm and his Master, and climbed up, as one finding strength and skill beyond his measure; and lo! now the midmost parts of the dragon came above him . . .

I repeat here my remarks in IV.186:

In the *Tale* (II.106) the band of seven clambered up the far side of the ravine in the evening and stayed there all night; at dawn of the second day, when the dragon moved to cross, Turambar saw that he had now only three companions, and when they had to climb back down to the stream-bed to come up under Glórund's belly these three had not the courage to go up again. Turambar slew the dragon by daylight . . . In Q the six all deserted Turambar during the first night . . . but he spent the whole of the following day clinging to the cliff; Glómund moved to pass over the ravine on the *second* night (my father clearly wished to make the dragon-slaying take place in darkness, but achieved this at first by extending the time Turambar spent in the gorge).

Curiously enough, in the text just given my father reverted, so far as the time-scale is concerned, to the story in the *Tale*, where Turambar spent the whole night in the ravine and the dragon moved to cross at the beginning of the next day (see further the commentary on §§329–32).

In the condensed account in Q nothing is said of the need to move along the river and then to climb up again to come under the dragon's belly ('The next evening . . . Glómund began the passage of the ravine, and his huge form *passed over Turambar's head*'); and here also it seems certain that my father went back to the *Tale*, where this is described in a way very similar to that in the draft manuscript of NE. In the *Tale* as in this draft there is no suggestion that the men had taken into account the possibility that the dragon might not cross at the point they had chosen (and therefore, in the final version, after attempting to climb they returned – as it must be assumed: it is not expressly stated – to the bottom of the ravine and waited); in both, they climbed up the far side of the gorge and clung beneath its brink, whence they had to climb down again to the water when the dragon moved. Dorlas' failure 'because of the reek' when he and Turambar came, in the riverbed, beneath the dragon corresponds to the failure of the three men in the *Tale*, who 'durst not climb the bank again' because 'the heat was so great and so vile the stench' (II.107).

[§§322–5]

The behaviour of Turambar's companions in the different versions can be set out thus:

The Tale

Three deserted during the night

The three others climbed down with Turambar to get beneath the dragon, but dared not climb up again

The Quenta

All six deserted during the (first) night (nothing is said of the need to change position)

Draft manuscript of NE

Two feared to cross the river and one (Albarth) was drowned in the crossing

Two more fled away during the night

The last (Dorlas) climbed down with Turambar to get beneath the dragon, but dared not climb up again

The revised and final story (NE pp. 133–4) is far better (and of course the version in GA, though very brief, is in agreement with it). By this time the passage in which Brandir defends himself against Dorlas (p. 152) had been emended to the final form (NE p. 129), except that Albarth (at first simply one of the five volunteers, but named because he fell and was drowned in the river) had become the kinsman of Brandir who rebukes Dorlas. There are now only two companions of Turambar, and the hard and boastful warrior Dorlas becomes the coward, while Albarth is the brave man who stays beside Turambar until he is struck by a falling stone. The development is a characteristic complex:

Brandir defends himself against Dorlas' scorn	Albarth defends Brandir against Dorlas' scorn
Turambar takes six companions	Turambar takes Dorlas and Albarth only as companions
One of these, Albarth, is drowned in the crossing; four flee; only Dorlas remains by Turambar	Dorlas flees Albarth remains by Turambar
Dorlas is drowned in the river	Albarth is drowned in the river

A curious detail in the final form of the story is worth remarking. In the new account, it occurs to Turambar that they are wasting their strength in climbing up the far side of the gorge *before* the dragon moves. It is not said that they descended from whatever point they had reached when he came to this realisation, and the passage concerning his dream 'in which all his will was given to

[§§322-5]

clinging' reappears from the earlier version (p. 153). But in the new story there was no need for them to cling: they could have, and surely would have, descended to the bottom and waited there. In fact, it is clear that this is what they did: it is said (NE p. 134) that when Glaurung moved to cross the ravine they were not standing right in his path, and Turambar at once 'clambered along the water-edge'. Thus the revised story still carries an unneeded trait from the earlier.

A draft slip, not fully legible, shows my father working out the new story:

Let Túrin slay dragon at nightfall. He reaches Nen Girith as sun is going down. He warns them that Glaurung will move in *dark*. He outlines his plan. They go down to Taiglin but there the heart fails his men, and they say: 'Lord, forgive us, but our hearts are not great enough for the venture. For [*illegible words*] the thought of those we have left.'

'What of me?' said Turambar. He dismissed them with scorn.

He goes on with Dorlas and Albarth.

This is an intermediate stage: there are other 'volunteers' beside Dorlas and Albarth, but they beg off before the crossing of the river. These others were abandoned.

This may seem much ado about a single episode, but it seems to me to illustrate in miniature the complex and subtle movement that is found in the history of the legends at large. It was, also, an episode of great importance: there are few 'monsters' to rival Glaurung, and my father strove to perfect the tale of how Túrin earned the title of *Dagnir Glaurunga*.

It remains to mention that in the final manuscript of NE *Albarth* was changed to *Torbarth*, the name in GA; but at all occurrences in NE of *Torbarth* it was changed later to *Hunthor*. In GA this further alteration was not made (it was of course adopted in *The Silmarillion*), but at the first occurrence only (§322) of *Torbarth* in GA my father pencilled above it *Gwerin*: on this name see further pp. 163–5.

§323   In the *Narn* (p. 132) it is told that Níniel and the people with her came to Nen Girith 'just at nightfall', but in the draft manuscript they reached the falls 'at the first breath of morning' (see commentary on §§329–32). In the draft manuscript, also, Brandir did not limp slowly after the others on his crutch, but 'took the small ambling horse that was trained to bear him, and he rode westward after Níniel and her companions. And many that saw him go had pity, for in truth he was well beloved by many.'

§324   As in GA, *Cabad-en-Aras* was corrected throughout, except where omitted by oversight, to *Cabed-en-Aras* on the final text of NE. The draft manuscript had *Mengas Dûr*, changed to *Cabad-en-*

Aras at the time of writing. In NE (p. 130) Turambar says of the ravine that over it, 'as you tell, a deer once leaped from the huntsmen of Haleth', and later (p. 140) Brandir says that Níniel 'leaped from the brink of the Deer's Leap'.

In NE (p. 130), when Turambar came to Nen Girith at sunset, he looked out over the falls, and seeing the spires of smoke rising by the banks of the Taiglin he said to his companions that this was good news, because he had feared that Glaurung would change his course and come to the Crossings, 'and so to the old road in the lowland'. I take this to be the old south road to Nargothrond, coming down from the Pass of Sirion and running through the western eaves of Brethil on its way to the Crossings; but the draft manuscript has here 'and so along the old road to Bar Haleth', against which my father wrote later: 'into deep Brethil'. *Bar Haleth* was written in above *Tavrobel* (struck out) on the map (see p. 186, §19). Beyond the fact that 'Tavrobel' was in the extreme east of Brethil it is not possible to be sure of its site. *Bar Haleth* was in turn crossed out. It seems certain therefore that this was a transient name for Ephel Brandir, which was marked in subsequently in the centre of Brethil; and 'the old road' in the draft manuscript distinct from that referred to in the final text.

§325 In NE it is told (p. 131) that from Nen Girith Turambar and his companions took the path to the Crossings, but 'before they came so far, they turned southward by a narrow track', and moved through the woods above the Taiglin towards Cabed-en-Aras. Mr Charles Noad has suggested that my sketch-map in *Unfinished Tales*, p. 149, should be modified, and the track shown to turn again *westward* to reach the Taiglin: thus 'The first stars glimmered in the East *behind* them'. See further p. 159, §333.

'So ended the last of the right kin of Haleth': 'right kin' must mean 'direct line'. But Torbarth was not the last, for Brandir, son of Handir son of Hundor son of Haleth, still lived.

§§329-32 The narrative of these paragraphs as first written in NE had many differences from the final text (pp. 135-7, beginning 'Now the screams of Glaurung came to the people at Nen Girith ...'), and I give the earlier text (which exists in two drafts); for the time-scale see commentary on §§322-5.

Now when the screams of Glaurung came to the folk at Nen Girith they were filled with terror; and the watchers beheld from afar the great breaking and burning that the Worm made in his throes, and deemed that he was trampling and destroying all those that had assailed him. Then those that had been most eager to come and see strange deeds were most eager to go, ere Glaurung should discover them. All therefore fled, either wild into the woods, or back towards Ephel Brandir.

[§§329–32]

But when Níniel heard the voice of the Worm, her heart died within her, and a shadow of her darkness fell on her, and she sat still, shuddering by Nen Girith.

The morning passed, and still she did not stir from the spot. So it was that Brandir found her. For he came at last to the bridge, spent and weary, having limped all the long way alone on his crutch; and it was seven leagues from Ephel Brandir. Fear had urged him on. For he met with some of those that fled back, and heard all that they had to tell. 'The Black Sword is surely dead, and all with him,' they said. But when he found that Níniel was not with them, and that they had left her behind in their terror, he cursed them and pressed on to Nen Girith, thinking to defend her or comfort her.

But now that he saw her still living, he found naught to say, and had neither counsel nor comfort, and stood silent looking on her misery with pity.

Time wore on, and the sun began to wester, and there came neither sound nor tidings. Brandir looking out could see no longer any smoke by the Taiglin. And suddenly he thought in his heart: 'Beyond doubt he is slain. But Níniel lives.' And he looked at her and his heart yearned towards her, and then he was aware that it was cold in that high place; and he went and cast his cloak about her, but she said naught to him. And he stood yet a while, and he could hear no sound but the voices of the trees and the birds and the water, and he thought: 'Surely the Worm is gone, and has passed into Brethil. He will overtake the hapless folk on the way.' But he pitied them no more: fools that had flouted his counsel. Nor his people waiting in Ephel Brandir: he had forsaken them. Thither Glaurung surely would go fast, and he would have time to lead Níniel away and escape. Whither he scarce knew, for he had never strayed beyond Brethil [*first draft only:* and though he knew of the Hidden Kingdom he knew little more than that its king loved not Men, and few were ever admitted]. But time was fleeting, and soon evening would come.

Then he went again to Níniel's side, and said: 'It groweth late, Níniel. What wouldst thou do?'

'I know not,' said she. 'For I am adread. But could I overcome my shuddering, I would arise and go, and seek my lord; though I fear that he is dead.'

Then Brandir knew not what to answer; and he said: 'All is strange. Who shall read the signs? But if he lives, would he not go to Ephel Brandir, where he left thee? And the bridge of Nen Girith doth not lie on the only road, or the straightest, thither from the place of battle.'

[§§329–32]

Then Níniel was roused at last, and she stood up, crying:
'Towards tidings I came hither, and yet all tidings I miss! Hath
some spell been laid on me that I linger here?' And she began to
hasten down the path from the bridge. But Brandir called to her:
'Níniel! Go not alone. I will go with thee. Thou knowest not what
thou may find. A healer thou mayest need. But if the dragon lies
there, then beware! For the creatures of Morgoth die hard, and
are dangerous in death.'

But she heeded him not and went now as though her blood
burned her, which before had been cold. And though he followed
as he could, because of his lameness she passed away until she
was out of his sight. Then Brandir cursed his fate and his weakness, but still he held on.

Night fell and all the woods were still; and the moon rose away
beyond Amon Obel, and the glades became pale. And Níniel ran
on; but as she came down from the upland towards the river it
seemed to her that she remembered the place, and feared it.

Thus Níniel passed the whole of the day at Nen Girith (in this earlier
version she and the people with her had come there 'at the first
breath of morning', commentary on §323, and Glaurung was slain
in the morning); when Brandir perceived that it was cold and cast
his cloak about her it was the second evening, whereas in the final
story it was the night of Glaurung's death (and no long time can
elapse between his death, Brandir's coming to Nen Girith, and
Níniel's running down to Cabed-en-Aras). A further important
divergence, among many other differences of detail, is that in the
earlier all the people fled from Nen Girith, leaving Níniel alone. But
from this point the draft manuscript and the final manuscript
become closely similar.

§332   In NE (p. 136), as also at the end of the earlier version given in
the commentary on §§329–32, 'the moon rose beyond Amon Obel'.
The sketch-map in *Unfinished Tales* (p. 149) is not well oriented: as
is seen from revisions made to the second map (and so reproduced
on my map to the published *Silmarillion*), Amon Obel was almost
due east of the Crossings of Taiglin.

§333   There are two points of detail to be mentioned in the text of
NE corresponding to this paragraph. The words concerning the
track that Brandir took to head off Níniel, 'went steeply down
southward to the river' (p. 137), were an editorial change from the
reading of the manuscript, which has 'went steeply down westward'. The change was made because it is expressly said here that it
was the path that Turambar and his companions had taken earlier:
cf. p. 131 'they turned southward by a narrow track'; but Mr
Noad's clearly correct suggestion (see p. 157, §325) makes this

emendation unnecessary. Secondly, in the words of Glaurung to Níniel at his death (p. 138) 'We meet again ere the end', 'ere the end' is a simple error for 'ere we end'.

§334 '[She] ran like a hunted deer, and came to Cabed-en-Aras': the name Cabed-en-Aras referred to the actual ravine in the Taiglin, and (as I suggested in *Unfinished Tales* p. 150, note 27) it may be supposed that the death-leap of Glaurung had carried him a good distance beyond the further cliff, so that Níniel had some way to run to the ravine. The wording of NE is clearer: 'Swiftly she came to the brink of Cabed-en-Aras'.

§335 *Cabad Naeramarth*: in an earlier form of this passage in NE (p. 138) the name was *Cabad Amarth* 'Leap of Doom'. In §§335, 346 *Cabad* was not corrected.

§§336–7 In Q there was no mention of Brandir's bringing the tidings to the waiting people. This was due to Q's compression, for it appears in the *Tale* (II.110); and his words in GA (deriving from NE) 'and those tidings are good' echo those in the *Tale*: 'and that is well; aye very well': in both, those who heard him thought that he was mad.

§§339–42 Q was here exceedingly compressed, saying only: 'he asked for Níniel, but none dared tell him, save Brandir. And Brandir distraught with grief reproached him; wherefore Túrin slew him ...' The complex scene in NE and GA goes back in a very general way to the *Tale* (II.111); there also Turambar calls Tamar (Brandir) 'Clubfoot', and it is this (as it appears) that leads him to tell all that he knows, which in turn incites Turambar to murder him, believing him to be lying out of malice.

§§346–7 In the *Tale* and Q the voice from the sword does not speak of Beleg or of Brandir. In NE as first written Turambar himself named them in his address to the sword: 'From no blood wilt thou shrink. Not from Beleg slain in madness, not from Brandir slain unjustly. That was a wicked deed, thou black sword. Do now a better and take Túrin Turambar! Wilt thou slay me swiftly?' And the voice from the blade replied: 'Thy blood will I gladly drink. For it is of the best, and sweeter will it seem than any that thou hast given me. Swift will I slay thee!' – echoing the words of Gurtholfin in the *Tale*, II.112; cf. also Q, IV.130.

§349 The sword was not broken in the *Tale* or in Q. – At the top of the manuscript page my father wrote hastily in pencil: 'Túrin should slay himself on Finduilas' tomb' (cf. *Unfinished Tales* p. 150, note 28).

The conclusion of NE (p. 146) in the manuscript actually reads: 'Thus endeth the tale of the Children of Húrin [*added:*] as it was told in the *Glaer nia* [*later* > *Narn i*] *Chîn Húrin*, the longest of all the lays of Beleriand.' The conclusion added afterwards to GA is thus almost exactly the same as that in NE, which does not however have the words 'and was made by Men'; with this cf. X.373.

NOTE 1

Variant forms at the end of the tale of
the Children of Húrin

There are, first, some rough draft texts that sketch out ideas for the dénouement of the tragedy; there can be no doubt that they were all abandoned in favour of the actual ending in NE and GA. One of them, beginning as in NE p. 143 immediately after the slaying of Brandir, reads as follows:

> now cursing Middle-earth and all the life of Men, now calling upon Níniel. But when at last the madness left him, he walked still in the wild bent and haggard, and pondered all his life in his thought, and ever Níniel's image was before him. And now with opened eye he saw her, remembering his father: there in woman's form was his voice and his face and the bend of his brows, and his hair like to gold, even as Túrin had the dark hair and the grey eyes, the [?pale cheek] and [*illegible words*] of Morwen his mother of the House of Bëor. Doubt could not be. But how had it chanced? Where then was Morwen? Had they never reached the H[idden] K[ingdom]? How had they met Glaurung? But no, he dared never seek Morwen.

I believe that this was a soon abandoned idea that Túrin could come, through his own reflections, to a recognition that what Brandir had said was true. It was displaced by the story of the coming of Mablung to the Crossings of Taiglin and meeting Túrin there.

In two related passages my father entertained the idea that Túrin met Morwen before his end. The first is very brief:

> And as he sat like a beggar-man near the Crossings of Taiglin, an old woman came by bowed on a stick; ragged she was and forlorn and her grey hair blew wild in the wind. But she gave him good-day, saying: 'And good day it is, master, for the sun is warm, and then hunger gnaws less. These are evil days for our likes: for I see by your bearing that, as I and so many, you have seen prouder days. In the summer we can drag on our lives, but who dare look beyond winter?'
>
> 'Whither go you, lady?' he said, 'for so methinks you were once wont to be called.'
>
> 'Nowhither,' she answered. 'I have long since ceased to seek what I missed. Now I took for naught but what will keep me over night to the next grey dawn. Tell me, whither goes this green road? Do any still dwell in the deep forest? And are they as fell as wanderers' tales tell?'

'What say they?' he asked.

This is followed on the manuscript page by 'now cursing Middle-earth and all the life of Men' &c., leading into a draft of the final version, where Mablung appears at the Crossings.

The second of these passages is longer, but only barely legible and in places altogether illegible. It begins in the same way as that just given, but Morwen's second speech ends at 'I look for naught beyond what will keep me through the cold night to next dawn.' Then Túrin speaks: 'I seek not either,' said he. 'For what I had is now lost utterly and is gone from Middle-earth for ever. But what would you seek?'

'What would an old woman seek,' said she, 'out in the wild, but her children, even if all say they be dead. I sought for a son once, but he went long ago. Then I sought for my daughter, but 'tis five years since she was lost in the wild. Five years is a long time for one young and fair – if the Worm did not get her, the Orcs have [*illegible*], or the [?cold heedless] wild.'

Then suddenly T[úrin]'s heart stood still. 'What like was your daughter, lady? Or what maybe was her name?'

The old woman told him that her daughter was tall, with golden hair and blue eyes, fleet-footed, a lover of all things that grow; '. . . Yet a little she leaped in her words, as her sire did also. Niënor daughter of Húrin she would have named herself, an you asked her. But maybe it would mean naught. For the name of Húrin was great [*illegible words*] All the realms [*illegible words*] are beaten down and mean folk or evil are lords. Yet you are of the older folk, I deem. I see by thy face that the old name meant somewhat to thee still.'

Túrin stared at her as a man that sees a ghost. 'Yea,' said he at last slowly. 'The name of Húrin of Hithlum and Morwen Baragund's daughter was known to me.

Of the remainder I can only read snatches:

and Morwen and her daughter went to the Hidden Kingdom [*illegible*] they say in Hithlum.' The old woman laughed bitterly. 'And what else did they say? That first Túrin went there and was used by the king in his border wars and lost, but came to Nargothrond and that Morwen went to seek him there with tardy aid of Thingol, but [*illegible words*] by the great drake Glaurung. [*illegible words*] Then she wept [*illegible words*]

This is clearly the beginning of another narrative route whereby Túrin might learn the truth, likewise abandoned before it was developed. – A pencilled note shows the entry of the 'Mablung-intervention':

Mablung searches and brings tidings to Thingol of Glaurung setting forth. This coincides with rumour (among orcs and wanderers) that the Black Sword has reappeared in Brethil. Mablung comes to Brethil (without orders from Thingol?) to warn Túrin and bring news of Niënor and Morwen.

Morwen should go back to Thingol and then depart as a beggar in the wild.

Lastly, and very remarkable, there is the following synopsis of the end of the story, written carefully on a slip, apparently over the same or similar text set down very roughly in pencil:

Turambar sets out. Asks for two companions. Dorlas volunteers, and speaks scorn of Brandir. Gwerin kinsman of Brandir volunteers. Brandir is embittered. Turambar bids Níniel stay at home.

When T[urambar] has gone Níniel insists on following. Brandir forbids but she takes no heed. Brandir appears to the Men of Brethil, but they will not obey him – they beg Níniel to remain, but as she will not, they will not restrain her by force. The wives of Dorlas and Gwerin go with her. Brandir follows after them.

The slaying of the Dragon may be told more or less as already done. But when Níniel reaches Nen Girith shuddering again takes her, and she can go no further. The wives also are not willing to go on – for they meet the scouts at Nen Girith and learn how near the Worm is . . . . . [*sic*]

When Túrin draws his sword out of Glaurung's belly, Glaurung's blood burns his sword hand; *also* Glaurung speaks to him, and says that Níniel is his sister. Túrin falls into a swoon of pain and horror.

The Dragon dies. Suddenly Níniel recovers her memory and all her past life is revealed to her. She sits aghast. Brandir sees her anguish, but believes that it is due to belief that Túrin has been slain – the dreadful cries of Glaurung have been heard at Nen Girith. Níniel gets up to flee, and Brandir thinking that she will really go in search of Túrin (while Glaurung is abroad) restrains her, saying *Wait!*

She turns to him, crying that this was ever his counsel, and to her sorrow she did not take it. But he may give that counsel once too often!

As indeed it proved. For at that moment Túrin appears. When the Dragon died his swoon also departed, but the anguish of the venom on his hand remained. He came, therefore, to Nen Girith for help, believing the scouts there. (It is Túrin that slays Dorlas on the way?)

As Turambar appears, Níniel gives a wail, crying: 'Túrin son of Húrin! Too late have we met. The dark days are gone. But night comes after!' 'How know you that name?' 'Brandir told me, and behold! I am Nienor. Therefore we must part.' And with that, ere any could hold her, she leapt over the fall of Nen Girith, and so ended, crying 'Water, water, wash me clean! Wash me of my life!'

Then the anguish of Túrin was terrible to see; and a mad fury took him, and he cursed Middle-earth and all the life of Men. And stooping over the falls, he cried in vain *Níniel, Níniel*. And he turned in wrath upon all those that were there, against his command; and all fled away from him, save only Brandir, who for ruth and horror could not move. But Túrin turned to him and said: 'Behold thy work, limping evil! Had Níniel remained, as I left her, and hadst thou not told my name, she might have been restrained from death. I could have gone away and left her, and she might have mourned for Turambar only.'

But Brandir cursed him, saying that their wedding could not have been hid; and that it was Túrin who wrought all this grief. 'And me thou hast shorn of all that I had, and would have – for thou art reckless and greedy!'

Then Túrin slew Brandir in his wrath. And repenting, he slew himself (using same words to the sword).

Mablung comes with news, and is heart-stricken. The Elves help the Halethrim to build a mound or memorial for the Children of Húrin – but N[íniel] was not there, and her body could not be found: mayhap Celebros bore it to Taiglin and Taiglin to the Sea.

A further simplification would be to make Brandir willing to go with Níniel, to guard her – for he thought Túrin would die.

This last sentence presumably refers to Brandir's attempt to stop Níniel from following Turambar from Ephel Brandir.

It seems impossible actually to demonstrate at what point in the evolution of the legend this was written, but that it is anyway as late as the rewritten, final form of the last part of the *Narn* is clear from such a detail as that *Celebros* is the name of the stream (see commentary on §317). I think that it belongs with the other passages given in this Note, in that it represents another, though far more drastic, attempt to reach the dénouement of Túrin's 'recognition' – this time from Niënor herself, who has learned the truth through no intermediary, but simply from the removal of the spell on her memory by the Dragon's death. But Mablung appears, though now after Túrin's death, and so I suspect that it is the latest of these attempts, and may very probably have *succeeded* the final form of the text. *Gwerin* as the name of Brandir's kinsman (Albarth, Torbarth, Hunthor) has appeared once before, pencilled over the first occurrence of Torbarth in GA (§322).

That my father should even have contemplated, to the extent of roughing out a synopsis, breaking so violently the superb interlocking narrative structure represented by the final text of the last part of the *Narn* is extraordinary and hard to fathom. Did he feel that it had become too evidently a 'structure', too complex in those interlocking movements, reports, forebodings, chances? The concluding note ('A *further simplification* would be ...') may support this. But it seems to me most probable that he was primarily concerned with the coming of Mablung (or indeed Morwen) as a *deus ex machina* at that very moment, bearer of the irrefutable proof, which he felt to be a serious weakness.

However this may be, the result is, I think, and granting that it is only represented by a rapid synopsis written in a certain way, far weaker; and since, apart perhaps from the pencilled name *Gwerin* in the *Grey Annals*, there is no other trace of it, it may be that he thought likewise.

NOTE 2

A further account of the Battle of Unnumbered Tears

The text of Chapter 20 in the published *Silmarillion* was primarily derived from the story in the *Grey Annals*, but elements were introduced from the old Chapter 16 in QS (V.307–13), and also from a third text. This is a typescript made by my father, and to all appearance made *ab initio* on his typewriter; it was explicitly intended as a component in the long prose Tale of the Children of Húrin (the *Narn*), but he had the manuscript of the *Grey Annals* in front of him, and for much of its length the new version remained so close to the *Annals* text that it can be regarded as scarcely more than a variant, although unquestionably much later. For this reason, and also because some of its divergent (additional) features had in any case been incorporated in the *Silmarillion* chapter, I excluded it from the *Narn* in *Unfinished Tales* (see pp. 65–6 and note 2 in that book), except for its end. There is however a major divergence in the *Narn* account which altogether contradicts the previous versions, and this is a convenient place to record it, together with some other details.

The text opens as follows (the typescript was a good deal corrected in ink, I think almost certainly very soon after it had been made, and I adopt these corrections silently except in certain cases).

Many songs are yet sung, and many tales are yet told by the Elves of the Nirnaeth Arnoediad, the Battle of Unnumbered Tears, in which Fingon fell and the flower of the Eldar withered. If all were now retold a man's life would not suffice for the hearing. Here then shall be recounted only those deeds which bear upon the fate of the House of Hador and the children of Húrin the Steadfast.

Having gathered at length all the strength that he could Maedros appointed a day, the morning of Midsummer. On that day the trumpets of the Eldar greeted the rising of the Sun, and in the east was raised the standard of the Sons of Fëanor; and in the west the standard of Fingon, King of the Noldor.

Then Fingon looked out from the walls of Eithel Sirion, and

his host was arrayed in the valleys and woods upon the east borders of Eryd-wethion, well hid from the eyes of the Enemy; but he knew that it was very great. For there all the Noldor of Hithlum were assembled, and to them were gathered many Elves of the Falas and [*struck out at once:* a great company] of Nargothrond; and he had great strength of Men. Upon the right were stationed the host of Dor-lómin and all the valour of Húrin and Huor his brother, and to them had come Hundar of Brethil, their kinsman, with many men of the woods.

Then Fingon looked east and his elven-sight saw far off a dust and the glint of steel like stars in a mist, and he knew that Maedros had set forth; and he rejoiced. Then he looked towards Thangorodrim, and behold! there was a dark cloud about it and a black smoke went up; and he knew that the wrath of Morgoth was kindled and that their challenge would be accepted, and a shadow fell upon his heart. But at that moment a cry went up, passing on the wind from the south from vale to vale, and Elves and Men lifted up their voices in wonder and joy. For unsummoned and unlooked-for Turgon had opened the leaguer of Gondolin, and was come with an army, ten thousand strong, with bright mail and long swords and spears like a forest. Then when Fingon heard afar the great trumpet of Turgon, the shadow passed and his heart was uplifted, and he shouted aloud: *Utulie'n aurë! Aiya Eldalië ar Atanatarni, utulie'n aurë!* (The day has come! Lo, people of the Eldar and Fathers of Men, the day has come!) And all those who heard his great voice echo in the hills answered crying: *Auta i lómë!* (The night is passing!)

It was not long before the great battle was joined. For Morgoth knew much of what was done and designed by his foes and had laid his plans against the hour of their assault. Already a great force out of Angband was drawing near to Hithlum, while another and greater went to meet Maedros to prevent the union of the powers of the kings. And those that came against Fingon were clad all in dun raiment and showed no naked steel, and thus were already far over the sands before their approach became known.

Then the heart of Fingon [> the hearts of the Noldor] grew hot, and he [> their captains] wished to assail their foes on the plain; but Húrin [> Fingon] spoke against this.

'Beware of the guile of Morgoth, lords!' he said. 'Ever his strength is more than it seems, and his purpose other than he reveals. Do not reveal your own strength, but let the enemy spend his first in assault on the hills. At least until the signal of Maedros is seen.' For it was the design of the kings that Maedros should march openly over the Anfauglith with all his strength, of Elves and of Men and of Dwarves; and when he had drawn forth, as he hoped, the main armies of Morgoth in answer, then Fingon should come on from the west, and so the might of Morgoth should be taken as between hammer and anvil and be broken to pieces; and the signal for this was to be the firing of a great beacon in Dorthonion.

But the Captain of Morgoth in the west had been commanded to draw out Fingon from his hills by whatever means he could.

It is most remarkable that in this *Narn* version there is no reference whatever to the hindering of Maedros by the guile of Uldor the Accursed; while on the other hand there is here the entirely new statement that a second and greater force left Angband to intercept Maedros and 'prevent the union of the powers of the kings' (contrast GA §222, where it is said that Morgoth 'trusted in his servants to hold back Maidros and prevent the union of his foes' – referring of course to the machinations of Uldor). Later in this narrative, the passage corresponding to the opening of GA §228 reads:

Then in the plain of Anfauglith, on the fourth day of the war, there began the Nirnaeth Arnoediad, all the sorrow of which no tale can contain. Of all that befell in the eastward battle: of the routing of Glaurung the Drake by the Naugrim of Belegost; of the treachery of the Easterlings and the overthrow of the host of Maedros and the flight of the Sons of Fëanor, no more is here said. In the west the host of Fingon retreated over the sands ...

Here 'the eastward battle' is spoken of as if it were altogether separate from the fighting in the west: there is no suggestion here that the host of Maedros finally came up and fell upon the rear of the enemy (GA §229). Finally, where in GA the meeting of Turgon and Húrin in the midst of the battle is followed (§229) by the coming of the host of Maidros, the *Narn* version reads:

And it is said that the meeting of Turgon with Húrin who stood beside Fingon was glad in the midst of battle. For a while then the hosts of Angband were driven back, and Fingon again began his retreat. But having routed Maedros in the east Morgoth had now great forces to spare, and before Fingon and Turgon could come to the shelter of the hills they were assailed by a tide of foes thrice greater than all the force that was left to them.

With these last words the *Narn* version returns to the GA text at §233. Thus my father, for whatever reason, had expunged the entire element of 'the machinations of Uldor' in delaying Maedros, and radically altered the course of the Battle of Unnumbered Tears by introducing the defeat and rout of the eastern host before any junction of the forces was achieved.

In *The Silmarillion* I preserved (inevitably) the story as told in the *Grey Annals*, but incorporated certain elements from the *Narn*, as may be seen from a comparison of the opening of the latter (pp. 165–6) with *The Silmarillion* pp. 190–1: the cloud and smoke over Thangorodrim, the great cry of Fingon, the 'dun raiment' of the force from Angband that came towards Hithlum. Some other minor points in this passage may be mentioned. The 'great company from Nargothrond' (see §221 and commentary) is corrected (p. 166); and the name of the leader of the men of Brethil, in GA Hundor son of Haleth the Hunter, is changed to Hundar: later in the text his father is said to be Halmir – an aspect of the extremely complex refashioning of the genealogies of the Edain which need not be entered into here (see pp. 236–8).

In GA (§222), following QS (§11), it was Fingon who was all for attacking at once the force from Angband on the plain, and Húrin who opposed it; this was followed in the *Narn*, but then corrected to make it Fingon who opposed the rashness of his captains. The change was perhaps made for probability's sake: such prudence and experience of Morgoth should lie rather with Fingon King of the Noldor than with Húrin, a Man of no more than thirty-one years. – Húrin (> Fingon) urged that the western host should wait in its positions 'at least until the signal of Maedros is seen'. In GA (§217) the occasion of the signal of Maidros to Fingon (not particularised as a beacon in Dorthonion) was to be the moment when the march of Maidros in open force over Anfauglith had incited the host of Morgoth to come forth from Angband; and owing to Uldor the Accursed the signal did not come. In the *Narn* Fingon with his far sight had actually seen that Maedros had set out, and it is also told that great force was on its way from Angband to meet him; but it is not said that the beacon was fired.

Other features of the story as told in *The Silmarillion* that are not found in GA are derived from the *Narn*. In the latter there is a more detailed account of the confrontation between the two hosts, and the riders of Morgoth come to the walls of the fortress at Eithel Sirion (here called *Barad Eithel*): thus whereas in GA Gwindor saw the slaughter of his brother Gelmir 'across the water', in the *Narn* he was 'at that point in the outposts'. The account of the western battle is very close indeed to that in GA, but the death of Fingon is differently and more fully told (see *The Silmarillion* p. 193): with the coming of Gothmog 'high-captain of Angband' Fingon was cut off from Húrin and Turgon, who were driven towards the Fen of Serech. The speeches of Turgon, Húrin, and Huor were scarcely changed from their form in GA (§§234–5), but the needed change in Huor's words to 'I shall never look on thy white walls *again*' was made (see the commentary on §§234–5). Lastly, in the *Narn* it is said that Húrin 'seized the axe of an Orc-captain and wielded it two-handed', and again Gothmog appears (see *The Silmarillion* p. 195).

In the account of the Mound of the Slain the *Narn* version names it *Haudh-en-Ndengin*, subsequently changed to *Haudh-en-Nirnaeth*.

The *Narn* text concludes with a remarkable elaboration of the confrontation of Húrin and Morgoth on the basis of GA §§244–8 (itself an elaboration of QS §§21–3); this was the only part of the text included in *Unfinished Tales* (pp. 66–8). As the speeches were typed they were set entirely in the second person singular, 'thou wert', 'knowest thou', etc.; but my father went through it changing every 'thou' and 'thee' to 'you', and the equivalent verb-forms – and changing 'Knowest thou' to 'Do you know' rather than 'Know you' (also 'puissant' to 'mighty'). In this form, of course, the text was printed in *Unfinished Tales*.

NOTE 3

A further account of the coming of Húrin and Huor to Gondolin

As in the case of the story of the Battle of Unnumbered Tears described in Note 2 above, there is also a version of that of Húrin and Huor in Gondolin found as a component of the *Narn*. This is even more closely based on the story in the *Grey Annals* §§161–6: while there are many small variations in the precise wording, virtually none are of any moment in respect of the narrative, until the end is reached, where a significant difference appears. This story was excluded from the *Narn* in *Unfinished Tales*, but its existence noted: p. 146, note 1. Before the end the only point worth mentioning is that Maeglin's words (GA §165) are here much fiercer: 'The king's grace to you is greater than ye know; and some might wonder wherefore the strict law is abated for two knave-children of Men. It would be safer if they had no choice but to abide here as our servants to their life's end.'

According to the story in GA, Húrin and Huor told when they returned to Dor-lómin that 'they had dwelt a while in honour in the halls of King Turgon', even though they would say nothing else. Against this my father noted on the GA typescript (p. 127, §166): 'They did not reveal Turgon's name'; and in the *Narn* version they refused altogether to declare even to their father where they had been. This version was adopted in the published *Silmarillion* (p. 159), with only a change at the end. Here the *Narn* text has:

Then Galion [> Galdor] questioned them no more; but he and many others guessed at the truth. For both the oath of silence and the Eagles pointed to Turgon, men thought.

The conclusion of the passage in *The Silmarillion* ('and in time the strange fortune of Húrin and Huor reached the ears of the servants of Morgoth') was taken from the GA version.

On these two (otherwise so closely similar) texts of the story see further p. 314.

PART TWO

THE LATER
QUENTA SILMARILLION

THE LATER *QUENTA SILMARILLION*

In Part Two I shall trace the development of the *Quenta Silmarillion*, in the years following the completion of *The Lord of the Rings*, from the point reached in Vol.X, p. 199; but the history now becomes (for the most part) decidedly simpler: much of the development can be conveyed by recording individually all the significant changes made to QS, and there is no need to divide it into two 'phases', as was done in Vol.X. The basic textual series is QS (so far as it went before its abandonment); the early amanuensis typescript 'LQ 1' of 1951, for which see X.141–3; and the late amanuensis typescript 'LQ 2' of about 1958, for which see X.141-2, 300.

In this latter part of the history the chapter-numbers become rather confusing, but I think that it would be more confusing to have none, and therefore I continue the numbering used in Vol.X, where the last chapter treated, *Of the Sun and Moon and the Hiding of Valinor*, was given the number 8.

9   OF MEN

This chapter was numbered 7 in the QS manuscript (for the text see V.245-7, §§81–7). The difference is simply due to the fact that the three 'sub-chapters' in QS numbered in Vol.V 3(a), 3(b), and 3(c) were in Vol.X called 3, 4, and 5 (see X.299). Few changes were made to the QS manuscript in later revision, and those that were made were incorporated in LQ 1. That typescript received no alterations, and is of textual value in only a few respects; the typist of LQ 2 did not use it, but worked directly from the old manuscript.

§81   'The Valar sat now behind the mountains and feasted' > 'Thus the Valar sat now behind their mountains in peace'.

§82   The placing of Hildórien 'in the uttermost East of Middle-earth that lies beside the eastern sea' was changed to: 'in the midmost parts of Middle-earth beyond the Great River and the Inner Sea, in regions which neither the Eldar nor the Avari have known'.

Many phrases have been used of the site of Hildórien. In the 'Annals' tradition it was 'in the East of the world' (IV.269, V.118, 125), but this was changed on the manuscript of AV 2 to 'in the midmost regions of the world' (V.120, note 13). In the *Quenta* it was 'in the East of East' (IV.99), and in QS, as cited above, 'in the uttermost East of Middle-earth': in my commentary on QS (V.248) I suggested that this last was not in contradiction with the changed reading of AV 2: 'Hildórien was in the furthest east of *Middle-earth*, but it was in the middle regions of the world; see *Ambarkanta* map IV, on which Hildórien is marked (IV.249).'

In the texts of the post-*Lord of the Rings* period there is the statement in the *Grey Annals* (GA) §57 that it was 'in the midmost regions of the world', as in the emended reading of AV 2; and there is the new phrase in the revision of QS, 'in *the midmost parts of Middle-earth* beyond the Great River and the Inner Sea' (with loss of the mention in the original text of 'the eastern sea'). This last shows unambiguously that a change had taken place, but it is very hard to say what it was. It cannot be made to agree with the old *Ambarkanta* maps: one might indeed doubt that those maps carried much validity for the eastern regions by this time, and wonder whether by 'the Inner Sea' my father was referring to 'the Inland Sea of Rhûn' (see *The Treason of Isengard* pp. 307, 333) – but on the other hand, in the *Annals of Aman* (X.72, 82) from this same period the Great Journey of the Elves from Kuiviénen ('a bay in the Inland Sea of Helkar') is described in terms that suggest that the old conception was still fully present. Can the Sea of Rhûn be identified with the Sea of Helkar, vastly shrunken? – Nor is it easy to understand how Hildórien 'in the midmost parts of Middle-earth' could be 'in regions which neither the Eldar nor the Avari have known'.

In LQ 2 most of the revised passage is absent, and the text reads simply: 'in the land of Hildórien in the midmost parts of Middle-earth; for measured time had come upon Earth ...' If this is significant, it must depend on a verbal direction from my father. On the other hand, the revision was written on the manuscript in two parts: 'in the midmost parts' in the margin and the remainder on another part of the page, where it would be possible to miss it; and I think this much the likeliest explanation.

§83   The opening of the footnote (V.245) was changed from 'The Eldar called them Hildi' to 'Atani they were called in Valinor, but the Eldar called them also Hildi'; and 'the birth of the Hildi' was changed to 'the arising of the Hildi'. For *Atani* see GA §57 and commentary. As frequently before, the typist of LQ 1 placed the footnote in the body of the text, where my father left it to stand; but it reappears as a footnote to LQ 2 – a first indication that the typescript was taken from the QS manuscript.

After 'those fathers of Men' (in which the *f* should not have been capitalised) was added 'the *Atanatardi*'. Here LQ 1 has *Atanatarni*, which was not corrected; while LQ 2 – based not on LQ 1 but on the manuscript – has *Atanatardi*. But the form *Atanatarni* occurs in the *Narn* text given in Note 2 to Part One: there Fingon before the beginning of the Battle of Unnumbered Tears cries *Aiya Eldalië ar Atanatarni* (p. 166). In GA §87, in a different passage, the form is

Atanatári (which was adopted in *The Silmarillion*); cf. also *Atana-tárion*, X.373.

§85 The sentence 'Only in the realm of Doriath, whose queen Melian was of divine race, did the Ilkorins come near to match the Elves of Kôr' was changed to: 'whose queen Melian was of the kindred of the [gods >] Valar, did the [Ekelli >] Sindar come near to match the [Elves of Túna >] Kalaquendi of the Blessed Realm.' On the term *Ekelli* 'the Forsaken' and its replacement by *Sindar* see X.169–70.

> *Eruman* > *Araman* (cf. X.123, 194).
> 'the ancient wisdom of their race' > '... of their folk'.

§86 'What befell their spirits after death' > 'What may befall ...' 'beside the Western Sea' > 'beside the Outer Sea' (see V.248, §86).

§87 'vanished from the earth' > 'vanished from the Middle-earth'.

To one or other copies of the LQ 2 typescript my father made a few changes. The chapter, typed without a number, was now numbered 'XI'. 'Gnomes' was changed to 'Noldor' at each occurrence, and in the first sentence of §85 'Dark-elves' to 'Sindar'. Against §82 he wrote: 'This depends upon an old version in which the Sun was first made after the death of the Trees (described in a chapter omitted).' I have already noticed this in X.299–300, and explained why he numbered the present chapter 'XI'. He also bracketed in pencil three passages in the account of the mortality of the Elves in §85: 'Yet their bodies were of the stuff of earth ... consumeth them from within in the courses of time'; 'days or years, even a thousand'; 'and their deserts'.

---

10   OF THE SIEGE OF ANGBAND

This chapter was numbered 8 in the QS manuscript, and the text is given in V.248–55, §§88–104. As in the preceding chapter, all post-*Lord of the Rings* revision was carried out on the QS manuscript: that is to say, no further revisions were made to the typescript LQ 1; and here again the late typescript LQ 2 was derived from the manuscript, not from LQ 1. In this chapter, on the other hand, by no means all the revisions made to the manuscript are found in LQ 1; and in the account that follows I notice all such cases. I do not notice the changes *Eruman* > *Araman*; *Tûn* > *Túna*; *Gnomes* > *Noldor*; *Thorndor* > *Thorondor*; *Bladorion* > *Ard-galen* (see p. 113, §44).

§88 The opening passage of the chapter in QS was rewritten on a slip attached to the manuscript – this slip being the reverse of a letter to my father dated 14 November 1951: but it was not incorporated into LQ 1. The introduction of this rider led the typist of LQ 2 to ignore the fact that a new chapter begins at this point, and to type *Of the Siege of Angband* as all of a piece with *Of Men*; subsequently my father inserted a new heading *Of the Siege of Angband* with the number 'XII' (on which see p. 175). The new opening reads:

As was before told Fëanor and his sons came first of the Exiles to Middle-earth, and they landed in the waste of Lammoth upon the outer shores of the Firth of Drengist. Now that region was so named, for it lay between the Sea and the walls of the echoing mountains of the Eryd Lómin. And even as the Noldor set foot upon the strand their cries were taken up into the hills and multiplied, so that a great clamour as of countless mighty voices filled all the coasts of the North; and it is said that the noise of the burning of the ships at Losgar went down the winds of the Sea as a tumult of great wrath, and far away all that heard that sound were filled with wonder.

Under the cold stars before the rising of the Moon Fëanor and his folk marched eastward, and they passed the Eryd Lómin, and came into the great land of Hithlum, and crossing the country of Dor-lómin they came at length to the long lake of Mithrim, and upon its north-shore they made their first camp in that region which was called by the like name.

There a host of the Orcs, aroused by the tumult of Lammoth, and the light of the burning at Losgar, came down upon them; and beside the waters of Mithrim was fought the first battle upon Middle-earth . . .

This is the story of Lammoth told (at about this same time) in the later *Tale of Tuor* (*Unfinished Tales* p. 23):

Tuor was now come to the Echoing Mountains of Lammoth about the Firth of Drengist. There once long ago Fëanor had landed from the sea, and the voices of his host were swelled to a mighty clamour upon the coasts of the North ere the rising of the Moon.

On the much later and apparently distinct story that Lammoth was so called because the echoes of Morgoth's cry were awakened by 'any who cried aloud in that land' see X.296, §17 and commentary, and *Unfinished Tales* p. 52. Both 'traditions' were incorporated in the published *Silmarillion*, pp. 80–1, 106.

At the end of this paragraph my father pencilled on the manuscript: 'He [Fëanor] gives the green stone to Maidros', but then noted that this was not in fact to be inserted; see under §97 below.

§90 'and they were unwilling to depart, whatever he might do' > '. . . whatever he might do, being held by their oath.' This addition is not present in LQ 1; while the typist of LQ 2, unable to read the first word, put 'They held by their oath', and this was allowed to stand. Cf. GA §50.

§91   'the Sun rose flaming in the West' > 'the Sun rose flaming above the shadows' (not in LQ 1).

'and good was made of evil, as happens still' removed.

§93   'the bright airs of those earliest of mornings' > 'the bright airs in the first mornings of the world.'

§94   A subheading was pencilled in the margin at the beginning of this paragraph: *Of Fingon and Maeðros* (apparently first written *Maidros*: see p. 115, §61). Not found in LQ 1, this was incorporated in LQ 2.

In the second sentence 'most renowned' > 'most honoured' (not in LQ 1).

To the words 'for the thought of his torment troubled his heart' was added (not in LQ 1): 'and long before, in the bliss of Valinor, ere Melkor was unchained, or lies came between them, he had been close in friendship with Maedros.' Cf. GA §61 and commentary (p. 115).

§95   'for the banished Gnomes!' > 'for the Noldor in their need!'

§97   A new page in the QS manuscript begins with the opening of this paragraph, and at the top of the page my father pencilled: 'The Green Stone of Fëanor given by Maidros to Fingon.' This can hardly be other than a reference to the *Elessar* that came in the end to Aragorn; cf. the note given under §88 above referring to Fëanor's gift at his death of the Green Stone to Maidros. It is clear, I think, that my father was at this time pondering the previous history of the *Elessar*, which had emerged in *The Lord of the Rings*; for his later ideas on its origin see *Unfinished Tales* pp. 248–52.

§98   '(Therefore the house of Fëanor were called the Dispossessed,) because of the doom of the Gods which gave the kingdom of Tûn [*later* > Túna] to Fingolfin, and because of the loss of the Silmarils' was changed (but the change is not present in LQ 1) to: '... (as Mandos foretold) because the overlordship passed from it, the elder, to the house of Fingolfin, both in Elendë and in Beleriand, and because also of the loss of the Silmarils.'

With the words 'as Mandos foretold' cf. AAm §153 (X.117); and on the content of the paragraph see p. 115, commentary on GA §§65–71.

§99   At the end of the paragraph, after 'he [Thingol] trusted not that the restraint of Morgoth would last for ever', was added: 'neither would he ever wholly forget the deeds at Alqualondë, because of his ancient kinship with [Elwë >] Olwë lord of the Teleri.' On the change of *Elwë* to *Olwë* see X.169–70.

§100   'in unexplored country' > 'in untrodden lands'.

§101   This passage on the finding of Nargothrond and Gondolin was expanded in three stages. The first alteration to QS replaced the sentence 'But Turgon went alone into hidden places' thus:

Yet Galadriel his sister went never to Nargothrond, for she remained long in Doriath and received the love of Melian, and abode with her and there learned great lore and wisdom. But the heart of Turgon remembered rather the white city of Tirion upon its hill, and its tower and tree, and he journeyed alone into hidden places . . .

Subsequently the whole of QS §101 was struck through and replaced by the following rider on a separate sheet. This was taken up into the first typescript LQ 1, but in a somewhat different form from the rider to the manuscript, which was followed in LQ 2 and is given here.

And it came to pass that Inglor and Galaðriel were on a time the guests of Thingol and Melian; for there was friendship between the lord of Doriath and the House of Finrod that were his kin, and the princes of that house alone were suffered to pass the girdle of Melian. Then Inglor was filled with wonder at the strength and majesty of Menegroth, with its treasuries and armouries and its many-pillared halls of stone; and it came into his heart that he would build wide halls behind everguarded gates in some deep and secret place beneath the hills. And he opened his heart to Thingol, and when he departed Thingol gave him guides, and they led him westward over Sirion. Thus it was that Inglor found the deep gorge of the River Narog, and the caves in its steep further shore; and he delved there a stronghold and armouries after the fashion of the mansions of Menegroth. And he called that place Nargothrond, and made there his home with many of his folk; and the Gnomes of the North, at first in jest, called him on this account Felagund, or 'lord of caverns', and that name he bore thereafter until his end. Yet Galaðriel his sister dwelt never in Nargothrond, but remained in Doriath and received the love of Melian, and abode with her, and there learned great lore and wisdom concerning Middle-earth.

The statement that 'Galaðriel dwelt never in Nargothrond' is at variance with what is said in GA §108 (p. 44), that in the year 102, when Nargothrond was completed, 'Galadriel came from Doriath and dwelt there a while'. – To this point the two forms of the rider differ only in a few details of wording, but here they diverge. The second form, in LQ 2, continues:

Now Turgon remembered rather the City set upon a Hill, Tirion the fair with its Tower and Tree, and he found not what he sought, and returned to Nivrost, and sat at peace in Vinyamar by the shore. There after three years Ulmo himself appeared to him, and bade him go forth again alone to the Vale of Sirion; and Turgon went forth and by the guidance of Ulmo he discovered the hidden vale of Tumladen in the encircling mountains, in the midst of which there was a hill of stone. Of this he spoke to none as yet, but returned to Nivrost, and there began in his secret counsels to devise the plan of a fair city [*struck out:* a memorial of Tirion upon Túna for which his heart still yearned in exile, and though he pondered much in thought he]

For this concluding passage LQ 1 returns to the first rewriting given at the beginning of this discussion of QS §101, 'But the heart of Turgon remembered rather the white city of Tirion upon its hill ...' The explanation of the differences in the two versions must be that a first form of the rider (which has not survived) was taken up into LQ 1, and that subsequently a second version was inserted into the QS manuscript in its place, and so used in LQ 2.

This replacement text for QS §101 is closely related to GA §§75–6 (p. 35); and since on its reverse side is a rejected draft for the replacement annal for the year 116 in GA (§§111–13, pp. 44–5), also concerned with Gondolin, it is clear that my father was working on the story of the origins of Nargothrond and Gondolin in both the *Silmarillion* and the *Annals* at the same time. See further pp. 198 ff.

§102   At the beginning of this paragraph a sub-heading *Of Dagor Aglareb* was pencilled on the manuscript, but this was not taken up in either typescript.

'the Blue Mountains' > 'Eredluin, the blue mountains'
'the second great battle' > 'the third great battle': see p. 116, §77.

A few corrections were made to one or the other, or to both, of the copies of LQ 2. In addition to those listed below, *Inglor* was changed to *Finrod*, and *Finrod* to *Finarphin* or *Finarfin*, throughout.

§92   *Túna > Tirion*
§98   '(the feud) was healed' > 'was assuaged'
§99   'Dark-elves of Telerian race' > 'Dark-elves, the Sindar of Telerian race'.
§100   At the beginning of this paragraph my father inserted a new chapter number and title: XIII *The Founding of Nargothrond and Gondolin*; and the next chapter, *Of Beleriand and its Realms*, was given in LQ 2 the number XIV.

Nivrost > Nevrast (and subsequently); the first appearance of the later form of the name (its appearance in the later *Tale of Tuor* was by editorial change).

§101   Against the name *Felagund* my father wrote this note: 'This was in fact a Dwarfish name; for Nargothrond was first made by Dwarves as is later recounted.' An important constituent text among the *Narn* papers is a 'plot-outline' that begins with Túrin's flight from Doriath and moves towards pure narrative in a long account of Túrin's relations with Finduilas and Gwindor in Nargothrond (which with some editorial development was given in *Unfinished Tales*, pp. 155–9). In this text the following is said of Mîm the Petty-dwarf:

> Mîm gets a certain curious liking for Túrin, increased when he learns that Túrin has had trouble with Elves, whom he detests. He says Elves have caused the end of his race, and taken all their mansions, especially Nargothrond (*Nulukhizidûn*).

Above this Dwarvish name my father wrote *Nulukkhizdīn* (this name was used, misspelt, in *The Silmarillion*, p. 230).

§104   *Glómund > Glaurung.* At the head of the page in QS my father wrote '*Glaurung* for *Glómund*', but the LQ typescript, as typed, has *Glómund* – whereas *Glaurung* appears already in the *Grey Annals* as written.

---

11   OF BELERIAND AND ITS REALMS

In Volume V (p. 407) I wrote as follows about the second *Silmarillion* map:

> The second map of Middle-earth west of the Blue Mountains in the Elder Days was also the last. My father never made another; and over many years this one became covered all over with alterations and additions of names and features, not a few of them so hastily or faintly pencilled as to be more or less obscure. ...
>
> The original element in the map can however be readily perceived from the fine and çareful pen (all subsequent change was roughly done); and I give here on four successive pages a reproduction of the map *as it was originally drawn and lettered.* ...
>
> The map is on four sheets, originally pasted together but now separate, in which the map-squares do not entirely coincide with the sheets. In my reproductions I have followed the squares rather than the original sheets. I have numbered the squares horizontally right across the map from 1 to 15, and lettered them vertically from A to M, so that each square has a different combination of letter and figure for subsequent reference. I hope later to give an account of all changes made to the map afterwards, using these redrawings as a basis.

This I will now do, before turning to the changes made to the chapter *Of Beleriand and its Realms.* On the following pages are reproduced the same four redrawings as were given in V.408–11, but with the subsequent alterations and additions introduced (those cases where I cannot interpret at all faint pencillings are simply ignored). Corrections to names (as *Nan Tathrin > Nan Tathren, Nan Dungorthin > Nan Dungortheb, Rathlorion > Rathloriel*) are replaced, not shown as corrections. It is to be remembered that, as I have said, all later changes were roughly done, some of them mere scribbled indications, and also that they were made at many different times, in pencil, coloured pencil, blue, black and red ink, and red, green and blue ball-point pen; so that the appearance of the actual map is very different from these redrawings. I have however retained the placing of the new lettering in almost all cases as accurately as possible.

There follows here a list, square by square, of features and names where some explanation or reference seems desirable; but this is by no means an exhaustive inventory of all later alterations and additions, many of which require no comment.

1   North-western section (p. 182)

(1) A 4–5   The mountain-chain is a mere zigzag line pencilled in a single movement, as also are the mountains on A 7 (extending east to the peaks encircling Thangorodrim on section 2, A 8).

(2) B 4 to C 4   The name *Dor-Lómen* was almost illegibly scribbled in; it seems to imply an extension of Dor-Lómen northwards.

(3) B 7 to C 7   The name beginning *Fen* is continued on Section 2, B 8 *of Rivil*, changed to *of Serech* (see p. 113, commentary on GA §44). An arrow, not inserted on the redrawing, points to three dots above the inflowing of Rivil as marking the Fen.

(4) C 1   I can cast no light on the name *Ened* of the island in the ocean.

(5) C 3   It seems probable that the name *Falasquil* referred to the small round bay, blacked in, on the southern shore of the great bay leading into the Firth of Drengist. On the remarkable reappearance of this ancient name see p. 344.

(6) C 4   The clearly-marked gap in the stream flowing into the Firth of Drengist represents its passage underground; with the name *Annon Gelyð* cf. *Annon-in-Gelydh* (the Gate of the Noldor) in the later *Tale of Tuor*, *Unfinished Tales* p. 18. The ravine of *Cirith Ninniach* is described in the same work (*ibid.* p. 23). The upper course of the stream is very faintly pencilled and uncertain, but it seems clear that it rises in the Mountains of Mithrim (*ibid.* p. 20).

(7) C 6   For the peak shaded in and marked *Amon Darthir*, with *Morwen* beside it, see *Unfinished Tales*, where it is told (p. 68) that the stream Nen Lalaith 'came down from a spring under the shadow of Amon Darthir', and (p. 58) that it 'came singing out of the hills past the walls of [Húrin's] house'.

(8) C 6 to D 7   For the river *Lithir* see p. 261.

(9) C 7   For the stream (Rivil) that flows into Sirion see Section 2, C 8.

(10) D 2–4   Both *Nevrast* and the *Marshes of Nevrast* were first

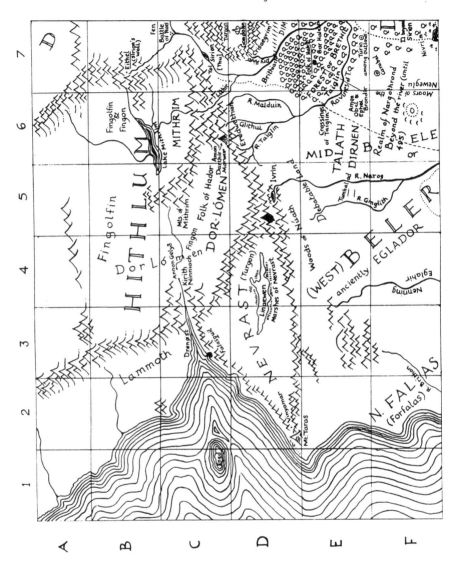

Sheet 1 North-west

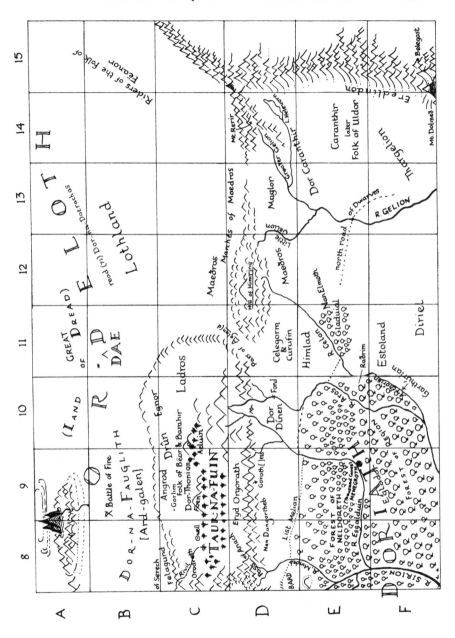

Sheet 2 North-east

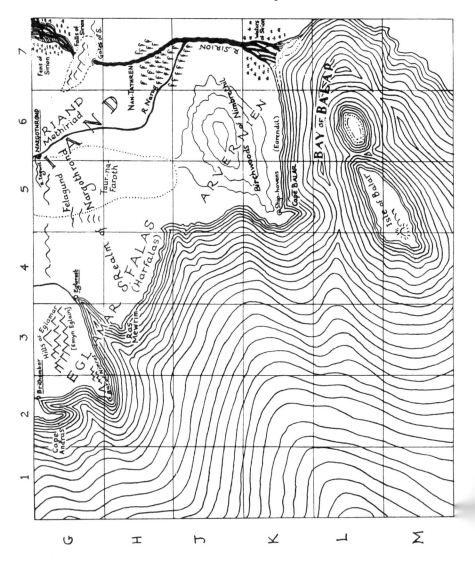

Sheet 3 South-west

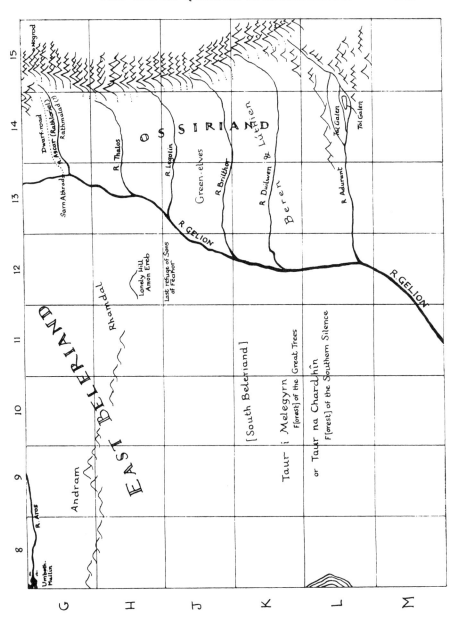

Sheet 4   South-east

written *Nivrost* (see p. 179, §100). On Lake Linaewen and the marshes see p. 192 and *Unfinished Tales* p. 25.

(11) D 6 For the river *Glithui* see *Unfinished Tales* p. 38 and note 16, and p. 68. In the first of these passages (the later *Tale of Tuor*) the name is *Glithui* as on the map, but in the second (the *Narn*) it is equally clearly *Gilthui*. For *Malduin* see *Unfinished Tales* p. 38 and *The Silmarillion* p. 205.

(12) D 7 The line of dots extending east from the Brithiach was struck out as shown; see Section 2, §38. For the ford of Brithiach see p. 228, §28.

(13) D 7 *Dim* is the first part of the name *Dimbard*: see Section 2, D 8.

(14) E 4 to F 4 *anciently Eglador*: *Eglador* was the original name of Doriath, 'land of the Elves' (see the *Etymologies*, V.356, stem ELED), and is so entered on the map (Section 2, F 9). For its later sense, 'land of the *Eglain*, the Forsaken People, the Sindar' see p. 189, §57; and here *Eglador* is used with a much wider reference: the western parts of Beleriand (see pp. 379–80). This is perhaps to be related to the statement in *The Tale of Years* (pp. 343–4), 'The foremost of the Eldar reach the coastlands of Middle-earth and that country which was after named Eglador' – to which however is added the puzzling phrase 'Thereof Beleriand was the larger part'.

(15) E 4 to D 5 *Woods of Núath*: see the later *Tale of Tuor* in *Unfinished Tales*, p. 36 and note 14.

(16) E 5 The name *Tumhalad* appears to be written twice, above and below the two short parallel lines shown. See pp. 139–40, commentary on GA §275.

(17) E 5-6 *Talath Dirnen* was first written *Dalath Dirnen*; see p. 228, §28.

(18) E 6 to F 6 South of the Crossings of Taiglin it is difficult to be sure, among various incomplete dotted lines, what was the course of the road to Nargothrond, but my father seems subsequently to have entered it as a straight line of short dashes as shown.

(19) E 6-7 From Ephel Brandir various lines, which I cannot certainly interpret and have not marked on the map, run west towards the Crossings of Taiglin. Possibly one line marks the road to the Crossings and another the course of Celebros. – *Tavrobel* on the map as originally lettered was struck out and replaced by *Bar Haleth* (also struck out), but no precise site is indicated. For *Bar Haleth* see p. 157, commentary on GA §324.

(20) E 7 *Folk of Haleth* clearly belongs to the first making of the map and should have been entered on the redrawing (V.408).

(21) F 2 The name *Forfalas* ('North Falas') seems not to occur

elsewhere; similarly with *Harfalas* ('South Falas'), Section 3, H 4.

(22)   F 4   The original name *R.Eglor* was struck out and replaced by *Eglahir*. Later the name *Nenning* was written in, but *Eglahir* was not struck out. See p. 117, commentary on GA §85.

(23)   F 5   For the dotted line on this square see §59 below.

(24)   F 6   The word 'or' refers to the name *Methiriad*, Section 3, G 6.

(25)   F 6   For the change of date from 195 to 495 see V.139, 407.

(26)   F 6–7   *Moors of the Neweglu*: among the *Narn* papers there are many texts concerned with the story of Mîm, and in these are found an extraordinary array of names for the Petty-dwarves: *Neweg, Neweglîn; Niwennog; Naug-neben, Neben-naug; Nebinnog, Nibennog, Nibinnogrim, Nibin-noeg; Nognith*. The name on the map, *Neweglu*, does not occur in the *Narn* papers.

(27)   F 7   The name of an isolated hill *Carabel* stands at the point where *Amon Rûdh* (the abode of Mîm) is shown on my map accompanying *The Silmarillion*. The name of the hill was changed many times: *Amon Garabel* > *Carabel*; *Amon Carab* (translated 'Hill of the Hat'); *Amon Narðol* and *Nardol* (cf. the beacon-hill *Nardol* in Anórien); *Amon Rhûg* 'the Bald Hill'; and *Amon Rûdh* of the same meaning.

(28)   F 7   For *Nivrim* see QS §110 (V.261).

2   North-eastern section (p. 183)

(29)   B 8   *(Fen) of Serech*: see Section 1, §3.

(30)   B 12 to A 13   'read (71) *Dor-na-Daerachas*': the number 71 oddly but certainly refers to the year 1971; the addition is very late, since it does not appear on the photocopy of the map used by my father c.1970 (see p. 330 and note 1, also p. 191, after §74).

(31)   B 12–13   *Lothland*: see p. 128, commentary on GA §§173–4.

(32)   C 9   The mountain named *Foen*: in a philological fragment of uncertain date it is stated that Dorthonion 'was called also *Taur-na-Foen*, the Forest of the Foen, for that was the name (which signifies "Long Sight") of the high mountain in the midst of that region.'

(33)   C 9–10   *Drûn*: cf. the later form of the *Lay of Leithian*, III.344, line 520: 'ambush in Ladros, fire in Drûn' (see commentary, III. 350).

(34)   C 10–11   For mentions of *Ladros* see p. 224 and §33 above; also *Unfinished Tales* p. 70, where Túrin is named 'heir of Dor-lómin and Ladros'.

(35)   C 11   On the left side of the square my father wrote Orodreth, subsequently striking it out. This placing of Orodreth's

territory goes back to the old story that of the sons of Finrod (Finarfin) on Dorthonion 'easternmost dwelt Orodreth, nighest to his friends the sons of Fëanor' (AB 1, IV.330).

(36)   C 12   *Maeðros* was corrected from *Maiðros*, so also on D 12; in the original *Marches of Maidros* the name was corrected to *Maedros*.

(37)   D 8   *bard* is the second element of *Dimbard* (see Section 1, D 7). The name is certainly written thus, with final *-d*, but elsewhere the form is always *Dimbar*.

(38)   D 8–9, E 9–10   The line of dots marked *List Melian* was struck out for some distance east of the Brithiach, as shown (see Section 1, D 7), and its discontinuous extension between Esgalduin and Aros was put in later and more roughly. On the significance of these dotted lines see p. 333, and for the name *List Melian* (the Girdle of Melian) see pp. 223, 228.

(39)   D 9   *Eryd Orgorath* seems to be written so, and above it apparently *Gorgorath*, but the forms are very hard to make out.

(40)   D 9   *Goroth[ ]ess*: the illegible letter in this otherwise totally unknown name (which was struck through) might be *r*.

(41)   D 9   For the bridge of Esgalduin marked on the published map (and named *Iant Iaur*) in the position equivalent to the S.E. corner of D 9 see pp. 332–3.

(42)   D 10   For *Dor Dínen* see pp. 194, 333.

(43)   D 10   The *Ford* over Aros can be shown to be a very late addition to the map: see p. 338, note 6.

(44)   D 11   *Pass of Aglon(d*: for the forms *Aglon* and *Aglond* see p. 338, note 3.

(45)   D 14   *Mt. Rerir*: in QS §114 (V.263) it is said that Greater Gelion came from Mount Rerir (the first occurrence of the name); about it were 'many lesser heights' (§118), and on its western slopes was built a Noldorin fortress (§142). The map was made before the emergence of Mount Rerir, and my father contented himself with writing the name against the not specially conspicuous mountain near the end of the line marking Greater Gelion.

(46)   E 8 to D 8   The name R. *Mindeb* was written on the map at its making but was inadvertently omitted from my redrawing (V.409).

(47)   E 11   *Himlad*: on the meaning of the name, and the reason for it, see p. 332 and note 4.

(48)   E 11   *Gladuial*: I have not found this name anywhere else.

(49)   E 11   *Raðrim*: the line directing the name to the wooded land between Aros and Celon is faintly pencilled on the map. *Raðrim* does not occur in any narrative text, but is found in

the *Etymologies* (V.382–3, stems RAD and RĪ): '*Radhrim* East-march (part of Doriath)'.

(50)   E 12–13, F 13   The words 'north road of Dwarves' are very faint and blurred, but this seems to be the only possible interpretation. On the extremely puzzling question of the Dwarf-roads in East Beleriand see pp. 334–6.

(51)   E 12   A word faintly pencilled across the upper part of this square could be interpreted as 'Marshes'.

(52)   F 9   *Eglador* pencilled under *Doriath*: see §14 above.

(53)   F 10   *Arthórien*: see pp. 112–13, commentary on GA §38; and the next entry.

(54)   F 10   *Garthúrian* (which could also be read as *Garthúrien*): in the text cited at §32 above it is said that 'the Noldor often used the name *Arthúrien* for Doriath, though this is but an alteration of the Sindarin *Garthúrian* "hidden realm".'

(55)   F 11   *Estoland*: the form is clear, but at all other occurrences of the name it is *Estolad*.

3   South-western section (p. 184)

(56)   G 2   *Cape Andras* is referred to in *Quendi and Eldar*, p. 379. Cf. *Andrast* 'Long Cape' in the extreme west of Gondor (Index to *Unfinished Tales*).

(57)   G 3 to H 3   The names *Eglamar* (as applied here) and *Emyn Eglain* (or *Hills of Eglamar*) are not found in any narrative text. *Eglamar* is one of the oldest names in my father's *legendarium*: together with *Eldamar* of the same meaning, 'Elf-home', it referred to the land of the Elves in Valinor, *Egla* being 'the Gnome name of the Eldar who dwelt in Kôr' (see I.251, II.338; also the *Etymologies*, V.356, stem ELED). The old names *Eglamar, Eglador, Eglorest* (> *Eglarest*), not abandoned, were afterwards related to the name by which the Sindar called themselves, *Eglath* 'the Forsaken People' (see X.85, 164). In *Quendi and Eldar* (p. 365) the etymology of *Eglain, Egladhrim* is given – though it is not the only one that my father advanced; and later in that essay (pp. 379–80) it is explained why these names were found in the Falas among the people of Círdan. (I cannot account for the application of the name *Eglamar* to Arthórien, the small land in the S.E. of Doriath between Aros and Celon, in the note cited on p. 112, commentary on GA §38.)

(58)   G 4   The name *Eglorest* of the map as originally made was not emended to the later form *Eglarest*.

(59)   G 5–6, H 5–6   The extent of the *Taur-na-Faroth* (or *High Faroth*) is marked out by the dotted line (extending somewhat north of Nargothrond on Section 1, F 5) as a very large region,

somewhat in the shape of a footprint: cf. the representation of the Hills of the Hunters on the first *Silmarillion* map (Vol.IV, between pp. 220 and 221). The dots outlining the more southerly part were cancelled, and rough lines (not represented in the redrawing) across G 5 (from left-centre to bottom-right) suggest a reduction in the extent of the highlands. See further §65 below.

(60)   G 5   The name *Ingwil* was not corrected to the later form *Ringwil* (see p. 197, §112).

(61)   G 6   I have not found the name *Methiriad* of 'Mid-Beleriand' elsewhere.

(62)   H 2   *Barad Nimras* replaced *Tower of Tindabel* (jumping the intervening name *Ingildon*): see p. 197, §120.

(63)   H 3   The coastline south-west of Eglarest was extended into a small cape named *Ras Mewrim*, a name not found elsewhere; in *Quendi and Eldar* (pp. 379–80) it is named *Bar-in-Mŷl* 'Home of the Gulls'.

(64)   H 4   *Harfalas*: see §21 above.

(65)   J 5-7, K 5-6   I have mentioned under §59 above that the dotted line marking the extent of the Taur-na-Faroth was later cancelled in its southern part; but the high country of *Arvernien* (clearly added to the map after the dotted line) is shown extending by a narrow neck to join the southern extremity of the Taur-na-Faroth as originally indicated: i.e., there is a great range of hills extending from near the southern coast, through this 'neck', to a little north of Nargothrond.

(66)   K 5-6   The name *Earendil* on K 6, though separated, very probably belongs with *Ship-havens* on K 5. Cf. the beginning of Bilbo's song at Rivendell:

Eärendil was a mariner
that tarried in Arvernien;
he built a boat of timber felled
in Nimbrethil to journey in ...

4   South-eastern section (p. 185)

(67)   G 8-9, H 8-11   The *Andram* is marked only as a faint pencilled line of small curves, more vague and unclear than in my redrawing.

(68)   G 11-13   A vaguely marked line of dashes (not represented on the redrawing) runs westward from just above *Sarn Athrad* on G 13: this perhaps indicates the course of the Dwarf-road after the passage of Gelion. This line bends gently north-west across G 12 and leaves G 11 at the top left corner, possibly reappearing on Section 2, F 10, where (if this is correct) it reached Aros just below the inflow of Celon. See p. 334.

(69)   G 14   The correction of *Rathlorion* to *Rathloriel* was an early

change (V.407). A name beneath, hastily pencilled, is very probably *Rathmalad* (cf. the name *Rathmallen* of this river in *The Tale of Years*, p. 353).

(70) H 11–12 *Rhamdal*: this spelling is found in QS §142 (beside *Ramdal* in §113, adopted in *The Silmarillion*) and in the *Etymologies*, V.390, stem TAL; cf. *ibid*. V.382, stem RAMBĀ, 'Noldorin *rhamb, rham*'.

(71) K 10–11 The scribbled named *South Beleriand* was struck out.

(72) K 9–11, L 9–11 For the name *Taur-im-Duinath* of the great forested region between Gelion and Sirion in the published *Silmarillion* and map see p. 193, §108.

(73) L 14–15 *Tol Galen*: the divided course of the river Adurant (whence its name, according to the *Etymologies*, V.349, stem AT(AT)) enclosing the isle of Tol Galen is shown in two forms. The less extensive division was drawn in ink (it seems that the oblong shape itself represents the island, in which case the area between it and the two streams is perhaps to be taken as very low-lying land or marsh); the much larger division, in which the northern stream leaves the other much further to the east and rejoins it much further to the west, was entered in pencil, together with the name. The name *Tol Galen* was written a third time (again in pencil) across the upper part of square M 14.

(74) L 14–15 The mountains on these squares, extending northward onto K 15, were pencilled in very rapidly, and those to the north of Tol Galen were possibly cancelled.

On line M at the foot of the map are these pencilled notes (again with the number 71, see p. 187, §30): 'These river-names need revision to etymologizable words. *Celon* should go. *Gelion* should be *Duin Dhaer*.' On these changes see pp. 336–7 and note 10.

I turn now to the development of the chapter *Of Beleriand and its Realms*. The great majority of the changes made to the text of QS (Chapter 9, V.258–66, §§105–21) are found in the early typescript LQ 1, but some are not, and appear only in LQ 2: these cases are noticed in the account that follows. I do not record the changes *Melko* > *Melkor*, *Helkaraksë* > *Helkaraxë*, *Bladorion* > *Ard-galen*, *Eglorest* > *Eglarest*.

§105 After the words 'in the ancient days' at the end of the first sentence the following footnote was added to QS. As usual, the typist of LQ 1 took up the footnote into the text, but it appears as a footnote in LQ 2, whose typist was again working directly from the manuscript.

These matters, which are not in the *Pennas* of Pengolod, I have added and taken from the *Dorgannas Iaur* (the account of the shapes of the lands of old that Torhir Ifant made and is kept in Eressëa), that those who will may understand more clearly, maybe, what is later said of their princes and their wars: quoth Ælfwine.

On the *Pennas* of Pengolod see V.201–4.

'These Melko built in the elder days' > 'These Melkor had built in ages past'

§106   *Hísilóme* was written in the margin of the manuscript against *Hithlum* in the text (the latter not struck out). This is not in LQ 1, but LQ 2 has 'Hithlum (Hísilómë)' in the text.

Eredlómin > *the Eryd Lammad*. This form (not in LQ 1) has not occurred before, and is not (I believe) found elsewhere: in §105 *Eredlómin* was left unchanged.

'And Nivrost was a pleasant land watered by the wet winds from the sea, and sheltered from the North, whereas the rest of Hithlum was open to the cold winds' was struck out and replaced by the following (which does not appear in LQ 1):

And Nivrost was by some held to belong rather to Beleriand than to Hithlum, for it was a milder land, watered by the wet winds from the Sea and sheltered from the North and East, whereas Hithlum was open to cold north-winds. But it was a hollow land, surrounded by mountains and great coast-cliffs higher than the plains behind, and no river flowed thence. Wherefore there was a great mere amidmost, and it had no certain shores, being encircled by wide marshes. Linaewen was the name of that mere, because of the multitude of birds that dwelt there, of such as love tall reeds and shallow pools. Now at the coming of the Noldor many of the Grey-elves (akin to those of the Falas) lived still in Nivrost, nigh to the coasts, and especially about Mount Taras in the south-west; for to that place Ulmo and Ossë had been wont to come in days of old. All that folk took Turgon for their lord, and so it came to pass that in Nivrost the mingling of Noldor and Sindar began sooner than elsewhere; and Turgon dwelt long in those halls that he named Vinyamar, under Mount Taras beside the Sea. There it was that Ulmo afterwards appeared to him.

This passage introduced a number of new elements: the topography of Nivrost (the high coast-cliffs are represented on the second map as originally drawn, p. 182), and Lake Linaewen (which appears also in the later *Tale of Tuor, Unfinished Tales* p. 25, with the same description of Nivrost as a 'hollow land'); the coming of Ulmo and Ossë to Mount Taras in the ancient days; and the conception that Sindarin Elves dwelt in Nivrost near the coast and especially about Mount Taras, and that they took Turgon to be their lord at the coming of the Noldor to Middle-earth. The later story that there were many Grey-elves among Turgon's people appears in the rewritten annal for the year 116 in GA (see §§107, 113 and the commentary on those passages).

The footnote in the QS manuscript 'Ilkorin name' to the sentence 'the great highland that the Gnomes first named Dorthonion' was struck out, and in the text 'Gnomes' was changed to 'Dark-elves'.

The extent of Dorthonion from west to east was changed from 'a hundred leagues' to 'sixty leagues'; on this change, made to bring the distance into harmony with the second map, see V.272.

§107   The length of Sirion from the Pass to the Delta was changed from 'one hundred and twenty-one leagues' to 'one hundred and thirty-one leagues'. The former measurement (see V.272) was the length of Sirion in a straight line from the northern opening of the Pass to the Delta; the new measurement is from Eithel Sirion to the Delta.

§108   A footnote was added to the first occurrence of *Eredlindon*:

Which signifieth the Mountains of Ossiriand; for the Gnomes [LQ 2 Noldor] called that land Lindon, the region of music, and they first saw these mountains from Ossiriand. But their right name was Eredluin the Blue Mountains, or Luindirien the Blue Towers.

This note, which may go back to a time near to the writing of QS, has been given and discussed in V.267, §108. The last five words were struck out on the manuscript and do not appear in LQ 1, the typist of which put the footnote into the body of the text and garbled the whole passage, which however remained uncorrected. The words 'quoth Ælfwine' were added to the manuscript at the end of the footnote, but appear only in LQ 2.

'a tangled forest' > 'Taur-im-Duinath, a tangled forest' (of the land between Sirion and Gelion south of the Andram; see under §113 below). On the second map this region is named *Taur i Melegyrn or Taur na Chardhin* (see p. 185).

'while that land lasted' > 'while their realm lasted'

§109   The extent of West Beleriand between Sirion and the Sea was changed from 'seventy leagues' to 'ninety-nine leagues', another change harmonising the distance with the second map (see V.272).

In 'the realm of Nargothrond, between Sirion and Narog' 'Sirion' was changed to 'Taiglin'.

§110   From the words 'first the empty lands' at the beginning of the paragraph all that followed in QS as far as 'Next southward lay the kingdom of Doriath' was struck out and replaced by the following on an attached rider:

first between Sirion and Mindeb the empty land of Dimbar under the peaks of the Crissaegrim, abode of eagles, south of Gondolin (though that was for long unknown); then between Mindeb and the upper waters of Esgalduin the no-land of Nan Dungorthin. And that region was filled with fear, for upon its one side the power of Melian fenced the north-march of Doriath, but upon the other side the sheer precipices of Ered Orgoroth [> Orgorath], mountains of terror, fell down from high Dorthonion. Thither Ungoliantë had fled from the whips of the Balrogs, and had dwelt there a while, filling the hideous ravines with her deadly gloom, and there still, when she had passed away, her foul broods lurked and wove their evil nets; and the thin waters that spilled from Ered Orgoroth [> Orgorath] were all defiled, and perilous to drink, for the hearts of those that tasted them were filled with shadows of madness and despair. All living things shunned that land, and the Noldor would pass through Nan Dungorthin only at great need, by paths nigh to the borders of Doriath, and furthest from the haunted hills.

But if one fared that way he came eastward across Esgalduin and Aros (and Dor Dínen the silent land between) to the North Marches of Beleriand, where the sons of Fëanor dwelt. But southward lay the kingdom of Doriath . . .

On the name Crissaegrim (which occurs, in the spelling Crisaegrim, in GA §161) see V.290, §147. In this passage is the first appearance of Dor Dínen 'the Silent Land' (added to the map p. 183, square D 10). The story that Ungoliantë dwelt in Nan Dungorthin when she fled from the Balrogs appears in the Annals of Aman (X.109, 123; cf. also X.297, §20).

'where he turned westward' (with reference to the river Esgalduin) > 'where it turned westward'.

§111   The marginal note to the name Thargelion 'or Radhrost' was changed to 'Radhrost in the tongue of Doriath.'

'This region the Elves of Doriath named Umboth Muilin, the Twilight Meres, for there were many mists' > 'This region the Noldor named Aelinuial and the Dark-elves Umboth Muilin, the Twilight Meres, for they were wrapped in mists', and the footnote giving the Gnomish names Hithliniath and Aelin-uial was struck out (thus LQ 1). Later emendation removed the words 'and the Dark-elves Umboth Muilin' (thus LQ 2).

§112   The opening word 'For' was changed to 'Now'; and in the following sentence 'Umboth Muilin' was changed to 'Aelin-uial'.

The passage beginning 'Yet all the lower plain of Sirion' was changed to read thus: 'Yet all the lower fields of Sirion were divided from the upper fields by this sudden fall, which to one looking from the south northward appeared as an endless chain of hills'. In the following sentence 'Narog came south through a deep gorge' > 'Narog came through these hills in a deep gorge'. (There is an error in the text of this sentence as printed (V.262): 'on its west bank rose' should read 'on its west bank the land rose'.)

§113   The last sentence of the paragraph (and the beginning of §114) was rewritten to read:

But until that time all the wide woods south of the Andram and between Sirion and Gelion were little known. Taur-im-Duinath, the forest between the two rivers, the Gnomes [LQ 2 Noldor] called that region, but few ever ventured in that wild land; and east of it lay the far green country of Ossiriand . . .

On *Taur-im-Duinath* see under §108 above.

§114   At the name *Adurant* there is a footnote to the text in QS, which like that in §108 may belong to a relatively early time (see my remarks in the commentary, V.268):

And at a point nearly midway in its course the stream of Adurant divided and joined again, enclosing a fair island; and this was called Tolgalen, the Green Isle. There Beren and Lúthien dwelt after their return.

§115   The opening sentence of the paragraph was rewritten thus: 'There dwelt the Nandor, the Elves of the Host of Dân, who in the beginning were of Telerian race, but forsook their lord Thingol upon the march from Cuiviénen . . .' On the first appearance of the name *Nandor*, a people originally from the host of the Noldor, see X.169, §28.

'Of old the lord of Ossiriand was Denethor': 'son of Dân' added after 'Denethor'. In the same sentence 'Melko' > 'Morgoth'.

It is notable that the phrase 'in the days when the Orcs were first made' was never altered.

At the end of the paragraph was added: 'For which reason the Noldor named that land Lindon', with a footnote '[The Country of Music >] The Land of Song' (see under §108 above); and '(Here endeth the matter taken from the *Dorgannas*)', on which see under §105 above.

§116   The whole of the latter part of this paragraph, from after the words 'But Turgon the wise, second son of Fingolfin, held Nivrost', was struck out and the following substituted (which does not appear in LQ 1):

(But Turgon the wise . . . held Nivrost), and there he ruled a numerous folk, both Noldor and Sindar, for one hundred years and sixteen, until he departed in secret to a hidden kingdom, as afterwards is told.

This passage belongs with the long replacement in §106 given above, which likewise does not appear in LQ 1.

§117   'But Angrod and Egnor watched Bladorion' > 'His younger brethren Angrod and Egnor watched the fields of Ard-galen'

§120   *Tindobel* (see V.270, commentary on QS §§119–20)   >
Ingildon (cf. GA §90 and commentary, p. 118).

★

These are all the changes (save for a very few of no significance) made
to the QS manuscript. A number of further changes were made to
the top copy of the late typescript LQ 2 (the carbon copy was not
touched).

The chapter-number 'XIV' was inserted (see p. 179, §100); and at
the head of the first page my father wrote: 'This is a geographical and
political insertion and may be omitted. It requires a map, of which I
have not had time to make a copy.' This sounds as if he were preparing
the LQ 2 typescript for someone to see it (cf. his words against §82 in
the chapter 'Of Men' in LQ 2: 'This depends upon an old version in
which the Sun was first made after the death of the Trees (described in
a chapter omitted)', p. 175); in which case the words here 'and may be
omitted' were much more probably advice to the presumed reader
than a statement of intention about the inclusion of the chapter in *The
Silmarillion*.

§105   *Ered-engrin* > *Eryd Engrin*

'(Utumno) . . . at the western end' > 'at the midmost'. This shift of
Utumno eastwards is implied in the hasty note pencilled on the LQ 2
text of Chapter 2, *Of Valinor and the Two Trees*, in which the story
entered that Angband also was built in the ancient days, 'not far
from the northwestern shores of the Sea' (see X.156, §12, and the
addition made to this paragraph, given below).

Eredwethion > *Erydwethrin* (and subsequently).

Eredlómin > *Erydlómin*. In LQ 2 §106 the name of the Echoing
Mountains is *Eryd Lammad*, following the change made to the QS
manuscript there (p. 192) but not here; and *Eryd Lammad* was
allowed to stand.

The passage 'Behind their walls Melkor coming back into Middle-
earth made the endless dungeons of Angband, the hells of iron,
where of old Utumno had been. But he made a great tunnel under
them . . .' was emended on LQ 2 to read:

Behind their walls Melkor had made also a fortress (after called
Angband) as a defence against the West, if any assault should
come from Valinor. This was in the command of Sauron. It was
captured by the Valar, and Sauron fled into hiding; but being in
haste to overthrow Melkor in his great citadel of Utumno, the
Valar did not wholly destroy Angband nor search out all its deep
places; and thither Sauron returned and many other creatures of
Melkor, and there they waited in hope for the return of their
Master. Therefore when he came back into Middle-earth Melkor
took up his abode in the endless dungeons of Angband, the hells
of iron; and he made a great tunnel under them . . .

§106   *Nivrost* > *Nevrast* (and subsequently; see p. 179, §100). The footnote to the first occurrence of *Nivrost* 'Which is West Vale in the tongue of Doriath' was struck out and replaced by the following:

> Which is 'Hither Shore' in the Sindarin tongue, and was given at first to all the coast-lands south of Drengist, but was later limited to the land whose shores lay between Drengist and Mount Taras.

§108   To the name *Taur-im-Duinath* (a later addition to QS, p. 193) a footnote was added: 'Forest between the Rivers (sc. Sirion and Gelion)'. This interpretation occurs in fact in a rewriting of the QS text at a later point: p. 195, §113.

§110   At the two occurrences of *Nan Dungorthin* in the long replacement passage in this paragraph given on p. 193–4 the later form *Nan Dungortheb* was substituted.

§111   *Damrod and Díriel* > *Amrod and Amras*, and in §118; cf. X.177.

The revised footnote against the name *Thargelion*, 'Radhrost in the tongue of Doriath' (p. 194), was struck out and not replaced (see under §118 below).

Cranthir > *Caranthir*, and in §118; cf. X.177, 181.

§112   *Taur-na-Faroth* > *Taur-en-Faroth* at both occurrences.

Ingwil (the torrent joining Narog at Nargothrond) > *Ringwil*.

Inglor > *Finrod* (and subsequently).

§117   *Finrod* > *Finarfin*

§118   At the end of the paragraph *Dor Granthir* > *Dor Caranthir*; in the footnote the same change was made, and *Radhrost* was replaced by *Talath Rhúnen*, the translation 'the East Vale' remaining. See under §111 above.

§119   'But Inglor was king of Nargothrond and overlord of the Dark-elves of the western havens; and with his aid Brithombar and Eglorest were rebuilt' was rewritten thus:

> But Finrod was king of Nargothrond and over-lord of all the Dark-elves of Beleriand between Sirion and the Sea, save only in the Falas. There dwelt still those of the Sindar who still loved ships and the Sea, and they had great havens at Brithombar and Eglarest. Their lord was Círdan the Shipbuilder. There was friendship and alliance between Finrod and Círdan, and with the aid of the Noldor Brithombar and Eglarest were rebuilt ...

Finrod (Inglor) now loses the overlordship of the Elves of the Falas, with the emergence of Círdan, but my father failed to correct the earlier passage in QS (§109) telling that 'the Dark-elves of the havens ... took Felagund, lord of Nargothrond, to be their king.' The statement here in §119 agrees with what is said in GA §85 (see also the commentary, p. 117).

§120   In the opening sentence of this paragraph the old name *Tindobel* had been changed to *Ingildon* (p. 196); it was now changed to *Nimras* (cf. *Barad Nimras*, the replacement of *Tower of Tindabel* on the second map, p. 190, §62.

Some of the changes made to LQ 2 were made also to the much earlier typescript LQ 1: *Ringwil* (§112), *Talath Rhúnen* (§118), *Nimras* (§120). In addition, *Dor Granthir* was corrected to *Dor Cranthir* (§118), and the passage concerning the lordship of the Falas (§119) was inserted, but still with the name *Inglor*: thus these changes were not made at the same time as those in LQ 2, which has *Dor Caranthir* and *Finrod*.

---

12   OF TURGON AND THE BUILDING OF GONDOLIN

This short chapter on three manuscript pages, with this title but without chapter-number, was inserted into the QS manuscript following *Of Beleriand and its Realms*.

At an earlier point in the manuscript (§101 in the chapter *Of the Siege of Angband*) a long rider was introduced on the subject of the foundation of Nargothrond by Inglor and the discovery of Gondolin by Turgon: see pp. 177–9. As I have explained there, this rider is extant in two partially distinct forms, the first in the early LQ 1 typescript series, and the second on a sheet inserted into the QS manuscript (whence it appears in the late typescript LQ 2). Without question the new chapter (which does not appear in the LQ 1 series) was written at the same time as the revised form of this rider to §101, and it is to this that the opening words of the new chapter ('It hath been told how by the guidance of Ulmo …') refer. (I have also noticed, p. 179, that on the reverse of this rider is a rejected draft for the replacement text of the year 116 in the *Grey Annals*, §§111–13; on this see below, at the end of the third paragraph of the text.)

There is no need to give *Of Turgon and the Building of Gondolin* in full, because, as will be seen shortly, a substantial part of it has been given already.

Of Turgon and the Building of Gondolin

It hath been told how by the guidance of Ulmo Turgon of Nivrost discovered the hidden vale of Tum-laden; and that (as was after known) lay east of the upper waters of Sirion, in a ring of mountains tall and sheer, and no living thing came there save the eagles of Thorondor. But there was a deep way under the mountains delved in the darkness of the world by waters that flowed out to join the stream of Sirion; and this Turgon found and so came to the green plain amid the mountains, and saw the island-hill that stood there of hard smooth stone; for the vale had been a great lake in ancient days. Then Turgon knew that he had found the place of his desire, and resolved there to build a fair city, a memorial of Tirion upon Túna, for which his heart still yearned in exile. But he returned to Nivrost, and remained there in peace, though he pondered ever in his thought how he should accomplish his design.

> The conclusion of this paragraph had already been used, but abandoned before it was completed, at the end of the rider to QS §101, p. 179.

Therefore, after the Dagor Aglareb, the unquiet that Ulmo set in his heart returned to him, and he summoned many of the hardiest and most skilled of his people and led them secretly to the hidden vale, and there they began the building of the city that Turgon had devised in his heart; and they set a watch all about it that none might come upon their work from without, and the power of Ulmo that ran in Sirion protected them.

> In this second paragraph my father was following and all but simply copying the revised annal for the year 64 in GA (§89); 'the hidden vale' was substituted for 'Gondolin' of GA because Turgon was now not to name his city until it was completed.

Now Turgon dwelt still for the most part in Nivrost, but it came to pass that at last the City was full-wrought, after two and fifty years of labour; and Turgon appointed its name, and it was called Gondolin [*in margin:* the Hidden Rock]. Then Turgon prepared to depart from Nivrost and leave his fair halls beside the Sea; and there Ulmo came to him once again and spake with him.

> From this point the new *Silmarillion* chapter follows almost word for word the replacement text of the annal for 116 in GA (§§111–13): the words of Ulmo to Turgon, and the departure from Vinyamar to Gondolin. The reason for this is simple: as I have noticed in the commentary on GA §113 (p. 120), my father wrote against the revised annal for 116: 'Set this rather in the *Silmarillion* and substitute a short notice' (the proposed 'short notice' is given *ibid.*).
>
> The text of the new chapter leaves that in the *Grey Annals* at the words 'passed the gates in the mountains and they were shut behind him'; the concluding words of GA §113 ('But Nivrost was empty of folk and so remained until the ruin of Beleriand') were not repeated here, but were brought in subsequently.

And through many long years none passed inward thereafter (save Húrin and Handir only sent by Ulmo); and the host of

Turgon came never forth again until the Year of Lamentation [*struck out, probably at the time of writing:* and the ruin of the Noldor], after three hundred and fifty years and more. But behind the circle of the mountains the folk of Turgon grew and throve, and they put forth their skill in labour unceasing, so that Gondolin upon Amon Gwareth became fair indeed and meet to compare even with Elven Tirion beyond the Sea. High and white were its walls, and smooth were its stairs, and tall and strong was the Tower of the King. There shining fountains played, and in the courts of Turgon stood images of the Trees of old, which Turgon himself wrought with elven-craft; and the Tree which he made of gold was named Glingal, and the Tree whose flowers he made of silver was named Belthil, and the light which sprang from them filled all the ways of the city. But fairer than all the wonders of Gondolin was Idril Turgon's daughter, she that was called Celebrindal the Silver-foot for the whiteness of her unshod feet, but her hair was as the gold of Laurelin ere the coming of Melkor. Thus Turgon lived long in bliss greater than any that hath been east of the Sea; but Nivrost was desolate, and remained empty of living folk until the ruin of Beleriand; and elsewhere the shadow of Morgoth stretched out its fingers from the North.

The opening sentence of this concluding section, with the reference to the entry of Húrin and Handir of Brethil into Gondolin, shows that it belongs with the original form of that story in the *Grey Annals* (§§149–50, and see the commentary, pp. 124–5); the later story that it was Húrin and his brother Huor appears in the long rider GA §§161–6.

This is the only account, brief as it is, of the actual city of Gondolin that my father wrote after that in Q (IV.139–40) – although there are also the notes that follow the abandoned text of the later *Tale of Tuor* (*Unfinished Tales* p. 56, note 31). That the Trees of Gondolin were images made by Turgon was stated in a footnote to Chapter 2 *Of Valinor and the Two Trees* in QS (see V.210–11; X.155), and this is repeated here – but with the addition that 'the light which sprang from them filled all the ways of the city'.

There is only one other text of the new chapter, the LQ 2 typescript, in which it is numbered 'XV' (see p. 196). To this my father made some corrections: *Nivrost* > *Nevrast* as in the preceding chapters; *Eryd Wethion* > *Eryd Wethrin*; *Handir* > *Huor* (see above); and *Amon Gwareth* > *Amon Gwared*. The marginal note rendering *Gondolin* as 'the Hidden Rock' was placed in a footnote in LQ 2, which my father then extended as follows:

Or so its name was afterwards known and interpreted; but its ancient form and meaning are in doubt. It is said that the name was given first in Quenya (for that language was spoken in Turgon's house), and was *Ondolindë*, the Rock of the Music of Water, for there were fountains upon the hill. But the people (who spoke only the Sindarin tongue) altered this name to *Gondolin* and interpreted [it] to mean Hidden Rock: *Gond dolen* in their own speech.

With the interpretation of Quenya *Ondolindë* as 'Rock of the Music of Water' cf. the early translation of *Gondolin* as 'Stone of Song' in the name-list to the tale of *The Fall of Gondolin* (II.216); and with the interpretation 'Hidden Rock' cf. the *Etymologies* in Vol.V, p. 355, stem DUL, where *Gondolin(n)* is said to contain three elements: 'heart of hidden rock'.

---

13 CONCERNING THE DWARVES

The reason for this title will be seen at the end of the chapter (pp. 213–14). To the original Chapter 10 *Of Men and Dwarfs* in the QS manuscript (V.272–6, §§122–31) only a few changes were made before a radical revision overtook it.

§122 'whom the Dark-elves named Naug-rim' > 'whom they named the Naug-rim', i.e. this became a Noldorin name for the Dwarves given to them by Cranthir's people.

§123 The marginal note 'quoth Pengolod' against the bracketed passage concerning the origin and nature of the Dwarves was struck out (see V.277–8, §123).

§124 'Nogrod, the Dwarfmine': above 'Dwarfmine' is pencilled 'Dwarrowdelf', and in the margin again 'Dwarrowdelf Nogrod was afar off in the East in the Mountains of Mist; and Belegost was in Eredlindon south of Beleriand.' At the head of the page, with a direction for insertion in the text after 'Belegost, the Great Fortress' the following is written very rapidly:

> Greatest of these was Khazaddûm that was after called in the days of its darkness Moria, and it was far off in the east in the Mountains of Mist; but Gabilgathol was on [the] east side of Eredlindon and within reach of the Elves.

In the text of QS as written *Nogrod* (which goes back to the old *Tale of the Nauglafring*) is a translation of *Khazaddûm*, and the meaning is 'Dwarfmine'; both Nogrod and Belegost (Gabilgathol) are specifically stated (QS §122) to have been 'in the mountains east of Thargelion', and were so placed in additions to the second map. In *The Lord of the Rings* Khazad-dûm is Moria, and Nogrod and Belegost are 'ancient cities in the Blue Mountains' (Appendix A, III). The notes in the margin of QS just given must represent an idea that was not adopted, whereby Belegost remained in Eredlindon, but *Nogrod / Khazad-dûm was removed to the Misty Mountains, and Nogrod became the ancient Elvish name of Moria.*

The statement in the first of these notes that 'Belegost was in Eredlindon *south of Beleriand*' is surprising: it seems to represent a reversion to the older conception of the place of the Dwarf-cities: see the Eastward Extension of the first *Silmarillion* map, IV.231, where the dwarf-road after crossing the Blue Mountains below Mount Dolmed turns south and goes off the map in the south-east corner, with the direction 'Southward in East feet of Blue Mountains are Belegost and Nogrod.'

§126   Against the words in the first sentence of the paragraph 'when some four hundred years were gone since the Gnomes came to Beleriand' my father noted: 'This must be removed to 300', changed to '310'. See p. 226, §1.

§127   'They were the first of Men that wandering west' > 'They were the first of Men that after many lives of wandering westward' *Gumlin* > *Galion* (see p. 123, §127).

§128   The footnote was changed to read:

It is recorded that this name was *Vidri* in the ancient speech of these Men, which is now forgotten; for afterwards in Beleriand they forsook their own speech for the tongue of the Gnomes. Quoth Pengolod.

In the sentence following the place of the footnote 'whom we call the Gnomes' was changed to '(whom we here call the Gnomes)'.

§129   'the lordship of Gumlin was in Hithlum' > 'the lordship of Galion was in Dorlómen'

Throughout the text the form *Dwarfs* (see V.277, §122) was changed to *Dwarves*.

★

The next step was the striking out of the entire text of Chapter 10 from the beginning as far as 'Hador the Goldenhaired' at the end of §125, and the substitution of a new and much enlarged form, carefully written and inserted into the QS manuscript. This has a few subsequent emendations (almost all made at the same time in red ink), and these are shown in the text that now follows. One of these emendations concerns the title itself. As the revised version was first written the title was *Of Dwarves and Men*, with a subtitle *Concerning the Dwarves* (but no subtitle where the section on Men begins). The title was struck out, and replaced by *Of the Naugrim and the Edain*; the subtitle *Concerning the Dwarves* was retained; and a new subtitle *Of the Edain* was inserted at the appropriate place.

In order not to interrupt the numbering of the QS text in Vol.V, for reference in the commentary that follows the text I number the paragraphs of the revised version from §1. – It will be seen that the opening paragraph repeats almost exactly that of QS (§122), but loses the original concluding sentence: 'For though the Dwarfs did not serve Morgoth, yet they were in some things more like to his people than to the Elves.'

Of the Naugrim and the Edain

Concerning the Dwarves

§1   Now in time the building of Nargothrond was completed, and Gondolin had been raised in secret; but in the days of the Siege of Angband the Gnomes had yet small need of hiding-places, and they ranged far and wide between the Western Sea and the Blue Mountains. And it is said that they climbed Eredlindon and looked eastward in wonder, for the lands of Middle-earth seemed wild and wide; but few ever passed over the mountains while Angband lasted. In those days the folk of Cranthir first came upon the Dwarves, whom they [> the Dark-elves] named the Naugrim; for the chief dwellings of that race were then in the mountains east of Thargelion, the land of Cranthir, and were digged deep in the eastern slopes of Eredlindon. Thence they journeyed often into Beleriand, and were admitted even into Doriath. There was at that time no enmity between Elves and Dwarves, but nonetheless no great love.

*Here are the words of Pengolod concerning the Naugrim**

§2   The Naugrim are not of Elf-kind, nor of Man-kind, nor yet of Melkor's breeding; and the Noldor in Middle-earth knew not whence they came, holding that they were alien to the Children, albeit in many ways like unto them. But in Valinor the wise have learned that the Dwarves were made in secret by Aulë, while Earth was yet dark; for he desired the coming of the Children of Ilúvatar, that he might have learners to whom he could teach his crafts and lore, and he was unwilling to await the fulfilment of the designs of Ilúvatar. Wherefore, though the Dwarves are like the Orcs in this: that they came of the wilfulness of one of the Valar, they are not evil; for they were not made out of malice in mockery of the Children, but came of the desire of Aulë's heart to make things of his own after the

---

* All that follows in the section 'Concerning the Dwarves' is written in a much smaller script than that of the opening paragraph.

pattern of the designs of Ilúvatar. And since they came in the days of the power of Melkor, Aulë made them strong to endure. Therefore they are stone-hard, stubborn, fast in friendship and in enmity, and they suffer toil and hunger and hurt of body more hardily than all other speaking-folk. And they live long, far beyond the span of Men, and yet not for ever. Aforetime the Noldor held that dying they returned unto the earth and the stone of which they were made; yet that is not their own belief. For they say that Aulë cares for them and gathers them in Mandos in halls set apart for them, and there they wait, not in idleness but in the practice of crafts and the learning of yet deeper lore. And Aulë, they say, declared to their Fathers of old that Ilúvatar had accepted from him the work of his desire, and that Ilúvatar will hallow them and give them a place among the Children in the End. Then their part shall be to serve Aulë and to aid him in the re-making of Arda after the Last Battle.

§3 Now these Fathers, they say, were seven in number, and they alone return (in the manner of the Quendi) to live again in their own kin and to bear once more their ancient names. Of these Durin was the most renowned in after ages, father of that Dwarf-kin most friendly to the Elves whose mansions were at Khazad-dûm.

§4 In the darkness of Arda already the Naugrim wrought great works, for they had, even from the first days of their Fathers, marvellous skill with metals and with stone, though their works had little beauty until they had met the Noldor and learned somewhat of their arts. And they gave their friendship more readily to the Noldor than to any others of Elves or Men, because of their love and reverence for Aulë; and the gems of the Gnomes they praised above all other wealth. But in that ancient time the Dwarves still wrought iron and copper rather than silver and gold; and the making of weapons and gear of war was their chief smith-craft. They it was that first devised mail of linked rings, and in the making of byrnies and of hauberks none among Elves or Men have proved their equals. Thus they aided the Eldar greatly in their war with the Orcs of Morgoth; though the Noldor believed that some of that folk would not have been loath to smithy also for Morgoth, had he been in need of their work or open to their trade. For buying and selling and exchange were their delight, and the winning of wealth thereby; and this they gathered rather to hoard than to use, save in further trading.

§5   The Naugrim were ever, as they still remain, short and squat in stature; they were deep-breasted, strong in the arm, and stout in the leg, and their beards were long. Indeed this strangeness they have that no Man nor Elf has ever seen a beardless Dwarf – unless he were shaven in mockery, and would then be more like to die of shame than of many other hurts that to us would seem more deadly. For the Naugrim have beards from the beginning of their lives, male and female alike; nor indeed can their womenkind be discerned by those of other race, be it in feature or in gait or in voice, nor in any wise save this: that they go not to war, and seldom save at direst need issue from their deep bowers and halls. It is said, also, that their womenkind are few, and that save their kings and chieftains few Dwarves ever wed; wherefore their race multiplied slowly, and now is dwindling.

§6   The father-tongue of the Dwarves Aulë himself devised for them, and their languages have thus no kinship with those of the Quendi. The Dwarves do not gladly teach their tongue to those of alien race; and in use they have made it harsh and intricate, so that of those few whom they have received in full friendship fewer still have learned it well. But they themselves learn swiftly other tongues, and in converse they use as they may the speech of Elves and Men with whom they deal. Yet in secret they use their own speech only, and that (it is said) is slow to change; so that even their realms and houses that have been long and far sundered may to this day well understand one another. In ancient days the Naugrim dwelt in many mountains of Middle-earth, and there they met mortal Men (they say) long ere the Eldar knew them; whence it comes that of the tongues of the Easterlings many show kinship with Dwarf-speech rather than with the speeches of the Elves.*

§7   In their own tongue the Dwarves name themselves Khuzûd [> Khazâd]; and the Dark-elves called them / the Naugrim [> Naug], the stunted. Which name the exiled Noldor also used [> likewise took for them], but called them also the Nyrn [*struck out:* of like meaning], and the Gonnhirrim masters of stone; and those who dwelt in Belegost they called the Ennfeng or Longbeards, for their beards swept the floor before their feet. The chief cities of the Khuzûd [> Khazâd] in the west of Middle-earth in those days were at Khazaddûm, and at

* [Marginal note] Thus the *Lammas.*

Gabilgathol and Tumunzahar, which are interpreted in the Gnomish tongue Nornhabar the Dwarrowdelf, and Belegost Mickleburg, and Nogrod the Hollowbold. Greatest of all the mansions of the Naugrim was Khazaddûm, that was after called in the days of its darkness Moria, but it was far off in the Mountains of Mist beyond the wide leagues of Eriador; whereas Belegost and Nogrod were upon the east side of Eredlindon and nigh to the lands of the Eldar. Yet few of the Elves, save Meglin of Gondolin, went ever thither; and the Dwarves trafficked into Beleriand, and made a great road that passed under the shoulders of Mount Dolmed and followed thence the course of Ascar, crossing Gelion at Sarn-athrad. There battle later befell; but as yet the Dwarves troubled the Elves little, while the power of the Gnomes lasted.

§8   *Here end the words that Pengolod spoke to me concerning the Dwarves*, which are not part of the *Pennas* as it was written, but come from other books of lore, from the *Lammas*, the *Dorgannas*, and the *Quentalë Ardanómion*: quoth Ælfwine.

Of the Edain

§9   It is reckoned that the first meeting of the Noldor and the Naugrim befell in the land of Cranthir Fëanor's son about that time when Fingolfin destroyed the Orcs at Drengist, one hundred and fifty-five years after the crossing of the Ice, and one hundred and five before the first coming of Glómund the dragon. After his defeat there was long peace, and it lasted for wellnigh two hundred years of the sun. During this time the fathers of the Houses of the Men of the West, the Atani [> Edain], the Elf-friends of old, were born in the land of Eriador east of the mountains: Bëor the Vassal, Haleth the Hunter, and Hador the Goldenhaired.

Here the revised part of QS Chapter 10 ends. It will be seen that while it was composed with the original QS text before him and with the actual retention of some of it, my father now introduced many new conceptions concerning the Dwarves. The long-enduring 'hostile' view has at last virtually vanished, with the loss of the sentence at the end of the first paragraph (see p. 203) – although in the original QS text the likeness of Orcs and Dwarves was subsequently (§123) spoken of only in terms of the analogous origin of the two races, each deriving from one of the Valar acting independently, and this remains in the revision. We learn now that:

– the Dwarves live far longer than Men (§2);

- they themselves believe that Aulë gathers them after their death into halls in Mandos set apart, and that after the Last Battle they will aid Aulë in the remaking of Arda (§2);
- there were Seven Fathers of the Dwarves, who are reincarnated in their own kin (after the manner of the Elves), bearing their ancient names (§3);
- Durin was the father of the Dwarf-kindred of Khazad-dûm, most friendly to the Elves (§3);
- the Dwarves were better disposed to the Noldor than to any others among Elves or Men on account of their reverence of Aulë (§4);
- the Dwarves are bearded from birth, both male and female (§5);
- Dwarf-women cannot be distinguished from the men by those of other race (§5);
- Dwarf-women are very few, and never go to war, nor leave their deep homes save at the greatest need (§5);
- few Dwarves ever wed (§5);
- the Dwarf-speech changes only very slowly, so that sundering of houses and realms does not greatly impair understanding between them (§6);
- Dwarves met Men in Middle-earth long before the Eldar met them, and hence there is kinship between Dwarf-speech and the languages of the Easterling Men (§6).

This revised version was of course a part of the 1951 revision. There are notable likenesses to what is said in the Appendices to *The Lord of the Rings* concerning the Dwarves: thus in Appendix A, III *(Durin's Folk)* there are references to the fewness of Dwarf-women, who remain hidden in their dwellings, to the indistinguishability of Dwarf-women from Dwarf-men to people of other races, and to the rarity of marriage (III.360); and in Appendix F (III.410) the slow changing of their tongue is described.

There follows now a commentary on particular points.

§1 The change made to the original QS text (p. 201, §122) of 'whom the Dark-elves named Naug-rim' to 'whom they [the Noldor] named the Naug-rim' was now reversed, by a subsequent emendation (later, in §7, the attribution of the name to the Dark-elves appears in the text as written).

§2 'And since they came in the days of the power of Melkor': i.e., before the awakening of the Elves, the Battle of the Gods, and the captivity of Melkor in Mandos.

§3 It is here that Durin of Khazad-dûm, 'most renowned' of the Seven Fathers of the Dwarves, enters *The Silmarillion*. It is not said here that Durin's people were the Longbeards; but his association with the Longbeards goes back in fact to *The Hobbit*, where at the end of the chapter *A Short Rest* Thorin says (in the text as originally published): 'He was the father of the fathers of *one of the two races of dwarves, the Longbeards,* and my grandfather's ancestor.' In the

Tale of the Nauglafring there were the two peoples, the Dwarves of Nogrod and the Dwarves of Belegost, and the latter were the Indrafangs or Longbeards; in the *Quenta* the same was true (or at least, no other peoples were mentioned), although the Longbeards had become the Dwarves of Nogrod (IV.104), and this remained the case in QS (§124).

In the present text two things are said on the subject. Durin was 'the father of that Dwarf-kin ... whose mansions were at Khazad-dûm' (§3); but (reverting to the *Tale of the Nauglafring*) the Longbeards were the Dwarves of Belegost (§7) – and this is said also both in the *Annals of Aman* and in the *Grey Annals* (see p. 108, §22). I am not altogether certain how to interpret this; but the simplest solution is to suppose that when my father wrote these texts he had forgotten Thorin's mention of Durin as the ancestor of the Longbeards in *The Hobbit* (or, less probably, that he consciously disregarded it), and the following considerations support it.

At the beginning of the section *Durin's Folk* in Appendix A (III) to *The Lord of the Rings* the reading of the First Edition was: 'Durin is the name that the Dwarves use for the eldest of the Seven Fathers of all their race', without mention of the Longbeards. Years later, on his copy of the second edition of *The Hobbit*, my father noted: 'Not so in *Silmarillion* nor see [*sic*] LR III p. 352' – this being a reference to the passage just cited from Appendix A in the First Edition: what was 'not so' was Thorin's reference to 'one of the two races of dwarves', become obsolete since the emergence of the conception of the Seven Fathers. At the same time he wrote on this copy many tentative phrases to replace Thorin's original words, such as 'the eldest of the Seven Fathers of the Dwarves', 'the father of the fathers of the eldest line of the Dwarf-kings, the Longbeards', before arriving at the final form as subsequently published, 'He was the father of the fathers of the eldest race of Dwarves, the Longbeards, and my first ancestor: I am his heir.' It was obviously consideration of Thorin's words in *The Hobbit* and the need for their correction that led him to alter the text of Appendix A, which in the Second Edition (1966) reads: 'Durin is the name that the Dwarves used for the eldest of the Seven Fathers of their race, *and the ancestor of all the kings of the Longbeards*', with the addition of a footnote reference to the passage in *The Hobbit*, now published in its corrected form.

Thus, circuitously, the Longbeards finally entered *The Lord of the Rings*, as the Dwarves of Khazad-dûm; but the texts of *The Silmarillion* and the *Annals* were never changed, and the Longbeards remained the Dwarves of Belegost.

§6   The marginal note 'Thus the *Lammas*' apparently refers specifically to the statement in the text concerning the kinship of languages of the Easterlings with Dwarf-speech. Cf. V.179 (*Lham-*

mas §9): 'the languages of Men are derived in part from them' (the tongues of the Dwarves); this was repeated in the footnote to QS §123, from which the present paragraph was developed, and which also has a marginal note 'So, the *Lhammas*'.

§7 The names and places of the Dwarf-cities now achieve almost their final form, and I recapitulate here the complex development:

QS original form, §124 (V.274)
> *Khazad-dûm* = *Nogrod* = *Dwarfmine* (in the Blue Mountains)
> *Gabilgathol* = *Belegost* = *Great Fortress*

QS original form emended, p. 201
> *Khazad-dûm* = *Nogrod* = *Dwarrowdelf*, later *Moria*
> *Gabilgathol* = *Belegost* = *Great Fortress*

QS revised version, §7
> *Tumunzahar* = *Nogrod* = *Hollowbold* (in the Blue Mountains)
> *Gabilgathol* = *Belegost* = *Mickleburg*
> *Khazad-dûm* = *Nornhabar* = *Dwarrowdelf*, later *Moria*

The Dwarvish name *Tumunzahar* of Nogrod appears in GA §19, but this is the first occurrence of the Elvish name *Nornhabar*.

Of the names of the Dwarves themselves, there first occur here *Gonnhirrim* masters of stone, and *Nyrn* (cf. *Nornwaith* in AAm, X.93, *Norn-folk* in GA §19, and the name *Nornhabar* of Khazad-dûm). *Naugrim* is now said to mean 'stunted', and *Nyrn* is 'of like meaning', though this statement was struck out; in the original text (§124) *Neweg* = 'stunted'. In addition, *Khuzûd* was subsequently changed to *Khazâd*, and *Naugrim* to *Naug*. I give here a summary of the development of these confusing names and forms:

Tale of the Nauglafring	*Nauglath*
Q	*Nauglir*
AB 1 (IV.311)	*Nauglar* (also in the List of Names, V.405: Dark-elvish name, adopted by the Gnomes)
QS (original form)	*Naugrim* (Dark-elvish name > (p. 201) Gnomish name) *Neweg* 'stunted' (Gnomish name)
QS (revised version)	*Naugrim* (> *Naug*) 'stunted' (Gnomish name > Dark-elvish name, adopted by the Gnomes) *Nyrn* (Gnomish name, 'stunted' – but this meaning rejected)
AAm	*Nauglath* > *Naugrim* *Nornwaith* (later rejected, X.106, §84)
GA	*Naugrim* *Norn-folk* (§19)

An important element in this revised section remains to be mentioned: at this stage the myth of the creation of the Dwarves lacked the element of the Fathers being laid to sleep, by the command of Ilúvatar, after their first arising. This is apparent from the text as it stands; and the entry of this element will be seen in a moment.

The next text was the typescript of the LQ 1 series, which followed the manuscript text exactly (but the changes of *Khuzûd* > *Khazâd* and *Naugrim* > *Naug* in §7 do not appear, nor in LQ 2), and after the first paragraph of the section *Of the Edain* (§9), where the revised version ends, followed the original text of QS, with the very few alterations that were made to it and which have been given on pp. 201–2.

The opening of 'the words of Pengolod [> Pengoloð] concerning the Naugrim' (§2) were struck out, long afterwards, on LQ 1, as far as 'the desire of Aulë's heart to make things of his own after the pattern of the designs of Ilúvatar.' Associated with the QS manuscript at this point are two pages headed 'Of Aulë and the Dwarves', enclosed in a paper wrapper bearing the words 'Amended Legend of Origin of Dwarves'; this begins as a good manuscript but breaks up into confusion and variant forms. A new text was written out fair in a late script of my father's, without title, and attached to LQ 1 as a replacement for the passage struck out; it begins thus, differing little from the rejected form:

> The Naugrim are not of the Elf-kind, nor of Man-kind, nor yet of Melkor's breeding; and the Noldor, when they met them in Middle-earth, knew not whence they came, holding that they were alien to the Children, although in many ways they resembled them. But here in Valinor we have learned that in their beginning the Dwarves were made by Aulë, while Earth was still dark; for Aulë desired the coming of the Children so greatly, to have learners to whom he could teach his lore and his crafts, that he was unwilling to await the fulfilment of the designs of Ilúvatar.

The remainder of the text will be found in the published *Silmarillion*, Chapter 2 *Of Aulë and Yavanna*, pp. 43–4, to its end at 'Then Aulë took the Seven Fathers of the Dwarves, and laid them to rest in far-sundered places; and he returned to Valinor, and waited while the long years lengthened.' There are a number of insignificant editorial alterations in the published text, and among them one point should be mentioned: my father was uncertain whether to use 'thou' or 'you' in the converse of Aulë with Ilúvatar (in one case he changed 'you may' to 'thou mayst' and then reverted to 'you may'). In the end he decided on 'you', whereas the published text has 'thou' throughout.

At the end of the insertion the chapter continues with 'Since they came in the days of the power of Melkor ...' (p. 204), but concomitantly with the introduction of the new form of the legend, in which the Fathers of the Dwarves were laid to sleep until after the awakening of the Elves and the imprisonment of Melkor, this was changed on LQ 1 to 'Since they were to come ...' The only other significant alteration made to LQ 1 was in the opening sentence of §3, which was changed to read: 'Now these Seven Fathers, they say, return to live again and to bear once more their ancient names.' It might be expected that my father would have made some change to the opening sentence of §4 after the entry of the new form of the legend, but he was evidently content with an internal shift of meaning: 'even from the first days of their Fathers' is to be understood as 'even from the first days of their Fathers when they awoke from their sleep'.

The earlier of the two texts of the inserted passage shows my father much exercised about the details of the making of the first Dwarves. Thus there are the following tentative and roughly-written passages:

(a)   But it is said that to each Dwarf Ilúvatar added a mate of female kind, yet because he would not amend the work of Aulë, and Aulë had yet made only things of male form, therefore the women of the Dwarves resemble their men more than all other [?speaking] races.

(b)   He wrought in secret in a hall under the mountains in Middle-earth. There he made first one Dwarf, the eldest of all, and after he made six others, the fathers of their race; and then he began to make others again, like to them but of female kind to be their mates. But he wearied, and when he [had] made six more he rested, and he returned to the seven fathers and he looked at them, and they looked at him, and whatever motion was in his thought that motion they performed. And Aulë was not pleased, but he began to teach them the language that he had designed for them, hoping thus to instruct them.
   But Ilúvatar knew all that was done, and in the very hour that the Eldest Dwarf first spoke with tongue, Ilúvatar spoke to Aulë; and Aulë

(c)   Aulë made one, and then six, and he began to make mates for them of female form, and he made six, and then he wearied. Thus he buried six pairs, but one (Durin) the eldest he laid alone.

(d)   And Aulë took the Seven Dwarves and laid them to rest under stone in far-sundered places, and beside each [of] them he laid a mate as the Voice bade him, and then he returned to Valinor.

(e)   Then Aulë took the Seven Dwarves and laid them to rest under stone in far-sundered places, and beside each he laid his mate, save only beside the Eldest, and he lay alone. And Aulë returned to Valinor and waited long as best he might. But it is not known when Durin or his brethren first awoke, though some think that it was at the time of the departure of the Eldar over sea.

With passage *(b)* cf. the essay on Orcs in Vol.X, p. 417:

But if [Melkor] had indeed attempted to make creatures of his own in imitation or mockery of the Incarnates, he would, like Aulë, only have succeeded in producing puppets: his creatures would have acted only while the attention of his will was upon them, and they would have shown no reluctance to execute any command of his, even if it were to destroy themselves.

In the final text, as printed in *The Silmarillion*, my father evidently abandoned the question of the origin of the female Dwarves, finding it intractable and the solutions unsatisfactory. Moreover in the finished form the element of the Eldest (Durin) being distinct from the others, and without mate, finds no place.

There is another version of the legend in the draft continuation (not sent) of a letter to Miss Rhona Beare dated 14 October 1958 *(The Letters of J. R. R. Tolkien* no.212); and here appears the idea of the one and the six, and the six mates of the six, making thirteen in all. I reprint the passage here, since it may not be readily available.

Aulë, for instance, one of the Great, in a sense 'fell'; for he so desired to see the Children, that he became impatient and tried to anticipate the will of the Creator. Being the greatest of all craftsmen he tried to *make* children according to his imperfect knowledge of their kind. When he had made thirteen,* God spoke to him in anger, but not without pity: for Aulë had done this thing *not* out of evil desire to have slaves and subjects of his own, but out of impatient love, desiring children to talk to and teach, sharing with them the praise of Ilúvatar and his great love of the *materials* of which the world is made.

The One rebuked Aulë, saying that he had tried to usurp the Creator's power; but he could not give independent *life* to his makings. He had only one life, his own derived from the One, and could at most only distribute it. 'Behold' said the One: 'these creatures of thine have only thy will, and thy movement. Though you have devised a language for them, they can only report to thee thine own thought. This is a mockery of me.'

Then Aulë in grief and repentance humbled himself and asked for pardon. And he said: 'I will destroy these images of my presumption, and wait upon thy will.' And he took a great hammer, raising it to smite the eldest of his images; but it flinched and cowered from him. And as he withheld his stroke, astonished, he heard the laughter of Ilúvatar.

---

* One, the eldest, alone, and six more with six mates.

'Do you wonder at this?' he said. 'Behold! thy creatures now live, free from thy will! For I have seen thy humility, and taken pity on your impatience. Thy making I have taken up into my design.' This is the Elvish legend of the making of the Dwarves; but the Elves report that Ilúvatar said thus also: 'Nonetheless I will not suffer my design to be forestalled: thy children shall not awake before mine own.' And he commanded Aulë to lay the fathers of the Dwarves severally in deep places, each with his mate, save Dúrin the eldest who had none. There they should sleep long, until Ilúvatar bade them awake. Nonetheless there has been for the most part little love between the Dwarves and the children of Ilúvatar. And of the fate that Ilúvatar has set upon the children of Aulë beyond the Circles of the world Elves and men know nothing, and if Dwarves know they do not speak of it.

It seems to me virtually certain that all this work on the later legend of Aulë and the Dwarves derives from the same time, and it is obvious that this letter belongs with the first or draft text from which extracts are given on pp. 211–12, preceding the final text attached to LQ 1 and printed in *The Silmarillion*. That text was incorporated in LQ 2 as typed, and for that typescript I have proposed (on wholly distinct grounds) 1958 as the approximate date (see X.141–2, 300). This, I think, fits well enough with the date of the letter (October 1958). It seems likely that my father revised the existing *Silmarillion* materials *pari passu* with the making of the typescript LQ 2, carried out under his guidance.

As already noticed (see p. 210), the original QS text (lightly emended) in the second part of the chapter, that concerned with the Edain, was followed in the early typescript LQ 1. At a later time the whole of the section on the Edain was struck through both on the QS manuscript (with the direction 'Substitute new form') and on LQ 1 (with the direction 'Cancel'). This new form was a typescript, made by my father himself, with the title *Of the Coming of Men into the West and the Meeting of the Edain and the Eldar*. In the LQ 2 series the section on the Dwarves, now much altered and expanded from its original form, was made into a separate chapter, on which my father inserted the number 'XVI' (following 'XV' *Of Turgon and the Building of Gondolin*, p. 200), retaining as title the original subtitle *Concerning the Dwarves* (p. 202). The new text of the second part, *Of the Coming of Men into the West*, then followed in LQ 2 as a further chapter and was given the number 'XVII'. I have followed this arrangement.

The complex textual evolution of the original chapter in QS can be displayed thus (the dates have been made definite except in one case).

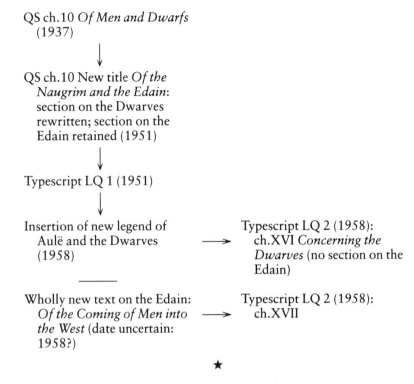

QS ch.10 *Of Men and Dwarfs*
(1937)

QS ch.10 New title *Of the
Naugrim and the Edain*:
section on the Dwarves
rewritten; section on the
Edain retained (1951)

Typescript LQ 1 (1951)

Insertion of new legend of
Aulë and the Dwarves
(1958)

Typescript LQ 2 (1958):
ch.XVI *Concerning the
Dwarves* (no section on the
Edain)

Wholly new text on the Edain:
*Of the Coming of Men into
the West* (date uncertain:
1958?)

Typescript LQ 2 (1958):
ch.XVII

★

It remains only to notice the changes made to LQ 2 *Concerning
the Dwarves*. The chief of these is a further revision of the names
of the Dwarves (see the table on p. 209). In §1 (p. 203) 'whom
the Dark-elves named the Naugrim' was struck out, and at every
occurrence the name *Naugrim* was replaced by *Dwarves* (except in the
heading to §2, where it was no doubt retained inadvertently). In §7 the
opening passage now read, both in LQ 1 and in LQ 2:

> In their own tongue the Dwarves name themselves Khuzûd; but
> the Dark-elves called them Naugrim, the stunted. Which name
> the exiled Noldor likewise took for them, but called them also the
> Nyrn ...

(The changes of *Khuzûd* to *Khazâd* and *Naugrim* to *Naug* made on
the manuscript did not appear in the typescripts as typed, see pp. 205,
210.) The passage was rewritten on LQ 2 thus:

> In their own tongue the Dwarves name themselves Khazâd; but
> the Grey-elves called them the Nyrn, the hard. This name the exiled
> Noldor likewise took for them, but called them also the Naugrim,
> the stunted folk ...

Other changes were: in §1, in the sentence 'few ever passed over the mountains', 'few' > 'none'; also *Cranthir* > *Caranthir*. In §7, in the sentence concerning Nornhabar, Belegost, and Nogrod, which were said to be interpretations 'in the Gnomish tongue' of the Dwarvish names, 'Gnomish' > 'Elvish'.

----

14   OF THE COMING OF MEN INTO THE WEST

The introduction of what very soon became an entirely new chapter – a massive extension of and departure from the 'traditional' history of the Edain – has been briefly described on p. 213. It emerges in a typescript (with carbon copy) made by my father: of antecedent draft material there is now no trace, but it seems to me very improbable that the text reached this form *ab initio*. It has in fact two titles: that typed as heading to the text is *Of the Coming of Men into the West and the Meeting of the Edain and the Eldar*, but on a separate title-page in manuscript it is called *Of the Coming of the Edain & their Houses and Lordships in Beleriand*.

The text was emended in ink on both copies almost identically; these changes were made, I feel sure, at much the same time as the original typing, and in the text that follows I adopt the emendations, but notice some of the original readings in the commentary. The separate title-page with the different title may belong with these, but I use here the other, in a shortened form *Of the Coming of Men into the West*, as was done in the published *Silmarillion*. The chapter (as emended) was incorporated in the typescript series LQ 2, as already mentioned, and subsequently given the number 'XVII'; perhaps (as with the new legend of Aulë and the Dwarves, see p. 213) it belongs to the period when the LQ typescript was being made (see p. 227, §13, and p. 229).

The text is found in the published *Silmarillion*, Chapter 17, but I have thought it best in this case to give the original in full. To show the editorial alterations and insertions in the published text takes much space, and it is difficult to make them clear, while the chapter is an essential companion to *The Wanderings of Húrin* in Part Three.

Of the Coming of Men into the West and the Meeting of the Edain and the Eldar

§1   Now it came to pass, when three hundred years and ten were gone since the Noldor came to Beleriand, in the days of the Long Peace, that Felagund journeyed east of Sirion and went hunting with Maglor and Maedros, sons of Fëanor. But he wearied of the chase and passed on alone towards the Mountains of Ered-lindon that he saw shining afar; and taking the

Dwarf-road he crossed Gelion at the ford of Sarn-athrad, and turning south over the upper streams of Ascar, he came into the north of Ossiriand.

§2   In a valley among the foothills of the Mountains, below the springs of Thalos, he saw lights in the evening, and far off he heard the sound of song. At this he wondered much, for the Green-elves of that land lit no fires, and they did not sing by night. At first he feared that a raid of Orcs had passed the leaguer of the North, but as he drew near he perceived that this was not so. For the singers used a tongue that he had not heard before, neither that of Dwarves nor of Orcs, and their voices were fair, though untutored in music.

§3   Then Felagund, standing silent in the night-shadow of the trees, looked down into the camp, and there he beheld a strange folk. They were tall, and strong, and comely, though rude and scantily clad; but their camp was well-ordered, and they had tents and lodges of boughs about the great fire in the midst; and there were fair women and children among them.

§4   Now these were a part of the kindred and following of Bëor the Old, as he was afterwards called, a chieftain among Men. After many lives of wandering out of the East he had led them at last over the Mountains, the first of the race of Men to enter Beleriand; and they sang because they were glad, and believed that they had escaped from all perils and had come to a land without fear.

§5   Long Felagund watched them, and love for them stirred in his heart; but he remained hidden in the trees until they had all fallen asleep. Then he went among the sleeping people, and sat beside their dying fire where none kept watch; and he took up a rude harp which Bëor had laid aside, and he played music upon it such as the ears of Men had not heard; for they had as yet no teachers in the art, save only the Dark-elves in the wild lands.

§6   Now men awoke and listened to Felagund as he harped and sang, and each thought that he was in some fair dream, until he saw that his fellows were awake also beside him; but they did not speak or stir while Felegund still played, because of the beauty of the music and the wonder of the song. Wisdom was in the words of the Elven-king, and the hearts grew wiser that hearkened to him; for the things of which he sang, of the making of Arda, and the bliss of Aman beyond the shadows of the Sea, came as clear visions before their eyes, and his Elvish speech was interpreted in each mind according to its measure.

§7   Thus it was that Men called King Felagund, whom they first met of all the Eldar, Wisdom, and after him they named his people The Wise.* Indeed they believed at first that Felagund was one of the gods, of whom they had heard rumour that they dwelt far in the West; and this was (some say) the chief cause of their journey. But Felagund dwelt among them and taught them true lore; and they loved him and took him for their lord, and were ever after loyal to the House of Finrod.**

§8   Now the Eldar were beyond all other peoples skilled in tongues; and Felagund discovered also that he could read in the minds of Men such thoughts as they wished to reveal in speech, so that their words were easily interpreted.† It was not long therefore before he could converse with Bëor; and while he dwelt with him they spoke much together. But when Felagund questioned Bëor concerning the arising of Men and their journeys, Bëor would say little; and indeed he knew little, for the fathers of his people had told few tales of their past and a silence had fallen upon their memory.

§9   'A darkness lies behind us,' Bëor said; 'and we have turned our backs on it, and we do not desire to return thither even in thought. Westwards our hearts have been turned, and we believe that there we shall find Light.'

§10   But Felagund learned from Bëor that there were many other Men of like mind who were also journeying westward. 'Others of my own kin have crossed the Mountains,' he said, 'and they are wandering not far away; and the Haladin, a people that speak the same tongue as we, are still in the valleys on the eastern slopes, awaiting tidings before they venture

* *Nóm* and [*Nómil* >] *Nómin* in the ancient language of this people (which afterwards was forgotten); for Bëor and his folk later learned the language of the Eldar and forsook their own, though they retained many names that came down to them [out of the past >] from their fathers.

** Thus Bëor got his name; for it signified Vassal in their tongue, and each of their chieftains after him bore this name as a title until the time of Bregolas and Barahir.

†It is said also that these Men had long had dealings with the Dark-elves of Middle-earth, and from them had learned much of their speech; and since all the languages of the Quendi were of one origin, the language of Bëor and his folk resembled the Elven-tongues in many words and devices.

further. There are also Men of a different speech, with whom we have had dealings at times. They were before us in the westward march, but we passed them; for they are a numerous people, and yet keep together and move slowly, being all ruled by one chieftain whom they call Marach.'

§11 Now the Nandor, the Green-elves of Ossiriand, were troubled by the coming of Men, and when they heard that a lord of the Eldar from over the Sea was among them they sent messengers to Felagund. 'Lord,' they said, 'if you have power over these new-comers, bid them to return by the ways that they came, or else to go forward. For we desire no strangers in this land to break the peace in which we live. And these folk are hewers of trees and hunters of beasts; therefore we are their unfriends, and if they will not depart we shall afflict them in all ways that we can.'

§12 Then by the advice of Felagund Bëor gathered all the wandering families and kindreds of his folk, and they removed over Gelion and took up their abode in the lands of Diriol, upon the east-banks of the Celon near to the borders of Doriath. But when after a year had passed Felagund wished to return to his own country, Bëor begged leave to come with him; and he remained in the service of the king while his life lasted. In this way he got his name Bëor, whereas his name before had been Balan; for Bëor signified Servant in the ancient tongue of his people. The rule of his folk he committed to his elder son Baran, and he did not return again to Estolad.*

Of the Kindreds and Houses of the Edain

§13 Soon after the departure of Felagund the other Men of whom Bëor had spoken came also into Beleriand. First came the Haladin; but meeting the unfriendship of the Nandor they turned north and dwelt in Radhrost, in the country of Caranthir son of Fëanor; and there for a time they had peace, though the people of Caranthir paid little heed to them. The next year, however, Marach led his people over the Mountains; and they were a tall and warlike folk, and they marched in ordered companies; and the Green-elves hid themselves and did not waylay them. And Marach hearing that the people of Bëor were dwelling in a green and fertile land, came down the Dwarf-road

---

* The Encampment. This was the name ever after of the land east of Celon and south of Nan Elmoth.

and settled his people in the country to the south and east of the dwellings of Baran son of Bëor. There was great friendship between the peoples, though they were sundered in speech, until they both learned the Sindarin tongue.

§14   Felagund himself often returned to visit Men; and many other Elves out of the westlands, both Noldor and Sindar, journeyed to Estolad, being eager to see the Edain, whose coming had long been foretold.* And Fingolfin, King of all the Noldor, sent messengers of welcome to them. Then many young and eager men of the Edain went away and took service with the kings and lords of the Eldar. Among these was Malach son of Marach, and he dwelt in Hithlum for fourteen years; and he learned the Elven-tongue and was given the name of Aradan.

§15   The Edain did not long dwell content in Estolad, for many still desired to go westwards; but they did not know the way: before them lay the fences of Doriath, and southward lay Sirion and its impassable fens. Therefore the kings of the three houses of the Noldor, seeing hope of strength in the sons of Men, sent word that any of the Edain that wished might remove and come to dwell among their people. In this way the migration of the Edain began: at first little by little, but later in families and kindreds, they arose and left Estolad, until after some fifty years many thousands had entered the lands of the kings.

§16   Most of these took the long road northwards, under the guidance of the Elves, until the ways became well known to them. The people of Bëor came to Dorthonion and dwelt in lands ruled by the House of Finrod. The people of Aradan (for Marach remained in Estolad until his death) for the most part went on westwards; and some came to Hithlum, but Magor son of Aradan and the greater number of his folk passed down Sirion into Beleriand and dwelt in the vales on the southern slopes of the Ered-wethion. A few only of either people went to Maedros and the lands about the Hill of Himring.

* *Atani* was the name given to Men in Valinor, in the lore that told of their coming; according to the Eldar it signified 'Second', for the kindred of Men was the second of the Children of Ilúvatar. *Edain* was the form of the name in Beleriand, and there it was used only of the three kindreds of the first Elf-friends. Men of other kind were called *Hravani* (or *Rhevain*), the 'Wild'. But all Men the Elves called *Hildi* [> *Hildor*], the Followers, or *Firyar*, the Mortals (in Sindarin *Echil* and *Firiath*).

§17   Many, however, remained in Estolad; and there was still a mingled people of Men living there long years after, until in the ruin of Beleriand they were overwhelmed or fled back into the East. For beside the old who deemed that their wandering days were over there were not a few who desired to go their own ways and feared the Eldar and the light of their eyes; and dissensions awoke among the Edain, in which the shadow of Morgoth may be discerned, for it cannot be doubted that he knew of the coming of Men and of their growing friendship with the Elves.

§18   The leaders of discontent were Bereg of the House of Bëor and Amlach one of the grandsons of Marach; and they said openly: 'We took long roads, desiring to escape the perils of Middle-earth and the dark things that dwell there; for we heard that there was Light in the West. But now we learn that the Light is beyond the Sea. Thither we cannot come where the gods dwell in bliss. Save one. For the Lord of the Dark is here before us, and the Eldar, wise but fell, who make endless war upon him. In the North he dwells, they say; and there is the pain and death from which we fled. We will not go that way.'

§19   Then a council and assembly of Men was called, and great numbers came together. And the Elf-friends answered Bereg, saying: 'Truly from the Dark King come all the evils from which we fled; but he seeks dominion over all Middle-earth, and whither now shall we turn and he will not pursue us? Unless he be vanquished here, or at least held in leaguer. Only by the valour of the Eldar is he restrained, and maybe it was for this purpose, to aid them at need, that we were brought into this land.'

§20   To this Bereg answered: 'Let the Eldar look to it! Our lives are short enough.' But there arose one who seemed to all to be Amlach son of Imlach, speaking fell words that shook the hearts of all that heard him: 'All this is but Elvish lore, tales to beguile new-comers that are unwary. The Sea has no shore. There is no Light in the West. You have followed a fool-fire of the Elves to the end of the world! Which of you has seen the least of the gods? Who has beheld the Dark King in the North? Those who seek the dominion of Middle-earth are the Eldar. Greedy for wealth they have delved in the Earth for its secrets and have stirred to wrath the things that dwell beneath it, as they ever have done and ever shall. Let the Orcs have the realm that is theirs, and we will have ours. There is room in the world, if the Eldar will let us be!'

§21   Then those that listened sat for a while astounded, and a shadow of fear fell on their hearts; and they resolved to depart far from the lands of the Eldar. But later Amlach returned among them and denied that he had been present at their debate or had spoken such words as they reported; and there was doubt and bewilderment among Men. Then the Elf-friends said: 'You will now believe this at least: there is indeed a dark Lord and his spies and emissaries are among us; for he fears us and the strength that we may give to his foes.'

§22   But some still answered: 'He hates us, rather, and ever more the longer we dwell here, meddling in his quarrel with the kings of the Eldar, to no gain of ours.' Many therefore of those that yet remained in Estolad made ready to depart; and Bereg led a thousand of the people of Bëor away southwards and they passed out of the songs of those days. But Amlach repented, saying: 'I now have a quarrel of my own with this Master of Lies which will last to my life's end'; and he went away north and entered the service of Maedros. But those of his people who were of like mind with Bereg chose a new leader and went back over the Mountains into Eriador and are forgotten.

§23   During this time the Haladin remained in Radhrost and were content. But Morgoth, seeing that by lies and deceits he could not yet wholly estrange Elves and Men, was filled with wrath and endeavoured to do Men what hurt he could. Therefore he sent out an orc-raid and passing east it escaped the leaguer and came in stealth back over the Mountains by the passes of the Dwarf-road and fell upon the Haladin in the southern woods of the land of Caranthir.

§24   Now the Haladin did not live under the rule of lords or many together, but each homestead was set apart and governed its own affairs, and they were slow to unite. But there was among them a man named Haldad who was masterful and fearless; and he gathered all the brave men that he could find, and retreated to the angle of land between Ascar and Gelion, and in the utmost corner he built a stockade across from water to water; and behind it they led all the women and children that they could save. There they were besieged, until they were short of food.

§25   Now Haldad had twin children: Haleth his daughter and Haldar his son; and both were valiant in the defence, for

Haleth was a woman of great heart and strength. But at last Haldad was slain in a sortie against the Orcs; and Haldar, who rushed out to save his father's body from their butchery, was hewn down beside him. Then Haleth held the folk together, though they were without hope; and some cast themselves in the rivers and were drowned. Seven days later, as the Orcs made their last assault and had already broken through the stockade, there came suddenly a music of trumpets, and Caranthir with his host came down from the north and drove the Orcs into the rivers.

§26   Then Caranthir looked kindly upon Men and did Haleth great honour, and he offered her recompense for her father and brother. And seeing, over late, what valour there was in the Edain, he said to her: 'If you will remove and dwell further north, there you shall have the friendship and protection of the Eldar and free lands of your own.'

§27   But Haleth was proud, and unwilling to be guided or ruled, and most of the Haladin were of like mood. Therefore she thanked Caranthir, but answered: 'My mind is now set, lord, to leave the shadow of the Mountains and go west whither others of our kin have gone.' When therefore the Haladin had gathered all that they could find alive of their folk who had fled wild into the woods before the Orcs, and had gleaned what remained of their goods in their burned homesteads, they took Haleth for their chief; and she led them at last to Estolad, and there they dwelt for a time.

§28   But they remained a people apart, and were ever after known to Elves and Men as the People of Haleth. Haleth remained their chief while her days lasted, but she did not wed, and the headship afterwards passed to Hardan son of Haldar her brother. Soon, however, Haleth desired to move westward again; and though most of her people were against this counsel, she led them forth once more; and they went without help or guidance of the Eldar, and passing over Celon and Aros they journeyed in the perilous land between the Mountains of Terror and the Girdle of Melian. That land was not yet so evil as it after became, but it was no road for mortal Men to take without aid, and Haleth only brought her folk through it with hardship and loss, constraining them to go forward by the strength of her will. At last they crossed over the Brithiach, and many bitterly repented their journey; but there was now no returning. Therefore in new lands they went back to their old life as best they could; and they dwelt in free homesteads in the woods of the Dalath Dirnen beyond Teiglin, and some wandered far into the realm of Nargothrond. But there were many who loved the Lady Haleth and wished to go whither she would and dwell under her rule; and these she led into the Forest of Brethil. Thither in the evil days that followed many of her scattered folk returned.

§29   Now Brethil was claimed as part of his realm by King Thingol, though it was not within the List Melian, and he would have denied it to Haleth; but Felagund, who had the friendship of Thingol, when he heard of all that had befallen the people of Haleth, obtained this grace for her: that she should dwell free in Brethil upon condition only that her folk should guard the Crossings of Teiglin against all enemies of the Eldar, and allow no Orcs to enter their woods. To which Haleth answered: 'Where are Haldad my father, and Haldar my brother? If the king fears a friendship between Haleth and those who devoured her kin, then the thoughts of the Eldar are strange to Men.' And Haleth dwelt in Brethil until she died; and her people raised a green mound over her in the heights of the Forest: Tûr Daretha, the Ladybarrow, Haudh-en-Arwen in the Sindarin tongue.

§30   In this way it came to pass that the Edain dwelt in the lands of the Eldar, some here, some there, some wandering, some settled in kindreds or small peoples. Nearly all learned soon the Grey-elven tongue, both as a common speech among themselves and because many were eager to learn the lore of the Elves. But after a time the Elf-kings, seeing that it was not good for Elves and Men to dwell mingled together without order, and that Men needed lords of their own kind, set regions apart where Men could lead their own lives, and appointed chieftains to hold these lands freely. No conditions were laid upon them, save to hold Morgoth as their foe and to have no dealings with him or his. They were the allies of the Eldar in war, but marched under their own leaders. Yet many of the Edain had delight in the friendship of the Elves and dwelt among them for so long as they had leave; and their young men often took service for a time in the hosts of the Kings.

§31   Now Hador Glorindol, son of Hathol, son of Magor, son of Malach Aradan entered the household of Fingolfin in youth, and was loved by the king. Fingolfin therefore gave to him the lordship of Dor-lómin, and into that land he gathered most of the people of his kin and became the mightiest of the chieftains of the Edain. In his house only the elven-tongue was spoken, though their own speech was not forgotten by his people.* But in Dorthonion the lordship of the people of Bëor and the country of Ladros was given to Boromir, son of Boron who was the grandson of Bëor the Old.

§32   The sons of Hador were Galdor and Gundor; and the sons of Galdor were Húrin and Huor; and the son of Húrin was Túrin the bane of Glaurung; and the son of Huor was Tuor, father of Eärendil the Blessed. And the son of Boromir was Bregor, whose sons were Bregolas and Barahir; and the daughters of the sons of Bregolas were Morwen the mother of Túrin, and Rían the mother of Tuor; but the son of Barahir was Beren One-hand who won the love of Lúthien Thingol's daughter and returned from the Dead; from them came Elwing the wife of Eärendil and all the Kings of Númenor after.

§33   All these were caught in the net of the Doom of the Noldor; and they did great deeds which the Eldar remember still among the histories of the Kings of old. And in those days the strength of Men was added to the power of the Noldor, and hope was renewed; and the people of the three houses of Men throve and multiplied. Greatest was the House of Hador Golden-head, peer of Elven-lords. Many of his people were like him, golden-haired and blue-eyed; they were tall and strong, quick to wrath and laughter, fierce in battle, generous to friend and to foe, swift in resolve, fast in loyalty, joyous in heart, the children of Ilúvatar in the youth of Mankind. But the people of the House of Bëor were dark or brown of hair; their eyes were grey and keen and their faces fair and shapely. Lithe and lean in body they were long-enduring in hardship. Of all Men they were most like the Noldor and most loved by them; for they were eager of mind, cunning-handed, swift in understanding, long in memory; and they were moved sooner to pity than to mirth, for the sorrow of Middle-earth was in their hearts. Like to them were the woodland folk of Haleth; but they were shorter and broader, sterner and less swift. They were less eager for lore, and used few words; for they did not love great concourse of men, and many among them delighted in solitude, wandering free in the greenwoods while the wonder of the

---

* From this speech came the common tongue of Númenor.

world was new upon them. But in the lands of the West their time was brief and their days unhappy.

§34 The years of the Edain were lengthened, according to the reckoning of Men, after their coming to Beleriand; but at last Bëor the Old died, when he had lived three and ninety years, for four and forty of which he had served King Felagund. And when he lay dead, of no wound or sickness, but stricken by age, the Eldar saw for the first time the death of weariness which they knew not in themselves, and they grieved for the swift loss of their friends. But Bëor at the last had relinquished his life willingly and passed in peace; and the Eldar wondered much at the strange fate of Men, for in all their lore there was no account of it and its end was hidden from them. Nonetheless the Edain of old, being of races eager and young, learned swiftly of the Eldar all such art and knowledge as they could receive, and their sons increased in wisdom and skill, until they far surpassed all others of Mankind, who dwelt still east of the Mountains and had not seen the Eldar and the faces that had beheld the Light.

★

I record here the few changes that were made to the LQ 2 typescript of the new chapter.

§1 *Felagund* > *Finrod Felagund*
§4 'had come to a land' > 'had come at last to a land'
§7 The second footnote was struck out (as it was also on the original typescript).
§12 *Diriol* > *Diriel* > *Amras*
§13 *Radhrost* > *Thargelion*, and again in §23.
§28 *Dalath Dirnen* > *Talath Dirnen*
§29 *List Melian*: 'Girdle of' written over the word *List* (which was not struck out).
§31 *Glorindol* > *Glórindol*
§33 'the wonder of the world' > 'the wonder of the lands of the Eldar'
'But in the lands of the West' > 'But in the realms of the West'

In addition, certain changes were made in pencil to the carbon copy only of the original typescript, and these were not taken up into LQ 2, nor were they added to it. They are as follows:

§16 'Magor son of Aradan' > 'Hador son of Aradan'
§29 *List Melian* > *Lest Melian*
   Tûr Daretha > *Tûr Haretha*
§31 'Now Hador Glorindol, son of Hathol, son of Magor, son of

Malach Aradan' was emended to read thus (the emendation was incorrectly made, but my father's intention is plain): 'Now Magor Dagorlind, son of Hathol, son of Hador Glorindal, son of Malach Aradan'

§32   'The sons of Hador' > 'The sons of Magor'

On the reversal of the places of Magor and Hador in the genealogy see p. 235.

Commentary

§1   'three hundred years and ten': the words 'and ten' were an addition. The original chapter in QS had 'four hundred', against which my father noted (p. 202, §126): 'This must be removed to 300', altering the date to '310'. This radical shift, putting back by ninety years the date of Felagund's meeting with Bëor (and so extending the lines of the rulers of the Edain in Beleriand by several generations), has been encountered in the opening of the *Athrabeth Finrod ah Andreth* (X.307 and third footnote).

§4   'Bëor the Old': the words 'the Old' were an addition, and 'as he was afterwards called' refer to 'Bëor' simply (see the second footnote to §7). – With 'After many lives of wandering out of the East' cf. the change made to the original QS chapter, p. 202, §127.

§7   The opening sentence of this paragraph as typed read:

Thus it was that Men called King Felagund, whom they first met of all the Eldar, *Sômar* that is Wisdom, and after him they named his people *Samûri* (that is the Wise).

As typed, the footnote was added to the word 'Wisdom', and read:

In the ancient language of the Edain (from which afterwards came the Númenórean tongue); but Bëor and his House later learned the language of the Eldar and forsook their own.

See V.275 (footnote) and p. 202, §128. – In 'the House of Finrod' *Finrod* = *Finarfin*. The footnote at this point in the text as typed read:

Thus Bëor got his name; for it signifies Vassal in the tongue of the Edain. But after Bëor all the children of his House bore Elvish names.

The revised footnote as given in the text printed was later struck out in pencil. See §12 in the text.

§9   The paragraph beginning 'But it was said afterwards ...' in the published *Silmarillion* between §9 and §10 of the original text was derived from the *Grey Annals*, §§79–80 (pp. 36–7).

§10   The reversal in the published *Silmarillion* of what is said in the original text (and cf. X.305) concerning the affinities of the languages of the Edain (so that the Haladin become 'sundered in speech' from the People of Bëor, and the tongue of the People of Marach becomes 'more like to ours') is based on late and very express statements of my father's. – In the present passage are the first occurrences of the names *Haladin* and *Marach*.

§12   The form *Diriol* seems not to occur elsewhere (see p. 225, §12). – Above the word 'Servant' my father pencilled 'Vassal', but then struck it through. – The region of *Estolad* was entered on the second map, but in the form *Estoland* (p. 189, §55).

§13   The heading *Of the Kindreds and Houses of the Edain* was an addition to the manuscript. Against the opening words 'Soon after the departure of Felagund' the date 311 was typed; 312 against the coming of the Haladin; and 313 against the coming of Marach and his people.

   Radhrost: Dark-elvish name of Thargelion. See p. 225, §13.

   Caranthir: the name as typed (twice) was *Cranthir*, emended to *Caranthir*, but later in the text (§23 and subsequently) *Caranthir* was the form as typed. This is an indication that the emendation of the text followed soon after its typing (p. 215), and may give support to the suggestion *(ibid.)* that *Of the Coming of Men into the West* belongs to the period when the LQ 2 typescript series was being made, since the change of *Cranthir* > *Caranthir* occurs as an emendation in *Of Beleriand and its Realms* in the LQ 2 series (p. 197, §111).

   On the statement that the peoples of Bëor and Marach were 'sundered in speech', omitted in the published text, see under §10 above.

§14   After the words 'dwelt in Hithlum' there followed in the typescript 'in the household of Fingolfin', which was struck out.

§15   Against the words 'some fifty years' the date 330–380 is typed in the margin.

§16   'the House of Finrod': see under §7 above. – The paragraph beginning 'It is said that in all these matters ...' in the published *Silmarillion* was derived from the *Grey Annals*, §§130–1 (pp. 49–50).

§18   With the speech of Bereg and Amlach compare the words of Andreth to Felagund in the *Athrabeth*, X.309–10.

§19   Against the first sentence of the paragraph the date 369 was added.

§20   After 'new-comers that are unwary' the text as typed read before emendation:

   Which of you has seen the Light or the least of the gods? Who has beheld the Dark King in the North? The Sea has no shore. There is no Light in the West, for we stand now in the West of the world.

§23   The form *Caranthir* appears here in the typescript as typed: see under §13 above. In the carbon copy a stroke was drawn through the *n* of *Caranthir*, sc. *Carathir*, and the same was done at the first occurrence of the name (§13) in the top copy.

§24   The siege of the Haladin behind their stockade is dated 375, typed in the margin.

§25   It is here that the Lady Haleth enters the history; Haleth the Hunter, Father of Men, who first appeared long before in the

Quenta as the son of Hador (when the 'Hadorian' and 'Halethian' houses were one and the same, see IV.104, 175), has now disappeared.

§27   Against the last sentence, referring to the sojourn of the Haladin in Estolad, the date 376–390 is typed in the margin.

§28   *Hardan* son of *Haldar*: the substitution of *Haldan* for *Hardan* in the published text was derived from a late change to a genealogical table of the Haladin (see p. 238).

Brithiach: the Ford of Brithiach over Sirion north of the Forest of Brethil had first appeared in the later *Tale of Tuor* (*Unfinished Tales* p. 41), and again in GA §161; see the map on p. 182, square D 7. – Against the sentence 'At last they crossed over the Brithiach' is the date 391.

Dalath Dirnen: the Guarded Plain east of Narog. The name first appears in the tale of Beren and Lúthien in QS (V.299), and was marked in on the second map, where it was subsequently changed to *Talath Dirnen* (p. 186, §17), as also on the LQ 2 typescript of the present text (p. 225, §28).

Teiglin: this was the form of the name adopted in the published *Silmarillion*; see pp. 309–10, at end of note 55.

§29   In the *Grey Annals* §132 (p. 50) the story had entered (under the year 422) that 'at the prayer of Inglor [Felagund] Thingol granted to Haleth's people to live in Brethil; for they were in good friendship with the woodland Elves' (Haleth here is of course Haleth the Hunter, who had entered Beleriand two years before).

List Melian, the Girdle of Melian: this name was entered on the second map (p. 183, D 8-9), and changed to *Lest Melian* on the carbon copy of the original typescript of the chapter (p. 225, §29).

Tûr Daretha: for the form *Tûr Haretha* in the published text see p. 225, §29. – The date of the death of the Lady Haleth is given in the margin: 420.

§31   In the newly devised history, Marach having displaced Hador Goldenhead as the leader of the people in the journey out of Eriador, Hador now appears as the descendant of Marach in the fourth generation; but the House of Hador retained its name (see IV.175). This is the first occurrence of the name *Glorindol*; but the later form *Lorindol* (adopted in the published *Silmarillion*) has been met with in the *Athrabeth* (X.305), and see pp. 233–5.

Marginal dates give Hador's years in Fingolfin's household as 405–415, and the granting to him of the lordship of Dor-lómin as 416.

The concluding sentence of the paragraph as typed read:

But in Dorthonion the lordship of the people of Bëor was given to Bregor son of Boromir . . .

The date of this gift, as typed in the margin, was 410. – 'The country of Ladros', in the emended version, was marked on the second map in the north-east of Dorthonion: p. 187, §34.

§32 For the remainder of its length *Of the Coming of Men into the West* returns to follow, with much rewriting and expansion, the form of the original chapter in QS. – *Galdor* first occurs here (otherwise than in later corrections), replacing *Galion* which itself replaced *Gumlin* (p. 123, §127).

The new genealogies of the Edain

My father's decision that the coming of the Edain over the Blue Mountains into Beleriand took place nearly a century earlier than he had supposed led to a massive overhauling of the chronology and the genealogies.

(i) The House of Bëor

From the new chapter it is seen that in the case of the Bëorians the original 'Father', Bëor the Old, remained, but four new generations were introduced between him and Bregolas and Barahir, who until now had been his sons. These generations are represented by Baran, Boron, Boromir, and Bregor (who becomes the father of Bregolas and Barahir), descendants in the direct line of Bëor the Old – though it is not actually stated that Boron was Baran's son, only that he was Bëor's grandson (§31). In the *Grey Annals* (§121) Bëor was born in the year 370, his encounter with Felagund took place in 400, the year in which his elder son Bregolas was born (§124), and he died in 450. In the new history he met Felagund in 310, departed with him in 311 (commentary on §13), and remained in his service for forty-four years until his death at the age of 93 (§34); from which his dates can be seen to be 262–355. His true name was *Balan* (§12); and it is stated in the second footnote to §7 that each of the chieftains of this people bore the name *Bëor* ('Vassal') as a title until the time of Bregolas and Barahir – though this note was afterwards struck out (commentary on §7). Boromir his great-grandson received the lordship of Dorthonion and Ladros in 410 (§31 and commentary).

There are two genealogical tables of the House of Bëor that relate closely to the new chapter and almost certainly belong to the same period (this is strongly suggested by the fact that a group of Elvish genealogies, closely resembling in form those of the Edain, is accompanied by notes dated December 1959). The two tables were obviously made at the same time. The first ('Bëor table I') was written neatly and clearly; it differs from the second in many of the dates and in its presentation of the descendants of Boron (grandson of Bëor the Old), thus:

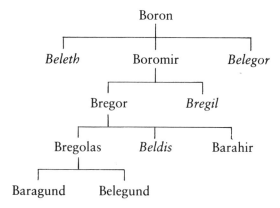

Names in italics show members of the House of Bëor who have not appeared before; of these Beleth, Bregil, and Beldis are marked on the table as daughters. Subsequent alterations, carried out in complex stages, brought the genealogy to the fuller form that it has in 'Bëor table II'; of these changes the most notable is the replacement of Boromir's daughter Bregil (who is moved down a generation) by *Andreth*, the first appearance of the name. The only other point to notice in table I is that Morwen was named *Eledhwen* (with *Eðelwen*, as in table II, added above).

Bëor table II took up all the changes made to I, and I have redrawn it on p. 231 in the form in which it was first made. The numerals added to certain of the names indicate the rulers of the House in their order. It is seen from this genealogy that Boron was indeed the son of Baran ('Bëor the Young'); and that Bereg the dissident (§18), in the text said only to be 'of the House of Bëor', was the son of Baranor son of Baran, and thus a great-grandson of Bëor the Old. It is seen also that the further extension of the House of Bëor that appears in the *Athrabeth Finrod ah Andreth* (X.305–6) was now present, with Andreth the sister of Bregor, and Belen the second son of Bëor the Old, father of Beldir (not previously named), father of Belemir the husband of Adanel. (Adanel is here said to be the daughter of Malach Aradan, son of Marach, whereas in the *Athrabeth* she is the sister of Hador Lorindol: on this see p. 235.)

A few changes were made subsequently, at different times, to Bëor table II, as follows:

- *(Bar Bëora)* added after 'The House of Bëor';
- Boron's dates changed to 315–408, and Boromir's birth to 338;
- the name *Saelin* pencilled beside *Andreth*, and also 'A[ndreth] the Wise';
- a remote descent from Beleth, sister of Baragund and Belegund, indicated, leading to *Erendis of Númenor*;

The House of Bëor

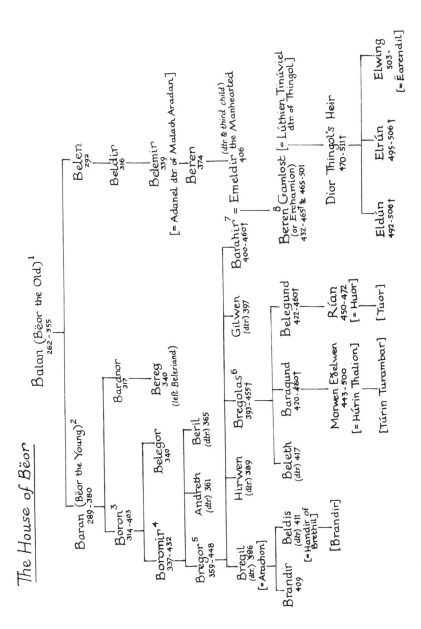

Balan (Bëor the Old)[1]
262-355

Baran (Bëor the Young)[2]
289-380

Belen
292

Bardnor
317

Beldir
316

Bereg
340
(left Beleriand)

Belemir
339
[= Adanel dtr. of Malach Aradan]

Boron[3]
314-403

Belegor
340

Beren
374

Beril
(dtr) 365

(dtr. & third child)

Boromir[4]
337-432

Andreth
(dtr) 361

Barahir[7] = Emeldir the Manhearted
400-460†   406

Bregor[5]
359-448

Hirwen
(dtr) 389

Gilwen
(dtr) 397

Beren Gamlost [= Lúthien Tinúviel
(or Erchamion)   dtr. of Thingol]
432-465† & 465-501

Bregil
(dtr) 386
[= Arachon]

Beldis
(dtr) 411
[= Handir of
Brethil]

Bregolas[6]
393-455†

Beleth
(dtr) 417

Belegund
422-460†

Dior Thingol's Heir
470-511†

Brandir
409

[Brandir]

Baragund
420-460†

Rían
450-472
[= Huor]

Eldún
492-506†

Elrún
495-506†

Elwing
503-
[= Eärendil]

Morwen Eðelwen
443-500
[= Húrin Thalion]

[Tuor]

[Túrin Turambar]

– a daughter *Hiril*, sister of Beren One-hand, given to Barahir and Emeldir.

On the name *Saelin* beside *Andreth* see p. 233. With the descent of Erendis of Númenor from Beleth daughter of Bregolas cf. *Aldarion and Erendis* in *Unfinished Tales*, p. 177, where it is said of Beregar the father of Erendis that he 'came of the House of Bëor': in my note on this (p. 214, note 10) I referred to her descent as given in the present genealogical table, but gave her ancestor's name wrongly as 'Bereth'.

Some of the later dates in the table differ from those in other sources. The first death of Beren is placed under 466 in the texts of *The Tale of Years*: 465 is a reversion to the date in AB 2 (see p. 131, §203). The second death of Beren, in the table dated 501, was placed in AB 2 in 503, while in *The Tale of Years* it is given as 505, then reverting to 503 (pp. 346, 348). In GA Bregolas was born in 400, Barahir in 402, Baragund in 424, and Belegund in 428 (these were the original dates going back to the earliest *Annals of Beleriand*, allowing for the extension by one and then by two centuries in subsequent versions; see the genealogical table in IV.315).

On the much changed date of the Second Kinslaying (here given as 511), in which Dior Thingol's heir was slain in fighting with the Fëanorians and his young sons Eldún and Elrún were taken and abandoned to starve in the forest, see *The Tale of Years*, pp. 345 ff.; it is plainly a mere inadvertence that in the same table the date of their death is given as 506, five years before that of Dior. In (later) sources Eldún and Elrún are twin brothers, born in the year 500 (see p. 257 and note 16 on p. 300; p. 349).

(ii) The House of Hador

In the old history of the Edain, now rejected, Hador the Goldenhaired, third of 'the Fathers of the Men of the West', was born in Eriador in 390, and came over the Blue Mountains into Beleriand in 420. Unlike the development in the House of Bëor, however, Hador (Glorindol, §31) retained his chronological place in the history (as will be seen shortly, his original birth-date remained the same), and his sons Galdor (< Galion < Gumlin) and Gundor; but with the much earlier date of 'the Coming of Men into the West' he was moved downwards in the genealogy, to become the ruler of the people in the fourth generation from Marach, under whose leadership they had entered Beleriand in 313 (commentary on §13). His father was Hathol, son of Magor, son of Malach, son of Marach (§31).

As with the House of Bëor, there are here also two genealogical tables closely related to the new conception. The earlier of these ('Hador table I') was made on my father's old typewriter using his 'midget type' (VIII.233). It was a good deal altered by revision of dates, and by additions, but these latter chiefly concern the extension of the genealogy to include the descendants of Húrin and Huor, with whom the table ended in the form as typed: the structure of the descent from the ancestor was far less changed than in the case of Bëor table I, and indeed the only addition here was the incorporation of Amlach, one of the leaders of discontent in Estolad, who is said in the text of the chapter (§18) to have been 'one of the grandsons of Marach'. Changes were also made to the names of the Haladin who appear in the genealogy.

A fair copy in manuscript ('Hador table II'), identical in appearance to the tables of the House of Bëor, followed, no doubt immediately, and this I have redrawn on p. 234, in the form in which it was made (i.e. omitting subsequent alterations). I notice here some points arising from these tables.

The date of Marach's entry into Beleriand differs by one year (314 for 313) from that given in the chapter (commentary on §13); table I had 315 altered to 314. In table I Marach's son Imlach, father of Amlach, is named *Imrach*.

In agreement with the genealogical tables of the House of Bëor, Adanel wife of Belemir is the daughter of Malach Aradan; in Hador table I it was said that Adanel 'wedded Belemir of the House of Bëor, and he joined the people of Aradan', the last words being struck out. It is also said in table I that Beren (I) was the fifth child of Adanel and Belemir; and that Emeldir was the third child of Beren.

In Hador table I there is the statement that 'the other children of Aradan' (i.e. beside Adanel and Magor) 'are not named in the Chronicles'. In table II a third child of Malach Aradan was named, however: 'Sael..th the Wise   344', together with the mention of 'others not concerned in these Chronicles'; *Sael..th* was first changed to *Saelon*, and then the name and the birth-date were struck out, so that the middle letters of the first name cannot be read. This was probably done at the time of the making of the table. *Saelon* appears in draft material for the *Athrabeth* (X.351–2) as the name of Andreth, replaced in the finished text (X.305) by *Saelind* ('the Eldar called her *Saelind*, "Wise-heart"'). In this sister of Magor and Adanel is seen, very probably, the first hint of the *Athrabeth*; subsequently, when my father perceived that the wise-women came of different houses of the Edain, with different 'lore and traditions' (X.305), he wrote *Saelin* and *Andreth the Wise* against the name *Andreth* in Bëor table II (p. 230). It seems a possibility that Adanel and Andreth were already present in the genealogies before their significance as 'wise-women' emerged.

In Hador table I Hador was named *Glorindol*, as in the text of the chapter (§31), emended to *Lorindol*, the form in table II. – I do not know why Gundor's death should be dated (in both I and II) a year later (456) than that of his father Hador. All the sources state that they both died at Eithel Sirion.

The 'double marriage' of Hador's daughter and elder son, named Glorwendil and Galion, to the son (Hundor) and daughter (unnamed)

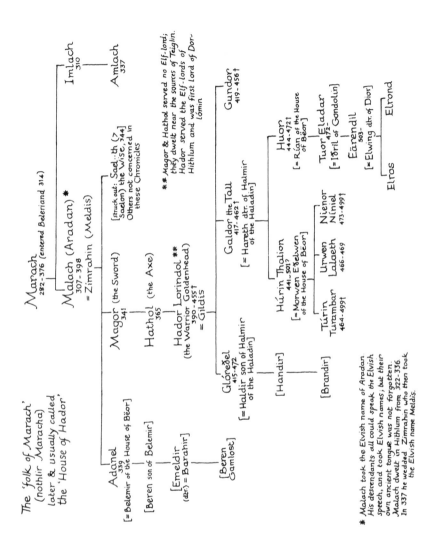

The 'folk of Marach'
(nothlir Maracha)
later & usually called
the "House of Hador"

Marach
282-376 (entered Beleriand 314)

Malach (Aradan) *
307-398
= Zimrahin (Meldis)

Imlach
310

Amlach
337

[struck out: Sadwith (?
Sadom) the Wise, 344]
Others not concerned in
these Chronicles

** Magor & Hathol served no Elf-lord;
they dwelt near the sources of Teiglin.
Hador served the Elf-lords of
Hithlum and was first lord of Dor-
lómin

Magor (the Sword)
341

Hathol (the Axe)
365

Hador Lorindol **
(the Warrior Goldenhead)
390-455†
= Gildis

Galdor the Tall
417-462†
[= Hareth dtr. of Halmir
of the Haladin]

Gundor
419-456†

Húrin Thalion
441-501?
[= Morwen Eðelwen
of the House of Bëor]

Huor
444-472†
[= Rían of the House
of Bëor]

Túrin
Turambar
464-499†

Urwen
Lalaeth
466-469

Nienor
Níniel
473-499†

Tuor Eladar
472-
[=Idril of Gondolin]

Eärendil
503-
[=Elwing dtr. of Dior]

Elros   Elrond

Adanel
339
[= Belemir of the House of Bëor]

[Beren son of Belemir]

[Emeldir
(dtr.) = Barahir]

[Beren
Camlost]

Glóreðel
415-472
[= Haldir son of Halmir
of the Haladin]

[Handir]

[Brandir]

* Malach took the Elvish name of Aradan.
His descendants all could speak the Elvish
speech, and took Elvish names; but their
own ancient tongue was not forgotten.
Malach dwelt in Hithlum from 322-336.
In 337 he wedded Zimrahin who then took
the Elvish name Meldis.

of Haleth the Hunter had already emerged in the *Grey Annals* (see the commentary on §§161, 171, pp. 126, 128). Now named Glóreðel and Galdor, the double marriage remains, but with the entire reconstitution of the People of Haleth the chronological place of Haleth the Hunter had been taken by *Halmir*: it is now his son *Haldir* and his daughter *Hareth* who marry Glóreðel and Galdor.*

The date of Húrin's death is given as '500?' in table I ('501?' in table II).

Tuor's name *Eladar* is translated 'Starfather' in table I, and in addition he is named *Ulmondil*; the form *Irildë* was added after *Idril* (so spelt): see II.343 and V.366–7 (stem KYELEP); and to Eärendil was added 'whose name was foretold by Ulmo'.

For *Urwen Lalaeth* see *Unfinished Tales* pp. 57–9.

In hasty pencillings on Hador table II the note saying that Magor and Hathol served no Elf-lord but dwelt near the sources of Teiglin, and that Hador was the first lord of Dor-lomin, was struck out; while at the same time *Hador Lorindol   first lord of Dorlómin* was written above *Magor (the Sword)*, and *Magor Dagorlind   the Sword   singer in battle* above *Hador Lorindol*. This reversal has been seen already in emendations made to the carbon copy only of the text of the chapter (pp. 225–6, §§16, 31–2 – where my father changed *Glorindol*, not to *Lorindol*, but to *Glorindal*). That this was not an ephemeral change is seen from the *Athrabeth*, where Adanel is the sister of Hador Lorindol, not of Magor.

I do not know of any statement elsewhere that bears on this change, but the words 'first lord of Dorlómin' that (so to speak) accompanied Hador's movement back by half a century are evidently significant, suggesting that my father had in mind to place Fingolfin's gift of the lordship of Dorlómin much earlier: he had said both in the text of the chapter and in the genealogical table that Malach (whose son was now Hador Lorindol) passed fourteen years in Hithlum. This change would not of itself entail the reversal of the names Magor and Hador; but the House of Hador was a name so embedded in the tradition that my father would not lose it even when Hador was no longer the first ruler in Beleriand, while on the other hand the importance and illustriousness of that house was closely associated with the lordship of Dorlómin – in other words, the name must accompany the first lordship. But it seems that he never wrote anything further on the matter, nor made any other alterations to the existing texts in the light of it.

The only other change made to Hador table II (it was made also to table I) was the writing of the name *Ardamir* above Eärendil.

---

* In table I the son of Halmir was still *Hundor*, and his daughter was *Hiriel*. *Hiriel* was changed to *Hareth*; and *Hundor* was changed to *Hundar* before reaching *Haldir*. See pp. 236–7.

(iii) The Haladin

This house of the Edain underwent the greatest change, since in this case the original 'Father' Haleth the Hunter disappeared, and of the Haladin (a name that first occurs in this new chapter, §10) it is said (§24) that they 'did not live under the rule of lords or many together'. The name *Haleth* now becomes that of the formidable Lady Haleth, daughter of Haldad, who had become the leader when the Haladin were attacked by Orcs in Thargelion. In the genealogical table of the House of Hador *Halmir* occupies the place in the history formerly taken by Haleth the Hunter, and it was his son and daughter who married the son and daughter of Hador Goldenhead.

A genealogical table of the Haladin exists in a single copy (preceded by rough workings in which the names were moved about in a bewildering fashion), this table being a companion, obviously made at the same time, to those of the Houses of Bëor and Hador. I give it on p. 237 as it was first made. As in the table of the Bëorians, the numerals against certain of the names refer to the leaders of the Haladin in sequence.

A particularly confusing element in the transformation of 'the People of Haleth' (who are confusing enough in any event) lies in the offspring of Halmir.

(1) In GA §212 (p. 70) it was told, in the annal for 468, that at the time of the Union of Maidros Haleth the Hunter 'gathered his folk in Brethil, and they whetted their axes; but he died of age ere the war came, and Hundor his son ruled his people' (in *The Silmarillion*, Chapter 20, p. 189, I retained this, substituting Halmir for Haleth the Hunter and Haldir for Hundor).

(2) I have noticed (p. 235, footnote) that in 'Hador table I' Halmir's son was still *Hundor*; and that this was changed to *Hundar* (found also in one of the constituent texts of the *Narn* as the name of the son) before reaching the final form *Haldir*.

(3) In the *Narn* version of the story of the Battle of Unnumbered Tears the leader of the men of Brethil is *Hundar* (pp. 166, 168).

(4) In a late alteration to the GA version of the story (see p. 133, commentary on §221) the sentence 'many of the woodmen came also with Hundor of Brethil' was changed to 'came also with Haldir and Hundar'.

(6) In the genealogical table of the Haladin both *Haldir*, son of Halmir and leader of the Haladin after his father's death, and his brother *Hundar*, are shown as having been slain in the Nirnaeth in the year 472.

It is seen therefore that when *Hundar* son of Halmir became *Haldir*, the name *Hundar* was not lost but was given to a brother of Haldir; and both went to the battle and both were slain. This is expressly stated in *The Wanderings of Húrin* (p. 281 and note 37); and indeed the line of Hundar is of great importance in that tale.

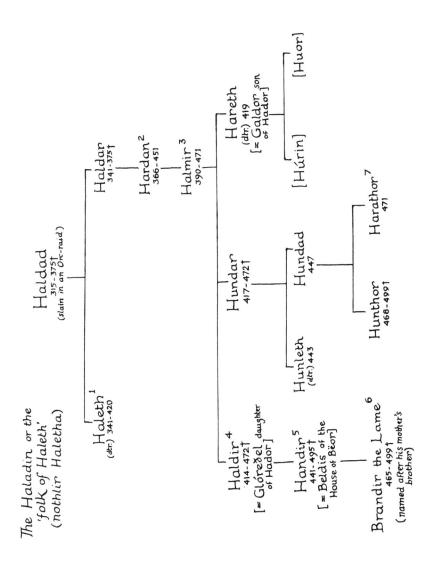

The Haladin or the
'folk of Haleth'
(nothlir Haletha)

Haldad
315–375†
(slain in an Orc-raid)

Haleth [1]
(dtr.) 341–420

Haldar
341–375†

Hardan [2]
366–451

Halmir [3]
390–471

Hareth
(dtr.) 419
[= Galdor son
of Hador]

[Húrin]   [Huor]

Hundar
417–472†

Hunleth
(dtr.) 443

Hundad
447

Harathor [7]
471

Hunthor
468–499†

Haldir [4]
414–472†
[= Glóreðel daughter
of Hador]

Handir [5]
441–495†
[= Beldis of the
House of Béor]

Brandir the Lame [6]
465–499†
(named after his mother's
brother)

Handir, son of Haldir, retained his name from far back; but the original story of his death in the battle of Tumhalad in 495 had been changed: he was slain in Brethil earlier in that year by 'Orcs that invaded his land' (GA §275). On his marriage with Beldis of the House of Bëor see p. 268.

Hunthor was Túrin's companion in the attack on Glaurung, killed by a falling stone (*Unfinished Tales*, p. 134); called *Torbarth* in GA (see p. 156).

Most of the later changes made to this table relate closely to the story of *The Wanderings of Húrin*, and these I neglect here. Of other alterations, one has been mentioned already (commentary on §28, p. 228): *Hardan* son of Haldar (twin brother of the Lady Haleth) was changed to *Haldan*, and this name was adopted in the published *Silmarillion*; but also pencilled against *Hardan* (either before or after the change to *Haldan*) is the name *Harathor* (the name repeated in his descendant, the seventh leader of the Haladin, four generations later). – The birth-dates of Hundar and Hareth were changed to 418 and 420; and Hundar's daughter *Hunleth* was an addition, though probably of the time of the making of the table.

Pencilled on a corner of the page is: '*Hal-* in old language of this people = head, chief. *bar* = man. *Halbar* = chieftain'; at the same time my father wrote '*b*' against the name *Haldar* (Haleth's brother) and perhaps very faintly struck out the '*d*' of this name: sc. *Halbar*. On this see p. 309.

---

15   OF THE RUIN OF BELERIAND AND THE FALL OF FINGOLFIN

We come now to Chapter 11 in QS, given in V.279–89. The text was not much emended on the manuscript, and I give such changes as were made in the form of notes referenced to the numbered paragraphs in Vol.V.

§134   *Bladorion* > *Ard-galen* and subsequently.
'fires of many colours, and the fume stank upon the air' > 'fires of many poisonous hues, and the fume thereof stank upon the air'
Dor-na-Fauglith > *Dor-no-Fauglith*
Dagor Vreged-úr > *Dagor Bragollach*
'the Battle of Sudden Fire' > 'the Battle of Sudden Flame' (and subsequently)

§137   'In that battle King Inglor Felagund was cut off from his folk and surrounded by the Orcs, and he would have been slain ...' > 'surrounded by the Orcs in the Fen of Serech betwixt Mithrim and Dorthonion, and there he would have been slain'. The *Fen of Rivil*, changed to *Fen of Serech*, was added to the second map (p. 181, §3), and the latter name occurs several times in GA.

§138   'fled now from Dorthonion' > 'fled away from Dorthonion'
'it was after called by the Gnomes Taur-na-Fuin, which is
Mirkwood, and Deldúwath, Deadly Nightshade' > 'it was after
called by the Dark-elves Taur-na-Fuin, which is Mirkwood, but by
the Gnomes Deldúwath, Deadly Nightshade'

§141   'Celegorn and Curufin ... sought harbour with their friend
Orodreth' > '... sought harbour with Inglor and Orodreth'. See
V.289, §141.

§142   'or the wild of South Beleriand' > 'nor to Taur-im-Duinath
and the wilds of the south'. On *Taur-im-Duinath* see p. 193, §108,
and p. 195, §113.

§143   'Sauron was the chief servant of the evil Vala, whom he had
suborned to his service in Valinor from among the people of the
gods. He was become a wizard of dreadful power, master of
necromancy, foul in wisdom' > 'Now Sauron, whom the Noldor
call Gorthú, was the chief servant of Morgoth. In Valinor he had
dwelt among the people of the gods, but there Morgoth had drawn
him to evil and to his service. He was become now a sorcerer of
dreadful power, master of shadows and of ghosts, foul in wisdom'.
On this passage, and the name *Gorthú*, see V.333, 338, and the
commentary on QS §143 (V.290).
   In the footnote to this paragraph *Tol-na-Gaurhoth > Tol-in-
Gaurhoth* (cf. GA §154 and commentary, pp. 54, 125).

§144   In 'for though his might is greatest of all things in this world,
alone of the Valar he knows fear' the words 'is' and 'knows' were
changed to 'was' and 'knew'.

§147   'for sorrow; but the tale of it is remembered, for Thorondor,
king of eagles, brought the tidings to Gondolin, and to Hithlum. For
Morgoth' > 'for their sorrow is too deep. Yet the tale of it is
remembered still, for Thorondor, king of eagles, brought the tidings
to Gondolin, and to Hithlum afar off. Lo! Morgoth'
   Gochressiel > Crisaegrim (see V.290, §147).

§149   'And most the Gnomes feared' > 'And ever the Gnomes feared
most'

§151   'Dwarfs' > 'Dwarves'

All these changes were taken up into the early typescript LQ 1 (in
which the footnotes to §§143, 156 were as usual incorporated in the
text, and so remained). LQ 1 received no emendation from my father,
not even the correction of misspelt names and other errors. These
errors reappear in the late typescript of the LQ 2 series, showing that
in this case the typist did not work from the manuscript. To the text in
LQ 2 my father gave the chapter-number 'XVIII' (see p. 215), and
made the following emendations.

§134   *Dor-no-Fauglith* (changed from *Dor-na-Fauglith* on the
manuscript, as noted above) > *Dor-nu-Fauglith*; a translation of the

name added in a footnote 'That is Land under Choking Ash'; and 'in the Noldorin tongue' (where LQ 1 had 'in the Gnomish tongue') > 'in the Sindarin tongue'.

Eredwethion > *Eredwethrin* (and subsequently)

§135   *Glómund* > *Glaurung* (and subsequently). See p. 180, §104.

§137   *Finrod* > *Finarfin* (this change was missed in §144).

'Bregolas, son of Bëor [the typescript has *Breor*, a mere error going back to LQ 1], who was lord of that house of men after his father's death' > 'Bregolas, son of Bregor ... after Boromir his father's death'. This accommodates the text to the new genealogy that came in with the new chapter *Of the Coming of Men into the West*. That was extant in the LQ 2 series, but for the present chapter my father gave the typist the old LQ 1 text to copy.

Inglor > *Finrod* (and subsequently)

'Barahir son of Bëor' > 'Barahir son of Bregor'

§138   *Taur-na-Fuin* > *Taur-nu-Fuin* (cf. GA §158 and commentary, pp. 56, 126).

§139   The name *Arthod* of one of the companions of Barahir had been misspelt *Arthrod* by the typist of LQ 1, and this error surviving into LQ 2 was not observed by my father. In GA (§159, p. 56) the name is *Arthad*, which was adopted in the published *Silmarillion*.

§140   *Gumlin* > *Galdor* and subsequently (see p. 229, §32); the intervening name *Galion*, appearing in GA (§127), was here jumped.

§141   'sought harbour with Inglor and Orodreth' (see p. 239, §141) > 'sought harbour with Finrod and Orodreth'

§142   *Cranthir* > *Caranthir*

Damrod and Díriel > *Amrod and Amras*

§143   'Now Sauron, whom the Noldor call Gorthú' (see p. 239, §143) > 'Now Sauron, whom the Sindar call Gorthaur'

'In Valinor he had dwelt among the people of the Valar, but there Morgoth had drawn him to evil and to his service' (see p. 239, §143; LQ 1 has 'gods'): this was struck out.

§147   In 'Morgoth goes ever halt of one foot since that day, and the pain of his wounds cannot be healed; and in his face is the scar that Thorondor made' the words 'goes', 'since', 'cannot', and 'is' were changed to 'went', 'after', 'could not', and 'was'. Cf. p. 239, §144.

§151   *Borlas and Boromir and Borthandos* > *Borlad and Borlach and Borthand*. In GA, in a passage extant in two versions, appear both *Borthandos* and *Borthand* (pp. 61, 64), the other names remaining as in QS. Here *Borlad* replaces *Borlas* and *Borlach* replaces *Boromir*, which latter had become the name of the fourth ruler of the People of Bëor.

§152   'Yet Haleth and his men' > 'Yet the People of Haleth'

Haleth > *Halmir* (and subsequently); at the first occurrence >

'Halmir Lord of the Haladin'. For *Halmir* see p. 236 and the genealogical table of the Haladin on p. 237.

§153 Since no alteration to this passage in QS had ever been made, at this late date the LQ 2 typescript still retained the old story that it was Haleth the Hunter and his fosterson Húrin who, hunting in the vale of Sirion in the autumn of the year of the Battle of Sudden Flame (455), came upon the entrance into Gondolin. That story had already been altered in the *Grey Annals* (§149), in that Húrin's companion had become Haleth's grandson Handir, and in a long rider inserted into the *Annals* (§§161–6, and see the commentary, pp. 126–7) it had been much further changed: Húrin's companion was now his brother Huor, and it was their presence (as fostersons of Haleth) among the Men of Brethil in the battle against the Orcs three years later (458) that led to their coming to Gondolin. The only alterations that my father made to the passage in LQ 2, however, were the replacement of *Gumlin* by *Galdor* and *Haleth* by *Halmir* – thus retaining the long since rejected story while substituting the new names that had entered with the chapter *Of the Coming of Men into the West*. This was obviously not his intention (probably he altered the names rapidly throughout the chapter without considering the content in this paragraph), and indeed he marked the passage in the margin with an X and noted against it 'This is incorrect story. See Annals and tale of Túrin'. This treatment may have been due to haste, or disinclination to deal with the text at that time; but it possibly implies uncertainty as to how he should relate the content of the *Quenta Silmarillion* at this point to the same material appearing in closely similar form both in the *Grey Annals* and in the *Narn*: see pp. 165 ff. In the published work the old text of QS §153 was replaced by that of GA §§161–6 (with a different ending: see p. 169).

Two alterations made hastily to the QS manuscript are not found in the typescripts. The first of these concerns the opening of §133: 'But when the sons of the sons of the Fathers of Men were but newly come to manhood'; this referred to the second generation after Bëor, Hador, and Haleth according to the old genealogies, i.e. Baragund, Belegund, Beren; Húrin, Huor; Handir of Brethil. When correcting the LQ 2 text my father had not observed the need to correct this in the light of the revised history of the Edain in Beleriand, and when he did recognise it he made the change only on the QS manuscript, thus:

> But when the fifth generation of Men after Bëor and Marach were not yet come to full manhood

Even so, the change is not quite as is to be expected; for in the fifth generation after Bëor and Marach were Bregolas, Barahir; Gundor, Galdor. There is of course no question that the men referred to are not these, but their sons – and even so the new reading 'not yet come to full manhood' is hardly suitable to Baragund and Belegund, who according to the changed dates in the genealogical table (pp. 231–2) were at this time 35 and 33 years old. At any rate it seems clear that 'fifth' was an error for 'sixth'.

The other alteration made to QS only, and obviously made much earlier than that just given, was an addition to the end of §137, after the words 'he [Felagund] gave to Barahir his ring'.

> But fearing now that all strong places were doomed to fall at last before the might of Morgoth, he sent away his wife Meril to her own folk in Eglorest, and with her went their son, yet an elvenchild, and *Gilgalad* Starlight he was called for the brightness of his eye.

Felagund's wife Meril has not been named before, nor any child of his; and this is the first appearance of Gil-galad from *The Lord of the Rings*. Another note on the subject is found in the QS manuscript near the opening of the 'short' (i.e. condensed) version of the tale of Beren and Lúthien (see V.293), pencilled rapidly at the foot of a page but clearly referring to the statement in the text that Felagund gave the crown of Nargothrond to Orodreth before his departure with Beren (*The Silmarillion* p. 170):

> But foreseeing evil he commanded Orodreth to send away his son Gilgalad, and wife.

This was struck out; and somewhat further on in the tale of Beren and Lúthien in the same version is a third hasty note, without direction for insertion but evidently referring to the passage in which Orodreth expelled Celegorn and Curufin from Nargothrond (*The Silmarillion* p. 176):

> But the Lady   wife of Inglor forsook the folk of Nargothrond and went with her son Gilgalad to the Havens of the Falas.

A blank space is here left for the name of Felagund's wife. In each of these mentions, taking them in sequence, her departure is displaced to a later point; but of course they need not have been written in that sequence (although the third presumably replaced the second, which was struck out). On the other hand it seems very unlikely that the three additions do not belong together, though there seems to be no way of discovering with certainty when they were written. – It may also be noticed that a later correction to the old AB 2 manuscript changed the sentence in the concluding annal (V.144) 'But Elrond the Half-elfin remained, and ruled in the West of the world' to 'But Elrond the Half-elven remained with Gilgalad son of Inglor Felagund who ruled in the West of the world.'

In this connection must be mentioned the passage in the *Grey Annals* §§108–9 (p. 44), where it is expressly stated that 'King Inglor Felagund had no wife', and that when Galadriel came to Nargothrond for the feast celebrating its completion in the year 102 she asked him why:

> ... but foresight came upon Felagund as she spoke, and he said:

'An oath I too shall swear and must be free to fulfill it and go into darkness. Nor shall anything of all my realm endure that a son should inherit.'

But it is said that not until that hour had such cold thoughts ruled him; for indeed she whom he had loved was Amárië of the Vanyar, and she was not permitted to go with him into exile.

Amárië appears again in GA, in both versions of the retelling of the story of Beren and Lúthien (§§180, 199), where it is said that Felagund dwells in Valinor with Amárië.

Later evidence makes it certain that the notes on the QS manuscript represent a rejected idea for the incorporation of Gil-galad into the traditions of the Elder Days; and the passage just cited from the *Grey Annals* is to be taken as showing that it had been abandoned. That Gil-galad was the son of Fingon (*The Silmarillion* p. 154) derives from the late note pencilled on the manuscript of GA (§157), stating that when Fingon became King of the Noldor on the death of Fingolfin 'his young son (?Findor) [*sic*] Gilgalad he sent to the Havens.' But this, adopted after much hesitation, was not in fact by any means the last of my father's speculations on this question.

THE LAST CHAPTERS OF THE *QUENTA SILMARILLION*

Of the next chapters in QS (12–15), the tale of Beren and Lúthien, there is almost nothing to add to my account in V.292 ff. A typescript in the LQ 1 series was made, but my father only glanced through it cursorily, correcting a few errors in the typing and missing a major one; from this it was copied in the LQ 2 series, which again he looked at in a cursory and uncomparative fashion: such old names as *Inglor* and *Finrod* were not changed to *Finrod* and *Finarfin*. The only change that he made to the LQ 2 text was at the very beginning (V.296), where against 'Noldor' he wrote in the margin 'Númenor', i.e. 'which is the longest save one of the songs of [the Noldor >] Númenor concerning the world of old.' With this cf. X.373.

The textual history of the following chapters (16 and 17) of the *Quenta Silmarillion* has been fully described in Vol.V (see especially pp. 293–4), and need not be repeated here. To Chapter 16, the story of the Battle of Unnumbered Tears, no further changes to the text as given in V.306–13 had been made (apart from those mentioned in V.313, §1) when the LQ 1 typescript was taken from it, and this my father did not correct or change at any point. Years later, the LQ 2 typescript was simply a copy of LQ 1, perpetuating its errors, and similarly neglected. Thus the confused account of Turgon's emergence from Gondolin, discussed in V.314–15, which had been resolved in the story as told in the *Grey Annals* (see p. 133, §221), remained in this text without so much as a comment in the margin.

With Chapter 17, the beginning of the story of Túrin (V.316–21), my father abandoned, in December 1937, the writing of the continuous *Quenta Silmarillion*. He had made no changes to the chapter when the last typescript of the LQ 1 series was taken from it, and this text he never touched. In this case he did indeed return later to the manuscript, making many additions and corrections (and rejecting the whole of the latter part of the chapter, V.319–21, §34–40); but this is best regarded as an aspect of the vast, unfinished work on the 'Saga of Túrin' that engaged him during the 1950s, from which no brief retelling suitable in scale to the *Quenta Silmarillion* ever emerged. LQ 2 was again a simple copy of LQ 1, by that time altogether obsolete.

Chapter 17 ended with Túrin's flight from Menegroth after the slaying of Orgof and his gathering of a band of outlaws beyond the borders of Doriath: 'their hands were turned against all who came in their path, Elves, Men, or Orcs' (V.321). The antecedent of this passage is found in Q *(Quenta Noldorinwa)*, IV.123; and from this point, in terms of the *Silmarillion* narrative strictly or narrowly defined, there is nothing later than Q (written, or the greater part of it, in 1930) for the rest of the tale of Túrin, and for all the story of the return of Húrin, the Nauglamír, the death of Thingol, the destruction of Doriath, the fall of Gondolin, and the attack on Sirion's Haven, until we come to the rewriting of the conclusion of Q which my father carried out in 1937.

This is not to suggest for a moment, of course, that he had lost interest in the later tales: 'Túrin' is the most obvious contradiction to that, while the later *Tale of Tuor* was undoubtedly intended to lead to a richly detailed account of the Fall of Gondolin, and *The Wanderings of Húrin* was not to end with his departure from Brethil, but to lead into the tale of the Necklace of the Dwarves. But the *Quenta Silmarillion* was at an end. I have said of the *Quenta Noldorinwa* (Q) in IV.76:

> The title ['This is the brief History of the Noldoli or Gnomes, drawn from the Book of Lost Tales'] makes it very plain that while Q was written in a finished manner, my father saw it as a compendium, a 'brief history' that was 'drawn from' a much longer work; and this aspect remained an important element in his conception of 'The Silmarillion' properly so called. I do not know whether this idea did indeed arise from the fact that the starting point of the second phase of the mythological narrative was a condensed synopsis (S) [the *Sketch of the Mythology*]; but it seems likely enough, from the step by step continuity that leads from S through Q to the version that was interrupted towards its end in 1937.

In these versions my father was drawing on (while also of course continually developing and extending) long works that already existed in prose and verse, and in the *Quenta Silmarillion* he perfected that characteristic tone, melodious, grave, elegiac, burdened with a sense of loss and distance in time, which resides partly, as I believe, in the literary fact that he was drawing down into a brief compendious history what he could also see in far more detailed, immediate, and dramatic form. With the completion of the great 'intrusion' and departure of *The Lord of the Rings*, it seems that he returned to the Elder Days with a desire to take up again the far more ample scale with which he had begun long before, in *The Book of Lost Tales*. The completion of the *Quenta Silmarillion* remained an aim; but the 'great tales', vastly developed from their original forms, from which its later chapters should be derived were never achieved.

It remains only to record the later history of the final element in QS, the rewritten conclusion of the *Quenta Noldorinwa*, which was given in V.323 ff. with such emendations as I judged to have been made very early and before the abandonment of work on QS at the end of 1937.

It is curious to find that a final typescript in the LQ 2 series of 1958(?) was made, in which the text of Q was copied from the words 'Húrin gathered therefore a few outlaws of the woods unto him, and they came to Nargothrond' (IV.132) to the end. It has no title, and apart from some corrections made to it by my father has no independent value: its interest lies only in the fact of its existence. The reason why it begins at this place in the narrative is, I think, clear (though not why it begins at precisely this point). At the time when my father decided to 'get copies made of all copyable material' (December 1957, see X.141–2) he provided the typist not only with the *Quenta Silmarillion* papers but also with (among other manuscripts) the *Grey Annals*. Thus the story of Túrin, in that form, was (or would be) secure in two typescript copies. But from the death of Túrin, if anything of the concluding parts of *The Silmarillion* was to be copied in this way, it had to be the text of Q: for there was nothing later (except the rewritten version of the conclusion). Yet in this text we are of course in quite early writing: for a single example among many, Q has (IV.139) 'For Turgon deemed, when first they came into that vale after the dreadful battle ...' – an explicit reference to the now long-discarded story of the foundation of Gondolin after the Battle of Unnumbered Tears; and so this appears in the late typescript. That was of course a mere *pis-aller*, an insurance against the possibility of a catastrophe, but its existence underlines, and must have underlined for my father, the essential and far-reaching work that still awaited him, but which he would never achieve.

The typist of LQ 2 was given the manuscript (see V.323) of the 1937 rewriting of the conclusion of Q, beginning 'And they looked upon the

Lonely Isle and there they tarried not'. Some of the later, roughly made emendations (see V.324) had already been made to the manuscript, but others had not. Up to the point where the rewritten text begins my father understandably paid no attention at all to the typescript, but the concluding portion he corrected cursorily – it is clear that he did not have the actual manuscript by him to refer to. These corrections are mostly no more than regular changes of name, but he made one or two independent alterations as well, and these are recorded in the notes that follow.

The corrections to the manuscript, carried out as it appears in two stages (before and after the making of the typescript), are mostly fairly minor, and a few so slight as not to be worth recording. I refer to the numbered paragraphs in V.324–34.

Changes of name or forms of name were: *Airandir* > *Aerandir* (§1); *Tûn* > *Tirion* (§3 and subsequently); *Kôr* > *Túna* (§4); *Lindar* > *Vanyar* (§§6, 26); *Vingelot* > *Vingilot* (§11, but not at the other occurrences); *Gumlin* > *Galion* (§16); *Gorthû* > *Gorthaur* (§30, see p. 240, §143); *Palúrien* > *Kementári* (§32); *Eriol* > *Ereol* (§33).

Fionwë was changed to *Eönwë* throughout, and 'son of Manwë' to 'herald of Manwë' in §5 (but in §6 'Fionwë son of Manwë' > 'Eönwë to whom Manwë gave his sword'); 'the sons of the Valar' became 'the host of the Valar' in §6, but 'the Children of the Valar' in §18, 'the sons of the Gods' in §20, and 'the sons of the Valar' in §§29, 32, were not corrected (see also under §15 below).

Other changes were:

§6 'Ingwiel son of Ingwë was their chief': observing the apparent error, in that Ingwiel appears to be named the leader of the Noldor (see V.334, §6), my father changed this to 'Finarphin son of Finwë': see IV.196, second footnote. In the typescript he let the passage stand, but changed *Ingwiel* to *Ingwion* (and also 'Light-elves' to 'Fair-elves', see X.168, 180).

§9 'Manwë' > 'Manwë the Elder King'

§12 'she let build for her' > 'there was built for her'

§13 'they took it for a sign of hope' > 'they took it for a sign, and they called it Gil-Orrain, the Star of high hope', with *Gil-Orrain* subsequently changed to *Gil-Amdir* (see X.320). The typescript had the revised reading, with *Gil-Orrain*, which my father emended to *Gil-Estel*; on the carbon copy he wrote *Orestel* above *Orrain*.

§15 'the Light-elves of Valinor' > 'the Light-elves in Valinor' 'the sons of the Gods were young and fair and terrible' > 'the host of the Gods were arrayed in forms of Valinor'

§16 'the most part of the sons of Men' > 'a great part of the sons of Men'

§17 'was like a great roar of thunder, and a tempest of fire' > 'was with a great thunder, and lightning, and a tempest of fire'

§18 'and in his fall the towers of Thangorodrim were thrown down'

> 'and he fell upon the towers of Thangorodrim and they were broken and thrown down'
'the chain Angainor, which long had been prepared' > 'the chain Angainor, which he had worn aforetime'

§20 'But Maidros would not harken, and he prepared ... to attempt in despair the fulfilment of his oath' > 'But Maidros and Maglor would not harken ...', with change of 'he' to 'they' and 'his' to 'their'.

§26 'and especially upon the great isles' > 'and upon the great isles'

§30 'and bears dark fruit even to these latest days' > 'and will bear dark fruit even unto the latest days'

'Sauron ... who served Morgoth even in Valinor and came with him' > '... who served Morgoth long ago and came with him into the world' (cf. the removal of the passage on this subject from the chapter *Of the Ruin of Beleriand*, p. 240, §143).

§31 'Túrin Turambar ... coming from the halls of Mandos' > 'Túrin Turambar ... returning from the Doom of Men at the ending of the world'. In the margin of the manuscript my father wrote 'and Beren Camlost' without direction for its insertion.

§32 'and she will break them [the Silmarils] and with their fire rekindle the Two Trees': this was emended on the carbon copy of the typescript only to: 'and he [Fëanor] will break them and with their fire Yavanna will rekindle the Two Trees'

Approximately against the last two sentences of the paragraph (from 'In that light the Gods will grow young again ...') my father put a large X in the margin of the manuscript.

Among these later changes were also the subheadings (*Of the Great Battle and the War of Wrath* at §15, *Of the Last End of the Oath of Fëanor and his Sons* at §20, and *Of the Passing of the Elves* at §26) which were noticed in the commentary on this text, V.336; I neglected however to mention there the introduction of a further subheading, *The Second Prophecy of Mandos*, at §31.

I said of this text in V.324: 'The very fact that the end of "The Silmarillion" still took this form when *The Lord of the Rings* was begun is sufficiently remarkable'. It seems much more remarkable, and not easy to interpret, that my father was treating it as a text requiring only minor and particular revision at this much later time. But his mode of emendation could sometimes be decidedly perfunctory, suggesting not a close, comparative consideration of an earlier text so much as a series of descents on particular points that struck his attention; and it may be that such later emendations as he made in this case are to be regarded rather in that light than as implying any sort of final approval of the content. But this text was peculiar in its inception, jumping forward from the beginning of the story of Túrin to the middle of a sentence much further on in the *Quenta*, and its later history does not diminish its somewhat mysterious nature.

PART THREE

THE WANDERINGS OF HÚRIN

AND OTHER WRITINGS
NOT FORMING PART
OF THE
QUENTA SILMARILLION

I
THE WANDERINGS OF HÚRIN

In *The Wanderings of Húrin* ('**WH**') it is not convenient to use the device of numbered paragraphs, and commentary (pp. 298 ff.) is here related to numbered notes in the text.

The earliest account of Húrin after his release by Morgoth is found in the *Tale of Turambar* (II.112–15, 135–6), leading to that in the *Sketch of the Mythology* (IV.32) and in Q (IV.132); see also AB 1 and AB 2 (IV.306, V.141). It is not necessary to say anything about these here, since in none of them is there any suggestion that Húrin returned to Hithlum (or went to Brethil) before he came to Nargothrond.

I have described (p. 103) how the manuscript of the *Grey Annals* (GA) ends with strange abruptness at the foot of a page, and said that 'it always seemed to me strange that my father should have abandoned the *Grey Annals* where he did, without at least writing the inscription that was carved on the stone'. At some later time (see *ibid.*) he entered roughly on the manuscript the inscription on the stone, and the words of conclusion to the tale, derived from the last part of the *Narn* (NE). The explanation of this was simple, when I discovered, misplaced among miscellaneous papers, manuscript pages that are very obviously the continuation of the *Grey Annals* (the first of these pages is indeed numbered continuously with the last page of the main manuscript); this continuation, it is plain, was already lost in my father's lifetime. The original conclusion was in fact exactly as in the addition made to GA when he presumed the original ending lost, except that the title of the work was then *Glaer nia Chîn Húrin*, as in NE (p. 160, §349). Subsequently my father had added the words 'and was made by Men', as in the conclusion added to GA (p. 103), and later again he changed the title to *Narn i Chîn Húrin*, as he did also in NE.

In the scarcely changing script of the main manuscript this 'lost' text stopped here, but was then continued on the same page in a different ink and script, with the date 500 twice written against this further entry and each time struck out.

It is said by some that Morwen on a time came in her witless wandering to that stone and read it, and died afterwards, though haply she did not understand the tale that it told, and in that was less tormented than Húrin. For all that Morgoth knew of the working of his curse Húrin knew also; but lies and malice were mingled with the truth, and he that sees through the eyes of Morgoth, willing or unwilling, sees all things crooked. [*Written in the margin later:* Some fate of Morwen must be devised. Did Morwen and Húrin meet again?]¹

At this point the ink and to a slight degree the style of the script change again. The following narrative is the first account of Húrin's release since the *Quenta* of 1930.

500

Especially Morgoth endeavoured to cast an evil light upon all that Thingol and Melian had done (for he hated and feared them most); and when at last he deemed the time ripe, in the year after the death of his children, he released Húrin from bondage and let him go whither he would. He feigned that in this he was moved by generosity to a defeated enemy, but in truth his purpose was that Húrin should further his malice. And little though Húrin trusted aught that Morgoth said or did, he went forth in grief, embittered by the lies of the Dark Lord.

Twenty-eight years Húrin was captive in Angband, and at his release was in his sixtieth year,² but great strength was in him still, in spite of the weight of his grief, for it suited the purpose of Morgoth that this should be so. He was sent under guard as far as the east-marches of Hithlum, and there he was let go free.

None that had known him [in] youth could mistake him still, though he had grown grim to look on: his hair and beard were white and long, but there was a fell light in his eyes. He walked unbowed, and yet carried a great black staff; but he was girt with his sword. Great wonder and dread fell on the land when it was noised in Hithlum that the Lord Húrin had returned. The Easterlings were dismayed, fearing that their Master would prove faithless again and give back the land to the Westrons, and that they would be enslaved in their turn. For watchmen had reported that Húrin came out of Angband.

'There was a great riding,' they said, 'of the black soldiers of Thangorodrim over the Anfauglith, and with them came this man, as one that was held in honour.'

Therefore the chieftains of the Easterlings dared not lay hands on Húrin, and let him walk at will. In which they were wise; for the remnant of his own people shunned him, because of his coming from Angband, as one in league and honour with Morgoth; and indeed all escaped captives were held in suspicion of spying and treachery in those days, as has been told. Thus freedom only increased the bitterness of Húrin's heart; for even had he so wished, he could not have roused any rebellion against the new lords of the land. All the following that he gathered was a small company of the homeless men and outlaws that lurked in the hills; but they had done no great deed against the Incomers since the passing of Túrin, some five years before.

Of Túrin's deeds in Brodda's hall Húrin now learned from the outlaws the true tale; and he looked on Asgon[3] and his men, and he said: 'Men are changed here. In thraldom they have found thrall hearts. I desire no longer any lordship among them, nor elsewhere in Middle-earth. I will leave this land and wander alone, unless any of you will go with me, to meet what we may. For I have no purpose now, unless I find chance to avenge the wrongs of my son.'

Asgorn[4] and six other desperate men were willing to go with him; and Húrin led them to the halls of Lorgan, who still called himself the Lord of Hithlum. Lorgan heard of their coming and was afraid, and he gathered other chieftains and their men in his house for defence. But Húrin coming to the gates looked on the Eastrons[5] in scorn.

'Fear not!' he said. 'I should have needed no companions, if I had come to fight with you. I am come only to take leave of the lord of the land. I have no liking for it any more, since you have defiled it. Hold it while you may, until your Master recalls you to the slave-tasks that fit you better.'

Then Lorgan was not ill-pleased to think that he would so soon and easily be rid of the fear of Húrin, without crossing the will of Angband; and he came forward.

'As you will, friend,' he said. 'I have done you no ill, and have let you be, and of this I hope you will bring a true tale, if you come again to the Master.'

Húrin eyed him in wrath. 'Friend me not, thrall and churl!' he said. 'And believe not the lies that I have heard: that I have ever entered into the service of the Enemy. Of the Edain am I and so remain, and there shall be no friendship between mine and yours for ever.'

Then hearing that Húrin had not after all the favour of Morgoth, or forswore it, many of Lorgan's men drew their swords to put an end to him. But Lorgan restrained them; for he was wary, and more cunning and wicked than the others, and quicker therefore to guess at the purposes of the Master.

'Go then, greybeard, to evil fortune,' he said. 'For that is your doom. Folly and violence and self-hurt are all the deeds of your kin. Fare you ill!'

'*Tôl acharn!*' said Húrin. 'Vengeance comes. I am not the last of the Edain, whether I fare ill or well.' And with that he departed, and left the land of Hithlum.

501

Of the wanderings of Húrin there is no tale told, until he came at last late in this year to Nargothrond. It is said that he had then gathered to him other fugitives and masterless men in the wild, and came south with a following of a hundred or more. But why it was that he went to Nargothrond is uncertain, save that so his doom and the fate of the Jewels led him. Some have said that

At this point the 'lost continuation' of the *Grey Annals* stops, at the foot of a page; but a further page is found, written in a wholly different script (a rapid italic that my father used quite frequently in the period after the publication of *The Lord of the Rings*), that clearly joins to the abandoned sentence 'Some have said that'. Together with the first extension of the Annals, that concerning Morwen (pp. 251–2), and then the narrative recounting Húrin's return to Hithlum, this page is a further and final link in the series of additions that were made at intervals whose length cannot be determined.

[Some have said that] maybe he knew not that Glaurung was dead, and hoped in his heart distraught to take vengeance on this evil thing – for Morgoth would conceal the death of Glaurung, if he could, both because the loss was a grief to him and a hurt to his pride, and because (from Húrin especially) he would conceal all that was most valiant or successful of Túrin's deeds. Yet this can scarce be so,[6] since the death of Glaurung was so bound up with the death of his children and revelation of their evil case; while the rumour of the assault of Glaurung upon Brethil went far and wide. Certainly Morgoth fenced men in Hithlum, as he was able, and little news came to them of events in other lands; but so soon as Húrin passed southward or met any wanderers in the wild he would hear tidings of the battle in the ravine of Taiglin.

More likely is it that he was drawn thither to discover news of Túrin; to Brethil he would not yet come, nor to Doriath.

He went first seeking a way into Gondolin, and the friendship of Turgon (which indeed would have been great); but he found it not. His doom was unwilling (for Morgoth's curse was ever upon him still); and moreover since the Nírnaeth Turgon had expended every art upon the hiding of his realm. It was then that Húrin finding

Here the text stops abruptly; but on the same page and clearly at the same time my father wrote the following:

Húrin goes to seek Gondolin. Fails. Passes by Brethil, and his anguish is increased. They will not admit him – saying that the Halethrim do not wish any more to become enmeshed in the shadow of his kin. But   ∧   [?new] Lord[7] gives the dragon-helm to Húrin. His heart is hot against Thingol. He passes it [Doriath] by and goes on to Nargothrond. Why? To seek news, plunder, – he had been an admirer of Felagund.

News of the fall of Nargothrond came to sons of Fëanor, and dismayed Maeðros, but did not all displease Celeg[orn] and Curufin. But when the news of the dragon's fall was heard, then many wondered concerning its hoard and who was the master? Some Orc-lord, men thought. But the Dwarves of [sic]   How did Mîm find it? He must come of a different race.[8]

These two pieces, especially the latter, are plainly a record of emerging ideas. In the first there is what is probably the earliest reference to the story that Húrin sought but failed to find the entrance to Gondolin. In the second appears a new articulation in the unwritten history of the Dragon-helm, together with other new detail (Húrin's admiration of Felagund, and the effect of the news of the fall of Nargothrond on the sons of Fëanor); and there is seen the first adumbration of a story of Húrin's adventures in Brethil before he went to Nargothrond.

Before coming to the fully achieved story of Húrin in Brethil there remains one further text to consider. When my father was engaged on his later work on the *Narn i Chîn Húrin* he made several plot-synopses arranged in annalistic form. Much of that material is not relevant here, since it is primarily concerned with the evolving story of Túrin; but one of them, which begins with the birth of Túrin, continues beyond his death and gives some account, though very brief, of Húrin after his release by Morgoth.

I give here the conclusion of this text (certainly somewhat later than any of the writings given thus far in Part Three), taking it up a little before the death of Túrin, since there are many interesting details in the annals for 490–9 bearing on the accounts given in NE and GA. The text was written legibly but very rapidly.

490-5

Túrin becomes a great captain in Nargothrond under the name of *Iarwaeth*, and is called *Mormegil* 'Black Sword'. [*Altered later to read:* Túrin becomes a great captain in Nargothrond. He only tells that he was lord of Cúarthol, and gives out his name as *Thuringud* the Hidden Foe; but is called *Mormegil* 'Black Sword'.

Gwindor reveals his true name to Finduilas, and Túrin is angry.[9]

494

Morgoth stirs up the Eastrons to greater hatred of Elves and Edain, and sends Orcs to aid them and impel them. Lorgan hearing of Niënor's beauty is eager to take her by force. Morwen and Niënor flee the land and come to Doriath. They seek news of Túrin.[10]

495

Tuor escapes from Hithlum by Cirith Ninniach and comes to Nivrost. He meets Gelmir and Arminas. Ulmo visits him on the shores by Mount Taras, and sends Voronwë to him. Tuor and Voronwë go to seek Gondolin which they reach in winter. Winter of 495–6 is the Fell Winter with ice and snow from November to March (5 months).

Gelmir and Arminas come to Nargothrond and bring warning of forces mustering in Narrow Land and under Erydwethian [*sic*]. They are rejected by Túrin.

Handir of Brethil slain in battle with the Orcs at the Crossings of Taeglin [*sic*]. His son Brandir the lame is chosen Chieftain, though many would have preferred his cousins Hunthor or Hardang.

Túrin and Orodreth defeated in Battle of Tum-halad by the dread of Glaurung. Gwindor also slain. Glaurung ravages Nargothrond, and cozens Túrin.

Túrin breaks his word to Gwindor to endeavour to save Finduilas, who is carried off. Instead under the spell of Glaurung he goes to Dorlómin to seek Morwen and Niënor.

Finduilas is slain by the Orcs near Crossings of Taeglin and buried by Men of Brethil in Haudh-en-Elleth.

Tuor sees Túrin near ravaged place of Eithil Ivrin but does not know who he is.

Glaurung takes possession of Nargothrond.[11]

496

Early in year Túrin comes to Dorlómin. He slays Brodda in his hall. Death of Sador. Túrin flies with Asgon and other outlawed Edain to the Mountains, and then leaves Dorlómin by himself. He comes at last to Brethil and learns of the fate of Finduilas.

Morwen and Niënor come to Nargothrond, but their escort (under Mablung) is scattered, and Morwen is lost in the wild, but Niënor is bewitched by Glaurung, and loses her memory, and runs into the wild.

Niënor comes to Brethil, and is called *Níniel*.[12]

496–

Under the name of *Turambar* Túrin becomes chief warrior of Brethil, and men give no heed to Brandir. Brandir falls in love with Níniel, but she loves Turambar.

497

Dior Halfelven weds Lindis of Ossiriand.[13]

498

Túrin weds Níniel (autumn).[14]

499

Glaurung assails Brethil. Túrin goes against him with Hunthor and Dorlas. Dorlas' heart fails and he leaves them. Hunthor is slain by a falling stone. Túrin slays Glaurung. Glaurung ere death reveals to Túrin and Niënor who they are. Túrin slays Brandir. Niënor casts herself into Taeglin. [*The following are separate additions to the text:*] Túrin slays Brandir and takes his own life. / Men of Brethil erect the *Talbor* or St[anding] Stone to their memory. / Mîm comes to Nargothrond and takes possession of the treasure.[15]

500

Elrún and Eldún twin sons of Dior are born.
Morgoth releases Húrin. Húrin goes to Hithlum.[16]

501

Húrin leaves Hithlum and with Asgon and six men goes down into the Narrow Land.

Húrin leaves his companions and seeks in vain an entrance to

Gondolin, but Morgoth's spies thus learn in what region it stands.

Húrin comes to the Stone and there finds Morwen, who dies. Húrin is put in prison by Hardang Chief of Brethil, but is aided by Manthor his kinsman (cousin of Hardang). In uprising Hardang and Manthor are slain and Obel Halad is burned. Húrin finds Asgon again and gathers other men and goes towards Nargothrond.[17]

502

Tuor weds Idril daughter of Turgon.

Húrin comes to Nargothrond and slays Mîm the petty-dwarf. He and his men carry off the treasure of Glaurung and bring it to Doriath. Húrin is admitted in pity.[18]

Here this plot-synopsis ends, at the foot of a manuscript page. I come now to the substantial complex of writing leading to a final text which my father ultimately entitled *The Wanderings of Húrin* (earlier *Of the Fate of Húrin and Morwen*). The final title seems not to be entirely apposite to the content of the work, which is wholly concerned with the story of Húrin in Brethil; it may have been intended to have a larger scope, to include the further story of Húrin told on the same scale, which was never written (see p. 310, note 57, and also the other title given below).

There is, first, a draft manuscript and associated rough workings (often of an extreme roughness). Many pages of the draft material are the backs of University documents dated 1954, others are documents from 1957. Secondly, there is a typescript made by my father on his later typewriter (see X.300), much emended in manuscript and with some substantial passages rejected and replaced by new material in typescript; and lastly an amanuensis typescript of virtually no independent value. The work can be placed with fair certainty towards the end of the 1950s.

My father's typescript, as typed, bore no title, but he wrote in ink on the top copy:

Of the Fate of Húrin and Morwen
Link to the Necklace of the Dwarves, 'Sigil Elu-naeth'
Necklace of the Woe of Thingol

The text opens thus:

So ended the tale of Túrin the hapless; and it has ever been held one of the worst of the deeds of Morgoth among Men in the ancient world. It is said by some that on a time Morwen came in her witless wandering to the graven stone, and knowing that her children were dead, though she understood not in what way their tale had ended, she sat beside the stone awaiting death; and there Húrin found her at last, as is after told. Less happy than hers was the lot of Húrin.

This passage derives, in its first sentence, from Q (IV.131), and then from the first continuation of the *Grey Annals* (pp. 251–2), with the addition that Húrin found Morwen beside the stone (cf. p. 258, annal 501). The passage was struck from the typescript and replaced by the following, written on a document dating from 1957:

So ended the tale of Túrin the Hapless, the worst of the works of Morgoth among Men in the ancient world. But Morgoth did not sleep nor rest from evil, and this was not the end of his dealings with the House of Hador, against which his malice was unsated, though Húrin was under his Eye, and Morwen wandered distraught in the wild.

Unhappy was the lot of Húrin.

At the head of this my father subsequently wrote *The Wanderings of Húrin*, and the final amanuensis typescript was given this title also (see p. 258). The typescript continues, from 'Less happy than hers was the lot of Húrin':

For all that Morgoth knew of the working of his malice Húrin knew also; but lies were mingled with the truth, and aught that was good was hidden or distorted. He that sees through the eyes of Morgoth, willing or unwilling, sees all things crooked.

It was Morgoth's special endeavour to cast an evil light upon all that Thingol and Melian had done, for he feared and hated them most; and when, therefore, he deemed the time ripe, in the year after the death of Túrin he released Húrin from bondage, bidding him go whither he would.

He feigned that in this he was moved by pity for an enemy utterly defeated, marvelling at his endurance. 'Such steadfastness,' he said, 'should have been shown in a better cause, and would have been otherwise rewarded. But I have no longer any use for you, Húrin, in the waning of your little life.' And he lied, for his purpose was that Húrin should still further his malice against Elves and Men, ere he died.

Then little though Húrin trusted aught that Morgoth said or did, knowing that he was without pity, he took his freedom and went forth in grief, embittered by the deceits of the Dark Lord. Twenty-eight years Húrin was captive in Angband . . .

In this passage my father was following, with some expansion, the continuation of the *Grey Annals* (p. 252); from this point he followed it almost without alteration as far as 'And with that he departed, and left the land of Hithlum' (p. 254).[19] There are thus two closely similar, and for most of their length all but identical, texts of this short narrative, which may be called 'Húrin in Hithlum'; but the first of them is the continuation of the *Annals*, and the second is the opening of a wholly new story of Húrin in Brethil – causing a postponement of the story of 'Húrin in Nargothrond', which in the event was never reached. Seeing then that the second text of 'Húrin in Hithlum' has an entirely distinct function, there is clearly no question of regarding the story of Húrin in Brethil as a further extension of the *Annals*. As will be seen, my father was very evidently no longer writing annals of Beleriand: that work was now abandoned – or possibly, in his intention, left in abeyance, until the new story had been completed on the scale that he found congenial.

I now give the further text of *The Wanderings of Húrin* (following from the words 'And with that he departed, and left the land of Hithlum'). The work is of peculiar complexity in this, that when my father was well advanced in the story he came to a clearer understanding (as he might have said) of the situation in Brethil at the time of Húrin's advent; and these new conceptions overtook it before it was completed in a primary form. In other words, the story grew and changed as he wrote, but in this case he did not abandon it and start again at the beginning: he returned to earlier parts of the story and reconstructed them. For the most part the text as actually typed could stand, but required continual emendation in respect of names and other details. It is not easy to find a perfectly satisfactory and readily comprehensible way of presenting this, but after much experimentation I concluded that the best method is to give as the text the final form achieved in the typescript, but to interrupt it (pp. 265 ff.) at the point where the new conceptions first appear and give an account of the development. Two passages are concerned: the revised form of the first is marked by single asterisks on pp. 262–3, and of the second by double asterisks on pp. 264–5.

It is said that the hunters of Lorgan dogged his footsteps and did not leave his trail until he and his companions went up into the mountains. When Húrin stood again in the high places he descried far away amid the clouds the peaks of the Crisaegrim, and he remembered Turgon; and his heart desired to come again to the Hidden Realm, if he could, for there at least he would be remembered with honour. He had heard naught of the things that had come to pass in Gondolin, and knew not that Turgon now hardened his heart against wisdom and pity, and allowed no one either to enter or to go forth for any cause whatsoever.[20] Therefore, unaware that all ways were shut beyond hope, he resolved to turn his steps towards the Crisaegrim; but he said nothing of his purpose to his companions, for he was still bound by his oath to reveal to no one that he knew even in what region Turgon abode.

Nonetheless he had need of help; for he had never lived in the wild, whereas the outlaws were long inured to the hard life of hunters and gatherers, and they brought with them such food as they could, though the Fell Winter had much diminished their store. Therefore Húrin said to them: 'We must leave this land now; for Lorgan will leave me in peace no longer. Let us go down into the vales of Sirion, where Spring has come at last!'

Then Asgon [21] guided them to one of the ancient passes that led east out of Mithrim, and they went down from the sources of the Lithir, until they came to the falls where it raced into Sirion at the southern end of the Narrow Land.[22] Now they went with great wariness; for Húrin put little trust in the 'freedom' that Morgoth had granted him. And rightly: for Morgoth had news of all his movements, and though for a while he was hidden in the mountains, his coming down was soon espied. Thereafter he was followed and watched, yet with such cunning that he seldom got wind of it. All the creatures of Morgoth avoided his sight, and he was never waylaid or molested.[23]

They journeyed southward on the west side of Sirion, and Húrin debated with himself how to part from his companions, at least for so long that he could seek for an entrance to Gondolin without betraying his word. At length they came to the Brithiach; and there Asgon said to Húrin: 'Whither shall we go now, lord? Beyond this ford the ways east are too perilous for mortal men, if tales be true.'

'Then let us go to Brethil, which is nigh at hand,' said Húrin. 'I have an errand there. In that land my son died.'

So that night they took shelter in a grove of trees, first outliers of the Forest of Brethil on its northern border only a short way south of the Brithiach. Húrin lay a little apart from the others; and next day before it was light he arose while they slumbered deep in weariness, and he left them and crossed the ford and came into Dimbar.

When the men awoke he was already gone far, and there was a thick morning mist about the river. As time passed and he did not return nor answer any call they began to fear that he had been taken by some beast or prowling enemy. 'We have become heedless of late,' said Asgon. 'The land is quiet, too quiet, but there are eyes under leaves and ears behind stones.'

They followed his trail when the mist lifted; but it led to the ford and there failed, and they were at a loss. 'If he has left us, let us return to our own land,' said Ragnir.[24] He was the youngest of the company, and remembered little of the days before the Nirnaeth. 'The old man's wits are wild. He speaks with strange voices to shadows in his sleep.'

'Little wonder if it were so,' said Asgon. 'But who else could stand as straight as he, after such woe? Nay, he is our right lord, do as he may, and I have sworn to follow him.'

'Even east over the ford?' said the others.

'Nay, there is small hope in that way,' said Asgon, 'and I do not think that Húrin will go far upon it. All we know of his purpose was to go soon to Brethil, and that he has an errand there. We are on the very border. Let us seek him there.'

'By whose leave?' said Ragnir. 'Men there do not love strangers.'

'Good men dwell there,' said Asgon, 'and the [Master >] Lord of Brethil is kin to our old lords.'[25] Nonetheless the others were doubtful, for no tidings had come out of Brethil for some years. 'It may be ruled by Orcs for all we know,' they said.

'We shall soon find what way things go,' said Asgon. 'Orcs are little worse than Eastrons, I guess. If outlaws we must remain, I would rather lurk in the fair woods than in the cold hills.'

Asgon, therefore, turned and went back towards Brethil; and the others followed him, for he had a stout heart and men said that he was born with good luck. Before that day ended they had come deep into the forest, and their coming was marked; for the Haladin were more wary than ever and kept close watch on their borders. In the [middle of the night >] grey of the morning, as all but one of the incomers were asleep, their camp was surrounded, and their watchman was held and gagged as soon as he cried out.

Then Asgon leapt up, and called to his men that they should draw no weapon. 'See now,' he cried, 'we come in peace! Edain we are out of [Mithrim > Hithlum >] Dorlómin.'

*'That may be so,' said the march-wardens. 'But the morn is dim. Our captain will judge you better when light is more.'

Then being many times outnumbered Asgon and his men were made prisoners, and their weapons were taken and their hands bound. Thus they were brought to Ebor their captain; and he asked their names and whence they came.

'So you are Edain of the North,' he said. 'Your speech bears you out, and your gear. You look for friendship, maybe. But alas! evil things have befallen us here, and we live in fear. Manthor my lord, Master of the North-march, is not here, and I must therefore obey the commands of the Halad, the Chieftain of Brethil. To him you must be sent at once without further question. There may you speed well!'

So Ebor spoke in courtesy, but he did not hope over much. For the new Chieftain was now Hardang son of Hundad. At the death of Brandir childless he had been made Halad, being of the Haladin, the kin of Haleth, from which all chieftains were chosen. He had not loved Túrin, and he had no love now at all for the House of Hador, in whose blood he had no part. Neither had he much friendship with Manthor, who was also of the Haladin.

To Hardang Asgon and his men were led by devious ways, and they were blindfolded. Thus at length they came to the hall of the Chieftains in Obel Halad;[26] and their eyes were uncovered, and the guards led them in. Hardang sat in his great chair, and he looked unkindly upon them.

'From Dorlómin you come, I am told,' he said. 'But why you come I know not.* Little good has come to Brethil out of that land; and I look for none now: it is a fief of Angband. Cold welcome you will find here, creeping in thus to spy out our ways!'

Asgon restrained his anger, but answered stoutly: 'We did not come in stealth, lord. We have as great craft in woods as your folk, and we should not so easily have been taken, if we had known any cause for fear. We are Edain, and we do not serve Angband but hold to the House of Hador. We believed that the Men of Brethil were of like sort and friendly to all faithful men.'

'To those of proved faith,' said Hardang. 'To be Edain is not enough alone. And as for the House of Hador it is held in little love here. Why should the folk of that House come here now?'

To that Asgon made no answer; for from the unfriendship of the [Master >] Chieftain he thought it best not to speak yet of Húrin.

'I see that you will not speak of all that you know,' said Hardang. 'So be it. I must judge as I see; but I will be just. This is my judgement. Here Túrin son of Húrin dwelt for a time, and he delivered the land from the Serpent of Angband. For this I give you your lives. **But he scorned Brandir, right Chieftain of Brethil, and he slew him without justice or pity. Therefore I will not harbour you here. You shall be thrust forth, whence you entered. Go now, and if you return it will be to death!'

'Then shall we not receive our weapons again?' said Asgon. 'Will you cast us back into the wild without bow or steel to perish among the beasts?'

'No man of Hithlum shall ever again bear weapon in Brethil,' said Hardang. 'Not by my leave. Lead them hence.'

But as they were haled from the hall Asgon cried: 'This is the justice of Eastrons not of Edain! We were not here with Túrin, either in good deed or evil. Húrin we serve. He lives still. Lurking in your wood do you not remember the Nirnaeth? Will you then dishonour him also in your spite, if he comes?'

'If Húrin comes, do you say?' said Hardang. 'When Morgoth sleeps, maybe!'

'Nay,' said Asgon. 'He has returned. With him we came to your borders. He has an errand here, he said. He will come!'

'Then I shall be here to meet him,' said Hardang. 'But you will not. Now go!' He spoke as in scorn, but his face whitened in sudden fear that some strange thing had happened boding yet worse to come. Then a great dread of the shadow of the House of Hador fell upon him, so that his heart grew dark. For he was not a man of great spirit, such as were Hunthor and Manthor, descendants of Hiril.

Asgon and his company were blindfolded again, lest they should espy out the pathways of Brethil, and they were led back to the North-march. Ebor was ill pleased when he heard of what had passed in Obel Halad, and he spoke to them more courteously.

'Alas!' he said, 'you must needs go forth again. But see! I return to you your gear and weapons. For so would my lord Manthor do, at the least. I would he were here! But he is the doughtiest man now among us; and by Hardang's command is Captain of the guards at the Crossings of Taiglin. There we have most fear of assault, and most fighting. Well, this much I will do in his stead; but I beg you, do not enter Brethil again, for if you do, we may feel constrained to obey the word of Hardang that has now gone out to all the marches: to slay you at sight.'

Then Asgon thanked him, and Ebor led them to the eaves of Brethil, and there wished them good speed.

'Well, thy luck has held,' said Ragnir, 'for at least we are not slain, though we came nigh it. Now what shall we do?'

'I desire still to find my lord Húrin,' said Asgon, 'and my heart tells me that he will come to Brethil yet.'

'Whither we cannot return,' said Ragnir, 'unless we seek a death swifter than hunger.'

'If he comes, he will come, I guess, by the north-march, between Sirion and [Taiglin >] Taeglin,' said Asgon. 'Let us go down towards the Crossings of [Taiglin >] Taeglin. There it is more likely that we may hear news.'

'Or bow-strings,' said Ragnir. Nonetheless they took Asgon's counsel, and went away westward, keeping such watch as they could from afar upon the dark eaves of Brethil.

But Ebor was troubled, and sent swiftly to Manthor reporting the coming of Asgon and his strange words concerning Húrin. But of this matter rumour now ran through all Brethil. And Hardang sat in Obel Halad in doubt, and took counsel with his friends.**

In the foregoing text two passages are replacements in the typescript of shorter passages that were rejected. The first of these, marked by asterisks at its beginning and end, runs from ' "That may be so," said the march-wardens' on p. 262 to ' "But why you come I know not" ' on p. 263. The rejected passage read as follows:

'Maybe,' answered the captain of the guards; 'but the morn is dim. Others shall judge you in a better light.'

Then, being many times outnumbered, Asgorn and his men were made prisoners, and their weapons were taken and their hands bound; and in this way they were brought at last before the new Master of the Haladin.

He was Harathor, brother of that Hunthor who perished in the ravine of Taeglin. By the childless death of Brandir he had inherited the lordship descending from Haldad. He had no love for the house of Hador, and no part in their blood; and he said to Asgorn, when the captives stood before him: 'From [Hithlum >] Dorlómin you come, I am told, and your speech bears it out. But why you come I know not.

For reference in the following pages I shall call this passage A 1 and its replacement A 2.

The second replacement passage, marked by two asterisks at

beginning and end, runs from 'But he scorned Brandir' on p. 264 to 'And Hardang sat in Obel Halad in doubt, and took counsel with his friends' on p. 265. Here the rejected passage read:

'... But he scorned Brandir, right Master of Brethil, and he slew him without justice or pity. For this I will take your freedom. You shall be held in bonds; and I shall not relent until good reason is shown me.'

Then he ordered them to be taken and shut in a cave and there to be guarded day and night. But as they were led away Asgorn cried: 'This is the justice of Eastrons not of Edain! We were not here with Túrin, either in good deed or evil. Húrin we serve, who still lives. Maybe lurking in your little wood you do not remember the Nirnaeth or his great deeds. Will you slay him to ease your griefs, if he comes?'

'If Húrin comes, do you say?' said Harathor. 'When Morgoth sleeps, maybe.'

'Nay,' said Asgorn. 'He has returned, and we came with him to your borders. He has an errand here, he said. He will come!'

'Then we will await him. And you shall too,' said Harathor, smiling grimly. But afterwards his heart misgave him, fearing that Asgorn spoke the truth and that some strange thing had happened, boding worse to follow. For he dreaded the shadow of the House of Hador, lest it should overwhelm his lesser folk, and he was not a man of great heart such as Hunthor his brother [*later* > such as the descendants of Haldir and Hiril his sister].

The rejected text then moved straight on to 'Now Húrin, coming into Dimbar' on p. 271. The passage just given I will call B 1 and its replacement B 2.

Among the draft manuscript papers is found the following text, which I will call 'C': in this my father reflected on the development of the story. Written very rapidly and roughly, with many abbreviations which I have expanded, it *preceded*, and was the basis for, the two replacement passages A 2 and B 2.

The Wanderings of Húrin.
? Where is to come in the revelation that Asgorn and company are in jail. They do not seem to fit, yet their coming to Brethil is needed to 'cast the shadow' by arousing fear and hatred in the heart of Harathor.

I suggest that the two jailings [i.e. that of Asgorn and his men and that of Húrin, told later] are too repetitive; and also Harathor is too fierce all at once. His doom is that because of the killing of Glaurung their lives are spared; but because of the killing of Brandir they are to be *thrust out*: he will have none of the House of Hador.

Asgorn says this is cruel treatment. He demands return of their weapons, 'or how else are they to live in the wild?' But Harathor says no man of Dorlómin shall bear a weapon in Brethil. Asgorn as they are led off asks if he will treat Húrin in like orkish manner. 'We will wait and see,' said Harathor.

[*This paragraph was struck out as soon as written*: [Manthor, captain >] The captain / of the Taiglin-guard returns their weapons, and bids them a fairly courteous farewell; but warns them that 'state of war' has been declared (which gives the Master / Warden right to issue orders to all under duty-rota) and that if they cross again into Brethil he or any other captain or watchman will shoot them. They go off but lurk in watch of the crossings, but miss Húrin, who entered out of Dimbar. Húrin should *not* enter by Taiglin-crossing, *nor* be found by Hauð-en-Elleth. (This has no significance in his case, and overworks the Hauð.)]

Asgorn and company are blindfolded as they are brought to Obel Halad and are put out *by the same way* as they entered (so as to learn no more of the ways of Brethil). They therefore lurk near the eaves in that region, and so miss Húrin who crossed the Brithiach and went to the Crossings of Taiglin.

The region nigh Brithiach and along Sirion for some way was the land of Manthor (brother of Hunthor who fell in the ravine). But Manthor, as one of the chief warriors and of the kin of the Haladin, was in command of the chief forces kept near the Crossings of Taiglin. (Manthor was not liked by Harathor, for many had wished to elect him Warden – it being . . . law to do so. And maybe Manthor too desired the Wardenship.) The captain of the guards near Brithiach was Enthor [> was therefore a chief henchman, called Ebor, of Manthor's (appointed by him)] younger brother of Hunthor and Manthor. So Manthor heard soon of what had happened: for all this family had been supporters and admirers of Túrin, and were proud of their *kinship* with the House of Hador. So Enthor [> Ebor] sent messengers to Manthor to tell him that Húrin might come, escaping from Angband.

In the last part of the *Narn* (NE) the emergence of Hunthor (< Torbarth) can be followed, from his origin in Albarth, at first simply one of those who volunteered to accompany Túrin to the attack on Glaurung and named only because he fell and was drowned at Cabed-en-Aras. In the first of these rejected passages (A 1, p. 265) the new lord of Brethil after the death of Brandir is Harathor, 'brother of that Hunthor who perished in the ravine of Taeglin'; and it is expressly said of him that 'he had no love for the house of Hador *and no part in their blood*'. These words, repeated in the revision A 2 (p. 263), are of great importance in the story.

An essential element in the older history of the People of Haleth was the intermingling of the line of their lords with that of the House of

Hador which came about through the 'double marriage' of Hador's son Galion with the daughter (unnamed) of Haleth the Hunter, and of his daughter Glorwendil with Haleth's son Hundor (GA §171 and commentary). This double marriage was preserved in the later transformed history of the Edain, when the genealogical place of Haleth the Hunter had been taken by Halmir (p. 236); the resulting relationships can be displayed thus:

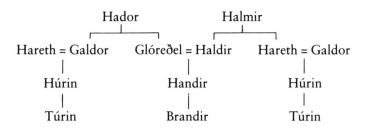

But the complexity was further increased by the introduction of another connection with the House of Bëor in the marriage of Beldis to Handir of Brethil (see the tables on pp. 231, 237):

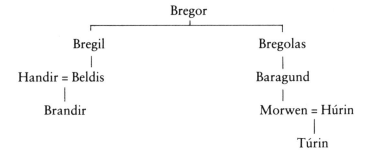

Thus Túrin was the second cousin of Brandir on the 'Hadorian' side, and he was also his second cousin on the Haladin side; while in the 'Bëorian' line he was Brandir's second cousin once removed – a genealogical situation to delight the heart of Hamfast Gamgee. Pointing out these relationships in an isolated note of this time, my father observed that 'Túrin would be more readily accepted by the Haladin when his true name and lineage were known or guessed', since he was akin to their lords in these ways. Harathor, on the other hand, 'had no love for the house of Hador and no part in their blood' (although he also was Túrin's second cousin, his great-aunt Hareth being Túrin's grandmother).

The genealogical table of the Haladin (p. 237) belongs to this stage: Harathor is shown as the seventh lord of the Haladin, succeeding

Brandir, and as the brother of Hunthor: they are the sons of Hundad, son of Hundar who died in the Nírnaeth.

The hostility of the new lord to the House of Hador was an essential idea in the story of Húrin in Brethil from the beginning; but in the last paragraph of the discussion C (p. 267) we see the emergence of a family within the larger clan who, on the contrary, took pride in their kinship with the House of Hador, and were thus divided in spirit from the new lord.

In C the significance of Hunthor is moved a stage further: he becomes the dead brother of Manthor (and must therefore, as will be seen in a moment, cease to be the brother of Harathor). Manthor had indeed already entered the story in the original drafting of WH, but he did not make his appearance until the discovery of Húrin beside the Hauð-en-Elleth (p. 275 in the final version), as captain of the guard in those parts; now in C he becomes a kinsman of Húrin, and an upholder of the values and virtues of the Edain. How his kinship with the House of Hador was introduced is seen from the correction made to the ending of the rejected passage B 1 (p. 266): '[Harathor] was not a man of great heart such as Hunthor his brother' > '... such as the descendants of Haldir and Hiril his sister'.* *Hiril* here enters the line of the People of Haleth, and the family tree is extended by a fourth child of Halmir: Haldir, Hundar, Hareth, and Hiril. In the replacement B 2 (p. 264) the phrase becomes 'he was not a man of great spirit, such as were Hunthor and Manthor, descendants of Hiril'. (That Manthor's mother was the daughter of Hiril is stated later in the text of WH, p. 289.)

In C Harathor was still so named, but he must have been on the point of receiving a new name, and must have already received a new lineage, separating him from those with 'Hadorian' sympathies, Hunthor and Manthor. The new name, *Hardang*, appears in the replacement text A 2 (p. 263) – and the occurrence of this name in the plot-sequence from the *Narn* papers shows incidentally that that text was written when my father's work on *The Wanderings of Húrin* was far advanced, if not completed. It is said there (p. 256) that when Brandir the Lame was chosen to be the Chieftain of Brethil 'many would have preferred his cousins Hunthor or Hardang', and (p. 258) that Manthor was a kinsman of Húrin and a cousin of Hardang.

This new 'family within the larger clan' was entered in roughly made alterations to the table of the Haladin (p. 237), of which I give the essentials in compressed form:

---

* Before Hiril was introduced as a second daughter of Halmir, his daughter Hareth was first named *Hiriel* (p. 235, footnote).

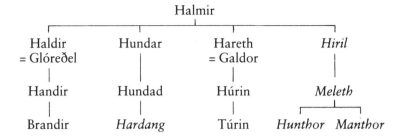

Hardang's birthdate is given as 470, Hunthor's as 467, and Manthor's as 469.

It also appears from C (p. 267) that a new conception of the social organisation of the Men of Brethil had entered, and with it a new meaning of the name *Haladin*: Manthor is said to be 'one of the chief warriors and of the kin of the Haladin', and that 'many had wished to elect him Warden'. In this connection, an isolated note (written on the reverse of that on the relationships of Túrin referred to on p. 268) states:

The title of the chieftains of Brethil should be not *lord* nor *Master*. They were elected from the family of Haldad – called the *Haladin*, that is 'wardens'. For *hal(a)* = in the old tongue of Bëor's house and Haldad's 'watch, guard'. *Halad* was a warden. (*Haldad* = watchdog.)

These new conceptions appear in the revision A 2 (p. 263), where Hardang is said to have been made *Halad*, 'being of the Haladin, the kin of Haleth, from which all chieftains were chosen'. It is also said, following the discussion in C, that Hardang was no friend to Manthor, 'who was also of the Haladin'. In contrast, in the first form of the passage (p. 265) Harathor is called 'the new Master of the Haladin', where *Haladin* clearly still means the whole people.

In the last paragraph of C (p. 267) a younger brother of Hunthor and Manthor appears, Enthor, 'captain of the guards near Brithiach' (in the additions made to the genealogical table of the Haladin this name *Enthor* was given to Hiril's husband, not otherwise named; and Meleth's husband is apparently named *Agathor*). The removal of the name Enthor in this sentence and substitution of 'a chief henchman, called Ebor, of Manthor's (appointed by him)' suggests that my father intended to cut out the words 'younger brother of Hunthor and Manthor', but omitted to do so; this is supported by the fact that Ebor, when he appears in the revision A 2 (p. 263), refers to 'Manthor my lord, Master of the North-march', who was not there. Manthor was not there because, as stated in C, he was 'in command of the chief forces kept near the Crossings of Taiglin'; Asgon and his companions entered Brethil from the north, near the Brithiach, and they left by the same way, meeting Ebor again and retrieving their weapons.

The only obscure point concerns the failure of Asgon's party to encounter Húrin on his return. My father was in two minds about this. The rejected fourth paragraph in C (p. 267) shows him (having decided that Asgorn and his men were not imprisoned) taking the view that they were ejected from Brethil near the Crossings: it is 'the captain of the Taiglin-guard' who restores their weapons; and they remain lurking in that neighbourhood. Thus they missed Húrin, 'who entered out of Dimbar' (i.e. came into Brethil from the north after crossing the Brithiach, as Asgorn had done). Húrin, he wrote, must *not* enter Brethil at the Crossings and be found lying beside the Hauð-en-Elleth (as the story was already in the draft manuscript).

But he at once, and understandably, thought better of this, and (in the fifth paragraph) retained the existing story that Húrin was found by the guards near the Crossings; he said now that Asgorn and his men were put out of Brethil in the same region as they entered, and that they lurked 'near the eaves in that region' – hence their failure to meet with Húrin. But in the replacement passage B 2 (p. 265) he has them decide not to stay near the north eaves of the forest, and they go down towards the Crossings.

I return now to the text, left at the end of the second passage of rewriting (B 2) on p. 265. It must be borne in mind that the typescript from this point belongs to the stage *before* the important alterations in the narrative entered in the two replacement passages discussed above. Thus for a long way 'the Master of Brethil' remains Harathor; the term *Halad* was not yet devised, and his dwelling was not yet named *Obel Halad*. Rather than rewrite the existing text after the new conceptions had arisen, my father found it sufficient to correct it. These corrections are very numerous but for the most part repetitive and systematic (as 'Master' to 'Halad' or 'Chieftain'), and to record each case in the text would make it unreadable. I have therefore ignored the rejected names and titles (this applies also to the short passage on pp. 263–4 between the two rewritten sections: here *Hardang* is in fact a correction on the typescript of *Harathor*).

Now Húrin, coming into Dimbar, summoned his strength and went on alone towards the dark feet of the Echoriad.[27] All the land was cold and desolate; and when at last it rose steeply before him and he could see no way to go further, he halted and looked about him in little hope. He stood now at the foot of a great fall of stones beneath a sheer rock-wall, and he did not know that this was all that was now left to see of the old Way of Escape: the Dry River was blocked and the arched gate was buried.[28]

Then Húrin looked up to the grey sky, thinking that by fortune he might once more descry the Eagles, as he had done long ago in his youth.[29] But he saw only the shadows blown from the East, and clouds swirling about the inaccessible peaks; and wind hissed over the stones. But the watch of the Great Eagles was now redoubled, and they marked Húrin well, far below, forlorn in the failing light. And straightaway Sorontar himself, since the tidings seemed great, brought word to Turgon.

But Turgon said: 'Nay! This is past belief! Unless Morgoth sleeps. Ye were mistaken.'

'Nay, not so,' answered Sorontar. 'If the Eagles of Manwë were wont to err thus, Lord, your hiding would have been in vain.'

'Then your words bode ill,' said Turgon; 'for they can mean only that even Húrin Thalion hath surrendered to the will of Morgoth. My heart is shut.' But when he had dismissed Sorontar, Turgon sat long in thought, and he was troubled, remembering the deeds of Húrin. And he opened his heart, and he sent to the Eagles to seek for Húrin, and to bring him, if they could, to Gondolin. But it was too late, and they saw him never again in light or in shadow.

For Húrin stood at last in despair before the stern silence of the Echoriad, and the westering sun, piercing the clouds, stained his white hair with red. Then he cried aloud in the wilderness, heedless of any ears, and he cursed the pitiless land: 'hard as the hearts of Elves and Men'. And he stood at last upon a great stone, and spreading wide his arms, looking towards Gondolin, he called in a great voice: 'Turgon, Turgon! Remember the Fen of Serech!' And again: 'Turgon! Húrin calls you. O Turgon, will you not hear in your hidden halls?'

But there was no answer, and all that he heard was wind in the dry grasses. 'Even so they hissed in Serech at the sunset,' he said. And as he spoke the sun went behind the Mountains of Shadow, and a darkness fell about him, and the wind ceased, and there was silence in the waste.

Yet there were ears that had heard the words that Húrin spoke, and eyes that marked well his gestures; and report of all came soon to the Dark Throne in the North. Then Morgoth smiled, and knew now clearly in what region Turgon dwelt, though because of the Eagles no spy of his could yet come within sight of the land behind the encircling mountains. This was the first evil that the freedom of Húrin achieved.[30]

As darkness fell Húrin stumbled from the stone, and fell, as one aswoon, into a deep sleep of grief. But in his sleep he heard the voice of Morwen lamenting, and often she spoke his name; and it seemed to him that her voice came out of Brethil. Therefore, when he awoke with the coming of day, he arose and returned; and he came back to the ford, and as one led by an unseen hand [he passed along the river Taeglin, until ere evening of the third day he reached the place >] he went along the eaves of Brethil, until he came in four days' journey to the Taeglin, and all his scanty food was then spent, and he was famished. But he went on like the shadow of a man driven by a dark wind, and he came to the Crossings by night, and there he passed over into Brethil.

The night-sentinels saw him, but they were filled with dread, so that they did not dare to move or cry out; for they thought that they saw a ghost out of some old battle-mound that walked with darkness about it. And for many days after men feared to be near the Crossings at night, save in great company and with fire kindled.

But Húrin passed on, and at evening of the sixth day he came at last to the place / of the burning of Glaurung, and saw the tall stone standing near the brink of Cabed Naeramarth.

But Húrin did not look at the stone, for he knew what was written there, and his eyes had seen that he was not alone. Sitting in the shadow of the stone there was a figure bent over its knees. Some homeless wanderer broken with age it seemed, too wayworn to heed his coming; but its rags were the remnants of a woman's garb. At length as Húrin stood there silent she cast back her tattered hood and lifted up her face slowly, haggard and hungry as a long-hunted wolf. Grey she was, sharp-nosed with broken teeth, and with a lean hand she clawed at the cloak upon her breast. But suddenly her eyes looked into his, and then Húrin knew her; for though they were wild now and full of fear, a light still gleamed in them hard to endure: the elven-light that long ago had earned her her name, Eðelwen, proudest of mortal women in the days of old.

'Eðelwen! Eðelwen!' Húrin cried; and she rose and stumbled forward, and he caught her in his arms.

'You come at last,' she said. 'I have waited too long.'

'It was a dark road. I have come as I could,' he answered.

'But you are late,' she said, 'too late. They are lost.'
'I know,' he said. 'But thou art not.'
'Almost,' she said. 'I am spent utterly. I shall go with the sun.
They are lost.' She clutched at his cloak. 'Little time is left,' she
said. 'If you know, tell me! How did she find him?'

But Húrin did not answer, and he sat beside the stone with
Morwen in his arms; and they did not speak again. The sun
went down, and Morwen sighed and clasped his hand and was
still; and Húrin knew that she had died.

So passed Morwen the proud and fair; and Húrin looked
down at her in the twilight, and it seemed that the lines of grief
and cruel hardship were smoothed away. Cold and pale and
stern was her face. 'She was not conquered,' he said; and he
closed her eyes, and sat on unmoving beside her as night drew
down. The waters of Cabed Naeramarth roared on, but he
heard no sound and saw nothing, and he felt nothing, for his
heart was stone within him, and he thought that he would sit
there until he too died.

Then there came a chill wind and drove sharp rain in his face;
and suddenly he was roused, and out of a black deep anger rose
in him like a smoke, mastering reason, so that all his desire was
to seek vengeance for his wrongs, and for the wrongs of his kin,
accusing in his anguish all those who ever had had dealings with
them.

He arose and lifted Morwen up; and suddenly he knew that it
was beyond his strength to bear her. He was hungry and old,
and weary as winter. Slowly he laid her down again beside the
standing stone. 'Lie there a little longer, Eðelwen,' he said, 'until
I return. Not even a wolf would do you more hurt. But the folk
of this hard land shall rue the day that you died here!'

Then Húrin stumbled away, and he came back towards the
ford of Taeglin; and there he fell beside the Hauð-en-Elleth, and
a darkness overcame him, and he lay as one drowned in sleep.
In the morning, before the light had recalled him to full waking,
he was found by the guards that Hardang had commanded to
keep special watch in that place.

It was a man named Sagroth who first saw him, and he
looked at him in wonder and was afraid, for he thought he
knew who this old man was. 'Come!' he cried to others that
followed. 'Look here! It must be Húrin. The incomers spoke
truly. He has come!'

'Trust you to find trouble, as ever, Sagroth!' said Forhend.

'The Halad will not be pleased with such findings. What is to be done? Maybe Hardang would be better pleased to hear that we had stopped the trouble at his borders and thrust it out.'

'Thrust it out?' said Avranc. He was Dorlas' son,[31] a young man short and dark, but strong, well-liked by Hardang, as his father had been. 'Thrust it out? Of what good would that be? It would come again! It can walk – all the way from Angband, if it is what you guess. See! He looks grim and has a sword, but he sleeps deep. Need he wake to more woe? [*Added:*] If you would please the Chieftain, Forhend, he would end here.'

Such was the shadow that now fell upon the hearts of men, as the power of Morgoth spread, and fear walked far and wide; but not all hearts were yet darkened. 'Shame upon you!' cried Manthor the captain, who coming behind had heard what they said. 'And upon you most, Avranc, young though you are! At least you have heard of the deeds of Húrin of Hithlum, or did you hold them only fireside fables? What is to be done, indeed! So, slay him in his sleep is your counsel. Out of hell comes the thought!'

'And so does he,' answered Avranc. 'If indeed he is Húrin. Who knows?'

'It can soon be known,' said Manthor; and coming to Húrin as he lay he knelt and raised his hand and kissed it. 'Awake!' he cried. 'Help is near. And if you are Húrin, there is no help that I would think enough.'

'And no help that he will not repay with evil,' said Avranc. 'He comes from Angband, I say.'

'What he may do is unknown,' said Manthor. 'What he has done we know, and our debt is unpaid.' Then he called again in a loud voice: 'Hail Húrin Thalion! Hail, Captain of Men!'

Thereupon Húrin opened his eyes, remembering evil words that he had heard in the drowse before waking, and he saw men about him with weapons in hand. He stood up stiffly, fumbling at his sword; and he glared upon them in anger and scorn. 'Curs!' he cried. 'Would you slay an old man sleeping? You look like Men, but you are Orcs under the skin, I guess. Come then! Slay me awake, if you dare. But it will not please your black Master, I think. I am Húrin Galdor's son, a name that Orcs at least will remember.'

'Nay, nay,' said Manthor. 'Dream not. We are Men. But these are evil days of doubt, and we are hard pressed. It is perilous here. Will you not come with us? At least we can find you food and rest.'

'Rest?' said Húrin. 'You cannot find me that. But food I will take in my need.'

Then Manthor gave him a little bread and meat and water; but they seemed to choke him, and he spat them forth. 'How far is it to the house of your lord?' he asked. 'Until I have seen him the food that you denied to my beloved will not go down my throat.'

'He raves and he scorns us,' muttered Avranc. 'What did I say?' But Manthor looked on him with pity, though he did not understand his words. 'It is a long road for the weary, lord,' he said; 'and the house of Hardang Halad is hidden from strangers.'

'Then lead me thither!' said Húrin. 'I will go as I can. I have an errand to that house.'

Soon they set forth. Of his strong company Manthor left most to their duty; but he himself went with Húrin, and with him he took Forhend. Húrin walked as he could, but after a time he began to stumble and fall; and yet he always rose again and struggled on, and he would not allow them to support him. In this way at last with many halts they came to the hall of Hardang in Obel Halad deep in the forest; and he knew of their coming, for Avranc, unbidden, had run ahead and brought the tidings before them; and he did not fail to report the wild words of Húrin at his waking and his spitting forth of their food.

So it was that they found the hall well guarded, with many men in the [fenced courtyard >] outer garth, and men at the doors. At the gate of the [court >] garth the captain of the guards stayed them. 'Deliver the prisoner to me!' he said.

'Prisoner!' said Manthor. 'I have no prisoner, but a man you should honour.'

'The Halad's words, not mine,' said the captain. 'But you may come too. He has words for you also.'

Then they led Húrin before the Chieftain; and Hardang did not greet him, but sat in his great chair and eyed Húrin up and down. But Húrin returned his gaze, and held himself as stiffly as he could, though he leaned on his staff. So he stood a while in silence, until at last he sank to the ground. 'Lo!' he said. 'I see that there are so few chairs in Brethil that a guest must sit on the floor.'

'Guest?' said Hardang. 'Not one bidden by me. But bring the old carl a stool. If he will not disdain it, though he spits on our food.'

Manthor was grieved at the discourtesy; and hearing one laugh in the shadow behind the great chair he looked and saw that it was Avranc, and his face darkened in wrath. 'Your pardon, lord,' he said to Húrin. 'There is misunderstanding here.' Then turning to Hardang he drew himself up. 'Has my company a new captain then, my Halad?' he said. 'For otherwise I do not understand how one who has left his duty and broken my command should stand here unrebuked. He has brought news before me, I see; but it seems he forgot the name of the guest, or Húrin Thalion would not have been left to stand.'

'The name was told to me,' answered Hardang, 'and his fell words also which bear it out. Such are the House of Hador. But it is the part of a stranger to name himself first in my house, and I waited to hear him. Also to hear his errand hither – since he says that he has one. But as for your duty, such matters are not dealt with before strangers.'

Then he turned towards Húrin, who sat meanwhile bent on the low stool; his eyes were closed, and he seemed to take no heed of what was said. 'Well, Húrin of Hithlum,' said Hardang, 'what of your errand? Is it a matter of haste? Or will you not perhaps take thought and rest and speak of it later more at your ease? Meanwhile we may find you some food less distasteful.' Hardang's tone was now more gentle, and he rose as he spoke; for he was a wary man, and [*struck out:* in his heart not over sure of his seat in the Master's chair; and] he had marked the displeasure on the faces of others beside Manthor.

Then suddenly Húrin rose to his feet. 'Well, Master Reed of the Bog,' he said. 'So you bend with each breath, do you? Beware lest mine blow you flat. Go take thought to stiffen you, ere I call on you again! Scorner of grey hairs, food-niggard, starver of wanderers. This stool fits you better.' With that he cast the stool at Hardang, so that it smote him on the forehead; and then he turned to walk from the hall.

Some of the men gave way, whether in pity or in fear of his wrath; but Avranc ran before him. 'Not so swift, carl Húrin!' he cried. 'At least I no longer doubt your name. You bring your manners from Angband. But we do not love orc-deeds in hall. You have assaulted the Chieftain in his chair, and a prisoner you now shall be, whatever your name.'

'I thank you, Captain Avranc,' said Hardang, who sat still in his chair, while some staunched the blood that flowed from his brow. 'Now let the old madman be put in bonds and kept close. I will judge him later.'

Then they put thongs about Húrin's arms, and a halter about his neck, and led him away; and he made no more resistance, for the wrath had run off him, and he walked as one in a dream with eyes closed. But Manthor, though Avranc scowled at him, put his arm about the old man's shoulder and steered him so that he should not stumble.

But when Húrin was shut in a cave [*struck out:* nigh to the one in which Asgorn and his men were still imprisoned] and Manthor could do no more to help him, he returned to the hall. There he found Avranc in speech with Hardang, and though they fell silent at his coming, he caught the last words that Avranc spoke, and it seemed to him that Avranc urged that Húrin should be put to death straightway.

'So, Captain Avranc,' he said, 'things go well for you today! I have seen you at like sports before: goading an old badger and having him killed when he bites. Not so swift, Captain Avranc! Nor you, Hardang Halad. This is no matter for lordly dealing out of hand. The coming of Húrin, and his welcome here, concerns all the folk, and they shall hear all that is said, before any judgement is given.'

'You have leave to go,' said Hardang. 'Return to your duty on the marches, until Captain Avranc comes to take command.'

'Nay, lord,' said Manthor, 'I have no duty. I am out of your service from today. I left Sagroth[32] in charge, a woodsman somewhat older and wiser than one you name. In due time I will return to my own marches.*[33] But now I will summon the folk.'

As he went to the door Avranc seized his bow to shoot Manthor down, but Hardang restrained him. 'Not yet,' he said. But Manthor was unaware of this (though some in the hall had marked it), and he went out, and sent all he could find that were

---

* For Manthor was a descendant of Haldad, and he had a little land of his own on the east march of Brethil beside Sirion where it runs through Dimbar. But all the folk of Brethil were freemen, holding their homesteads and more or less land about them of their right. Their Master was chosen from the descendants of Haldad, out of reverence for the deeds of Haleth and Haldar; and though as yet the mastership had been given, as if it were a lordship or kingdom, to the eldest of the eldest line, the folk had the right to set anyone aside or to remove him, for grave cause. And some knew well enough that Harathor had tried to have Brandir the Lame passed over in his own favour.

willing to go as messengers to bring together all the masters of homesteads and any others that could be spared. [*Struck out:* It was the custom of the Haladin[34] that in all matters other than war the wives were also summoned to counsel and had equal voices with the husbands.]

Now rumour ran wild through the woods, and the tales grew in the telling; and some said this, and some that, and the most spoke in praise of the Halad and set forth Húrin in the likeness of some fell Orc-chieftain; for Avranc was also busy with messengers. Soon there was a great concourse of folk, and the small town [35] about the Hall of the Chieftains was swelled with tents and booths.[36] But all the men bore arms, for fear lest a sudden alarm should come from the marches.

When he had sent out his messengers Manthor went to Húrin's prison, and the guards would not let him enter. 'Come!' said Manthor. 'You know well that it is our good custom that any prisoner should have a friend that may come to him and see how he fares and give him counsel.'

'The friend is chosen by the prisoner,' the guards answered; 'but this wild man has no friends.'

'He has one,' said Manthor, 'and I ask leave to offer myself to his choice.'

'The Halad forbids us to admit any save the guards,' they said. But Manthor who was wise in the laws and customs of his people replied: 'No doubt. But in this he has no right. Why is the incomer in bondage? We do not bind old men and wanderers because they speak ill words when distraught. This one is imprisoned because of his assault upon Hardang, and Hardang cannot judge his own cause, but must bring his grievance to the judgement of the Folk [*struck out:* and some other must sit in the chair at the hearing]. Meanwhile he cannot deny to the prisoner all counsel and help. If he were wise he would see that he does not in this way advance his own cause. But maybe another mouth spoke for him?'

'True,' they said. 'Avranc brought the order.'

'Then forget it,' said Manthor. 'For Avranc was under other orders, to remain on his duty on the marches. Choose then between a young runagate, and the laws of the Folk.'

Then the guards let him in to the cave; for Manthor was well esteemed in Brethil, and men did not like the [masters >] chieftains who tried to overrule the folk. Manthor found Húrin sitting on a bench. There were fetters on his ankles, but his hands were unbound; and there was some food before him untasted. He did not look up.

'Hail, lord!' said Manthor. 'Things have not gone as they should, nor as I would have ordered them. But now you have need of a friend.'

'I have no friend, and wish for none in this land,' said Húrin.

'One stands before you,' answered Manthor. 'Do not scorn me. For now, alas! the matter between you and Hardang Halad must be brought to the judgement of the Folk, and it would be well, as our law allows, to have a friend to counsel you and plead your case.'

'I will not plead, and I need no counsel,' said Húrin.

'You need this counsel at least,' said Manthor. 'Master your wrath for the time, and take some food, so that you may have strength before your enemies. I do not know what is your errand here, but it will speed better, if you are not starved. Do not slay yourself while there is hope!'

'Slay myself?' cried Húrin, and he staggered up and leant against the wall, and his eyes were red. 'Shall I be dragged before a rabble of wood-men with fetters upon me to hear what death they will give me? I will slay myself first, if my hands are left free.' Then suddenly, swift as an old trapped beast, he sprang forward, and before Manthor could avoid him he snatched a knife from his belt. Then he sank down on the bench.

'You could have had the knife as a gift,' said Manthor, 'though we do not deem self-slaughter a noble deed in those who have not lost their reason. Hide the knife and keep it for some better use! But have a care, for it is a fell blade, from a forge of the Dwarves. Now, lord, will you not take me for your friend? Say no word; but if you will now eat with me, I will take that for yea.'

Then Húrin looked at him and the wrath left his eyes; and together they drank and ate in silence. And when all was finished, Húrin said: 'By your voice you have overcome me. Never since the Day of Dread have I heard any man's voice so fair. Alas! alas! it calls to my mind the voices in my father's house, long ago when the shadow seemed far away.'

'That may well be,' said Manthor. 'Hiril my foremother was sister of thy mother, Hareth.'

'Then thou art both kin and friend,' said Húrin.

'But not I alone,' said Manthor. 'We are few and have little wealth, but we too are Edain, and bound by many ties to your people. Your name has long been held in honour here; but no news of your deeds would have reached us, if Haldir and Hundar had not marched to the Nirnaeth. There they fell, but [seven >] three of their company returned, for they were succoured by Mablung of Doriath and healed of their wounds.[37] The days have gone dark since then, and many hearts are overshadowed, but not all.'

'Yet the voice of your Chieftain comes from the shadows,' said Húrin, 'and your Folk obey him, even in deeds of dishonour and cruelty.'

'Grief darkens your eyes, lord, dare I say it. But lest this should prove true, let us take counsel together. For I see peril of evil ahead, both to thee and to my folk, though maybe wisdom may avert it. Of one thing I must warn thee, though it may not please thee. Hardang is a lesser man than his fathers, but I saw no evil in him till he heard of thy coming. Thou bringest a shadow with thee, Húrin Thalion, in which lesser shadows grow darker.'

'Dark words from a friend!' said Húrin. 'Long I lived in the Shadow, but I endured it and did not yield. If there is any darkness upon me, it is only that grief beyond grief has robbed me of light. But in the Shadow I have no part.'

'Nevertheless, I say to thee,' said Manthor, 'that it follows behind thee. I know not how thou hast won freedom; but the thought of Morgoth has not forgotten thee. Beware.'

'Do not dote, dotard, you would say,' answered Húrin. 'I will take this much from you, for your fair voice and our kinship, but no more! Let us speak of other things, or cease.'

Then Manthor was patient, and stayed long with Húrin, until the evening brought darkness into the cave; and they ate once more together. Then Manthor commanded that a light should be brought to Húrin; and he took his leave until the morrow, and went to his booth with a heavy heart.

The next day it was proclaimed that the Folkmoot for Judgement should be held on the morning following, for already five hundred of the headmen had come in, and that was by custom deemed the least number which might count as a full meeting of the Folk. Manthor went early to find Húrin; but the guards had been changed. Three men of Hardang's own household now stood at the door, and they were unfriendly.

'The prisoner is asleep,' their leader said. 'And that is well; it may settle his wits.'

'But I am his appointed friend, as was declared yesterday,' said Manthor.

'A friend would leave him in peace, while he may have it. To what good would you wake him?'

'Why should my coming wake him, more easily than the feet of a jailer?' said Manthor. 'I wish to see how he sleeps.'

'Do you think all men lie but yourself?'

'Nay, nay; but I think that some would fain forget our laws when they do not suit their purpose,' answered Manthor. Nonetheless it seemed to him that he would do little good to Húrin's case if he debated further, and he went away. So it was that many things remained unspoken between them until too late. For when he returned day was waning. No hindrance was now offered to his entry, and he found Húrin lying on a pallet; [added:] and he noted with anger that he now had fetters also upon his wrists with a short chain between them.

'A friend delayed is hope denied,' said Húrin. 'I have waited long for thee, but now I am heavy with sleep and my eyes are dimmed.'

'I came at mid-morning,' said Manthor, 'but they said that thou wert sleeping then.'

'Drowsing, drowsing in wanhope,' said Húrin; 'but thy voice might have recalled me. I have been so since I broke my fast. That counsel of thine at least I have taken, my friend; but food doth me ill rather than good. Now I must sleep. But come in the morning!'

Manthor wondered darkly at this. He could not see Húrin's face, for there was little light left, but bending down he listened to his breathing. Then with a grim face he stood up and took up under his cloak such food as remained, and went out.

'Well, how did you find the wild man?' said the chief guard.

'Bemused with sleep,' answered Manthor. 'He must be wakeful tomorrow. Rouse him early. Bring food for two, for I will come and break fast with him.'[38]

The next day, long before the set time at mid-morn, the Moot began to assemble. Almost a thousand had now come, for the most part the older men [struck out: and women],[39] since the watch on the marches must still be maintained. Soon all the Moot-ring was filled. This was shaped as a great crescent, with seven tiers of turf-banks rising up from a smooth floor delved back into the hillside. A high fence was set all about it, and the only entry was by a heavy gate in the stockade that closed the open end of the crescent. In the middle of the lowest tier of seats was set [added:] the Angbor or Doom-rock, / a great flat stone upon which the Halad⁴⁰ would sit. Those who were brought to judgement stood before the stone and faced the assembly.

There was a great babel of voices; but at a horn-call silence fell, and the Halad entered, and he had many men of his household with him. The gate was closed behind him, and he paced slowly to the Stone. Then he stood facing the assembly and hallowed the Moot according to custom. First he named Manwë and Mandos, after the manner which the Edain had learned from the Eldar, and then, speaking the old tongue of the Folk which was now out of daily use, he declared that the Moot was duly set, being the three hundred and first Moot of Brethil, called to give judgement in a grave matter.

When as custom was all the assembly cried in the same tongue 'We are ready', he took his seat upon the [stone >] Angbor, and called in the speech of Beleriand⁴¹ to men that stood by: 'Sound the horn! Let the prisoner be brought before us!'⁴²

The horn sounded twice, but for some time no one entered, and the sound of angry voices could be heard outside the fence. At length the gate was thrust open, and six men came in bearing Húrin between them.

'I am brought by violence and misuse,' he cried. 'I will not walk slave-fettered to any Moot upon earth, not though Elven-kings should sit there. And while I am bound thus I deny all authority and justice to your dooms.' But the men set him on the ground before the Stone and held him there by force.

Now it was the custom of the Moot that, when any man was brought before it, the Halad should be the accuser, and should first in brief recite the misdeed with which he was charged. Whereupon it was his right, by himself or by the mouth of his friend, to deny the charge, or to offer a defence for what he had done. And when these things had been said, if any point was in doubt or was denied by either side, then witnesses were summoned.

Hardang,⁴³ therefore, now stood up and turning to the assembly he began to recite the charge. 'This prisoner,' he said, 'whom you see before you, names himself Húrin Galdor's son, once of Dorlómin, but long in Angband whence he came hither. Be that as it may.'[44]

But hereupon Manthor arose and came before the Stone. 'By your leave, my lord Halad and Folk!' he cried. 'As friend to the prisoner I claim the right to ask: Is the charge against him any matter that touches the Halad in person? Or has the Halad any grievance against him?'

'Grievance?' cried Hardang, and anger clouded his wits so that he did not see Manthor's trend. 'Grievance indeed! This is not a new fashion in headgear for the Moot. I come here with wounds new-dressed.'

'Alas!' said Manthor. 'But if that is so, I claim that the matter cannot be dealt with in this way. In our law no man may recite an offence against himself; nor may he sit in the seat of judgement while that charge is heard. Is not this the law?'

'It is the law,' the assembly answered.

'Then,' said Manthor, 'before this charge is heard some other than Hardang son of Hundad must be appointed to the Stone.'

Thereupon many names were cried, but most voices and the loudest called upon Manthor. 'Nay,' said he, 'I am engaged to one part and cannot be judge. Moreover it is the Halad's right in such a case to name the one who should take his place, as doubtless he knows well.'

'I thank you,' said Hardang, 'though I need no self-chosen lawman to teach me.' Then he looked about him, as if considering whom he should name. But he was in a black anger and all wisdom failed him. If he had named any of the headmen there present, things might have gone otherwise. But in an evil moment he chose, and to all men's wonder he cried: 'Avranc Dorlas' son! It seems that the Halad needs a friend also today, when lawmen are so pert. I summon you to the Stone.'

Silence fell. But when Hardang stepped down and Avranc came to the Stone there was a loud murmuring like the rumour of a coming storm. Avranc was a young man, not long wedded, and his youth was taken ill by all the elder headmen that sat there. [For he was not loved for himself. >] And he was not loved for himself; for though he was bold, he was scornful, as was Dorlas his father before him. / And dark tales were [struck out: still] whispered concerning Dorlas [struck out: his father, who had been Hardang's close friend]; [45] for though naught was known for certain, he was found slain far from the battle with

Glaurung, and the reddened sword that lay by him had been the sword of Brandir.[46]

But Avranc took no heed of the murmur, and bore himself airily, as if it were a light matter soon to be dealt with.

'Well,' he said, 'if that is settled, let us waste no more time! The matter is clear enough.' Then standing up he continued the recital. 'This prisoner, this wild man,' he said, 'comes from Angband, as you have heard. He was found within our borders. Not by chance, for as he himself declared, he has an errand here. What that may be he has not revealed, but it cannot be one of good will. He hates this folk. As soon as he saw us he reviled us. We gave him food and he spat on it. I have seen Orcs do so, if any were fools enough to show them mercy. From Angband he comes, it is clear, whatever his name be. But worse followed after. By his own asking he was brought before the Halad of Brethil – by this man who now calls himself his friend; but when he came into hall he would not name himself. And when the Halad asked him what was his errand and bade him rest first and speak of it later, if it pleased him, he began to rave, reviling the Halad, and suddenly he cast a stool in his face and did him great hurt. It is well for all that he had nothing more deadly to hand, or the Halad would have been slain. As was plainly the prisoner's intent, and it lessens his guilt very little that the worst did not happen, for which the penalty is death. But even so, the Halad sat in the great chair in his hall: to revile him there was an evil deed, and to assault him an outrage.

'This then is the charge against the prisoner: that he came here with evil intent against us, and against the Halad of Brethil in special (at the bidding of Angband one may guess); that gaining the presence of the Halad he reviled him, and then sought to slay him in his chair. The penalty is under the doom of the Moot, but it could justly be death.'

Then it seemed to some that Avranc spoke justly, and to all that he had spoken with skill. For a while no one raised a voice upon either side. Then Avranc, not hiding his smile, rose again and said: 'The prisoner may now answer the charge if he will, but let him be brief and not rave!'

But Húrin did not speak, though he strained against those that held him. 'Prisoner, will you not speak?' said Avranc, and still Húrin gave no answer. 'So be it,' said Avranc. 'If he will not speak, not even to deny the charge, then there is no more to do.

The charge is made good, and the one that is appointed to the Stone must propound to the Moot a penalty that seems just.'

But now Manthor stood up and said: 'First he should at least be asked why he will not speak. And to that question reply may be made by his friend.'

'The question is put,' said Avranc with a shrug. 'If you know the answer give it.'

'Because he is fettered [*added:* hand and foot],'[47] said Manthor. 'Never before have we dragged to the Moot in fetters a man yet uncondemned. Still less one of the Edain whose name deserves honour, whatsoever may have happened since. Yes, "uncondemne⌐" I say; for the accuser has left much unsaid that this Moot must hear before judgement is given.'

'But this is foolishness,' said Avranc. 'Adan or no, and whatever his name, the prisoner is ungovernable and malicious. The bonds are a needed precaution. Those who come near him must be protected from his violence.'

'If you wish to beget violence,' answered Manthor, 'what surer way than openly to dishonour a proud man, old in years of great grief. And here is one now weakened by hunger and long journeying, unarmed among a host. I would ask the folk here assembled: do you deem such caution worthy of the free men of Brethil, or would you rather that we used the courtesy of old?'

'The fetters were put on the prisoner by the order of the Halad,' said Avranc. 'In this he used his right for the restraint of violence in his hall. Therefore this order cannot be gainsaid save by the full assembly.'

Then there went up a great shout 'Release him, release him! Húrin Thalion! Release Húrin Thalion!' Not all joined in this cry, yet there were no voices heard on the other side.

'Nay, nay!' said Avranc. 'Shouting will not avail. In such a case there must be a vote in due form.'

Now by custom in matters grave or doubtful the votes of the Moot were cast with pebbles, and all who entered bore with them each two pebbles, a black and a white for *nay* and for *yea*. But the gathering and counting would take much time, and meanwhile Manthor saw that with each moment the mood of Húrin grew worse.

'There is another way more simple,' he said. 'There is no danger here to justify the bonds, and so think all who have used their voice. The Halad is in the Moot-ring, and he can remit his own order, if he will.'

'He will,' said Hardang, for it seemed to him that the mood of the assembly was restive, and he hoped by this stroke to regain its favour. 'Let the prisoner be released, and stand up before you!'

Then the fetters were struck off Húrin's hands and feet. Straightway he stood up, and turning away from Avranc he faced the assembly. 'I am here,' he said. 'I will answer my name. I am Húrin Thalion son of Galdor Orchal,[48] Lord of Dorlómin and once a high-captain in the host of Fingon King of the North-realm. Let no man dare to deny it! That should be enough. I will not plead before you. Do as you will! Neither will I bandy words with the upstart whom you permit to sit in the high seat. Let him lie as he will! [*Struck out*: But if my friend wishes to speak and to set forth the truth of what has chanced, let him do so. Listen who will!]

'In the name of the Lords of the West, what manner of folk are you, or to what have you become? While the ruin of Darkness is all about you will you sit here in patience and hear this runagate guard ask for a doom of death upon me – because I broke the head of an insolent young man, whether in a chair or out of it? He should have learned how to treat his elders before you made him your Chieftain forsooth.

'Death?' 'Fore Manwë, if I had not endured torment for twenty years and eight, if I were as at the Nirnaeth, you would not dare to sit here to face me. But I am not dangerous any longer, I hear. So you are brave. I can stand up unbound to be baited. I am broken in war and made tame. Tame! Be not too sure!' He lifted up his arms and knotted his hands.

But here Manthor laid a restraining hand on his shoulder, and spoke earnestly in his ear. 'My lord, you mistake them. Most are your friends, or would be. But there are proud freemen here too. Let me now speak to them!'

Hardang and Avranc said naught, but smiled one to another, for Húrin's speech, they thought, did his part no good. But Manthor cried: 'Let the Lord Húrin be given a seat while I speak. His wrath you will understand better, and maybe forgive, when you have heard me.

'Hear me now, Folk of Brethil. My friend does not deny the main charge, but he claims that he was misused and provoked beyond bearing. My masters [*struck out*: and good wives],[49] I was captain of the march-wardens that found this man asleep by the Hauð-en-Elleth. Or asleep he seemed, but he lay rather in weariness on the brink of awaking, and as he lay he heard, as I fear, words that were spoken.

'There was a man called Avranc Dorlas' son, I remember, as one of my company, and he should be there still, for such were my orders. As I came behind I heard this Avranc give counsel to the man who had first found Húrin and guessed at his name. Folk of Brethil, I heard him speak thus. "It would be better to slay the old man asleep and prevent further trouble. And so the Halad would be pleased," said he.

'Now maybe you will wonder less that when I called him to full waking and he found men with weapons all about him, he spoke bitter words to us. One at least of us deserved them. Yet as for despising our food: he took it from my hands, and he did not spit upon it. He spat it forth, for it choked him. Have you never, my masters, seen a man half-starved who could not swallow food in haste though he needed it? And this man was in great grief also and full of anger.

'Nay, he did not disdain our food. Though well he might, if he had known the devices to which some who dwell here have fallen! Hear me now and believe me, if you may, for witness can be brought. In his prison the Lord Húrin ate with me, for I used him with courtesy. That was two days ago. But yesterday he was drowsed and could not speak clearly, nor take counsel with me against the trial today.'

'Little wonder in that!' cried Hardang.

Manthor paused and looked at Hardang. 'Little wonder indeed, my lord Halad,' he said; 'for his food had been drugged.'

Then Hardang in wrath cried out: 'Must the drowsy dreams of this dotard be recited to our weariness?'

'I speak of no dreams,' answered Manthor. 'Witness will follow. But since against custom I am challenged while I speak, I will answer now. I took away from the prison food of which Húrin had eaten some. Before witnesses I gave it to a hound, and he lies still asleep as if dead. Maybe the Halad of Brethil did not contrive this himself, but one who is eager to please him. But with what lawful purpose? To restrain him from violence, forsooth, when he was already fettered and in prison? There is malice abroad among us, Folk of Brethil, and I look to the assembly to amend it!'

At this there was great stir and murmur in the Moot-ring; and when Avranc stood up calling for silence, the clamour grew greater. At last when the assembly had quieted a little Manthor said: 'May I now continue, for there is more to be said?'

'Proceed!' said Avranc. 'But let your wind be shortened. And I must warn you all, my masters, to hear this man warily. His good faith cannot be trusted. The prisoner and he are close akin.'

These words were unwise, for Manthor answered at once: 'It is so indeed. The mother of Húrin was Hareth daughter of Halmir, once Halad of Brethil, and Hiril her sister was the mother of my mother. But this lineage does not prove me a liar. More, if Húrin of Dorlómin be akin to me, he is kinsman of all the House of Haleth. Yea, and of all this Folk. Yet he is treated as an outlaw, a robber, a wild man without honour!

'Let us proceed then to the chief charge, which the accuser has said may bear the penalty of death. You see before you the broken head, though it seems to sit firm on its shoulders and can use its tongue. It was hurt by the cast of a small wooden stool. A wicked deed, you will say. And far worse when done to the Halad of Brethil in his great chair.

'But my masters, ill deeds may be provoked. Let any one of you in thought set himself in the place of Hardang son of Hundad. Well, here comes Húrin, Lord of Dorlómin, your kins-man, before you: head of a great House, a man whose deeds are sung by Elves and Men. But he is now grown old, dispossessed, grief-laden, travel-worn. He asks to see you. There you sit at ease in your chair. You do not rise. You do not speak to him. But you eye him up and down as he stands, until he sinks to the floor. Then of your pity and courtesy you cry: "Bring the old carl a stool!"

'O shame and wonder! He flings it at your head. O shame and wonder rather I say that you so dishonour your chair, that you so dishonour your hall, that you so dishonour the Folk of Brethil!

'My masters, I freely admit that it would have been better, if the Lord Húrin had shown patience, marvellous patience. Why did he not wait to see what further slights he must endure? Yet as I stood in hall and saw all this I wondered, and I still wonder and I ask you to tell me: How do you like such manners in this man that we have made Halad of Brethil?'

Great uproar arose at this question, until Manthor held up his hand, and suddenly all was still again. But under cover of the noise Hardang had drawn near to Avranc to speak with him, and surprised by the silence they spoke too loud, so that Manthor and others also heard Hardang say: 'I would I had not hindered thy shooting!'[50] And Avranc answered: 'I will seek a time yet.'

But Manthor proceeded. 'I am answered. Such manners do not please you, I see. Then what would you have done with the caster of the stool? Bound him, put a halter on his neck, shut him in a cave, fettered him, drugged his food, and at last dragged him hither and called for his death? Or would you set him free? Or would you, maybe, ask pardon, or command this Halad to do so?'

Thereupon there was even greater uproar, and men stood up on the turfbanks, clashing their arms, and crying: 'Free! Free! Set him free!' And many voices were heard also shouting: 'Away with this Halad! Put him in the caves!'

Many of the older men who sat in the lowest tier ran forward and knelt before Húrin to ask his pardon; and one offered him a staff, and another gave him a fair cloak and a great belt of silver. And when Húrin was so clad, and had a staff in hand, he went to the [added: Angbor] Stone and stood up on it, in no wise as a suppliant, but in mien as a king; and facing the assembly he cried in a great voice: 'I thank you, Masters of Brethil here present, who have released me from dishonour. There is then justice still in your land, though it has slept and been slow to awake. But now I have a charge to bring in my turn.

'What is my errand here, it is asked? What think you? Did not Túrin my son, and Nienor my daughter, die in this land? Alas! from afar I have learned much of the griefs that have here come to pass. Is it then a wonder that a father should seek the graves of his children? More wonder it is, meseems, that none here have yet ever spoken their names to me.

'Are ye ashamed that ye let Túrin my son die for you? That two only dared go with him to face the terror of the Worm? That none dared go down to succour him when the battle was over, though the worst evils might thus have been stayed?

'Ashamed ye may be. But this is not my charge. I do not ask that any in this land should match the son of Húrin in valour. But if I forgive those griefs, shall I forgive this? Hear me, Men of Brethil! There lies by the Standing Stone that you raised an old beggar-woman. Long she sat in your land, without fire, without food, without pity. Now she is dead. Dead. She was Morwen my wife. Morwen Eðelwen, the lady elven-fair who bore Túrin the slayer of Glaurung. She is dead.

'If ye, who have some ruth, cry to me that you are guiltless, then I ask who bears the guilt? By whose command was she thrust out to starve at your doors like an outcast dog?

'Did your Chieftain contrive this? So I believe. For would he not have dealt with me in like manner, if he could? Such are his gifts: dishonour, starvation, poison. Have you no part in this? Will you not work all his will? Then how long, Masters of Brethil, will you endure him? How long will you suffer this man called Hardang to sit in your chair?'

Now Hardang was aghast at this turn, and his face went white with fear and amazement. But before he could speak, Húrin pointed a long hand at him. 'See!' he cried. 'There he stands with a sneer on his mouth! Does he deem himself safe? For I am robbed of my sword; and I am old and weary, he thinks. Nay, too often has he called me a wild man. He shall see one! Only hands, hands, are needed to wring his throat full of lies.'

With that Húrin left the Stone and strode towards Hardang; but he gave back before him, calling his household-men about him; and they drew off towards the gate. Thus it appeared to many that Hardang admitted his guilt, and they drew their weapons, and came down from the banks, crying out upon him.[51]

Now there was peril of battle within the hallowed Ring. For others joined themselves to Hardang, some without love for him or his deeds, who nonetheless held to their loyalty and would at least defend him from violence, until he could answer before the Moot.

Manthor stood between the two parties and cried to them to hold their hands and shed no blood in the Moot-ring; but the spark that he had himself kindled now burst to flame beyond his quenching, and a press of men thrust him aside. 'Away with this Halad!' they shouted. 'Away with Hardang, take him to the caves! Down with Hardang! Up Manthor! We will have Manthor!' And they fell upon the men that barred the way to the gate, so that Hardang might have time to escape.

But Manthor went back to Húrin, who now stood alone by

the Stone. 'Alas, lord,' he said, 'I feared that this day held great peril for us all. There is little I can do, but still I must try to avert the worst evil. They will soon break out, and I must follow. Will you come with me?'

Many fell at the gate on either side ere it was taken. There Avranc fought bravely, and was the last to retreat. Then as he turned to flee suddenly he drew his bow and shot at Manthor as he stood by the Stone. But the arrow missed in his haste and hit on the Stone, striking fire beside Manthor as it broke. 'Next time nearer!' cried Avranc as he fled after Hardang.

Then the rebels burst out of the Ring and hotly pursued Hardang's men to the Obel Halad, some half mile away. But before they could come there Hardang had gained the hall and shut it against them; and there he was now besieged. The Hall of the Chieftains stood in a garth with a round earthwall all about it rising from a dry outer dyke. In the wall there was only one gate, from which a stone-path led to the great doors. The assailants drove through the gate and swiftly surrounded all the hall; and all was quiet for a while.

But Manthor and Húrin came to the gate; and Manthor would have a parley, but men said: 'Of what use are words? Rats will not come out while dogs are abroad.' And some cried: 'Our kin have been slain, and we will avenge them!'

'Well then,' said Manthor, 'allow me at least to do what I can!'

'Do so!' they said. 'But go not too near, or you may receive a sharp answer.'

Therefore Manthor stood by the gate and lifted up his great voice, crying out to both sides that they should cease from this kin-slaying. And to those within he promised that all should go free who came forth without weapons, even Hardang, if he would give his word to stand before the Moot the next day. 'And no man shall bring any weapon thither,' he said.

But while he spoke there came a shot from a window, and an arrow went by the ear of Manthor and stood deep in the gate-post. Then the voice of Avranc was heard crying: 'Third time shall thrive best!'

Now the anger of those without burst forth again, and many rushed to the great doors and tried to break them down; but there was a sortie, and many were slain or hurt, and others also in the garth were wounded by shots from the windows. So the assailants being now in mad wrath brought kindlings and great store of wood and set it by the gate; and they shouted to those within: 'See! the sun is setting. We give you till nightfall. If you do not come forth ere then, we will burn the hall and you in it!' Then they all withdrew from the garth out of bowshot, but they made a ring of men all round the outer dyke.

The sun set, and none came from the hall. And when it was dark the assailants came back into the garth bearing the wood, and they piled it against the walls of the hall. Then some bearing flaming pine-torches ran across the garth to put fire in the faggots. One was shot to his death, but others reached the piles and soon they began to blaze.

Manthor stood aghast at the ruin of the hall and the wicked deed of the burning of men. 'Out of the dark days of our past it comes,' he said, 'before we turned our faces west. A shadow is upon us.' And he felt one lay a hand on his shoulder, and he turned and saw Húrin who stood behind him, with a grim face watching the kindling of the fires; and Húrin laughed.

'A strange folk are ye,' he said. 'Now cold, now hot. First wrath, then ruth. Under your chieftain's feet or at his throat. Down with Hardang! Up with Manthor! Wilt thou go up?'

'The Folk must choose,' said Manthor. 'And Hardang still lives.'

'Not for long, I hope,' said Húrin.

Now the fires grew hot and soon the Hall of the Haladin was aflame in many places. The men within threw out upon the faggots earth and water, such as they had, and great smoke went up. Then some sought to escape under its cover, but few got through the ring of men; most were taken, or slain if they fought.

There was a small door at the rear of the hall with a jutting porch that came nearer to the garth-wall than the great doors in front; and the wall at the back was lower, because the hall was built on a slope of the hillside. At last when the roof-beams were on fire, Hardang and Avranc crept out of the rear-door, and they reached the top of the wall and stole down into the dyke, and they were not marked until they tried to climb out. But then with shouts men ran upon them, though they did not know who they were. Avranc flung himself at the feet of one that would seize him, so that he was thrown to the ground, and Avranc sprang up and away and escaped in the mirk. But another cast a spear at Hardang's back as he ran, and he fell with a great wound.

When it was seen who he was, men lifted him up and laid him before Manthor. 'Set him not before me,' said Manthor, 'but before the one he misused. I have no grudge against him.'

'Have you not?' said Hardang. 'Then you must be sure of my death. I think that you have always begrudged that the Folk chose me to the chair and not you.'

'Think what you will!' said Manthor and he turned away. Then Hardang was aware of Húrin who was behind. And Húrin stood looking down on Hardang, a dark form in the gloom, but the light of the fire was on his face, and there Hardang saw no pity.

'You are a mightier man than I, Húrin of Hithlum,' he said. 'I had such fear of your shadow that all wisdom and largesse forsook me. But now I do not think that any wisdom or mercy would have saved me from you, for you have none. You came to destroy me, and you at least have not denied it. But your last lie against me I cast back upon you ere I die. Never' — but with that blood gushed from his mouth, and he fell back, and said no more.

Then Manthor said: 'Alas! He should not have died thus. Such evil as he wrought did not merit this end.'

'Why not?' said Húrin. 'He spoke hate from a foul mouth to the last. What lie have I spoken against him?'

Manthor sighed. 'No lie wittingly maybe,' he said. 'But the last charge that you brought was false, I deem; and he had no chance to deny it. I would that you had spoken to me of it before the Moot!'

Húrin clenched his hands. 'It is not false!' he cried. 'She lies where I said. Morwen! She is dead!'

'Alas! lord, where she died I do not doubt. But of this I judge that Hardang knew no more than I till you spoke. Tell me, lord: did she ever walk further in this land?'

'I know not. I found her as I said. She is dead.'

'But, lord, if she came no further, but finding the Stone there sat in grief and despair by the grave of her son, as I can believe, then . . .'

'What then?' said Húrin.

'Then, Húrin Hadorion, out of the darkness of your woe know this! My lord, so great a grief, and so great a horror of the things that there came to pass is upon us that no man and no woman since the setting up of the Stone has ever again gone nigh to that place. Nay! the Lord Oromë himself might sit by that stone with all his hunt about him, and we should not know. Not unless he blew his great horn, and even that summons we should refuse!'

'But if Mandos the Just spake, would you not hear him?' said Húrin. 'Now some shall go thither, if you have any ruth! Or would you let her lie there till her bones are white? Will that cleanse your land?'

'Nay, nay!' said Manthor. 'I will find some men of great heart and some women of mercy, and you shall lead us thither, and we will do as you bid. But it is a long road to wend, and this day is now old in evil. A new day is needed.'

The next day, when the news that Hardang was dead went abroad, a great throng of people sought for Manthor, crying that he must be Chieftain. But he said: 'Nay, this must be laid before the full Moot. That cannot be yet; for the Ring is unhallowed, and there are other things more pressing to do. First I have an errand. I must go to the Field of the Worm and the Stone of the Hapless, where Morwen their mother lies untended. Will any come with me?'

Then ruth smote the hearts of those that heard him; and though some drew back in fear, many were willing to go, but among these there were more women than men.

Therefore at length they set off in silence on the path that led down along the falling torrent of Celebros. Wellnigh eight leagues was that road, and darkness fell ere they came to Nen Girith,[52] and there they passed the night as they could. And the next morning they went on down the steep way to the Field of Burning, and they found the body of Morwen at the foot of the Standing Stone. Then they looked upon her in pity and wonder; for it seemed to them that they beheld a great queen whose dignity neither age nor beggary nor all the woe of the world had taken from her.

Then they desired to do her honour in death; and some said: 'This is a dark place. Let us lift her up, and bring the Lady Morwen to the Garth of the Graves and lay her among the House of Haleth with whom she had kinship.'

But Húrin said: 'Nay, Niënor is not here, but it is fitter that she should lie here near her son than with any strangers. So she would have chosen.' Therefore they made a grave for Morwen above Cabed Naeramarth on the west side of the Stone; and when the earth was laid upon her they carved on the Stone: *Here lies also Morwen Eðelwen*, while some sang in the old tongue the laments that long ago had been made for those of their people who had fallen on the March far beyond the Mountains.

And while they sang there came a grey rain and all that desolate place was heavy with grief, and the roaring of the river was like the mourning of many voices. And when all was ended they turned away, and Húrin went bowed on his staff. But it is said that after that day fear left that place, though sorrow remained, and it was ever leafless and bare. But until the end of Beleriand women of Brethil would come with flowers in spring and berries in autumn and sing there a while of the Grey Lady who sought in vain for her son. And a seer and harp-player of Brethil, Glirhuin, made a song saying the Stone of the Hapless should not be defiled by Morgoth nor ever thrown down, not though the Sea should drown all the land. As after indeed befell, and still the Tol Morwen stands alone in the water beyond the new coasts that were made in the days of the wrath of the Valar. But Húrin does not lie there, for his doom drove him on, and the Shadow still followed him.

Now when the company had come back to Nen Girith they halted; and Húrin looked back, out across Taeglin towards the westering sun that came through the clouds; and he was loth to return into the Forest. But Manthor looked eastward and was troubled, for there was a red glow in the sky there also.[53]

'Lord,' he said, 'tarry here if you will, and any others who are weary. But I am the last of the Haladin and I fear that the fire which we kindled is not yet quenched. I must go back swiftly, lest the madness of men bring all Brethil to ruin.'

But even as he said this an arrow came from the trees, and he stumbled and sank to the ground. Then men ran to seek for the bowman; and they saw a man running like a deer up the path towards the Obel, and they could not overtake him; but they saw that it was Avranc.

Now Manthor sat gasping with his back to a tree. 'It is a poor archer that will miss his mark at the third aim,' he said.

Húrin leaned on his staff and looked down at Manthor. 'But thou hast missed thy mark, kinsman,' he said. 'Thou hast been a valiant friend, and yet I think thou wert so hot in the cause for thyself also. Manthor would have sat more worthily in the chair of the Chieftains.'

'Thou hast a hard eye, Húrin, to pierce all hearts but thine own,' said Manthor. 'Yea, thy darkness touched me also. Now alas! the Haladin are ended; for this wound is to the death. Was not this your true errand, Man of the North: to bring ruin upon us to weigh against thine own? The House of Hador has conquered us, and four now have fallen under its shadow: Brandir, and Hunthor, and Hardang, and Manthor. Is that not enough? Wilt thou not go and leave this land ere it dies?'

'I will,' said Húrin. 'But if the well of my tears were not utterly dried up, I would weep for thee, Manthor; for thou hast saved me from dishonour, and thou hadst love for my son.'

'Then, lord, use in peace the little more life that I have won for thee,' said Manthor. 'Do not bring your shadow upon others!'

'Why, must I not still walk in the world?' said Húrin. 'I will go on till the shadow overtakes me. Farewell!'

Thus Húrin parted from Manthor. When men came to tend his wound they found that it was grave, for the arrow had gone deep into his side; and they wished to bear Manthor back as swiftly as they could to the Obel to have the care of skilled leeches. 'Too late,' said Manthor, and he plucked out the arrow, and gave a great cry, and was still. Thus ended the House of Haleth, and lesser men ruled in Brethil in the time that was left.

But Húrin stood silent, and when the company departed, bearing away the body of Manthor, he did not turn. He looked ever west till the sun fell into dark cloud and the light failed; and then he went down alone towards the Hauð-en-Elleth.

Both my father's typescript and the amanuensis typescript end here, and this is clearly the designed conclusion of 'Húrin in Brethil'; but in draft manuscript material there are some suggestions (very slight) as to the course of the narrative immediately beyond this point.[54] There are also a few other brief writings and notes of interest.[55]

My father never returned to follow the further wanderings of Húrin.[56] We come here to the furthest point in the narrative of the Elder Days that he reached in his work on *The Silmarillion* (in the widest sense) after the Second War and the completion of *The Lord of the Rings*. There are bits of information about the succeeding parts – not much – but no further new or revised narrative; and the promise held out in his words (p. 258) 'Link to the Necklace of the Dwarves, *Sigil Elu-naeth*, Necklace of the Woe of Thingol' was never fulfilled. It is as if we come to the brink of a great cliff, and look down from highlands raised in some later age onto an ancient plain far below. For the story of the Nauglamîr and the destruction of Doriath, the fall of Gondolin, the attack on the Havens, we must return through more than a quarter of a century to the *Quenta Noldorinwa* (Q), or beyond. The huge abruptness of the divide is still more emphasised by the nature of this last story of the Elder Days, the Shadow that fell upon Brethil.[57] In its portrayal of the life of Brethil into which Húrin came for its ruin, the intricacies of law and lineage, the history of ambition and conflicting sentiment within the ruling clan, it stands apart. In the published *Silmarillion* I excluded it, apart from using Húrin's vain attempt to reach Gondolin and his finding of Morwen dying beside the Standing Stone. Morwen's grave is made by Húrin alone; and having made it, 'he passed southwards down the ancient road that led to Nargothrond'.

To have included it, as it seemed to me, would have entailed a huge reduction, indeed an entire re-telling of a kind that I did not wish to undertake; and since the story is intricate I was afraid that this would produce a dense tangle of narrative statement with all the subtlety gone, and above all that it would diminish the fearful figure of the old man, the great hero, Thalion the Steadfast, furthering still the purposes of Morgoth, as he was doomed to do. But it seems to me now, many years later, to have been an excessive tampering with my father's actual thought and intention: thus raising the question, whether the attempt to make a 'unified' *Silmarillion* should have been embarked on.

NOTES

1 With the beginning of this passage cf. Q (IV.131): 'Some have said that Morwen, wandering woefully from Thingol's halls, when she found Nienor not there on her return, came on a time to that stone and read it, and there died.' – For the abandoned idea that it was Túrin who met Morwen in her wandering see pp. 161–2.

2 Húrin was born in 441 (GA §141). – At this point the first side of the 'lost manuscript' ends. The text on the reverse was struck through and replaced by a new text on a new sheet, all but identical in content but finely written – suggestive of confidence in this further extension of the *Grey Annals*.

3 Asgon reappears here, without introduction, from NE (*Unfinished Tales* p. 109), one of the men who fled with Túrin from Brodda's hall; in the condensed account in GA (§297) he was not named.

4 The spellings *Asgorn* here, but *Asgon* in the preceding paragraph (see note 3), are clear. See note 21.

5 The term *Eastron* has not been used before.

6 'Yet this can scarce be so': i.e., ignorance of Glaurung's death can scarcely be the reason for Húrin's going to Nargothrond.

7 The space marked by a caret evidently awaited the name of the new Lord of Brethil.

8 'He must come of a different race': is this the first reference to the Petty-dwarves?

9 *(Annal 490–5)* The name *Iarwaeth* has appeared in GA §268 (see also p. 142, commentary on §277, at end), but *Thuringud* 'the Hidden Foe' is found nowhere else: cf. Finduilas' name for Túrin, *Thurin* 'the Secret', *Unfinished Tales* pp. 157, 159).

10 *(Annal 494)* The statements that Morgoth stirred up the Eastrons (see note 5) to greater hatred of the Elves and Edain, and that Lorgan sought to take Niënor by force, are entirely new. In GA (§274) it is clear that Morwen and Niënor left Dor-lómin because the lands had become more safe.

11 *(Annal 495)* *Cirith Ninniach*, the final name of the Rainbow Cleft, is found in the later *Tale of Tuor* (*Unfinished Tales* p. 23), where also the meeting of Tuor with Gelmir and Arminas is recounted (pp. 21–2); the name was added to the map (p. 182, square C 4). On the story of their coming to Nargothrond and its relation to the *Grey Annals* see pp. 141–2, commentary on §277. It may be mentioned here that in another 'plot-synopsis' concerning Túrin my father referred to the two Elves by the names Faramir and Arminas, adding in a note: 'Faramir and Arminas were later Eärendil's companions on voyage'.

The 'Narrow Land' is the Pass of Sirion. The form *Erydwethian* occurs in the typescript text of 'Gelmir and Arminas' (p. 142).

'[Handir's] son Brandir the lame is chosen Chieftain, though many would have preferred his cousins Hunthor or Hardang': there has been no previous suggestion of a disagreement over the succession to Brandir; judging by the outspokenness of the people of Brethil as recorded in NE, they would surely have used it against Brandir if they had known of it. – The name *Hunthor* replaced *Torbarth* as that of the 'kinsman of Brandir', who died at Cabed-en-Aras, in NE (this change was not made in GA: see p. 156). He appears in the genealogical table of the Haladin (p. 237), but his descent had by this time been changed: for this, and for Hardang, another cousin, see pp. 268–70.

The defeat of Tum-halad has not previously been attributed to 'the dread of Glaurung', nor has it been said that Túrin gave his word to Gwindor that he would endeavour to save Finduilas.

On the form *Haudh-en-Elleth* see p. 148, §301.

The story that Tuor and Voronwë saw Túrin journeying northward at Eithil Ivrin has appeared in an inserted annal entry in GA (§299), but no more was said there than that 'they saw

Túrin pass, but spoke not with him'. For the fullest account see the later *Tale of Tuor, Unfinished Tales* pp. 37–8.

12 *(Annal 496)* The death of Sador in the fighting in Brodda's hall is told in NE *(Unfinished Tales* p. 108), where also Asgon of Dor-lómin first appears (p. 109).

13 *(Annal 497)* Lindis of Ossiriand: no mention has been made before of the wife of Dior Thingol's heir. See further *The Tale of Years*, pp. 349–51.

14 *(Annal 498)* In GA (§319) Túrin and Níniel were married 'at the mid-summer' of 498, and she conceived in the spring of 499.

15 *(Annal 499)* Of course Glaurung did not reveal to Túrin 'who he was': he did not need to. But this is without significance: it was a short-hand when writing very fast (in the same annal my father wrote 'Nargothrond' for 'Brethil' and 'Tuor' for 'Túrin'), and means that it was through the words of Glaurung that Túrin and Niënor came to know that they were brother and sister.

The name *Talbor* of the memorial stone raised at Cabed-en-Aras has not been given before.

For previous mentions of Mîm and the treasure of Nargothrond, and his death at the hand of Húrin, see the *Tale of Turambar*, II.113–14; the *Sketch of the Mythology*, IV.32; the *Annals of Beleriand* (AB 1 and AB 2), IV.306 and V.141; and Q, IV.132 and commentary IV.187–8.

16 *(Annal 500)* The names *Elrún* and *Eldún* of the sons of Dior appear in emendations made to Q (IV.135) and AB 2 (V.142 and note 42), replacing *Elboron* and *Elbereth*. It has not been said that they were twin brothers (in the *Genealogies* associated with AB 1, of which some extracts were given in V.403, their birth-dates were three years apart, 192 and 195, – later 492, 495: these latter are found in the genealogical table of the House of Bëor, p. 231).

In AB 2 (following AB 1) Húrin was released by Morgoth in the year 499 (IV.306, V.141), and 'he departed and sought for Morwen'; in the continuation of GA (p. 252) the year was 500, as here.

17 *(Annal 501)* In AB 2 (following AB 1) Húrin and his companions (described simply as 'men'; in Q, IV.132, as 'a few outlaws of the woods') came to Nargothrond in 500 (see note 16), whereas in this text, after his visit to Brethil, he sets out for Nargothrond in 501 and comes there in 502. The earlier sources do not say that he found Morwen (cf. the note written against the first continuation of GA, p. 252: 'Some fate of Morwen must be devised. Did Morwen and Húrin meet again?'), nor do they know of his attempting to return to Gondolin (see the end of the continuation of GA, pp. 254–5, where this is first referred to, though without mention of the discovery by Morgoth's spies of the region where Gondolin lay).

The story of Húrin in Brethil was now in existence and probably in its final form (see p. 269). – A first mention of Obel Halad, replacing Ephel Brandir, is found in a note pencilled on the typescript of NE (p. 148, §302).

18 *(Annal 502)* In AB 2 Tuor wedded Idril in 499 (V.141); the date in *The Tale of Years* is (with some hesitation) 502 (pp. 346 ff.). On the bringing of the treasure of Nargothrond to Doriath see IV.188.

19 Only the following points in the WH version need be noted. After the words (p. 252) 'it suited the purpose of Morgoth that this should be so' my father added to the typescript later: 'and the needs of his body had been well served to this end'; and 'unless I find chance to avenge the wrongs of my children' (where GA has 'the wrongs of my son', p. 253) was changed to 'unless I find chance to hear more news of my kin, or to avenge their wrongs, if I may.' Where the GA continuation has Asgon and then Asgorn (note 4), WH has *Asgorn*, corrected to *Asgon*, and further on in the narrative *Asgon* as typed (see note 21). *Eastrons* of GA is here *Easterlings*. On the amanuensis typescript Húrin's words *Tôl acharn* were corrected to *Tûl acharn*.

20 The passage recounting Húrin's ignorance of what had happened in Gondolin to his crossing the Brithiach into Dimbar was a good deal changed at the time of typing, though for the most part this was a matter of rearrangement. Here the text as first typed read:

He knew not the things that had come to pass there, since Tuor brought thither the message of Ulmo, as is yet to be told; and now Turgon, refusing the counsel of the Lord of Waters, allowed none to enter or to go forth for any cause whatsoever, hardening his heart against pity and wisdom.

Tuor had reached Gondolin in 495 (GA §299).

21 *Asgon* was an emendation of the name as typed, *Asgorn*. This was a regular change, until the form *Asgon* appears in the text as typed: I print *Asgon* throughout, except in passages that were rejected before the name was changed.

22 Here the text as first typed read:

Húrin came down from the sources of the Lithir, which fell tumbling into Sirion and was held to be the south bounds of the Narrow Land. There Sirion was already too wide and deep to cross, and too perilous for any but the young and hardiest to swim; so Húrin and his men journeyed on, seeking the fords of the Brithiach.

The name *Lithir* was written against a river already shown on the original form of the second map: p. 182, squares C 6 to D 7.

23 At this point there followed in the draft manuscript and in the typescript as first typed: 'and though this seemed to him to bode evil rather than good, after a time he grew less heedful.'

24 The name *Ragnir* is found also as that of a blind servant of Morwen's in Dor-lómin (*Unfinished Tales* p. 71). In a rejected phrase in the draft manuscript this companion of Asgon's is called 'Ragnir the tracker'.

25 Asgon supposed that the Lord of Brethil was still Brandir the Lame. Cf. what is said of Brandir's successor Hardang a little further on: 'he had no love now at all for the House of Hador, in whose blood he had no part.'

26 On *Obel Halad* see note 17.

27 *Echoriad*: the Encircling Mountains about Gondolin. The form *Echoriath* in the published *Silmarillion* derives from the later *Tale of Tuor*; but *Echoriad* here is much later.

28 The old story in the tale of *The Fall of Gondolin* (II.189) that those of the fugitives from the sack of Gondolin who fled to the Way of Escape were destroyed by a dragon lying in wait at its outer issue, a story that survived into Q (IV.144), had been abandoned, and was excluded from *The Silmarillion* on the basis of the present passage: see II.213, second footnote, and IV.194.

29 Cf. GA §161 (p. 57), of the escape of Húrin and Huor into Dimbar forty-three years before this time: they 'wandered in the hills beneath the sheer walls of the Crisaegrim. There Thorondor espied them, and sent two Eagles that took them and bore them up ...'

30 At this point in the draft manuscript my father wrote:

Later when captured and Maeglin wished to buy his release with treachery, Morgoth must answer laughing, saying: Stale news will buy nothing. I know this already, I am not easily blinded! So Maeglin was obliged to offer more – to undermine resistance in Gondolin.

Almost exactly the same note is found on the slip giving information about the new meaning of the name *Haladin* (p. 270); but here, after the words 'undermine resistance in Gondolin', my father continued: 'and to compass the death of Tuor and Eärendel if he could. If he did he would be allowed to retain Idril (said Morgoth).'

Thus the story in Q was changed (IV.143):

[Meglin] purchased his life and freedom by revealing unto Morgoth the place of Gondolin and the ways whereby it might be found and assailed. Great indeed was the joy of Morgoth ...

Both the present passage in WH (telling that Morgoth learned from Húrin's wandering 'in what region Turgon dwelt') and that from Q were used in the published *Silmarillion* (pp. 228, 242), 'the *very* place of Gondolin' for 'the place of Gondolin' being an editorial addition.

31 There was a series of alterations to the names of the men of Manthor's company near the Crossings of Taeglin (and some

speeches were reassigned among the speakers). In the draft manuscript the names were *Sagroth*; *Forhend* son of Dorlas; and his friend *Farang*. In the typescript as typed they were *Sagroth*; *Forhend*; and his friend *Farang* son of Dorlas. The son of Dorlas is the one who plays an important part in the story. By emendation to the typescript the statement that Farang was the friend of Forhend was removed, and – further on in the narrative – the name *Farang* became *Faranc*; then, near the end of WH, it became *Avranc*, and this name was substituted throughout the text from his first appearance. I print throughout the final formulation only.

32 *Sagroth* was here emended to *Galhir*, but later *Sagroth* was reinstated. Galhir was perhaps intended to be another member of Manthor's company, rather than a replacement of the name *Sagroth*.

33 The footnote at this point was typed at the same time as the text. The statement concerning Manthor's domain in the east of Brethil preceded that in the text C (p. 267): 'The region nigh Brithiach and along Sirion for some way was the land of Manthor'. Haldar was the son of Haldad, founder of the line, and twin brother of the Lady Haleth (p. 221, §25). With the last sentence cf. the plot-synopsis, p. 256: 'Brandir the lame is chosen Chieftain, though many would have preferred his cousins Hunthor or Hardang.' The whole footnote was struck through (before the emendation of *Harathor* to *Hardang*).

34 The term *Haladin* is used here, in a sentence that was rejected rather than corrected, in the original sense of the whole 'People of Haleth'.

35 With the use of the word *town* cf. p. 148, §302.

36 The word *booth* is used in the old sense of 'a temporary dwelling covered with boughs of trees or other slight materials' (O.E.D.). My father may well have had in mind the Norse word *búð*, used in the Sagas especially of the temporary dwellings at the Icelandic parliament, and regularly rendered 'booth' in translations.

37 It is said also in the *Narn* plot-synopsis, of which a part is given on pp. 256–8, but at an earlier point (the year 472), that Haldir and Hundar were slain in the Nírnaeth, and that 'three only of their men were left alive, but Mablung of Doriath healed their wounds and brought them back.' See further pp. 236–7.

38 The draft manuscript has here:
  'He must be wakeful tomorrow. It may be that better food is needed. Take care, or maybe the guards will have to stand before the Folk also.'
  'What do you mean by that?' said the leader.
  'Unriddle it as you will,' said Manthor.

39 'and women' derives from the draft manuscript. Cf. the passage

struck out on p. 279, concerning the summoning of wives to counsel according to the customs of Brethil.

40   Here and often subsequently *Halad* is an emendation of *Warden*; see the statement cited on p. 270, where *Halad*, plural *Haladin*, is translated 'warden(s)'. I give *Halad* in all these cases and do not record the changes.

41   There seems not to have been any specific reference previously to the passing out of common use of the old speech of the People of Haleth (where the draft manuscript has 'the old tongue of the Haladin', and also 'Moot of the Haladin'), and its replacement by 'the speech of Beleriand'.

42   The draft manuscript has here a passage depending on the story, still in being, of the captivity of Asgorn (Asgon) and his men (cf. the rejected sentence in the typescript, p. 278: Húrin was shut in a cave 'nigh to the one in which Asgorn and his men were still imprisoned'):

'Let the first prisoners be brought before us!' Then Asgorn and his companions were led in, with their hands bound behind them.

At that there was much murmuring; and [an old man >] Manthor stood up. 'By your leave, Master and Folk,' he said. 'I would ask: why are these men in bonds?'

There is then a note: 'Harathor should conceal the fact that Asgorn &c. are still in durance, and Manthor should reveal why.' Here the text stops, and begins on a new page with a draft for the changed story as found in the typescript text.

43   At this point the name *Hardang*, for *Harathor*, appears in the text as typed.

44   The draft manuscript has 'Be that as it may —', i.e. Hardang's sentence was interrupted by Manthor.

45   An addition to the draft manuscript says: 'He [Dorlas] had also been Harathor's friend, and a scorner of Brandir while Harathor desired to oust him.' That Dorlas had been a friend of Hardang (Harathor) has been mentioned earlier, at the first appearance of Dorlas' son Avranc (p. 275): 'well-liked by Hardang, as his father had been.'

46   In the story of Dorlas' death in the last part of the *Narn* (NE) as told in the manuscript, Brandir retained his sword. It is said subsequently in that text that 'Brandir, seeing his death in Túrin's face, drew his small sword and stood in defence'; and Túrin 'lifted up Gurthang and struck down Brandir's sword, and smote him to death.' By changes made to the much later amanuensis typescript of NE the story was altered to that given in *Unfinished Tales*: Brandir cast down his sword after the slaying of Dorlas (p. 139), facing Túrin 'he stood still and did not quail, though he had no weapon but his crutch', and the words 'struck down

Brandir's sword' were removed (p. 143). It seems to me unlikely that my father would have made these changes, whereby Túrin's murder of Brandir becomes even worse, in order to make Dorlas' reputation seem more murky in the rumours current in Brethil: I believe that he made them precisely because he wished so to represent Túrin in his encounter with Brandir – in which case, of course, the changes to the NE typescript had already been made when the present passage was written. Subsequently it was bracketed, from 'And dark tales were whispered concerning Dorlas', presumably implying doubt about its inclusion; and the matter is not referred to again.

47 'hand and foot': an addition had been made earlier (p. 282) concerning the further fettering of Húrin on his wrists.

48 *Galdor Orchal*: 'Galdor the Tall'. The 'title' has not previously appeared in Elvish form.

49 With the rejected words 'and good wives' cf. note 39.

50 'I would I had not hindered thy shooting': see p. 278.

51 The story of the events in the Moot-ring was told in the draft manuscript (written in ink over a pencilled text) in fairly close accord with the final form to the point where Húrin cries out on Harathor (as is still the name): 'Only hands, hands, are needed to wring such a throat full of lies'. Then follows:

With that, in a fury, Húrin sprang off the Stone and made for Harathor. But Harathor fled before him, calling on his household men to gather round him; and at the gate he turned, crying: 'It is a lie that he speaks, Men of Brethil. He raves as ever. I knew naught of this till now!' In this he spoke the truth; but too late. In their wrath few of the assembly believed him.

(In the original pencilled text Harathor said more in his defence, using the argument given in the final form to Manthor (pp. 294–5): 'None of the Folk go ever to that stone, for the place is accursed. Not till now have I or any man or woman of the Folk heard tale of her coming to the stone.') At this point in the superimposed text in ink my father stopped, and wrote: 'Do not allow Harathor to defend himself. He flies in fear – and so seems to most of the Folk to acknowledge his guilt.'

From here onwards the draft manuscript becomes chaotic. The pencilled text, in part illegible, continues, interspersed here and there with later passages written in ink, to the end of the story, but the 'layers' are so confused that a coherent development can scarcely be deduced. It seems, however, that at this stage the story of the siege and burning of the Hall of the Chieftains had not entered. The rout of Harathor and his supporters from the Moot-ring seems to have been followed at once by Manthor's reproaches to Húrin – a defence of the conduct of the Men of Brethil towards Túrin, and a denial that Harathor could have

known anything of the coming of Morwen, which in turn leads at
once to the expedition to Cabed Naeramarth and the burial of
Morwen. In his words to Húrin Manthor declares himself to be
now 'the last of the Haladin', but there seems to be no indication
of the fate of Harathor. See further note 53.

A new draft text, very roughly written but coherent, takes up at
the opening of Húrin's speech to the assembly (p. 290): this was
the text from which the final form was closely derived.

52   In NE (*Unfinished Tales* p. 136) it was 'five leagues at the least'
from Ephel Brandir to Nen Girith; in an earlier draft of that
passage it was seven leagues (commentary on GA §§329–32, p.
158).

53   The end of the original draft manuscript (see note 51) is partly
illegible, but after the burial of Morwen 'they return and see red
fire. The Obel is burning as the rebels assault the ... But as they
make their way an arrow comes out of the wood and Manthor
falls.' This suggests that the burning of the Hall of the Chieftains
originally followed the burial of Morwen, and that when that
burning became a central event in the story the red glow in the
sky seen from Nen Girith was retained as the sign of a further
eruption of rioting on the following day. This is supported by the
conclusion of the second draft manuscript, given in note 54 (at
end); but the matter is very uncertain.

54   The end of the original draft manuscript (see notes 51, 53) after
the death of Manthor, pencilled over by my father to make it
clearer but with a gap where there is a word, or words, that he
could not interpret, reads thus:

   A few men fearing the end of Brethil and desiring to flee further
   from Morgoth – having no homes or lands of their own – are
   willing to go with Húrin. They depart – and fall in [*sic*] But
   now Húrin seems to pick up strength and youth – vengeance
   seems to have heartened him, and he [   ] and walks now
   strongly. They pass into the woods and gather the last fugitives
   of the wood-men (the kin of the folk of Brethil).
      Asgorn they choose for captain, but he treats Húrin as lord,
   and does as he will[s]. Whither shall we go? They must
   [?know] a place of refuge. They go towards Nargothrond.

Another, isolated page gives this version of the end:

   For a while he stood there grim and silent. But Manthor looked
   back and saw red light far away. 'I must return,' he said. The
   party begins to go back wearily towards Obel Halad.
      An arrow slays Manthor. – The voice of Faranc [*see note 31*]
   cries: 'Third time thriven. At least you shall not sit in the Chair
   you coveted.' They give chase but he escapes in the dark.

The Moot Ring has been 'unhallowed'. The confederation breaks up. Men go each to their own homesteads. Húrin must depart. He gathers a few men who despair now of defending Brethil from the growing strength of Morgoth [and] wish to fly south. At the Taiglin crossing they fall in with Asgon, who has heard rumour of the wild deeds in Brethil, and of Húrin's coming, and are now venturing back into the land to seek him. Asgon greets him – and is glad that Harathor has been punished. Angered that no one had told Húrin of their coming.

They go on and gather fugitive 'wood-men'. They elect Asgon captain but he ever defers to Húrin. Whither to go? Húrin elects to go to Nargothrond. Why?

The references to 'wood-men' ('kin of the folk of Brethil') in these passages are no doubt to the men who dwelt in the woodland south of the Taeglin, described in the *Narn* (*Unfinished Tales* p. 85, and thereafter called 'the Woodmen'):

There before the Nirnaeth many Men had dwelt in scattered homesteads; they were of Haleth's folk for the most part, but owned no lord, and they lived both by hunting and by husbandry, keeping swine in the mast-lands, and tilling clearings in the forest which were fenced from the wild. But most were now destroyed, or had fled into Brethil, and all that region lay under the fear of Orcs, and of outlaws.

These hasty sketches of Húrin's immediate movements after leaving Brethil agree with what is said in the plot-synopsis (p. 258): 'Húrin finds Asgon again and gathers other men and goes towards Nargothrond'. The question 'Why?' of his decision to go there reappears from the final addition to the end of the *Grey Annals* (p. 255), which probably did not long precede the writing of *The Wanderings of Húrin*.

The second draft manuscript (see note 51, at end) continues on from the point where the typescript text ends, though with a line drawn across the page beneath the words 'he went down alone towards the Hauð-en-Elleth'. I give this partly illegible conclusion from the death of Manthor.

... and plucked out the arrow, and gave a great cry, and lay still.

Then they wept, and they took him up, and prepared to bear him back, and they took no more heed of Húrin. But he stood silent, and turned soon away; the sun was gone down into cloud and the light failed, and he went down alone towards the Hauð-en-Elleth.

[Thus befell the ruin of Brethil. For >] Now it is said that / those who ... with Hardang were not all caught, and others came in hearing the news, and there was fighting in the Obel, and a great burning, until all was well nigh destroyed [*see note 53*]. But when the madness [*written above:* wrath] of men had cooled they made peace, and some said: 'What hath bewitched us? Surely Húrin begot all this evil, and Hardang and Avranc were more wise. They would have kept him out if they could.' So they chose Avranc to be their chief, since none of the House of Haleth were left, but [?? he wielded no] such authority and reverence as the Chieftains before, and the Folk of Brethil fell back again to be more like their kinsmen in the [?open] woods – each minding his own houselands and little ... and their ... was loosened.

But some misliked this and would not serve under Avranc and made ready to depart, and they joined Húrin.

55 The following brief writing on the subject of Manthor is another 'discussion' like the text 'C' (pp. 266–7) and no doubt belongs to much the same time. Here as there the name is *Harathor*, but I suggested (p. 269) that he must have been on the point of receiving a new name, and on the same page as the present passage appear the workings leading to the name *Hardang*.

The page begins with a draft for the last words of Húrin and Manthor at Nen Girith, closely similar to the ending both in the second draft manuscript (on which see note 51, at end) and in the final typescript (pp. 296–7). I believe that the present form was the first, and that my father set it down experimentally, as it were, and then proceeded to explain and justify it, as follows (the many contractions of words and names are expanded):

I think it would be good to make Manthor a less merely 'good' character. For so his extremely zealous and cunning espousal of Húrin's cause would better be explained. Certainly he has a great natural concern for 'courtesy' – sc. civilized behaviour *and* mercy, and he would have been angry at the treatment of Húrin whoever he was. But (a) he was *proud* of his kinship with the House of Hador; (b) he had desired the Wardenship – and many had wanted to elect him. He was of the senior line, but by a daughter (Hiril). But though so far descent had been by eldest son, it had been laid down by Haleth (and Haldar her brother) that daughters and their descendants were to be eligible for election. The descendants of Hundar: Hundad, Harathor had not been men of mark or gallantry.

So plainly Manthor was also using the coming of Húrin to further his ambition – or rather, the shadow of Húrin fell on him, and awoke the ambition (dormant). Note: Manthor never raises the matter of Húrin's *errand*, or (as was fairly plain) that Húrin came with ill-will, especially towards the rulers of Brethil and the 'anti-Túrin' party.

Mention should be made in the tale of Túrin (dwelling in Brethil and death) – à propos of Hunthor? – of Manthor and the friendship of his branch for Túrin and reverence for the House of Hador.

There was some ill-feeling between the branches: on the one side akin to the House of Hador (via Glóreðel and via Hareth and Hiril) and [on the other] the line of Hundar.

This enlarges and defines some of the things said in the last paragraph of the discussion in the text 'C' (p. 267), where the friendship for Túrin among the descendants of Hiril, and pride in their kinship with the House of Hador, were referred to, and the idea that Manthor 'desired the Wardenship' referred to as a possibility.

An isolated slip, headed *Names*, has the following notes:

The *Haladin* name of people directly descended from Haldar Haleth's brother (by male or female line), a family or *'nothlir'* from which the Chieftains or *Halbars* of Brethil were chosen by the Folk.
For *halad* sg. 'chieftain' ..... *halbar*.
The Chieftain after Brandir was *Hardang*.
His evil-counsellor friend to be *Daruin*.
Dorlas > *Darlas*
Dar = mastery, lordship
bor = stone. The Stone in the Ring was the *halabor*. The Standing Stone was the *Talbor*.

The word *halbar* 'chieftain', to be substituted for *halad*, appears in a note pencilled on the genealogical table of the Haladin, where also the name *Haldar* was apparently altered to *Halbar*: see p. 238. The name *Talbor* of the Standing Stone appears also in an addition to the *Narn* plot-synopsis (p. 257), but the stone in the Moot-ring is named *Angbor* 'Doom-rock' in additions to the typescript text of WH (see p. 283). These new names, and *Darlas* for *Dorlas*, *Daruin* for *Avranc*, must represent a further group of substitutions subsequent to the final text of WH, although it is odd in that case that *Hardang* should be included.

Following these notes on the same slip of paper are notes on the name *Taeglin*; these were struck out, but virtually the same notes in more finished form are found on another slip:

Taeglin(d) better *Taeglind*
*taika (√*taya* mark, line, limit > *tayak*) *mære*, boundary, limit, boundary line.
linde 'singer / singing', name (or element in names) of many rivers of quick course that make a rippling sound.

mære is an Old English word of the same meaning. – It seems that the form chosen for the published *Silmarillion* should have been *Taeglin* rather than *Teiglin* (see p. 228, §28).

56 Some interesting remarks of my father's concerning *The Wanderings of Húrin* are found on the back of one of the slips on which Professor Clyde Kilby wrote comments and criticisms of the work:

> The criticisms seem to me largely mistaken – no doubt because this is a fragment of a great saga, e.g. Thingol and Melian are mentioned as objects of Morgoth's malice, because Húrin's next exploit will be to bring ruin to Doriath. The outlaws are not a 'device', but already accounted for – and play a part in the story of Túrin when he came to Dor Lómin. Húrin does pick them up again and they are the nucleus of the force with which he goes to Nargothrond and slays Mîm and seizes the gold of the dragon.
>
> As for 'too little action,' 'too much speech', I have re-read this quite impersonally after many years when I had practically forgotten it – the speeches are bitter and pungent and in themselves exciting. I thought the whole business from the entry of Húrin not only moving but very exciting.

The reference to Thingol and Melian arose from Professor Kilby's taking exception to their only being mentioned in one place (p. 259). The response that his remarks (written, I believe, in 1966) elicited is particularly interesting in that they show that the story of Húrin's seizing the treasure of Nargothrond was still fully in being, although my father never even approached it again. Very striking is his phrase, 'Húrin's next exploit will be to bring ruin to Doriath'.

57 On the amanuensis typescript my father pencilled, beneath *The Wanderings of Húrin*: 'I   *The Shadow Falls on Brethil*'. At the beginning of his discussion of the story in text C (p. 266) he said of Asgorn and his men that 'their coming to Brethil is needed to "cast the shadow" by arousing fear and hatred in the heart of Harathor.' It may be therefore that the subheading *The Shadow Falls on Brethil* was intended to refer only to the first part of the story of Húrin in Brethil. On the other hand, he introduced no other sub-headings into the body of the text, and it seems equally possible that he meant this as the title of the whole story, 'II' to be the next stage of Húrin's 'wanderings', *Húrin in Nargothrond*.

II
ÆLFWINE AND DÍRHAVAL

In *Unfinished Tales* (p. 146) I referred to the existence of an 'introductory note' to the *Narn i Chîn Húrin*, found in different forms, and I
gave a very condensed and selective account of the content. The two
versions are in fact more distinct than this suggests, and here I print
them both in full. One of them is a clear manuscript written with
almost no hesitations or alterations (whether at the time or later): this,
which I will call 'A', clearly preceded the other, and I give it first. The
numbered notes will be found on p. 315.

Túrin Turumarth[1]

Here begins that tale which Ælfwine made from the *Húrinien*:
which is the longest of all the lays of Beleriand now held in
memory in Eressëa. But it is said there that, though made
in Elvish speech and using much Elvish lore (especially of
Doriath), this lay was the work of a Mannish poet, Dírhavel,
who lived at the Havens in the days of Ëarendel and there
gathered all the tidings and lore that he could of the House of
Hador, whether among Men or Elves, remnants and fugitives
of Dorlómin, of Nargothrond, or of Doriath. From Mablung
he learned much; and by fortune also he found a man named
Andvír, and he was very old, but was the son of that Andróg
who was in the outlaw-band of Túrin, and alone survived the
battle on the summit of Amon Rûdh.[2] Otherwise all that time
between the flight of Túrin from Doriath and his coming to
Nargothrond, and Túrin's deeds in those days, would have
remained hidden, save the little that was remembered among
the people of Nargothrond concerning such matters as Gwindor
or Túrin ever revealed. In this way also the matter of Mîm and
his later dealings with Húrin were made clear. This lay was all
that Dírhavel ever made, but it was prized by the Elves and
remembered by them. Dírhavel they say perished in the last raid
of the sons of Fëanor upon the Havens. His lay was composed
in that mode of verse which was called *Minlamad thent / estent*.[3]
Though this verse was not wholly unlike the verse known to
Ælfwine, he translated the lay into prose (including in it, or

adding in the margins as seemed fit to him, matter from the Elvish commentaries that he had heard or seen); for he was not himself skilled in the making of verse, and the transference of this long tale from Elvish into English was difficult enough. Indeed even as it was made, with the help of the Elves as it would seem from his notes and additions, in places his account is obscure.

This version into 'modern' English, that is forms of English intelligible to living users of the English tongue (who have some knowledge of letters, and are not limited to the language of daily use from mouth to mouth) does not attempt to imitate the idiom of Ælfwine, nor that of the Elvish which often shows through especially in the dialogue. But since it is even to Elves now 'a tale of long ago', and depicts high and ancient persons and their speech (such as Thingol and Melian), there is in Ælfwine's version, and clearly was in Dírhavel's day, much archaic language, of words and usage, and the older and nobler Elves do not speak in the same style as Men, or in quite the same language as that of the main narrative; there are therefore here retained similar elements. It is for this reason that, for example, Thingol's speech is not that of our present day: for indeed the speech of Doriath, whether of the king or others, was even in the days of Túrin more antique than that used elsewhere. One thing (as Mîm observed) of which Túrin never rid himself, despite his grievance against Doriath, was the speech he had acquired during his fostering. Though a Man, he spoke like an Elf of the Hidden Kingdom,[4] which is as though a Man should now appear, whose speech and schooling until manhood had been that of some secluded country where the English had remained nearer that of the court of Elizabeth I than of Elizabeth II.

The second text ('B') is very much briefer, and was composed on the typewriter which my father used for several of the *Narn* texts, and other writings such as the chapter *Of the Coming of Men into the West.*

Many songs are yet sung and many tales are yet told by the Elves in the Lonely Isle of the Nirnaeth Arnoediad, the Battle of Unnumbered Tears, in which Fingon fell and the flower of the Eldar withered. But here I will tell as I may a Tale of Men that Dírhaval[5] of the Havens made in the days of Eärendel long ago.

Narn i Chîn Húrin he called it, the Tale* of the Children of Húrin, which is the longest of all the lays that are now remembered in Eressëa, though it was made by a man.

For such was Dírhaval. He came of the House of Hador, it is said, and the glory and sorrow of that House was nearest to his heart. Dwelling at the Havens of Sirion, he gathered there all the tidings and lore that he could; for in the last days of Beleriand there came thither remnants out of all the countries, both Men and Elves: from Hithlum and Dor-lómin, from Nargothrond and Doriath, from Gondolin and the realms of the Sons of Fëanor in the east.

This lay was all that Dírhaval ever made, but it was prized by the Eldar, for Dírhaval used the Grey-elven tongue, in which he had great skill. He used that mode of Elvish verse which is called [*long space left in typescript*] which was of old proper to the *narn*; but though this verse mode is not unlike the verse of the English, I have rendered it in prose, judging my skill too small to be at once *scop* and *walhstod*.[6] Even so my task has been hard enough, and without the help of the Elves could not have been completed. I have not added to Dírhaval's tale, nor omitted from it anything that he told; neither have I changed the order of his history. But on matters that seemed of interest, or that were become dark with the passing of the years, I have made notes, whether within the tale or upon its margins, according to such lore as I found in Eressëa.

That A preceded B, at whatever interval (but I do not think that it was long), is seen, among other considerations, from the use of the old name 'the *Húrinien*' in the opening sentence of A (whereas in B it is called *Narn i Chîn Húrin*). This name had appeared years before in QS Chapter 17, *Of Túrin Turamarth or Túrin the Hapless*: 'that lay which is called *iChúrinien*, the Children of Húrin, and is the longest of all the lays that speak of those days' (V.317). (For *Húrinien* beside *iChúrinien*, and my reason for substituting *Hîn* for *Chîn* in *Unfinished Tales*, see V.322.)

It is possible to state with certainty at what period these pieces were written. I said in *Unfinished Tales* (p. 150): 'From the point in the story where Túrin and his men established themselves in the ancient dwelling of the Petty-dwarves on Amon Rûdh there is no completed narrative on the same detailed plan [as in the preceding parts], until the *Narn* takes up again with Túrin's journey northwards after the fall

---

* [*footnote to the text*] *narn* among the Elves signifies a tale that is told in verse to be spoken and not sung.

of Nargothrond': from the existing materials I formed a brief narrative in *The Silmarillion*, Chapter 21, and gave some further citations from the texts in *Unfinished Tales*, pp. 150–4. Now the story of Túrin and Beleg in Mîm's hidden dwelling on Amon Rûdh and the short-lived 'Land of Bow and Helm', Dor-Cúarthol, belongs (like all the rest of the huge extension of this part of the 'Túrins Saga') to the period after the publication of *The Lord of the Rings*; and the mention in text A of the man Andvír, 'the son of that Andróg who was in the outlaw-band of Túrin, and alone survived the battle on the summit of Amon Rûdh' (see note 2) shows that this story was fully in being (so far as it ever went) when A was written – indeed it seems likely enough that A belongs to the time when my father was working on it.

It is therefore very notable that at this relatively late date he was propounding such a view of the 'transmission' of the *Narn i Chîn Húrin* (in contrast to the statement cited in X.373, that 'the three Great Tales must be Númenórean, and derived from matter preserved in Gondor': the second of the 'Great Tales' being the *Narn i Chîn Húrin*). Striking also is the information (in both texts) that the verse-form of Dírhaval's lay bore some likeness to the verse known to Ælfwine (meaning of course the Anglo-Saxon alliterative verse), but that because Ælfwine was no *scop* (see note 6) he translated it into (Anglo-Saxon) prose. I do not know of any other statement bearing on this. It is tempting to suspect some sort of oblique reference here to my father's abandoned alliterative *Lay of the Chidren of Húrin* of the 1920s, but this may be delusory.

The second version B, in which the introductory note becomes a preface by Ælfwine himself, rather than an 'editorial' recounting of what Ælfwine did, was clipped to and clearly belonged with a twelve-page typescript composed *ab initio* by my father and bearing the title 'Here begins the tale of the Children of Húrin, *Narn i Chîn Húrin*, which Dírhaval wrought.' This text provides the opening of the *Narn* in *Unfinished Tales* (pp. 57–8), and continues into the story of Húrin and Huor in Gondolin (omitted in *Unfinished Tales*) which was based very closely indeed on the version in the *Grey Annals* and is described on pp. 169–70 (then follows the story of Túrin's sister Lalaeth and of his friendship with Sador Labadal, ending with the riding away of Húrin to the Battle of Unnumbered Tears, which is given in *Unfinished Tales* pp. 58–65). It is very difficult to interpret, in the story of the visit to Gondolin, the close similarity or (often) actual identity of wording in Dírhaval's lay with that of the version in the *Grey Annals*. The same question arises, despite a central difference in the narrative, in the case of the *Narn* version of the Battle of Unnumbered Tears and that in the *Annals* (see pp. 165 ff.). The *Narn* text is not linked, as is the Gondolin story, to the name of Dírhaval; but it is a curious fact that it begins (p. 165) 'Many songs are yet sung, and many tales are yet told by the

Elves of the Nirnaeth Arnoediad, the Battle of Unnumbered Tears, in which Fingon fell and the flower of the Eldar withered' – for this is identical to the opening of Ælfwine's preface (text B, p. 312), except that the latter has 'are yet told by the Elves *in the Lonely Isle*'.

NOTES

1 In the old *Tale of Turambar* the Gnomish form of *Turambar* was *Turumart*, and in Q *Turumarth*, where however it was changed to *Turamarth*, as it was also in QS (V.321). *Turumarth* here must represent a reversion to the original form.

2 Andvír son of Andróg appears nowhere else. It is expressly stated in a plot-outline of this part of the *Narn* that Andróg died in the battle on the summit of Amon Rûdh (see *Unfinished Tales* p. 154). The wording here is plain, and can hardly be taken to mean that it was Andvír (also a member of the outlaw-band) who alone survived.

3 The name of the verse is clearly *Minlamad thent / estent*: *Minlamed* in *Unfinished Tales* p. 146 is erroneous.

4 Cf. the 'linguistic excursus' in the *Grey Annals*, p. 26, where there is a reference to the speech of the Grey-elves becoming the common tongue of Beleriand and being affected by words and devices drawn from Noldorin – 'save in Doriath where the language remained purer and less changed by time'.

5 The name is perfectly clearly *Dírhavel* in A, but is typed *Dírhaval* in B, which being the later should have been adopted in *Unfinished Tales*.

6 Against *scop* my father noted: 'O.English = poet', and against *walhstod* 'O.English = interpreter' (on the carbon copy 'interpreter / translator').

III
MAEGLIN

The tale of Isfin and Eöl and their son Meglin (in the earliest form of his name) had long roots, and I have set out its earlier history in concise form on pp. 121–2, §§117–20. As the text of the *Grey Annals* was first written the form of the story in AB 2 was repeated: Isfin left Gondolin in the year before the Battle of Unnumbered Tears, and twenty-one years later Meglin was sent alone to Gondolin (GA original annals 471 and 492, pp. 47, 84). It was at that stage that a full tale of Meglin and how he came to Gondolin was first written.

This was a clear manuscript of 12 sides, fairly heavily emended both at the time of writing and later; it belongs in style very evidently with the *Annals of Aman*, the *Grey Annals*, the later *Tale of Tuor*, and the text which I have called the *End of the Narn* ('NE', see p. 145), and can be firmly dated to the same time (1951). It was on the basis of this work that revised annals concerning the story were introduced into GA (years 316, 320, and 400, pp. 47–8), as noticed earlier (p. 123); these were written on a page from an engagement calendar for November 1951 (p. 47).

An amanuensis typescript with carbon copy was made many years later, as appears from the fact that it was typed on my father's last typewriter. This typescript took up almost all of the emendations made to the manuscript. For the present purpose I shall call the manuscript of 1951 'A' and the late typescript 'B', distinguishing where necessary the top copy as 'B(i)' and the carbon as 'B(ii)'.

The B text was corrected and annotated in ball-point pen, and so also was the carbon copy – but not in the same ways; the original manuscript A also received some late emendations, which do not appear in B as typed. Moreover, a great deal of late writing in manuscript from the same time was inserted into B(i), with other similar material, overlapping in content, found elsewhere; for this my father used scrap paper supplied to him by Allen and Unwin, and two of these sheets are publication notes issued on 19 January 1970 – thus this material is very late indeed, and it is of outstanding difficulty.

Although the typescript B was also very late, as evidenced by the typewriter used, details of names show that the manuscript A had actually reached many years earlier the form from which it was typed; it seems very probable that my father had it typed in order to provide a copy on which substantial further change and annotation could be carried out c.1970. Only those few changes to A made in ball-point pen and not taken up into B belong to the final period of work on the story.

To set out in detail the evolution of all this material would take a very great deal of space, and for much of its length involve the simple repetition of Chapter 16 *Of Maeglin* in the published *Silmarillion*. In this case, therefore, I shall use that chapter as the text for reference, and concentrate chiefly on the very late work, which has many notable features that of their nature could have no place in the published book. I shall refer in this account to the paragraphs in *The Silmarillion*, numbering them for convenience of internal reference, and giving the opening words of each for ease of identification. It should be noted here that the *Silmarillion* text takes up emendations from both the top copy (B(i)) and carbon (B(ii)) of the typescript, and that in cases (which are numerous) where they differ in the rewriting of original passages the published text is often an amalgam of both.

The Title
The manuscript A as written had no title; later my father pencilled on it *Of Meglin*, changing this to *Of Isfin and Glindûr*. The typescript B has the title (as typed) *Of Maeglin*, with the subtitle *Sister-son of Turgon, King of Gondolin*. At the head of the first page of B(i) my father wrote that the text is 'An enlarged version of the coming of Maeglin to Gondolin, to be inserted in FG in its place', and noted also that 'FG = Fall of Gondolin'. This can only be a reference to the abandoned *Tale of Tuor* (entitled *Of Tuor and the Fall of Gondolin*, but retitled *Of Tuor and his Coming to Gondolin* for inclusion in *Unfinished Tales*), which belongs to the same period as the manuscript A. Thus at this very late date my father was still holding to the hope of an entirely rewritten story of the Fall of Gondolin, of which so little had actually been done (and those parts some twenty years before). The only evidence that he at any time considered the story of Maeglin as a possible component in the *Quenta Silmarillion* is the word *Silmarillion* with a query pencilled against the opening paragraphs of the manuscript; and this was struck out.

§1   *Aredhel Ar-Feiniel, the White Lady of the Noldor...*
Here, and throughout B(i), *Isfin* was changed to *Areðel*; and in the margin against the first occurrence my father wrote:
This name is derived from the oldest (1916) version of FG. It is now quite unacceptable in form, unsuitable to the position and character of Turgon's sister, and also meaningless.
Presumably he meant that since no etymology of *Isfin* was feasible it was on that account unsuitable to be the name of Turgon's sister (cf. II.344, where the original explanation of the name as 'snow-locks' or 'exceeding-cunning' is given, and the present note is referred to). Also written in the margin is '? *Rodwen* = High Virgin Noble' and

'*Rodwen Los* in Golodh. .' (last letters illegible; the word 'Virgin' is also not perfectly clear).

At the top of the first page of the carbon B(ii) the notes on the name are different. Here my father wrote: 'Name *Isfin* must be changed throughout to *Feiniel* (= White Lady)'. Against this he wrote an X, and 'Change *Isfin* to *Aredhel* (Noble-elf)'. Whereas in B(i), as I have noted, *Isfin* was changed to *Areðel* throughout, in B(ii) *Isfin* was merely circled, except in two cases where it was replaced by *Feiniel*, and in one case where it was replaced by *Ar-Feiniel*. My father was correcting the top copy and the carbon independently but at (more or less) the same time, very probably because he had the one in one place and the other in another. In the published *Silmarillion* I combined them as *Aredhel Ar-Feiniel*, although there is no warrant for this; they were evidently competing names, and the notes at the head of the carbon copy cited above suggest that *Areðel (Aredhel)* was his final choice.

The name *Nivrost* was changed on both copies of B to *Nevrost* (not *Nevrast*, the usual later form).

In the manuscript A it was said of Isfin that she longed to 'hunt' in the forests, emended to 'walk' and thus appearing in B. With this cf. the rider inserted into the passage in QS concerning the princes of the Noldor, where it is told that in Valinor Isfin 'loved much to ride on horse and to hunt in the forests, and there was often in the company of her kinsmen, the sons of Fëanor'. Subsequently *Isfin* in this passage was changed to *Írith* (see X.177, 182); this name is found in *Quendi and Eldar* (see p. 409 and note 34).

The published text uses 'you' forms throughout. In A 'thou' forms were used throughout, but in the passage (§5) in which the march-wardens of Doriath address Isfin the 'thou' forms were altered to the 'polite' plural. *Noldor* was changed to *Ñoldor* throughout B(i).

In A, the text begins with the date 316.

§4   *And Turgon appointed three lords of his household . . .*

On B(i) only, my father pencilled with reference to these opening words the names *Glorfindel, Egalmoth,* and *Ecthelion,* and also 'On etymologies of *Egalmoth* and *Ecthelion* see note'. This note is written on the same typescript page and its reverse, but is very hard to read:

These names are also derived from primitive FG, but are well-sounding and have been in print. They are late popular forms of archaic *Ægamloth, Ægthelion.* Note *amloth* is said (where?) to be probably not S[indarin]. Q **ambalotse* 'uprising-flower' – referring to the flower or floreate device used as a crest fixed to point of a tall . . . helmet. Name therefore = pointed helm-crest.

Ecthelion must be similarly from *Aegthelion.* Latter element is a derivative of √*stel* 'remain firm'. The form with prefix '*sundóma*', *estel*, was used in Q and S for 'hope' – sc. a temper of mind, steady, fixed in purpose, and difficult to dissuade and unlikely to fall into despair or abandon its purpose. The unprefixed *stel-* gave [? S verb] *thel* 'intend, mean, purpose, resolve, will'. So Q ? *þelma* 'a fixed idea, . . ., will.'

The illegible word in 'a tall . . . helmet' might possibly be 'archaic'. The word *sundóma* is an important term in the analysis of Quendian phonological structure. Very briefly indeed, the Quendian consonantal 'base' or *sundo* was characterised by a 'determinant vowel' or *sundóma*: thus the *sundo* KAT has a medial *sundóma* 'A', and TALAT has the *sundóma* repeated. In derivative forms the *sundóma* might be placed before the first consonant, e.g. ATALAT; thus *estel* beside *stel* in this note.

On the words 'These names . . . have been in print' (referring to the Ruling Stewards of Gondor named Egalmoth and Ecthelion) see II.211–12 and footnote, where the present note is referred to; for my remark there that my father 'subsequently decided against naming Aredhel's escort' see p. 328.

§5   *But when she came to the Ford of Brithiach . . .*
'his kinsfolk of the house of Finarfin': B still has *Finrod* here, and the change to *Finarfin* was made on B(ii) only.

In A and B the march-wardens said to Isfin: 'The speediest way is by the East Road from Brithiach through eastern Brethil, and so along the north-march of this Kingdom, until you pass Esgalduin and Aros, and so come to the woods behind the Hill of Himring.' In B(ii) only, 'Esgalduin and Aros' was changed to 'the Bridge of Esgalduin and the Ford of Aros'.

In the published text 'the lands that lie behind the Hill of Himring' seems to be a mere error for 'the woods . . .' which was not observed.

§6   *Then Aredhel turned back . . .*
A and B have 'the Eryd Gorgoroth', but on B(ii), and also on A at the same time, this was changed to 'the haunted valleys of the Gorgorath'; similarly A and B 'Dungorthin' > 'Nan Dungortheb' on A and B(ii).

The original form of this paragraph was not changed on B(i), but was rewritten on B(ii). This rewriting did not significantly change the sense, but added that the companions of 'Feiniel' (see under §1 above) 'had no choice but to follow her, for they were not permitted to restrain her by force', and that when they returned to Gondolin 'Turgon said to them: "At least I should be glad that three whom I trust and love were not led to death by the wilfulness of one."' These additions were not included in the published text.

§7   *But Aredhel, having sought in vain for her companions . . .*
Where the published text has 'she held on her way' the original text, preserved in B(i), has 'she held to the East Road'; in B(ii) this was emended to 'At last she found the East Road again'. In B(ii) the name

Celon was at both occurrences in the paragraph circled for correction, and at the second the name *Limhir* was written above (see p. 337).

Of Isfin's coming to the land of Himlad (a name which first occurs in this story) the original text of A and B read:

... at that time they [Celegorm and Curufin] were from home, riding with Cranthir, east in Thargelion. But the folk of Celegorm welcomed her, and did all that she asked; and for a while she had great joy in the freedom of the woods. And ever she would ride further abroad, often alone, save it were for hounds that she led, seeking for new paths ...

This was rewritten on B(i) to the form it has in the published text. In a first stage of the rewriting the phrase 'save it were for hounds that she led' was bracketed with the note: 'Omit unless the presence of dogs is afterwards of importance'; in the second stage it was omitted. Against the *o* of *Thargelion* my father wrote *a* (sc. *Thargelian*), with a query. In B(ii) the rewriting was different, retaining more of the original text, including the reference to hounds; *Thargelion* was changed here also to *Thargelian*, without a query (on the latter form see pp. 336–7).

§8   *In that wood in ages past ...*

On B(i) my father wrote the following note in the margin of the typescript against the first occurrence in the story of the name Eöl, which he bracketed:

Another name from prim[itive] FG – meaningless then and now. But it was not intended to have any meaning in Q[uenya] or S[indarin]. For Eöl was said to be a 'Dark Elf', a term then applied to any Elves who had not been willing to leave Middle-earth – and were then (before the history and geography had been organized) imagined as wandering about, and often ill-disposed towards the 'Light-Elves'. But it was also sometimes applied to Elves captured by Morgoth and enslaved and then released to do mischief among the Elves. I think this latter idea should be taken up. It would explain much about Eöl and his smithcraft. (I think the name might stay. It isn't really absolutely necessary that names should be significant.)

In the old tale of *The Fall of Gondolin* Eöl was not in fact called 'the Dark Elf', although in the soon abandoned *Lay of the Fall of Gondolin* (III.146) he is called 'dark Eöl', and it is said that 'the Dark Elves were his kindred that wander without home'. In the *Sketch of the Mythology* (IV.34) he was called 'the Dark Elf Eöl', and so also in the *Quenta* (IV.136); in AB 1 (IV.301) he is 'Eöl a Dark-elf', and in AB 2 (V.136) 'Eöl the Dark-elf' – so also in all the entries in GA. I do not think that 'Dark-elves' had ever been used in the sense referred to in this note, that of 'darkened Elves', Elves ensnared and corrupted by Morgoth. The words 'I think this latter idea should be taken up. It would explain much about Eöl and his smithcraft' were the basis for an abandoned sketch of Eöl's history given below.

The original text had 'Of old he was of the kin of Thingol, but he loved him not, and when the Girdle of Melian was set about the Forest of Region he fled thence to Nan Elmoth.' In a passage of the 'Túrins Saga' which was excluded in *Unfinished Tales* (p. 96 and note 12) because it had been used in *The Silmarillion* (pp. 201–2), it is told that Eöl gave the sword Anglachel which he had made 'to Thingol as fee, which he begrudged, for leave to dwell in Nan Elmoth'.

Against the words 'but he loved him not' my father wrote in the margin of the carbon copy, B(ii): 'Because Thingol was friendly with the Noldor before they left Middle-earth' (cf. X.172). On B(i) he emended the words 'he loved him not' to 'he was ill at ease in Doriath', and on an inserted page he roughed out a new story about Eöl. This is in two versions, which are however largely identical. The first reads:

but he was restless and ill at ease in Doriath, and when the Girdle of Melian was set about the Forest of Region where he dwelt he departed. It is thought (though no clear tale was known) that he was captured by orks and taken to Thangorodrim, and there became enslaved; but owing to his skills (which in that place were turned much to smithcraft and metalwork) he received some favour, and was freer than most slaves to move about, and so eventually he escaped and sought hiding in Nan Elmoth (maybe not without the knowledge of Morgoth, who used such 'escaped' slaves to work mischief among the Elves).

The second version begins:

and when he heard that Melian would put a Girdle about Doriath that none could pass . . . . . without the leave of the king or of Melian herself, he left the Forest of Region where he had dwelt and sought for a place to dwell. But since he did not love the Noldor he found it hard to find a place where he would be unmolested. It was believed afterwards (though no certain tale was known) that in his wandering he was captured [*&c. as in the first version*]

This is possibly compatible with the story that Eöl gave Anglachel to Thingol as fee to dwell in Nan Elmoth. It would be interesting to know why my father wished thus to change Eöl's history – or rather, why he wished to attribute Eöl's skill in metals to a time of slavery in Angband; but in any event he thought better of it, for in a scribbled note beside the two versions of the story he said that this would not do, being too repetitive of the later history of Maeglin, and that Eöl's skill was derived from the Dwarves.

§9   *Now the traffic of the Dwarves . . .*

The opening of this paragraph read as follows in A:

Now the traffic of the Dwarves followed two roads, the northern of which, going towards Himring, passed nigh Nan Elmoth, and there Eöl would meet the Enfeng and hold converse with them. And, as their friendship grew, he would at times go and dwell as a guest in the deep mansions of Belegost.

The only emendation to A was the replacement of the old term *Enfeng* (Longbeards, the Dwarves of Belegost, see pp. 108, 207–8) by *Anfangrim*, here first appearing. In B(ii) 'the deep mansions of Belegost' was changed to '... of Nogrod or Belegost'; adopting this in the published text I altered in consequence *Anfangrim* 'Longbeards' to the general term *Naugrim*.

In the following passage A had originally:

There he learned much of metalwork, and came to great skill therein; and he devised a metal hard and thin and yet pliable, and it was black and shining like jet. *Rodeöl*, the metal of Eöl, he named it, and he was clad therein, and so escaped many wounds.

The name of the metal was changed many times. First *Rodeöl* was altered to *Glindûr*, then to *Targlîn* and *Morlîn*; then (apparently) back to *Glindûr*, and finally to *Maeglin*, the form in B.

The idea that the name of Eöl's son was derived from that of the metal is found in the revised annal for 320 in GA (p. 48): 'Eöl named him Glindûr, for that was the name of the metal of Eöl'; subsequently *Glindûr* was changed to *Maeglin* both as the name of the metal and as the name of the son (as also in A: see under §10 below).

The passage was left as it stood in B(i), but at the head of the first page of B(ii) my father wrote: 'The metal must *not* have same name as Maeglin'; and he emended the text to the form that it has in the published *Silmarillion*, with the name of the metal *galvorn*. (Following 'whenever he went abroad' the words 'and so escaped many wounds' were omitted in *The Silmarillion*, apparently through inadvertence.)

To the passage 'But Eöl ... was no Dwarf, but a tall Elf of a high kin of the Teleri' my father wrote on the manuscript A (only) a note beginning with the words 'Not in revision' – which probably means that what follows is not in the corrections made to the copies of the typescript ('the revision'). In this note my father was copying a very faint and illegible form of it on the same page, and trying to interpret his own writing; I give it exactly as it stands:

Eöl should not be one of Thingol's kin, but one of the Teleri who refused to cross the Hithaeglir. But [later] he and a few others of like mood, averse to concourse of people, ... [had] crossed the [Mts] long ago and come to Beleriand.

Against this note he wrote 'but the relationship to Thingol would have point', and the date 1971.

Aredhel Ar-Feiniel: B(ii) has here *Ar-Feiniel* (emended from *Isfin*); see p. 318.

§10   *It is not said that Aredhel was wholly unwilling ...*

In the margin of the manuscript at the mention of the birth of Eöl's son my father wrote later the date 320 (cf. p. 48, §119). The sentence in A as originally written read:

After some years Isfin bore to Eöl a son in the shadows of Nan

Elmoth, and he was named Meglin by his father, for he was dark and supple, as the metal of Eöl.

The fact that the metal was originally named *Rodeöl* in A (see under §9 above) but the son *Meglin* (the original name) seems to suggest that the idea that the son was named from the metal only arose after the initial writing of the manuscript, despite the words 'for he was dark and supple, as the metal of Eöl'. The changing forms of the son's name in A were *Meglin* > *Targlin* > *Morlin* > *Glindûr* and finally *Maeglin*.

The sentence in this form (with the name *Maeglin*, as of the metal also) was preserved in B(i); but in B(ii), the text on which my father declared that the same name must not be used both of Eöl's son and Eöl's metal and changed that of the latter to *galvorn*, he altered it to the form in the published text, in which Aredhel secretly gave her son the Noldorin name *Lómion* 'Child of the Twilight', and Eöl named him *Maeglin* (interpreted 'Sharp Glance', see p. 337) when he was twelve years old.

§12 *Yet it is said that Maeglin loved his mother better...*

'Turgon ... had no heir; for Elenwë his wife perished in the crossing of the Helcaraxë': here A has 'Turgon ... had no heir: for his wife, Alairë, was of the Vanyar and would not forsake Valinor'. On the page of jottings that concludes the abandoned later *Tale of Tuor* (see *Unfinished Tales* p. 56) a note which I did not include says that 'Alairë remained in Aman'. That this was the case because she was a Vanya is reminiscent of the story of Amárië, beloved of Felagund, who was a Vanya, 'and was not permitted to go with him into exile' (p. 44, §109). The typescript B as typed has *Alairë*, but on both A and B(ii), not on B(i), my father corrected (presumptively in 1970) the name to *Anairë*. The substitution of *Elenwë* in *The Silmarillion* was based on the Elvish genealogies of 1959 (see pp. 229, 350), where *Anairë* (defined as a Vanya 'who remained in Túna') was later corrected to '*Elenwë* who perished in the Ice'; on the same table at the same time *Anairë* was entered as the wife of Fingolfin, with the note that she 'remained in Aman'.

In a note added to the typescript of the *Annals of Aman* (X.128, §163) my father said that in the crossing of the Helkaraxë 'Turgon's wife was lost and he had then only one daughter and no other heir. Turgon was nearly lost himself in attempts to rescue his wife – and he had less love for the Sons of Fëanor than any other'; but Turgon's wife is not named.

§13 *In the telling of these tales...*

Golodhrim: A had *Noldor*, changed immediately to *Goloðrim* (*Golodhrim* B).

In this paragraph, and in §14, the name of Eöl's son (see under §§9, 10 above) passed through these forms in A: *Morleg* (which has not occurred before) > *Morlin* > *Glindûr* > *Maeglin*.

§§14 ff.   *It came to pass that at the midsummer* ...

Against the opening sentence in A my father later wrote the date 400 (cf. p. 48, §120). The original text, preserved unchanged in both copies of B, read here:

And it came to pass that the Dwarves bade Eöl to a feast in Nogrod, and he rode away. Then Maeglin went to his mother and said: 'Lady, let us depart while there is time! What hope is there in the wood for thee or for me? Here we are held in bondage, and no profit more shall I find in this place. For I have learned all that my father or the [Nornwaith >] Naugrim have to teach, or will reveal to me; and I would not for ever dwell in the dark woods with few servants, and those skilled only in smith-craft. Shall we not go to Gondolin? Be thou my guide, and I will be thy guard.'

Then Isfin was glad, and looked with pride upon her son. 'That indeed I will do, and swiftly,' she said; 'and no fear shall I have upon the road with a guard so valiant.'

Therefore they arose and departed in haste, as secretly as they might. But Eöl returned, ere his time, and found them gone; and so great was his wrath that he followed after them, even by the light of day.

(For *Nornwaith*, replaced by *Naugrim*, see p. 209.) At this point there are two earlier versions of the text in A, both struck through. The first reads:

But Morleg had also mistrusted his father, and he took cunning counsel, and so he went not at once by the East Road, but rode first to Celegorm and found him in the hills south of Himring. And of Celegorm he got horses surpassing swift, and the promise of other aid. Then Morleg and Isfin passed over Aros and Esgalduin far to the north where they spilled from the highlands of Dorthonion, and turned then southward, and came to the East Road far to the west. But Celegorm and Curufin waylaid the East Road and its ford over Aros, and denied it to Eöl, and though he escaped from them in the darkness he was long delayed.

The next version reads:

For his servants reported to him that they had fled to the fords of the East Road over Aros and Esgalduin. But they were two days ahead, and had taken the swiftest of his horses, and hard though he pursued them, he came never in sight of them, until they passed over the Brithiach and abandoned their horses. But there by ill fate he saw them even as they took the secret path, which lay in the course of the Dry River; and he followed them with great stealth, step by step, and came upon them even in the darkness of the great vault where the Guards of the Way kept watch unceasing. Thus he was taken, even as they, by the Guards

It is interesting to see the intervention of Celegorm and Curufin in the story here, removed at once but reappearing many years later.

On the page carrying these rejected passages there follow very
rapidly pencilled notes outlining the further course of the story:
   After they entered he entered. Taken by guards. Claims to be Isfin's
   husband. Words to Turgon. Isfin acknowledges it. Turgon treats Eöl
   with honour. Eöl draws a bow and shoots at Morleg in the King's
   hall, saying that his own son shall not be filched. But Isfin sets
   herself in way and is wounded. While Eöl is in prison Isfin dies
   of venom. Eöl condemned to death. Taken to the precipice of
   Caragdar. Morleg stands by coldly. They hurl him over the precipice
   and all save Idril approve.
After the rejection of the passages given above my father wrote a final
version, beginning again at 'even by the light of day' on p. 324:
   even by the light of day; for his servants reported to him that they
   had ridden to the East Road and the ford over Aros. But they were
   two days ahead, and hard though he pursued them, and had the
   swiftest steed, he came never in sight of them, until they [came
   under the shadows of the Crisaegrim, and sought for the secret
   path >] reached the Brithiach, and abandoned their horses.
The text then continues as in *The Silmarillion* §23 (paragraph
beginning *Then Eöl rode off in haste* . . .).
   The final text of A was preserved in the typescript B, and in neither
the top copy nor the carbon did my father change it (except for 'a
feast' > 'a midsummer feast' in the latter). From here onwards, in fact,
there were no further emendations or annotations made to the carbon
copy B(ii), and this text no longer concerns us. But in B(i) my father
inserted into the typescript a long text on separate pages; and this
appears to be the last piece of substantial *narrative* that he wrote on
the Matter of the Elder Days – it cannot be earlier than 1970 (see
p. 316). It begins at the words 'It came to pass that at the midsummer', and continues through the flight of Maeglin and Aredhel, Eöl's
pursuit, and the intervention of Curufin: *The Silmarillion* pp. 134–6,
§§14–23, where it joins the original A text at 'until they reached the
Brithiach, and abandoned their horses'.
   As has been seen (p. 317) this story of Maeglin was not written to
stand as an element in the *Quenta Silmarillion*; and the detail of the
narrative in this very late interpolation was somewhat reduced in the
published text, chiefly by the removal of all the precise timing and
numbering of days and a return to the manner of the original simpler
and more remote narrative. The chief omissions and consequent
alterations are as follows.
   §14   *and he rode away*. Original text: 'and he rode away, though he
thought it likely that in his absence Maeglin might seek to visit the
sons of Fëanor in spite of his counsels, and he secretly ordered his
servants to keep close watch on his wife and son.'
   Therefore he said to Aredhel: 'Therefore when Eöl had been gone
some days Maeglin went to his mother and said:'

§§15–16   *and telling the servants of Eöl that they went to seek the sons of Fëanor* ...: 'Therefore that night as secretly as they could they made provision for a journey, and they rode away at daybreak to the north-eaves of Nan Elmoth. There as they crossed the slender stream of Celon they spied a watchman, and Maeglin cried to him: "Tell your master that we go to visit our kin in Aglon." Then they rode on over the Himlad to the Fords of Aros, and then westward along the Fences of Doriath. But they had tarried overlong. For on the first night of the three days feast, as he slept, a dark shadow of ill foreboding visited Eöl, and in the morning he forsook Nogrod without ceremony and rode homeward with all speed. Thus he returned some days earlier than Maeglin had expected, coming to Nan Elmoth at nightfall of the day after their flight. There he learned from his watchman that they had ridden north less than two days before and had passed into the Himlad, on their way to Aglon.

'Then so great was Eöl's anger that he resolved to follow them at once; so staying only to take a fresh horse, the swiftest that he had, he rode away that night. But as he entered the Himlad he mastered his wrath ...'

Against *Celon* is written *? Limhir* (see under §7 above).

§16   *Curufin moreover was of perilous mood; but the scouts of Aglon had marked the riding of Maeglin and Aredhel* ...: 'Curufin was a man of perilous mood. So far they had left him [Eöl] free to go his ways, but could if they wished confine him within the bounds of Nan Elmoth and cut him off from his friendship with Dwarves, of which Curufin was jealous. Things proved little better than he feared; for the scouts of Aglon ...'

And before Eöl had ridden far ...: 'So ere Eöl had ridden half the way over Himlad he was waylaid by well-armed horsemen, who forced him to go with them to their lord Curufin. They reached his camp about noon; and he greeted Eöl with little courtesy.'

§19   *It is not two days since they passed over the Arossiach* ...: 'Nearly two days ago they were seen to pass the Fords of Aros, and to ride swiftly westward.' For the name *Arossiach* introduced into the published text see p. 338, note 2.

§22   *to find a kinsman thus kindly at need*: 'to find one's nephew so kindly at need.' On this alteration see §23 below.

By the laws of the Eldar I may not slay you at this time: here there is a footnote in the original: 'Because the Eldar (which included the Sindar) were forbidden to slay one another in revenge for any grievance however great. Also at this time Eöl had ridden towards Aglon with no ill intent, and it was not unjust that he should seek news of Areðel and Maeglin.'

§23   *for he perceived now that Maeglin and Aredhel were fleeing to Gondolin*: 'For he saw now that he had been cheated, and that his wife and son were fleeing to Gondolin, and he had been delayed, so that it was now more than two days since they crossed the Fords.'

This narrative is followed by various notes. One of these is a genealogical table:

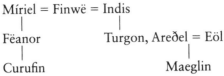

To this is added: 'So Curufin was half-nephew of Turgon and Areðel. Eöl was uncle by marriage of Curufin, but that was denied as a "forced marriage".' This genealogy is the basis for Eöl's words cited under §22 above, 'to find one's nephew so kindly at need'; but it is of course entirely wrong. The correct genealogy is:

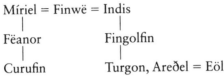

Curufin was not Eöl's nephew (through Areðel), but his cousin (by marriage). It is a strange error, one might say unprecedented, since it is not a mere casual slip.

On another page is the following long, rapidly written, and remarkably elaborate discussion of the motives of Celegorm and Curufin.

The meeting between Eöl and Curufin (if not too long an interruption) is good, since it shows (as is desirable) Curufin, too often the villain (especially in the Tale of Tinúviel), in a better and more honourable light – though still one of dangerous mood and contemptuous speech. Curufin of course knew well of Eöl's hatred of the Noldor, and especially of Fëanor and his sons, as 'usurpers' (though in this case unjust, since the lands occupied by the 5 sons had not been peopled before by the Sindar). Also he knew of Eöl's friendship with the Dwarves of Nogrod (indeed Eöl could not have journeyed alone across E. Beleriand to Nogrod unless allowed by the 5 sons), among whom he had tried with some success to stir up unfriendliness to the Noldor. Which was a grievance to the 5 sons, who had, before Eöl's coming to Nan Elmoth, had much profit from the help of the Dwarves. Curufin also knew that Eöl's wife was of the Noldor, indeed he had long known who she was, and now shrewdly guessed that she was [?seeking] to escape from her husband at last. Curufin could have slain Eöl (as he greatly wished!) and no one beyond the few men with him at his camp (who would never have betrayed him) would ever have heard of it – or much mourned it. In Elmoth it would simply be learned that Eöl had ridden in pursuit of Areðel and never come back, and there were perils enough upon the road to account for that. But this would have been in Eldarin law and sentiment *murder*; Eöl came alone, on no errand of mischief at that time, but in distress. Also [he] had answered Curufin's contempt and insults soberly or indeed with courtesy (whether it were ironic or not). Also and more cogently he was one of the Eldar, and not so far as was known under any shadow of Morgoth – unless that vague one which afflicted many others of the Sindar (? due to whispers inspired by Morgoth) – jealousy of the Noldor. Which was dangerous (whatever the faults of their rebellion) since if Morgoth had not been followed by the Exiles, it seems clear that all the Sindar would soon have been destroyed or enslaved.

An important point not made clear is Curufin and Celegorm's earlier action in the matter of Areðel. She had actually stayed with them, and made no secret of who she was – indeed they knew her well from of old. Why did they not send word to Gondolin? Her escort though valiant chiefs would seem to have been so bewildered and daunted by the horrors of the valleys west of Esgalduin that they had never reached the Bridge of Esgalduin or come near to Aglond. This makes it necessary, I think, *not* to name the most eminent and bravest chieftains (Glorfindel, Egalmoth, and Ecthelion) as her escort. The answer then to the above question is this: the perils of Dungorthin etc. were universally dreaded by the Eldar, and not least by the sons of Fëanor, to him [*read* whom] refuge southward into Doriath was utterly closed. It had, of course, been expressly forbidden by Turgon that Areðel should go that way. Only her wilfulness had done this. Her escort plainly endured to the utmost of their strength the perils in their search, and so doubtless in fact aided her escape, by drawing to themselves the chief attention of the evil creatures. Now there had [been] since Gondolin was 'closed' no communication at all between the sons of Fëanor and Turgon. It was known of course that any of these sons (or any fully accredited messengers) bearing tidings of Areðel would at once have been admitted. But Areðel had evidently told Curufin (and later Celegorm of whom she was most fond) enough of herself, to understand that she had escaped from Gondolin by her own will and was glad to dwell [with] them and be free. Now they could only get word to Gondolin by facing evil perils, which only her rescue from misery would have seemed to them sufficient reason. Moreover while she was happy and at ease they delayed – believing that even if Turgon was informed he would only have demanded her return (since his permission to her to depart was void after her disobedience). But before they had made up their minds she was again lost, and it was a long time before they knew or even guessed what had become of her. This they did eventually when Areðel again began to visit the borders of Nan Elmoth, or stray beyond them. For they held a constant watch on Nan Elmoth, mistrusting the doings and goings of Eöl, and their scouts espied her at times riding in the sunlight by the wood-eaves. But now it seemed too late [to] them; and they all [? read they thought that all] they would get for any peril would be the rebuke or wrath of Turgon. And this [they] wished in no way to receive. For they were now under a shadow of fear, and beginning to prepare for war again ere the strength of Thangorodrim became insuperable.

In this piece there are major difficulties, and also some minor points to mention. (1) It is said that Curufin 'knew of Eöl's friendship with the Dwarves of Nogrod': in the narrative Eöl's visits were to Belegost, changed on B(ii) to 'Nogrod or Belegost' (see under §9 above), but already in A the feast to which he had gone at the time of the flight of his wife and son was held at Nogrod (§14). Elsewhere among these late 'Maeglin' writings it is said of Eöl: 'Lately he had visited Nogrod often; he had become very friendly with the Dwarves of Nogrod, since those of Belegost to the north had become friends of Caranthir son of Fëanor.' (2) The pass is here named *Aglond*, though in the interpolated narrative itself it is named *Aglon*; see p. 338, note 3. (3) For the naming of Aredhel's escort, here rejected, see under §4 above. (4) The reference to *Dungorthin* rather than *Dungortheb* is a casual reversion to the old and long-enduring name.

(5) The *five* sons of Fëanor are three times mentioned, but I cannot explain this. It does not seem credible that the Seven Sons of Fëanor, so deeply rooted and so constantly recurring in the tradition, should become five by a mere slip of forgetfulness, as in the omission of Fingolfin from the genealogy (p. 327). By this time the story had entered that one of the twin brothers Damrod and Díriel, later Amrod and Amras, the youngest of Fëanor's sons, died in the burning of the ships of the Teleri at Losgar, because he 'had returned to sleep in his ship': this was stated in a pencilled note on the typescript of the *Annals of Aman* (X.128, §162), although no consequential alteration to any text was ever made. Possibly my father had come to believe that both Amrod and Amras died in the burning ship.

(6) Lastly, the concluding sentence of the discussion, concerning the preparation for war by Celegorm and Curufin, is surprising. The Siege of Angband ended very suddenly at midwinter of the year 455. Between the rout of Glaurung in 260 and the Battle of Sudden Flame there was (in the words of the *Grey Annals*, p. 46) 'the long peace of wellnigh two hundred years. In that time there was naught but affrays on the north-marches ...' It is true that in 402 (p. 49) there was 'fighting on the north-marches, more bitter than there had been since the routing of Glaurung; for the Orcs attempted to pierce the pass of Aglon'; while in 422 (p. 50) Fingolfin 'began to ponder an assault upon Angband', which came to nothing, because 'most of the Eldar

were content with matters as they were and slow to begin an assault in which many must surely perish'. But Maeglin and Aredhel fled to Gondolin from Nan Elmoth in 400. There has nowhere been any indication that the sons of Fëanor were beginning to prepare for war 55 years before the Dagor Bragollach, with which the Siege of Angband ended.

For the remainder of the narrative there are very few alterations to the top copy B(i) of the typescript, and I notice only the following: §35 *It was appointed that Eöl should be brought* ...: at the end of the paragraph my father added:

For the Eldar never used any poison, not even against their most cruel enemies, beast, ork, or man; and they were filled with shame and horror that Eöl should have meditated this evil deed.

From this point also the published text follows the original very closely, and the small amount of editorial alteration in no way affects the narrative.

I have mentioned (p. 316) that in addition to the very late emendations and annotations, recorded above, made to the text of *Maeglin* there is also much further material from the same time. These writings are primarily concerned with the geography, times, and distances of the journeys on horseback, but they are complicated and confused, often repeating themselves with slight differences of calculation, and in part virtually illegible. They contain however many curious details about the geography and the ways taken by travellers in those regions.

To set out this material in ordered form, treating it page by page and attempting to trace the development in sequence, is not possible, and if it were possible unnecessary. My father himself noted: 'These calculations of times in Eöl's journeys though interesting (and sufficient to establish their possibility) are not really necessary in the narrative – which seems credible as it stands even when faced by a map.' What follows is a discussion with some citation of what can be learned (and still more, of what can not be learned) of the roads in East Beleriand. The numbered notes are found on pp. 338–9.

Associated with this material are rather pale photocopies of the North-east and South-east sections of the map. These photocopies were taken when the map had received almost all the alterations that were ever made to it;[1] and my father used the copies, not the original, to indicate features arising from his reconsideration and development of the story of Maeglin c.1970. Since the tracks are far more readily understood visually than by description, the redrawing of the North-east section (p. 183) is reproduced again on p. 331 with the alterations shown; the markings on the South-east section are few and easily understood from a description, and for these reference is made to the redrawing on p. 185.

My father had stated in a note on the back of the original 'second

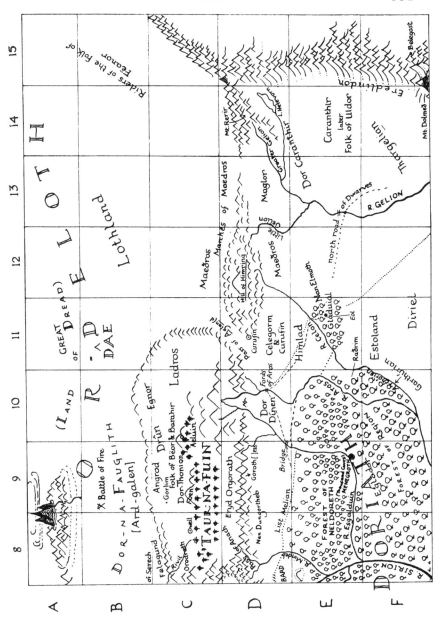

Sheet 2 North-east (with additions)

map' (see V.272) that the scale is 50 miles to 3·2 cm, which is the length of the sides of the squares. On the back of one of these photocopies, however, he wrote: 'The centimetre reckoning on the original map is unnecessary, clumsy, and inaccurate. Actually 2 squares of 1·25 [inches] each = 100 miles. ... The scale is therefore 40 miles to an inch. 50 miles to 1·25 inches = one square.' Although he did not precisely say so here, it looks to me as if he made the original grid on the basis of inches, but subsequently interpreted it as if it were in centimetres.

The East Road. In the original text of *Maeglin* (p. 319, §5) the march-wardens of Doriath said to Isfin that 'the speediest way is by the East Road from Brithiach through eastern Brethil, and so along the north-march of this Kingdom, until you pass Esgalduin and Aros, and so come to the woods behind the Hill of Himring', which was not altered when the corrections were made to the text long afterwards, except by changing 'Esgalduin and Aros' to 'the Bridge of Esgalduin and the Ford of Aros' on one copy. In §6, she 'sought' the 'road' between the Mountains of Terror and the north fences of Doriath, and in §7 'she held to the East Road, and crossed Esgalduin and Aros', changed on one copy to 'At last she found the East Road again ...' In one of the rejected passages in the manuscript A given under §§14 ff on p. 324 it is said that 'Morleg [Maeglin] went not at once by the East Road, but rode first to Celegorm', while in the second rejected passage *(ibid.)* '[Eöl's] servants reported to him that they had fled to the fords of the East Road over Aros and Esgalduin'; in the third form (p. 325) 'his servants reported to him that they had ridden to the East Road and the ford over Aros.'

From all these passages it is clear that when he wrote the original text of *Maeglin* in 1951 my father conceived of an East–West road running from the ford of Brithiach between the Mountains of Terror and the northern borders of Doriath, and across the rivers Esgalduin and Aros; and the fact that the first of these passages was allowed to stand in both typescripts seems to show that he still retained this conception in 1970. The only difference seems to be the introduction of a bridge, rather than a ford, over Esgalduin. That this was certainly the case is seen from the following passage:

Eöl's house (in the middle of Elmoth) was about 15 miles from the northmost point of the wood beside Celon. From that point it was about 65 miles N.W. to the Ford of Aros.[2] At that time Curufin was dwelling at the S.E. corner of the Pass of Aglond[3] about 45 miles N.E. from the Ford of Aros. The Himlad (cool-plain) behind Aglond and Himring, between the northern courses of the Rivers Aros and Celon, he claimed as his land.[4] He and his people naturally kept watch on the Ford of Aros; but they did not prevent the few hardy travellers (Elves or Dwarves) that used the road West – East past the

north fences of Doriath. (Beyond the Ford was an entirely unin-
habited region between the mountains north [? *read* in the north,]
Esgalduin and Aros and Doriath: not even birds came there. It was
thus called *Dor Dhínen* the 'Silent Land'.)[5]

Beyond the Aros (some 25 miles) lay the more formidable
obstacle of the Esgalduin in which no fordable point was to be
found. In the 'peaceful days' before the return of Morgoth and
Ungoliant, when Doriath's north borders were the mountains of
Fuin (not yet evil), the West – East road passed over the Esgalduin
by a bridge outside the later fence of Melian. This stone-bridge,
the *Esgaliant* or *Iant Iaur* (old bridge) was still in existence, and
watched by the wardens of Doriath, but its use by Eldar was not
hindered. It was necessary therefore to fugitives crossing Aros to
turn S.W. to the bridge. From there they would keep as close as they
could to the Fences of Doriath (if Thingol and Melian were not
hostile to them). At the time of this story, though many evils lurked
in the Mountains the chief peril lay in passing Nan Dungortheb
from which clouds and darkness would creep down almost to the
Fences.

Turning to the photocopy of the map, Eöl's house was marked in
Nan Elmoth as shown in my redrawing (p. 331). A line in green ball-
point pen connects his house to a point on the northern border of the
wood beside the river; and from here a green dotted line (represented
as a line of dashes in the redrawing) runs across the Himlad to the
'Fords of Aros', marked in red ball-point pen.[6] The green dots then
run S.W. to the bridge over Esgalduin, this being labelled 'Bridge'
simply (*Esgaliant* or *Iant Iaur* in the text just cited).[7] Beyond the Iant
Iaur the green dots continue S.W. for a short way and then stop: they
are not shown in relation to the *List Melian* (the Girdle of Melian).

It is stated in a note on the photocopy map that this green line marks
the 'track of Maeglin and his mother, fleeing to Gondolin'. In the light
of the text just cited, it is also the line of the East–West road from the
Ford of Aros to the Iant Iaur; but otherwise the course of the road is
not represented. The dotted line along the edge of Neldoreth is named
on the map *List Melian,* and does not mark a road. Westward this line
was indeed extended beyond Mindeb to the Brithiach, but these dots
were struck out (p. 188, §38); eastwards it was extended between
Esgalduin and Aros, and then between Aros and Celon, and this seems
to represent the continuation of the *List Melian.*

On account of these obscurities I excluded from the text of the
chapter *Of Maeglin* in *The Silmarillion* the references to the 'East
Road' and rephrased the passages; but on the map accompanying the
book I marked in its course. This seems now to have been the wrong
thing to do in both cases: for there certainly was an East Road, but its
course is unclear and its destination unknown. Beyond Aros going east

there is no indication of where it went: it is said in the passage cited above that it and the bridge by which it passed over Esgalduin were ancient works deriving from the 'peaceful days' before the return of Morgoth: it was not a road made by the Noldor for communication between the western realms and the Fëanorians. There is also no justification for marking it as turning S.E. after the Fords of Aros. Beyond Esgalduin going west it is said in this passage that travellers 'would keep as close as they could to the Fences of Doriath', which does not sound like the following of a beaten road.

The Dwarf-roads. Equally obscure is the question of the Dwarf-roads in Eastern Beleriand. In the earliest *Annals of Beleriand* (AB 1, IV.332) it was said that 'the Dwarves had of old a road into the West that came up along Eredlindon to the East and passed westward in the passes south of Mount Dolm and down the course of the River Ascar and over Gelion at the ford Sarn Athrad and so to Aros.' This agrees exactly with the (revised) course of the road on the 'Eastward Extension' of the first *Silmarillion* map (see IV.231, 336). It is seen from the central (original) part of the first map that it crossed Celon and Aros west of Nan Elmoth (which of course did not at that time yet exist) and so ran in a W.S.W. direction to the Thousand Caves (between pp. 220 and 221 in Vol.IV). But the course of the ancient route of the Dwarves after the passage of Sarn Athrad was never marked in on the second map – unless the vague line described in the notes on the map, p. 190, §68, is correctly interpreted as the Dwarf-road. If that is so, then its course had been changed to cross Aros much further to the south, and then to run northwards through the Forest of Region to Menegroth. But better evidence is provided in the late *Quenta Silmarillion* chapter *Of the Coming of Men into the West*, pp. 218–19, where it is said that 'Marach ... came down the Dwarf-road and settled his people in the country to the south and east of the dwellings of Baran son of Bëor': this was Estolad, 'the name ever after of the land east of Celon and south of Nan Elmoth'. On the disuse of the old Dwarf-road(s) into Beleriand after the coming of the Noldor see p. 121, commentary on GA §114.

It was said already in the original text of *Maeglin* (p. 321, §9) that 'the traffic of the Dwarves followed two roads, the northern of which, going towards Himring, passed nigh Nan Elmoth'. This was not altered in the late work on *Maeglin*; and on the primary map (already present when the photocopy was made) a line of faintly pencilled dots marked 'north road of Dwarves' (see p. 189, §50) runs E.S.E. from near Nan Elmoth, crosses Gelion some way south of the confluence of its arms, and then turns southward, running more or less parallel to the river. There is no trace of its course west or north of Nan Elmoth, and it is impossible to be sure whether any further continuation southwards or eastwards is marked beyond the point where it ends in my redrawing (p. 183).

The *Maeglin* papers do not resolve the course of this 'north road of the Dwarves', because (although all obviously belong to the same time) they evidently represent different conceptions.

(i) Writing of Eöl's journey to Nogrod, my father said:

From Elmoth to Gelion the land was, north of the Andram and the Falls below the last Ford over Gelion[8] (just above the inflow of the River Ascar from the Mountains), mostly rolling plain, with large regions of big trees without thickets. There were several beaten tracks made originally by Dwarves from Belegost and Nogrod, the best (most used and widest) being from the Little Ford past the north of Elmoth and to the Ford of Aros, it crossed the Bridge of Esgalduin but went no further for, if the Dwarves wished to visit Menegroth

This text then becomes altogether illegible. At the mention of 'the last Ford over Gelion' he added a note that the name *Sarn Athrad* of this ford must be changed to *Harathrad* 'South Ford', 'in contrast to the much used northern ford where the river was not yet very swift or deep, nearly due east of Eöl's house (72 miles distant)'; and against *Harathrad* here he wrote *Athrad Daer* ('the Great Ford').[9]

The implication seems to be that Eöl crossed Gelion at the northern ford, but this is not actually stated. There are two alterations to the photocopies of the map that relate to what is said here. One is the marking of a crossing over Gelion on square E 13 (p. 331), just above the point where the dotted line 'north road of Dwarves' crosses the river on the primary map, but without any track leading to this crossing. The other is at the ford of Sarn Athrad on the South-east section (p. 185), where on the photocopy my father wrote the name anew over the existing name, circled it, and wrote beside it *Harathrad*.

Beyond this nothing can be said of the north road of the Dwarves, and there is no indication in map or text of where, or indeed whether, it joined the 'south road'. It is indeed very puzzling that this northerly road, which in the text of *Maeglin* is said to have gone 'towards Himring' (as is to be expected: leading to territories of the Sons of Fëanor), is in the citation (i) just given said to pass the Ford of Aros and the Bridge of Esgalduin: for these crossings were on the East Road to the Brithiach (pp. 332–3). And apart from this, why should this road turn westward, and why should it go no further than the Bridge of Esgalduin?

(ii) On another page my father said that the journey from Eöl's house to Nan Elmoth in the direction of Nogrod was

through wilds (but not generally in difficult country for horses) without any made roads, but along a beaten track made by Dwarvish traders to the Sarn Athrad (the last point where the River

Gelion could be crossed) meeting the Dwarf-road up to and through the high pass in the mountains leading to Nogrod.

Here there is no mention of the northern ford, or indeed of the northern road; and it seems to be implied that Eöl would necessarily cross at Sarn Athrad (still so called, not Harathrad); moreover it is said that Eöl riding from Nan Elmoth to Nogrod took 'a beaten track made by Dwarvish traders' to Sarn Athrad that *met* the Dwarf-road up to the high pass.

In addition to the green dotted line entered on the photocopy of the map and stated to be the track of Maeglin and Aredhel fleeing from Nan Elmoth (p. 333), lines of red dots (represented on my redrawing as lines of closely-spaced dots) run from Nan Elmoth to the Ford of Aros, and also south-east from Nan Elmoth (p. 331). On the South-east section in the photocopy (see the redrawing of the primary map on p. 185) this red dotted line continues straight on across square G 13 to Sarn Athrad, and then coincides with the Dwarf-road up into the mountains, already present on the primary map. There is no note on the photocopy to explain what these lines represent, but there can be no doubt that they mark the journeys of Eöl (even though the dots continue all the way to the Ford of Aros, whereas he was arrested in his pursuit of Maeglin and Aredhel by the riders of Curufin 'ere he had ridden half the way over Himlad', p. 326, §16). Thus the line running from Nan Elmoth to Sarn Athrad clearly corresponds to what is said in citation (ii).

The absence of any really clear and full statement – indeed the suggestion that my father's ideas on the subject had not reached any stability, and the extreme doubtfulness of some of the markings on the map, led me to omit the course of the Dwarf-roads on the published map.

Apart from the matter of roads, there are some notes on names in these papers that show my father's dissatisfaction with old names already seen in the cases of *Isfin* and *Eöl* (pp. 317, 320): here those in question are *Gelion* and *Celon* (cf. his note on the primary map, p. 191, where he said that 'these river-names need revision to etymologizable words').[10] In notes in different places he proposed (in sequence) *Gelduin, Gevilon, Gevelon*, and also *Duin Daer* (cf. *Duin Dhaer* in the note on the primary map just referred to); *Gevelon* is derived from Dwarvish *Gabilān* 'great river'. On the back of one of the photocopies of the map he wrote:

The land east of it [the river] is Thorewilan [the *a* is underlined]. The Dwarvish name was also often translated *Duin Daer*. The name *Gabilān* was by the Dwarves given only to the River south of the Falls where (after the junction of the River with the Asgar coming from the Mountains) it became swift and was steadily increased in volume by the inflow of five more tributaries.

The name *Thargelion* on the primary map was changed to *Thargelian* (with the *a* underlined: p. 331): the latter form has appeared in emendations to the typescripts of *Maeglin* (p. 320). The form *Asgar* appeared in the 1930s (beside *Ascar*), see IV.209; cf. the *Etymologies*, V.386, stem SKAR: 'N[oldorin] *asgar, ascar* violent, rushing, impetuous'.

The substitution of the name *Limhir* for *Celon* has appeared as a proposal in one of the typescripts of *Maeglin* (p. 320), and among the 'geographical' papers is the following note:

Celon is too hackneyed a river-name. *Limhir* (the clear / sparkling river) – repeated in L.R. as were not unnaturally other names from Beleriand – is more suitable for the river, a tributary of the Aros and a clear *slender* stream coming down from the Hill of Himring.

The name *Limhir* does not occur in *The Lord of the Rings*, unless my father was referring to the Limlight, of which he said in *Guide to the Names in The Lord of the Rings* (*A Tolkien Compass*, ed. Lobdell, p. 188): 'The spelling -*light* indicates that this is a Common Speech name; but leave the obscured element *lim-* unchanged and translate -*light*: the adjective *light* here means "bright, clear".'

Lastly, it remains to mention the etymology of *Maeglin* found among these papers.

mik pierce: **mikrā* sharp-pointed (Q *miχa*, S **megr*): 'strong adjective' *maikā* sharp, penetrating, going deep in – often in transferred sense (as Q *hendumaika* sharp-eye, S *maegheneb* > *maecheneb*).

glim gleam, glint (usually of fine slender but bright shafts of light). Particularly applied to light of eyes; not Q. S *glintha-* glance (at), *glînn*.

From these two is derived the name *Maeglin*, since Maeglin had, even more than his father, very bright eyes, and was both physically very keen-sighted and mentally very penetrant, and quick to interpret the looks and gestures of people, and perceive their thoughts and purposes. The name was only given to him in boyhood, when these characteristics were recognized. His father till then was contented to call him *Iôn*, son. (His mother secretly gave him a N. Quenya name *Lómion* 'son of twilight'; and taught Maeglin the Quenya tongue, though Eöl had forbidden it.)

This development of the story of Maeglin from the form in which he had written it twenty years before seems to have been the last concentrated work that my father did on the actual narratives of the Elder days. Why he should have turned to this legend in particular I do not know; but one sees, in his minute consideration of the possibilities of the story, from the motives of the actors to the detail of terrain, of roads, of the speed and endurance of riders, how the focus of his vision of the old tales had changed.

NOTES

1 The words 'read (71) *Dor-na-Daerachas*' were added to the primary map later: see p. 187, §30, and note 6 below.

2 In another passage among these papers the Ford(s) of Aros are called *Arossiach*; this name was adopted on the map accompanying *The Silmarillion* and introduced into the text.

3 The text has 'at the S.W. corner', but this was a slip of the pen. It is stated elsewhere in these papers that the dwelling of Curufin and Celegorm was on a low hill at the S.E. corner of the Pass of Aglond, and on the photocopy map *Curufin* is marked with a circle on the most westerly of the lower heights about the Hill of Himring (p. 331, square D 11). – The form *Aglond* occurs in the discussion of the motives of Celegorm and Curufin (p. 328), beside *Aglon* in the interpolated narrative of Eöl's encounter with Curufin. On the map the name is written *Aglon(d*, which I retained on my redrawing (V.409) of the map as first made and lettered, in the belief that the variant *lond* was an original element. Although it looks to be so, it may be that the *(d* was added much later.

4 My father noted here: 'In spite of what Eöl said, it had in fact not been inhabited by Sindar before the coming of the Noldor'; and also that the name 'cool-plain' derived from the fact that 'it was higher in its middle part and felt often the chill northern airs through Aglon. It had no trees except in its southern part near the rivers.' In another place it is said that 'Himlad rose to a swelling highland at its centre (some 300 feet high at its flat top)'.

5 For the first mention of Dor Dínen (so spelt, as also on the map, not Dor Dhínen) see p. 194.

6 The primary map had no crossing marked on the Aros when the photocopy was made. The word *Ford* was put in after, or at the same time as, *Fords of Aros* was entered on the photocopy.

7 The name *Iant Iaur* was adopted from this text in *The Silmaril-lion*, both on the map and in a mention of 'the stone bridge of Iant Iaur' in Chapter 14, *Of Beleriand and its Realms*, p. 121 (for the original passage see p. 194).

8 The falls in Gelion below Sarn Athrad have not been referred to before, and indeed in QS Chapter 9 *Of Beleriand and its Realms* (V.262–3, §113; *The Silmarillion* p. 122) their existence is denied: 'Gelion had neither fall nor rapids throughout his course'.

9 On another page the following names are proposed as replacements for *Sarn Athrad*: '*Athrad i-Nogoth* [> *Negyth*] or *Athrad Dhaer*, "Ford of the Dwarves" or "Great Ford"'.

10 The fact that the note on the primary map (p. 191) saying that the names *Celon* and *Gelion* need to be changed bears (like the

addition of *Dor-na-Daerachas*, p. 187, §30) the number '71', clearly meaning the year 1971, suggests that all the late work on *Maeglin* belongs to that year. My father died two years later.

IV
OF THE ENTS AND THE EAGLES

This brief text belongs to the late, or last, period of my father's work, and must be dated at the earliest to 1958–9, but may well be later than that. The original draft is extant, a manuscript on two sides of a single sheet, written at great speed with very little correction in a script that is just legible. It is titled *Anaxartamel*.

This was followed by a text made on my father's later typewriter (see X.300) that expanded the first draft, but from which scarcely anything of any significance in that draft was excluded. It bears no title. In the published *Silmarillion* it was used to form the second part of Chapter 2 *Of Aulë and Yavanna*, pp. 44–6, beginning at the words 'Now when Aulë laboured in the making of the Dwarves ...' This was of course a purely editorial combination.

The published text followed the typescript with very little deviation, except in the matter of 'thou' and 'you' forms, about which my father was initially uncertain, as he was also in the text concerning Aulë and the Dwarves which forms the first part of the chapter in the published *Silmarillion* (see p. 210). In the manuscript draft he used 'you' throughout; in the typescript he used both 'you' and 'thy, hast' in the opening paragraphs, but then 'you, your' exclusively, subsequently correcting the inconsistencies. As in the first part of the chapter 'thou, thee, thy' forms were adopted in the published work.

There are two amanuensis typescripts, independent of each other, taken from the typescript after all corrections had been made. They have no textual value, except that on one of them my father pencilled the title *Of the Ents and the Eagles*, and on the other the title *Anaxartaron Onyalië*.

NOTES

In these notes, which are largely confined to differences of reading, the original draft is called A, the typescript B, and the published text S.

When Yavanna went to Manwë (p. 45) 'she did not betray the counsel of Aulë': the meaning of this is that Yavanna did not reveal anything to Manwë of the making of the Dwarves; in the first part of the chapter (p. 43) 'fearing that the other Valar might blame his work, he wrought in secret', and the intervention of Ilúvatar (who 'knew what was done') was directly to Aulë. The word *betray* in S is an editorial alteration of *bewray* in A and B.

'But the *kelvar* can flee or defend themselves, whereas the *olvar* that grow cannot' (p. 45): in B there is a marginal note against *kelvar*, 'animals, all living things that move', which was omitted in S. In A these words were not used, but a blank space was left where *kelvar* stands in B. Immediately following this, A has: 'Long in the growing, swift in the felling, and unless they pay toll with fruit upon the bough little mourned at the ending, as even among the Valar I have seen'; in B the last phrase became 'as I have seen even among the Maiar in Middle-earth', but this was at once rejected. The final text of the passage is as in S.

In Yavanna's following words beginning 'I lifted up the branches of great trees ...' B has 'and some sang to Eru amid the wind and the rain and the glitter of the Sun'; the last words were omitted in S on account of the implication that the Sun existed from the beginning of Arda.

In the passage describing Manwë's experience of the renewal of the Vision of the Ainur (p. 46; entirely lacking in A) the text of B as typed read: 'but it was not now remote, for he was himself in the midst, and yet he saw that all was upheld by the hand of Eru and that too was within', subsequently changed to the reading of S (in which *Eru* > *Ilúvatar*).

In the words of Eru recounted by Manwë to Yavanna on Ezellohar the sentence 'For a time: while the Firstborn are in their power, and while the Secondborn are young' was bracketed for exclusion in B, but was retained in S.

In Manwë's last speech, 'In the mountains the Eagles shall house, and hear the voices of those who call upon us' was first written in B: '... and hear the voices of those who call upon me, and of those who gainsay me.'

At the end of a draft letter dated September 1963, of which a passage is cited on p. 353, my father added in a very rough note (given in *Letters* p. 335):

No one knew whence they (Ents) came or first appeared. The High Elves said that the Valar did not mention them in the 'Music'. But some (Galadriel) were [of the] opinion that when Yavanna discovered the mercy of Eru to Aulë in the matter of the Dwarves, she besought Eru (through Manwë) asking him to give life to things made of living things not stone, and that the Ents were either souls sent to inhabit trees, or else that slowly took the likeness of trees owing to their inborn love of trees.

With the words 'the Ents were either souls sent to inhabit trees' cf. the words of Eru in the text (p. 46): 'When the Children awake, then the thought of Yavanna will awake also, and it will summon spirits from afar, and they will go among the *kelvar* and the *olvar*, and some will dwell therein ...' It seems likely enough that the note on the draft letter and the writing of *Anaxartaron Onyalië* belong to much the same time.

V
THE TALE OF YEARS

The Tale of Years was an evolving work that accompanied successive stages in the development of the *Annals*. I have given it no place hitherto in *The History of Middle-earth* (but see X.49), because its value to the narrative of the Elder Days is very small until towards the end of the later (post-*Lord of the Rings*) version, when it becomes a document of importance; but here some very brief account of it must be given.

The earliest form is a manuscript with this title that sets out in very concise form the major events of the Elder Days. The dates throughout are in all but perfect accord with those given in the pre-*Lord of the Rings* texts 'The Later Annals of Valinor' and 'The Later Annals of Beleriand' (AV 2 and AB 2). Since this *Tale of Years* was obviously written as an accompaniment to and at the same time as those versions of the *Annals*, adding nothing to them, I did not include it in Volume V.

Much later a new version of *The Tale of Years* was made, and this alone will concern us here. It very clearly belongs with the major work on the *Annals* carried out in 1951(–2), issuing in the last versions, the *Annals of Aman* and the *Grey Annals*. My father subsequently made a typescript text of it, but this obviously belongs to the same period.

The manuscript of this version as originally written was a very good clear text, but it was heavily corrected, interpolated, and rewritten in many stages; and since it was my father's working chronology during that period the dates, more especially in the first or Valinórean part, were changed so often, with bewildering movements back and forth, as to make the evolution of the chronology extremely difficult to understand. The important point, so far as the Valinórean part is concerned, is that the dates in the manuscript of *The Tale of Years* as originally written were essentially the same as those in the *Annals of Aman* as originally written; while modification to that chronology went together step by step in the two texts. In the case of AAm I noted (X.47–8) that with so many alterations to the dates it was impracticable to do more than give the final chronology, and in the case of *The Tale of Years* the evolution is even more complex. In the result, the latter work is of very little independent value in this part; there are however a small number of matters that should be recorded.

In the manuscript as it was originally written the Elder Days began with the Awakening of the Elves: 'Here begin the Elder Days, or the First Age of the Children of Ilúvatar'; but 'the Elder Days' was struck out and does not appear in the typescript. Further on in *The Tale of Years* there is recorded a difference in application of the term 'Elder Days' in respect of their ending (a difference not, to my knowledge, found elsewhere): after the entry for V.Y.1500 'Fingolfin and Inglor cross the Straits of Ice' (this being the date in the *Grey Annals*, p. 29) it is said in the manuscript:

> Here end the Elder Days with the new reckoning of time, according to some. But most lore-masters give that name also to the years of the war with Morgoth until his overthrow and casting forth.
> So far did Quennar Onótimo compile this count and compute the years.
> Here follows the continuation which Pengoloð made in Eressëa.

In the typescript text this was retained, but with this difference: 'Here end the Elder Days, with the new reckoning of Time, according to the Lore-masters of Valinor. But the Lore-masters of the Noldor give that name also to the years of the war with Morgoth ...'

Quennar Onótimo appears in the *Annals of Aman* (see X.49), where he is cited as the source for the passage on the reckoning of time. This passage was marked for transference to *The Tale of Years*, and appears in manuscript pages (one of which is reproduced as the frontispiece to Vol.X, *Morgoth's Ring*) of a new opening of the work written in forms so splendid that it is not surprising that it did not proceed very far.

The authorship of the *Annals* underwent many changes. In the earliest *Annals of Valinor* (AV 1, IV.263) Pengolod is named as the author, and also of the *Annals of Beleriand* (AB 1), but the conception soon entered that Rúmil was the author of the first part of AV and that the work was only completed by Pengolod: in AV 2 Rúmil's part ends with the return to Valinor of those Noldor, led by Finrod (Finarfin), who did not continue the northward journey after the Doom of Mandos (see V.116, 123). In the first form of the opening of the *Annals of Aman* (X.48) it is said that they 'were written by Quennar i Onótimo, who learned much, and borrowed much also, from Rúmil; but they were enlarged by Pengoloð'. In the second version of the opening, however, Rúmil alone is named: 'Here begin the Annals of Aman, which Rúmil made'. In the fine manuscript pages of the opening of *The Tale of Years* referred to above there is no ascription of authorship (apart from the naming of Quennar Onótimo as the author of the passage on the reckoning of time).

A few points of content in this part remain to be mentioned. In the entry for 1125 (cf. X.83) the manuscript reads: 'The foremost of the Eldar reach Beleriand. They are filled with a great fear of the Sea and for long refuse to go further. Oromë departs to Valinor to seek counsel.' This was not emended, but in the typescript this entry appears in its place: 'The foremost of the Eldar reach the coastlands of Middle-earth and that country which was after named Eglador.

Thereof Beleriand was the larger part.' This is apparently to be related to one of the entries *Eglador* added to the map: see p. 186, §14; but the concluding phrase is mysterious.

In this connection, the entry for the year 1150 reads thus in the manuscript: 'The Teleri of Olwë's host at length also depart over Sea. The friends of Elwë remain behind: these are the Eglath, the Forsaken, or the Sindar (the Grey-elves).' The form *Eglath* is found in the annal for this year in AAm (X.85); but on the manuscript of *The Tale of Years* it was emended subsequently to *Eglim*, while in the typescript the form is *Eglir*: it seems that neither of these occur elsewhere (see pp. 365, 379).

Lastly, the entry for 1497 begins with the words 'Morgoth from a new stronghold at Angband assails the Grey-elves of Beleriand.' At this stage the story was still that Angband was built on the ruins of Utumno (see GA §35 and commentary, pp. 15, 111). My father pencilled on the typescript (referring to the interval since Morgoth's return from Valinor in 1495): 'Too small a time for Morgoth to build Angband', and also 'Time too small, should be 10 at least or 20 Valian Years'. This would have required substantial modification of the chronology; and it seems conceivable that this consideration was a factor in the emergence of the later story that Utumno and Angband were distinct fortresses in different regions, both built by Morgoth in ancient days (X.156, §12).

Of the latter or Beleriandic part of *The Tale of Years* there is little to say until the last entries are reached. The chronology agrees closely with that of the *Grey Annals*, including the revised stories of the origins of Gondolin and of Eöl, and the brief entries (agreeing with GA in such names as *Galion* for *Galdor* and *Glindûr* for *Maeglin*) add nothing to the major text. There is in fact only one point that need be noticed: in the entry for 495 my father added to the manuscript 'Tuor leaves Dorlómin, dwells a year at Falasquil.' The last five words were subsequently struck out. *Falasquil* was the name of the cove in the sea-coast where Tuor dwelt for a while in the tale of *The Fall of Gondolin* (II.152); and it was written also onto the map (see p. 181, §5). It seems quite likely that both these additions were made at the time when my father was writing the later *Tale of Tuor*, and had been rereading the old tale (as he clearly did, II.203); but *Falasquil* does not appear in the later *Tuor*.

Subsequent very cursory emendation of the typescript brought in the radically changed legend of the Coming of the Edain, revision of names to later forms, and additions to the story of Túrin.

But from the point where the *Grey Annals* were abandoned *The Tale of Years* becomes a major source for the end of the Elder Days, and indeed in almost all respects the only source deriving from the time following the completion of *The Lord of the Rings*, woefully inadequate as it is. As the manuscript was originally made (in which condition I will distinguish it as 'A') the entries from 500 to the end, very brief, followed the first (pre-*Lord of the Rings*) version of *The Tale of Years* (see p. 342) closely: my father clearly had that in front of him, and did no more than make a fair copy with fuller entries, introducing virtually no new matter or dates not found in AB 2 (V.141–4). It will make things clearer, however, to give the text of the entries for those years as they were first written.

500   Birth of Ëarendil in Gondolin.

501   Making of the Naugla-mír. Thingol quarrels with the Dwarves.

502   The Dwarves invade Doriath. Thingol is slain and his realm ended. Melian returns to Valinor. Beren destroys the Dwarf-host at Rath-lóriel.

506   The Second Kin-slaying.

507   The Fall of Gondolin. Death of King Turgon.

508   The gathering of the remnants of the Elves at the Mouths of Sirion is begun.

524   Tuor and Idril depart over Sea.

525   The voyages of Ëarendil begun.

529   The Third and Last Kin-slaying.

533   Ëarendil comes to Valinor.

540   The last free Elves and remnants of the Fathers of Men are driven out of Beleriand and take refuge in the Isle of Balar.

547   The host of the Valar comes up out of the West. Fionwë son of Manwë lands in Beleriand with great power.

550–597   The last war of the Elder Days, and the Great Battle, is begun. In this war Beleriand is broken and destroyed. Morgoth is at last utterly overcome, and Angband is unroofed and unmade. Morgoth is bound, and the last two Silmarils are regained.

597   Maidros and Maglor, last surviving sons of Fëanor, seize the Silmarils. Maidros perishes. The Silmarils are lost in fire and sea.

600   The Elves and the Fathers of Men depart from Middle-earth and pass over Sea.
    Here ends the First Age of the Children of Ilúvatar.

The only points of any significance in which this differs from what was said in AB 2 or the original version of *The Tale of Years* that accompanied it are the additions in the entry 540 of the statement that when 'the last free Elves' took refuge in the Isle of Balar they were accompanied by 'remnants of the Fathers of Men', and in the entry 600 that the Fathers of Men departed from Middle-earth with the Elves and passed over the Sea.

In the next stage, which I will call 'B', many corrections and interpolations and alterations of date were made to A; I give here the text in this form, so far as is necessary.

501   Return of Húrin.
502   After seven years' service Tuor weds Idril of Gondolin.
      Making of the Naugla-mír. Thingol quarrels with the Dwarves.
503   Birth of Ëarendil in Gondolin.
      The Dwarves invade Doriath. Thingol is slain and his realm ended. Melian takes Nauglamír to Beren and Lúthien and then returns to Valinor. Celegorm and Curufin destroy the Dwarf-host at Sarn-athrad in Rath-lóriel; and are wroth to find the Silmaril not there. Dior goes to Doriath.
505   (Spring) Second death of Beren, and Lúthien dies also. Dior Thingol's heir wears Silmaril [struck out: and returns to Doriath].
509   (Spring) Second Kinslaying. Last warning of Ulmo to Gondolin.
510   The fall of Gondolin at Midsummer. Death of King Turgon.
511   The gathering of the remnants of the Elves at the Mouths of Sirion is begun.

In the remaining entries some of the dates were altered but very few changes were made to the content; the text of A need not therefore be repeated.

533   The date of Ëarendil's coming to Valinor was changed several times, apparently > 536 > 540 > 542.
547   The coming of the host of the Valar was moved to 545.
550–597   The dates of 'the last war of the Elder Days' were changed to 545–587, and after the last words of the original entry the following was added: 'Ancalagon is cast down by Ëarendil and all save two of the Dragons are destroyed.'
597   This entry was changed to 587.
600   This final entry was changed to 590, and the following was added to it: 'Morgoth is thrust from Arda into the Outer Dark.'

'Here ends the First Age of the Children of Ilúvatar' was changed to: 'Here end the Elder Days with the passing of Melkor, according to the reckoning of most lore-masters; here ends also the First Age . . .'

The hastily made alterations and additions to the entry 503 (502 in A) introduced major new turns into the story as it had been told in all the versions: the tale of *The Nauglafring* (II.238), the *Sketch of the Mythology* (IV.33), the *Quenta* (IV.134), and AB 2 (V.141). There it was Beren, after his return from the dead, who with his host of Elves ambushed the Dwarves at Sarn-athrad, and took from them the Nauglamír in which was set the Silmaril; now it becomes Celegorm and Curufin who fought the battle at Sarn-athrad – but the Silmaril was not there, because Melian had taken it from Menegroth to Beren and Lúthien in Ossiriand. In the old tale, Gwendelin (Melian), coming to the Land of the Dead that Live after the battle, was wrathful when she saw Lúthien wearing the Necklace of the Dwarves, since it was made of accursed gold, and the Silmaril itself was unhallowed from its having been set in Morgoth's crown; while in the *Sketch* (probably) and in the *Quenta* (explicitly) it was Melian who told Beren of the approach of the Dwarves coming from Doriath and enabled the ambush to be prepared (her warning afterwards, when the Necklace of the Dwarves had been recovered, against the Silmaril being retained).

The entrance of Celegorm and Curufin into the story seems to have arisen in the act of emending the text; for my father first added to the original entry ('Beren destroys the Dwarf-host at Rath-lóriel') the words 'and is wounded in battle', referring to Beren (cf. the *Tale*, II.237: 'Beren got many hurts'). He then at once changed 'Beren destroys' to 'Celegorm and Curufin destroy' and 'is wounded in battle' to 'are wroth to find the Silmaril not there'.

In the original entry in A 'at Rath-lóriel' was just a slip for 'in'; but the replacement 'at Sarn-athrad in Rath-lóriel' is strange, for Sarn-athrad was not a ford over that river (Ascar) but over Gelion, and so remained in the latest writing, though the name was changed (see p. 335).

In 505, the striking out of Dior's return to Doriath preceded its inclusion under 503. There has never been any mention of a further warning of Ulmo (509) since the coming of Tuor to Gondolin. On the addition in 545–587 concerning Ancalagon see V.329, §18; and with the reference to the end of the Elder Days 'according to the reckoning of most lore-masters' cf. p. 343.

The third stage was the striking out of the whole manuscript from the year 400 almost to the end, and its replacement by a new version ('C'), which I give here for the same period, from the return of Húrin from Angband: this is a clear text with some later changes to the dates (changes which largely return the dates to those in B).

501   Return of Húrin from captivity. He goes to Nargothrond and seizes the treasure of Glaurung.

502   Making of the Nauglamír. Thingol quarrels with the Dwarves.

503   The Dwarves of Belegost and Nogrod invade Doriath. Thingol is slain, and his realm ended. The Dwarves carry off the Dragon-gold, but Melian escaped and carried off the Nauglamír and the Silmaril, and brought it to Beren and Lúthien. Then she returned to Valinor; but Lúthien wore the

Silmaril. Now Curufin and Celegorm hearing of the sack of Menegroth ambushed the Dwarves at the fords of Ascar and defeated them; but the Dwarves cast the gold into the river, which was after named Rathlóriel. Great was the chagrin of the Sons of Fëanor to discover that the Silmaril was not with the Dwarves; but they dared not assail Lúthien.

Dior goes to Doriath and endeavours to reestablish the realm.

504 [> 502] Tuor wedded Idril Celebrindal Turgon's daughter of Gondolin.

505 [> 503] Birth of Earendil Half-elven in Gondolin (Spring). Here a messenger brought the Silmaril by night to Dior in Doriath, and he wore it; and by its power Doriath revived for a while. But it is believed that in this year Lúthien and Beren passed away, for they were never heard of again on earth: mayhap the Silmaril hastened their end, for the flame of the beauty of Lúthien as she wore it was too bright for mortal lands.

511 [> 509] The Second Kinslaying. The Sons of Fëanor assail[ed] Dior, and he was slain; slain also were Celegorm and Curufin and Cranthir. Eldún and Elrún sons of Dior were left in the woods to starve. Elwing escaped and came with the Silmaril to the Mouths of Sirion. Ulmo sends a last warning to Gondolin, which now alone is left; but Turgon will have no alliance with any after the kinslaying of Doriath. Maeglin Eöl's son, sister-son of Turgon, was taken in the hills, and betrayed Gondolin to Morgoth.

512 [> 510] The Fall of Gondolin. Death of King Turgon.

513 [> 511] Tuor and Idril bring Earendil and the remnant of Gondolin to the Mouths of Sirion.

527 [> 530] Earendil weds Elwing. Unquiet of Ulmo comes upon Tuor. Tuor and Idril depart over Sea, and are heard of no more on earth.

528 [> 530 > 534] Voyages of Earendil begin.

[Added entry:] 528 [> 532] Elros and Elrond twin sons of Earendil born.

532 [> 534 > 538] The Third and Last Kinslaying. The Havens of Sirion destroyed and Elros and Elrond sons of Earendel taken captive, but are fostered with care by Maidros. Elwing carries away the Silmaril, and comes to Earendel [> Earendil] in the likeness of a bird.

536 [> 540 > 542] Earendil comes to Valinor.

Here the replacement text C comes to an end. In the entries 400–499 in C (not given here) this text is so close in every date and detail of narrative to the Grey Annals as to be scarcely an independent document; and *The Tale of Years* was beginning to turn in on itself, so to speak, and to become 'Annals' again. In the entries given above, where we reach narrative not treated in GA and where AB 2 is otherwise the latest source, it is much to be regretted that my father did not allow this tendency even fuller scope, and did not extend into a more substantial narrative of Celegorm and Curufin at Sarn Athrad, the revival of Doriath, and the Second Kinslaying.

I add a few notes on particular points.

503 The ford at which the Dwarves were ambushed, not now itself named, is still over Ascar, not Gelion (see p. 347). The statement that the Dwarves 'cast the gold into the river' is at variance with the story told in the *Sketch* and the *Quenta* (where this was done by Beren and the Green-elves), and was perhaps a conscious return to the tale of *The Nauglafring* (II.237), in which the gold fell into the river with the bodies of the Dwarves who bore it, or else was cast into the water by Dwarves seeking to reach the banks.

505 With the changed dating of this entry the whole narrative of the invasion of Doriath, the battle at the ford, the coming of Dior to Doriath, the deaths of Beren and Lúthien, and the bringing of the Silmaril to Dior, is comprised within the single year 503. – The brief revival of Doriath under Dior has not before been associated with the Silmaril; cf. what is said of its presence at the Havens of Sirion (pp. 351, 354). On the probable association of the Silmaril with the deaths of Beren and Lúthien (though of an entirely different nature from that suggested here) see IV.63, 190.

511 On the fate of Dior's sons cf. AB 2 (V.142), where it is told that they 'were taken captive by the evil men of Maidros' following, and they were left to starve in the woods; but Maidros lamented the cruel deed, and sought unavailingly for them.' – It seems possible that 'Turgon will have no alliance with any' was intended to be 'no alliance with any son of Fëanor'; cf. the *Quenta* (IV.140): 'Tidings Turgon heard of Thorndor concerning the slaying of Dior, Thingol's heir, and thereafter he shut his ear to word of the woes without; and he vowed to march never at the side of any son of Fëanor.'

528 (added entry) On the statement that Elros and Elrond were twins see V.152. It is stated in *The Line of Elros* (*Unfinished Tales* p. 218) that Elros was born 58 years before the Second Age began: this agrees with the changed date here (532) and the end of the First Age in 590 (p. 346).

Finally, we come to stage 'D', the typescript of *The Tale of Years*; but before turning to the entries beginning with the return of Húrin there are two pencilled entries on the typescript at a slightly earlier point which must be noticed:

497 Dior weds   of the Green-elves > Dior weds Nimloth.
500 Birth of the twin sons of Dior, Elrún and Eldún.

In connection with the first of these, there is an isolated note (it was written in fact on the back of the single page concerning the Dragon-helm of Dorlómin referred to on pp. 140, 143):

Dior born (in Tol Galen?) c.470. He appears in Doriath after its ruin, and is welcomed by Melian with his wife Elulin of Ossiriand.

On this note see p. 353, year 504. The fourth letter of *Elulin* is not perfectly certain. – In addition, the name of Dior's wife is also given as *Lindis*: see pp. 351, 353.

The name *Nimloth* was adopted in the published *Silmarillion* (see p. 234, where she is said to be 'kinswoman of Celeborn') on account of its appearance in the series of Elvish genealogies which can be dated to December 1959 (p. 229). This table gives the descendants of Elwë (Thingol) and of his younger brother Elmo, of whom it is said that he was 'beloved of Elwë with whom he remained.' On one side of the table (descent from Elwë) the wife of Dior Eluchil (Thingol's heir) is Nimloth 'sister of Celeborn'. Similarly on the other side, Elmo's son is Galaðon, and Galaðon has two sons, Galathil and Celeborn 'prince of Doriath', and a daughter Nimloth, wife of Dior Eluchil. But on the same table Nimloth wife of Dior also appears as the daughter of Galathil (thus in the first case she was the second cousin of Dior, and in the latter the third cousin of Elwing). It is clear from rough pencillings on this page that my father was uncertain about this, and it looks as if Nimloth as niece of Celeborn was his second thought. I referred to this genealogy in *Unfinished Tales*, p. 233, but did not mention the alternative placing of Nimloth as Celeborn's sister.

On the second of these late additions to the typescript, the birth of Eldún and Elrún in the year 500, see pp. 257 and 300, note 16.

I give now the text of the typescript of *The Tale of Years* in its concluding entries. At the end the typescript becomes manuscript, and it is convenient to distinguish the two parts as 'D 1' and 'D 2'.

501   Húrin is released from captivity. He goes to Nargothrond and seizes the treasure of Glaurung. He takes the treasure to Menegroth and casts it at the feet of Thingol.

502   The Nauglamír is wrought of the treasure of Glaurung, and the Silmaril is hung thereon. Thingol quarrels with the Dwarves who had wrought for him the Necklace.

503   The Dwarves of Belegost and Nogrod invade Doriath. King Elu Thingol is slain and his realm ended. Melian escapes and carries away the Nauglamír and the Silmaril, and brings them to Beren and Lúthien. She then forsook Middle-earth and returned to Valinor.

Curufin and Celegorm, hearing of the sack of Menegroth, ambushed the Dwarves at the Fords of Ascar as they sought to carry off the Dragon-gold to the mountains. The Dwarves were defeated with great loss, but they cast the gold into the river, which was therefore after named Rathlóriel. Great was the anger of the sons of Fëanor to discover that the Silmaril was not with the Dwarves; but they dared not to assail Lúthien. Dior goes to Doriath and endeavours to recover the realm of Thingol.

In this year, or according to others in the year before, Tuor wedded Idril Celebrindal Turgon's daughter of Gondolin; and in the spring of the year after was born in Gondolin Eärendil Halfelven. [*This paragraph was struck out later with the words* Must be placed in 502.]

In the autumn of this year a messenger brought by night the Silmaril to Dior in Doriath.

Here the typewritten text D 1 ends abruptly near the head of a page, but is continued in very rough manuscript for some distance (D 2), though not so far as the end of version C (which itself did not go by any means so far as B).

503 Elwing the White daughter of Dior born in Ossiriand.

504 Dior returns to Doriath, and with the power of the Silmaril restores it; but Melian departed to Valinor. Dior now publicly wore the Nauglamír and the Jewel.

505 The sons of Fëanor hearing news of the Silmaril that it is in Doriath hold council. Maidros restrains his brethren, but a message is sent to Dior demanding the Jewel. Dior returns no answer.

506 Celegorn inflames the brethren, and they prepare an assault on Doriath. They come up at unawares in winter.

506–507 At Yule Dior fought the sons of Fëanor on the east marches of Doriath, and was slain. There fell also Celegorn (by Dior's hand) and Curufin and Cranthir. The cruel servants of Celegorn seize Dior's sons (Elrún and Eldún) and leave them to starve in the forest. (Nothing certain is known of their fate, but some say that the birds succoured them, and led them to Ossir.) [*In margin*: Maidros repenting seeks unavailingly for the children of Dior.] The Lady Lindis escaped with Elwing, and came hardly to Ossir, with the Necklace and the Jewel. Thence hearing the rumour she fled to the Havens of Sirion.

509 Maeglin captured by spies of Melkor (Sauron?).

510 Midsummer. Assault and sack of Gondolin, owing to treachery of Maeglin who revealed where it lay.

511 Exiles of Gondolin (Tuor, Idril and Eärendil &c.) reach Sirion, which now prospers in the power of the Silmaril.

512 Sons of Fëanor learn of the uprising of the New Havens, and that the Silmaril is there, but Maidros forswears his oath.

525   The Unquiet of Ulmo came upon Tuor and he built a ship Ëarámë, and departed into the West with Idril (and Voronwë?) and is heard of in no tale since. Eärendil wedded Elwing and became Lord of the men of the Havens.

527   Torment fell upon Maidros and his brethren (Maglor, Damrod and Diriel) because of their unfulfilled oath.

Here the text ends, halfway down the last page. A commentary on it follows.

501   In the original story of Húrin's coming to Menegroth in the *Tale of Turambar* (II.114–15) he with his 'band' or 'host' of 'wild Elves' brought the treasure of Nargothrond in a huge assemblage of sacks and boxes, and they 'cast down that treasury at the king's feet.' So also in the *Sketch of the Mythology* (IV.32) 'Húrin casts the gold at Thingol's feet', without however any indication of how the gold was brought to Doriath; but in the *Quenta* (IV.132) 'Húrin went unto Thingol and sought his aid, and the folk of Thingol bore the treasure to the Thousand Caves' (on the unsatisfactory nature of this version see IV.188). In AB 2 (V.141) 'Húrin brought the gold to Thingol.' See further p. 258.

503   Against 'The Dwarves of Belegost and Nogrod invade Doriath' my father pencilled an X and the single word 'cannot': i.e., the Dwarves *could not* pass the Girdle of Melian. In the old sources the protective magic was defeated by the device of a treacherous Elf (in the *Tale*) or Elves (in the *Sketch* and the *Quenta*); but since the *Quenta* the question had never again come to the surface. In this connection there is a page of rough notes, such as my father often made when meditating on a story at large, concerned with the 'Túrins Saga' (such as 'An account of Beleg and his bow must be put in at the point where Túrin first meets him', and 'Túrin must be *faithless* to Gwindor – for his character is throughout that of a man of good will, kind and loyal, who is carried away by emotion, especially wrath ...'); and among these and written at the same time, though entirely unconnected, is the following:

> Doriath cannot be entered by a hostile army! Somehow it must be contrived that Thingol is lured outside or induced to go to war beyond his borders and is there slain by the Dwarves. Then Melian departs, and the girdle being removed Doriath is ravaged by the Dwarves.

The word 'cannot' may well have been written against the entry for 503 in *The Tale of Years* at the same time as this.

The story that it was Celegorm and Curufin who ambushed the Dwarves at 'the Fords of Ascar' is repeated without change from the previous version C (p. 348). There is a passing reference to a similar story (for in this case it was Caranthir, not Celegorm and Curufin) in the post-*Lord of the Rings* text *Concerning Galadriel and Celeborn*. This was published in *Unfinished Tales* in a 'retold', somewhat selective form for the purposes of that section of the book; and in the passage (p. 235) saying that Celeborn had no love for any Dwarves, and never forgave them for their part in the destruction of Doriath ('passing over Morgoth's part in this (by angering of Húrin), and Thingol's own faults'), my father proposed rather than stated that only the Dwarves of Nogrod took part in the assault, and that they were 'almost entirely destroyed by Caranthir'.

This was not, however, his final view, as it appears. In a letter of 1963 (*Letters* no.247, p. 334) he wrote that he could 'foresee' one event in the Elder Days in which the Ents took a part:

> It was in Ossiriand ... that Beren and Lúthien dwelt for a while after Beren's return from the Dead. Beren did not show himself among mortals again, except once. He intercepted a dwarf-army that had descended from the mountains, sacked the realm of Doriath and slain King Thingol, Lúthien's father, carrying off a great booty, including Thingol's necklace upon which hung the Silmaril. There was a battle about a ford across one of the Seven Rivers of Ossir, and the Silmaril was recovered ... It seems clear that Beren, who had no army, received the aid of the Ents – and that would not make for love between Ents and Dwarves.

In this it is also notable that the old story that the Dwarves took the Nauglamír from Menegroth reappears (see pp. 346–7).

Beneath the *-lóriel* of *Rathlóriel* my father wrote in pencil: *lórion* (*Rathlórion* was the original form of this river-name), but he struck this out and then wrote *mallen*, sc. *Rathmallen* (cf. *Rathmalad* (?) on the map, p. 191, §69).

504 Dior's return to Doriath has been given already under 503 in D 1, the typescript part of the text. – In the B and C versions (pp. 346–7) Melian brought the Silmaril to Beren and Lúthien in Ossiriand and then departed to Valinor, and this is said also in D 1 (p. 350). The present entry in D 2, a year later, repeats that Melian went to Valinor, and the suggestion is that she was in Doriath when Dior came; cf. the note cited on p. 350: 'Dior ... appears in Doriath after its ruin, and is welcomed by Melian'. This seems clearly to have been the story in AB 1 (IV.307) and AB 2 (V.141–2). But it is impossible to be certain of anything with such compressed entries.

506–507 *Ossir*: Ossiriand. – On Maidros' unavailing search for Elrún and Eldún see p. 349, year 511.

The Lady Lindis: Lindis appears elsewhere as the name of Dior's wife (see p. 257). The sentence 'Thence hearing the rumour she fled to the Havens of Sirion' presumably means that Lindis heard the rumour that the survivors of Gondolin had reached the Havens (an event recorded in this text under the year 511).

510 The story that the site of Gondolin was revealed to Morgoth by Maeglin was later changed: see pp. 272–3 and note 30.

511   Cf. the *Quenta* (IV.152): 'for them seemed that in that jewel lay the gift of bliss and healing that had come upon their houses and their ships'; also AB 2 (V.143).

512   That Maidros 'forswore his oath' was stated in AB 2 (V.142); in this and the following entries my father was following that text very closely (indeed D 2 is based upon it throughout).

525   The suggestion that Voronwë was the companion of Tuor and Idril on their voyage into the West is notable. He (Bronweg / Voronwë) was originally Eärendil's fellow-mariner (IV.38, 150). Cf. Tuor's words to him in the later *Tale of Tuor* (*Unfinished Tales* p. 33): 'far from the Shadow your long road shall lead you, and your hope shall return to the Sea.'

It would be interesting to know when this manuscript conclusion D 2 was written. It looks as if it belongs with some of the alterations and additions made to the typescript in earlier entries, particularly those pertaining to the story of Túrin, and in these there are suggestions that they derive from the period of my father's work on the *Narn*. But this is very uncertain; and if it is so, it is the more remarkable that he should have based these entries so closely on the old pre-*Lord of the Rings* annals.

★

A note on Chapter 22 Of the Ruin of Doriath
in the published Silmarillion

Apart from a few matters of detail in texts and notes that have not been published, all that my father ever wrote on the subject of the ruin of Doriath has now been set out: from the original story told in the *Tale of Turambar* (II.113–15) and the *Tale of the Nauglafring* (II.221 ff.), through the *Sketch of the Mythology* (IV.32–3, with commentary 61–3) and the *Quenta* (IV.132–4, with commentary 187–91), together with what little can be gleaned from *The Tale of Years* and a very few later references (see especially pp. 352–3). If these materials are compared with the story told in *The Silmarillion* it is seen at once that this latter is fundamentally changed, to a form for which in certain essential features there is no authority whatever in my father's own writings.

There were very evident problems with the old story. Had he ever turned to it again, my father would undoubtedly have found some solution other than that in the *Quenta* to the question, How was the treasure of Nargothrond brought to Doriath? There, the curse that Mîm laid upon the gold at his death 'came upon the possessors in this wise. Each one of Húrin's company died or was slain in quarrels upon the road; but Húrin went unto Thingol and sought his aid, and the folk of Thingol bore the treasure to the Thousand Caves.' As I said in IV.188, 'it ruins the gesture, if Húrin must get the king himself to send for the gold with which he is *then* to be humiliated'. It seems to me most likely (but this is mere speculation) that my father would have reintroduced the outlaws from the old *Tales* (II.113–15, 222–3) as the bearers of the treasure (though not the fierce battle between them and the Elves of the Thousand Caves): in the scrappy writings at the end of *The Wanderings of Húrin* Asgon and his companions reappear after the disaster in Brethil and go with Húrin to Nargothrond (pp. 306–7).

How he would have treated Thingol's behaviour towards the Dwarves is impossible to say. That story was only once told fully, in the *Tale of the Nauglafring*, in which the conduct of Tinwelint (precursor of Thingol) was wholly at variance with the later conception of the king (see II.245–6). In the *Sketch* no more is said of the matter than that the Dwarves were 'driven away without payment', while in the *Quenta* 'Thingol ... scanted his promised reward for their labour; and bitter words grew between them, and there was battle in Thingol's halls'. There seems to be no clue or hint in later writing (in *The Tale of Years* the same bare phrase is used in all the versions: 'Thingol quarrels with the Dwarves'), unless one is seen in the words quoted from *Concerning Galadriel and Celeborn* on p. 353: Celeborn in his view of the destruction of Doriath ignored Morgoth's part in it 'and Thingol's own faults'.

In *The Tale of Years* my father seems not to have considered the problem of the passage of the Dwarvish host into Doriath despite the Girdle of Melian, but in writing the word 'cannot' against the D version (p. 352) he showed that he regarded the story he had outlined as impossible, for that reason. In another place he sketched a possible solution *(ibid.)*: 'Somehow it must be contrived that Thingol is lured outside or induced to go to war beyond his borders and is there slain by the Dwarves. Then Melian departs, and the girdle being removed Doriath is ravaged by the Dwarves.'

In the story that appears in *The Silmarillion* the outlaws who went with Húrin to Nargothrond were removed, as also was the curse of Mîm; and the only treasure that Húrin took from Nargothrond was the Nauglamír – which was here supposed to have been made by Dwarves for Finrod Felagund, and to have been the most prized by him of all the hoard of Nargothrond. Húrin was represented as being at last freed from the delusions inspired by Morgoth in his encounter with Melian in Menegroth. The Dwarves who set the Silmaril in the Nauglamír were already in Menegroth engaged on other works, and it was they who slew Thingol; at that time Melian's power was withdrawn from Neldoreth and Region, and she vanished out of Middle-earth, leaving Doriath unprotected. The ambush and destruction of the Dwarves at Sarn Athrad was given again to Beren and the Green

Elves (following my father's letter of 1963 quoted on p. 353, where however he said that 'Beren had no army'), and from the same source the Ents, 'Shepherds of the Trees', were introduced.

This story was not lightly or easily conceived, but was the outcome of long experimentation among alternative conceptions. In this work Guy Kay took a major part, and the chapter that I finally wrote owes much to my discussions with him. It is, and was, obvious that a step was being taken of a different order from any other 'manipulation' of my father's own writing in the course of the book: even in the case of the story of The Fall of Gondolin, to which my father had never returned, something could be contrived without introducing radical changes in the narrative. It seemed at that time that there were elements inherent in the story of the Ruin of Doriath as it stood that were radically incompatible with 'The Silmarillion' as projected, and that there was here an inescapable choice: either to abandon that conception, or else to alter the story. I think now that this was a mistaken view, and that the undoubted difficulties could have been, and should have been, surmounted without so far overstepping the bounds of the editorial function.

PART FOUR

QUENDI
AND
ELDAR

QUENDI AND ELDAR

The title *Quendi and Eldar* clearly belongs properly to the long essay that is printed here, though my father used it also to include two other much briefer works, obviously written at much the same time; one of these, on the origin of the Orcs, was published in *Morgoth's Ring* (see X.415, where a more detailed account is given). *Quendi and Eldar* is extant in a typescript with carbon copy that can be fairly certainly dated to the years 1959–60 *(ibid.)*; and both copies are preceded by a manuscript page that in addition to the following preamble gives a parallel title *Essekenta Eldarinwa*.

> Enquiry into the origins of the Elvish names for Elves and their varieties clans and divisions: with Appendices on their names for the other Incarnates: Men, Dwarves, and Orcs; and on their analysis of their own language, Quenya: with a note on the 'Language of the Valar'.

My father corrected the two copies carefully and in precisely the same ways (except for a few later pencilled alterations). The text printed here follows the original very closely, apart from very minor changes made for consistency or clarity, the omission of a passage of extremely complex phonology, and a reorganisation of the text in respect of the notes. As often elsewhere in his later writings, my father interrupted his main text with notes, some of them long; and these I have numbered and collected at the end, distinguishing them from my own numbered notes by referring to them in the body of the text as *Note 1, Note 2*, &c., with a reference to the page on which they are found. Also, and more drastically, I have omitted one substantial section from Appendix D (see p. 396). This was done primarily for reasons of space, but the passage in question is a somewhat abstract account of the phonological theories of earlier linguistic Loremasters and the contributions of Fëanor, relying rather allusively on phonological data that are taken for granted: it stands apart from the content of the work at large (and entered, I suspect, from the movement of my father's train of thought rather than as a planned element in the whole).

Also for reasons of space my commentary is kept to a severe minimum. Abbreviations used are PQ (Primitive Quendian), CE (Common Eldarin), CT (Common Telerin), Q (Quenya), T (Telerin), Ñ (Ñoldorin), S (Sindarin), V (Valarin).

QUENDI AND ELDAR

Origin and Meanings of the Elvish words referring to *Elves* and their varieties. With Appendices on their names for other Incarnates.

A.   The principal linguistic elements concerned.

1.   *KWENE

(a) PQ **kwene* 'person' (m. or f.). CE **kwēn* (*-kwen*), pl. **kwenī*, 'person' (m. or f.), 'one', '(some)body'; pl. 'persons', '(some) people'.

(b) PQ and CE **kwende*, pl. **kwendī*. This form was made from **kwene* by primitive fortification of the median *n* > *nd*. It was probably at first only used in the plural, in the sense 'people, the people as a whole', sc. embracing all the three original clans.

(c) **kwendjā* adj. 'belonging to the **kwendī*, to the people as a whole'.

2.   *ELE   According to Elvish legend this was a primitive exclamation, 'lo!' 'behold!' made by the Elves when they first saw the stars. Hence:

(a) CE **el*, **ele*, **el-ā*, 'lo!' 'look!' 'see!'

(b) CE **ēl*, pl. **eli*, *ēli*, 'star'.

(c) CE **elen*, pl. **elenī*, 'star', with 'extended base'.

(d) CE **eldā*, an adjectival formation 'connected or concerned with the stars', used as a description of the **kwendī*. According to legend this name, and the next, were due to the Vala Oromë. They were thus probably at first only used in the plural, meaning 'star-folk'.

(e) CE **elenā*, an adjectival form made from the extended stem **elen*, of the same meaning and use as **eldā*.

3.   *DELE

(a) A verbal base **dele*, also with suffix **del-ja*, 'walk, go, proceed, travel'.

(b) **edelō*, an agental formation of primitive pattern: 'one who goes, traveller, migrant'. A name made at the time of the Separation for those who decided to follow Oromë.

(c) **awa-delo*, **awā-delo*, ?**wā-delō*. Old compounds with the element **awa* 'away' (see below). A name made in Beleriand for those who finally departed from Middle-earth.

4. *HEKE Probably not in origin a verbal base, but an adverbial element 'aside, apart, separate'.

(a) PQ *heke* 'apart, not including'.

(b) PQ and CE verbal derivative, transitive: *hek-tā* 'set aside, cast out, forsake'.

(c) PQ *hekla* 'any thing (or person) put aside from, or left out from, its normal company'. Also in personal form *heklō* 'a waif or outcast'; adjectival forms *heklā* and *hekelā*.

The element *AWA, appearing in 3(c) above, referred to movement away, viewed from the point of view of the thing, person, or place left. As a prefix it had probably already developed in CE the form *au-. The form *awā was originally an independent adverbial form, but appears to have been also used as a prefix (as an intensive form of *awa-, *au-). The form *wā- was probably originally used as a verbal stem, and possibly also in composition with verbal stems.

In the Eldarin languages this stem made contact in form with other elements, distinct in origin and in sense. *ABA 'refuse', 'say nay (in refusal or denial)': this is the source of the CE *abar, pl. *abarī 'a refuser', one who declined to follow Oromë. *WO in forms *wō and *wo- (the latter only as a prefix): this was a dual adverb 'together', referring to the junction of two things, or groups, in a pair or whole. The plural equivalent was *jō, *jōm, and as a prefix *jo, *jom. *HO in forms *hō and *ho: this was an adverb 'from, coming from', the point of view being outside the thing referred to.

The principal derivatives in form (their use is discussed below) of the CE words given above were as follows:

*KWEN

QUENYA 1(a) *quēn*, pl. *queni*; unstressed, as a pronoun or final element in a compound, *quen*.

1(b) *Quendi*. The sg. *quende* (not much used) was made in Quenya from *Quendi*, on the model of other nouns in -*e*, the majority of which formed their plurals in -*i*. There were also two old compounds: *Kalaquendi* 'Light-elves' and *Moriquendi* 'Dark-elves'.

1(c) *Quendya*, which remained in the Vanyarin dialect, but in Ñoldorin became *Quenya*. This was only used with reference to language.

TELERIN   1(a) *pen* as a pronoun, and -*pen* in a few old compounds.
   1(b) *Pendi*, plural only. Also in the compounds *Calapendi* and *Moripendi*.
   1(c) Not found.

SINDARIN   1(a) *pen*, usually mutated *ben*, as a pronoun. Also -*ben*, -*phen* in a few old compounds.
   1(b) Not found. The compounds *Calben* (pl. *Celbin*) and *Morben* (pl. *Moerbin*, *Morbin*) must certainly have descended from the same source as those mentioned above, but their final element was evidently altered to agree with the compounds of **kwen*. The unaltered derivatives would have been **Calbend*, **Moerbend*; but though final -*nd* eventually became -*n* in Sindarin, this change had not occurred in the early records, and no cases of -*bend* are found. In addition, the form *Morben* (without affection[1] of the *o*) shows either an alteration to **mora-* for *mori-*, after **kala-*, or more probably substitution of S *morn-* from **mornā*, the usual S adjectival form.
   1(c) Not found.

*EL

QUENYA   2(a) *ela!* imperative exclamation, directing sight to an actually visible object.
   2(b) *ēl*, pl. *ēli*, 'star' (poetic word).
   2(c) *elen*, pl. *eleni* (occasionally in verse *eldi*), 'star'. The normal word for a star of the actual firmament. The pl. form *eleni*, without syncope, is re-formed after the singular.
   2(d) *Elda* only used as a noun, chiefly in the pl. *Eldar*. See also (Quenya) 3(b) below.
   2(e) *Elda* as above. As an adjective referring to stars the form used was *elenya*.

TELERIN   2(a) *ela!* as in Quenya.
   2(b) *ēl*, pl. *ēli*. The ordinary word for 'star'.
   2(c) *elen*, pl. *elni*. An archaic or poetic variant of the preceding.
   2(d) *Ella*. An occasional variant of *Ello*, which was the normal form of the word. This shows contact with the products of **edelō*: see further under (Telerin) 3.
   2(e) Not found. The form would have been **Elna*.

SINDARIN   2(a) *elo!* An exclamation of wonder, admiration, delight.

2(b) Not found.

2(c) *êl*, pl. *elin*, class-plural *elenath*. An archaic word for 'star', little used except in verse, apart from the form *elenath* 'all the host of the stars of heaven'.

2(d) *Ell-*, only used in the m. and f. forms *Ellon*, *Elleth*, elf-man, elf-woman; the class-plural *El(d)rim*; and final *-el*, pl. *-il*, in some old compounds: see (Sindarin) 3(b).

2(e) *Elen*, pl. *Elin*, with class-plural *Eledhrim*, Elf, Elves. *dhr* is < *n-r* in secondary contact. On usage see further below.

*DEL

QUENYA 3(a) *lelya-* 'go, proceed (in any direction), travel'; past tense *lende*. This form is due to the early change in Q of initial *d* > *l*. The change was regular in both Vanyarin and Ñoldorin dialects of Quenya. It occurs occasionally also in Telerin languages, though this may be due rather to *d/l* variation in PQ, for which there is some evidence. A notable example being *de/le* as pronominal elements in the 2nd person.

In Q *del-* seems to have become *led*, by dissimilation. The past form clearly shows *led*, while *lelya* may also be derived from *ledja*, since *dj* became *ly* medially in Quenya.

3(b) *Eldo*. An archaic variant of *Elda*, with which it coalesced in form and sense. *Eldo* cannot however be directly descended from *edelō*. Its form is probably due to a change *edelo* > *eledo*, following the change in the verb. The change of initial *d* > *l* was early and may have preceded syncope, and the loss of feeling for the etymological connexions of the word, which finally resulted in the blending of the products of 2 and 3. Unchanged *edelō* would by syncope have given *eðlo* > *ello* (which is not found). See, however, under Sindarin for reasons for supposing that there may have been a variant form *edlō* (with loss of *sundóma*):[2] this could have produced a Quenya form *eldo*, since transposition of *dl* in primary contact to the favoured sequence *ld* not infrequently occurred in the pre-record period of Quenya.

3(c) *Aurel* < *aw(a)delo*. *Oärel* < *awādelo*. In the Vanyarin dialect *Auzel* and *Oäzel*. *Oärel (Oäzel)* were the forms commonly used in Q. The plurals took the forms *-eldi*. This shows that the ending *-el* was associated with the noun *Elda*. This was facilitated by a normal development in Q morphology: a word of such a form independently as *eldā*, when used as the final element in a compound of early date, was shortened to *elda, pl. *eldī > *eld, *eldī > historic Q -el, -eldi. In addition öar was in actual use in Q as an adverbial form derived from *AWA (see below): a fact which also accounts for the selection of öarel, öazel.

TELERIN   3(a) delia 'go, proceed'. Past tense delle.

3(b) Ello. The usual form, preferred to Ella, from which, however, it did not differ in sense. Both *edelō and *edlō regularly became ello in Telerin.

3(c) Audel, pl. Audelli. This shows the same association with -el, the shortened form in composition of ella, ello, as that seen in Q.

SINDARIN   3(a) Not found.

3(b) Edhel, pl. Edhil. The most used word in Sindarin; but only normally used in these forms. As noted above under (Sindarin) 2(d) the m. and f. forms were Ellon, Elleth; and there was also a class-plural Eldrim, Elrim (ll-r in secondary contact > ldr, later again simplified). As suggested under (Quenya) 3(b), there may have been a variant *edlō, which would regularly give ell- in Sindarin. Since this shorter form would be most likely to appear in compounds and extended forms, it would account for the limitation of Sindarin ell- to such forms as Ellon, Elleth, Eldrim. It would also account for the blending of the products of stems 2 El and 3 Del in Sindarin, as well as in Quenya. The form -el, pl. -il also occurs in some old compounds (especially personal names), where it may be due also to a blending of *elda and *edlo. In later compounds -edhel is used.

3(c) Ódhel, pl. Ódhil; beside later more usual Gódhel, Gódhil. Also a class-plural Ódhellim, Gódhellim. Ódhel is from *aw(a)delo, and the exact equivalent of Q Aurel, T Audel. Gódhel could be derived from *wādelo: S initial *wā- > gwǭ > go. But since it appears later than Ódhel, and after this term had become specially applied to the Exiled Ñoldor, it seems most probable that it took g- from the old clan-name Golodh, pl. Goelydh, which it practically replaced. Golodh was the S equivalent of Q Ñoldo, both from PQ *ñgolodō.

*HEK

QUENYA   4(a) heka! imperative exclamation 'be gone! stand aside!'. Normally only addressed to persons. It often appears in the forms hekat sg. and hekal pl. with reduced pronominal affixes of the 2nd person. Also hequa (? from *hek-wā) adverb and preposition 'leaving aside, not counting, excluding, except'.

4(b) *hehta-*, past tense *hehtane*, 'put aside, leave out, exclude, abandon, forsake'.

4(c) *hekil* and *hekilo* m., *hekile* f.: 'one lost or forsaken by friends, waif, outcast, outlaw'. Also *Hekel*, pl. *Hekeldi*, re-formed to match *Oärel*, especially applied to the Eldar left in Beleriand. Hence *Hekelmar* and *Hekeldamar*, the name in the language of the loremasters of Aman for Beleriand. It was thought of as a long shoreland beside the Sea (cf. *Eglamar* under Sindarin below).

TELERIN   4(a) *heca!* For Q *hequa* the T form is *heco* (? < *hek* + *au*).

4(b) *hecta-* 'reject, abandon'.

4(c) *hecul*, *heculo*. Also with special reference to those left in Beleriand, *Hecello*; *Heculbar* or *Hecellubar*, Beleriand.

SINDARIN   PQ *h-* only survived in the dialects of Aman. It disappeared without trace in Sindarin. *hek* therefore appears as *ek*, identical in form with PQ *eke* 'sharp point'.

4(a) *ego!* 'be off!' This is from *hek(e) ā: ā* the imperative particle, being originally independent and variable in place, survived in S as *ō* > *o*, though this now always followed the verb stem and had become an inflexion.

4(b) *eitha-*. This is in the main a derivative of PQ *ek-tā*, and means 'prick with a sharp point', 'stab'; but the sense 'treat with scorn, insult' (often with reference to rejection or dismissal) may show the effect of blending with PQ *hek-ta*. To say to anyone *ego!* was indeed the gravest *eithad*.

4(c) *Eglan*, mostly used in the plural *Eglain*, *Egladhrim*. The name that the Sindar gave to themselves ('the Forsaken') as distinguished from the Elves who left Middle-earth. *Eglan* is < an extended adjectival form *heklanā*. The older shorter form (*hekla* or *heklā*) survives in a few place-names, such as *Eglamar* (cf. *Hekelmar*, etc.), *Eglarest*. These are shown to be old from their formation, with the genitival element preceding: *ekla-mbar*, *ekla-rista*.

*AWA

QUENYA   *au-* as a verbal prefix: < either *au* or *awa*; as in *au-kiri-* 'cut off'. The point of view was in origin 'away from the speaker or the place of his thought', and this distinction is usually preserved in Q. Thus *aukiri* meant 'cut off, so that a portion is lost or no longer available', but *hókiri* (see below) meant 'cut off a required portion, so as to have it or use it'.

öa, öar. Adverbs: < **awā;* the form *öar* shows addition of the ending *-d* (prehistoric *-da*) indicating motion to or towards a point. The form *awā* appears originally to have been used either of rest or motion, and *öa* can still be so used in Q. This adverbial *öa, öar* was occasionally used as a prefix in compounds of later formation. Though, as has been shown, in *Oäreldi,* the most commonly used, the *r* is in fact of different origin.

The verb *auta-* 'go away, leave (the point of the speaker's thought)' had an old 'strong' past tense *anwe,* only found in archaic language. The most frequently used past and perfect were *vāne, avānie,* made from the stem **wā;* together with a past participle form *vanwa.* This last was an old formation (which is also found in Sindarin), and was the most frequently used part of the verb. It developed the meanings 'gone, lost, no longer to be had, vanished, departed, dead, past and over'. With it the forms *vāne* and *avānie* were specially associated in use and meaning. In the more purely physical sense 'went away (to another place)' the regular forms (for a *-ta* verb of this class) *öante, öantie* were used. The form perfect *avānie* is regularly developed from **a-wāniiē,* made in the prehistoric period from the older perfect form of this type **awāwiiē,* with intrusion of *n* from the past (the forms of past and perfect became progressively more closely associated in Quenya). The accent remained on the *wā,* since the augment or reduplication in verbal forms was never accented even in the retraction period of Quenya (hence no form **öanie* developed: contrast *öante* < **áwa-n-tē*). The form *vānie* appearing in verse has no augment: probably a phonetic development after a preceding vowel; but such forms are not uncommon in verse.

SINDARIN   The only normal derivative is the preposition *o,* the usual word for 'from, of'. None of the forms of the element **awa* are found as a prefix in S, probably because they became like or the same as the products of **wō, *wo* (see next). The form *Ódhel* is isolated (see above, Sindarin 3(c)). As the mutations following the preposition *o* show, it must prehistorically have ended in *-t* or *-d*. Possibly, therefore, it comes from **aud,* with *d* of the same origin as that seen in Q *öar* (see above). Some have thought that it received the addition -t (at a period when *au had already become ǭ > o) by association with *et 'out, out of'. The latter retains its consonant in the form ed before vowels, but loses it before consonants, though es, ef, eth are often found before s, f, th. o, however, is normally o in all positions, though od appears occasionally before vowels, especially before o-. The influence of *et > ed is therefore probably only a late one, and does not account for the mutations.

TELERIN   The Telerin forms are closely similar to those of Quenya in form and meaning, though the development *áua > öa does not occur, and v remains w in sound. Thus we have prefix au-, adverb au or avad; verb auta- with past participle vanua, and associated past and perfect vāne and avānie; and in physical senses vante, avantie.

*WO

QUENYA   This does not remain in Q as an independent word. It is however a frequent prefix in the form ó- (usually reduced to o- when unstressed), used in words describing the meeting, junction, or union of two things or persons, or of two groups thought of as units. Thus: o-mentie (meeting or junction of the directions of two people) as in the familiar greeting between two people, or two companies each going on a path that crosses that of the other: Elen síla lúmenna omentielvo![3] 'A star shines upon the hour of the meeting of our ways.' (Note 1, p. 407)

This prefix was normally unstressed in verbs or derivatives of verbs; or generally when the next following syllable was long. When stressed it had the form ó-, as in ónoni 'twins', beside the adj. onóna 'twin-born', also used as a noun 'one of a pair of twins'.

TELERIN   use does not materially differ; but in form the w- (lost in Quenya before ō) is retained: prefix vō, vo-. (Note 1, p. 407)

SINDARIN   In the prefix gwa-, go- 'together, co-, com-'. The dual limitation was no longer made; and go- had the senses both of *wo and *jo. *jo, *jom- disappeared as a living prefix. gwa- occurred only in a few S dissyllables, where it was stressed, or in their recognizable derivatives: e.g. gwanūn 'a pair of twins', gwanunig one of such a pair. These were mostly of ancient formation, and so retained their dual significance. gwa- is regularly developed from *wo > *wa >

gwa, when stressed in prehistoric Sindarin. *go-* is from **wo* > *gwo* > *go*, when primitively unstressed; and also from *gwa-* > *go-*, when it became again unstressed. Since PQ **wā* (one of the forms of *AWA) would also have produced *gō-*, *go-*, or *gwa-* if primitively shortened (e.g. before two consonants), while **au* would have produced *o-*, the same as the frequent initially mutated form of *go-* 'together', the prefixal forms of *AWA were lost in Sindarin.

*HO

QUENYA   This was evidently an ancient adverbial element, occurring principally as a proclitic or enclitic: proclitic, as a prefix to verb stems; and enclitic, as attached to noun stems (the usual place for the simpler 'prepositional' elements in PQ). Hence Quenya *hō-* (usually so, even when it had become unstressed), as a verb prefix. It meant 'away, from, from among', but the point of view was outside the thing, place, or group in thought, whereas in the derivatives of *AWA the point in thought was the place or thing left. Thus Q *hōkiri-* 'cut off', so as to have or use a required portion; whereas *aukiri-* meant 'cut off' and get rid of or lose a portion. *hōtuli-* 'come away', so as to leave a place or group and join another in the thought or place of the speaker; whereas *au* could not be used with the stem *tul-* 'come'.

As a noun enclitic *-hō* became *-ō*, since medial *h* was very early lost without trace in CE. This was the source of the most used 'genitive' inflexion of Quenya. Properly it was used partitively, or to describe the source or origin, not as a 'possessive', or adjectivally to describe qualities; but naturally this 'derivative genitive' (as English *of*) could be used in many circumstances that might have possessive or adjectival implications, though 'possession' was indicated by the adjectival suffix *-va*, or (especially in general descriptions) by a 'loose compound'. Thus 'Orome's horn' was *róma Oroméva* (if it remained in his possession); *Orome róma* would mean 'an Orome horn', sc. one of Orome's horns (if he had more than one); but *róma Oroméo* meant 'a horn coming from Orome', e.g. as a gift, in circumstances where the recipient, showing the gift with pride, might say 'this is Orome's horn'. If he said 'this *was* Orome's horn', he would say *Oroméva*. Similarly *lambe Eldaron* would not be used for 'the language of the Eldar' (unless conceivably in a case where the whole language was adopted by another people), which is expressed either by *Elda-lambe* or *lambe Eldaiva*. *(Note 2, p. 407)*

There remained naturally many cases where either possessive-adjectival or partitive-derivative genitives might be used, and the tendency to prefer the latter, or to use them in place of the former, increased. Thus *alkar Oromëo* or *alkar Oroméva* could be used for 'the splendour of Oromë', though the latter was proper in a description of Oromë as he permanently was, and the former of his splendour as seen at the moment (proceeding from him) or at some point in a narrative. 'The Kings of the Eldar' might be either *i arani Eldaron* or *i arani Eldaive*, though the former would mean if accurately used 'those among the Eldar who were kings' and the latter 'those (kings) in a particular assembly who were Elvish'. In such expressions as 'Elwe, King of the Sindar (people), or Doriath (country)' the derivative form was usual: *Elwe, Aran Sindaron*, or *Aran Lestanórëo*.

TELERIN   The Telerin use of the prefix *ho-* was as in Quenya. The inflexion was *-o*, as in Quenya, but it did not receive *-n* addition in the plural. It was more widely used than in pure Quenya, sc. in most cases where English would employ the inflexion *-s*, or *of*; though the possessive, especially when it concerned a single person or possessor, was expressed without inflexion: either with the possessor placed first (the older usage), or (possibly under the influence of the genitival or adjectival expressions which were placed second) following the possessed. In the latter case, the appropriate possessive suffix ('his, hers, its, their') was usually appended to the noun. So *Olue cava*; or *cava Olue*, usually *cavaria Olue* (sc. 'the house of him, Olwe'); = 'Olwe's house'. The last form was also used in Quenya with proper names, as *köarya Olwe*. Both languages also used the adjectival possessive suffixes in a curious way, attaching them to adjectives attributed to proper names (or names of personal functions, like 'king'): as *Varda Aratarya*, 'Varda the Lofty, Varda in her sublimity'. This was most usual in the vocative: as in *Meletyalda*, or fuller *Aran Meletyalda* (literally 'your mighty' or 'king your mighty'), more or less equivalents of 'Your Majesty'. Cf. Aragorn's farewell: *Arwen vanimalda, namárie!*[4]

SINDARIN   Since initial *h-* disappeared in Sindarin *hō* would have become *ū* and so, clashing with the negative *ū*, naturally did not survive. *ho as a proclitic might have given o; but it does not occur as a verbal prefix, although it possibly contributed to the Sindarin preposition o (see under *Awa, Sindarin) which is used in either 'direction', from or to the point of view of the speaker. Since all final vowels disappeared in Sindarin, it cannot be determined whether or not this language had in the primitive period developed inflexional -ō. Its presence in Telerin of Aman makes its former presence in Sindarin probable. The placing of the genitive noun second in normal Sindarin is also probably derived from inflexional forms. Compounds of which the first element was 'genitival' were evidently in the older period still normal, as is seen in many place- and personal names (such as Egla-mar), and was still in more limited use later, especially where the first element was or was regarded as an adjective (as Mordor 'Land of Darkness' or 'Dark Land'). But genitival sequences with the possessor or qualifier second in the later period also became fixed compounds: as Dóriath, for Dôr Iâth 'Land of the Fence'.

*ABA

Though this became a verbal stem, it is probably derived from a primitive negative element, or exclamation, such as *BA 'no!' It did not, however, deny facts, but always expressed concern or will; that is, it expressed refusal to do what others might wish or urge, or prohibition of some action by others. As a verbal stem it developed the form *aba- (with connecting vowel a in the aorist); as a particle or prefix the forms *aba, *bā, and *abā.

QUENYA   In Quenya the verb ava- was little used in ordinary language, and revealed that it was not in origin a 'strong' or basic verbal stem by having the 'weak' past form avane. In ordinary use it was replaced by the compound vā-quet (váquetin, váquenten) 'to say no', sc. 'to say I will not', or 'do not', 'to refuse' or 'to forbid'.

As a prefix the form used was usually ava-, the force of which can be observed in avaquétima 'not to be said, that must not be said', avanyárima 'not to be told or related', as contrasted with úquétima 'unspeakable', that is, 'impossible to say, put into words, or unpronounceable', únyárima 'impossible to recount', sc. because all the facts are not known, or the tale is too long. Compare also Avamanyar 'those who did not go to Aman, because they would not' (an equivalent of *Avari*) with *Úamanyar* 'those who did not in the event reach Aman' (an equivalent of *Hekeldi*).

As a particle (the form of this stem most used in ordinary language) the Quenya form was usually *vá!* This was an exclamation or particle expressing the will or wish of the speaker, meaning according to context 'I will not' or 'Do not!' Note that it was not used, even in the first person, in a statement about the speaker's future action, depending on foresight, or a judgement of the force of circumstances. It could sometimes, as seen in *váquet-* (above), be used as a verbal prefix.

A longer form *áva* or *avá* (stressed on the last syllable), which shows combination with the imperative particle *ā*, was commonly used as a negative imperative 'Don't!', either used alone or with an uninflected verbal stem, as *áva kare!* 'Don't do it!' Both *vá* and *áva* sometimes received verbal pronominal affixes of the first singular and first plural exclusive: as *ávan, ván, ványe* 'I won't', *avamme, vamme* 'we won't'.

An old derivative of *aba-* as a quasi-verbal stem was *abaro* > CE *abar. This was an old agental formation, as seen also in *Teler*, pl. *Teleri*, made with the suffix *-rŏ*, added to *ómataina*.[5] (Other forms of this suffix were *-rō* added to stem, with or without *n*-infixion; and *-rdŏ* > *rd*.) *abar thus meant 'recusant, one who refuses to act as advised or commanded'. It was specially applied to (or first made to describe?) the section of the Elves who refused to join in the Westward March: Q *Avar*, pl. *Avari*.

TELERIN The Telerin use was closely similar to that of Quenya. The forms were the same, except that Telerin preserved CE *b* distinct from *v* or *w*: hence the prefix was *aba-* (*abapétima* 'not to be said'); the particle *bá*; the exclamation *abá*. The verbal form, however, was in normal use: *aban* 'I refuse, I will not'. In a negative command only the uninflected *abá* was used: *abá care* 'don't do it!'

SINDARIN In Sindarin the following forms are found. *baw!* imperious negative: 'No, no! Don't!' *avo* negative adverb with verbs, as *avo garo!* 'don't do it'; sometimes used as a prefix: *avgaro* (< *aba-kar ā*). This could be personalized in the form *avon* 'I won't', *avam* 'we won't': these were of course not in fact derived from *avo*, which contained the imperative -*o* < **ā*, but from the verb stem **aba*, with inflexions assimilated to the tense stems in -*ā*; but no other parts of the verb survived in use, except the noun *avad* 'refusal, reluctance'. Derived direct from *baw!* *(*bā)* was the verb *boda-* 'ban, prohibit' *(*bā-ta)*.

(With the uses of this stem, primary meaning 'refuse, be unwilling', to form negative imperatives, cf. Latin *nōlī*, *nōlīte*.)

B. Meanings and use of the various terms applied to the Elves and their varieties in Quenya, Telerin, and Sindarin.

Quenya

1. *quén*, pl. *queni*, person, individual, man or woman. Chiefly used in the unstressed form *quen*. Mostly found in the singular: 'one, somebody'; in the pl. 'people, they'. Also combined with other elements, as in *aiquen* 'if anybody, whoever', *ilquen* 'everybody'. In a number of old compounds -*quen*, pl. *queni* was combined with noun or adjective stems to denote habitual occupations or functions, or to describe those having some notable (permanent) quality: as -*man* in English (but without distinction of sex) in *horseman, seaman, workman, nobleman*, etc. Q *roquen* 'horseman, rider'; *(Note 3, p. 407) kiryaquen* 'shipman, sailor'; *arquen* 'a noble'. These words belong to everyday speech, and have no special reference to Elves. They were freely applied to other Incarnates, such as Men or Dwarves, when the Eldar became acquainted with them.

2. *Quendi* Elves, of any kind, including the Avari. The sg. *Quende* was naturally less frequently used. As has been seen, the word was made when the Elves as yet knew of no other 'people' than themselves. The sense 'the Elvish people, as a whole', or in the sg. 'an Elf and not some other similar creature', developed first in Aman, where the Elves lived among or in contact with the Valar and Maiar. During the Exile when the Ñoldor became re-associated with their Elvish kin, the Sindar, but met other non-Elvish people, such as Orcs, Dwarves, and Men, it became an even more useful term. But in fact it had ceased in Aman to be a word of everyday use, and remained thereafter mainly used in the special language of 'Lore': histories or tales of old days, or learned writings on peoples and

languages. In ordinary language the Elves of Aman called themselves *Eldar* (or in Telerin *Elloi*): see below.

There also existed two old compounds containing **kwendī*: **kala-kwendī* and **mori-kwendī*, the Light-folk and the Dark-folk. These terms appear to go back to the period before the Separation, or rather to the time of the debate among the Quendi concerning the invitation of the Valar. They were evidently made by the party favourable to Oromë, and referred originally to those who desired the Light of Valinor (where the ambassadors of the Elves reported that there was no darkness), and those who did not wish for a place in which there was no night. But already before the final separation **mori-kwendī* may have referred to the glooms and the clouds dimming the sun and the stars during the War of the Valar and Melkor,[6] so that the term from the beginning had a tinge of scorn, implying that such folk were not averse to the shadows of Melkor upon Middle-earth.

The lineal descendants of these terms survived only in the languages of Aman. The Quenya forms were *Kalaquendi* and *Moriquendi*. The *Kalaquendi* in Quenya applied only to the Elves who actually lived or had lived in Aman; and the *Moriquendi* was applied to all others, whether they had come on the March or not. The latter were regarded as greatly inferior to the *Kalaquendi*, who had experienced the Light of Valinor, and had also acquired far greater knowledge and powers by their association with the Valar and Maiar.

In the period of Exile the Ñoldor modified their use of these terms, which was offensive to the Sindar. *Kalaquendi* went out of use, except in written Ñoldorin lore. *Moriquendi* was now applied to all other Elves, except the Ñoldor and Sindar, that is to Avari or to any kind of Elves that at the time of the coming of the Ñoldor had not long dwelt in Beleriand and were not subjects of Elwë. It was never applied, however, to any but Elvish peoples. The old distinction, when made, was represented by the new terms *Amanyar* 'those of Aman', and *Úamanyar* or *Úmanyar* 'those not of Aman', beside the longer forms *Amaneldi* and *Úmaneldi*.

3. *Quendya*, in the Ñoldorin dialect *Quenya*. This word remained in ordinary use, but it was only used as a noun 'the Quendian language'. *(Note 4, p. 407)* This use of *Quendya* must have arisen in Aman, while *Quendi* still remained in general use. Historically, and in the more accurate use of the

linguistic Loremasters, *Quenya* included the dialect of the Teleri, which though divergent (in some points from days before settlement in Aman, such as **kw* > *p*), remained generally intelligible to the Vanyar and Ñoldor. But in ordinary use it was applied only to the dialects of the Vanyar and Ñoldor, the differences between which only appeared later, and remained, up to the period just before the Exile, of minor importance.

In the use of the Exiles *Quenya* naturally came to mean the language of the Ñoldor, developed in Aman, as distinct from other tongues, whether Elvish or not. But the Ñoldor did not forget its connexion with the old word *Quendi*, and still regarded the name as implying 'Elvish', that is the chief Elvish tongue, the noblest, and the one most nearly preserving the ancient character of Elvish speech. For a note on the Elvish words for 'language', especially among the Ñoldorin Lore-masters, see Appendix D (p. 391).

4. *Elda* and *Eldo*. The original distinction between these forms as meaning 'one of the Star-folk, or Elves in general', and one of the 'Marchers', became obscured by the close approach of the forms. The form *Eldo* went out of use, and *Elda* remained the chief word for 'Elf' in Quenya. But it was not in accurate use held to include the Avari (when they were remembered or considered); i.e. it took on the sense of *Eldo*. It may, however, have been partly due to its older sense that in popular use it was the word ordinarily employed for any Elf, that is, as an equivalent of the *Quende* of the Loremasters. When one of the Elves of Aman spoke of the *Eldalie*, 'the Elven-folk', he meant vaguely all the race of Elves, though he was probably not thinking of the Avari.

For, of course, the special kinship of the *Amanyar* with those left in Beleriand (or *Hekeldamar*) was remembered, especially by the Teleri. When it was necessary to distinguish these two branches of the *Eldar* (or properly *Eldor*), those who had come to Aman were called the *Oäzeldi*, Ñ *Oäreldi*, for which another form (less used) was *Auzeldi*, Ñ *Aureldi*; those who had re-mained behind were the *Hekeldi*. These terms naturally be-longed rather to history than everyday speech, and in the period of the Exile they fell out of use, being unsuitable to the situation in Beleriand. The Exiles still claimed to be *Amanyar*, but in practice this term usually now meant those Elves remaining in Aman, while the Exiles called themselves *Etyañgoldi* 'Exiled Ñoldor', or simply (since the great majority of their clan had come into exile) *Ñoldor.* All the subjects of Elwë they called *Sindar* or 'Grey-elves'.

Telerin

1. The derivatives of *KWEN were more sparingly represented in the Telerin dialects, of Aman or Beleriand. This was in part due to the Common Telerin change of *kw* > *p, (Note 5, p. 407)* which caused **pen* < **kwen* to clash with the PQ stem *PEN 'lack, be without', and also with some of the derivatives of *PED 'slope, slant down' (e.g. **pendā* 'sloping'). Also the Teleri felt themselves to be a separate people, as compared with the Vanyar and Ñoldor, whom taken together they outnumbered. This sentiment began before the Separation, and increased on the March and in Beleriand. In consequence they did not feel strongly the need for a general word embracing all Elves, until they came in contact with other non-Elvish Incarnates.

As a pronoun enclitic (e.g. in *aipen*, Q *aiquen; ilpen*, Q *ilquen*) **kwen* survived in Telerin; but few of the compounds with *pen* 'man' remained in ordinary use, except *arpen* 'noble (man)', and the derived adjective *arpenia.*

Pendi, the dialectal equivalent of Q *Quendi*, survived only as a learned word of the historians, used with reference to ancient days before the Separation; the adjective **Pendia* (the equivalent of *Quendya*) had fallen out of use. *(Note 6, p. 408)* The Teleri had little interest in linguistic lore, which they left to the Ñoldor. They did not regard their language as a 'dialect' of Quenya, but called it *Lindārin* or *Lindalambe.* Quenya they called *Goldōrin* or *Goldolambe*; for they had few contacts with the Vanyar.

The old compounds in Telerin form *Calapendi* and *Moripendi* survived in historical use; but since the Teleri in Aman remained more conscious of their kinship with the Elves left in Beleriand, while *Calapendi* was used, as *Kalaquendi* in Quenya, to refer only to the Elves of Aman, *Moripendi* was not applied to the Elves of Telerin origin who had not reached Aman.

2. *Ello* and *Ella.* The history of the meanings of these words was almost identical with that of the corresponding *Elda* and *Eldo* in Quenya. In Telerin the *-o* form became preferred, so that generally T *Ello* was the equivalent of Q *Elda.* But *Ella* remained in use in quasi-adjectival function (e.g. as the first element in loose or genitival compounds): thus the equivalent of Q *Eldalie* was in T *Ellālie.*

In contrast to the *Elloi* left in Beleriand those in Aman were in histories called *Audel*, pl. *Audelli*. Those in Beleriand were the *Hecelloi* of *Heculbar* (or *Hecellubar*).

Sindarin

1. Derivatives of **KWEN* were limited to the sense: pronominal 'one, somebody, anybody', and to a few old compounds that survived. PQ **kwende*, **kwendī* disappeared altogether. The reasons for this were partly the linguistic changes already cited; and partly the circumstances in which the Sindar lived, until the return of the Ñoldor, and the coming of Men. The linguistic changes made the words unsuitable for survival; the circumstances removed all practical need for the term. The old unity of the Elves had been broken at the Separation. The Elves of Beleriand were isolated, without contact with any other people, Elvish or of other kind; and they were all of one clan and language: Telerin (or Lindarin). Their own language was the only one that they ever heard; and they needed no word to distinguish it, nor to distinguish themselves.

As a pronoun, usually enclitic, the form *pen*, mutated *ben*, survived. A few compounds survived, such as *rochben* 'rider' (m. or f.), *orodben* 'a mountaineer' or 'one living in the mountains', *arphen* 'a noble'. Their plurals were made by *i*-affection, originally carried through the word: as *roechbin*, *oerydbin*, *erphin*, but the normal form of the first element was often restored when the nature of the composition remained evident: as *rochbin*, but always *erphin*. These words had no special association with Elves.

Associated with these compounds were the two old words *Calben (Celbin)* and *Morben (Moerbin)*. On the formal relation of these to Quenya *Kalaquendi* and *Moriquendi* see p. 362. They had no reference to Elves, except by accident of circumstance. *Celbin* retained what was, as has been said, probably its original meaning: all Elves other than the Avari; and it included the Sindar. It was in fact the equivalent (when one was needed) of the Quenya *Eldar*, Telerin *Elloi*. But it referred to Elves only because no other people qualified for the title. *Moerbin* was similarly an equivalent for Avari; but that it did not mean only 'Dark-*elves*' is seen by its ready application to other Incarnates, when they later became known. By the Sindar anyone dwelling outside Beleriand, or entering their realm from outside, was called a *Morben*. The first people of this kind to be met were the *Nandor*, who entered East Beleriand over the passes of the Mountains before the return of Morgoth; soon after his return came the first invasions of his Orcs from the North.[7] Somewhat later the Sindar became aware of Avari, who had crept in small and secret groups into Beleriand from the South. Later came the Men of the Three Houses, who were friendly; and later still Men of other kinds. All these were at first acquaintance called *Moerbin*. *(Note 7, p. 408)* But when the Nandor were recognized as kinsfolk of Lindarin origin and speech (as was still recognizable), they were received into the class of *Celbin*. The Men of the Three Houses were also soon removed from the class of *Moerbin*. *(Note 8, p. 408)* They were given their own name, *Edain*, and were seldom actually called *Celbin*, but they were recognized as belonging to this class, which became practically equivalent to 'peoples in alliance in the War against Morgoth'. The Avari thus remained the chief examples of *Moerbin*. Any individual Avar who joined with or was admitted among the Sindar (it rarely happened) became a *Calben*; but the Avari in general remained secretive, hostile to the Eldar, and untrustworthy; and they dwelt in hidden places in the deeper woods, or in caves. *(Note 9, p. 408)* *Moerbin* as applied to them is usually translated 'Dark-elves', partly because *Moriquendi* in the Quenya of the Exiled Ñoldor usually referred to them. But that no special reference to Elves was intended by the Sindarin word is shown by the fact that *Moerbin* was at once applied to the new bands of Men (Easterlings) that appeared before the Battle of the Nírnaeth. *(Note 9, p. 408)* If in Sindarin an Avar, as distinct from other kinds of *Morben*, was intended, he was called *Mornedhel*.

2. *Edhel*, pl. *Edhil*. In spite of its ultimate derivation (see p. 360) this was the general word for 'Elf, Elves'. In the earlier days it naturally referred only to the Eldarin Sindar, for no other kind was ever seen; but later it was freely applied to Elves of any kind that entered Beleriand. It was however only used in these two forms.

The masculine and feminine forms were *Ellon* m. and *Elleth* f. and the class-plural was *Eldrim*, later *Elrim*, when this was not replaced by the more commonly used *Eledhrim* (see below). The form without the m. and f. suffixes was not in use, and survived only in some old compounds, especially personal names, in the form *el*, pl. *il*, as a final element.

The form *Elen*, pl. *Elin* was only used in histories or the works of the Loremasters, as a word to include all Elves (Eldar and Avari). But the class-plural *Eledhrim* was the usual word for 'all the Elvish race', whenever such an expression was needed.

All these words and forms, whatever their etymologies (see above), were applicable to any kind of Elf. In fact *Edhel* was properly applied only to Eldar; *Ell-* may have a mixed origin; and *Elen* was an ancient general word. *(Note 10, p. 410)*

3. The Sindar had no general name for themselves as distinct from other varieties of Elf, until other kinds entered Beleriand. The descendant of the old clan name **Lindāi* (Q *Lindar*) had fallen out of normal use, being no longer needed in a situation were all the *Edhil* were of the same kind, and people were more aware of the growing differences in speech and other matters between those sections of the Elves that lived in widely sundered parts of a large and mostly pathless land. They were thus in ordinary speech all *Edhil*, but some belonged to one region and some to another: they were *Falathrim* from the sea-board of West Beleriand, or *Iathrim* from Doriath (the land of the Fence, or *iath*), or *Mithrim* who had gone north from Beleriand and inhabited the regions about the great lake that afterwards bore their name. *(Note 11, p. 410)*

The old clan-name **Lindāi* survived in the compound *Glinnel*, pl. *Glinnil*, a word only known in historical lore, and the equivalent of Quenya *Teleri* or *Lindar*; see the Notes on the Clan-names below. All the Sindarin subjects of King Elu-Thingol, as distinguished from the incoming Ñoldor, were sometimes later called the *Eluwaith*. *Dúnedhil* 'West-elves' (the reference being to the West of Middle-earth) was a term made to match *Dúnedain* 'West-men' (applied only to the Men of the Three Houses). But with the growing amalgamation, outside Doriath, of the Ñoldor and Sindar into one people using the Sindarin tongue as their daily speech, this soon became applied to both Ñoldor and Sindar.

While the Ñoldor were still distinct, and whenever it was desired to recall their difference of origin, they were usually called *Ódhil* (sg. *Ódhel*). This as has been seen was originally a name for all the Elves that left Beleriand for Aman. These were also called by the Sindar *Gwanwen*, pl. *Gwenwin* (or *Gwanwel, Gwenwil*) 'the departed': cf. Q *vanwa*. This term, which could not suitably be applied to those who had come back, remained the usual Sindarin name for the Elves that remained in Aman.

Ódhil thus became specially the name of the Exiled Ñoldor. In this sense the form *Gódhel*, pl. *Gódhil* soon replaced the older form. It seems to have been due to the influence of the clan-name *Golodh*, pl. *Goelydh*; or rather to a deliberate blending of the two words. The old clan-name had not fallen out of memory (for the Ñoldor and the Sindar owing to the great friendship of Finwe and Elwe were closely associated during their sojourn in Beleriand before the Departure) and it had in consequence a genuine Sindarin form (< CE *ñgolodō). But the form *Golodh* seems to have been phonetically unpleasing to the Ñoldor. The name was, moreover, chiefly used by those who wished to mark the difference between the Ñoldor and the Sindar, and to ignore the dwelling of the Ñoldor in Aman which might give them a claim to superiority. This was especially the case in Doriath, where King Thingol was hostile to the Ñoldorin chieftains, Fëanor and his sons, and Fingolfin, because of their assault upon the Teleri in Aman, the people of his brother Olwe. The Ñoldor, therefore, when using Sindarin, never applied this name *(Golodh)* to themselves, and it fell out of use among those friendly to them.

4. *Eglan*, pl. *Eglain*, *Egladrim*. This name, 'the Forsaken', was, as has been said, given by the Sindar to themselves. But it was not in Beleriand a name for all the Elves who remained there, as were the related names, *Hekeldi*, *Hecelloi*, in Aman. It applied only to those who wished to depart, and waited long in vain for the return of Ulmo, taking up their abode on or near the coasts. There they became skilled in the building and management of ships. Círdan was their lord.

Círdan's folk were made up both of numbers of the following of Olwe, who straying or lingering came to the shores too late, and also of many of the following of Elwe, who abandoned the search for him and did not wish to be separated for ever from their kin and friends. This folk remained in the desire of Aman for long years, and they were among the most friendly to the Exiles.

They continued to call themselves the *Eglain*, and the regions where they dwelt *Eglamar* and *Eglador*. The latter name fell out of general use. It had originally been applied to all western Beleriand between Mount Taras and the Bay of Balar, its eastern boundary being roughly along the River Narog. *Eglamar*, however, remained the name of the 'Home of the Eglain': the sea-board from Cape Andras to the headland of Bar-in-Mŷl

('Home of the Gulls'),[8] which included the ship-havens of Círdan at Brithonbar[9] and at the head of the firth of Eglarest.

The *Eglain* became a people somewhat apart from the inland Elves, and at the time of the coming of the Exiles their language was in many ways different. *(Note 12, p. 411)* But they acknowledged the high-kingship of Thingol, and Círdan never took the title of king.[10]

*Abarī

This name, evidently made by the Eldar at the time of the Separation, is found in histories in the Quenya form *Avari*, and the Telerin form *Abari*. It was still used by the historians of the Exiled Ñoldor, though it hardly differed from *Moriquendi*, which (see above) was no longer used by the Exiles to include Elves of Eldarin origin. The plural *Evair* was known to Sindarin loremasters, but was no longer in use. Such Avari as came into Beleriand were, as has been said, called *Morben*, or *Mornedhel*.

C. The Clan-names,
with notes on other names for divisions of the Eldar.

In Quenya form the names of the three great Clans were *Vanyar*, *Ñoldor*, and *Lindar*. The oldest of these names was *Lindar*, which certainly goes back to days before the Separation. The other two probably arose in the same period, if somewhat later: their original forms may thus be given in PQ as **wanjā*, **ñgolodō*, and *lindā / glindā*. *(Note 13, p. 411)*

According to the legend, preserved in almost identical form among both the Elves of Aman and the Sindar, the Three Clans were in the beginning derived from the three Elf-fathers: *Imin*, *Tata*, and *Enel* (sc. One, Two, Three), and those whom each chose to join his following. So they had at first simply the names *Minyar* 'Firsts', *Tatyar* 'Seconds', and *Nelyar* 'Thirds'. These numbered, out of the original 144 Elves that first awoke, 14, 56, and 74; and these proportions were approximately maintained until the Separation.[11]

It is said that of the small clan of the *Minyar* none became Avari. The *Tatyar* were evenly divided. The *Nelyar* were most reluctant to leave their lakeside homes; but they were very cohesive, and very conscious of the separate unity of their Clan (as they continued to be), so that when it became clear that their chieftains Elwe and Olwe were resolved to depart and would have a large following, many of those among them who had at first joined the Avari went over to the Eldar rather than be separated from their kin. The Ñoldor indeed asserted that most of the *'Teleri'* were at heart *Avari*, and that only the *Eglain* really regretted being left in Beleriand.

According to the Ñoldorin historians the proportions, out of 144, that when the March began became Avari or Eldar were approximately so:

Minyar 14:   *Avari* 0   *Eldar* 14
Tatyar 56:   *Avari* 28   *Eldar* 28
Nelyar 74:   *Avari* 28   *Eldar* 46 > *Amanyar Teleri* 20;
    Sindar and Nandor 26

In the result the Ñoldor were the largest clan of Elves in Aman; while the Elves that remained in Middle-earth (the *Moriquendi* in the Quenya of Aman) outnumbered the Amanyar in the proportion of 82 to 62.[12]

How far the descriptive Clan-names, *wanjā*, *ñgolodō*, and *lindā* were preserved among the Avari is not now known; but the existence of the old clans was remembered, and a special kinship between those of the same original clan, whether they had gone away or remained, was still recognized. The first Avari that the Eldar met again in Beleriand seem to have claimed to be Tatyar, who acknowledged their kinship with the Exiles, though there is no record of their using the name *Ñoldo* in any recognizable Avarin form. They were actually unfriendly to the Ñoldor, and jealous of their more exalted kin, whom they accused of arrogance.

This ill-feeling descended in part from the bitterness of the Debate before the March of the Eldar began, and was no doubt later increased by the machinations of Morgoth; but it also throws some light upon the temperament of the Ñoldor in general, and of Fëanor in particular. Indeed the Teleri on their side asserted that most of the Ñoldor in Aman itself were in heart Avari, and returned to Middle-earth when they discovered their mistake; they needed room to quarrel in. For in contrast the Lindarin elements in the western Avari were friendly to the Eldar, and willing to learn from them; and so close was the feeling of kinship between the remnants of the Sindar, the Nandor, and the Lindarin Avari, that later in Eriador and the Vale of Anduin they often became merged together.

Lindar (Teleri)[13]

These were, as has been seen, much the largest of the ancient clans. The name, later appearing in Quenya form as *Lindar* (Telerin *Lindai*), is already referred to in the legend of 'The Awakening of the Quendi', which says of the Nelyar that 'they sang before they could speak with words'. The name **Lindā* is therefore clearly a derivative of the primitive stem **LIN* (showing reinforcement of the medial N and adjectival *-ā*). This stem was possibly one of the contributions of the Nelyar to Primitive Quendian, for it reflects their predilections and associations, and produces more derivatives in Lindarin tongues than in others. Its primary reference was to melodious or pleasing sound, but it also refers (especially in Lindarin) to water, the motions of which were always by the Lindar associated with vocal (Elvish) sound. The reinforcements, either medial *lind-* or initial *glin-*, *glind-*, were however almost solely used of musical, especially vocal, sounds produced with intent to please. It is thus to the love of the Nelyar for song, for vocal music with or without the use of articulate words, that the name *Lindar* originally referred; though they also loved water, and before the Separation never moved far from the lake and waterfall[14] of Cuiviénen, and those that moved into the West became enamoured of the Sea. *(Note 14, p. 411)*

In Quenya, that is, in the language of the Vanyar and Ñoldor, those of this clan that joined in the March were called the *Teleri*. This name was applied in particular to those that came at last and latest to Aman; but it was also later applied to the Sindar. The name *Lindar* was not forgotten, but in Ñoldorin lore it was chiefly used to describe the whole clan, including the Avari among them. *Teleri* meant 'those at the end of the line, the hindmost', and was evidently a nickname arising during the March, when the Teleri, the least eager to depart, often lagged far behind. *(Note 15, p. 411)*

Vanyar

This name was probably given to the First Clan by the Ñoldor. They accepted it, but continued to call themselves most often by their old numerical name *Minyar* (since the whole of this clan had joined the Eldar and reached Aman). The name referred to the hair of the Minyar, which was in nearly all members of the clan yellow or deep golden. This was regarded as a beautiful feature by the Ñoldor (who loved gold), though they were themselves mostly dark-haired. Owing to intermarriage the golden hair of the Vanyar sometimes later appeared among the Ñoldor: notably in the case of Finarfin, and in his children Finrod and Galadriel, in whom it came from King Finwë's second wife, Indis of the Vanyar.

Vanyar thus comes from an adjectival derivative **wanjā* from the stem **WAN*. Its primary sense seems to have been very similar to English (modern) use of 'fair' with reference to hair and complexion; though its actual development was the reverse of the English: it meant 'pale, light-coloured, not brown or dark', and its implication of beauty was secondary. In English the meaning 'beautiful' is primary. From the same stem was derived the name given in Quenya to the Valie *Vána* wife of Orome.

Since the Lindar had little contact with the Vanyar either on the March or later in Aman, this name was not much used by them for the First Clan. The Amanyar Teleri had the form *Vaniai* (no doubt taken from the Ñoldor), but the name appears to have been forgotten in Beleriand, where the First Clan (in lore and history only) were called *Miniel*, pl. *Mínil*.

Ñoldor

This name was probably older than *Vanyar*, and may have been made before the March. It was given to the Second Clan by the others. It was accepted, and was used as their regular and proper name by all the Eldarin members of the clan throughout their later history.

The name meant 'the Wise', that is those who have great knowledge and understanding. The Ñoldor indeed early showed the greatest talents of all the Elves both for intellectual pursuits and for technical skills.

The variant forms of the name: Q *Ñoldo*, T *Goldo*, S *Golodh (Ngolodh)*, indicate a PQ original **ñgolodō*. This is a derivative of the stem **NGOL* 'knowledge, wisdom, lore'. This is seen in Q *ñóle* 'long study (of any subject)', *iñgole* 'lore', *ingolmo* 'loremaster'. In T *góle*, *engole* had the same senses as in Q but were used most often of the special 'lore' possessed by the Ñoldor. In S the word *gûl* (equivalent of Q *ñóle*) had less laudatory associations, being used mostly of secret knowledge, especially such as possessed by artificers who made wonderful things; and the word became further darkened by its frequent use in the compound *morgul* 'black arts', applied to the delusory or perilous arts and knowledge derived from Morgoth. Those indeed among the Sindar who were unfriendly to the

Ñoldor attributed their supremacy in the arts and lore to their learning from Melkor-Morgoth. This was a falsehood, coming itself ultimately from Morgoth; though it was not without any foundation (as the lies of Morgoth seldom were). But the great gifts of the Ñoldor did not come from the teaching of Melkor. Fëanor the greatest of them all never had any dealings with Melkor in Aman, and was his greatest foe.

Sindar

Less commonly the form *Sindel*, pl. *Sindeldi*, is also met in Exilic Quenya. This was the name given by the Exiled Ñoldor (see Note 11) to the second largest of the divisions of the Eldar. *(Note 16, p. 412)* It was applied to all the Elves of Telerin origin that the Ñoldor found in Beleriand, though it later excluded the Nandor, except those who were the direct subjects of Elwe, or had become merged with his people. The name meant 'the Grey', or 'the Grey-elves', and was derived from *THIN, PQ *thindi 'grey, pale or silvery grey', Q *þinde*, Ñ dialect *sinde*.

On the origin of this name see Note 11. The Loremasters also supposed that reference was made to the hair of the Sindar. Elwe himself had indeed long and beautiful hair of silver hue, but this does not seem to have been a common feature of the Sindar, though it was found among them occasionally, especially in the nearer or remoter kin of Elwe (as in the case of Círdan).[15] In general the Sindar appear to have very closely resembled the Exiles, being dark-haired, strong and tall, but lithe. Indeed they could hardly be told apart except by their eyes; for the eyes of all the Elves that had dwelt in Aman impressed those of Middle-earth by their piercing brightness. For which reason the Sindar often called them *Lachend*, pl. *Lechind* 'flame-eyed'.[16]

Nandor

This name must have been made at the time, in the latter days of the March, when certain groups of the Teleri gave up the March; and it was especially applied to the large following of Lenwe, *(Note 17, p. 412)* who refused to cross the Hithaeglir.[16] The name was often interpreted as 'Those who go back'; but in fact none of the Nandor appear to have returned, or to have rejoined the Avari. Many remained and settled in lands that they had reached, especially beside the River Anduin; some turned aside and wandered southwards. *(Note 18, p. 412)* There was, however, as was later seen, a slow drift westward of the Moriquendi during the captivity of Melkor, and eventually groups of the Nandor, coming through the Gap between the Hithaeglir and Eryd Nimrais, spread widely in Eriador. Some of these finally entered Beleriand, not long before the return of Morgoth.[17] These were under the leadership of Denethor, son of Denweg (see Note 17), who became an ally of Elwe in the first battles with the creatures of Morgoth. The old name *Nandor* was however only remembered by the Ñoldorin historians in Aman; and they knew nothing of the later history of this folk, recalling only that the leader of the defection before the crossing of the dread Hithaeglir was named Lenwe (i.e. Denweg). The Sindarin loremasters remembered the Nandor as *Danwaith*, or by confusion with the name of their leader *Denwaith*.

This name they at first applied to the Nandor that came into Eastern Beleriand; but this people still called themselves by the old clan-name **Lindai*, which had at that time taken the form *Lindi* in their tongue. The country in which most of them eventually settled, as a small independent folk, they called *Lindon* (< **Lindānā*): this was the country at the western feet of the Blue Mountains (Eryd Luin), watered by the tributaries of the great River Gelion, and previously named by the Sindar *Ossiriand*, the Land of Seven Rivers. The Sindar quickly recognized the *Lindi* as kinsfolk of Lindarin origin (S *Glinnil*), using a tongue that in spite of great differences was still perceived to be akin to their own; and they adopted the names *Lindi* and *Lindon*, giving them the forms *Lindil* (sg. *Lindel*) or *Lindedhil*, and *Lindon* or *Dor Lindon*. In Exilic Quenya the forms used (derived from the Sindar or direct from the Nandor) were *Lindi* and *Lindon* (or *Lindóne*). The Exiled Ñoldor also usually referred to the Eryd Luin as *Eryd Lindon*, since the highest parts of that range made the eastern borders of the country of Lindon.

These names were however later replaced among the Sindar by the name 'Green-elves', at least as far as the inhabitants of Ossiriand were concerned; for they withdrew themselves and took as little part in the strife with Morgoth as they could. This name, S *Laegel*, pl. *Laegil*, class-plural *Laegrim* or *Laegel(d)-rim*, was given both because of the greenness of the land of Lindon, and because the *Laegrim* clothed themselves in green as an aid to secrecy. This term the Ñoldor translated into Quenya *Laiquendi*; but it was not much used.

Appendix A. Elvish names for Men.

The first Elves that Men met in the world were Avari, some of whom were friendly to them, but the most avoided them or were hostile (according to the tales of Men). What names Men and Elves gave to one another in those remote days, of which little was remembered when the Loremasters in Beleriand made the acquaintance of the After-born, there is now no record. By the Dúnedain the Elves were called *Nimîr* (the Beautiful).[18]

The Eldar did not meet Men of any kind or race until the Ñoldor had long returned to Beleriand and were at war with Morgoth. The Sindar did not even know of their existence, until the coming of the Nandor; and these brought only rumour of a strange people (whom they had not themselves seen) wandering in the lands of the East beyond the Hithaeglir. From these uncertain tales the Sindar concluded that the 'strange people' were either some diminished race of the Avari, or else related to Orcs, creatures of Melkor, bred in mockery of the true Quendi. But the Ñoldor had already heard of Men in Aman. Their knowledge came in the first place from Melkor and was perverted by his malice, but before the Exile those who would listen had learned more of the truth from the Valar, and they knew that the newcomers were akin to themselves, being also Children of Ilúvatar, though differing in gifts and fate. Therefore the Ñoldor made names for the Second Race of the Children, calling them the *Atani* 'the Second Folk'. Other names that they devised were *Apanónar* 'the After-born', and *Hildor* 'the Followers'.

In Beleriand *Atan*, pl. *Atani*, was the name most used at first. But since for a long time the only Men known to the Ñoldor and Sindar were those of the Three Houses of the Elf-friends, this name became specially associated with them, so that it was seldom in ordinary speech applied to other kinds of Men that came later to Beleriand, or that were reported to be dwelling beyond the Mountains. The Elf-friends *(Note 19, p. 412)* were sometimes called by the Loremasters *Núnatani* (S *Dúnedain*), 'Western Men', a term made to match *Dúnedhil*, which was a name for all the Elves of Beleriand, allied in the War (see p. 378). The original reference was to the West of Middle-earth, but the name *Núnatani, Dúnedain* was later applied solely to the Númenóreans, descendants of the *Atani*, who removed to the far western isle of *Númenóre*.

Apanónar 'the After-born' was a word of lore, not used in daily speech. A general term for Men of all kinds and races, as distinct from Elves, was only devised after their mortality and brief life-span became known to the Elves by experience. They were then called *Firyar* 'Mortals', or *Fírimar* of similar sense (literally 'those apt to die'). *(Note 20, p. 412)* These words were derived from the stem *PHIRI* 'exhale, expire, breathe out', which had no original connexion with death.[19] Of death, as suffered by Men, the Elves knew nothing until they came into close association with the *Atani*; but there were cases in which an Elf, overcome by a great sorrow or weariness, had resigned life in the body. The chief of these, the departure of Míriel wife of King Finwe, was a matter of deep concern to all the Ñoldor, and it was told of her that her last act, as she gave up her life in the body and went to the keeping of Mandos, was a deep sigh of weariness.

These Quenya names were later adapted to the forms of Sindarin speech: *Atan > Adan*, pl. *Edain*; *Firya > Feir*, pl. *Fîr* (with *Firion* m.sg., *Firieth* f.sg.), class-plural *Firiath*; *Fírima > Fíreb*, pl. *Fírib*, class-plural *Firebrim*. These forms, which cannot for historical reasons have been inherited from CE, but are those which the words if inherited would have taken, show that they were adapted by people with considerable knowledge of both tongues and understanding of their relations to one another; that is, they were probably first made by the Ñoldor for use in Sindarin, when they had adopted this language for daily use in Beleriand. *Fíreb* as compared with *Fírima* shows the use of a different suffix, *(Note 21, p. 412)* since the S equivalent of Q *-ima* (**-ef*) was not current. *Apanónar* was rendered by *Abonnen*, pl. *Eboennin*, using a different participial formation from the stem *ONO* 'beget, give birth to'. *Hildor*, since the stem *KHILI* 'follow' was not current in Sindarin, was rendered by *Aphadon*, pl. *Ephedyn*, class-plural *Aphadrim*, from S *aphad-* 'follow' < **ap-pata* 'walk behind, on a track or path'.

Appendix B. Elvish names for the Dwarves.

The Sindar had long known the Dwarves, and had entered into peaceful relations with them, though of trade and exchange of skills rather than of true friendship, before the coming of the Exiles. The name (in the plural) that the Dwarves gave to themselves was *Khazâd*, and this the Sindar rendered as they might in the terms of their own speech, giving it the form *chaðǫd > *chaðaud > Hadhod. (Note 22, p. 412) Hadhod, Hadhodrim was the name which they continued to use in actual intercourse with the Dwarves; but among themselves they referred to the Dwarves usually as the Naugrim 'the Stunted Folk'. The adjective naug 'dwarf(ed), stunted', however, was not used by itself for one of the Khazād. The word used was Nogoth, pl. Noegyth, class-plural Nogothrim (as an occasional equivalent of Naugrim). (Note 23, p. 413) They also often referred to the Dwarves as a race by the name Dornhoth 'the Thrawn Folk', because of their stubborn mood as well as bodily toughness.

The Exiles heard of the Dwarves first from the Sindar, and when using the Sindarin tongue naturally adopted the already established names. But later in Eastern Beleriand the Ñoldor came into independent relations with the Dwarves of Eryd Lindon, and they adapted the name Khazād anew for use in Quenya, giving it the form Kasar, pl. Kasari or Kasāri. (Note 24, p. 413) This was the word most commonly used in Quenya for the Dwarves, the partitive plural being Kasalli, and the race-name Kasallie. But the Sindarin names were also adapted or imitated, a Dwarf being called Nauko or Norno (the whole people Naukalie or Nornalie). Norno was the more friendly term. (Note 25, p. 413)

The Petty-dwarves. See also Note 7. The Eldar did not at first recognize these as Incarnates, for they seldom caught sight of them in clear light. They only became aware of their existence indeed when they attacked the Eldar by stealth at night, or if they caught them alone in wild places. The Eldar therefore thought that they were a kind of cunning two-legged animals living in caves, and they called them Levain tad-dail, or simply Tad-dail, and they hunted them. But after the Eldar had made the acquaintance of the Naugrim, the Tad-dail were recognized as a variety of Dwarves and were left alone. There were then few of them surviving, and they were very wary, and too fearful to attack any Elf, unless their hiding-places were approached too nearly. The Sindar gave them the names Nogotheg 'Dwarf-let', or Nogoth niben 'Petty Dwarf'.[20]

The great Dwarves despised the Petty-dwarves, who were (it is said) the descendants of Dwarves who had left or been driven out from the Communities, being deformed or undersized, or slothful and rebellious. But they still acknowledged their kinship and resented any injuries done to them. Indeed it was one of their grievances against the Eldar that they had hunted and slain their lesser kin, who had settled in Beleriand before the Elves came there. This grievance was set aside, when treaties were made between the Dwarves and the Sindar, in consideration of the plea that the Petty-dwarves had never declared themselves to the Eldar, nor presented any claims to land or habitations, but had at once attacked the newcomers in darkness and ambush. But the grievance still smouldered, as was later seen in the case of Mîm, the only Petty-dwarf who played a memorable part in the Annals of Beleriand.

The Ñoldor, for use in Quenya, translated these Sindarin names for the Petty-dwarves by *Attalyar* 'Bipeds', and *Pikinaukor* or *Pitya-naukor*.

The chief dwellings of the Dwarves that became known to the Sindar (though few ever visited them) were upon the east side of the Eryd Luin. They were called in the Dwarf-tongue *Gabilgathol* and *Tumunzahar*. The greatest of all the mansions of the Dwarves, *Khazad-dûm*, beneath the Hithaeglir far to the east, was known to the Eldar only by name and rumour derived from the western Dwarves.

These names the Sindar did not attempt to adapt, but translated according to their sense, as *Belegost* 'Mickleburg'; *Novrod*, later *Nogrod*, meaning originally 'Hollowbold'; and *Hadhodrond* 'Dwarrowvault'.[21] *(Note 26, p. 414)* These names the Ñoldor naturally used in speaking or writing Sindarin, but for use in Quenya they translated the names anew as *Túrosto*, *Návarot*, and *Casarrondo*.

Appendix C. Elvish names for the Orcs.

The opening paragraphs of this Appendix have been given in *Morgoth's Ring* p. 416 and are not repeated here. The words that now follow, 'these shapes and the terror that they inspired', refer to the 'dreadful shapes' that haunted the dwellings of the Elves in the land of their awakening.

For these shapes and the terror that they inspired the element chiefly used in the ancient tongue of the Elves appears to have been *RUKU. In all the Eldarin tongues (and, it is said, in the Avarin also) there are many derivatives of this stem, having such ancient forms as: *ruk-*, *rauk-*, *uruk-*, *urk(u)*, *runk-*, *rukut/s*, besides the strengthened stem *gruk-*, and the elaborated *guruk-*, *ñguruk. (Note 27, p. 415)* Already in PQ that word must have been formed which had in CE the form **rauku* or **raukō*. This was applied to the larger and more terrible of the enemy shapes. But ancient were also the forms *uruk, urku/ō*, and the adjectival *urkā* 'horrible'. *(Note 28, p. 415)*

In Quenya we meet the noun *urko*, pl. *urqui*, deriving as the plural form shows from **urku* or **uruku*. In Sindarin is found the corresponding *urug*; but there is in frequent use the form *orch*, which must be derived from **urkō* or the adjectival **urkā*.

In the lore of the Blessed Realm the Q *urko* naturally seldom occurs, except in tales of the ancient days and the March, and then is vague in meaning, referring to anything that caused fear to the Elves, any dubious shape or shadow, or prowling creature. In Sindarin *urug* has a similar use. It might indeed be translated 'bogey'. But the form *orch* seems at once to have been applied to the Orcs, as soon as they appeared; and *Orch*, pl. *Yrch*, class-plural *Orchoth* remained the regular name for these creatures in Sindarin afterwards. The kinship, though not precise equivalence, of S *orch* to Q *urko, urqui* was recognized, and in Exilic Quenya *urko* was commonly used to translate S *orch*, though a form showing the influence of Sindarin, *orko*, pl. *orkor* and *orqui*, is also often found.

These names, derived by various routes from the Elvish tongues, from Quenya, Sindarin, Nandorin, and no doubt Avarin dialects, went far and wide, and seem to have been the source of the names for the Orcs in most of the languages of the Elder Days and the early ages of which there is any record. The form in Adunaic *urku, urkhu* may be direct from Quenya or Sindarin; and this form underlies the words for Orc in the languages of Men of the North-West in the Second and Third Ages. The Orcs themselves adopted it, for the fact that it referred to terror and detestation delighted them. The word *uruk* that occurs in the Black Speech, devised (it is said) by Sauron to serve as a lingua franca for his subjects, was probably borrowed by him from the Elvish tongues of earlier times. It referred, however, specially to the trained and disciplined Orcs of the regiments of Mordor. Lesser breeds seem to have been called *snaga*.[22]

The Dwarves claimed to have met and fought the Orcs long before the Eldar in Beleriand were aware of them. It was indeed their obvious detestation of the Orcs, and their willingness to assist in any war against them, that convinced the Eldar that the Dwarves were no creatures of Morgoth. Nonetheless the Dwarvish name for Orcs, *Rukhs*, pl. *Rakhâs*, seems to show affinity to the Elvish names, and was possibly ultimately derived from Avarin.

The Eldar had many other names for the Orcs, but most of these were 'kennings', descriptive terms of occasional use. One was, however, in frequent use in Sindarin: more often than *Orchoth* the general name for Orcs as a race that appears in the Annals was *Glamhoth*. *Glam* meant 'din, uproar, the confused yelling and bellowing of beasts', so that *Glamhoth* in origin meant more or less 'the Yelling-horde', with reference to the horrible clamour of the Orcs in battle or when in pursuit – they could be stealthy enough at need. But *Glamhoth* became so firmly associated with Orcs that *Glam* alone could be used of any body of Orcs, and a singular form was made from it, *glamog*. (Compare the name of the sword *Glamdring*.)

Note. The word used in translation of Q *urko*, S *orch*, is Orc. But that is because of the similarity of the ancient English word *orc*, 'evil spirit or bogey', to the Elvish words. There is possibly no connexion between them. The English word is now generally supposed to be derived from Latin *Orcus*.

The word for Orc in the now forgotten tongue of the Druedain in the realm of Gondor is recorded as being (? in the plural) *gorgûn*. This is possibly derived ultimately from the Elvish words.

Appendix D.
*Kwen, Quenya, and the Elvish (especially Ñoldorin)
words for 'Language'.

The Ñoldorin Loremasters state often that the meaning of *Quendi* was 'speakers', 'those who form words with voices' – *i karir quettar ómainen*. Since they were in possession of traditions coming down from ancient days before the Separation, this statement cannot be disregarded; though the development of sense set out above may also stand as correct.

It might be objected that in fact no stem **KWEN* clearly referring to speech or vocal sound is found in any known Elvish tongue. The nearest in form is the stem **KWET* 'speak, utter words, say'. But in dealing with this ancient word we must go back to the beginnings of Elvish speech, before the later organisation of its basic structure, with its preference (especially in stems of verbal significance) for the pattern X-X(-), with a fixed medial consonant, as e.g. in stems already exemplified above, such as *Dele, *Heke, *Tele, *Kala, *Kiri, *Nuku, *Ruku, etc. A large number of monosyllabic stems (with only an initial consonant or consonant group) still appear in the Eldarin tongues; and many of the dissyllabic stems must have been made by elaboration of these, just as, at a later stage again, the so-called *kalat- stems were extended from the disyllabic forms: *kala > *kalat(a).

If we assume, then, that the oldest form of this stem referring to vocal speech was *KWE, of which *KWENE and *KWETE were elaborations, we shall find a striking parallel in the forms of *KWA. This stem evidently referred to 'completion'. As such it survives as an element in many of the Eldarin words for 'whole, total, all', etc. But it also appears in the form *KWAN, and cannot well be separated from the verb stem *KWATA, Q quat- 'fill'. The assumption also helps to explain a curious and evidently archaic form that survives only in the languages of Aman: *ekwē, Q eque, T epe. It has no tense forms and usually receives no pronominal affixes, (Note 29, p. 415) being mostly used only before either a proper name (sg. or pl.) or a full independent pronoun, in the senses say / says or said. A quotation then follows, either direct, or less usually indirect after a 'that'-conjunction.

In this *ekwē we have plainly a last survivor of the primitive *KWE. It is again paralleled by a similar formation (though of different function) from *KWA: *akwā. This survives in Quenya only as aqua 'fully, completely, altogether, wholly'. (Note 30, p. 415) Compare the use of -kwā in the formation of adjectives from nouns, such as -ful in English, except that the sense has been less weakened, and remains closer to the original meaning of the stem: 'completely'. (Note 31, p. 415)

In Quenya the form eques, originally meaning 'said he, said someone' (see Note 29) was also used as a noun eques, with the analogical plural equessi, 'a saying, dictum, a quotation from someone's uttered words', hence also 'a saying, a current or proverbial dictum'.

We may therefore accept the etymology of *kwene, *kwēn that would make its original meaning 'speaking, speaker, one using vocal language'. It would indeed be natural for the Elves, requiring a word for one of their own kind as distinguished from other creatures then known, to select the use of speech as a chief characteristic. But once formed the word must have taken the meaning 'person', without specific reference to this talent of the Incarnates. Thus *nere, *nēr 'a male person, a man' was derived from *NERE referring to physical strength and valour, but it was possible to speak of a weak or cowardly nēr; or indeed to speak of a dumb or silent kwēn.

It might therefore still be doubted that in the derivative *kwendī the notion of speaking was any longer effectively present. The statement of the Loremasters cannot, however, be dismissed; while it must be remembered that the Elves were always more deeply concerned with language than were other races. Up to the time at least of the Separation, then, *Kwendī must still have implied 'we, the speaking people'; it may indeed have primarily applied to concourses for discussion, or for listening to speeches and recitations. But when the Elves came to know of other creatures of similar forms, and other Incarnates who used vocal language, and the name *Kwendī, Quendi was used to distinguish themselves from these other kinds, the linguistic sense must have been no longer present in ordinary language.

With regard to the word Quenya: an account is given above of the way in which this word became used first in Aman for Elvish speech, (Note 32, p. 416) and then for the dialects of the Eldar in Aman, and later for the language of the Vanyar and Ñoldor, and finally in Middle-earth for the ancient tongue of the Ñoldor preserved as a language of ritual and lore. This is historically correct, whatever may be the ultimate etymology of Quenya before the Eldar came to Aman. The view taken above (p. 360) is that it is derived from an adjective *kwendjā formed upon the stem *kwende (of which *kwendi was the plural), meaning 'belonging to the Quendi or Elves'.

Pengolodh the Loremaster of Eressëa says, in his Lammas or Account of Tongues, that Quenya meant properly 'language, speech', and was the oldest word for this meaning. This is not a statement based on tradition, but an opinion of Pengolodh; and he appears to mean only that Quendya, Quenya is actually never recorded except as the name of a language, and that language was the only one known to exist when this word was first made.

In any case it is clear that Quenya was always in fact

particular in its reference; for when the Ñoldorin Loremasters came to consider linguistic matters, and required words for speech or vocal language in general, as a mode of expression or communication, and for different aspects of speech, they made no use of the element *kwen, quen or its derivatives.

The usual word, in non-technical use, for 'language' was *lambē, Q and T lambe, S lam. This was undoubtedly related to the word for the physical tongue: *lambā, Q and T lamba, S lam. It meant 'tongue-movement, (way of) using the tongue'. (Note 33, p. 416) This use of a word indicating the tongue and its movements for articulate language no doubt arose, even in a period when all known speakers spoke substantially the same language, from elementary observation of the important part played by the tongue in articulate speaking, and from noticing the peculiarities of individuals, and the soon-developing minor differences in the language of groups and clans.

Lambe thus meant primarily 'a way of talking', within a common generally intelligible system, and was nearer to our 'dialect' than to 'language'; but later when the Eldar became aware of other tongues, not intelligible without study, lambe naturally became applied to the separate languages of any people or region. The Loremasters, therefore, did not use lambe as a term for language or speech in general. Their terms were derived from the stem *TEÑ 'indicate, signify', from which was formed the already well-known word *tenwe > Q tengwe 'indication, sign, token'. From this they made the word tengwesta 'a system or code of signs'. Every 'language' was one such system. A lambe was a tengwesta built of sounds (hloni). For the sense Language, as a whole, the peculiar art of the Incarnates of which each tengwesta was a particular product, they used the abstract formation tengwestie.

Now *TEÑ had no special reference to sound. Ultimately it meant 'to point at', and so to indicate a thing, or convey a thought, by some gesture, or by any sign that would be understood. This was appreciated by the Loremasters, who wished for a word free from any limitations with regard to the kind of signs or tengwi used. They could thus include under tengwesta any group of signs, including visible gestures, used and recognized by a community.

They knew of such systems of gesture. The Eldar possessed a fairly elaborate system, (Note 34, p. 416) containing a large number of conventional gesture-signs, some of which were as 'arbitrary' as those of phonetic systems. That is, they had no more obvious connexion with self-explanatory gestures (such as pointing in a desired direction) than had the majority of vocal elements or combinations with 'echoic' or imitative words (such as *māmā, Q máma 'sheep', or *k(a)wāk, Q quáko 'crow').

The Dwarves indeed, as later became known, had a far more elaborate and organized system. They possessed in fact a secondary tengwesta of gestures, concurrent with their spoken language, which they began to learn almost as soon as they began learning to speak. It should be said rather that they possessed a number of such gesture-codes; for unlike their spoken language, which remained astonishingly uniform and unchanged both in time and in locality, their gesture-codes varied greatly from community to community. And they were differently employed. Not for communication at a distance, for the Dwarves were short-sighted, but for secrecy and the exclusion of strangers.

The component sign-elements of any such code were often so slight and so swift that they could hardly be detected, still less interpreted by uninitiated onlookers. As the Eldar eventually discovered in their dealings with the Naugrim, they could speak with their voices but at the same time by 'gesture' convey to their own folk modifications of what was being said. Or they could stand silent considering some proposition, and yet confer among themselves meanwhile.

This 'gesture-language', or as they called it iglishmêk, the Dwarves were no more eager to teach than their own tongue. But they understood and respected the disinterested desire for knowledge, and some of the later Ñoldorin loremasters were allowed to learn enough of both their lambe (aglâb) and their iglishmêk to understand their systems.

Though a lambe was thus theoretically simply a tengwesta that happened to employ phonetic signs, hloníti tengwi, the early loremasters held that it was the superior form, capable of producing a system incalculably more subtle, precise and extensive than any hwerme or gesture-code. When unqualified, therefore, tengwesta meant a spoken language. But in technical use it meant more than lambe. The study of a language included not only lambe, the way of speaking (that is what we should call its phonetics and phonology), but also its morphology, grammar, and vocabulary.

The section omitted from Appendix D (see p. 359) begins here. The remainder of the text, which now follows, was all included in this Appendix.

Before he turned to other matters Fëanor completed his alphabetic system, and here also he introduced a change in terms that was afterwards followed. He called the written representation of a spoken *tengwe* (according to his definition)[23] a *tengwa*. A 'letter' or any individual significant mark had previously been called a *sarat*, from *SAR 'score, incise' > 'write'.[24] The Fëanorian letters were always called *tengwar* in Quenya, though *sarati* remained the name for the Rúmilian letters. Since, however, in the mode of spelling commonly used the full signs were consonantal, in ordinary non-technical use *tengwar* became equivalent to 'consonants', and the vowel-signs were called *ómatehtar*. When the Fëanorian letters were brought to Beleriand and applied (first by the Ñoldor) to Sindarin, *tengwa* was rendered by its recognized Sindarin equivalent *têw*, pl. *tîw*. The letters of the native S alphabet were called *certh*, pl. *cirth*. The word in Exilic Quenya *certa*, pl. *certar* was an accommodated loan from Sindarin; there was no such word in older Quenya. The Sindarin *certh* is probably from *kirtē 'cutting', a verbal derivative of a type not used in Quenya, the form of which would in any case have been *kirte, if inherited.

Though Fëanor after the days of his first youth took no more active part in linguistic lore and enquiry, he is credited by tradition with the foundation of a school of *Lambengolmor* or 'Loremasters of Tongues' to carry on this work. This continued in existence among the Ñoldor, even through the rigours and disasters of the Flight from Aman and the Wars in Beleriand, and it survived indeed to return to Eressëa.

Of the School the most eminent member after the founder was, or still is, Pengolodh,[25] an Elf of mixed Sindarin and Ñoldorin ancestry, born in Nevrast, who lived in Gondolin from its foundation. He wrote both in Sindarin and in Quenya. He was one of the survivors of the destruction of Gondolin, from which he rescued a few ancient writings, and some of his own copies, compilations, and commentaries. It is due to this, and to his prodigious memory, that much of the knowledge of the Elder Days was preserved.

All that has here been said concerning the Elvish names and their origins, and concerning the views of the older loremasters, is derived directly or indirectly from Pengolodh. For before the overthrow of Morgoth and the ruin of Beleriand, he collected much material among the survivors of the wars at Sirion's Mouth concerning languages and gesture-systems with which, owing to the isolation of Gondolin, he had not before had any direct acquaintance. Pengolodh is said to have remained in Middle-earth until far on into the Second Age for the furtherance of his enquiries, and for a while to have dwelt among the Dwarves of Casarrondo (Khazad-dûm). But when the shadow of Sauron fell upon Eriador, he left Middle-earth, the last of the *Lambengolmor*, and sailed to Eressëa, where maybe he still abides.

Note on the 'Language of the Valar'

Little is said in Ñoldorin lore, such as has been preserved, concerning the 'language of the Valar and Maiar'; though it has been supposed above that the application of *Quenya* to the speech of the Elves in Aman was due to the contrast between the tongue of the Valar and the tongue of the Elves, which they had before supposed to be the only language in the world. Considering the interest of the Ñoldor in all matters concerning speech this is strange. Pengolodh indeed comments upon it and offers explanations. What he says in the beginning of his *Lammas* is here summarized; for his comment contains all that is now known of the matter.

'Even if we had no knowledge of it,' he says, 'we could not reasonably doubt that the Valar had a *lambe* of their own. We know that all members of their order were incarnated by their own desire, and that most of them chose to take forms like those of the Children of Eru, as they name us. In such forms they would take on all the characters of the Incarnates that were due to the co-operation of *hröa* with indwelling *fëa*, for otherwise the assumption of these forms would have been needless, and they arrayed themselves in this manner long before they had any cause to appear before us visibly. Since, then, the making of a *lambe* is the chief character of an Incarnate, the Valar, having arrayed them in this manner, would inevitably during their long sojourn in Arda have made a *lambe* for themselves.

'But without argument we know that they did so; for there are references to the *Lambe Valarinwa* in old lore and histories, though these are few and scattered. Most of these references appear to be derived, by tradition of mouth, from "the Sayings of Rúmil" *(I Equessi Rúmilo)*, the ancient sage of Tirion, concerning the early days of the Eldar in Aman and their first dealings with the Valar. Only part of these *Equessi*[26] were preserved in the memory of the *Lambengolmor* during the dark years of the Flight and the Exile. All that I can find or remember I have here put together.'

The information that Pengolodh then gives is here set out more briefly. His preliminary points are these. Few of the Eldar ever learned to speak Valarin, even haltingly; among the people as a whole only a small number of words or names became widely known. Fëanor indeed, before the growth of his discontent, is said to have learned more of this tongue than any others before his time, and his knowledge must at any rate have far surpassed the little that is now recorded; but what he knew he kept to himself, and he refused to transmit it even to the *Lambengolmor* because of his quarrel with the Valar.

Our knowledge *(Note 35, p. 416)* is therefore now limited (1) to statements of the 'ancients' that certain words in Quenya were actually derived from Valarin; (2) to the occasional citation of words and names purporting to be Valarin (neither adopted in Quenya nor adapted to it), though undoubtedly recorded with only approximate accuracy, since no signs or letters not already known in the Elvish alphabets are employed; (3) to statements that certain names (especially those of the Valar or of places in Valinor) were translations of the Valarin forms. In cases (1) and (3) the actual Valarin words are not always indicated.

With regard to group (1) Pengolodh cites a 'Saying' of Rúmil: 'The Eldar took few words from the Valar, for they were rich in words and ready in invention at need. But though the honour which they gave to the Valar might have caused them to take words from their speech, whether needed or not, few words of Valarin could be fitted to Elvish speech without great change or diminution. For the tongues and voices of the Valar are great and stern, and yet also swift and subtle in movement, making sounds that we find hard to counterfeit; and their words are mostly long and rapid, like the glitter of swords, like the rush of leaves in a great wind or the fall of stones in the mountains.'

Pengolodh comments: 'Plainly the effect of Valarin upon Elvish ears was not pleasing.' It was, he adds, as may be seen or guessed from what survives, filled with many consonants unfamiliar to the Eldar and alien to the system of their speech.[27]

The examples that Pengolodh gives are as follows.

(1) (a) words

Ainu 'one of the "order" of the Valar and Maiar, made before Eä'. Valarin *ayanūz*. It was from this *ainu* that in Quenya was made the adjective *aina* 'holy', since according to Quenya derivation *ainu* appeared to be a personal form of such an adjective.

aman 'blessed, free from evil'. Chiefly used as the name of the land in which the Valar dwelt. V form not given; said to mean 'at peace, in accord (with Eru)'. See *Manwe*.

aþar, Ñ *asar* 'fixed time, festival'. V *aþāra* 'appointed'.

axan 'law, rule, commandment'. V *akašān*, said to mean 'He says', referring to Eru.

indil 'a lily, or other large single flower'. V *iniðil*.

mahalma 'throne'. V *maχallām* (adapted to Quenya), properly one of the seats of the Valar in the *Máhanaxar* or 'Doom Ring'. The element *maχan*, said to mean 'authority, authoritative decision', was also used in the form *Máhan*, one of the eight chiefs of the Valar, usually translated as *Aratar*.

miruvóre, miruvor 'a special wine or cordial'. V *mirubhōzē-*; said to be the beginning of a longer word, containing the element *mirub-* 'wine'.[28]

telluma 'dome', especially the 'Dome of Varda' over Valinor; but also applied to the domes of the mansion of Manwe and Varda upon Taniquetil. V *delgūmā*, altered by association with Q *telume*. See Note 15.

Pengolodh also cites the colour-words, which he says may be found in ancient verse, though they are used only by the Vanyar, 'who, as Rúmil reports, adopted many more words than did the Ñoldor':

ezel, ezella 'green'. See *Ezellohar*.

nasar 'red'; *ulban* 'blue'. V forms not given.

tulka 'yellow'. See *Tulkas*.

(b) names

Aule V *Aʒūlēz* (meaning not given).

Manwe Reduction and alteration to fit Quenya, in which words of this shape, ending in *-we*, were frequent in personal names. V *Mānawenūz* 'Blessed One, One (closest) in accord with Eru'. Oldest Q forms *Mánwen, Mánwe*.

Tulkas V *Tulukhastāz*; said to contain V elements *tulukha(n)* 'yellow', and *(a)šata-* 'hair of head': 'the golden-haired'.

Osse, Orome   On these two names, the only ones that became known to the Eldar before they reached Aman, see note below.

Ulmo   Like *Manwe*, a reduction and alteration to fit Quenya, in which the ending *-mo* often appeared in names or titles, sometimes with an agental significance: *Ulmo* was interpreted as 'the Pourer' < *UL 'pour out'. The V form is given as *Ul(l)ubōz*, containing the element *ul(l)u* 'water'.

Osse and Orome. Orome was the first of the Valar that any of the Eldar saw. Osse they met in Beleriand, and he remained long upon the coasts, and became well known to the Sindar (especially to the Eglain). Both these names therefore have Sindarin forms. To *Osse* corresponds S *Yssion* or *Gaerys*; to *Orome* the S *Araw*. The V forms are given as *Oš(o)šai* (said to mean 'spuming, foaming'); and *Arǫmēz*.

The first name was evidently adopted in the form *Ossai*, which became naturally Q *Osse*. In S *Ossai* would become *ossī* > *ussi* > *yssị* to which the ending (of male names) *-on* was added; or else the adjective **gairā* 'awful, fearful' was prefixed, producing *Gaerys*. The latter was more often used by the inland Teleri. **gairā* is from **gay-* 'astound, make aghast', which was also used in the oldest Eldarin word for the Sea: **gayār*, Q *ëar*, S *gaear*.

Arǫmēz evidently, as was pointed out by Fëanor, contained the open *a*-like *ǫ* (which did as a matter of later observation occur frequently in Valarin). This was treated as was the Eldarin *ǫ*, so that the Sindarin development was > **arāmē* > *arǫmæ* > *araum(a)* > *arauɱ*, *arauv* > *araw*. (In North Sindarin or Mithrim, where the diphthongization of *ō* and the opening of intervocalic *m* did not occur, the form produced was *Arum*; cf. the North Sindarin transformation of the Exilic Ñoldorin name *Hísilóme* > *Hithlum*.) The Quenya form with *Orome* for **Arome* < **Arōmē*, may show assimilation of the initial *o* to the following *ō* before the retraction of the normal Q accent to the first syllable; but Pengolodh says that it was due to the association of the name with the native Q **rom*, used of the sound of trumps or horns, seen in the Q name for the great horn of Orome, the *Vala-róma* (also in Q *romba* 'horn, trumpet', S *rom*).

'The Eldar,' he says, 'now take the name to signify "horn-blowing" or "horn-blower"; but to the Valar it had no such meaning. Now the names that we have for the Valar or the

Maiar, whether adapted from the Valarin or translated, are not right names but titles, referring to some function or character of the person; for though the Valar have right names, they do not reveal them. Save only in the case of Orome. For it is said in the histories of the most ancient days of the Quendi that, when Orome appeared among them, and at length some dared to approach him, they asked him his name, and he answered: *Orome*. Then they asked him what that signified, and again he answered: *Orome. To me only is it given; for I am Orome.* Yet the titles that he bore were many and glorious; but he withheld them at that time, that the Quendi should not be afraid.'

Nahar, the name of Orome's horse. 'Otherwise it was,' says Pengolodh, 'with the steed upon which the Lord Orome rode. When the Quendi asked his name, and if that bore any meaning, Orome answered: *"Nahar*, and he is called from the sound of his voice, when he is eager to run".' But the V form that is recorded by Rúmil was *næχærra*.

Ezellohar (also translated as *Koron Oiolaire, Korollaire*), the Green Mound upon which grew the Two Trees. V *Ezellōχār.*

Máhanaxar, the 'Doom-ring' in which were set the thrones of the Valar whereon they sat in council (see *mahalma* above, p. 399). Reduced and altered from V *māχananaškād.* Also translated as *Rithil-Anamo.*

(2) Valarin words and names, recorded but not adopted.
(a) words
uruš, rušur 'fire'.
ithīr 'light'.
ul(l)u 'water'.
šebeth 'air'.

(b) names
Arda: V *Apāraphelūn* (said to mean 'appointed dwelling'). Arda Unmarred: *Apāraphelūn Amanaišāl*; Arda Marred: *Apāraphelūn Dušamanūðān.*
Telperion: V *Ibrīniðilpathānezel.*
Laurelin: V *Tulukhedelgorūs.*
Ithil 'moon': V *Phanaikelūth.* Said to mean 'bright mirror'.
Anar 'Sun': V *Apāraigas.* Said to mean 'appointed heat'.

At the end of this short list Pengolodh cites another *eques* of Rúmil, which might seem contrary to that already quoted above: 'Let none be surprised who endeavour to learn somewhat of the tongue of the Lords of the West, as have I, if they find therein many words or parts of words that resemble our own words for the same or similar meanings. For even as they took our form for love of us, so in that form their voices would be likely to light upon similar *tengwi*.'

Upon this Pengolodh comments: 'He knew not of Men or of Dwarves. But we who have dwelt among Men know that (strange though that seems to some) the Valar love them no less. And for my part I perceive a likeness no less, or indeed greater, between the Valarin and the tongues of Men, notably the language of the Dúnedain and of the Children of Marach (sc. Adunaic). Also in general manner it resembles the tongues of the Kasāri; though this is not to be wondered at, if the tradition that they have is true that Aule devised for them their tongue in its beginning, and therefore it changes little, whereas the *iglishmēk* which they made for themselves is changeable.'

(3) [Cf. p. 398: 'statements that certain names (especially those of the Valar or of places in Valinor) were translations of the Valarin forms']

Arda   Q *arda* (< **gardā*, S *gardh*) meant any more or less bounded or defined place, a region. Its use as a proper name for the World was due to V *Apāraphelūn*.

Aratar 'the Supreme', was a version of the V *māχanāz*, pl. *māχanumāz* 'Authorities', also adapted as *Māhan*, pl. *Māhani*.

Eä 'All Creation', meaning 'it is', or 'let it be'. Valarin not recorded.

Ambar 'the Earth', meaning 'habitation'. Though the Eldar often used *Arda* in much the same sense, the proper meaning of *Ambar* was the Earth only, as the place where the Aratar had taken up their dwelling, and the Incarnate were destined to appear.[29]

Eru 'the One'. *Ilúvatar* was, however, a name made by the Eldar (when they had learned of Eru from the Valar), which they used more often than *Eru*, reserved for the most solemn occasions. It was made from *ilúve* 'allness, the all', an equivalent of *Eä*, and *atar* 'father'.

Varda 'the Sublime'. V form not given.

Melkor 'He who arises in Might', oldest Q form **mbelekōro*. V form not given.

Námo 'Judge'; usually called by the Eldar *Mandos*, the place of his dwelling.

Irmo 'Desirer'; usually called by the name of his dwelling *Lórien*.

Este 'Repose'. (*SED: CE *esdē* > *ezdē*, Q *Este*, T *Ēde* (as names only); S *îdh* 'rest, repose'.)

Vala 'has power' (sc. over the matter of Eä), 'a Power'; pl. *Valar*, 'they have power, the Powers'. Since these words are from the point of Q structure verbal in origin, they were probably versions of V words of verbal meaning. Cf. *axan* (p. 399), *Eä*; and also Q *eques*.

Atan, pl. *Atani* 'Men', meaning 'the Second, those coming next'. The Valar called them in full 'the Second Children of Eru', but the Quendi were 'the first Children of Eru'. From these terms the Q *Minnónar* 'First-born' and *Apanónar* 'After-born' were imitated; but Q *Eruhin*, pl. *Eruhíni* 'Children of Eru', or 'Elves and Men', is a translation of the Valarin expression 'Children of Eru' (of which the actual Valarin form is not recorded, probably because the V equivalent of *Eru* is nowhere revealed). Besides the form *-hin*, *-híni* only used in composition after a parental name, Q has *hína* 'child', and *hina* only used in the vocative addressing a (young) child, especially in *hinya* (< *hinanya*) 'my child'. S has *hên*, pl. *hîn*, mostly used as a prefix in patronymics or metronymics: as *Hîn Húrin* 'The Children of Húrin'. These words are derivatives of stem *khin*: *khīnā* (in composition *khīna* > Q *-hin*), and *khinā*.

Kalakiryan 'the Cleft of Light', the pass in the Pelóri not far from the north side of Taniquetil through which the Light of the Trees in Valinor flowed out to the shores of Aman.

Taniquetil, the highest of the mountains of the Pelóri, upon which were the mansions of Manwë and Varda. The name was properly only that of the topmost peak, meaning High-Snow-Peak. The whole mountain was most often called by the Eldar *(Oron) Oiolosse*, '(Mount) Everwhite' or 'Eversnow'. There were many names for this mountain in Quenya. A variant or close equivalent of *Taniquetil* was *Arfanyaras(se)*. The Sindarin forms of the names were made by the Noldor, for the Sindar knew nothing of the land of Aman except by report of the Exiles: e.g. *Amon-Uilos* and *Ras-Arphain*.

Pelóri 'the fencing, or defensive Heights'. The mountains of Aman, ranging in a crescent from North to South, close to the western shores.

On this list Pengolodh comments: 'These are all that I can find in old lore or remember to have read or heard. But the list is plainly incomplete. Many of the names once known and used, whether they be now found in the surviving histories or passed over, must have belonged to the first or the last group. Among those that are still remembered I note *Avathar*, the name of the dim and narrow land between the southern Pelóri and the Sea in which Ungoliante housed. This is not Elvish. There are also the names *Nessa*, the spouse of Tulkas, and *Uinen* the spouse of Osse. These too are not Elvish, so far as cán now be seen; and since the names *Tulkas* and *Osse* come from Valarin, the names of their spouses may also represent titles in the Valarin tongue, or such part of them as the Eldar could adapt. I say "so far as can now be seen", for there is no certainty in this matter without record. It is clear that some, or indeed many, of these adoptions and translations were made in very early days, when the language of the Eldar was otherwise than it became before the Exile. In the long years, owing to the restlessness and inventiveness of the Eldar (and of the Ñoldor in particular), words have been set aside and new words made; but the names of the enduring have endured, as memorials of the speech of the past. There is also this to consider. When words of Elvish tongue had been used to make the names of things and persons high and admirable, they seem to have been felt no longer suitable to apply to lesser things, and so passed from the daily speech.

'Thus we see that *vala* is no longer used of any power or authority less than that of the Valar themselves. One may say *Ā vala Manwe!* "may Manwe order it!"; or *Valar valuvar* "the will of the Valar will be done"; but we do not say this of any lesser name. In like manner *Este* or *Ēde* is the name only of the spouse of Lórien, whereas the form that that word has in Sindarin *(îdh)* means "rest", such as even a tired hound may find before a fire.' *(Note 36, p. 416)*

The reasons that Pengolodh gives or surmises for the scanty knowledge of Valarin preserved in Ñoldorin lore are here summarized. Some have already been alluded to.

Though Valarin had many more sounds than Eldarin, some alien to the Eldarin style and system, this only imposed any real difficulty upon the borrowing of words and their adaptation to Eldarin. To learn Valarin was probably not beyond the powers of the Eldar, if they had felt the need or desire to do so;

references to the difficulty of Valarin are mainly due to the fact that for most of the Eldar learning it was an ungrateful and profitless task.

For the Eldar had no need to learn the language of Valinor for the purposes of communication; and they had no desire either to abandon or to alter their own tongue, which they loved and of which they were proud. Only those among them, therefore, who had special linguistic curiosity desired to learn Valarin for its own sake. Such 'loremasters' did not always record their knowledge, and many of the records that were made have been lost. Fëanor, who probably knew more of the matter than any of the younger generations born in Aman, deliberately withheld his knowledge.

It was probably only in the very early days that the Eldar heard Valarin much spoken, or had opportunity for learning it, unless by special individual effort. The Teleri had little immediate contact with the Valar and Maiar after their settlement on the shores. The Ñoldor became more and more engrossed with their own pursuits. Only the Vanyar remained in constant association with the Valar. And in any case the Valar appear quickly to have adopted Quenya.

All the orders of Eru's creatures have each some special talent, which higher orders may admire. It was the special talent of the Incarnate, who lived by *necessary* union of *hröa* and *fëa*, to make language. The Quendi, first and chief of the Incarnate, had (or so they held) the greatest talent for the making of *lambe*. The Valar and Maiar admired and took delight in the Eldarin *lambe*, as they did in many other of the skilled and delicate works of the Eldar.

The Valar, therefore, learned Quenya by their own choice, for pleasure as well as for communication; and it seems clear that they preferred that the Eldar should make new words of their own style, or should translate the meanings of names into fair Eldarin forms, rather than [that] they should retain the Valarin words or adapt them to Quenya (a process that in most cases did justice to neither tongue).

Soon after the coming of the Vanyar and Noldor the Valar ceased to speak in their own tongue in the presence of the Eldar, save rarely: as for instance in the great Councils, at which the Eldar were sometimes present. Indeed, it is said that often the Valar and Maiar might be heard speaking Quenya among themselves.

In any case, to speak of the early days of the settlement at Tirion, it was far easier and swifter for the Valar to learn Quenya than to teach the Eldar Valarin. For in a sense no *lambe* was 'alien' to the Self-incarnate. Even when using bodily forms they had less need of any *tengwesta* than had the Incarnate; and they had made a *lambe* for the pleasure of exercising the powers and skills of the bodily form, and (more remotely) for the better understanding of the minds of the Incarnate when they should appear, rather than for any need that they felt among themselves. For the Valar and Maiar could transmit and receive thought directly (by the will of both parties) according to their right nature;[30] and though the use of bodily form (albeit assumed and not imposed) in a measure made this mode of communication less swift and precise, they retained this faculty in a degree far surpassing that seen among any of the Incarnate.

At this point Pengolodh does not further discuss this matter of the transmission and reception of thought, and its limitations in any order of creatures. But he cites, as an example of the speed with which by its aid a *tengwesta* may be learned by a higher order, the story of the Finding of the Edain. According to this the Ñoldorin king, Finrod, quickly learned the tongue of the folk of Bëor whom he discovered in Ossiriand, for he understood in large measure what they meant while they spoke. 'Now Finrod,' he says, 'was renowned among the Eldar for this power which he had, because of the warmth of his heart and his desire to understand others; yet his power was no greater than that of the least of the Maiar.'[31]

Pengolodh concludes as follows. 'In the histories the Valar are always presented as speaking Quenya in all circumstances. *(Note 37, p. 417)* But this cannot proceed from translation by the Eldar, few of whose historians knew Valarin. The translation must have been made by the Valar or Maiar themselves. Indeed those histories or legends that deal with times before the awaking of the Quendi, or with the uttermost past, or with things that the Eldar could not have known, must have been presented from the first in Quenya by the Valar or the Maiar when they instructed the Eldar. Moreover this translation must have concerned more than the mere words of language. If we consider the First History, which is called the *Ainulindalë*: this must have come from the Aratar themselves (for the most part indeed from Manwe, it is believed). Though it was plainly put into its present form by Eldar, and was already in that form when it was recorded by Rúmil, it must nonetheless have been from the first presented to us not only in the words of Quenya, but also according to our modes of thought and our imagination of the visible world, in symbols that were intelligible to us. And these things the Valar understood because they had learned our tongue.'

Author's Notes to Quendi and Eldar

Note 1 (p. 367; referred to in two passages)
Distinguish *yomenie* 'meeting, gathering' (of three or more coming from different directions). The Telerin form was: *ēl sīla lūmena vomentienguo*.

Note 2 (p. 369)
It was a later development in Quenya, after the elements *-ō* and *-vā* had become inflexions, applicable to all nouns, to pluralize *-o* by the addition of the plural sign *-n*, when added to a plural stem (as by natural function it could be): as *lasseo* 'of a leaf', *lassio* > *lassion* 'of leaves'. Similarly with *-va*; but this was and remained an adjective, and had the plural form *-ve* in plural attribution (archaic Q *-vai*); it could not, however, indicate plurality of source, originally, and the Q distinction *Eldava* 'Elf's' and *Eldaiva* 'Elves'' was a Q innovation.

Note 3 (p. 372)
roquen is < *roko-kwēn* with Quenya syncope, *roko* being an older simpler form of the stem, found in some compounds and compound names, though the normal form of the independent word 'horse' had the fortified form *rokko*. These compounds being old were accented as unitary words and the main stress came on the syllable preceding *-quen*: *kirya:quen, kirya:queni*.

Note 4 (p. 373)
That is, elliptically for *Quenya lambe*, as *English* for *English language*. When historians needed a general adjective 'Quendian, belonging to the Elves as a whole', they made the new adjective *Quenderin* (on the model of *Eldarin, Ñoldorin*, etc.); but this remained a learned word.

Note 5 (p. 375)
This change took place far back in Elvish linguistic history; possibly before the Separation. It is in any case common to the Telerin of Aman, Sindarin, and Nandorin.

Note 6 (p. 375)

The Ñoldorin Loremasters record that *Pendi* was used by the Teleri only of the earliest days, because they felt that it meant 'the lacking, the poor' (*PEN), with reference to the indigence and ignorance of the primitive Elves.

Note 7 (p. 377)

The Dwarves were in a special position. They claimed to have known Beleriand before even the Eldar first came there; and there do appear to have been small groups dwelling furtively in the highlands west of Sirion from a very early date: they attacked and waylaid the Elves by stealth, and the Elves did not at first recognize them as Incarnates, but thought them to be some kind of cunning animal, and hunted them. By their own account they were fugitives, driven into the wilderness by their own kin further east, and later they were called the *Noegyth Nibin*[32] or Petty-dwarves, for they had become smaller than the norm of their kind, and filled with hate for all other creatures. When the Elves met the powerful Dwarves of Nogrod and Belegost, in the eastern side of the Mountains, they recognized them as Incarnates, for they had skill in many crafts, and learned the Elvish speech readily for purposes of traffic. At first the Elves were in doubt concerning them, believing them to be related to Orcs and creatures of Morgoth; but when they found that, though proud and unfriendly, they could be trusted to keep any treaties that they made, and did not molest those who left them in peace, they traded with them and let them come and go as they would. They no longer classed them as *Moerbin*, but neither did they ever reckon them as *Celbin*, calling them the *Dornhoth* ('the thrawn folk') or the *Naugrim* ('the stunted people'). [See further on the Petty-dwarves pp. 388–9.]

Note 8 (p. 377)

Though *Morben* might still be applied to them by any who remained hostile to Men (as were the people of Doriath for the most part); but this was intended to be insulting.

Note 9 (p. 377; referred to in two passages)

The implication that as opposed to *Celbin* the *Moerbin* were allies of Morgoth, or at least of dubious loyalty, was, however, untrue with regard to the Avari. No Elf of any kind ever sided with Morgoth of free will, though under torture or the stress of great fear, or deluded by lies, they might obey his commands: but this applied also to *Celbin*. The 'Dark-elves', however, often were hostile, and even treacherous, in their dealings with the Sindar and Ñoldor; and if they fought, as they did when themselves assailed by the Orcs, they never took any open part in the War on the side of the Celbin. They were, it seems, filled with an inherited bitterness against the Eldar, whom they regarded as deserters of their kin, and in Beleriand this feeling was increased by envy (especially of the Amanyar), and by resentment of their lordliness. The belief of the Celbin that, at the least, they were weaker in resistance to the pressures or lies of Morgoth, if this grievance was concerned, may have been justified; but the only case recorded in the histories is that of Maeglin, the son of Eöl. Eöl was a Mornedhel, and is said to have belonged to the Second Clan (whose representatives among the Eldar were the Ñoldor).[33] He dwelt in East Beleriand not far from the borders of Doriath. He had great smith-craft, especially in the making of swords, in which work he surpassed even the Ñoldor of Aman; and many therefore believed that he used the morgul, the black arts taught by Morgoth. The Ñoldor themselves had indeed learned much from Morgoth in the days of his captivity in Valinor; but it is more likely that Eöl was acquainted with the Dwarves, for in many places the Avari became closer in friendship with that people than the Amanyar or the Sindar. Eöl found Írith,[34] the sister of King Turgon, astray in the wild near his dwelling, and he took her to wife by force: a very wicked deed in the eyes of the Eldar. His son Maeglin was later admitted to Gondolin, and given honour as the king's sisterson; but in the end he betrayed Gondolin to Morgoth. Maeglin was indeed an Elf of evil temper and dark mind, and he had a lust and grudge of his own to satisfy; but even so he did what he did only after torment and under a cloud of fear. Some of the Nandor, who were allowed to be Celbin, were not any better. Saeros, a counsellor of King Thingol, who belonged to a small clan of Nandor living in eastern Doriath, was chiefly responsible for the driving into outlawry of Túrin son of Húrin. Túrin's mother was named Morwen 'dark maiden', because of her dark hair, and it was one of Saeros' worst insults to call her Morben. For that Túrin smote him in the king's hall.[35]

This resentment on the part of the Avari is illustrated by the history of PQ *kwendī. This word, as has been shown, did not survive in the Telerin languages of Middle-earth, and was almost forgotten even in the Telerin of Aman. But the Lore-masters of later days, when more friendly relations had been established with Avari of various kinds in Eriador and the Vale of Anduin, record that it was frequently to be found in Avarin dialects. These were numerous, and often as widely sundered from one another as they were from the Eldarin forms of Elvish speech; but wherever the descendants of *kwendī were found, they meant not 'Elves in general', but were the names that the Avari gave to themselves. They had evidently continued to call themselves *kwendī, 'the People', regarding those who went away as deserters – though according to Eldarin tradition the numbers of the Eldar at the time of the Separation were in the approximate proportion of 3:2, as compared with the Avari (see p. 381). The Avarin forms cited by the Loremasters were: kindi, cuind, hwenti, windan, kinn-lai, penni. The last is interesting as showing the change kw > p. This might be independent of the Common Telerin change; but it suggests that it had already occurred among the Lindar before the Separation. The form penni is cited as coming from the 'Wood-elven' speech of the Vale of Anduin, and these Elves were among the most friendly to the fugitives from Beleriand, and held themselves akin to the remnants of the Sindar.

Note 10 (p. 378)
It is not surprising that the Edain, when they learned Sindarin, and to a certain extent Quenya also, found it difficult to discern whether words and names containing the element el referred to the stars or to the Elves. This is seen in the name Elendil, which became a favourite name among the Edain, but was meant to bear the sense 'Elf-friend'. Properly in Quenya it meant 'a lover or student of the stars', and was applied to those devoted to astronomical lore. 'Elf-friend' would have been more correctly represented by Quen(den)dil or Eldandil.

Note 11 (p. 378)
Lake Mithrim, meaning originally 'Lake of the Mithrim'. Mithrim was a name given to them by the southern-dwellers, because of the cooler climate and greyer skies, and the mists of the North. It was probably because the Noldor first came into contact with this northerly branch that they gave in Quenya the name Sindar or Sindeldi 'Grey-elves' to all the Telerin inhabitants of the Westlands who spoke the Sindarin language.[36] Though this name was also later held to refer to Elwe's name Thingol (Sindikollo) 'Grey-cloak', since he was acknowledged as high-king of all the land and its peoples. It is said also that the

folk of the North were clad much in grey, especially after the return of Morgoth when secrecy became needed; and the Mithrim had an art of weaving a grey cloth that made its wearers almost invisible in shadowy places or in a stony land. This art was later used even in the southern lands as the dangers of the War increased.

Note 12 (p. 380)
The language of Mithrim was also a marked dialect; but none of the dialects of Sindarin differed widely enough to interfere with intercourse. Their divergences were no greater than those that had arisen between the Quenya as spoken by the Vanyar, and as spoken by the Ñoldor at the time of the Exile.

Note 13 (p. 380)
For the late PQ *gl-* as an initial variation of *l-* see General Phonology.[37] Though this Clan-name has **glind-* in Sindarin, the *g-* does not appear in Amanya Telerin, nor in Nandorin, so that in this case it may be an addition in Sindarin, which favoured and much increased initial groups of this kind.

Note 14 (p. 382)
For this reason the most frequently used of the 'titles' or secondary names of the Lindar was *Nendili* 'Water-lovers'.

Note 15 (p. 382)
A simple agental formation (like **abaro* > **abar* from **ABA*) from the stem **TELE*, the primary sense of which appears to have been 'close, end, come at the end': hence in Q *telda* 'last, final'; *tele-* intransitive verb 'finish, end', or 'be the last thing or person in a series or sequence of events'; *telya* transitive verb 'finish, wind up, conclude'; *telma* 'a conclusion, anything used to finish off a work or affair'. This was possibly distinct from **tel-u* 'roof in, put the crown on a building', seen in Q *telume* 'roof, canopy'. (This was probably one of the earliest Quendian words for the heavens, the firmament, before the increase of their knowledge, and the invention of the Eldarin word *Menel*. Cf. *Telumehtar* 'warrior of the sky', an older name for *Menelmakil*, Orion.) The word *telluma* 'dome, cupola' is an alteration of *telume* under the influence of Valarin *delgūmā*: see p. 399. But **telu* may be simply a differentiated form of **TELE*, since the roof was the final work of a building; cf. *telma*, which was often applied to the last item in a structure, such as a coping-stone, or a topmost pinnacle.

Note 16 (p. 384)
See above, p. 381. The proportion, per 144, of the Eldar
remaining in Middle-earth was reckoned at 26, of which about
8 were Nandor.

Note 17 (p. 384)
Lenwe is the form in which his name was remembered in
Ñoldorin histories. His name was probably **Denwego*, Nandorin *Denweg*. His son was the Nandorin chieftain *Denethor*.
These names probably meant 'lithe-and-active' and 'lithe-and-
lank', from **dene-* 'thin and strong, pliant, lithe', and **thara-*
'tall (or long) and slender'.

Note 18 (p. 384)
The name *Nandor* was a derivative of the element **dan*, **ndan-*
indicating the reversal of an action, so as to undo or nullify its
effect, as in 'undo, go back (the same way), unsay, give back (the
same gift: not another in return)'. The original word **ndandō*,
therefore, probably only implied 'one who goes back on his
word or decision'.

Note 19 (p. 386)
In Q *Eldameldor*, S *Elvellyn*. That is, 'Elf-lovers'. The words
Quendili, *Eldandili* (see Note 10), though not excluding
affection and personal loyalties, would have implied also deep
concern with all lore relative to the Elves, which was not
necessarily included in the words *meldor*, *mellyn* 'lovers,
friends'.

Note 20 (p. 387)
That is, to die by nature, of age or weariness, and inevitably, not
only (as the Elves) of some grievous hurt or sorrow.

Note 21 (p. 387)
S *-eb* is from **ikwā*, CT **-ipā*, probably related to the Q *-inqua*.
Cf. S *aglareb* 'glorious', Q *alkarinqua*. Both are probably
related to the element **kwa*, **kwa-ta* seen in Eldarin words for
'full'.

Note 22 (p. 388)
S *ch* was only an approximation; the Dwarvish *kh* was in fact
a strong aspirate, not a spirant. Similarly at the time of the
borrowing Sindarin did not possess either the sound *z* or long *ā*.
This does not mean that the Elves could not imitate or acquire
sounds alien to their native speech. All the Elves had great skill
in language, and far surpassed Men in this matter. The Ñoldor

were the chief linguists of the Elves, but their superiority was shown not so much in the acquisition of new tongues as in their love of language, their inventiveness, and their concern with the lore of language, and the history and relations of different tongues. In adopting a word for use in their own tongue (which they loved) Elves fitted it to their own style for aesthetic reasons.

Note 23 (p. 388)

These words are derived from the stem *NUKU 'dwarf, stunted, not reaching full growth or achievement, failing of some mark or standard', seen in *nuktā-, Q *nuhta-* 'stunt, prevent from coming to completion, stop short, not allow to continue', S *nuitha-* of similar senses. An adjectival formation was *naukā, from which were derived S *naug*, Q *nauka*, especially applied to things that though in themselves full-grown were smaller or shorter than their kind, and were hard, twisted or ill-shapen. *Nogoth* is probably from some such form as *nukotto/a 'a stunted or ill-shapen thing (or person)'.

Note 24 (p. 388)

The Q *h* had become too weak to represent aspirate *kh* which was therefore rendered by *k*. Final *d* had become *r*, and this change was recognized in the adaptation. Medial $z < s$ had become *r* in the Noldorin dialect of Q except when an adjacent syllable, or (as here) the same syllable, already contained an *r*.

Note 25 (p. 388)

Norno is a personalized form of the adjective *norna* 'stiff, tough', the Q equivalent of S *dorn*. Both are from the stem *DORO 'dried up, hard, unyielding'. With the frequent initial enrichment $d > nd$ this appears in PQ *ndorē 'the hard, dry land as opposed to water or bog > land in general as opposed to sea; a land (a particular region with more or less defined bounds)'. Hence S *dôr* (*-ndor > -nor, -nnor*) 'land'. In Q this word became confused or blended with the distinct *nōrē from the stem *ONO (see p. 387), 'family, tribe or group having a common ancestry, the land or region in which they dwelt'. Thus Q *nóre* was generally used for 'land' associated with a particular people, and the old *ndorē survived only in name-compounds: as *Valinóre < *Valinōrē 'the people and land of the Valar', beside *Valinor, Valandor*. A particular land or region was in Q *arda*; 'land' as opposed to water or sea was *nór* (< *ndōro*) as opposed to *eär*. The Q forms *norna, Norno* may also contain *nd-*, though S *dorn* does not; but this is probably one of the cases in which Q initial *d* became *n-*, not *l-*, by assimilation to an *n* occurring later in the word.

Note 26 (p. 389)

Novrod was the oldest form, and appears in the earlier annals, beside the variant *Grodnof*. These contain the CE elements **nāba* 'hollow', and *(g)rotā* 'excavation, underground dwelling'. *Novrod* retains the older Eldarin (and the Dwarvish) order with the adjectival element first. At the time of its making **nāba-grota* had no doubt already reached its archaic S form **nǫv-ʒrot* > *novrod*. *Grodnof* has the same elements in the later more usual Sindarin order. The form *Nogrod* which later became usual is due to the substitution of *Nog-*, taken as a form of *Naug* 'dwarf' (with the usual change of *au* > *o*), after the element *Nov-* had become obscure. The adjective **nāba* > *nǫv*, *nǫf* only remained current in the Northern dialect, where the name *Novrod* originated. In the other dialects *nǫv*, as a stressed independent word, proceeded to *nauv* > *naw* (with the usual loss of final *v* after *au*, *u*), and this word ceased to be used in current speech. *Novrod* in earlier annals is sometimes found glossed *Bar-goll* 'hollow dwelling', using the more current adjective *coll* < **kuldā*.

Hadhodrond uses the adapted form *Hadhod* = *Khazād*. The element *rond* is not related to *grod*, *-rod*. The latter is from **groto* 'dig, excavate, tunnel'. S *rond*, Q *rondo* are from **rono* 'arch over, roof in'. This could be applied both to natural and to artificial structures, but its view was always from below and from the inside. (Contrast the derivatives of **tel*, **telu* mentioned in Note 15.) CE **rondō* meant 'a vaulted or arched roof, as seen from below (and usually not visible from outside)', or 'a (large) hall or chamber so roofed'. It was still often applied pictorially to the heavens after the Elves had obtained much greater knowledge of 'Star-lore'. Cf. the name *Elrond* 'Star-dome' (*Elros* meant 'Star-glitter'). Cf. also S *othrond* applied to an underground stronghold, made or enlarged by excavation, containing one or more of such great vaulted halls. *othrond* is < S *ost+rond*. CE **ostō*, Q *osto*, S *ost*, is derived from **soto* 'shelter, protect, defend', and was applied to any fortress or stronghold made or strengthened by art. The most famous example, after the great dwelling of Elwe at Menegroth, was *Nargothrond* < *Narog-ost-rond* ('the great underground burg and halls upon the River Narog'), which was made by Finrod, or completed and enlarged by him from the more primitive dwellings made by the Petty-dwarves.

Though distinct in origin the derivatives of *groto* and *rono* naturally came into contact, since they were not dissimilar in shape, and a *rondō* was usually made by excavation. Thus S *groth* < *grottā* (an intensified form of *grod* < *grotā*) 'a large excavation' might well apply to a *rond*. *Menegroth* means 'the Thousand Caves or Delvings', but it contained one great *rond* and many minor ones.

Note 27 (p. 390)
(ñ)guruk is due to a combination of *(g)ruk* with *NGUR 'horror', seen in S *gorth*, *gorthob* 'horror, horrible', and (reduplicated) *gorgor* 'extreme horror'.

Note 28 (p. 390)
Some other derivatives are in Quenya: *rukin* 'I feel fear or horror' (constructed with 'from' of the object feared); *ruhta-* 'terrify'; *rúkima* 'terrible'; *rauko* and *arauko* < *grauk-*) 'a powerful, hostile, and terrible creature', especially in the compound *Valarauko* 'Demon of Might', applied later to the more powerful and terrible of the Maia servants of Morgoth. In Sindarin appear, for instance, *raug* and *graug*, and the compound *Balrog* (equivalents of Q *rauko*, etc.); *groga-* 'feel terror'; *gruitha* 'terrify'; *gorog* (< *guruk*) 'horror'.

Note 29 (p. 392)
Affixes appear in *equen* 'said I', *eques* 'said he / she', used in reporting a dialogue.

Note 30 (p. 392)
ekwē was probably a primitive past tense, marked as such by the 'augment' or reduplicated base-vowel, and the long stem-vowel. Past tenses of this form were usual in Sindarin 'strong' or primary verbs: as *akāra* 'made, did' > S *agor*. *akwā*, however, was probably not verbal, but an extension or intensification of *kwā*, used adverbially.

Note 31 (p. 392)
In Eldarin languages this is usually found in the forms *-ikwā* or *-ukwā*, or with nasal infixion *-iñkwā*, *-uñkwā*. The vowels *i*, *u* were probably derived from the terminations of nouns or other stems to which *kwā* was added, but the dissyllabic suffixal forms had become quite independent of this origin. The forms using *u* were mainly applied to things heavy, clumsy, ugly or bad.

Note 32 (p. 393)

Little is said in Ñoldorin lore concerning the language of the Valar and Maiar; but on this point a note is added at the end of this Appendix (pp. 397 ff.).

Note 33 (p. 394)

lamba is derived from *LABA 'move the tongue, lick', and may be referred to *lab-mā (with a suffix frequent in the names of implements): the group *bm* > *mb* in CE and possibly earlier. *lambe* is probably from *lab-mē, denoting the action of *LABA, or the use of the *lambā. (Cf. *JULU 'drink', *julmā, Q *yulma*, S *ylf* 'drinking-vessel'; *julmē, Q *yulme*, 'drinking, carousal'.) These words have no original connexion with *LAMA which refers to sounds, especially to vocal sounds, but was applied only to those that were confused or inarticulate. It was generally used to describe the various cries of beasts. Hence the word *laman(a), *lamān, Q *laman*, pl. *lamni* or *lamani*; S *lavan*, pl. *levain*, 'animal', usually only applied to four-footed beasts, and never to reptiles or birds. (This may be compared with *kwene 'user of articulate speech'.) The Sindarin *glam* < *glamb* / *glamm* (p. 391) is an elaboration of *LAM.

Note 34 (p. 394)

In genuine independent use mainly employed between persons out of earshot: the Elves had astonishingly acute eyesight at a distance. These 'signals' were really distinct from the gestures (especially those of the hands) made as concomitants to speech and additions to tone-changes for the conveyance of feeling, though some of the gestures in both systems were similar. The Elves made considerable use of the concomitant gestures, especially in oration or recitation.

Note 35 (p. 398)

By which Pengolodh meant the knowledge available in Middle-earth. The *Lammas* was composed in Eriador.

Note 36 (p. 404)

Other later Loremasters conjectured that *Nessa* was in fact Elvish in form (though archaic, on Pengolodh's own principle), being < *neresā, a feminine adjectival formation from *NER, meaning 'she that has manlike valour or strength'. They also would remove *Taniquetil* from the group of 'translations'. *Arfanyarasse*, they say, is the translation: 'high (i.e. noble, revered) – shining white – peak', but *Taniquetil* is an adaptation, though one that has probably greatly altered the original in the attempt to give the name some kind of Eldarin significance: ? high white point. As they say, *ta-* does not mean 'lofty' in Eldarin, though it may remind one of *tára* 'tall, high' (*TAR); *nique* does not refer to snow, but to cold; and Q *tilde*, -*til* is not a mountain peak, but a fine sharp point (mostly used of small and slender things). For *nique* cf. Q *niku-* 'be chill, cold (of weather)'; *nique* 'it is cold, it freezes'; *ninque* 'chill, pallid', *nixe* 'frost', *niquis*, *niquesse* 'frost-patterns' (the latter by association with *quesse* 'feather').

Most significant, they cite from an ancient legend of the Flight the tale that as the mists of Araman wrapped the distant mountains of Valinor from the sight of the Ñoldor, Fëanor raised his hands in token of rejection and cried: 'I go. Neither in light or shadow will I look upon you again, *Dahanigwishtilgūn.*' So it was recorded, though the writers of the histories no longer knew what he meant. For which reason the strange word may have been ill transmitted. But even so it still bears some likeness to *Taniquetil*, though it can no longer be analysed. (In a few versions, say the Loremasters, it is written *dāhanigwiš-telgūn.*) They also cite *Fionwe* [read *Eönwe*?] (the herald of Manwe) as another name for which no Elvish etymology is known.

Note 37 (p. 406)
Usually in a formal and elevated style. Often, when there were differences, rather according to the Vanyarin manner than the Ñoldorin, for the Vanyar were most in their company; though the Ñoldorin writers have sometimes substituted their own forms.

Editorial Notes

1 'affection': mutation (of the vowel *o* caused by the following *i* in *Mori(quendi)*).
2 *sundóma*: see p. 319.
3 *omentielvo*: this was typed *omentielmo*, subsequently changed to *omentielvo*. The same change was made in the Second Edition of *The Fellowship of the Ring* (p. 90).
4 *The Fellowship of the Ring* p. 367 (at the end of the chapter *Lothlórien*); First Edition *vanimalda*, Second Edition *vanimelda*.
5 The term *ómataina* or 'vocalic extension' is used of the addition to the 'base' of a final vowel identical to the *sundóma* (p. 319).
6 'The glooms and the clouds dimming the sun and the stars': an explicit reference, it seems, to some form of the changed astronomical myth adumbrated in Text II of the section 'Myths

Transformed' in *Morgoth's Ring*. In that text my father raised the question 'how can the Eldar be called the "Star-folk"?' if the Sun is 'coeval with the Earth' (X.375); and proposed a complex story (X.377–8) in which the darkening of the world by Melkor, who brought up vast glooms to shut out all vision of the heavens, is a chief element. See further pp. 423–4.

7   'The first people of this kind to be met were the Nandor': this strangely contradicts the history recorded in the *Annals* (GA §19, p. 9; also AAm §84, X.93), according to which the Dwarves first entered Beleriand in Valian Year 1250, and the building of Menegroth was achieved before the coming of Denethor, leader of the Nandor, in 1350 (pp. 11–13). The following statement here that the first invasions of the Orcs followed Morgoth's return is an equally striking contradiction of the *Annals*: according to GA §27 Orcs entered Beleriand in 1330 (cf. also X.106, §85): 'Whence they came, or what they were, the Elves knew not then, deeming them to be Avari, maybe, that had become evil and savage in the wild.'

8   'from Cape Andras to the headland of Bar-in-Mŷl': *Cape Andras* was entered on the map (p. 184, square G 2), but the headland to the south (itself an extension of the coastline as originally drawn) is there called *Ras Mewrim* (p. 190, §63). The name in the present text was typed *Bar-in-Gwael*; the translation 'Home of the Gulls' was added at the same time as the change to *Bar-in-Mŷl* (by a later pencilled change on one copy *-in-* > *-i-*).

9   *Brithonbar*, not *Brithombar*, is the form typed, and not corrected.

10 With this passage on the subject of the Eglain cf. p. 189, §57, and pp. 343–4. The concluding sentence 'But they acknowledged the high-kingship of Thingol, and Círdan never took the title of king' differs from the *Annals*, where Círdan either acknowledged Felagund of Nargothrond as overlord, or else was (as it seems) an independent Lord of the Falas 'yet ever close in friendship with Nargothrond' (GA §85, and commentary p. 117).

11 For the legend of *Imin*, *Tata*, and *Enel* see pp. 420 ff.

12 The story found in the *Annals of Aman* of the kindreds of Morwë and Nurwë, who refused the summons of the Valar and became the Avari (X.81–2, 88, 168), had been abandoned.

13 The name *Lindar* 'Singers' of the Teleri has appeared in the 'Glossary' to the *Athrabeth Finrod ah Andreth* (X.349); it was for long the name of the First Kindred, the later Vanyar.

14 On the waterfall of Cuiviénen see p. 424.

15 In other late writing Círdan is said to have been of the kin of Elwë, but I have not found any statement of the nature of the kinship.

16 *Lenwë* has replaced the long-standing name *Dân* of Denethor's

father; from this text it was adopted in *The Silmarillion*.

17   The statement that the Nandor entered Beleriand 'not long before the return of Morgoth' is another remarkable contradiction of the *Annals* (cf. note 7 above). Earlier (p. 377) it is said that they came 'before the return of Morgoth', which no doubt implies the same. But in GA §31 there is a marvellous evocation of 'the long years of peace that followed after the coming of Denethor', and they were indeed long: from 1350 to 1495, 145 Valian Years, or 1389 Years of the Sun. I am at a loss to explain these profound changes in the embedded history.

18   On the Adunaic word *Nimir* 'Elf' see *The Drowning of Anadûnê* (Vol.IX, Index II, p. 473).

19   *Fírimar*: the old form was *Fírimor* (QS §83, V.245, footnote). An account of the development of meaning in the verb *fírë* is given in connection with *Fíriel*, the later name of Míriel, in X.250.

20   The name *Nogoth niben* was adopted in *The Silmarillion* (in the plural, *Noegyth nibin*: see Note 7 to the present text, p. 408); the word *nogoth* of the Dwarves has not occurred before (see note 32 below). For other names and name-forms of the Petty-dwarves see p. 187, §26.

21   In the revision of the QS chapter on the Dwarves the Sindarin name of Khazad-dûm was *Nornhabar*, translated 'Dwarrowdelf' (p. 206). 'Dwarrowdelf' is found also in *The Fellowship of the Ring*; in the present text the Sindarin name was typed *Hadhodrûd* and translated 'Dwarrowmine', but the change to *Hadhodrond* 'Dwarrowvault' was made immediately. *Hadhodrond* was adopted in *The Silmarillion*.

22   Cf. Appendix F to *The Lord of the Rings*, p. 409: 'The lesser kinds were called, especially by the Uruk-hai, *snaga* "slave".'

23   Fëanor held that, in spite of the usual mode of spelling, vowels were each independent *tengwi* or word-building elements.

24   On one copy only a later pencilled correction changed *SAR to *SYAR.

25   At the head of the page is a pencilled note on one copy only: 'Change *Pengolodh* to *Thingódhel*'.

26   For the word *equessi* see p. 392. Both in that passage and in the present one the word was typed *Equeri* and then corrected.

27   For the old conception in the *Lhammas* of the 1930s, according to which the origin of all Elvish speech was in the language of the Valar (communicated to the Elves by Oromë), see V.168, 192–3.

28   In *The Road Goes Ever On*, p. 61, the name *miruvórë* (occurring in *Namárië*) is said to be of Valarin origin.

29   Cf. Note 2 on the Commentary on the *Athrabeth Finrod ah Andreth* (X.337), where it is said that 'Physically Arda was what we should call the Solar System', and that in Elvish traditions 'the principal part of Arda was the Earth (*Imbar* "the Habitation") ...

so that loosely used Arda often seems to mean the Earth'. For *Ambar* see the references given in X.359, note 12.

30   Cf. AAm §164 (X.129): 'without voices in silence [the gods] may hold council one with another', and the passage cited from *The Return of the King* in my note on that passage (X.135).

31   Cf. the late QS chapter *Of the Coming of Men into the West*, p. 217: 'Felagund discovered ... that he could read in the minds of Men such thoughts as they wished to reveal in speech, so that their words were easily interpreted.'

32   *Noegyth Nibin* was a correction of the name typed, *Nibinn..g*, probably *Nibinnoeg* (see p. 187, §26). The notes being interspersed in the text, this note was written before the passage on p. 388 was reached.

33   It is curious that – as in the original text of *Maeglin*, where he was 'of the kin of Thingol' – in my father's very late work on the story Eöl becomes again 'one of the Eldar' (p. 328), though consumed with hatred of the Noldor; whereas here he is a *Mornedhel* (one of the Avari), and moreover of the aboriginal Second Clan.

34   The name *Írith* is found as a correction (made after the publication of *The Lord of the Rings*) of the old name *Isfin* in QS §42 (X.177). When my father worked on the *Maeglin* story c.1970 he appears to have forgotten *Írith*, for his notes at that time express dissatisfaction with the 'meaningless' name *Isfin* as if it had never been replaced (pp. 317–18).

35   Saeros' insulting of Túrin by calling his mother Morwen *Morben* was a development in the story (see QS §39, V.321, and *Unfinished Tales* p. 80) that could only arise, of course, with the emergence of the words *Calben* and *Morben*.

36   Neither the interpretation of *Mithrim* as the name of a people (for the old etymology see V.383–4, stem RINGI) nor this explanation of the name *Sindar* have been met before.

37   'General Phonology': my father was not here referring to any specific, completed work.

APPENDIX

The legend of the Awaking of the Quendi
(Cuivienyarna)

It is said in *Quendi and Eldar*, p. 380:

According to the legend, preserved in almost identical form among both the Elves of Aman and the Sindar, the Three Clans were in the beginning derived from the three Elf-fathers: *Imin*, *Tata*, and *Enel* (sc. One, Two, Three), and those whom each chose to join his following. So they had at first simply the names *Minyar* 'Firsts', *Tatyar* 'Seconds', and *Nelyar* 'Thirds'. These numbered, out of the

original 144 Elves that first awoke, 14, 56, and 74; and these proportions were approximately maintained until the Separation.
A form of this legend is found in a single typescript with carbon copy.
On one copy my father wrote (and similarly but more briefly on the
other): 'Actually written (in style and simple notions) to be a surviving
Elvish "fairytale" or child's tale, mingled with counting-lore'. Corrections to either copy are taken up in the text that follows.

While their first bodies were being made from the 'flesh of Arda'
the Quendi slept 'in the womb of the Earth', beneath the green
sward, and awoke when they were full-grown. But the First
Elves (also called the Unbegotten, or the Eru-begotten) did not
all wake together. Eru had so ordained that each should lie
beside his or her 'destined spouse'. But three Elves awoke first of
all, and they were elf-men, for elf-men are more strong in body
and more eager and adventurous in strange places. These three
Elf-fathers are named in the ancient tales *Imin*, *Tata*, and *Enel*.
They awoke in that order, but with little time between each; and
from them, say the Eldar, the words for one, two, and three
were made: the oldest of all numerals.*

Imin, Tata and Enel awoke before their spouses, and the first
thing that they saw was the stars, for they woke in the early
twilight before dawn. And the next thing they saw was their
destined spouses lying asleep on the green sward beside them.
Then they were so enamoured of their beauty that their desire
for speech was immediately quickened and they began to 'think
of words' to speak and sing in. And being impatient they could
not wait but woke up their spouses. Thus, the Eldar say, the first
thing that each elf-woman saw was her spouse, and her love for
him was her first love; and her love and reverence for the
wonders of Arda came later.

Now after a time, when they had dwelt together a little, and
had devised many words, Imin and Iminyë, Tata and Tatië, Enel
and Enelyë walked together, and left the green dell of their
waking, and they came soon to another larger dell and found
there six pairs of Quendi, and the stars were again shining in the
morrow-dim and the elf-men were just waking.

Then Imin claimed to be the eldest and to have the right of

* [footnote to the text] The Eldarin words referred to are *Min*, *Atta*
(or *Tata*), *Nel*. The reverse is probably historical. The Three had no
names until they had developed language, and were given (or took)
names after they had devised numerals (or at least the first twelve).

first choice; and he said: 'I choose these twelve to be my companions.' And the elf-men woke their spouses, and when the eighteen Elves had dwelt together a little and had learned many words and devised more, they walked on together, and soon in another even deeper and wider hollow they found nine pairs of Quendi, and the elf-men had just waked in the starlight.

Then Tata claimed the right of second choice, and he said: 'I choose these eighteen to be my companions.' Then again the elf-men woke their spouses, and they dwelt and spoke together, and devised many new sounds and longer words; and then the thirty-six walked abroad together, until they came to a grove of birches by a stream, and there they found twelve pairs of Quendi, and the elf-men likewise were just standing up, and looking at the stars through the birch boughs.

Then Enel claimed the right of third choice, and he said: 'I choose these twenty-four to be my companions.' Again the elf-men woke their spouses; and for many days the sixty Elves dwelt by the stream, and soon they began to make verse and song to the music of the water.

At length they all set out together again. But Imin noticed that each time they had found more Quendi than before, and he thought to himself: 'I have only twelve companions (although I am the eldest); I will take a later choice.' Soon they came to a sweet-smelling firwood on a hill-side, and there they found eighteen pairs of Quendi, and all were still sleeping. It was still night and clouds were in the sky. But before dawn a wind came, and roused the elf-men, and they woke and were amazed at the stars; for all the clouds were blown away and the stars were bright from east to west. And for a long time the eighteen new Quendi took no heed of the others, but looked at the lights of Menel. But when at last they turned their eyes back to earth they beheld their spouses and woke them to look at the stars, crying to them *elen, elen!* And so the stars got their name.

Now Imin said: 'I will not choose again yet'; and Tata, therefore, chose these thirty-six to be his companions; and they were tall and dark-haired and strong like fir-trees, and from them most of the Ñoldor later were sprung.

And the ninety-six Quendi now spoke together, and the newly-waked devised many new and beautiful words, and many cunning artifices of speech; and they laughed, and danced upon the hill-side, until at last they desired to find more companions. Then they all set out again together, until they came to a lake dark in the twilight; and there was a great cliff about it upon the east-side, and a waterfall came down from the height, and the stars glittered on the foam. But the elf-men were already bathing in the waterfall, and they had waked their spouses. There were twenty-four pairs; but as yet they had no formed speech, though they sang sweetly and their voices echoed in the stone, mingling with the rush of the falls.

But again Imin withheld his choice, thinking 'next time it will be a great company'. Therefore Enel said: 'I have the choice, and I choose these forty-eight to be my companions.' And the hundred and forty-four Quendi dwelt long together by the lake, until they all became of one mind and speech, and were glad.

At length Imin said: 'It is time now that we should go on and seek more companions.' But most of the others were content. So Imin and Iminyë and their twelve companions set out, and they walked long by day and by twilight in the country about the lake, near which all the Quendi had awakened – for which reason it is called Cuiviénen. But they never found any more companions, for the tale of the First Elves was complete.

And so it was that the Quendi ever after reckoned in twelves, and that 144 was for long their highest number, so that in none of their later tongues was there any common name for a greater number. And so also it came about that the 'Companions of Imin' or the Eldest Company (of whom came the Vanyar) were nonetheless only fourteen in all, and the smallest company; and the 'Companions of Tata' (of whom came the Ñoldor) were fifty-six in all; but the 'Companions of Enel' although the Youngest Company were the largest; from them came the Teleri (or Lindar), and they were in the beginning seventy-four in all.

Now the Quendi loved all of Arda that they had yet seen, and green things that grew and the sun of summer were their delight; but nonetheless they were ever moved most in heart by the Stars, and the hours of twilight in clear weather, at 'morrow-dim' and at 'even-dim', were the times of their greatest joy. For in those hours in the spring of the year they had first awakened to life in Arda. But the Lindar, above all the other Quendi, from their beginning were most in love with water, and sang before they could speak.

It seems that my father had resolved (at least for the purpose of this 'fairy-tale') the problem of the name 'Star-folk' of the Elves (see p. 417, note 6) in a beautifully simple way: the first Elves awoke in the late night under skies of unclouded stars, and the stars were their earliest memory.

In *Quendi and Eldar* (p. 382) my father wrote of 'the lake and waterfall of Cuiviénen', and this is explained in the *Cuivienyarna*: 'they came to a lake dark in the twilight; and there was a great cliff about it upon the east-side, and a waterfall came down from the height, and the stars glittered on the foam.' Through so many years he was returning to Gilfanon's Tale in *The Book of Lost Tales* (I.232):

Now the places about Koivië-néni the Waters of Awakening are rugged and full of mighty rocks, and the stream that feeds that water falls therein down a deep cleft ... a pale and slender thread, but the issue of the dark lake was beneath the earth into many endless caverns falling ever more deeply into the bosom of the world.

INDEX

Elements in this book have greatly taxed my limited powers as an index-maker: notably, the reconstitution of the genealogy of the ruling house of the people of Brethil, introducing extremely complex movements of closely similar names, but also in such matters as the Dwarf-cities or the terms in different languages for 'Eldar', 'Elves'. I have found it often impossible within a short space to give an adequate indication of the bearings and relations of names, and my brief explanatory identifications cannot in such cases be pressed.

Whereas in the texts themselves I have very largely followed my father's very variable usage in respect of capitalisation, hyphenation, separation of elements, or placing of a diaeresis (*Ëarendil, Eärendil*), in the index I employ constant forms (and such devices as the combination of *Eryd-* and *Ered-* in the names of mountain-ranges in a single entry). For 'voiced *th*' I use '*dh*' (*Aredhel*) rather than 'ð' (*Areðel*).

Names appearing in the genealogical tables of the houses of the Edain are included, as also are those on the maps (pp. 182–5), these latter being indicated by asterisks; but names on the map repeated on p. 331 are not, unless additional or altered.

In the entries relating to Part Four (*Quendi and Eldar*) names of languages, as *Quenya, Sindarin,* or *Common Eldarin,* include the many instances where abbreviations are used in the text. No Valarin names are recorded in the index, and only exceptionally the 'deduced' or 'unrecorded' name-forms marked in the text by asterisks.

Names occurring in the titles or sub-titles of chapters, etc. are only exceptionally included.

Abari See *Avari.*
Abonnen See *Apanónar.*
Adan See *Edain.*
Adanel 'Wise-woman' of the People of Marach. 230–1, 233–5
Adûnaic 390, 402, 419
Adurant, River In Ossiriand. 13, *185, 191, 195
Ælfwine 192–3, 206, 311–12, 314–15
Aelin-uial 194. See *Hithliniath, Umboth Muilin, Twilight Meres.*
Aeluin See *Tarn-aeluin.*
Aerandir Companion of Eärendil on his voyages; earlier form *Airandir.* 246

Ened   Island in the Ocean west of Drengist. 181, *182
Enel   'Three', the third of the Fathers of the Elves. 380, 418, 420–3; *Companions of Enel* 423. See *Nelyar.*
Enelyë   Spouse of Enel. 421
Enemy, The   17, 29, 31, 50, 55, 59, 118, 166, 253
Enfeng   'Longbeards', Dwarves of Belegost. 10–13, 75, 108, 134, 321–2, *Ennfeng* 205, *Enfengs* 112; of Nogrod 75, 108, 134. See *Anfangrim, Indrafangs, Longbeards.*
English   312, 368–9, 372, 383, 392, 407; *(Old) English* 309, 312–15, 391–2. See *Anglo-Saxon.*
Enthor   Younger brother of Hunthor and Manthor. See 267, 270.
Ents   341, 353, 356; *Shepherds of the Trees* 356
Eöl   47–8, 71, 84, 121–3, 127, 139, 316, 320–30, *331, 332–3, 335–8, 344, 348, 409, 420. See *Dark-elves.*
Eönwë   Herald of Manwë. 246, 417. (Replaced *Fionwë*, son of Manwë.)
Ephel Brandir   Dwellings of the Men of Brethil on Amon Obel. 89, 92, 96–7, 145, 148, 151–2, 157–8, 164, *182, 186, 301, 306; *the Ephel* 97. See *Bar Haleth, Obel Halad.*
Erchamion   'One-handed', name of Beren. 51, 231
Ered-   (in names of mountain-ranges) See *Eryd-.*
Erendis of Númenor   230, 232
Ereol, Eriol   246
Eressëa   See *Tol Eressëa.*
Eriador   13, 39, 48–9, 60–1, 64, 109–10, 123, 128–9, 206, 221, 228, 232, 381, 385, 397, 410, 416
Eru   130, 341, 399, 402–3, 405, 421; *Eru-begotten* (the first Elves) 421; *the One* 212, 402. See *Children of Eru.*
Eruhíni   Children of Eru (singular *Eruhin*). 403
Eruman   Earlier name of Araman. 115, 175
Eryd (Ered) Engrin   6, 104, 196. See *Iron Mountains.*
Eryd (Ered) Gorgoroth   319, ~ *Gorgorath* 129, 188, *the Gorgorath* 319; ~ *Orgoroth* 15, 129, 194, ~ *Orgorath* 61, 64, 129, *183, 188, 194. See *Mountains of Terror.*
Eryd Lammad   See *Eryd Lómin.*
Eryd (Ered) Lindon   49, 105, *183, 193, 201–3, 206, 215, 334, 385, 388. See *Blue Mountains, Eryd Luin, Ossiriand.*
Eryd (Ered) Lómin   17, 38, 117, 176, 192, 196; *Eryd Lammad* 192, 196. See *Echoing Mountains.*
Eryd (Ered) Luin   5, 7, 10, 13, 32, 38–9, 60, 104, 108, 117, 179, 193, 385, 389. See *Blue Mountains, Eryd Lindon, Luindirien.*
Eryd (Ered) Nimrais   110, 385. See *White Mountains.*
Eryd (Ered) Orgoroth   See *Eryd Gorgoroth.*
Eryd (Ered) Wethrin   17–18, 38, 40, 46, 60, 74, 85, 113–14, 117, 196, 200, 240; earlier ~ *Wethion* 45, 74, 89, 91, 113, 120, 134,

Feiniel 'White Lady' (318), Turgon's sister, wife of Eöl. 318–19; *Ar-Feiniel* 317–18, 322. See *Isfin, Írith, Aredhel.*

Feir, plurals *Fîr, Firiath* Sindarin, = Quenya *Firya(r)* 'Mortal(s)'. 219, 387

Felagund King of Nargothrond; name used alone or with *Inglor, Finrod* (2). 35, 38, 44, 48–9, 52, 59, 62–3, 65–7, 88, 94, 116–17, 120, 123–4, 129–31, 135, 147, 149, 178–9, *183–4, 197, 215–19, 223, 225–9 , 238, 242–3, 255, 323, 355, 418, 420; said to be a Dwarvish name 179; as father of Gilgalad, see *Gilgalad;* his wife 44, 242; his ring 52, 59, 65, 242; *the Doors of Felagund* 84, 86, 143, 149. *Lord of Caves* 35, ~ *Caverns* 178

Fell Winter, The The winter of the year 495, after the fall of Nargothrond. 88, 93, 256, 261

Fell Year, The The year (455) of the Battle of Sudden Flame. 52, 125

Fen of Rivil, Fen of Serech See *Rivil, Serech.*

Field of the Worm, Field of Burning At Cabed Naeramarth. 295

Fifth Battle of Beleriand 71, 133. See *Battle of Unnumbered Tears* (formerly the Fourth Battle).

Finarfin Later name of Finrod (1), son of Finwë. 115, 130, 142, 179, 188, 197, 226, 240, 243, 319, 343, 383; *Finarphin* 179, 246

Findor See *Gilgalad.*

Finduilas Daughter of Orodreth King of Nargothrond. 83–5, 87–9, 91–2, 95, 101, 138–43, 147–8, 160, 180, 256–7, 299

Fingolfin (including references to his house and people) 17, 21, 23, 25–6, 29–34, 36, 38, 40, 43, 45–6, 49–50, 52, 54–6, 72–3, 75, 77, 114–15, 117, 121, 124–6, 134, 136, 177, *182, 195, 206, 219, 223, 227–8, 235, 243, 323, 327, 329, 343, 379; his wife *Anairë* 323

Fingon 31, 38, 46–7, 52, 56, 59–60, 70–7, 115, 117, 122, 124, 128, 133–4, 165–8, 174, 177, *182, 243, 287, 312, 315; as father of Gilgalad, see *Gilgalad.*

Finrod (1) Earlier name of Finarfin. (Most references are to his children or his house.) 22, 31–4, 38, 40, 42–4, 49, 52, 54, 67, 83, 115, 119, 130, 142, 178–9, 188, 197, 217, 219, 226–7, 240, 243, 319, 343. *Finrodian* (language) 22

Finrod (2) Later name of Inglor (see 65, 130); references include *Finrod Felagund.* 65, 130, 179, 197–8, 225, 240, 243, 355, 383, 406, 414; *Finrod Inglor* 130. See *Felagund.*

Finwë 6–8, 21, 33–4, 41, 62, 67, 246, 327, 379, 383, 387

Fionwë Son of Manwë. 6, 105, 246, 345; Herald of Manwë 417. See *Eönwë.*

Fíreb, plurals *Fírib, Firebrim* Sindarin, = Quenya *Fírima(r)* 'Mortal(s)'. 387

Firiath 'Mortals', see *Feir.*

Fíriel Name given to Míriel wife of Finwë. 419

Fírima(r) 'Mortal(s)'. 387, 419; *Fírimor* 419. See *Fíreb.*

First Age 342, 345–6, 349

Gochressiel   The Encircling Mountains about Gondolin. 239. See *Echoriad.*

God 212

Gódhel, plurals *Gódhil, Gódhellim*   (Sindarin) The Exiled Noldor. 364, 379. See *Ódhel.*

Gods   42, 55, 65, 175, 177, 217, 220, 227, 240, 246–7, 420; Battle of the Gods 207, People ~ 239, Sons ~ 246

Goldo   (Telerin) = *Noldo.* 383. *Goldorin, Goldolambë*, Telerin names of Quenya. 375

Golodh, plurals *Goelydh, Golodhrim*   Sindarin form of *Noldo.* 323, 364, 379 383

Gondolin   5, 18, 22–3, 25–8, 35, 40, 44–5, 47–8, 53, 55, 57(–8), 68, 70, 72–6, 84, 91, 110, 116, 118–23, 125–7, 133, 135–6, 139, 146, 166, 169, 177, 179, *182, 193, 198–201, 203, 206, 234, 239, 241, 243–5, 254–6, 258, 260–1, 272, 298, 300–2, 313–14, 316–17, 319, 324, 326, 328, 330, 333, 344–8, 351, 353, 356, 396–7, 409; translated *the Hidden Rock* 199–201; *the Guarded City, ~ Realm* 53, 57, *the Hidden City, ~ Kingdom, ~ Realm* 56–7, 91, 195, 260. *Lay of the Fall of Gondolin* 121, 320; the tongue of Gondolin 22–3, 25–8, and its population 25–8, 40, 44–5, 55–6, 119, 126; etymology 201. See *Ondolindë.*

Gondor   189, 314, 319, 391

Gonnhirrim   'Masters of stone', the Dwarves. 205, 209

Gorgûn   Name of the Orcs in the language of the Druedain. 391

Gorlim the Unhappy   Companion and betrayer of Barahir. 56, 59, *183

Gorothress(?)   See *183, 188

Gorsodh   Name of Sauron 'in Beleriand'. 54

Gorthaur   Sindarin name of Sauron. 240, 246; replacing *Gorthú* (Noldorin name) 239–40, 246

Gothmog   18 ('Lord of the Balrogs'), 168 ('High-captain of Angband'), 169

Great, The   212. See *Aratar.*

Great Battle   (at the end of the Elder Days) 345. See *Last Battle.*

Great Fortress   108, 201, 209. See *Belegost, Mickleburg.*

Great Gulf   6, 104–5, 109

Great March   (of the Eldar) 122; *the March* 13, 20–1, 23, 106, 195, 373, 375, 381–4, 390; *the Westward March* 371; *Marchers* 374; *Great Journey* 174

Great River   13, 109, 173–4; *Vale of the ~* 13. See *Anduin.*

Great Sea   6, 8, 91, 104–7, 111. See *(The) Sea, Western Sea.*

Great Tales   314

Green-elves   13, 16, 21, 28, 39, 111–12, 118, *185, 216, 218, 349, 355–6, 385. See *Danas, Laegel, Nandor.*

Green Mound   (of the Two Trees) 401. See *Ezellohar, Korollairë.*

Green Stone   See *Elessar.*

Harathor   (1) Proposed replacement of *Hardan*. 238.   (2) Chieftain of the Haladin when Húrin came to Brethil (replaced by *Hardang*). 237–8, 265–71, 278, 303–5, 307–8, 310

Harathrad   The 'South Ford', Sarn Athrad. 335–6. See *Athrad Daer*, *Sarn Athrad*; *Northern Ford*.

Hardan   Son of Haldar and father of Halmir; second chieftain of the Haladin. 222, 228, 237–8. See *Haldan*, *Harathor* (1).

Hardang   Chieftain *(Halad)* of the Haladin when Húrin came to Brethil (replaced *Harathor* (2)). 256, 258, 263–6, 269–71, 274–81, 283–4, 287–95, 297, 299, 302–4, 307–9

Hareth   Daughter of Halmir, wife of Galdor, and mother of Húrin. 234–5, 237–8, 268–70, 280, 289, 309. See *Hiriel*.

Harfalas   *184, 187, 190; *South Falas* *184, 187

Hathaldir   Companion of Barahir. 56

Hathol   Father of Hador in the revised genealogy. 223, 225, 232, 234 ('the Axe'), 235; later, son of Hador 226, (235)

Haudh-en-Arwen   The burial-mound of the Lady Haleth. 223. See *Tûr Haretha*.

Haudh-en-Elleth   The burial-mound of Finduilas. 95, 148, 256, 267, 269, 271, 274, 288, 297, 299, 307; earlier *Haudh-en-Ellas* 92–3, 95, 99, 101, 148; *Mound of the Elf-maid* 148

Haudh-en-Ndengin   The Mound of the Slain in Anfauglith. 169; *Haudh-na-Dengin* 72, 79, 133; other variants 79; *Haudh-en-Nirnaeth* 169 . See *Hill of Slain*.

Havens   (1) Of the Falas (see *Brithombar*, *Eglarest*). 5, 8, 16, 34, 56, 77, 80, 89, 104, 107, 111, 117, 135, 197, 242–3.   (2) The *Ship-havens* at Cape Balar. *184, 190.   (3) Of Sirion: see *Sirion*.

Hecelloi; Heculbar   See *Hekeldi; Hekelmar*.

Hekeldi   Quenya name of the Eldar who remained in Beleriand. 365, 371, 374, 379; singular *Hekel* 365. Telerin *Hecello*, plural *Hecelloi*, 365, 376, 379

Hekelmar   Quenya name of Beleriand. 365; also *Hekeldamar* 365, 374. Telerin *Heculbar* and *Hecellubar* 365, 376

Helevorn   Lake in Thargelion. 34, 45, 121, *183

Helkar   The Inland Sea. 174

Helkaraxë   6, 29, 191, 323; *Helkaraksë* 191. See *Grinding Ice*.

Hidden City, Hidden Realm   See *Gondolin*; *Hidden Kingdom*, see *Gondolin* and *Doriath*; *Hidden Way* (into Gondolin) 48

High Elves   341

High Faroth   35, 116, 189. See *Taur-en-Faroth*, *Hills of the Hunters*,

High Speech (of the West)   21, 26–7, 44; *High Tongue (of Valinor)*   25

Hildor   'The Followers', Men. 219, 386–7; earlier form *Hildi* 31, 174, 219. See *Aphadon*, *Echil*.

Hildórien   The region where Men awoke. 30, 114, (site of) 173–4

373, 411; *Primitive Quendian* (abbreviated PQ) 359–61, 363–5, 368, 375–6, 380, 382–4, 390, 409, 411, 413
Quendil, Quendendil   'Elf-friend'. 410; plural *Quendili* 412
Quennar (i) Onótimo   Eldarin loremaster. 343
Quentalë Ardanómion   Unknown work of learning referred to by Ælfwine. 206
Quenta (Noldorinwa)   The *Quenta Silmarillion* (references in the texts only). 27–8, 32, 38, 48, 59, 117, 120
Quenya (= *Quenya lambë* 407) 22–3, 145, 201, 318–20, 337, 359, 361–78, 380–5, 387–400, 402–3, 405–7, 410–17; original and Vanyarin form *Quendya* 361, 373, 375, 393

Radhrim   'East-march', Doriath beyond Aros. *183, 188–9. Cf. *Nivrim*.
Radhrost   'East Vale', Thargelion. 194, 197, 218, 221, 225, 227. Cf. *Nivrost* 'West Vale' (entry *Nevrast*), and see *Talath Rhúnen*.
Radhruin   Companion of Barahir. 56, 126. Earlier name *Radros* 126
Ragnir   (1) Servant of Morwen. 302. (2) Companion of Asgon. 262, 265, 302
Ragnor   Companion of Barahir. 56
Ramdal   See *Rhamdal*.
Ras-Arphain   Sindarin name of Taniquetil. 403. See *Arfanyarassë*; *Amon Uilos*.
Ras Mewrim   Cape south-west of Eglarest. *184, 190, 418. See *Bar-in-Mŷl*.
Rathlóriel, River   (also *Rathloriel*) Name given to the Ascar: 'Bed of Gold'. 180, *185, 190, 345–8, 351, 353; earlier name *Rathlorion* 180, 190, 353; late names *Rathmalad, Rathmallen* *185, 191, 353
Region   The southern forest of Doriath 7, 11, 15–16, 106, 112, *183, 321, 334, 355; *Region over Aros* 112
Rerir, Mount   Source of Greater Gelion. 34, *183, 188
Rhamdal   'Wall's End' in East Beleriand. *185, 191; *Ramdal* 191. See *Andram*.
Rhevain   See *Hravani*.
Rhûn, Sea of   174
Rían   Mother of Tuor. 52, 56, 71, 79, 126, 133, 135, 224, 231, 234
Ringil   Fingolfin's sword. 55
Ringwil, River   Tributary stream of Narog. 190, 197–8. (Replaced *Ingwil*.)
Rithil-Anamo   The Doom-ring of the Valar. 401. See *Máhanaxar*.
Rivendell   190
Rivil   Tributary stream of Sirion. 72, 113, 181, *183; *Rivil's Well* 59, 113, *183; *Fen of Rivil* 113, 181, 238 (see *Serech*).
Road Goes Ever On, The   419
Roads   In Brethil 157, 186; to Nargothrond 157, 186, 398. *The East*

Star-folk Elves (for the original linguistic elements and the development of meaning see 360, 362–3, 374). 360, 374, 418, 423

Stars, The (including references to *starlight*) 6–7, 9, 14, 30, 47, 105–6, 108, 110–11, 113, 176, 360, 373, 410, 417, 421–4; *the great stars* 5; Elvish words for 'star' 360, 362–3; *'Star-lore'* 414

Stone of the Hapless, Standing Stone See *Talbor*.

Sun, The 20–1, 24, 26, 30–1, 47, 110, 113–14, 175, 177, 196, 341, 373, 417–18, 423; *the Daystar* 30; *Years of the Sun* (8, 16), 20, 22, 24, 27, 30, 206, 419. See *Anar*.

Swarthy Men 60 (described), 61, 64, 74, 127. See *Easterlings, Eastrons*.

Tad-dail Petty-dwarves. See *Levain tad-dail*.

Taiglin, River 49, 57, 66, 88–9, 92, 97–8, 100, 103, 139, 147, 151, 153, 156–8, (159), 160, 164, *182, 193, 254, 265, 267, 271. Later forms *Teiglin* 147, 223, 228, 234–5, 310; *Taeglin* 257, 265, 267, 273, 296, 307, 309, *Taeglind* (and etymology) 309. On the forms of the name see 309–10.

    Crossings of Taiglin (Teiglin, Taeglin), also *the Crossings*, 92–3, 95, 99, 101, 141, 147–8, 157, 159, 161, *182, 186, 223, 256, 264–5, 267, 270–1, 273, 302, 307; *Ford of Taeglin* 274

Talath Dirnen 85, 140, *182, 186, 225, 228; earlier form *Dalath Dirnen* 140, 186, 223, 225, 228. See *Guarded Plain*.

Talath Rhúnen Name replacing *Radhrost* (Thargelion). 197–8

Talbor The stone of Túrin and Niënor at Cabed Naeramarth. 257, 300, 309. *The Standing Stone* 257, 274, 290, 295, 298, 309; *Stone of the Hapless* 295–6; other references to the Stone 103, 251, 258–9, 273–4, 294–6, 298. See *Tol Morwen*.

Tamar Precursor of Brandir in the *Tale of Turambar*. 160

Taniquetil 'High-Snow-Peak', properly the highest peak of the mountain Oiolossë. 399, 403, 416–17 (origin of the name). See *Arfanyarassë, Ras-Arphain*.

Taras, Mount 44, *182, 192, 197, 256, 379

Targlin Rejected name of (1) Maeglin, 323; (2) the metal of Eöl, 322 (see *Galvorn*).

Tata 'Two', the second of the Fathers of the Elves. 380, 418, 420–2; *Companions of Tata* 423. See *Tatyar*.

Tatië Spouse of Tata. 421

Tatyar Elves of the Second Clan. 380–1, 420

Taur-en-Faroth The highlands west of Narog. 197; earlier form *Taur-na-Faroth* 116, *184, 189–90, 197. See *High Faroth, Hills of the Hunters*.

Taur-im-Duinath 'Forest between the Rivers' (Sirion and Gelion). 191, 193, 195, 197, 239. See next entries.

Taur-i-Melegyrn 'Forest of the Great Trees', a name of *Taur-im-Duinath*. *185, 193